"I SHALL GIVE YOU
THE REA-TRAITOR . . ."

Roake, war leader of the Rea clan, whirled to face his mother, Akras. "I shall give you the traitor. I shall give you the home vessel. I shall give you the relaweed, the Rea-star, and the kree'va. Give me the time to complete my plans."

"Your plans?" demanded Akras. "Have you assumed the leadership of the clan?"

"My plans serve you and the Rea," answered Roake. "If you had wanted blind servility, Mother, you would have named Tagran your war leader."

Ares, Akras' younger son, rose abruptly to his feet and drew his gleaming clan-knife. "Do not mock the clan leader, Brother, or I shall slay you along with the Rea-traitor."

Roake ignored his brother's threat, but he bent one knee to touch the floor, assuming the position of obedience, and he addressed Akras earnestly. "Let me finish what I have begun, or the traitor *will* win again. If I fail to fulfill my vows to you, if the traitor does escape, I shall offer myself willingly to my brother's anxious blade. Let me use the daar'va, Mother."

"It is the war leader's tool. Use it as you must. But show me the stolen Rea treasures before this day ends, Roake, or Ares will be war leader by the next dawn!"

THE INQUISITOR

CHERYL J. FRANKLIN

DAW BOOKS, INC.
DONALD A. WOLLHEIM, FOUNDER
375 Hudson Street, New York, NY 10014

ELIZABETH R. WOLLHEIM
SHEILA E. GILBERT
PUBLISHERS

First Printing, May 1992

1 2 3 4 5 6 7 8 9

DAW TRADEMARK REGISTERED
U.S. PAT. OFF. AND FOREIGN COUNTRIES
—MARCA REGISTRADA
HECHO EN U.S.A.

PRINTED IN THE U.S.A.

For Armandita,
who would certainly be an alien relations expert
in another universe

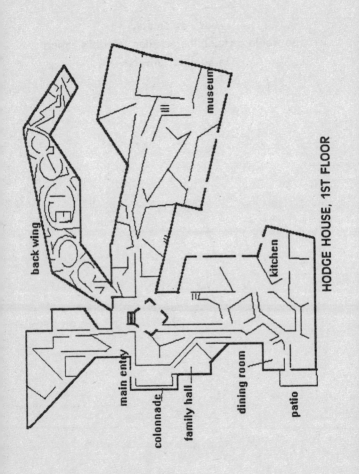

back wing

museum

main entry

colonnade

family hall

dining room

kitchen

patio

HODGE HOUSE, 1ST FLOOR

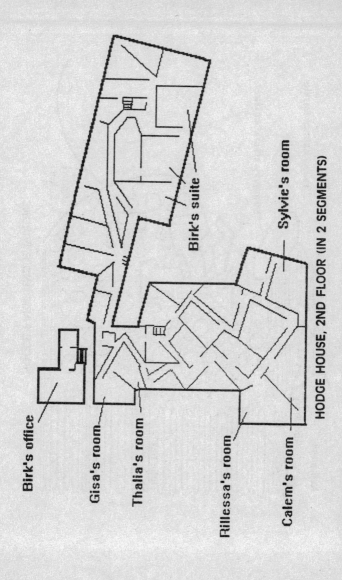

HODGE HOUSE, 2ND FLOOR (IN 2 SEGMENTS)

Birk's suite

Birk's office

Gisa's room

Thalia's room

Rillessa's room

Calem's room

Sylvie's room

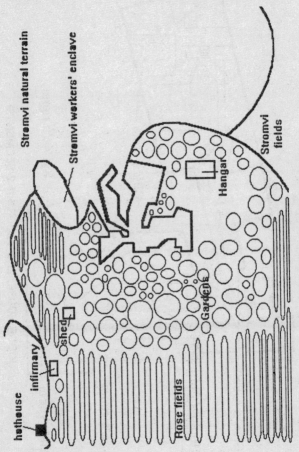

HODGE FARM AND ENVIRONS

Stromvi natural terrain

Stromvi workers' enclave

Stromvi fields

Hangar

Gardens

Rose fields

shed

infirmary

hothouse

PROLOGUE

The ships will come soon. The long quarantine ends. Death-watch, started so long ago by a frightened young-ling, has nearly completed its grim cycle.

My people still tell many of the old stories. The children speak of tall, ghostly demons and dark giants with serpentine hands, mingling the traits of forgotten Consortium races into imagined monsters. Their fabled creatures rise in the air and sweep across the surface lands. The children's thoughts seldom delve into their species' earthen cradle.

In my childhood, our stories lived—with us—in the caves, tunnels, and burrows. Each root spike had a parable of purpose. The core clay was a stubborn old man, taking pleasure from perversity. Every cavern had its nymph, good or evil, fair or frightful.

I once dreamed of a cavern nymph. The Deetari may guide their life-choices by such vivid seeings, but we Stromvi left the mystics' path in our early history. We are too sensible, we claim. Nonetheless, I have always remembered my singular childhood vision with an uneasy suspicion that it was indeed a dream of prophecy.

I visualize the past and see the nymph's richly patterned hide. I feel her subtle scent, as delicate as the pale, fragile lace of fire-lily roots. She stands firmly on four legs, her upper torso raised proudly. The complex sheen of layered resins covers her in a sparkling of elusive blue and glossy violet, such as the people of my childhood found most pleasing. Bands of plaited magi reeds encircle her ankles and wrists, and the gleaming petals of silver-lilies crown her as gently as the soft dawn sky that I miss so deeply.

She still reaches compellingly into senses that I have not possessed for many spans of time. As the dream

9

began, I felt awed by her, though she looked much like a woman of my people. When I walked toward her, she grew until she stood as tall as the great cavern in which she waited. A graceful, luminous veil of living, growing root tendrils draped her, bestowing their rich gifts of varied resins.

She became even taller, bruising the blossoms of her crown against the ragged umber clay above her. She reached toward me with the cupped hands of welcome, but dagger-sharp nails emerged, steaming with resin-cutting acid. She expanded, her strong limbs bloating and scraping the stone-pocked walls. Like the venom sacs of an osang snake, stretching as the poison fills them, her sense nodules bulged across her head.

Her pruning teeth thrust forward, and they darkened with decay. Her milky-lidded eyes broadened and smeared, and her nostrils thinned in distortion. I watched her serene face become sickly, as her primary mouth twisted, one corner rising upward from the serrated rows of teeth. The pruning jaw of the lower mouth continued its forward motion, tearing the mouth folds and the skin from her neck ridge, leaving a raw, bloodless wound. The stretching continued, until she consisted only of thin, translucent, colorless skin, her head and torso and limbs all of one single piece like a tawdry, painted balloon. She exploded, and I awoke.

I dreaded sleep for many nights after that disquieting dream. I feared inside my haunted head, until my teeth clattered in wordless despair. I felt the dread crawling inside of me. I could not even speak of the dream, because it held such terror.

I did not understand why the horror of this dream refused to leave me. I did not know why a dream so brief and simple, so quickly gone awry, could hurt so hard and long. Even now, it frightens me—a little less sharply but still with potency. The images rise easily in my mind, despite all the spans that have passed, and I feel the same terror and know that I am still a child before the hollow queen of my people's nearly forgotten past.

I have never had but that one true nightmare, and it came only once, yet it has never faded. After all that I have witnessed and endured, the nightmare remains the source of the deepest fears within me. It retains a subtle power over my life, reminding me of all the explosive evils that may lie hidden within apparent loveliness and peace. I never even told my beloved Ngev of the nightmare's existence; I never told my honored parents.

I feel the loneliness of their loss tonight. My own life seems fragile to me. My honored father would tell me to stop moping over imagined specters and enjoy the beauty of a warm, clear evening. I shall try, honored father, but your foolish Ngina tends to drift between the past and present these days. Your foolish daughter is a very old woman.

The second moon will soon cross in front of her brother and shadow his face with her disorderly profile. The younglings prepare their wish-rods beside the steaming, golden pools, awaiting the propitious moment. In my own youth, we cast our wishes into the wide, lilac trumpet throats of the panguulung, treading cautiously among the panguulung beds' fleshy gray-green leaves, avoiding the delicate violet flowers and deceptively succulent fruit. Our wishes were borne by the barbed arrows of silver-lily seeds, but our excitement was the same as that of these present younglings. Not everything has changed.

The ashes of my Ngev lie beneath that clear, rich pond. The sweetness of his hide-scent seems still to linger against me. Such lush, vigorous warmth is unknown to Stromvi's recent children, for the changes have altered both our scents and our scent-perceptions. The lighter, daintier substitutes are not unpleasant, but they seem shallow to me. None of these strong, young men could ever please me like my Ngev, and it is not age that has numbed my interests. I have taken younger mates and loved them well, but none of them could ever touch my senses with fullness, for I am of a different time. Any of my sisters, had they survived, would understand.

The moon crossing has begun. I no longer move swiftly, or I would join those younglings and cast my own wish. My sons and daughters would click disparagingly at their mother's folly, but my grandchildren would approve my gesture, mistaking it for a sign of rebellion against age. My great-grandchildren do not know what to think of me under any circumstances, for they are too far removed from the world of my youth, and they fear me slightly for my strangeness. I am the last who truly remembers.

These children with their wish-rods know nothing of the suffering, nothing of the sacrifices, nothing of the anguish we endured in order to adapt. They are unfettered by the past because we succeeded. They have a future to fashion into high wonders or the simplicity cherished by their ancestors. When I am gone, the final relic of the old world will unite with the fire and the wind of the new creation—my father's creation. I am a little sorry that the old custom will no longer serve, for I would prefer an earthen shroud.

The second moon looks dark against her brother. I cast my wish, though I have no rod, and the silver-lilies have not bloomed for many spans: Let me live until the long quarantine ends, just one more season. I have never lost my wistful eagerness to travel to all the planets of the vast Consortium, but I would settle for a visit with our neighbors on Deetari.

I wonder if the Deetari matriarch would welcome me as a prophetess. I have the age, experience, and rank to earn the title. My revered father would laugh to think of his flighty daughter as a figure of honor.

I do not know if anyone beyond this small planet remembers me. Old Nod still glows across the galaxy, measuring the spans in the night sky, but his persistent brilliance gives scant comfort. The news has been sparse in recent years. The lives of my alien friends, bonded to me by shared calamity, diverged from my humble struggles long ago. The quarantine has made off-world communication a clumsy, infrequent process.

When the quarantine ends, the Calongi will come to restore the old ties. These children around me will be as astounded by the Calongi as newly welcomed members of the Consortium. I am the most alien being my children have ever encountered (outside of stories that they half-disbelieve), and I represent New Stromvi's own beginning.

I must survive to greet the Calongi. I must give my memories to the Prili data gatherers, who alone may have the skills to accurately preserve my view of our history. I have retained all my father's journals and hoarded every eloquent remnant of Hodge's Folly. I have even saved the Rea-star.

I am not important in myself. Whatever briefly pivotal role I may have played in my youth, I have been no more significant than the least of my brave people since that distant time. For many reasons, I wish that I were not the last. I feel unworthy. The sustaining confidence that grew from hard survival has abandoned me. Or is it only memory of my honored father that makes me as uncertain as a child again? I loved him, but he still intimidates me.

The moon shifts beyond her brother's range, and the younglings leave the pools in slow, formal cadence. The reed-pipes sing hauntingly. I can see one of the wish-rods, trapped by a resin bubble and unable to sink beneath the golden surface of the pool. Whose wish, I wonder, lies thus trapped? It could be mine. The resin bubble has a disturbing, distorting potency like the cavern nymph of my nightmare.

A Soli once advised me to assume my proper authority over that terrible dream and conquer it. He did not tell me how to achieve this miracle. I suppose it seemed a simple thing to him, who had mastered so much that should have been impossible.

I do not know why I told that strange Soli of my dream. Perhaps I knew that he would understand the horror. He had confronted a hollow queen.

We called him Jase. He was my father's friend—and mine, I think. The story of the Change begins and ends with him. But no: The Change begins and ends with Birk, for Birk's arrogance made Akras hollow, and Birk's arrogance made Jase whole.

PART I:

The Seeds of Anger

CHAPTER 1

Birkaj knew his crime. Disobedience, more than the actual slaying of the Rea clan leader, had made him a fugitive. He had forfeited his clan-rights, but he would yield nothing of what he had taken. He knew the smugglers and their routes and bases, for the Rea clan prospered by raiding such lawless worlds and beings. The Rea clan could not retract that boon of knowledge from Birkaj, any more than it could take from him the spans of warrior's training. Not even Raskannen's formidable death-curse had the power to nullify the past.

If asked, Birkaj would have said that he shared his people's passionate beliefs in the power of an Essenji's life and death, but Birkaj had a cynical pragmatism that few of his people possessed. Other Rea might preach a creed of freedom, but their bonds of clanship imposed more restrictions than Consortium law. Birkaj believed only in himself.

The largest surviving group of true Essenji, the Rea clan had preserved their racial distinctions by extensive, deliberate inbreeding. The Rea occasionally strengthened the genetic pool with a few captive Soli, but the Rea took care to dilute the presence of dominant Soli genes. Most Essenji, less determined than the Rea, had been reabsorbed into the Soli species from which the Essenji were originally derived. The Rea let go of nothing easily: not clan customs, not clan members, not clan treasures.

Birkaj turned the Rea-star in his hands, feeling the sharp edges of the rubies' settings. The Rea had honed the metal tines deliberately, for the starburst symbolized the keenness of the Rea people, as well as the power of the Rea clan leader. The impracticality of the brooch's magnificent design was itself characteristic of both the

Rea clan and the Essenji species. Most Essenji indulged in romantic extremism.

Birkaj of the Rea had the knowledge, the equipment, enough Rea jewels to invest, and above all, the ruthless energy to succeed among the lawless. If a young Soli like Per Walis could use smuggler's origins to establish an independent trade network, a Rea warrior could surely achieve as much. Birkaj did not need the clan; so he told himself. He almost believed his arrogant claim, except when he thought of Akras.

All of the loneliness, all of the hurt of a man who has lost his claims on clan and family, all had tightened into a strangled memory of Akras—and not solely because she was only child and heir of the Rea clan leader, Raskannen. Birkaj recalled her now with a curse on his lips, driven by the embittering power of betrayal: Akras, whose name meant "beauty" among the Essenji. She was gifted with the beauty of her name, the strength and lithe grace of her extraordinary species, and the secure pride of knowing that her people cherished her.

In Akras, all of the purest physical traits of the Essenji had bred true. The characteristic Essenji musculature, which contributed significantly to the general beauty of the Essenji people, achieved exceptional definition beneath Akras' pale gold skin. Her eyes were amber fire. The black center stripe of her long hair was wide between the silken silver that blurred into a fine fur as it reached the shoulders. Akras wore her hair loose, for the Rea braided their hair only for battle.

In the distorting mirror of Birkaj's mind, Akras donned the entire, exquisite richness of the Rea clan's greatest glories, and all of the perfection of the Essenji species fulfilled itself in her. An idealized image of Akras troubled Birkaj, remaining incongruously intact among the rubble of his broken ambitions for the Rea clan. Nothing had transpired as he had intended.

Any ambitious young man of the Rea might have appreciated Birkaj's fundamental obsession. Akras had often chosen a young warrior of her people, loving him utterly, until her favor shifted to another: Even bestowed briefly, the love of Akras gave added status to a Rea man. Eventually, all Rea had agreed, Akras would select one of her lovers as husband and war leader.

Birkaj had known the lightness of her attachments when he sought to win her. He had mocked Tagran's earnest longings. He had derided Zagare's childish refusal to accept the transience of her intense passions. Birkaj had approved Akras' wisdom in discarding such men as possible war leaders. He had waited deliberately for her to learn of weakness before concluding that she was ready to learn of strength.

Akras had not disappointed Birkaj. She had accepted his attentions eagerly. She *had* chosen him. She had later called him traitor, but it was Akras who had betrayed her lover's trust.

Angrily, Birkaj broke the reverie that drifted toward personal guilt. Anger rose easily as he thought about Zagare, the man Akras had finally selected as husband. Akras claimed her truest vengeance against Birkaj unconsciously: Birkaj continued to desire her with the jealous intensity that only another Essenji might understand. He might claim the dearest Rea treasures, but somehow Akras and the Rea themselves had eluded him, and that loss seared all Rea honor from him.

The ship's proximity alarm rang softly, and Birkaj snarled to himself. He thrust the Rea-star back into its lua-hide case and stowed the case beneath the command console. He tapped the console to enlarge the display of the approaching vessel. The crimson starburst emblem along the great vessel's gleaming hull blazed on his display screen.

A larger, brighter blaze overwhelmed the softer images, and Birkaj clung to his chair as his ship jerked to avoid the deadly fire. The Rea vessel turned, following the quick maneuver of Birkaj's ship precisely, and the second bolt missed by a narrower margin. Birkaj shouted at the Rea, knowing that his ship would convey his message in the next, brief instant between dodging attacks: "Only a coward lets a machine fight his battles for him, Zagare. You are weak, and you have no honor. You disgrace the Rea."

Birkaj's ship lurched again, and a warning code flashed on the console, indicating the severity of the strain on the small ship's resources. The past ten millispans of dodging the well-armed Rea vessel had nearly drained Birkaj's power reserves. His cunning, however, had not faltered, and his determination had increased along with his resentment.

Birkaj had eluded the Rea for over a span, but he had accepted the inevitability of direct conflict. He had killed Raskannen and fled with the Rea-star and the kree'va, the two great emblems of the Rea clan leader's authority. Birkaj assuaged a brief pang of Rea honor by reminding himself that he had not chosen to fight his people. By forcing him to battle for his life, they had left him no option but ruthlessness.

The automatic defenses of Birkaj's ship enabled him to escape two more attacks, though the Rea fire had darkened the ship's tough shield-skin, and the ship shuddered from stress. The display of the Rea vessel resumed its clarity as the attacks abruptly ceased. The small ship steadied, though it maintained alert mode, as programmed by its captor. Birkaj waited, smiling slightly, imagining Zagare's dilemma of honor. Zagare was a capable warrior, but he had no gift of leadership.

Zagare's deep voice filled Birkaj's ship: "How does a traitor, thief, and murderer dare speak of Rea honor?"

Birkaj answered carefully, allowing himself no fear or nervousness, for such weaknesses were unworthy of a Rea warrior: "You accuse without proof, betrayer of friends. Let the Rea people judge between us in a legal contest—or do you fear that my strength will show the truth?"

"You have no truth in you," said Akras in her satiny voice, and Birkaj experienced a contradictory shiver of pleasure at hearing her, even in her furious contempt of him.

"Have you forgotten so much, my Akras?" asked Birkaj gently, and he imagined that her unwilling memories argued in his favor.

Zagare answered tersely, "I have forgotten nothing."

"Then accord me my due rights," retorted Birkaj, his moment of softness vanquished by the hard, proud confidence of a Rea warrior. "Face me, Zagare, and challenge me lawfully for the rights you have usurped as Rea war leader."

"Dock your ship in the lower bay," snapped Zagare. "You do not deserve the truce of faith given by a code that you mock, but your dishonor will not sully the clan.

You claim your *rights* only in desperation, but I shall grant them. I shall execute you lawfully and relish the privilege."

Birkaj adjusted his ship's controls to initiate entry into the larger vessel. He deactivated the warning chime, for he trusted the blindness of Zagare's honor. Zagare was a fool.

As his ship entered the bay, Birkaj readied the kree'va, the clan leader's counterpart of the daar'va, the great weapon of the Rea war leader. In his span of exile, Birkaj had devoted much time to a study of the ancient device. Unlike the Rea-star, the kree'va served as a very practical tool of power, though legends of its destructive potential had long made it an emblem of authority rather than an actual element of Rea aggression.

The daar'va could rearrange the existing chemical compounds in gases or liquids, creating deadly concentrations or voids of critical elements, generating lattices of moisture or minute particles to reflect or scatter signals according to the wielder's programming, and generally disrupting sensitive systems. The kree'va incorporated an energy-to-matter conversion capability, which enabled it to create new elements as well as shift those that were already present. Neither system had sufficient power to affect the stability of solids significantly but either system could produce radical changes in an existing environment: some temporary, some self-perpetuating.

For the past two generations of Rea, vague tales of the kree'va's dangers had kept all but the clan leader from experimenting with it. Birkaj set the kree'va's controls with vicious force, still enraged by the custom that he had defied so irrevocably. He acknowledged no guilt in himself: Raskannen had refused to understand, refused to behave sensibly, refused to lead the Rea to their deserved greatness.

Damona had begun to listen, but Damona's death had left Raskannen deaf, weakened by unseemly mourning for his war-leader wife. Raskannen, serving as both clan leader and war leader after losing Damona, had been unwilling even to consider Birkaj's ambitions for the Rea. Birkaj was convinced that he would now be war leader, if Raskannen had remained strong. Raskannen's shortsightedness had forced Birkaj to defy tradition and

study the kree'va for himself. Raskannen, finding Birkaj
with the kree'va, had struck first. Birkaj had certainly
not intended to slay Raskannen, clan leader and father
of the adored Akras. How could Akras believe such dishonor of her lover?

But she had believed. Worse, she had accepted Zagare
as clan mate and war leader. She was clan leader now,
and the Rea obeyed her. The Rea obeyed Zagare. It was
intolerable. However, Zagare's rule would not last much
longer.

Birkaj smiled as the great Rea vessel enclosed his ship.
The bay pressurized, and the Rea guards arrived, armed
with traditional clan-knives and dark energy guns. Zagare, his narrow, ivory face intense beneath his black
and silver mane, led the guards himself. The war leader's
red cloak swung in cadence with his gait. The reflected
light of the war-star cast ruby shadows on his smooth
chin.

Birkaj traced the second spiral arm of the kree'va's
controller. The scarlet spiral began to glow. Zagare approached Birkaj's ship and glared impatiently at its
sealed door. Birkaj traced the fourth spiral arm, the
third, and the fifth. Each began to glow, until the first
spiral pulsed, and a deafening roar filled the lower bay
of the Rea vessel.

Birkaj withdrew his hand quickly from the kree'va,
startled by the waves of sound that beat from the device.
His earlier experiments had disrupted photonic circuits,
as he had intended, but had produced no such audio
effect. Birkaj's perfect confidence faltered slightly as he
realized he knew less about the kree'va than he had
imagined. He had relied on the imperviousness of his
small ship's relatively primitive electronics, for the materials used in the old designs were less sensitive to the
kree'va's readjustments. The kree'va could protect its
wielder within a programmed radius, but perhaps that
result, too, was unpredictable. Birkaj touched several of
his ship's controls, activating clocks and meters and other
harmless functions to assure himself that his ignorance
had not sabotaged the electronics that he still needed.

The kree'va's thunder faded, but even its wake sufficed
to drown Zagare's furious shout against Birkaj's treachery. Birkaj saw the Rea move in an eerie, silent panto-

mime. The atmosphere inside the shuttle bay began to alter. Waves of minor but lethal changes emanated from the kree'va-directed field that flowed slowly outward from Birkaj's ship.

The Rea guards stumbled from the pain inflicted by the kree'va's manipulations, but some reached the body of the Rea vessel. Zagare stood farthest from escape and nearest to the deadliness. Stricken and suffocating, Zagare tugged the ruby starburst from his cloak and flung it through the closing doors. If he mouthed a death-curse, no one heard. The doors of the shuttle bay merged and sealed.

Birkaj nodded in approval. Zagare was dead. That morsel of vengeance was complete. Birkaj doubted that the inner bay doors would suffice to save the entire Rea vessel, but at least the doors still functioned. The Rea clan could conceivably survive. Birkaj had upheld his own honor by granting them a chance.

Birkaj refused to mourn family and friends among the Rea, for they had turned from him unanimously. He hoped that Akras would live, though he exulted at her defeat. He wanted her to recognize the Rea's conqueror. He wanted her to know her folly in choosing Zagare over Birkaj.

Birkaj waited for a dozen microspans before he let the killing design of the kree'va fade. He traced a simpler code onto the kree'va's panel, and the outer bay doors melted apart. The vacuum of space inhaled Zagare's body and dismantled it.

Birkaj reactivated his ship's controls and left the derelict Rea vessel. He made no claim of conquest, thereby expressing scorn for the people who had chosen such an ineffectual war leader as Zagare. The insult would injure more deeply than the deaths.

Birkaj's ship's sensors detected a distant Bercali cruiser shifting course toward the malfunctioning Rea vessel in the hope of making a salvage claim. The prospect of the crude Bercali turning the proud Rea home into a prison barge repulsed Birkaj, but he made no effort to discourage the boarding. The Rea had betrayed him; they deserved any dishonor that might befall them.

*   *   *

The daar'va recognized its cousin, the weapon that Birkaj turned against the Rea, but the clan leader understood the magnitude of Birkaj's treachery without the daar'va's aid. The monitors of the Rea vessel carried the entire disaster as it occurred, until the kree'va's field reached some vital system and caused the monitors to fail. Rea guards, who maintained a constant watch for enemies or choice victims, found their warning screens registering their own Rea ship as optimum target. When the screens darkened, many of the guards wondered if their ship had commenced self-destruction.

Rea warriors, accustomed to a sophisticated vessel that tended itself, continuously fumbled as they tried to maintain the vast, dying ship by manual operation. Seasoned Rea warriors enacted their emergency duties slowly, even their stern discipline impaired by the shock of attack by one of their own kindred. The Rea had condemned Birkaj, but they had not imagined that he could use the kree'va against his own clan.

On the clan leader's monitor, Akras watched Zagare die, and she whispered his killer's name. Only the warrior Tagran heard her, for only Tagran had remained with her in the small, stark command room after Zagare left to claim Birkaj as prisoner. Zagare had not considered this exercise of Rea justice worthy of the customary war contingent at readiness beside the clan leader. Akras had not disputed his decision, though she had stayed in the command room, and she had not forbidden Tagran to remain with her. Zagare would have left the command room empty, for the sophisticated Rea vessel defended itself quite effectively against such small opponents as Birkaj—except when the opponent wielded a weapon like the kree'va within the Rea vessel's own sphere of protection.

Tagran laid his hand on Akras' smooth shoulder, but Akras only continued to stare at the clan leader's console, as if she were trapped by the same silent vacuum that consumed her husband's body. Tagran grieved for Akras' pain, though he had predicted Zagare's failure as a war leader. Tagran knew Birkaj, as Tagran had known Zagare, for all three men had trained together and studied together since childhood. Zagare had often bested Birkaj in the games of direct combat; in every contest that required strategy or guile, Birkaj had won. Tagran had tried to give warning to the senior warriors, but they had dismissed his words as jealousy. He found scant satisfaction in being proven right.

Akras' gold-and-fire eyes had a distant focus, and they did not seem to follow the furor of activity that her monitor portrayed. "Akras," murmured Tagran, trying to draw her from the unnatural trance that seemed to have drowned her vital spirit. "You are clan leader, and this is not the time for mourning" he reminded her, for he was a warrior as well as her friend.

She pulled rigidly away from his hand. She touched the broadcast activator. "Prepare the tactical ships for escape," ordered Akras sharply, and her rich voice ran through the wide halls of the Rea vessel. "War guards, report to the command room." Her own monitor became blank, and she let her hand fall heavily to her side.

"Escape ships?" demanded Tagran. "You cannot abandon the home vessel!" He would never have questioned Raskannen or Damona, but the instincts of Rea obedience did not transfer easily to Akras of the bright smiles and teasing laughter. He loved her with a silent intensity, but he could not think of her as clan leader. Akras was made for beauty, like the crimson silk she wore instead of warrior's leather.

"My father taught me what a clan leader must know about the kree'va," answered Akras grimly, "and the clan cannot remain on this ship and survive."

Tagran could not reply. Akras was still Akras: slim and fair and fiery. But something about her had shifted in the past few moments. Something in her had grown cold.

The doors slid open. The war guards, six strong Rea men and women in tough, burnished lua-leather kilts and coppery breastplates, entered the command room. "We cannot remain here," announced Akras with a quickening of her voice. "We must escape this vessel and this vicinity, before we become crippled prey for a Bercali prison galley. We have a little time, since the Rea-traitor does not understand the kree'va well enough to have created a rapid change. Gather your war teams and go to your assigned ships. We must survive to avenge ourselves."

The war guards' hesitation troubled Tagran, making him recognize his own temerity in disputing a clan leader's orders. Obedience made the clan strong, and that strength had made them free. Akras must demand obedience; it was her right, and it was her duty. The clan had no other leader left.

Kaspar, a senior warrior whose hair was more white than black and silver, spoke reasonably, "Akras, the kree'va has already rendered the corridors near the ship bays lethal. Even if we wished to reach the escape ships, we have only enough protective suits to transfer thirty warriors at a time, and we have less gear for the children. We cannot abandon the home vessel. We must gather the clan in the upper level, until the kree'va's effects have passed."

"Do you understand nothing, Kaspar?" snapped Akras with growing urgency. "We have insufficient protective gear to remain *here*. The upper level offers no lasting defense against the kree'va. Whatever we do, many of us will die, and we shall all suffer the kree'va's poison. We must leave this ship while we are still alive and able to escape the Bercali, because we shall be too ill to fight them. Issue the reserves of adaptation fluid to those who have no other adequate protection."

"Our fluid supplies will be exhausted," protested Kaspar, and a glimmer of impatience marked the glance he exchanged with the senior guard beside him.

In swift fury, Akras leapt from her chair and pressed her bronze-handled knife against Kaspar's throat. She demanded coldly, "Waster of time, have you forgotten that my father is dead, and I am clan leader now?" All of the warriors fell silent, staring at a young woman who had never before showed interest in any conquest that was not romantic. Kaspar's mouth gaped in shock. Even Tagran, who knew her best of any in that room, found himself stunned by this stern, strong stranger dressed in Akras' flowing crimson silks. "I am clan leader, and I shall be obeyed."

Kaspar grunted, "Of course, clan leader."

Akras nicked his ear deliberately, as she released him. Kaspar pressed his hand against the ear to staunch the blood, but a new respect had replaced impatience in his expression: This minor blood-letting was the sort of warning gesture that Raskannen might have made. Tagran could see a similar transformation of attitude take cautious hold in each of the other guards, and he wondered if any of them shared a measure of his own disquiet.

When Akras resumed her interrupted commands, all of her listeners were attentive. "We shall take the tactical ships and regather at the last haven's coordinates. We shall assess our damages and rebuild from that point," she hissed, and those who watched her would never again think of her as clan leader's daughter; she was clan leader, and she would be obeyed. "Move swiftly!" Kaspar and the other guards saluted her and strode determinedly from the room. "Tagran, you will take charge of the daar'va."

The daar'va's care was the war leader's duty, and for a moment Tagran saw his dreams fulfilled. "Come with me, Akras," he urged. "This room is unsafe, and the command console no longer functions."

"Because we were children together, Tagran, do not think I shall expect less obedience from you." Akras raised her gleaming dagger before her eyes and held it, pointing upward. "Do you serve me, Tagran?"

Tagran understood her: He would never be war leader, but he could stand at Akras' side. He was not bitter, for he had never truly expected more from her. "Yes, clan leader," he answered dutifully.

"Before you take the daar'va to the escape ship, go to the suite I shared with Zagare. Tell Sorana to bring my son to me now." Tagran bowed and obeyed.

* * *

Silently, Akras watched Tagran depart. The doors did not close behind him, for the kree'va's impairments had reached into another of the ship's central control systems. Moving numbly, Akras used her knife's handle to smash the inoperative access panel for the emergency equipment. She pried open the cupboard. Only Damona's protection suit hung there, for Raskannen had relied on the adaptation fluid contained in the silver box that rested on the cupboard floor.

Sheathing her clan-knife at her waist, Akras removed the carefully designed, well-sealed box that protected the precious adaptation fluid, the last remnant of Raskannen's hoard. She touched the cipher lock to release the lid. Raskannen's own cache of fluid was a much purer, more potent blend than even the best smugglers were generally able to supply, since Consortium control of adaptation fluid was strict. Raskannen had paid the Cuui a small fortune for the illegal fluid, but Raskannen had not begrudged the cost. Smugglers' fluid were usually far less pure than Consortium fluids, and none were strong enough to satisfy an addict. Raskannen had been an addict for the last five spans of his life: A dubious gift of Rea prosperity.

"Raskannen called you his Freedom," murmured Akras, raising a golden packet of the fluid to the light. The lights flickered ominously.

"Clan leader, I have brought your son." Sorana, a young Rea breeder, stood uneasily at the door. With some contempt, Akras recognized Sorana's eagerness to make her own escape and see her charge returned to the clan leader's care. Akras nodded curtly, and Sorana laid the child on the console. "Go to your ship," ordered Akras quietly, and Sorana bowed and left without further delay.

Akras placed the silver box beside her son. Again she unsheathed her knife and raised it over the console. She turned the point of the knife downward.

Her son, just half a span old, followed the brightness of the blade with his pale eyes. Akras lowered the knife, until it touched the silver down along the boy's neck. She shaved a streak of the tentative mane, baring the ivory skin. She pressed the point of the knife against that skin, restraining the child to prevent him from writhing away from her. Amber blood beaded and trickled, and the child wailed.

With a bitter cry, Akras raised the knife high above her head. "To what dishonor have you brought me, Birkaj?" she groaned. Ruthlessly, she turned the dagger against her own face and silken hair, scarring herself with the violent marks of a solemn death-hunt.

She kicked the remnants of her sheared hair impatiently from her sandaled feet. She shed her crimson silks, now stained with her blood. She took the protective suit and hastily dressed herself in it, carefully adjusting the suit to protect her unborn child. Before she sealed the suit, she removed from the silver box all four measures of Raskannen's potent adaptation fluid and the single measure of lesser fluid that had been Damona's. She fitted Damona's fluid pouch with an injector patch and pressed the device against her neck. She jerked slightly as the stinging inoculation spread through her veins. She completed dressing.

She fitted one of Raskannen's pouches of adaptation fluid for injection. She pressed the injector against her son's neck. He shrieked as the fierce fire of an addict's measure of adaptation fluid filled him and set its unyielding claim upon him. With care, she resealed the box that held the remaining fluid, and she stowed the box in her backpack.

Akras wrapped her crying, struggling son tightly in his blanket, and she took him in her arms. With her face butchered, bleeding, and unrecognizable, she stared at her own reflection in the polished metal of the command room's walls. "I shall regain my honor," she vowed, "when I have destroyed the Rea-traitor, as he has destroyed me." She stared at her son. "And you will lead me to the victory."

CHAPTER 2

We Stromvi have never understood the warring ways. My Ngev was a strong man, but he would never have used his strength against any of his people. My honored father was stern and strict, and all of us lived in awe of him, but we never feared him. We could never have conceived of any Stromvi using a child as a tool of vengeance.

Essenji were bred for the most warlike characteristics of their Soli kindred: In Essenji terms, Akras was strong. Akras salvaged a dying remnant of her clan—for few of them escaped Birkaj's vicious blow undamaged. She forced them to survive, and she forced them to remain proud Rea, despite their losses. When she could not steal sufficient cures or other supplies for them, she bargained with the same lawless beings the Rea had always used and despised as prey. She traded her own treasures and skills first, asking nothing of her warriors that she did not sacrifice herself. Akras had ample gifts of determination and cunning, and she employed all she possessed according to the Essenji's purest concepts of greatness. The Essenji ideal was always flawed.

At first, the effort of clan survival must have consumed the clan's full energies. As Akras re-created the Rea, her vision of restored strength and prosperity must have seemed gloriously inspired to her people. I prefer to believe that her people did not truly understand her ultimate intentions, the hoarded secret that sustained her with its poisonous promise.

Span upon span of murderous plotting: What Stromvi could imagine such cruel warping of maternal care? The sons of Akras would know praise for physical prowess and clever battle-senses, but they would not know gentleness or love. They would not see their mother smile except in victory over a fallen foe. The Rea claimed to honor personal freedom, but the tyranny of Akras' powerful obsession enslaved her entire clan.

Akras' sons would learn their harsh lessons well, for their clan leader/mother filled her children with her adamant purpose and her pride. In predatory patience, Akras measured each cherished possession that the Reatraitor amassed, for these defined the scope of what she would steal from him. The sons would find the Reatraitor and destroy him by the same lingering, intolerable pain he had bequeathed to their mother. The sons of Akras would destroy the life and then destroy the man, Birkaj, and neither son knew that Zagare was not the father of them both.

*   *   *

Birk Hodge arrived on Stromvi in the year when I first emerged from the cavern of my birth. The impression of his coming has endured through the spans, though it seemed a simple, unexceptional event in itself. I have come to believe that the incidents we need most to remember will embed themselves in the memory, regardless of their apparent unimportance at the time of occurrence. It is right that I, who alone can remember the end, should also remember the beginning.

The Stromvi of that time was mostly flat, but our rich plant life provided considerable contour. The depth of the vine mass varied, depending on the type of vine that dominated a particular patch. The leaves of ubiquitous thorn vines, lacy or thick and pulpy, wore fanciful violet traceries across the green. Most thorn vines produced flowers in shades of blue, followed by clusters of pink or green berries. Many Stromvi plants were epiphytes; many of these resembled the colorful orchids that bloom here still. Vine seedlings grew everywhere, covered by tough fibrous caps that helped the seedlings push through the vine mass to reach the sunlight.

The blue, violet, and deep green tones predominated on my Stromvi, but shades of lavender, pink, and pale yellow-green were not uncommon. The sky varied in color (depending on the time of day) from pale pink to lilac to blue. The sunlight tended to be diffuse due to the high resin content in the air. When Birk Hodge arrived, the sky was a misty lavender.

My honored mother carried me carefully across the fine moss of the tunnel mouth, for the resin coating of my hide was still too thin to thwart the thorns and poisons of Stromvi's uncertain surface. My mother raised her strong upper torso tall to hold me and to enable me to see across the vine mass, though my distant view was lined by seven-meter-tall lily spikes and the violet rapiers of magi reeds. I still spotted the hovercraft quickly, for my eyes had youth's flexibility. I trembled and buried my head in the thick, warm folds of my mother's neck ridge. I recall the spicy reassurance of her resin-scents.

I heard the steady clicking of my people and knew they found no cause to fear, but the surface world's openness was still new and awful to me. The shining hovercraft approached from terrifying distances of emptiness, and I dreaded it. My hind teeth, small and recently formed, clattered my distress.

My mother tried to comfort me into silence. The hovercraft settled heavily into a bed of cling weeds, until the pilot dome of the ship's ivory shell barely cleared the thick foliage. Though the ship's door slid open, the weeds impeded the exit of the man who had come to claim his chosen realm. I had never seen a man of any species but my own. His white thatch of hair fascinated me and distracted me from my complaints.

I could not understand his words, for I was very young and did not yet know the Consortium's trade speech. Mister Birk's pride and confidence, however, required no such uncertain form of communication. The scent of his ambition had crossed the still smooth skin of my head. I did not understand completely what I perceived, but I recognized a new authority in my life.

I dreamed that night of the hollow cavern nymph.

*   *   *

I cannot gauge the length of Mister Birk's journey from Rea to Hodge Farm. With ironic unity of vision, both he and Akras initially pursued much the same course to rebuild their shattered lives. Both exploited the Rea knowledge of smugglers' names and smugglers' lairs, but Mister Birk made a point of becoming known as a growing power among the lawless, while Akras used mystery and secrecy to veil her clan's advancement. Akras' method succeeded more slowly, but she eventually surpassed Mister Birk in her terrible influence, reaching a tier above him without ever letting him learn that the Rea yet survived.

I am not adept at estimating the age of those who are not Stromvi, and I never thought to ask when I had the opportunity. As a youngling, I had little interest in the ages of Mister Birk's children, for they seemed disdainful and disinterested in any Stromvi. I have imagined that Akras developed her slow vengeance for thirty spans, for that is considered a reasonable age of maturity for many of the species which are similar to the Soli, and the sons of Akras were indeed strong warriors by the time I met them.

To me, those strange, bipedal creatures, whom we long knew only as Soli, were as much a part of my world as silver-lilies and osang snakes. By the time I emerged from the caverns of my own volition, Mister Birk and his Soli workmen had cleared a plot of Stromvi land down to the clay. The scar on my planet was small, and I was too young and simple to question it. Others of my people grumbled, until my honored father sanctioned the project openly.

My father's curiosity as a horticulturist may have led him to appreciate the Hodge experiment with Soli flora, or he may have known (or deduced) more about Birk Hodge than he ever told me. He may have feared the consequences of refusal. The Consortium's inquisitors would form their own conclusions eventually, but I do not share their understanding of perfect Sesserda Truth.

My honored father's reasons did not matter to the people of the Ngenga Valley, who trusted him implicitly: His word sufficed. The Stromvi in other enclaves made no complaint. I realized only in later spans how far my honored father's influence extended.

Within our local year (a length of time slightly longer than the Calongi span), Hodge Farm occupied the largest part of the Ngenga Valley. Within the second year, Mister Birk completed the monstrosity that he called a house, and most of the local people worked his fields instead of their own. He brought his house servants from Deetari, for no Stromvi would enter that foolish Soli-style dwelling.

Mister Birk's son and daughter joined him shortly after the serving staff arrived. I never saw their Soli mother, but I did not question the reasons for her absence, until the time of change made me doubt all that I had accepted previously as true. Since the Soli genes dominated, Calem and Sylvie had no obvious Essenji traits, and Mister Birk had deliberately altered his own appearance. In any case, I did not subject the people—either the species or the individuals—to existential consideration. I was never introspective or philosophically inclined as a child.

As a youngling, I recognized only dimly that the Stromvi environment was naturally uncomfortable for a species as alien as the Soli. Although adaptation fluid enables its users to live in virtually any Consortium environment, the fluid guarantees only health, not comfort, in severe climes. Until unpleasant personal experience educated me regarding the fluid's limitations, I did not fully realize the improbability of an honest Soli trades-man (such as I long considered Mister Birk to be) choosing to live on Stromvi.

Mister Birk created Hodge Farm for his own dark, compelling reasons, while Akras watched, prepared, and waited with unholy patience: This much I heard from Akras herself, and I trusted her in this matter, though in little else. I have never doubted her pain. When she spoke of her past, her eerily self-absorbed voice acknowl-edged her private, tormented reality with unwavering conviction. Even I felt the power of her absolute belief in her own vision.

In its relativley brief existence, Hodge Farm became well known among those who cherish the rare flowers that originated on planets outside the Consortium's bounds. I would credit my honored father as the primary reason for such success, but I must admit that Mister Birk provided the impetus and initial inspiration. We Stromvi had previously traded only our vine weavings for Consortium goods.

Flower breeding may seem an odd vocation for a for-mer Rea warrior, smuggler, and pirate, but exotic flow-ers are affordable chiefly by the very rich and very powerful. Mister Birk knew whom to cultivate. He had patterned his ambitions after the single Soli who shared (with two Cuui) the ability to produce and market adaptation fluid outside of Consortium control. The Soli's name was Per Walis, and his concubines enjoyed Soli roses.

Those who doubt that such purveyors of injustice could coexist with the Consortium should recall that I knew these people, and I witnessed the results of their terrible schemes. They live on the fringes of the Consortium, trying to snatch pieces of the Consortium's privileges without yielding to Consortium law. Few of them succeed for long, but the lawless aspirants are numerous, and Consortium law respects even the cultures of those uncivilized Level VII's—up to a point. Rarely do the schemes of Level VII's impinge on the rights of a Level V people, such as Stromvi. Level VII's generally attack their own peers or the Level VI's of like species.

I understand why the Calongi confer special honor on those who are capable of teaching the least civilized Consortium members, the Level VI's, and the high honor is not accorded solely for facing the real dangers of Level VI and Level VII crime. The constant exposure to uncivilized ideas is itself unsettling. My revered father knew more about Mister Birk and the Rea than anyone outside their clan, and my father confided much in me before the end. To my sorrow, even he acknowledged the possibility that his own concepts of justice may have suffered from familiarity with Birk Hodge. The legatee of the infamous Mirelle of Attia told me chilling stories of her own family and Per Walis. Am I less wise for having listened to her all those spans ago?

I have missed Tori, Mirelle's great-granddaughter, despite her uncomfortable ability to make truth seem fluid and inconstant. When I met her, Tori was little more than a youngling herself, but she had lived so much more vividly than I—as a youngling, I was foolish enough to envy her. I considered Tori a friend, though I did not claim to understand her. I did not expect to understand a Soli.

As I have aged and watched my children's children grow, I have often wished that I could tell Tori how much her friendship meant to me. Perhaps my alienness

from my own people has made me feel closer to the
friends of my youth, irrespective of species or even civilization level. Without Tori's candor in those final days
before the change, I would have been unable to fulfill
my purpose of remembering. Life-purpose, after all,
makes us civilized. On this, at least, my honored father
and the Calongi agreed.

CHAPTER 3

They had named her Victoria, either from a peculiar sense of humor or from stubborn optimism, but they had abbreviated the name early to Tori, apparently abandoning their initial hopes for her. Tori had little clear notion of who "they" were—Mama was only Mama. As a child, Tori had found the plurality of reference mildly disturbing. No one had ever been willing to enlighten Tori regarding "their" identities, and she had stopped asking at an early age. She concluded eventually that "they" had included Great-grandmama Mirelle, but she preferred not to speculate further.

Tori's peculiarly matriarchal genealogy included no official secondary name except Mirelle, as it excluded any reference to male participation in the act of her creation. For most of her life, Uncle Per had supplied her with both the needs and luxuries of existence, but Tori did not mistake his purpose for fatherly concern. He was her mother's patron, and the terms of Tori's care through childhood were specified succinctly in the written contract of patronage.

Beyond childhood, the extent of Uncle Per's obligations became nebulous. Nothing would require him to permit Tori's return after her stormy departure two spans ago. Even if the inquisitors did not sentence her to penitential service on some unpleasant, isolated Consortium world, she would be little more than a penurious refugee.

Tori suppressed her sigh, for inquisition had made her very leery of giving outward indications of her thoughts or feelings, even when sitting in apparent solitude. The peculiarities of Tiva disorder made her unconscious physical reactions much less predictable—hence, less informative—than those of a normal Soli woman, but gestures and facial expressions still required conscious control.

She had known about her rare Tiva condition, of course, or she would never have attempted the impossible feat of trying to circumvent Consortium justice. She had concealed truth from the extraordinary perceptions of four Calongi inquisitors, but the improbability of what she had done astounded her.

The inquisitors could still judge her guilty. They still controlled her future and her life. Without a verdict, she would never be free of them, and she doubted that she would be free at all once the verdict was complete.

The fifth inquisitor would come soon. His meticulous arrangement of this meeting revealed nothing of his conclusions or his progress in evaluating Tori's case. He had already devoted a full local month to the precise, indefatiguable inquisitor's process of examining her, observing her with that nerve-racking Calongi thoroughness, and evaluating both her perceptions of truth and the absolute Truth of Sesserda. She thought she should have gained confidence with each Calongi who informed her that no clear verdict had become manifest. Each new inquisitor, however, made her more aware of the isolation she had imposed on herself; each new process of inquisition made her own knowledge of truth a little harder to bear.

Tori stared at the wallpaper's watery print, the landlady's faded effort at gentility. The blues, composed of old, imperfect dyes, had become uneasy shades of pink. Yellowed stains marred the wall's lower half. Only a hint remained of the mural's scene of shallow-running ships with their ghostly, ballooning sails. The ships appeared empty, for the blurring of time had stolen the detail from any figures that might once have crossed that pallid sea.

Tori had thought it would be easier to hear the verdict in the relatively familiar surroundings of her landlady's parlor. She had remembered the room as disheveled but benign. She had thought the inquisitor's offer to come to her this time might be an act of kindness. She should have known better, she concluded with a shudder. This room, worn and unkept, was made for fear.

Fear is for fools, Victoria. Fear is never for us.

"Yes, Great-grandmama," replied Tori to the image in her mind. She tightened her small, finely boned fists in her lap. She raised her head slightly, and she forced herself to see another room, more than half her life ago:

a clean, pale, elegant room; herself, a dark-haired, restless child with thin legs dangling from the edge of a high, stiff chair; the proud, exquisitely ageless woman who was Great-grandmama Mirelle. That single, uncannily memorable meeting with her infamous great-grandmother remained the strongest image that Tori's mind could summon to overcome the present.

"I'm glad that you don't fear me, Victoria," murmured the recollection of Great-grandmama Mirelle with the famous half-smile and clear, green eyes that seemed perpetually suggestive of exotic secrets. "Rosalinde has always feared me."

A young, frightened woman in a dilapidated room duplicated Mirelle's half-smile, but in her memory she became again the dark-haired girl who answered with an incongruously mature cynicism, "Mama has pretended to be helpless and mindless for so long, she has forgotten how to be anything else."

"Rosalinde has her wiles, but she has never been as independent as I hoped. I overestimated her father's intelligence." Mirelle shrugged, grace blending with sensuality in even that small movement. The girl observed, recalling lessons that made such mannerisms instinctive. "Adele wanted him, and I made the mistake of indulging her."

"Did Grandmama fear you?"

"Adele did not fear anyone."

"Did you kill her?"

Mirelle arched one finely tilted eyebrow. "Adele died of her own scheming, not of mine. Who suggested to you that I killed my own daughter?"

The girl shrugged. The gesture, despite her immaturity, bore a remarkable similarity to Mirelle's. "Your enemies never live long, do they? Everyone knows that you argued with Grandmama before she died."

"Does 'everyone' know why we argued?" asked Mirelle.

"Grandmama accused you of murdering her first daughter."

"Adele's first daughter died unborn," said Mirelle very softly.

"Grandmama said you opened the incubator and tried to substitute your own clone, but someone stopped you before you could finish."

"Adele was never able to admit that her child was defective," sighed Mirelle, but the half-smile did not waver. "You are precocious, Victoria, but you should be more cautious with your speculations. Full cloning is illegal in the Consortium, and destroying one's own granddaughter would require a particularly hardened attitude. Do you believe that I am capable of such actions?"

"Mama says you're capable of anything that you consider necessary."

"I am a survivor," admitted Mirelle, "but you must believe that I have done nothing for reasons of cruelty, even against those who have treated me most harshly. Never allow anyone to make you ashamed of me, Victoria. . . ." Her smile became pensive, as she added, ". . . or of yourself."

"Uncle Per says you're very rich and very powerful."

"I am very powerful, and I've been very rich as often as I've been very poor." She touched the clear, sparkling stones of the choker at her neck. "Your Uncle Per would be disappointed to learn how few of my jewels are real these days. The cost of survival increases significantly with every passing span, and the cost of perpetuity is higher still."

"You're not very poor now, are you?" asked the girl with a faint frown, for Great-grandmama had always been described to her in terms of invincibility.

"No," laughed Mirelle. "You have no concept of poverty, do you, Victoria? I hope you never learn that lesson for yourself. When you remember it some day, be proud of what you have achieved."

"How shall I remember something I've never learned?"

"Has it never happened to you before?" asked Mirelle solemnly.

"No," replied the girl in puzzlement.

Mirelle's eyes closed briefly, and a fleeting frustration made the fine contours of her face seem indomitable. The enticing sense of softness returned quickly. "Never mind, Victoria. At least the cost of your education hasn't been wasted. I'm pleased that you seem to have benefitted as I hoped, despite Per's unfortunate efforts to make you dependent on him. You must never depend on anyone but yourself, Victoria. Don't repeat my mistakes." The girl swung her legs with childish impatience at an injunction she considered irrelevant, and Mirelle sighed, "You are so young. Did I wait too long?"

"If you had visited us earlier, I would have been younger still."

"I was advised not to visit you at all," replied Mirelle, "because the future should not envy the past, and the present should not be burdened with the future. I heeded that advice, until I reminded myself that I know you better than anyone else, and I knew that you would be strong enough to face me and learn from me. We are alike, Victoria. We are both survivors."

A young woman in a room with stained wallpaper echoed, "We are both survivors," and she tried to believe in that fragment of a cryptic conversation. Greatgrandmama had never clarified her purpose for that visit, and she had died shortly thereafter. Tori still felt that something significant had been left unsaid and incomplete: something, perhaps, that could have averted the misery of the present or, at least, could have enabled her to feel less oppressively alone.

The door beside the faded mural, its automated mechanism long broken, squeaked open. Master Omi, the most recent of Tori's five inquisitors, entered. She had heard that he was a musician by profession, and the nearby planet where he was to perform now awaited the end of this unusually difficult inquisition. *Little disruptions trouble many lives,* thought Tori, *because of Arnod, because of me.* She wondered if her Calongi inquisitor resented the interruption of his personal plans, or if his species' religious tenets of Sesserda made the duty of inquisition a source of satisfaction to him. Deciphering any emotion in a Calongi was generally a futile effort for those Consortium members defined by the Calongi as "less civilized."

Covered by the layered cape of varied length appendages, attached in rings at the neck and mid-torso, the Calongi appeared unrelievedly dark and grim, though a faint iridescence seemed to follow his graceful movements. Individually, the outer arms resembled thin, smoothly tapered cylinders, but collectively they gave a distinct illusion of solid, velvety fabric, broken only by the golden collar of neck tendrils. Well over two meters in height, Master Omi was the tallest of the five Calongi who had questioned Tori, and the two prominent eye-mounds atop his large head barely cleared the doorway. The short, gold cilia on the ridges above his eyes bent to avoid the lintel.

The Calongi nose and mouth were placed like the corresponding Soli parts, but the angular, uptilted Calongi nose contributed significantly to the species' general appearance of arrogance. Master Omi's blue sense triangles, situated at each side of his head, were unusually pronounced, and the matrix of blue sensor patches covering the dark skin of the large back-skull, the braincase, was exceptionally orderly. The Calongi's eyes, each a blue orb surrounding a catlike slit, did not turn obviously toward his subject of inquisition, but Tori did not mistake that lack of focus for inattentiveness. Sight was only one of the ninety-six Calongi senses.

"As my honored colleagues informed me, your case is unusual, Miss Mirelle," observed Master Omi in a very even voice, courteously constrained to accommodate the limited senses of a Soli woman. "I have never encountered a victim of Tiva disorder before. It is, of course, a rare condition, and I have little regular contact with species below Civilization Level III. Criminal inquisition is very rarely required for beings above Level VI." The quiet remark carried no weight of condemnation, but its detached assumption of superiority emphasized the relentless force that was Consortium justice.

The Calongi—and a few, exceptional members of other species—fulfilled their Sesserda faith by performing inquisitions, as needed. The inquisitors judged many issues in the Consortium, a very small percentage of which involved crimes, deliberate offenses against fellow beings. Most judgments involved discernment of the rightness of a given goal or course of action, often for an entire planet or people. Requests for individual judgments were always honored for Level V and above, since such beings did not make frivolous demands. A Level VI needed to provide substantiating evidence or testimony. Tori wondered how many of her argumentative neighbors had united to accuse her.

"I didn't choose to be born with Tiva disorder," answered Tori, hoping that she sounded as poised and sure of herself as Great-grandmama Mirelle, "just as I didn't choose to find my husband murdered."

Master Omi did not reply. He stood in a protracted silence that Tori made no effort to interrupt, though every added microspan of waiting exacerbated her nervousness. The Calongi would observe her according to his own judgment and timing, and she had learned that any effort to distract him would be ignored or turned to her own discomfort. She counted the faded threads of the weaving that covered the arm of her chair.

"Sesserda Truth creates Consortium law, which produces Consortium peace," said Omi at last, "and only the uncivilized fail to respect the Calongi species-purpose that makes that law possible."

" 'Respect creation,' " replied Tori, "is the basic premise of Sesserda, isn't it?" She hated these inevitable philosophical digressions, but she had also learned that the implicit moral condemnations ended faster if she responded to them.

The Calongi inclined his head in an acknowledgment tailored to the Soli woman's culture and perceptions. "Respect for Consortium law is the crucial difference between Level VI Consortium members and their species' Level VII counterparts, to whom Consortium freedom and the benefits of Consortium science and arts are, of course, denied."

"We all know why inquisitors don't need walls to imprison their subjects," answered Tori dryly. "Not even a marginally civilized Level VI like me jeopardizes Consortium membership lightly."

Master Omi's cold voice became ominously stern, and it seemed to shake the walls though he did not speak loudly: "Direct defiance of Sesserda judgment in an official inquisition constitutes a very severe Consortium offense."

He uses a Calongi vocal trick to provoke a betraying reaction from me, Tori told herself, but the fear inside her tightened despite her awareness of his technique. The true inquisition was beginning again; she had hoped that it had ended. "Tiva disorder is a physical abnormality," answered Tori, "not an indication of defiance." When Omi became silent again, she wondered helplessly what new factor he had added to the weight against her.

Tori had been raised by nominal Consortium members of distinctly non-Consortium origins, but *she* had been educated according to Consortium standards. Tori had long recognized the rarity of her own upbringing, finely divided between outward Consortium membership and private lawlessness, but until inquisition, she had not appreciated the precariousness of such a position. Tiva disorder allowed her to deceive the Calongi to a certain extent, but it did nothing to mitigate the Calongi's intimidating effect. Her apparent ability to evade Consortium justice perversely made her feel more guilty, and she had the unsettling suspicion that the inquisitors were cognizant of that particular reaction.

"Judgment of the crime against Arnod Conaty will remain incomplete," decreed Master Omi with toneless, terrible dispassion, and Tori had to shake herself to hear his words as anything but condemnation. "Your files, Miss Mirelle, will contain the fact of inquisition without resolution."

"The inquisition is ended?" asked Tori uncertainly. This sudden decree, though she had heard it four times before, still stunned her. Master Omi's words were the best that she could have expected to hear, but they left her with an aching sense of abandonment. Consortium justice should be perfect; Consortium justice should be complete; or Uncle Per was right, and Consortium justice was only Calongi conceit.

"This is my final verdict," answered Master Omi.

"Will you hand my case to another inquisitor now?"

"Five is sufficient for this purpose."

The breath seemed to catch in Tori's throat, for inquisition had relentlessly dictated her life for the half-span since Arnod had died. Somewhere before inquisition, a more innocent Tori had existed: not a particularly content young woman, but someone who had imagined that her Consortium privileges were irrevocable. "Am I free to leave here?"

"You are as free as your capabilities allow." As Master Omi turned to leave, his outer arms swayed, revealing just a glimmer of the brightly iridescent limbs beneath the dark drapery. He moved soundlessly into the dingy hall and out of Tori's view.

Tori felt too leaden to rise from the chair. Instead of

relief, doubts filled her. She had no money, thanks to
Arnod. She had no job, thanks to the uncertain outcomes
of five inquisitions. She had no purpose.

The landlady, a stringy Soli woman who had enjoyed
Arnod's insincere flattery, thrust her pinched face into
the room. "Master Omi tells me your inquisition has
ended. I'd appreciate your leaving now," she said
brusquely. With a nervous, sputtering gesture, the landlady patted the tight, red curls that covered her head
thickly. "I've another tenant waiting for that apartment
of yours."

Tori made a conscious effort to appear unflustered,
although she had not even considered where she might
go once the inquisitors freed her. "How could I bear to
leave a place with so many fond memories?" asked Tori,
donning her best imitation of Mirelle's irony.

"I suppose you're cold enough to want to stay living
where your husband was murdered," said the landlady
sourly.

Tori's smile had a bitter twist, but she pulled herself
to her feet and joined the landlady in the doorway. Tori
experienced an odd sense of confronting a newly diminished world. Tori was not tall, but the landlady had acquired a significant stoop since Arnod's death: Inquisition
had aged even those who had endured only its fringes.
Tori tried to remember the woman's small, friendly gifts
of fruits and gossip in kindlier days. "You're disappointed that the inquisitors didn't find me guilty, aren't
you?"

"Calongi know best about guilt," conceded the landlady grudgingly, "but they don't say I have to trust you."

With a pretense of calm amusement, Tori smiled at
the woman. "I'll leave in a few days. I need to make
some travel arrangements first." She did not wait to hear
the landlady's further opinions, none of which were likely
to be positive.

As Tori moved down the hall, the landlady's nephew
slouched out of one of the apartments and crossed his
arms, liberally covered with machine grease. "Did Auntie
throw you out yet?" he demanded. He was a gangly
young Soli, who had always leered openly at Tori prior
to inquisition.

"Do you ever plan to repair the light panel in my living

room?" countered Tori with a cool gaze designed to make the recipient feel self-conscious and very young. In fact, he was older than Tori.

His expression became an ugly mix of discomfort and resentment. "I'm not entering that apartment while you live there."

"You needn't worry," answered Tori. "I only kill my husbands." She regretted her sarcasm when the young man retreated back into the apartment with the haste of very real consternation. "I was not found guilty," she protested belatedly, but he had closed the door and did not hear her.

* * *

On an early morning, fifteen millispans after her inquisition's end, Victoria Mirelle leaned against the white stone wall above the northern edge of Per Walis' estate. The morning smelled of sage and dust, the dryness so sharp that it cut through the inner passages of her body and burned her thirsty skin. She moistened her lips, but they felt hard and rough, and she rubbed the fleeting dampness from them before the air could steal it. The songs of the gray windbirds sounded shrill and demented. A plume of blue smoke rose above the uneven hills which hid the town.

Mama had greeted her very briefly last night, offering a nervous, dutiful kiss and a concerned suggestion as to possible patrons. In the repentant dawn, Tori regretted her own sharp retort, which had rekindled all the prickly feelings of the past. Rosalinde Mirelle was impervious to the barbs or blandishments of nearly anyone but Uncle Per and her own daughters, and Tori did not relish being part of the exception. Toward Lila, Mama's weakness took the form of excessive indulgence; toward Tori, Mama's sensitivity had always carried an unpleasant resemblance to the fear Mama had otherwise reserved solely for Great-grandmama Mirelle.

Tori unlatched the iron hook of the low gate. The rough timbers that formed the stairs down the slope were worn and twisted, and dark steel spikes had been driven through them, deep into the ground, to secure the uncertain footing. The stairway curved, veering slightly to the left. A narrow stretch of unclaimed, indeterminate soil divided the lowest step from the manicured expanse of clipped grass.

The barren ground felt harsh against her feet, and she leapt nimbly toward the lawn. The air shuddered as Tori crossed the unseen barrier and reentered Uncle Per's estate. The sudden scent of moisture shocked her, though she had spent far more of her life within the estate's sheltering bubble than outside in the planet's natural desert dryness. She shivered slightly and hurried across the lawn to the warmer woods.

Amber leaves dappled the mirror of a dusty rose dawn. The pond, circled by a ring of trees, defied disturbance, but a dragonfly touched dainty legs to the surface, and the mirror quivered. An orange sithrin unfolded its long wings and glided among trees the color of its vivid camouflage. The troubled air hummed through the sithrin's back-comb, as if protesting the presence of such alien life on Arcy.

A breeze, ripe with the tart odor of fallen autumn berries, transformed the pond's serene surface into a ladder work of dark shadows and bright sunlight, and the soft colors of the new morning fused with the garish desperation of the dying summer. On a planet without perceptible changes of season, the artifice seemed disrespectful.

Tori rocked forward on her feet, and she spread her arms, as if she would take flight with the sithrin and the dragonflies. She shook her thick, dark hair, tangled by too much prowling through the brush, leafy arches, and hollows of the garden's unkempt perimeter. An impish quickening of reckless eagerness peered from her green eyes, but the eagerness retreated hastily, battered by the resurgent habit that recent experience had built.

Reckless enthusiasm had cost too high a price when it alit on Arnod Conaty. Even here in the overly guarded refuge of Uncle Per's gardens, inescapable memories woven tightly from skeins of grief, frustration, and regret cast their pall across her. Tori lifted her chin, defying the past: Determination still maintained its spark within her. She had survived Arnod and the shame he had heaped upon her. She had survived the realization of his death. She had even survived the Calongi inquisition.

The awareness of survival had added an untamed, unconquerable quality to a face that had once seemed too meticulously formed to shelter any substance of thought or emotion. Tori had inherited the lissome beauty of Mirelle in uncannily complete measure, but she had nothing of the helpless quality that characterized her mother and half-sister. Nothing about the family trade offended her more than the pretense of submissiveness. Nothing frustrated her more than the true helplessness that had now forced her return to Per Walis' protection.

Never depend on anyone but yourself, Victoria.

"I know, Great-grandmama," murmured Tori. "But how shall I live when no Soli in the Consortium will hire me, shelter me, or endure my company? Only someone as uncivilized as Uncle Per seems likely to accept an unacquitted subject of inquisition."

Tori let her arms drop heavily to her sides, and she thrust her hands into the wide pockets of the wine-colored jacket that hung to her knees. With strong strides, she crossed the uneven ground to the pond's edge. Her bare feet skidded on a patch of rotting brown berries, and the soft mud at the pond's edge engulfed her toes. The pond retained its illusion of balmy summer, for a heated spring fed the water's depths at Uncle Per's command. The water butterflies required a carefully controlled environment, which deviated pleasantly from the temperature variations of the estate's synthetic seasons.

"What are you thinking, Tori?" demanded the girl who sat cross-legged on the graying, bentwood bench beside the pond.

Tori's wind-reddened lips curled into a smile of irony that robbed her of her look of youthful innocence. A similar expression adorned the most valued of Mirelle's portraits. "I was thinking how much I love this place and how much I hate it."

"Why do I even talk to you? I never understand you," complained the girl on the bench, and she stretched her knit cap across her auburn bangs and peered at Tori from the cap's shadow.

"You seem to understand Uncle Per," replied Tori, "which bests any achievement of mine."

"You try too hard to understand him, when you should simply appreciate him."

Tori exhaled in a ragged laugh. "I have trouble appreciating hypocrites, Lila."

"Don't start again," sighed Lila.

Tori turned from the pond to glance sidelong at her half-sister. "Uncle Per claims to respect Consortium law, but his ideas of justice are restricted to anything that serves him. This estate, which he calls a preserve, is an offense against every aspect of this planet's native life. Uncle Per prides himself on being a civilized member of the Consortium, but he still refers to his species as 'human' instead of 'Soli,' as if he had never taken the vow of membership, as if he still identified himself more closely with lawless 'humans' than with fellow Consortium beings, as if the rest of the Consortium's members were somehow inferior to him. I don't know how many people's lives he regularly destroys, but I know that his concept of a life-purpose consists of maximizing his personal comfort at the expense of anyone or anything else. If Consortium justice were as perfect as the Calongi pretend, Uncle Per would be the inquisitors' subject." *But I am the one they dissect,* Tori thought bitterly, *because Sesserda Truth is pure but pitiless, and Uncle Per is far too cautious to let accusations rise against him.*

"I was glad when I heard that you were coming home," grumbled Lila, "because I've been lonely, but you've become very poor company. I don't know why you blame your failures on Uncle Per. He doesn't owe you anything. You chose to leave us and live in poverty, instead of waiting for Mama to arrange a sensible contract of patronage for you. Uncle Per didn't need to accept your unrepentant request to return."

"Mama has pleased him for many spans," replied Tori dryly. "She is an uncommonly skillful concubine, and Uncle Per still hopes that I may inherit both the family gifts and his personal patronage."

"You're disgusting and unfair." Lila unfurled her long legs. Dry leaves crackled beneath the weight of her slim feet. "Don't forget that Mama expects you to accompany us into town this morning. She's already invited two prospective patrons here, and you certainly won't impress them with those rags that you call a wardrobe. A patron would be more likely to want me, and I'm not even old enough yet to be legally available." Lila began to walk up the slope toward the house, her movements as delicate as her youthful features.

"If I wanted a patron, I could negotiate my own contract!" shouted Tori, but Lila pretended not to hear the pained retort. Tori sloshed the mud from her feet and climbed the crumbling slope to the level path. She slumped onto the bench that Lila had vacated and considered how wretchedly she had mangled her life.

Tori could remember impersonally that day when she had first met Arnod in the town, but she could not even imagine how she had actually felt at the time. He had paid attention to her and not to Mama or Lila, but Tori could not fathom why his interest in her had mattered. A surplus of masculine attention had pursued her since the first time she smiled at a man—not because of her own charms, she felt sure, but for the notoriety of the family that she represented. Perhaps that was the reason he had attracted her: Arnod in his unabashed ignorance had never heard of Mirelle of Attia.

With a pang of embarrassment, Tori recalled writing a maudlin letter to Mama about loving Arnod Conaty too much to live without him. In a brief moment of panic, Tori considered running to the house to awaken Mama and to learn the letter's fate. Calmer reasoning revived, and Tori decided that the letter could not even cause much harm to her ego at this point. Having been stripped emotionally bare by the inquisitors, Tori concluded that she had no pride left to injure.

Arnod had abused and taken advantage of Tori from the day they left Arcy, and Tori could no longer feel anything more charitable toward him than sporadic pity for his weaknesses. She would have preferred to convince herself that she had only married Arnod in order to escape from Arcy and Uncle Per, but she knew that she had not been nearly that smart. At some inconceivable time, she had actually believed that Arnod cared about her: about her, Tori, and not about Mirelle.

"Worst of all," she murmured to the pond, "I had to prove myself more civilized than my family: I had to insist on a legal life-marriage rather than a contract of patronage." She picked up a clump of soft, russet berries and hurled them into the pond. She watched the ripples that told of water butterflies rushing toward the fruit. "If not for that ghastly silenen thong, I might have spent the rest of my spans slaving to support him and enduring his boastful infidelities."

She wanted to be glad that Arnod was dead, but she could only feel sorry that nothing had occurred as she had hoped. She wanted to be completely free of him, but he tormented her even from the fiery tomb of an alien sun. She had crawled back to Mama and Uncle Per in desperation because the Sesserda justice of the Calongi inquisitors would not let her escape herself. Lila, whose deepest thoughts generally concerned her own welfare, was right: Uncle Per deserved more gratitude than Tori had given him.

"He worries that I've observed too much over the spans and drawn the correct conclusions about his unlawful business dealings," muttered Tori to herself, but she remained ashamed of her recent attitude. Despite his many flaws of character, Uncle Per had always been kind to his concubines and their children.

In a rueful mood, Tori sprang to her feet and climbed toward the house. She overtook Lila, who had stopped within the arbor to stare through a narrow opening in the thick, green vines and yellow berry clusters. Peering through the tangle at her sister's side, Tori could see a narrow segment of Mama's rose garden. A bulky, mottled blue-and-violet shape with six stout legs waddled across Tori's view, and Tori jumped slightly in surprise.

The strange, vaguely reptilian being drew himself upright to a height of a meter and a half, and Tori realized that the front two limbs were actually arms. Shovel-shaped hands ended in fingers that appeared to be partially retractable, each finger tipped by a nail that looked wickedly sharp and strong. The hands, as well as the front feet had opposing thumbs, and the being was using all four of the front limbs in a dexterous process of measuring the garden plot and simultaneously marking in a small notebook.

"It's only a Stromvi," whispered Lila, relishing her moment of superior knowledge. "He delivered the new roses, and he's overseeing the planting."

"Why are you spying on him?" asked Tori, matching her sister in conspiratorial softness. "I thought you shared Uncle Per's loathing for all-things-not-Soli."

"I'm not spying on the Stromvi." Lila pulled her sister over to the better vantage point. "I'm spying on *him*."

Lila indicated a trim, muscular man, who seemed to be a Soli, though his shock of hair was as startlingly white as his shirt and trousers. His deeply tanned face, strong and ageless, had a subtly golden tinge. The man conversed with the Stromvi, who folded his thick arms and nodded his massive, violet head solemnly. Even without the evidence of the Stromvi's respectful attention, the Soli conveyed the absolute confidence of an established leader.

"Who is he?" asked Tori, relinquishing her view reluctantly, as Lila reclaimed her original position. Lila's surreptitious watching seemed childish, but Tori admitted that the man was a compelling and unexpected figure to find on Uncle Per's secluded, jealously guarded estate—almost as unexpected as the Stromvi.

"His name is Birk Hodge," answered Lila, oblivious to the ridiculous spectacle that she presented, hunched before a peephole in an overgrown arbor. "He sells us roses. The Stromvi works for him. Wonderful, isn't he?"

"Why don't you go talk to him, instead of creeping through the bushes to observe him secretly?"

"Mama would turn me into rose mulch! You know how she's always felt about us talking to day workers, and your little escapade has made her that much worse."

Tori answered impatiently, "You're not a child, Lila." Reminders of Arnod were unbearable; remembrance was too bitter. "Neither am I." Tori strode from the arbor and headed toward the two men, Soli and Stromvi. The mottled Stromvi sensed her first, lifting his broad head and testing the air to identify the approaching scent.

A knot of nervousness formed in Tori's stomach, but she raised her chin proudly and approached the men without hesitation. She concentrated on the Stromvi's hide patterns, which were far brighter and more intricate than she had first realized: Interlocking diamonds and chevrons covered a smooth hide, richly contoured with knobs and thick joint ridges. The hide had an almost jewellike depth of light, as if the Stromvi's entire body were encased in layers in sapphire and amethyst, occasionally punctuated with emerald.

"You need not fear me," said the Stromvi, sparing

Tori the awkwardness of arriving so determinedly with nothing to say. His two shining black eyes, though seemingly undersized for his bulk, brimmed with kindly earnestness.

"I don't fear you," replied Tori, gaining courage from the denial.

The Stromvi issued a low, rhythmic series of clicking sounds from his throat, and thick lids slowly covered and uncovered the sympathetic eyes. Birk Hodge smiled and murmured, "The Stromvi people are generally very sensitive to the scents of Soli emotions, but perhaps Ngoi is confused by his recent adaptation inoculation."

Ngoi murmured a courteous agreement, and he sighed expressively in a deep, rasping rush of spicy breath: "I apologize for making personal comments irresponsibly. I have no manners."

"I apologize for my thoughtless reaction," answered Tori. The Stromvi bared a fearsome expanse of teeth: Very long, very close fitting, very numerous, the white teeth seemed to dominate the massive, knobbed head. Tori recoiled instinctively, before she realized that the Stromvi was merely imitating a Soli smile. She began to laugh at herself in embarrassment. "I apologize again. We live an inexcusably sheltered existence on Arcy."

"As we do on Stromvi," replied Birk Hodge. His eyes—an amber color with golden highlights—seemed to be making a very thorough assessment of Tori, but the inspection was too impersonal to be offensive. "Are you the lady whose discriminating taste in gardens has brought us here?"

"The roses are for Rosalinde Mirelle," answered Tori, her cheeks warming with resentment against Uncle Per's advice to deny her own family name whenever possible—until inquisition had faded measurably into the past. "I'm only a visitor here." *And I'm an unwelcome visitor, a visitor who has attracted too much official Consortium attention, a visitor awaiting Mama's imminent orders to leave on the arm of an unknown patron.* The recklessness in Tori roused defiantly at thought of that nameless patron whom she would be expected to coddle and embrace. "I was a junior administrator on Desda-3 until recently, but someone close to me died there, and I couldn't stay any longer. Would you be interested in hiring me, Mister Hodge?"

Birk Hodge seemed amused. The Stromvi, Ngoi, leaned forward to peer at Tori more closely, milky inner lids blinking across his black eyes. He clicked a sound that Tori imagined was surprise. Birk Hodge, despite a slightly cynical smile, responded soberly, "Have you any experience in horticulture?"

"No," answered Tori with forthright calm, "but I learn quickly, and I work hard."

"Did Per Walis ask you to speak to me?" asked Birk Hodge, and his amber eyes narrowed keenly.

"No," replied Tori quickly, wondering if Birk Hodge knew the dubious nature of Uncle Per's business ventures. "The idea was entirely my own." She presumed that a seller of roses would prefer to remain detached from Uncle Per's superficially legitimate enterprises, although Uncle Per did attract unhealthy interest from unexpected quarters. . . .

Birk's pensive nod reassured Tori only slightly. "You make an intriguing offer." Ngoi clicked briefly, but Birk raised a hand, and the Stromvi fell silent. "Do you know anything about the planet Stromvi?"

"Nothing."

"I thought not. Are you always this impulsive?"

"I seize promising opportunities when they arise," declared Tori firmly, and she displayed a confident smile.

"How would our mutual host, Per Walis, react if I accepted your offer?"

Uncle Per would react with less horror than Mama will feel, thought Tori, forbidding herself a very undignified urge to giggle. "He would be pleased that I had found fruitful employment."

The Stromvi touched her arm with the back of his hand. His skin felt cool and slick. "Mister Hodge is teasing you, young female," he informed her gently. "Soli do not adapt easily to my beautiful planet. You would not care to live there."

"I'm afraid that Ngoi is correct," admitted Birk, though his glance toward Ngoi carried a hint of irritation.

Tori shrugged. "The risk is mine. Consider my offer, Mister Hodge. You know where to find me: Ask for Tori Mir—." She amended quickly, "Tori Darcy." Most of

Uncle Per's dependents adopted the surname of Darcy. She was not sure that Uncle Per would appreciate her use of the name, but the Darcys of Arcy were so numerous that "Darcy" was nearly useless for identifying a specific individual. *Anyway,* reasoned Tori with a trace of smugness, *it was Uncle Per's idea that I use a name other than Mirelle.*

She left the two men watching her: the Soli with pensive amusement, the Stromvi with an unmistakable element of concern. When she had passed beyond the rise that separated the rose garden from the house, she sat on the soft, green lawn, pulled her fingers through her tangled hair, and began to laugh at her own outrageous nerve. Lila would be furious with envy.

CHAPTER 4

Scanning a carefully gathered file on Per Walis, Birk Hodge stopped at a picture of one of the most infamous concubines in Consortium history, and he began to smile. His memory had not betrayed him. He had seen the girl before. She was the image of Mirelle.

He continued scanning the file until he found the picture of Rosalinde Mirelle and her two daughters. An annotation said: Lila, age nine; Victoria, age fourteen. The picture, which had appeared in a local Arcy journal, was five spans old. The mother and the youngest daughter shared the same auburn hair and delicate form; the mother even seemed to have that daughter's childlike prettiness. The older girl, however, had Mirelle's striking coloring. Although she seemed just as delicately built as her sister, a sureness of posture and a directness in her green gaze left an impression of underlying steel.

Birk could recognize individual features of Mirelle in all three of her descendants, but only the older girl, Victoria, struck him as a worthy inheritor of Mirelle's legend. Victoria Mirelle was unquestionably Tori Darcy. The ramifications of the girl's improbable offer became even more intriguing to him.

Birk knew a great deal about the Mirelle family because he had spent a great deal of time studying Per Walis, seeking Walis' weaknesses. The concubines had offered the obvious point of access to the estate, for Per Walis indulged his concubines, particularly his favorites, such as Rosalinde Mirelle. A craving for exotic roses had been accommodated easily with the aid of Stromvi's gifted horticulturists.

Walis' fondness for expensive concubines had surprised Birk, though Per Walis' personal habits were recognized far more widely than the nature of Per Walis' business.

Birk understood a desire for heirs, but that did not seem to be the focus of Walis' interests. The concubines appeared to be simply a weakness, astonishing to Birk in a man of Per Walis' particular form of success.

Birk had followed Per Walis' career for many spans, of course, for Per Walis was the model upon whom Birk had based his ambitions since leaving the Rea. Over the spans, Birk had gained increasing appreciation for Per Walis' achievements. Birk had even attributed genius to Per Walis, since Birk had been unable to rise to Per Walis' level of influence, let alone surpass the Soli. As a smuggler, Birk had never even managed to meet anyone more significant than Per Walis' hirelings. Hodge Farm Roses had provided the long-sought introduction, where direct approaches had failed.

Birk gloated over his fellow smugglers, who had never discovered the true simplicity of reaching the unreachable Per Walis. Birk had only contempt for legitimate Consortium businessmen, who had never sought to exploit Stromvi's lucrative fount of opportunities. Stromvi's atmosphere was uncomfortable, but the people were absurdly compliant and cooperative. The good will of Per Walis was simply the most satisfying acquisition in an impressive string of Hodge Farm successes. Birk had never considered that exploitation of the Stromvi people might be viewed as uncivilized by educated Consortium members. Birk Hodge did not think in such terms.

To Birk, the most unexpected result of the Hodge Farm experiment had been the magnitude of the demand for the legitimate merchandise, which Birk had intended only as a means of access and as camouflage for illegal trade. The honest profits from the sale of a few custom-hybridized roses to Per Walis exceeded the past half-span's worth of less honorable takings and made the smuggling jobs that much easier to conceal. Since establishing Hodge Farm, Birk had lived quite extravagantly on the lawful proceeds, allowing him to stash his less orthodox earnings for a safe future.

Birk understood why few of the lawless ever profited simultaneously from legal and illegal trade: The hazards of masquerading as a Consortium member were real. The Calongi seldom exercised their civilization's full power, but the lawless told stories of entire planets that had

disappeared after treading too carelessly on Consortium
bounds of tolerance. Even Birk, though he posed as a
Consortium tradesman, did not try to claim the rights of
a true member. Since he had never taken the oath to
obey Consortium law, he depended on smugglers' fare
and smugglers' methods, enhanced only slightly by the
legitimate member-status of his children. Birk knew of
only one significant dealer in unlawful merchandise who
actually dared assume the full privileges—and risks—of
Consortium membership, and Birk envied Walis' courage
in making that great, dangerous lie.

Birk had found Per Walis to be an unimpressive little
man in person, but he admired the intelligent pragmatism
that characterized Walis' professional interests. Walis
knew his limits and never pressed them to the point of
attracting official Consortium attention. He also had the
foresight to eliminate sources of formal complaint before
such individuals could become troublesome.

Because of that ruthless practicality, dealings of any
sort with Per Walis did carry an element of personal hazard, but no mere Soli could intimidate an Essenji warrior
of the Rea clan. Extending a policy of caution toward
the powerful Calongi was good sense. Fearing a Soli,
even a man of Per Walis' influence, was absurd.

Fear was itself a contemptible thing. What Rea women
would slink behind the bushes like that auburn-haired
Soli girl, badly concealing her curiosity? Birk admired
the sister, Victoria, more for her bold approach in stating
what she wanted than for her remarkable resemblance to
the original Mirelle. She had surprised him; that was also
to her credit.

Birk wondered if fortune or design had led her to him.
In either case, the next move required careful thought.
Some legal trouble had reputedly driven the young
woman back to Arcy after a span's absence, and she
had obviously changed her name. Both facts were mildly
troubling, and Birk could not request Victoria Mirelle's
official Consortium record, since access to Prili data files
was the privilege of only true Consortium members. Birk
would never entrust such a delicate inquiry to either of
his children. Nonetheless, as daughter of Per Walis' favorite concubine and as great-granddaughter of Mirelle
of Attia, Miss Tori Darcy could not be dismissed lightly.

Birk contemplated the possibilities with growing satisfaction. Hodge Farm had provided a meeting with Per Walis, but Tori Darcy could open an entirely new level of opportunity. Birk had always intended to rival Per Walis, but Per Walis could be a formidable ally.

Birk presumed that Tori would seek a contract of patronage from him, since concubinage was her family's well-established and deservedly-profitable profession. The prospect appealed to him—the legends of Mirelle tantalized even the Essenji—but every legal Consortium contract carried a risk to a man whose only Consortium documents were falsified. The licensing of Hodge Farm had required delicate handling and considerable, expensive help from a talented Cuui forger.

Birk had no intention of entering into any valid Consortium agreement, which—if challenged—would commit him implicitly and irrevocably to Consortium law. Birk enjoyed the protection and profitability of Consortium society. He did not mean to shackle his own actions with the Calongi code of justice.

The idea of patronage disturbed him on an emotional level as well, though that was an issue that he refused to acknowledge. He had taken a Soli woman once before and regretted it. No Soli woman could ever be Akras.

No, he would evade the issue of patronage, at least until he could assure himself that Miss Darcy shared her family's tolerance for a successful independent. She had shown no impatience to discuss patronage, likely assuming that she could gain better contractual terms by delaying and encouraging desire to grow. Perhaps she had not yet decided how far she would commit herself. Perhaps she was measuring the degree of lawlessness that Birk Hodge would condone; Birk's smile returned at that thought.

A hesitant knock at the door of Birk's cabin interrupted his musings and caused him to replace his smile with a snarl of frustration. He did not like sharing his ship, though he needed workers to support his businessman's role. He disciplined his expression into blandness before releasing the door's lock.

The young Soli man still held his hand poised to knock again. He let the arm fall self-consciously, combing his fingers through his straight black hair, as if that gesture had been his original purpose. Thick, curling brows tilted expressively above blue eyes, mocking their owner's nervousness with a whimsy of their own.

"What do you want, Squire?" asked Birk mildly. He used the subtly taunting epithet that his son, Calem, had devised for the young man, the embarrassed scion of an ancient aristocracy.

"I want to talk to you about a message I received from Sylvie. She asked me not to communicate with her again while she is at the university."

Birk answered impatiently, "I do not dictate my children's lives." He did not intend to discuss the message, which he had sent in Sylvie's name. Since Sylvie had refused to terminate her attachment to Calem's friend, Birk had taken charge. Sylvie would learn that her father did not tolerate defiance, even from her.

The Squire replied dryly, "I thought you dictated everyone's lives, Mister Hodge."

"If sarcasm were a more marketable commodity, you might amount to something, Squire. Unfortunately, you mistake a caustic tongue for a weapon of strength."

The Squire crossed his lean arms, tanned by the potent Stromvi sun. "You told Sylvie to stay away from me, didn't you?"

"I asked you to educate my son, not court my daughter." Calem had always disappointed Birk, for he resembled his unlamented Soli mother, but Sylvie's attempted defection had been a blow. Birk would not relate any such personal sentiments to this presumptuous young man, who had inspired Sylvie's rebellion. Birk had hoped for worthy heirs, but he had never found another Akras to provide them. He had not even found another Essenji.

"I am your son's friend and your guest, not a hired worker," retorted the Squire, showing a glint of sensitive pride. "When Calem asked me to take his place on this journey, I agreed willingly. I did not expect you to treat me like your exploited Stromvi, while your son enjoys his holiday on Esprit-2 at my expense."

"For a bright young man, you have very little common sense. Did you come here to complain or to seek a favor from me?"

"Why have you ordered Sylvie to reject my messages to her?"

"Because you are weak-willed and devoid of ambition. My daughter needs strength around her, since she has none herself."

"I should have thought you had sufficient ambition for your entire family."

Birk smiled coldly. "You're lazy and ineffectual, but you're not unobservant. You may use that as my recommendation for your next employer. You're not returning to Hodge Farm."

"You can't fire me because I don't work for you. You may abandon me here, but don't expect to control my future. I shall see Sylvie and Calem when I please."

Irritated by the Squire's impertinence, Birk dropped his shallow pretense of civility. "Don't try to cross me, Squire, for you have no hope of surviving conflict with me. You will not return to Hodge Farm now or in the future. You will not see Sylvie or communicate with her in any way. You defied me once and turned my own daughter against me, but I shall not let her remain so misled. Because you have served me for a time, I am allowing you to leave unpunished, but do not mistake me for a forgiving man." Birk grabbed the Squire's wrist and squeezed it tightly, crushing the tendons. The young man cried out in protest. "I have destroyed far worthier enemies than you, Squire. I shall not tolerate a second offense." With a quick, apparently effortless gesture, Birk threw the young man hard against the far wall of the ship's narrow corridor.

The young man recovered himself stiffly, but he remained slightly hunched over his abused wrist. His blue eyes glared. "You've a damnable nerve," growled the Squire furiously. "I could demand official Consortium judgment against you for this attack. Sylvie and Calem would support my claim."

"Even if my children were treacherous enough to speak against me, no Calongi would condemn me for defending my daughter," scoffed Birk. "Your accusation is infantile and displays your ignorance of reality. That temper of yours makes you stupid. Leave my sight, or I shall break you now and discard the pieces." Birk made a slight, threatening motion in the Squire's direction, and the Squire scurried down the hall with a muttered curse.

Birk closed the door as he said, "You would not survive against the least of the Rea."

Birk frowned, for he had yielded to anger. He had not intended to clarify his position regarding the Squire until after the completion of the present job. The Squire was a useful worker.

Birk returned to the narrow desk that unfolded from the wall above his bunk, and he stared at the data film on which his transactions with Per Walis had been recorded. He had already passed the film through the scanner, and his account had been increased accordingly. But what use was the amassing of greater wealth and power without heirs capable of appreciating it? He had wanted to increase the might of the Rea, not provide toys and baubles for the likes of Calem, or for Sylvie and her pathetic Squire. Additional children appeared impossible, for Birk had used imperfect, illegal adaptation fluid too liberally for too many spans, and he had no intention of bequeathing his fortune to anyone but his own blood-kin.

Despite occasional rumors, all of his specific inquiries over the past spans indicated that he was the last of the Rea clan. He had buried the kree'va after concluding that it had extinguished his people. He had cursed the device, forgetting that it had merely obeyed his own command.

Birk shook himself mentally, disgusted with his sense of defeat. The Squire was a useless fool and nothing more. He did not represent any failure on the part of Birk Hodge. Birk began to word his approach to Per Walis on the delicate subject of expanded business dealings. A joint interest in Miss Tori Darcy might provide an excellent opening for discussion. . . .

CHAPTER 5

Tori seated herself on a rough timber step that became a little more buried by sand with every passing span. She had stood here this morning without a future. The yellow Arcy sun had now passed its zenith.

Since receiving a terse note of acceptance from Birk Hodge, Tori had been struggling to adjust to the reality of what she had begun. She saw Uncle Per crossing the lawn toward her, but she did not rise to meet him. She hugged her knees and wished that she could leave Arcy without this confrontation.

Per Walis had the padded look of many Soli men whose youthful muscles had turned to fat. He wore his brown hair clipped almost to his skull, and his trace of a mustache seemed to be little more than a smudge. His eyes were very dark and seemed to have no depth. His conventional Soli clothing always seemed rumpled, though platinum buttons adorned his blue silk shirt, and the fabric of his trousers was fine Atiri wool.

Uncle Per was panting slightly by the time he reached Tori, for his weight was approaching its cyclical peak again. He sank awkwardly to the step beside her, but there was no clumsiness in his brisk greeting: "Birk Hodge tells me that you have decided to become a horticulturist."

"I've accepted a job at Hodge Farm," answered Tori, wondering what she would do if Uncle Per actually ordered her not to leave Arcy. Contradicting Uncle Per was not a pastime to be practiced often.

Uncle Per nodded and rubbed his hands together thoughtfully. "I've dealt indirectly with Birk Hodge in the past. He may not be an ideal employer for you."

"He's willing to hire me."

Uncle Per examined Tori with a sardonic candor that

made her blush. "I'm sure he's very willing," answered Uncle Per, "because he's ambitious, but you can do better. I could negotiate an excellent contract of patronage for you, Tori, despite your recent indiscretion."

" 'Indiscretion' is a fine euphemism for a murdered husband."

"You could transform a patron's concerns into sympathy. Tell him of Conaty's cruelty to you, and you'll stir your patron's protective instincts."

"I know Great-grandmama's techniques," replied Tori a trifle bitterly, "but I don't want to use them. You still don't understand, do you? I married Arnod because I loathed having you arrange suitable lovers for me and letting me imagine that they came to me on their own. I made a mistake in trusting Arnod, but at least the mistake wasn't choreographed by you and Mama. I am so tired of being expected to relive the life of Great-grandmama Mirelle!"

"You are more like her than you realize. You have the same potential."

"But I do not have her limitations, unless I let you and Mama bind me in them. Great-grandmama had no education but what she gave herself on that lawless, independent planet where she was born. She learned her trade out of necessity, and I suppose I would have done the same, given her lack of alternatives. I have other choices."

"Such as what?" asked Uncle Per, and though his smile looked kindly it felt cruel. "Inquisition on a charge of murder is not a recommended means of establishing any traditional Consortium career. Your family is remarkably gifted in a very ancient, very proud craft, and you should not despise your natural attributes."

"Concubinage is hardly an accepted Sesserda life-purpose. It's a craft built on lust and lies. It's *wrong*, Uncle Per."

Per Walis sighed, but his smile lingered. "I thought you would surely have outgrown such naive ideas by now." He patted her hand. "You're still a child in many ways. We may have sheltered you too much. Perhaps a span or so with a man like Birk Hodge will be good for you. Your mother will be disappointed, but I'll speak to her."

Surprised by Uncle Per's easy capitulation, Tori forbore to retort about the "naïveté" of Calongi religious principles that were fundamental to Consortium law. "Thank you, Uncle Per," she murmured.

"I'll expect you to write regularly and tell us all about Hodge Farm." Uncle Per at his most congenial could allay nearly anyone's suspicions, but Tori found herself wondering why Uncle Per seemed so satisfied. Uncle Per shunned official Consortium attention zealously, but he had not suggested that her presence at his estate could present an immediate problem. "I've had some curiosity about this rose farm since Hodge began it," continued Per Walis with a slight, considering nod. "You know how much your mother admires roses."

"Are you interested in hearing about Hodge Farm or in seeing me depart?"

"You should follow Mirelle's example and learn to hide such cynicism, Tori." Uncle Per heaved himself to his feet. "Come to the house and talk to your mother. I don't like to see the two of you in conflict."

"Mama and I are always in conflict. I'll only hurt her feelings if I talk to her now."

"You'll hurt her more if you leave without a word. Come along." He extended his hand.

Tori accepted his warm, fleshy grip reluctantly. Even as a child, she had not relished being touched by Uncle Per. He always seemed to prolong the physical contact far too long.

True to precedent, Uncle Per continued to hold Tori's hand as they crossed the estate gardens to reach the low, sprawling house. When Mama emerged from an arched doorway, Uncle Per put his arm around Tori's waist. Mama's expression tightened briefly. Tori and Rosalinde Mirelle agreed on very little, but they had long shared an underlying dread that Uncle Per would transfer his attention from Rosalinde to her oldest daughter.

Rosalinde wore a sheer, flowery morning robe that showed her shapely figure to advantage. The rose scent of her perfume was potent, and her smile made silent promises to Uncle Per. Uncle Per released Tori and greeted Rosalinde with an intimate caress. Tori waited patiently to see if passion would, as usual, take precedence over maternal concern.

Rosalinde surprised her daughter. Or perhaps it was Uncle Per who decided to postpone his pleasure, for he separated from Rosalinde with only a trace of hesitation. "I've given Tori my approval," said Per simply. Without a glance at Tori, Uncle Per entered the house.

Rosalinde rubbed her bare arms. "I wish Per had let the summer last a little longer."

"Maybe you should leave the estate more often," suggested Tori. "The rest of Arcy is warm enough."

"The Arcy climate is terrible for the skin." Rosalinde felt her taut jawline, hunting for any sign of wrinkles or sagging flesh, though periodic injections of various conditioning fluids made her look no older than Tori. "You shouldn't take walks outside the estate. There's no reason to age yourself prematurely."

"You won't need to worry about the drying of my skin much longer, Mama. I'm told that Stromvi is very humid."

Rosalinde glanced toward the house, as if hoping that Uncle Per would return and rescue her from unpleasantness. "I promised your great-grandmother that I would give you every advantage in establishing yourself." Her soft voice broke. "You're not making this easy for me."

"You've given me everything, just as you promised. I'm grateful, Mama, but I can't stay here," said Tori, feeling resentful of the guilt that Mama could always tap.

"You're just like Mirelle," said Rosalinde, becoming the tragic, helpless victim, "so stubborn and superior. You chose to hurt yourself, but you don't understand how much you hurt the rest of us."

"Please, Mama, don't cry."

"You could have a fine patron to protect you, but no. You're too civilized to be a concubine like me. You have to marry a man who abuses you so much that you finally kill him. You have to take a job with a stranger on some primitive world I've never heard of."

"Mister Hodge is willing to hire me for honest work, Mama."

"And how long will it be until he abuses you? You don't know him. Every time you debase yourself, you hurt me and your sister. You hurt your Uncle Per. You're thoughtless, Tori."

"I'm sorry, Mama." The guilt became unbearable because its substance was emotion without reason. Tori ran back into the garden, wishing she could run all the way to Stromvi.

* * *

The trip to Stromvi was not entirely what Tori had expected. The process of travel was itself fairly predictable: The Hodge ship was smaller than the commercial vessels that Tori had taken previously, but the serene, enclosed environment was equally effective at protecting its passengers from any knowledge of external realities. The surprise to her was that the Hodge ship carried only an unfriendly Jiucetsi pilot, Birk Hodge himself, Ngoi, and Tori—and Birk Hodge rarely appeared. Ngoi hinted that family troubles had placed Birk Hodge in a sullen mood. It was Ngoi who made Tori feel welcome.

She was given a cabin that still betrayed the traces and habits of a previous tenant. The programmable command sequences, by which the cabin could communicate with the rest of the ship, had been organized meticulously. Several books on horticulture contained the thin-film overlays and comments of diligent study. Each book wore a Hodge Farm rose embossed in its pale, leathery cover. Ngoi offered to remove the coarse, strikingly colored weavings that covered the walls and bed, but Tori declined. Ngoi seemed pleased that she enjoyed the weavings; he explained with some pride that they were Stromvi designs. When she asked Ngoi who had occupied the room, the Stromvi clicked incomprehensibly and shrugged.

"He was a Soli friend of Mister Birk's son," admitted Ngoi after a little more prodding.

"Mister Hodge has a son and a daughter, doesn't he?" asked Tori.

"Calem and Sylvie." As he spoke, Ngoi also clicked the pattern that Tori had come to recognize as affirmation. "Both are university students. They are seldom on Stromvi now. I hope you will not feel lonely on my planet, Miss Tori. You and Mister Birk will be the only Soli living at Hodge Farm, and Mister Birk often travels to market his products."

Tori smiled, appreciating Ngoi's concern. She did not

try to explain that she wanted only to escape the past, and that her compulsion overwhelmed all other reasoning. "How do you click and speak at the same time?"

"An inner set of jaws controls the click speech." Ngoi stretched open his primary mouth, revealing hundreds of teeth in staggered rows. The set of inner jaws widened independently, and an array of smaller, flatter teeth lined the passage to the throat. Ngoi clicked a rapid pattern with the inner teeth, closed the outer mouth, and issued his startling smile. "I will try to teach you to understand the click speech, if you like. It is a useful thing to know on Stromvi."

"I would like to learn it," answered Tori. Something almost forgotten awakened inside of her. She felt the difference, but only later did she recognize the source as hope.

She passed much of the trip learning simple click patterns from Ngoi. She tried to imitate the rhythms by tapping, but she could not duplicate the subtle sound shifts that Ngoi controlled by using different portions of his jaws. She learned enough to appreciate that the Stromvi language had more complexity than she had first thought.

Attempts to speak to the Jiucetsi pilot were hopeless. Though he clearly heard ship signals, he made no response to any of Tori's greetings, making her wonder if he understood Consortium Basic at all. Ngoi obviously disliked the Jiucetsi, who was apparently one of a corps of independent pilots that Birk Hodge occasionally employed as backups for automated ship systems. Ngoi intimated that the Jiucetsi was a retired soldier who had known Birk for many spans. The Jiucetsi had only two arms instead of the three that were more common for his species, but Ngoi did not know if the lack was the result of accident or nature.

"He does not stay on Stromvi," said Ngoi, and that comment apparently excused the Jiucetsi from any lasting significance in Ngoi's perspective.

Birk Hodge continued to puzzle Tori. When he did emerge from hiding, he was charming and affable to her, but he barely acknowledged Ngoi. Tori had seen him leaving in the Jiucetsi's company, but the two men never exchanged a word in her presence. She had made one remark to Birk about the books in her cabin, inquiring whether she might use them.

Birk had snarled, "Does Ngoi know that Hodge books were brought on this ship without my permission?"

Tori had replied quickly, "I'm sure that Ngoi wouldn't defy your orders, Mister Hodge." Placating Birk Hodge had required another full millispan of her best conciliatory efforts.

By the time they approached Stromvi ten millispans later, Tori had reached the phase of doubt that so often followed her impulsive decisions. She knew nothing about Birk Hodge. She knew little about the planet Stromvi, and Ngoi's meager descriptions were not encouraging. "You never learn, Victoria," she muttered, as the Hodge ship landed at Stromvi's single, unsophisticated spaceport. She applied an inoculation patch to her arm and winced at the momentary burning of adaptation fluid.

Tori joined Birk Hodge in the exit lock. Ngoi had already ridden the platform down to the planet's surface. The Jiucetsi would not debark, for he would take the ship to its berth at the major port on the neighboring planet of Deetari. The outer doors of the ship opened, filling the lock with Stromvi atmosphere, and Tori began to choke on the thick, stinging resin. A wave of dizziness made her reach for support, and Birk steadied her. "The first adaptation to Stromvi is the worst," he assured her. "Soli are seldom ill for more than a few days."

Tori tried to reply but abandoned the effort. She stepped onto the platform and endured its motion as it lowered her to the Stromvi surface. The night sky shrouded everything beyond the flat landing field. Conscious only of an umimpressive, nearly deserted port complex, Tori followed Birk Hodge to the silver hovercraft that would take them to Hodge Farm. Ngoi's warnings about his world's peculiar atmosphere now seemed far too mild.

Tori's short flight to Hodge Farm was a misery. She tried once to glimpse the Stromvi landscape by night. The rush of unidentifiable, luminous streaks beneath the hovercraft aggravated her nausea. Adaptation fluid would not allow its recipient the relief of actual illness, but Tori felt close to death. She had traveled often enough to carry her own supply of adaptation fluid, but she had never experienced such a severe reaction to environmental change.

As Birk Hodge landed the hovercraft, dim blue light flowed in from the windows. Tori ventured another look outside, but she could see only a patch of landing yard and the outline of a boxy hangar against a dark backdrop. "Welcome to the Ngenga Valley," clicked Ngoi.

"Please don't ask for my opinion yet," muttered Tori, although the cessation of the hovercraft's movement had already improved her outlook. She was able to clamber out of her chair and down the hovercraft's steps without assistance, leaving the lading platform for Ngoi's bulk.

The ground felt spongy. The stars were a misty blur. Even the slim, opposing crescents of the planet's two moons seemed blurred. Gentle sounds of Stromvi click-speech wafted through the humid darkness. Except for the painful pungency of the resinous atmosphere, Stromvi gave Tori an initial impression of softness.

Ngoi rested his cool hand on her arm. "I shall see you tomorrow, Miss Tori. I shall greet my own family now."

Tori smiled at him. "Tomorrow," she echoed. She wished that she could accompany Ngoi instead of Birk Hodge.

Birk emerged from the hovercraft carrying only a woven drawstring bag. "Good. You're adapting well," he said on observing Tori's steady stance. "I'll have Thalia bring your luggage." Ngoi vanished into the darkness.

Birk led Tori across the hangar yard toward a dim, ivory monster of a house, an overwhelming amalgam of Soli architecture and design. The structure was impressive but not particularly attractive. Tori decided to reserve further opinion until she could examine the house in daylight.

They circled the house to enter through a wide colonnade at the top of a short flight of stone stairs. Shadowy roses added familiar fragrance to the strangeness of the night. Entering the Hodge house disoriented Tori completely. Crystal panels seemed to rise in front of her at the least probable locations, and distorted echoes surrounded her.

"I'll ask my housekeeper to prepare a guest room for

you to use tonight," said Birk, maneuvering easily through the strange maze of hallways. "We'll discuss long-term arrangements after you're settled."

"I'm ready for a night's sleep, even if it is morning by my personal reckoning." Tori stopped, because a manicured young Soli woman had appeared from a gap between crystal panels.

The young woman was pretty but not beautiful, well-proportioned but not striking, expensively attired but oddly colorless. Her expression suggested a temper at odds with her sophisticated veneer. She did not seem to notice Tori. "Where is he?" she demanded of Birk. "Where did you send him?"

Birk Hodge smiled at her, disregarding both her questions and her anger. "Miss Darcy, this is my daughter, Sylvie. She seems to have obtained an unexpected leave from university." Tori nodded slightly, deciding that friendly overtures would be futile at present.

Sylvie glanced impatiently at Tori. "Did you exchange my Squire for *her?*"

Birk answered evenly, "Miss Darcy will be working for me."

"You lied to me," accused Sylvie, while Tori hoped this family squabble did not typify relations at Hodge Farm. "You lied to him *about* me. How could you hurt me this way? When I told you my decision, I trusted you to respect my right to choose for myself."

A young, pale, languid man emerged from the blue shadows farther down the hallway. "Father respects no one but himself, Sylvie. Haven't I warned you for spans? Just because you've always been his favorite, you thought you could defy him. I'm really quite proud of you for making the attempt, but you and the Squire were both overmatched." The young man appraised Tori and extended his hand to her. "I'm Calem Hodge. Personally, I find you a distinct improvement over Sylvie's Squire."

Tori accepted the handshake reluctantly. The heat was too oppressive to make any physical contact appealing. Calem's heavy grip dragged at her spirits, and his pointed reluctance to release her hand did not improve her mood. Calem's clinging reminded her of Uncle Per, yet she lacked the energy to pull free.

Calem gazed at her with open appreciation. Tori could

not help but categorize him as a "type," defined to her by Mama in one of Mama's rare maternal efforts: The type who wore arrogance as a shield for insecurity, not because of any real inadequacy, but because of an unmet need for external approval. Calem's "type" was particularly easy for a concubine to manage, since a shaky ego devoured encouragement like a starveling.

Birk Hodge watched his son critically, as if awaiting some predictable failure. "Come to my office later, Calem, and we'll reevaluate the progress of your education," said Birk, "since the Squire will no longer be available to serve as a crutch for your laziness."

Calem gave his father a look of bored tolerance, but he released Tori's hand. Sylvie snapped, "I haven't changed my mind about him, Daddy. I'll find him and tell him how you deceived us both."

Birk answered impatiently, "The Consortium is vast, and your Squire is very small and insignificant. He is gone, and I advise you to forget him quickly. There are far too many *useful* young men I'd like you to cultivate."

"If it's any help, Sylvie," offered Calem, "I know the names of most of the universities that the Squire considers 'adequate.' He's a perpetual student. You're sure to find him enrolled in some esoteric program." Calem's contribution struck Tori as fairly useless, considering the large number of Consortium universities open to Soli students, but she certainly did not intend to add her opinion to the argument.

Sylvie seemed surprised by even such token support from her brother. Her face acquired the same puckered expression that usually preceded Mama's rare, honest tears. "Thank you, Calem." Sylvie returned to the room from which she had appeared.

"You really have outdone yourself this time," said Calem to his father. "Sylvie and the Squire would never have lasted. They have nothing in common. Sylvie's infatuated, and the Squire fancies the idea of rescuing a helpless maiden from a domineering ogre. Now, you've transformed them into star-crossed lovers. Unless you've killed him, the Squire will be back."

Birk replied ominously, "Cowards don't cross me twice."

"No," murmured Calem, his expression bitter. "I don't suppose we do."

"If you don't mind, Mister Hodge," interrupted Tori, manufacturing a winning smile for Birk, "I'd like to see that guest room."

"Of course," replied Birk graciously. Calem shrugged and followed his sister.

As Tori accompanied Birk, the house's strange echoes carried Calem's voice to her briefly: "At least someone seems to be able to handle our dear father. We'll see how long she lasts."

CHAPTER 6

A very disgruntled Soli scrubbed the warehouse walls for his Calongi employers. The Nikli who shared the night shift had again disappeared before the work was half complete. The Soli's arms ached, his hands burned from the astringent cleanser, and the unfairness of the Nikli's shirking rankled more deeply because the incomparably just Calongi did not seem to notice it. The situation was not what the Soli had intended to achieve by requesting training in the Calongi religious philosophy of Sesserda.

He could not quite recapture the reasons for his initial request. His circumstances had changed uncomfortably since that time, less than a hundred millispans ago, when Birk Hodge had thrown one taunt too many at him. Advanced Soli training programs had courted the Squire eagerly in the past, and he had not particularly valued their attentions. His family, never deeply interested in any practical form of education, had encouraged scholarship as a necessary attribute of civilized behavior, not as a means of achieving life-purpose.

In truth, Birk's accusations of laziness had not been unwarranted or unprecedented, but Birk's hard delivery had stung the young man's pride more than all the blandishments of kindlier beings. Leaving Arcy with a sprained wrist and an uncertain future, the Squire had found himself confronted by a very humbling dose of reality: He had never tried to establish life-purpose; he had dabbled in many fields, but he had never persisted at anything; he feared Birk Hodge. Having an orderly mind, the Squire decided that his major flaws must be addressed in proper sequence. While he did feel some guilt for relegating Sylvie to the final stage, he was honest enough to admit that the relationship had begun to deteriorate even before Birk Hodge's intervention.

The Squire's newly conceived goals—the same ambitions that Birk Hodge mocked—burst into life at impractical heights. The Calongi discouraged him from the start, though his official records qualified him to enter any Level VI program of study. Soli senses were too limited, the Calongi said, for any advanced Sesserda mastery; the most gifted Soli could never achieve more than bottom rank. Sesserda was a religion to be lived, not a set of rules to be studied and recited by rote for the amusement of Soli psuedo-intellectuals.

Calongi never denied a Consortium member the right to study Sesserda. A few Calongi schools had been designed for just such stubborn Level VI aspirants as the Squire. The Calongi accepted him, though they told him he was foolish.

"Supreme arrogance," mumbled the young man who scrubbed the wall, chastising both the Calongi and himself for disbelieving their warnings. He was not enjoying the additional lessons in humility. He could imagine Birk Hodge's scornful reaction.

The Squire paused to rub a cramp from his shoulder. The completed wall gleamed at him softly. He threw the scrub rag into the bucket, too tired even to grumble against the mandated use of primitive cleaning tools for a task that Xiani engineers could have easily automated. He gathered the bucket and mop and moved to the next pastel segment of the corridor.

He squeezed the thin green liquid from the rag and began to clean an aqua wall with wide circles of motion. He tried not to think of how many corridors he had already finished and how many yet awaited him. The Nikli's absence more than doubled the work, for the Nikli species could nearly match the Calongi in multitasking control of their varied limbs.

The Squire bent to soak the rag again, and he snagged his thumb on the pail's rough seam. A trickle of his red blood muddied the cleaning fluid, and the Squire cursed as the astringent burned deep into the cut, blistering the edges. He grimaced at the thin streaks of inflammation spreading rapidly from the minor wound, belatedly recalling an injunction to wear protective gloves when using the most potent cleansers. Suviki chemists guaranteed that their cleaning solvents would not prove fatal to Con-

sortium members; no one guaranteed that the products
might not be unpleasantly toxic to such a susceptible species as the Soli.

"Maybe Birk Hodge was right," he muttered to himself. "I should have tried selling sarcasm, since I certainly
don't seem destined to gain renown as a Sesserda scholar.
I can't even wash Calongi walls successfully."

He left his work and tools and headed for the night
dispensary, hoping that someone there would know how
to treat a stupid Soli for whatever toxin the Calongi
cleanser contained. In a warehouse filled with Calongi
medical supplies, surely there would be an appropriate
antidote somewhere. His entire hand was beginning to
burn, the fingers curling involuntarily in reaction to the
pain.

As he passed the supply closet, he heard a crash that
made him jump with unwarranted guilt. He nearly expected to see a Calongi master appear and berate him
for allowing such a noise to disturb the tranquillity of a
Calongi building. He flung the door open to see the bipedal Nikli kick a fallen paint pot into the corner.

Blue paint splattered the Nikli's silver kilt and leathery
brown skin. The taloned hands of the Nikli's long-arms
scraped at the paint irritably. At the middle of his broad,
barrel-shaped chest, the short arms of his mid-claws were
crossed and held close to the body, gripping a metallic
box. "How nice of you to arrive so promptly, y'Lidu,"
said the irritated Squire.

The Nikli's faceted eyeband shimmered darkly, and
the heavy forward prong of his antlers slammed against
the Soli's head. The Nikli dragged the stunned Soli
through the pool of spilled paint and shoved him behind
a mound of folded rags. Glancing cautiously into the corridor, the Nikli exited the closet and closed the door
carefully behind him.

The Squire did not try to move for many microspans
because his head felt shattered by the Nikli's inexplicable
attack, and the poison in his hand made his reactions all
the more sluggish. The janitors of the dawn shift would
surely find him, even if no one noticed his abandoned
work and came in search of him sooner. He was afraid
even to touch his head to probe the extent of damage.

"I knew y'Lidu didn't like me, but this is absurd." He

tugged a rag from the stack that covered him and dabbed gingerly at the tender side of his head. "I wonder which point of the famous Nikli conscience-above-consciousness I offended this time." The white rag became mottled with crimson blood and broken black hairs, but the skull seemed to be intact. "*My* consciousness informs me that I've been assigned to scrub a warehouse in the company of a raving lunatic. Sesserda wisdom probably equates my Soli imperfections with a Nikli's minor flaw of murderous rage." He sighed at the bloodied rag, "Perhaps the Calongi are right in considering Level VI enclaves almost as dangerous as the war zones of the lawless."

He tried to lift himself to his feet by grasping the closet's ventilation grate, but the grate came loose in his one good hand, fell, and nearly smashed his head a second time. "This is not my night," he muttered. He frowned as a small, gray canister dropped from the grate and landed in his lap. He turned the grate to view its inner side. An uneven patch of half-set cement showed where the canister had broken free.

"Madmen and martyrs," he whispered. He tried to envision an innocent explanation, but he was far too well educated to achieve such naive comfort. The Nikli life-purpose was social conscience, but the Nikli were as subject to Level VI irrationality as the Soli. The Squire recognized the Nikli's purpose with a slow, rising horror. "I've been working side by side with a blasted terrorist."

The softly hissing canister had evidently been emitting its imperceptible deadliness since the Nikli's hasty departure. The Soli tried to replace the seal, but the canister's design did not accommodate him. He considered throwing the canister in the garbage chute, but he reasoned grimly that destruction of the canister would only hasten the distribution of the canister's poisonous contents.

His thoughts began to rush, impelled by the first significant danger he had ever known. The Nikli people were prone to philosophical extremism, but they were a very competent race. Any terrorist capable of progressing this far in an attack against Calongi employed sophisticated tools. The canister had surely been designed to emit a poison that could incapacitate a Calongi, at least temporarily, and Calongi were nearly indestructible. Any poison that could impede a Calongi would certainly kill a Soli, for Soli were a relatively fragile species.

He had already inhaled too much of the gas to survive. This was undoubtedly why y'Lidu had not taken the trouble to silence his Soli coworker more permanently. Y'Lidu did not need to waste time on the Squire, assured of the Squire's death and contemptuous of the same weakness of spirit that Birk Hodge had derided.

The Squire grunted, "A plague on them both." He astonished himself with the clarity of purpose that engulfed him. He could not undo the damage. He could possibly minimize its extent by moving the canister promptly to the one tightly sealed chamber in the facility.

Urgency gave him new strength, denying his injuries. He tucked the canister into a pocket of his work apron, and he scrambled from his undignified position in the closet. He struck the alarm panel outside the closet door, but the panel remained dark and unresponsive, and he did not pause to investigate the reasons. He assumed that y'Lidu, having succeeded at the nearly impossible task of concealing his goals from the Calongi, would be equally capable in the matter of sabotaging an alarm system. The Soli continued down the corridor at a rapid pace, striking every alarm panel as he passed, hoping that the Nikli might have missed one circuit, but all of the panels remained dark and silent.

The plasma vault, where replacement supplies of Calongi bodily fluids were stored, was closed but never locked. Its own deadly atmosphere protected it from anyone but a Calongi. Dire warnings in Calongi, Consortium Basic, and a hundred other languages and symbolisms outlined the heavy double doors and whispered in a hundred voices. The mechanical bar that usually crossed the doors dangled from one end. The Soli breathed deeply, then pressed through six such sets of doors. Each barrier closed automatically behind him.

Y'Lidu lay on the floor beneath the far shelves of the wide room, a willing martyr to the cause that an aberration of his Nikli conscience had decreed. His sharp midclaws still clutched the silver box. Above him, rows of golden vials gleamed with the soft iridescence of their contents, the purest form of relanine, lifeblood of Calongi and the most dangerous of narcotics to virtually all other Consortium species. Minute traces of relanine gave the potency to adaptation fluid.

The vials could not contain the fluid completely; it seeped through any seal that did not violate its purity and make it too unstable for Calongi transfusions. Even the massive, carefully crafted vault doors allowed relanine vapors to escape. The inner vault was saturated. Stored in such quantities, the relanine filled the air of the vault and penetrated quickly into any creature so foolish as to enter.

Though he held his breath, refusing to inhale, the Squire could feel the tingling that signified danger. He placed the still hissing canister on a shelf beside the relanine. The poison of relanine writhed with the poison from the terrorist's design, and the air sparkled in iridescent waves.

The Squire crossed to y'Lidu and pried the box from the Nikli's claws. The Nikli's narrow eyeband flickered, and the talons of the Nikli's long-arms tore suddenly across the Squire's leg. The gasp of relanine-saturated air choked the Squire, and the Nikli pinned him against the floor.

"You will be privileged to join me in martyrdom, stupid Soli," laughed y'Lidu, intoxicated both by his zealous cause and by the relanine that was killing him. "We shall prove the dangers of storing Calongi medical supplies on a planet of multiple races. The Calongi sneer at us, but I shall show them Nikli greatness."

"Martyrdom has never been one of my aspirations," muttered the Squire. His tongue seemed thick and uncooperative, but a part of him had begun to feel insanely euphoric. The relanine had burned all lesser toxins from his lungs and cut hand, and it had begun its own strange work inside of him. "What do you wager that the Calongi manage to halt the relanine contamination before it escapes the warehouse? They do anticipate trouble from us Level VI children, after all."

The Nikli tapped the box with one dark, closely trimmed claw. "The initial explosion will carry the shards of relanine vials halfway across the continent."

"You might have told me not to bother cleaning the corridors tonight."

The Nikli began to laugh, a deep, rumbling sound that

became a gasping, retching effort to survive. Y'Lidu convulsed away from the Squire, who snatched the explosive device and ran from the vault on unsteady, agonized legs. The Squire careened through the corridors without conscious goal, intent only on a panicky need to prevent the effects of the Nikli's bomb from touching the relanine vault.

The relanine had spread through the orifices of the Squire's head to reach the brain, and his nervous system reassembled itself at relanine's capricious commands. Sensations, both familiar and strange, raced in a maddening sequence, each trying to confound the others. A moment of exquisite joy blurred into revulsion, followed by a resurgence of anguish.

He did not know where he ran or even that he continued to move. He could not sort perceptions that seemed to have expanded beyond those he had always known. His Soli senses seemed numb from the assault. The sockets of his eyes burned so fiercely that he was sure that the optical nerves were destroyed along with all of the surrounding flesh.

He knew when he was no longer alone, but he could not name the sense that provided that information. He was aware of being carried, but no perception of touch or equilibrium informed him. He counted days and nights without being able to identify the method he employed to measure the passage of time. He did not truly sleep, but he did not awaken. He wondered why he continued to live and who had come to prevent the Nikli's planned destruction, but neither those concerns nor any others could stimulate emotion in him.

He counted one hundred and seventeen local days before he *heard* again. A clatter and a formless rumble identified themselves within his brain. He moved his mouth; no sound emerged, but he felt the muscles stretch, and he tasted a sweet-pungent flavor like crystallized ginger. He knew that a voice tried to reach him, and he knew the speaker as Ukitan, honored Calongi master, though he did not remember where that renowned being had entered his life. He sensed the rich, layered harmonies in the Calongi's voice and wondered why he had never before recognized the subtle music of Calongi speech.

"Open your eyes, Soli-lai," ordered Ukitan. "You control your senses. They do not control you."

Stunned by the honorific form of command, the Squire obeyed. A smear of iridescent light rewarded his effort. He squinted to resolve the blur into definition, and he saw and knew Ukitan, but he also realized that his vision had redefined itself, encompassing a bewildering new range of frequencies. The velvety cloak of the Calongi's many specialized appendages no longer seemed dark, idle, and concealing. Patterns of warmth defined the active limbs and shifted according to the unique complexity of Calongi multibrained control.

"You must learn to control your new perceptions," chided Ukitan gently, "or the distraction of them will drive you mad."

"Terrorist?" asked the Squire, and he heard new shadings in his own hoarse croaking.

"Our facilities are better protected than either you or y'Lidu evidently realized. Such unfortunate incidents are not unprecedented among Level VI students, though Sesserda aspirants seldom attempt such large-scale violence. We were concerned about y'Lidu's suitability." In Ukitan's momentary pause, the Squire sensed the unspoken addendum: The concern had relegated y'Lidu to a humble task beside an equally uncertain Soli candidate. "Y'Lidu did not survive."

"Relanine?" whispered the Squire, certain that he should be as dead as y'Lidu.

"You were thoroughly contaminated. Various large gashes on your body accelerated the relanine's penetration, and the rapidity of the absorption may have saved you. It certainly helped you to reach the watchman despite the severity of your injuries."

As he spoke, Ukitan ran probing, delicate tendrils across the Squire's neck and head, and the Squire felt the precision of the pressure shifts that tested him. With a dexterous hand, Ukitan manipulated a light-directed syringe above the Squire's chest. Though the process occurred within a nanospan, the Squire felt the injection's penetration as distinctly as if time had slowed to make him dwell in full awareness of every instant. A surging pulse of tingling warmth began to flow through him, and it maintained its rhythm with his heartbeat.

"Your body defied probabilities and adapted success-fully," observed Ukitan. "You are the first of your spe-cies to survive such drastic relanine toxicity. We honor you for risking yourself in order to protect your fellow students. None of us predicted that such determination lay within you."

The Squire tried to laugh, but his lungs ached with the effort. "A good day's work?" he asked wryly.

"As a noble gesture, yes. In a practical sense, your sacrifice was unnecessary to us and very costly to you, Soli-lai."

The painful noble gesture had no purpose, concluded the Squire ruefully. *I was foolish to think that the Calongi could have needed a mere Soli's help.*

Ukitan voiced the soothing Calongi undertones that persuaded lesser species so capably. Unaffected, the Squire awaited the grim reason for Ukitan's gentle ma-nipulations. "Your survival required a biochemical ad-justment to accommodate the addictive properties of pure relanine."

"Addictive. . . ."

"You felt the injection that I gave you just now. We have attached a device to your heart that will maintain the necessary level of relanine inside you, as long as you replenish the implant's supply at regular intervals. A guide filament directs the relanine into the implant's cav-ity. Your heart's action controls the issuance. One of our physicians, Agurta-lai, grew the implant for you."

"Calongi tissue inside me?"

"No other substance can contain relanine effectively, and your biochemistry has adapted to a state that is rela-tively compatible with ours. Even contact with our living blood cells would cause you only discomfort instead of death. The frequency of your injections will vary, de-pending on external conditions, but the implant should not inconvenience you excessively. We shall ensure that adequate relanine is available to sustain you in the maxi-mum possible comfort, of course."

"Thank you so much," grunted the Squire, unsure of whether to express gratitude or devastation. He could observe Ukitan's kindly efforts to convey calm, and he regretted his own detachment from them.

"Since we have little data on Soli in the area of extreme relanine addiction, we cannot predict the severity of the long-term effects. Both the Suviki chemists and the Abalusi medical technicians have already requested the opportunity to examine you, Soli-lai."

I am dead, after all, he concluded grimly, *and the eager scientists of a dozen species already rush to perform the autopsy.* "Why do you address me as 'Soli-lai'?"

"Because you are a singularly honored member of your species. We honor you for the intent of your gesture, as well as for the potential that we perceive in you now."

"I am no longer strictly a Soli, am I, Ukitan-lai?"

"There are those who say that even the use of adaptation fluid makes all Consortium members part-Calongi."

"You don't honor me for being a fool, who made a meaningless sacrifice. Relanine addiction isn't admirable. You address me with an honorific title, because I am truly part-Calongi now."

"Life-purpose may follow a winding course, Soli-lai," replied Ukitan, "but we shall discuss philosophy further when you are better rested." When his student recognized the answer as evasion, Ukitan's pulse patterns signaled unspoken acknowledgment.

The Squire perceived both the subtle pulse signal and the emotion that accompanied it, though he could scarcely define the origins of his own observation. "I make you uncomfortable, Ukitan-lai."

Ukitan showed respect for the student by responding indirectly, as he might to a fellow Calongi, "We shall transfer you to the school on Calong-4. You will advance much farther in Sesserda rankings than we predicted."

"You predicted for a Soli student, who surely died in an unfortunate accident. I am not that student."

"Perceptions and wisdom often increase in unison."

CHAPTER 7

The Squire first visited Stromvi in my sixth year, the third year of Hodge Farm. His colors were dark, where Mister Birk, Jeffer, and Mister Birk's children were pale. I did not otherwise distinguish the Squire among the Soli. The colors of all Soli seem bland to me, and I was far too critical of any strangeness in my childhood.

My honored mother chided me for my intolerance, but I think she never truly approved of any alien herself. She only came to respect the Squire in later spans, after the accident that changed him into something that was both more and less than a Soli man. He did not call himself Squire then, of course. He had become Jase Sleide.

The Soli inquisitor: My memories of him hold such bittersweet potency. We Stromvi all knew him when he returned to Stromvi, though he had changed since he lived among us in his first youth. His own species saw him as a stranger. He did not try to amend their perceptions of him. He had come for other reasons.

We Stromvi allowed him his small deception, and I imagine that he was grateful to us, though he would not have objected had we announced his former name freely. After all these spans of respecting his choice to disassociate himself from his past, I no longer even remember the name he used when he first lived on Stromvi, before he became the Squire, before he became Jase Sleide.

Perhaps the Calongi will tell me his former name when they arrive, for they have always known the truth about him. Their answer would please an old Stromvi woman, who still likes to imagine that her memory is sound. The answer would also please the Prili when I give them my recollections of the past, for they value thoroughness. I remember other details so clearly that I must wonder if Jase employed some odd, exotic Sesserda method on me in my youth—to force me to remember or to force me to forget.

I shall not convey that particular doubt to the Prili, lest it taint their belief of me in the vital subjects. The Prili may fashion their own suspicions about Jase, if they so wish. Jase can certainly defend himself, if he still lives. I am somehow confident that he has survived, though the relanine may have transformed him unrecognizably by now.

It is not for Jase that I must relate my view of Old Stromvi's final drama. He and his Calongi colleagues are content with their own perceived Truth. Perhaps I should likewise be content with that Sesserda Truth that all Consortium members honor. Perhaps Tori Darcy long ago infected me with her uncivilized doubts about the perfection of Consortium justice. I shall not allow Consortium history to record my noble father as a villain, as others may have depicted him. I must relate the deeds I witnessed and the truths my honored father conveyed to me in his final spans.

My father loved Stromvi above all else. Those who believe that he destroyed a Consortium world do not perceive clearly, and I would argue the point even with a Calongi. My honored father was a gifted horticulturist among a people who knew their world intimately. He understood the complex needs of our planet's intricate ecology, and he took extreme measures because no easier course would serve. He destroyed nothing but the blighted harvest of a hollow, mocking queen.

PART II

First Harvest

CHAPTER 8

Tagran observed his clan leader impassively, attentive to her commands. He felt the ache of encroaching age today, for the spans had been hard. Even standing in his customary place at his clan leader's side had tired him, though he would never have admitted such weakness. His fatigue made him nostalgic.

Akras was the clan leader whom Tagran would obey even to the taking of his own life, but Tagran had difficulty remembering the nature of the love she had inspired in her youth. Her laughter had begun to sour when her father died at her lover's hand. Her softness had become rigidity when her people lost their might, both symbolic and actual, to the treachery of that same lover. Her gentleness had drowned in bitter dreams of vengeance against him whom she had once deemed great and honorable.

This later Akras, a hard, solemn woman whose iron-gray braid hung between the shaved emblems of revenge, used her remaining grace for purposes of stealth. She trusted no one who contradicted her in any slight issue that related to her vengeful goals: Destroy Birkaj, Rea-traitor, murderer, and thief; regain the kree'va, the Rea-star, and the great home vessel that the Rea had been forced to abandon; restore the honor of the Rea clan, though the surviving Rea consisted of barely two hundred warriors, rather than the stalwart legions of Akras' youth. Akras obeyed her profane inspiration with unswerving purity of purpose. She expected no less of her clan.

Tagran had often tried to identify the point at which the clan's goals had shifted from renewal to vengeance alone. For so many spans, the effort to endure and rebuild had consumed his own attentions. When he realized that Akras had again made the clan a significant power among the lawless, he had been surprised. He had seen no significant outward evidence of increased prosperity. Smugglers did not recognize the Rea clan by name or know its warriors. Roake had simply cited the need to request more of his addict's fluid from Per Walis, and Tagran had idly evaluated the rising cost of Roake's habit. Only a significant independent could afford to escalate such an addiction.

Tagran still had difficulty accepting Roake as war leader. Tagran had long fulfilled the majority of the position's functions, though Akras had never awarded him the title. Tagran held strong opinions regarding the actions that the war leader should take. He did not doubt Roake's capability, but Roake's methods disturbed him. Stubborn devotion could blind Tagran to Akras' faults, but her obsession showed too clearly in her sons.

Several of the Rea shared Tagran's uneasiness. Some of the warriors had regarded Tagran as war leader in truth and disliked seeing him supplanted, even by the clan leader's eldest son. Others, whose memories were long, whispered that the younger son, Ares, had the purer lineage and deserved to claim his father's rights. No one spoke of Roake's resemblance to the Rea-traitor, but Tagran was not the only senior warrior to observe it.

However, the senior Rea warriors were few now, the numbers diminishing with each span. Most of the younger clan members enjoyed Roake's leadership. Roake's energy and eloquence inspired them. The Rea-traitor was an irritating rival to be conquered. If honor could be salvaged by his defeat, so much the better.

Both Roake and Ares were capable warriors, but Tagran saw their fathers reflected more clearly with every passing span. Tagran believed that Akras had recognized the same bitter truth. She took pride in Ares, the son of Zagare, but she acknowledged Roake as the better tactician, Roake as the ablest fighter, Roake as the most crucial element of her clan's recent success. Both sons respected their mother as clan leader. They made no pretense of loving her. She did not love them.

With his feet aching and his back growing stiff, Tagran felt regret for the spans that now separated him from

Raskannen's spirited daughter. Whether Birkaj's treachery had changed her, or she had disappeared beneath the burden of sustaining the clan, she had become as scarred as her face. Her coldness had made Ares' vengeful anger keener, and Akras encouraged his anger, telling him that it made him strong. Akras encouraged Roake's hard rationality, telling him that it would make him powerful.

Akras' lightless gaze revealed nothing, but Tagran required no assurance of her satisfaction: her plans approached fulfillment. The Rea-traitor had been made vulnerable and would soon realize his lethal predicament. She had positioned her Soli pawn within the top level organization of Per Walis himself, and the Rea-traitor had accepted the tantalizing bait. The Bercali vermin had entered a similar trap of greed, and it would close around them inescapably, cleansing the home vessel in the first step of purification. Every aspect of the Rea-traitor's life would unravel, and every thing and creature dear to him would suffer.

Roake always presented his plans in terms of honor rather than revenge, and even Tagran had felt his clan spirit revive a little with the sound of the past's nobler ideals. Proud words, too long unheard, might have come from Raskannen's mouth: The Rea must have honor in order to have freedom; no law but Rea honor bound a member of the Rea clan, but that honor must be paramount; no one could be allowed to profit from attack against the Rea, for concession meant weakness, and weakness meant a loss of freedom. After so many spans of desperate struggle, Roake's promises of true, honorable victory assumed a mythic significance to the clan. Only a dozen of the oldest Rea wore the ritual scars indicative of conquest, for no actual wars had been fought since Birkaj's great betrayal. The younger Rea grew eager; the older Rea polished their pride, even as they doubted.

All would be redeemed. All would be restored. The Rea would return to glory, blazing even brighter than before. So Roake promised; so the people believed. Tagran wished that he could share that vision. For a moment, Tagran's expression softened, recalling the Rea of his youth.

The arrival of Roake and Ares interrupted Tagran's

wistful reverie with the painful reality of the present. The brothers entered together at their clan leader's command. Roake, slightly taller than Ares, wore the war leader's red cloak, fastened by the ruby war-star that had lain so long unused. Over lua-leather vest and kilt, Ares' cloak was black like Tagran's. Both young men were impressive warriors, as true to the Essenji's physical ideal as their mother. The army of an ancient Soli civilization had inspired the Rea's battle attire. Those long-dead soldiers might easily have mistaken Akras' sons for deities of war.

Roake and Ares had been arguing before they entered the cramped cabin where their clan leader awaited them. Tagran recognized their stiffness toward each other. Tagran knew them well, though he had never once spoken to either on a personal level. Obedient to Akras' wishes, Tagran had always distanced himself from her sons, though he had instructed them in many of the warriors' skills and codes.

Tagran had pitied them as boys, isolated by their mother's will from any clan companionship. With maturity, Roake had broken some of the barriers of his own rank. He had taken two wives, though Tagran doubted that those young women knew anything of their husband's inner thoughts. Ares' attachments never amounted to more than an occasional liaison. Excessive inbreeding had made Ares unstable in many ways, but Tagran actually liked him better than the arrogant Roake. Tagran had always preferred temperamental Zagare to scheming Birkaj.

"That Soli woman has seen Ares," growled Roake, and Akras frowned. A Rea warrior should await his clan leader's command to speak. Roake's pride had grown stronger as *his* plans fulfilled themselves. The latent legacy of the Rea-traitor's independence fueled Tagran's uneasiness.

Akras did not censure Roake. She nodded at Ares. "What has occurred?"

Ares answered with crisp obedience, "The wife of the Rea-traitor's son recognized the Bori. She does not know what the Bori concealed."

"The Rea-traitor will know," snapped Roake. "He will know he is threatened if the woman speaks. You were careless, brother. You let the Bori grow hungry, and its camouflage faltered."

"The Stromvi environment is harsh even for the Bori," retorted Ares, "and Wotan came late to the rendezvous because you failed to inform him that the Deetari supply ship was making an extra trip to Stromvi this decispan."

Roake answered with disgust, "If a Rea pilot cannot evade detection by a supply ship, we should not be trading in relaweed."

Akras intervened sternly, "Did you examine the field, Ares?"

Ares nodded. "The seedlings are established. The Stromvi workers think they have planted a Soli herb as another Hodge Farm experiment."

"We knew that much from Febro," muttered Roake, "who values his life too much to deceive us. There was no need for Ares to visit the planet himself. He has jeopardized everything by letting that woman see him." Tagran concurred silently, though he disapproved of Roake for disputing the clan leader's judgment in sending Ares.

"The vengeance belongs to the Rea," answered Akras, her hard, amber eyes narrowing in anger, "and we shall witness it in full." Tagran tried to shift position imperceptibly. The depths of Akras' bitterness had made him increasingly uncomfortable of late. "Mister Febro is a useful tool, but his kind is bought and sold too easily. He serves us well as agent in our dealings with Per Walis, but I shall not entrust him with Rea honor. Do not forget our greater purpose, Roake. I shall see the Rea-traitor destroyed."

Among the clan, thought Tagran grimly, *it is Roake who speaks of great purpose and Rea honor. Roake understands expediency too well.*

Roake growled, "The woman will warn him prematurely, unless we stop her now. We can eliminate her as a danger, but the need should not exist. She is an unnecessary victim, and only a fool destroys a Consortium member so carelessly."

Akras declared sharply, "She is aligned with the Rea-traitor."

Ares drew his clan-knife and turned its bronze hilt toward Akras in the proper warrior's offering. Tagran sensed the trembling of Ares' uncertain temper beneath the quiet words: "I shall eliminate the Soli woman my-self. Our overall plan will not suffer."

Roake snapped, "If you kill her, the Rea-traitor will be warned as clearly as if we announced ourselves."

"I have more subtlety than you think, my brother." Akras touched the proffered hilt, accepting his gesture. Ares saluted her as he resheathed the knife.

"You take needless risks, Ares—like our clan leader." Roake paced the floor in front of Tagran.

"Where is your warrior's calm?" demanded Akras, and Roake stopped his restless walking and stared at her coldly. Alone among the Rea, Roake could stand unin-timidated before the clan leader's displeasure. His self-assurance was another of the uncomfortable reminders of Birkaj.

"I have laid the plans too carefully to abandon them now," said Roake with crisp pride. "The traitor's daugh-ter feels the beginning of her humiliation. The son is already ours to claim, though he is too stupid to perceive his danger. We shall destroy everyone who has value to the traitor." Roake persisted, "Let me finish the work I have begun, clan leader, as we planned—without further improvisations that could impede the ultimate success."

Like his mother, thought Tagran, *Roake fixes on an idea and maintains it with absolute discipline. Like his father, he pursues his ambitions with a cunning that cre-ates its own blindness.*

Roake continued, "The traitor's possessions, workers, and servants will soon be made useless to him. He will see his life unravel, and he will be unable to stop the process or escape it. I shall eradicate every facet of his unmerited contentment, and he will see and know that he has nothing." Roake glared at his brother, whose slight smile relished an awareness of the greater honor. Roake acknowledged grudgingly, "The privilege of the actual kill will be yours, Ares, as we agreed."

"As our clan leader decreed," said Ares, taunting the brother he envied.

"The traitor may welcome death," answered Roake, "when I have finished."

Forestalling a serious clash, Akras murmured softly, "The Rea-traitor is ours again, as he will soon discover. You have delivered him to me, Roake, and I am pleased." The conflict between the brothers would not end here; Tagran did not doubt that Akras would use her sons' rivalry, as she used every facet of her resources. Akras' lips became tight and stern. "But do not defy me again, Roake. I can complete my death-vow without you."

Ares fingered the copper clasp that fastened his dark cloak, where Roake wore the war leader's emblem. Roake did not observe his brother's gesture, but Tagran saw, and Akras' thin lips smiled grimly. Roake's work, the long preparation, was nearly done. The time for Zagare's son to claim his own vengeance drew near.

CHAPTER 9

The two men met in silence, each reaching the arched stone bridge in full awareness of the other's approach. They paused together at the top of the bridge, and each bent briefly to appreciate the swiftness of the meandering stream below them. The golden clouds of evening covered one sun, but enough clear, deeply blue sky remained to let the second sun's light perform a fiery dance on the water's surface. The water's scent was sweet.

The Soli man appeared small and slight beside the Calongi, whose rippling cloak of outer limbs and tendrils savored the many delicately contrived perceptions of his water garden. The Soli was a dark, slender man, who seemed to be a rather ordinary representative of his race—except for his eyes, which had an oddly iridescent sheen instead of any consistent color. The slanting light of evening burnished his skin and forced the sharp angles of his features into prominence.

The Calongi spoke first, as was proper to his high rank. "You recall a story from your childhood," he remarked mildly, for he was an advanced Sesserda adept, and the acuity of his observations was lauded as extraordinary even among his own people.

"I recall a fable of two men who met upon a bridge and fought a duel of honor," murmured the Soli, accustomed to the keenness of Calongi perceptions. "Their swords determined justice."

"Your people cherish their heroes."

The Soli laughed softly in self-deprecation. "As a species, we Soli have always esteemed our warriors above our intellectuals, even when we have claimed otherwise." He sighed, as if the weight of his entire species' sins oppressed him. "We value the destroyers above the creators, though destruction is so much easier to achieve.

Our history chronicles tangible, material power. Our driest historians conspire to elevate the violent, the selfish and the ruthless to lasting prominence."

"Power may dictate history without defining the limits of respect," answered the Calongi, offering encouragement with the shadings of his many-layered voice.

The Soli shook his head, but his expression lost some of its pensive sorrow, gaining instead a trace of humor. "You are indulging my arrogant moodiness, Ukitan-lai, instead of berating me, as I deserve. Your statement may hold true among the more civilized races of the Consortium, but we Soli are still a primitive lot. Our obsession with physical prowess, blind assurance, and unreasoning determination shows how little we have evolved from the hunters and warriors of our past. We glorify the renegade, the rebel, and the scoundrel, while we often vilify the conscientious, the dutiful, and the obedient. Conscious development could do our species abundant good."

"If one accepts the Hlalegi perspective, yes."

"I know: Conscious development might also negate our native gifts, if one prefers the view of the Iloni naturalists. You, my noble friend, simply accept us Soli as a child-species. Do you Calongi never speculate among yourselves regarding our future purpose among the larger order of life? Or do you despair of us ever increasing our civilization level at all?"

"Few species advance collectively." Ukitan, honored Sesserda master and noble inquisitor, shifted the warmth patterns of his neck tendrils in an implicit elaboration that only another Sesserda adept would have the skills to perceive. "You have established the precedent for your people to follow, Jase-lai."

Jase inclined his head in a faint, wry acknowledgment of his unique Soli status. "Civilization advancement by relanine addiction doesn't seem likely to gain wide popularity. Your extraordinary tribute to my odd talents has placed me in a very ambivalent position in many respects."

"We bestow honors and privilege strictly according to our perceptions of Sesserda justice, as you know."

"And Calongi perceptions comprise justice on more worlds than I have ever counted. I do esteem you greatly,

Ukitan-lai, and I respect your people for upholding Sesserda Truth even at your own inconvenience. The effort of keeping me alive has cost you far more than your researchers will ever recover from their studies of me, and I know how many Consortium beings resent the advancement of a humble Soli to Sesserda's third rank."

"Such resentment is uncivilized. Many more beings enjoy the skills that your honored status represents, for you advise them capably in the presence of beings who would be intimidated by a Calongi master. You have found your own true purpose, Jase-lai, which proves that we judged wisely in the manner in which we rebuilt and trained you. To find your proper life-purpose is a gift that few individuals achieve, and the accomplishment is more remarkable since your species remains so far from discerning a collective vision."

"One might say that a need to analyze behavioral patterns has taken residence in my blood. I offer advice on alien relations out of compulsion, not generosity, and I was always too vocally opinionated for my own good." The Soli traced the grain of the living wood that formed the bridge's railing. "This bridge stood here before any member of my species touched our own world's moon, but many Soli behave as if we were the most civilized beings in the universe."

"The egocentricity of childhood," murmured Ukitan, "is a common phase of species development. Your particular life-purpose bodes well for Soli advancement."

"My obsession with alien cultures is an ironic byproduct of the relanine contamination, no more controllable than my erratic internal clock."

"Relanine altered your time sense considerably. The Tani philosophers find it the most interesting aspect of your addiction."

"The Tani wait like eager morticians to see if my perception of finer time increments results in a proportional reduction of my life span."

"I have often found the Tani to be a ghoulish species," admitted Ukitan. He transitioned to the topic that the Soli had evaded, "You do not need to make this journey, Jase-lai."

The Soli folded his arms, and a ripple of iridescence ran across the supple, tawny fabric that clothed him, a second skin designed to help slow the dissipation of the relanine in his system. "You think I fear to confront my own people, Ukitan-lai?"

"You have avoided contact with Soli since the contamination."

"No Soli have requested my services until now."

"This is not a request for advice on an interspecies contract negotiation. This is a request for an inquisitor, which should not have been directed at any specific individual."

"These particular people were friends once."

"The request was not placed on that basis. It was aimed at the Sesserda adept, Jase Sleide, by one who knows of you only a few misleading facts from random Prili data files. These people will be unable to view you as a friend, even if you chose to identify yourself with your past. You have altered in far more than your name, Jase-lai."

Jase frowned slightly, for Ukitan seldom voiced his opinions so directly. Ukitan preferred Sesserda subtleties, and his present mood indicated a depth of concern that dismayed the Soli. "I do not particularly want them to remember me, Ukitan-lai, but *I* must remember them. I owe a friendship-debt, and I must repay it even if the recipients do not realize who serves their need." He gestured toward the stream. "You have also taught me to recognize strong life currents, Ukitan-lai. Will you tell me that I have been summoned back to Stromvi on the basis of coincidence?"

"Life currents may be beneficial or treacherous. You have never used the inquisitor's skills in earnest, Jase-lai. You will suffer on many levels."

Jase's certainty wavered, but he dismissed his doubts. He had judged the need according to proper Sesserda methods. He trusted his discernment. "Do you doubt the validity of your own judgment, Ukitan-lai? You awarded me my Sesserda rank."

"The doubts are your own. I relate the truth that I perceive in you."

"I thank you for your reading, honored friend." The appreciation was sincere, though only a silent Sesserda litany allowed Jase to overcome a twinge of resentment against the teasing of unnecessary worries.

"I have revealed nothing to astonish you," remarked Ukitan, placidly approving the Soli's control of response. "The conflicts inside you exist and must be resolved eventually, but you need not hasten the healing process."

"So you advised me when I first attempted this journey, and you judged wisely, but nearly five spans have passed since that time." *Five spans that constitute my life,* added Jase in silence, knowing that the Calongi would follow his thoughts. *The very frenetic, very concentrated life of Jase Sleide, who sprang full-grown into Sesserda awareness with only an uneasy recollection of a disassociated youth and childhood.*

"An inquisition may not provide the optimum method of making peace with your past," murmured Ukitan, his neck tendrils shifting appreciatively as an evening flower opened and added its distant scent to the garden. "You could repay your friendship-debt by less painful means."

Jase watched a cloud shadow cross the rippling stream. He answered slowly, "I must go to Stromvi as inquisitor, Ukitan-lai. I have discerned this truth reluctantly, but I am confident of its validity." As he spoke, he accepted his own statement.

"Then you must go," agreed Ukitan, acknowledging the inarguable certainty of Sesserda judgment. "Will you leave today?"

"Tomorrow."

"Mintaka-lai wishes to hear your opinion of her new summer-song. She wants an alien perspective."

"Her request honors me. I shall seek her immediately." The two men, drastically dissimilar in physical attributes, exchanged the bows of parting friends. The slight gesture accommodated their differences and made them, for the moment, similar.

CHAPTER 10

The new bicolor hybrid had grown tall this year, shooting long canes upward toward the sun. The second blooming had begun, and ivory buds crowned the mass of dark green foliage. Only one bud had opened enough to reveal the powder blue streaking of the petals near the calyx. Less spicy than richly sweet, the fragrance resembled the perfume of the plant's ancestral rose more closely than most of the Hodge hybrids.

Tori ran her gloved fingers searchingly along the leathery stem. Thorns had accompanied so many of the experiments with ancient scents and forms. Any sharp imperfections, marring the smoothness of the canes, would defer the marketing of the hybrid once again, since none of the other blue-and-whites had met with Nguri's approval. Tori frowned, feeling a protrusion near the base of a new growth region, but a closer inspection of the roughness betrayed only a badly trimmed shoot.

"Ngela," she called and pointed toward the hybrid's base, making a clipping motion in the air. The Stromvi nodded his broad and knobby head, extending his sharp pruning teeth in a wicked grin. Tori had never decided which form of Stromvi smile looked more menacing: The baring of the primary mouth's formidable armament, or the display of the pruning teeth, the twin fanged claws that thrust forward so alarmingly from the hide sheath of the lower "mouth." She had concluded only that the Stromvi's inability to issue both smiles at once was a blessing.

Tori collected her basket and carried her inspection gear across the mossy field to the first year roses. She keyed the location entry in her notebook, summoning the breeding history and recent growth status for the next block of roses. Two of the bushes were flagged for inspection.

"Watch out for the rainbow hybrid on the end," cautioned Nguri. "Few thorns, but very small and sharp."

The elderly Stromvi emerged from the thick rose hedge, raised his upper body to an upright stance, and ambled toward Tori. She rubbed mud from the great knob of his neck ridge. The jewel tones of his aged, resin-thickened hide sparkled through the dark clay. "You've been burrowing again," she accused him. "You should leave the hard work for the younglings, Nguri!"

"Someone must teach them to differentiate between rich soil and core clay," grumbled Nguri, clicking disapproval, "and that lazy *clickikuk* Ngoi finds no time to spare these days."

The Stromvi word for "idler" lost much of its pejorative sense in translation, but Tori understood the force of its intent. "Nguri," she chided, "you shouldn't show such a lack of respect for a fellow Stromvi senior."

"Birk's useless son," continued Nguri, "infects my workers by bad example."

"Calem hasn't been idle, and Ngoi's been working hard for him."

"Ngoi is neglecting his serious duties."

"He and Calem are testing new products. I'd have thought you'd be interested in their results."

"They did not request my advice."

"And you felt insulted," said Tori, "so you refused even to visit their field." Nguri grunted, which amounted to an admission. Tori teased, "You'll have to become less predictable, Nguri, or Calem will circumvent your advice in everything."

"You view his selfish schemings too lightly."

Silenced for a moment by Nguri's unusual gloom, Tori added the next growth reading to her notebook. She could not believe that Calem's influence caused as much harm as Nguri claimed, or as little impact as Birk imagined, but she knew that Nguri dominated the people of the Ngenga Valley at least as thoroughly as Birk Hodge. Tori occasionally speculated that Birk's authority was as shallow as his ownership of the Ngenga surface lands, though she knew that Stromvi and Soli alike would have scoffed at her opinions.

Tori murmured soothingly, "Even if Calem doesn't show you the respect you deserve, his example is a temporary condition. He plans to leave after his sister's wedding."

"He has stayed six months awaiting the occasion," growled Nguri, and his hind teeth clicked a uniquely Stromvi expression of disgust. "Birk listens to you, Tori. Tell him to push his disgraceful son out into the Consortium and let the Calongi find a purpose for him. I tell Birk, but Birk thinks I am only an old complainer."

"You are an old complainer," laughed Tori fondly.

Nguri hunched his lower back, acknowledging Tori's accusation with a total absence of contrition. He continued his stubborn criticism, "Calem exerts more energy in circumventing work than the work itself would require. He is lazy, greedy, and selfish." He pronounced the ultimate Consortium insult, "Calem has no purpose."

"Birk says the same and worse," replied Tori with a shrug.

"Birk grumbles, but he continues to support the *clickikuk*!" Nguri straightened and pushed his head close to Tori's face, peering at her nearsightedly. "Calem and Sylvie both know how badly their father wants blood heirs. While they remain childless but capable of producing children, Birk will never disown them, as they deserve."

"You know I can't see you at that range," complained Tori absently. She did not want to comment on the Hodge family's mutual abuses and dependencies. She retreated a pace, so as to bring Nguri into better focus. The disparate visual ranges of Stromvi and Soli sometimes required compromise. "I shall try to exert some more effective influence on Birk than your cantankerous growls," promised Tori, "but I doubt that Birk will react as you wish. Birk is seldom open-minded where his children are concerned."

"He is entirely blind where his children are concerned," retorted Nguri. "He is as poor a parent as their irresponsible mother, whom none of us has seen these many spans."

"Whereas you are a model of objectivity toward your children," remarked Tori very seriously.

"I do not encourage them to flout all civilized behavior!"

Tori turned to hide a smile, for Nguri's children often bemoaned their father's unrelenting strictness. Tori pushed her broad-brimmed hat, woven of Stromvi fibers, to the back of her head, and she stretched her face upward toward the warm sun, its milky light diffuse from the humid Stromvi atmosphere. "I'd like to see Calem go—just to spare us all from Rillessa's hysterical fantasies about 'It' watching her with passionate designs on her person! I shall burn three flames of joy as soon as Sylvie's wedding is in the past."

"Sylvie's wedding *will* pass," muttered Nguri, "and Sylvie will disappear for at least half a span—until she tires of her Harrow and crawls home for her father's sympathy and the financial backing to attract another husband."

"The immediate future concerns me more than the duration of Sylvie's current infatuation. When Harrow returns here to his beloved polygamist, we'll be overrun with helpless Soli, sick and querulous from their initial adaptation to Stromvi."

"I shall disappear into the deep caverns until they depart."

"You may have that luxury," sighed Tori, "but I'm expected to serve as social coordinator." She rubbed another smear of clay from Nguri's neck, wondering where he had managed to accumulate so much hard soil. "I do wish Birk hadn't insisted that the wedding occur here. It's not as if a marriage were a rare event in Sylvie's life. Is this her fourth or fifth husband?"

"Fifth," answered Nguri, "but Harrow's friends are potential customers, much valued by Birk." He leaned appreciatively into Tori's messaging gesture. His shoulder joints, stiffened by age and the early morning's exertion, did not allow him to reach his neck ridges easily.

"I doubt that Harrow's economic connections are worth the cost to us in aggravation," observed Tori wryly, "since they're probably as shallow as Harrow's salesmanship. You think Calem presents a problem? Sylvie's wedding will bring all serious work to a complete halt for at least a month."

"Harrow's salesmanship has impressed Birk," said Nguri, clicking his hind teeth pensively, "and Birk does know how to identify the people who can further Hodge fortunes."

"I sometimes think Birk was raised by a Cuui trader," agreed Tori with a grimace. She could have elaborated on Birk's resemblance to another successful trader of her acquaintance: Per Walis. She could also have remarked on her strong suspicion that Harrow Febro's most significant "friends" were employed by Uncle Per.

A span ago, Tori had visited Arcy for the first time since accepting the job at Hodge Farm. She had argued with Mama almost immediately, for Mama could speak of nothing but the spans that Tori was wasting without a contract of patronage. Lila, now comfortably established with a rich Soli patron of her own, had not troubled to keep her promised meeting with her sister. Only Uncle Per had greeted Tori effusively, and he had proceeded to question her in depth about both Birk Hodge and Harrow Febro. On returning to Hodge Farm, Birk had demonstrated a very similar interest in Uncle Per, though Birk and Uncle Per met regularly to discuss Mama's ever-expanding rose garden. Tori had pretended ignorance to both men, and she had hated herself for distrusting them equally.

Abandoning such depressing thoughts, Tori tapped Nguri's massive jaw and replaced her hat with a brisk gesture. "Can you reach the trunk of that breeder in the next row, Nguri? I need to compare the core growth with the yearlings' numbers."

"Helpless Soli," teased Nguri, "daunted by a few thorns. Hand me your meter."

Relieved that Nguri had abandoned his earlier grimness, Tori responded cheerfully, "If I had four legs, three hundred teeth, and a hide that could dull a diamond saw, I might give you some competition for your title as Stromvi's foremost horticulturist, my friend."

"If you had four legs, adequate teeth, and a decent skin, I would take you as one of my wives and increase the average intelligence of my collective offspring by a factor of ten."

"Your offspring are bright enough."

Nguri clicked in amiable contradiction. "Never again would I take a wife for beauty only. Ngeta has a terrible temper. I was very foolish as a youngling."

"Your compliment overwhelms me," answered Tori with exaggerated sweetness and a mocking curtsy, "but I doubt that Ngeta would appreciate it."

Nguri blinked his black eyes, sharing her ironic humor. The Stromvi elder could recognize Soli concepts of beauty without sharing Soli tastes. "If you were Stromvi, you could give even my Ngeta cause for jealousy."

"I don't have the humility in me to be a lesser wife to anyone." She pulled the meter from her basket and placed it in Nguri's broad hand. His fingers extended to close across it.

"Not even as wife to Birk?" asked Nguri slyly.

Tori cuffed him—with gentle care to spare her own hand. "Have you no respect for your employer?"

Nguri grinned with his primary mouth. "I have greater respect for your cleverness, Soli female."

The outstanding cleverness that led me from Uncle Per to a man very like him, thought Tori. *And they are both better than Arnod. . . .*

Nguri thrust his head and arms past the young roses and into the thick mass of old growth behind them. Tori could hear him biting off dead branches as he moved. "Ngoi has been neglecting the pruning as well," he grumbled, his mood again subdued. Nguri clamped the meter into place, waited for its reading to stabilize, and pulled his long torso back into the open air. "Too much more of this neglect," declared Nguri solemnly, "and we shall start losing valuable breeding stock. These grand old bushes need constant attention just to survive."

Tori nodded. No one argued with Nguri where the roses were concerned. "I'll mention the problem to Birk."

"And you will speak to him about Calem, also. You will remember?"

"I'll remember, Nguri." *Nguri could be right about Calem's intentions to linger,* mused Tori without much happiness. Despite Calem's outspoken disinterest in his father's work and Rillessa's general loathing for Stromvi, the couple seemed to have established themselves at Hodge Farm for much more than the duration of a ceremonial marriage. Calem's experiment might be unproductive, as Nguri seemed to think, but it did set a disturbing precedent for further efforts.

Pensively, Tori watched Nguri's rolling gait as he lumbered further into the gardens by paths that only Stromvi could negotiate easily. She respected Nguri, and his concern today seemed to run deeper than usual. She also had her own reasons for wanting Calem and Rillessa gone. The couple distrusted Tori's motives in remaining at Hodge Farm, and they made their feelings known. She did not want to lose her job because of the jealous avarice of Birk's heirs.

One of Nguri's youngest children pushed her broad head cautiously out of a resin tunnel. "Is he gone?" she whispered nervously.

"Yes, Ngina," answered Tori with a smile, and the young Stromvi used her powerful arms to pull herself out of the tunnel. The thick ridges and knobs of a mature Stromvi were still small and smooth on Ngina, but a tapestry pattern of blue and deep violet had begun to replace the taupe mottling of adolescence. The Stromvi considered Ngina an exceptionally pretty child, and she promised to become as favored as her mother, Ngeta, who was Nguri's senior wife. Tori thought that Nguri was very proud of Ngina in his gruff way, but Ngina shared her siblings' awe of him.

"Would you tell my honored father that I have cleared the last resin tunnel on this side of the Farm?" asked Ngina brightly.

"You could have told him yourself."

"And invite him to inspect my work and quiz me and tell me that I disgrace him by my ignorance? No, thank you." Ngina shook a clot of mud from her right foreleg, and she admired the sheen of blue resin catching the light and enhancing the emerging colors of her hide.

"He wouldn't try to teach you if he didn't respect your abilities."

"I already know more about root plantings, resin cultures, and soil chemistry than any other youngling in the Ngenga Valley."

"And your father knows more than anyone on the planet. Be patient with him, Ngina-li."

"Tell him to be patient with me!"

"I'll tell him that you're an irresponsible chatterer unless you trim that cling weed for me."

Ngina dove between the hedgerows and snapped her

knife-sharp pruning teeth dutifully. She emerged, gnawing the severed vine absently. "I am exceedingly responsible, Miss Tori. I am working entirely of my own
volition today. Ngoi never gave us any orders at all this
morning."

"I think Birk needs to have a talk with Ngoi," sighed
Tori. Perhaps Nguri was right about Calem's influence.
Ngoi had never been exceptionally skilled, but he had
always been a competent work leader until the last few
months. He was also a friend, who had grown disturbingly distant since starting that mysterious crop experiment
with Calem. "How often has Ngoi failed to give you
assignments?"

"Three or four times," answered Ngina. She raised her
head suddenly, tasting the air, and then she scurried back
to the tunnel. "I forgot to check the east hedge for dew
worms," she announced hurriedly, and she dove beneath
the ground.

Tori turned to seek the reason for Ngina's hasty retreat. When she saw Sylvie approaching, she regretted
that she lacked the physical equipment to follow Ngina.
She chided herself for the uncharitable thought.

Sylvie arrived in the breathless haste that she maintained insistently despite the heavy Stromvi atmosphere.
"The lace-pinks will bloom in time for the wedding,
won't they?" demanded Sylvie, her pert face furrowed
with worry. "I've centered all the color plans around the
lace-pinks."

"They will attain absolute perfection on the day of the
ceremony," answered Tori with careful patience. "Nguri
knows his craft. He predicts the behavior of his charges
very accurately, and the lace-pinks are among the most
reliable performers. Stop worrying, Sylvie."

Sylvie pushed damp strands of pale brown hair away
from her brow. "Harrow will expect perfection," she
sighed. "His friends will expect perfection."

"So will your father," answered Tori dryly, "but he's
not fretting about the performance of his roses." Tori
tested a new shoot. A thorn snagged her gloves, and she
tagged the bush for regrafting.

"I know. Daddy is worried about my performance. I
feel like a sacrificial lua cub."

"I thought you adored Harrow," said Tori, wishing

that Sylvie would not confide in her so readily. Nothing inspired self-pity as effectively as its example in another.

"I adore all my husbands," answered Sylvie with a rueful smile, "for a little while."

Unable to think of a tactful response to this patent truth, Tori replied with an understanding nod that was only half sincere. She caught sight of Ngora beginning to approach but diving back into the hedge on noticing Sylvie. Few Stromvi actively disliked Sylvie, but few felt comfortable with her. Tori empathized with the Stromvi attitude. There was something stunted about Sylvie, as if a promising beginning had gone awry.

"Have you seen Rillessa this morning?" asked Sylvie. "I need to show her the wedding dance again. Calem has no patience for teaching her."

"I haven't been inside the house at all today."

"I suppose I'll have to drag her from her room again," grumbled Sylvie. "Honestly, I think that woman is losing her pitiful, little mind. All this nonsense about being watched has begun to pall."

"Rillessa misses her work. She enjoyed gathering dry data for Prili statisticians."

"The Calongi are right. Family success should not be a substitute for individual productivity." With this hypocritical decree, Sylvie fanned her loose, white shift around her knees to manufacture a faint breeze. "This day is going to be stifling. I hope we have cooler weather for the wedding. Are you joining us for luncheon?"

"Am I expected?" asked Tori, mildly startled by the request. Tori generally stayed in the field with the Stromvi workers between dawn and dusk. She shared a midday meal of manna, the basic food devised by Suviki biochemists to meet the nutritional needs of nearly all Consortium species. The partaking of common food, said Calongi wisdom, promoted unity and peace.

"Please come, Tori. Daddy is much more congenial in your presence, and I want him in a good mood before the wedding guests arrive. He's been in a wretched temper ever since I sent Harrow to buy my wedding gift from that jeweler on Calqui. From the way Daddy's acting, you would think I'd told Harrow to spend Daddy's money on my present." Sylvie touched Tori's glove-encased wrist lightly and announced with the characteristic Hodge presumption, "I'll tell Thalia to prepare a place for you."

Before Tori could reply, Sylvie had hurried back toward the main house. Tori grimaced, contemplating the prospect of Calem's bitter insults, Rillessa's contagious nervousness, and Sylvie's wheedling. Sylvie and Calem rarely visited Hodge Farm simultaneously, and neither had stayed for more than a month in the last five spans. Tori did not relish the current exception. Birk alone was sufficiently difficult to handle. Tori had learned to appreciate the peace of Hodge absences the first time she had been left with only Stromvi and Deetari at Hodge Farm.

Tori's initial years on Stromvi seemed blissfully simple now, though she had struggled to impress Birk with her value to him and to overcome Nguri's suspicions of her motives in seeking employment on Stromvi. Her goals had shifted slightly when she realized that Birk had hired her only to solidify connections with Uncle Per. Tori had never intended to use her uneasy relationship with Uncle Per for advancement of her own plans. She would not have sought to work for a man who wanted such close ties to Uncle Per. By the time she began to understand Birk, however, she had learned to value Stromvi too much to want to leave.

Tori did not know the extent or legitimacy of Birk's business with Uncle Per, and she carefully maintained her ignorance. Hodge Farm produced legal products of exceptional quality, and Hodge Farm was the only aspect of Birk's business that concerned her. Speculation would have been easy: about Birk, about Harrow Febro, about Calem's experiments. As a child, Tori had learned far more than she wanted to know about Uncle Per. She did not plan to repeat *that* mistake.

She might have felt more need to know and interfere, if she had believed that her presence at Hodge Farm actually contributed significantly to Birk's *other* business dealings. Uncle Per's dubious obligation to her ended at the border of Arcy's atmosphere. Tori made sure that she had established herself firmly as part of Hodge Farm, before Birk recognized the limitations of Uncle Per's interest in his concubines' children.

She had achieved her escape from Arcy, and she had

shown herself capable of more than her hereditary profession. She was reasonably content with her chosen purpose, though the arrival of Birk's children had made Hodge Farm distinctly less pleasant. Tori murmured to the lavender sky, "I may light *five* flames of joy when Sylvie's wedding is past."

When Tori had completed her inspection of the first-year roses, she returned to the supply cottage. She stowed her basket, gloves, hat, and heavy apron in the locker and climbed the stairs to the loft, her home for the last five local years—nearly six spans by standard Consortium reckoning.

Since the Stromvi could not climb stairs easily, Nguri had installed an old, rusty gong at the base of the stairs in order to let the Stromvi workers summon Tori. Most of her visitors—Stromvi or Soli or Deetari—ignored the gong. They simply clicked or shouted or whistled for her, according to species' preference. The only formality at Hodge Farm confined itself to the main house, a rambling, two-story structure of ornate indulgence that Stromvi derided and Birk prized.

Tori smiled wryly, considering Birk Hodge and assessing her own reflection with sardonic resignation. Nguri was uncomfortably astute. Tori was quite confident that she could influence Birk, if she chose to use the methods she had been bred and trained to apply. She did not particularly relish the potential. She held a flowered shawl in front of her and pushed her dark hair away from her face. The brilliant silk complemented her vivid coloring admirably. "Great-grandmama would be proud of the resemblance," she murmured.

She could control Birk. She had learned him quite well enough. He admired strength and despised weakness; she was happy to play to that preference. His aesthetic tastes were nearly nonexistent, aside from mimicry of what others preferred; Mirelle's great-granddaughter certainly did not need to worry about appealing to the majority of her species. Birk was also one of the loneliest men Tori had ever met, at once dependent on his children and contemptuous of them. Tori had occasionally wondered why a man who placed such value on family had such a dearth of acknowledged kindred. Consortium members always had the choice of belonging somewhere.

Tori grimaced, reminded of her own ambivalent feelings toward anything that resembled family. She exchanged dutiful letters with Mama and Lila, but she was glad to remain distant, enjoying the excuse of Stromvi's harshness for Soli adaptation. She would be pleased never to see Uncle Per again, and her brief marriage to Arnod had been nothing but disaster. Tori felt closer to Nguri and the other Stromvi than to her own family, though she had never confided the turmoil of her past or present emotions to anyone at Hodge Farm. Tori felt safe on Stromvi, largely because no one questioned her too deeply. For once, she had found a place where she wanted to stay. How far she would commit herself in order to remain on Stromvi was another matter.

In fleeing the family legacy on benign Arcy, she had trapped herself neatly within temptation's confines on the Soli-inhospitable planet of Stromvi. "You could have a comfortably secure future," Tori informed her reflection, "away from any recollection of Arnod or inquisition. You've pretended blindness to worse than Birk." *If I could ever decide what I really wanted*, mused Tori, *at least one of Nguri's prophecies could easily come true.*

"I wish I liked Birk as well as I like Nguri," sighed Tori a little wistfully. She shook her head, letting her hair fall back to her shoulders. She scolded herself, "Don't be a fool, Victoria. As Great-grandmama often proved, practicality does not require affection."

She dressed carefully in shirt and full trousers of deep, Stromvi-neutral green to create the right impression of a hard-working, upright young woman dedicated to the Consortium ideal of universal productivity. As long as she could pretend that the past did not exist, the pose was easy enough. She was good at her job as general Hodge Farm assistant, handling all the miscellaneous tasks that came more easily to a Soli than a Stromvi. She was good at most jobs, and she had certainly tried enough of them in a span of trying to sustain Arnod Conaty's profligate habits. "Dear Arnod," she murmured, "may his treacherous soul endure the icy purgatory of Uccula. He only had to die for his sins. He condemned me to live for them."

Tori's rebuke mocked herself more than Arnod Conaty. Nguri might teasingly disparage his own selection of mates, but Tori doubted that any Stromvi could conceive of the cruel self-absorption of a man like Arnod. "Nguri's high opinion of my intelligence would fall abysmally if he knew the history of my late husband," she informed herself with an acrid laugh.

Disciplining herself to a much less cynical attitude, Tori left her loft to walk across the garden to the main house. The beauty of the varied roses approaching the peak of their season helped submerge hard memories. Tori enjoyed working for Birk Hodge. In such peaceful moments, she almost wished that she could fix her current life in a resin casting: the friendly bickerings with Nguri and the other Stromvi, the shared excitement when a new hybrid received approval, the constant hope of expanding the realm of scents and forms that made so many Consortium species prize Hodge roses.

Tori had not expected to become sincerely attached to the Stromvi people. She had not expected Birk Hodge to accept her ridiculous offer without even requesting her official Consortium records. She wished that she could convince herself that her past would remain decently interred, but the recent, sustained visits by Calem and Sylvie had roused all her deepest worries from long slumber.

Impulsive risks had never daunted her, but she loathed this steady sense that her comfortable life was corroding from beneath her. She knew the decision that she must make, if she truly valued her life on Stromvi. She could work productively in many fields, but she could only ensure her future security by obtaining a contract of patronage. That was one maternal lesson that Tori had finally begun to accept after spans of rebellion.

Birk was a more palatable choice than Uncle Per, but Birk might not remain long available to her. Both Calem and Sylvie had a jealous interest in their father's fortunes, and they had both made cutting comments about the passing spans and Tori's continued presence at Hodge Farm. Unless Tori acted soon, Sylvie and Calem would certainly uncover the reasons for the Hodge Farm assistant's low employability quotient in Consortium files. They could cite her record as a blot against Hodge Farm. Birk would need considerable incentive to ignore any factor that might damage business.

Tori shrugged. The thin, silken fabric of her tailored

shirt clung to her shoulders instead of sliding smoothly across her skin, for the strength of the humid summer had begun to fill the day insistently. She gave a passing thought to concern that the potent heat might burn the more fragile, primitive roses, but she knew that Nguri could be trusted to see that any vulnerable species were protected. She must ask Birk if he had heard how long the early heat wave was expected to last.

CHAPTER 11

"Where is the harvest?" demanded the angry man again. Ngoi clicked a refusal to reply. His captor understood the meaning, if not the words. "Who ordered you to burn the field?"

Ngoi tried to straighten himself, but the pain was too great. The burning field had spread explosively, fed by Stromvi resin. Ngoi had little experience with any form of fire, and Birk's chemical fire—not a Consortium blend, for it wore no Suviki seal—had been unexpectedly potent. Ngoi hoped that he had contained the fire before the silver ship arrived and spewed forth these warriors, the minions of demonic retribution.

Ngoi accepted the retribution as just, though he knew nothing of its origins. He knew his own guilt. He had relied too heavily on his personal judgment, never consulting with any of the other Stromvi seniors. He had allowed Calem to develop the field unsupervised, because he had felt sympathy for Calem, always so belittled by Birk. Master Nguri and several other seniors had long predicted that Ngoi's trusting nature would eventually reap disaster.

"Where is the harvest?" repeated the fierce young man, who seemed to command this well-armed troop. The warriors were not Soli, for the scents and colors were wrong, but the visual differences were relatively small. One of the warriors applied cruel pressure to the burn holes in Ngoi's hide.

Ngoi grunted, "Soli *herbs* do not belong on Stromvi." Calem had called them herbs. Birk had used a more ominous name, which had no Soli origin: *relaweed*. Ngoi had not required further explanation of Calem's crime.

On recognizing how Calem had used him, Ngoi had also experienced an emotion that was strange to him:

distrust of those who were not Stromvi. Ngoi's new suspicions touched the father just as darkly as the son. Instead of leaving the first seed harvest in Calem's storage shed, as Birk had ordered, Ngoi had moved the parcels to one of the old, hidden southern tunnels. He had intended to notify the other Stromvi seniors himself, as soon as the field was destroyed, but the warriors had thwarted his plans.

He hoped the harvest was safe. He would have felt better if he had been able to hide the harvest more thoroughly. Still, the compromise had been necessary. In the shallow tunnel, one of the Stromvi younglings would surely find the parcels and report their presence to the seniors. Soli searched less efficiently for treasures beneath the ground.

Ngoi assumed that these vicious warriors were Calem's thwarted customers, but Ngoi cared chiefly that further damage to Stromvi be prevented. These warriors valued their precious harvest. The Stromvi seniors would be well equipped to negotiate a peaceful settlement.

If only the pain would ease enough to let him think clearly. . . . Some of the chemical fire had surely penetrated beneath the resin layers and was eating its way inside of him. Had that been Birk's intention? To destroy at once the evidence of evil and the only Stromvi who knew the evil's name?

Such thoughts were unworthy, but honor became hard to remember as the pain became intense. If he could reach the burning regions, he could remove the damaged flesh before its fire spread. But the warriors had bound his arms and legs. Perhaps he could extend his pruning teeth far enough to stop the fire. He would decide and act quickly, if the warriors would only turn away from him for a moment. The pain was growing worse. It burned like his guilt, and both must be excised.

"Where did you hide the *herbs*, old man?" asked the questioner, adopting a friendly, reasonable tone. "We know you harvested most of the first crop, because we've watched your progress."

"You didn't watch closely enough, Ares," snapped a new voice. All of the warriors turned toward the tall, red-cloaked man who entered.

A blighted vine must be destroyed without hesitation,

thought Ngoi, confusedly remembering one of Master Nguri's stern rules. In the instant of the warriors' distraction, Ngoi's sharp pruning teeth tore the guilty fire from his agonized sinew and bone.

*   *   *

With her back pressed tightly against her bedroom wall, Rillessa watched the window closely, trying to catch sight of *It*. She was sure that she had glimpsed *It* when she first awoke, but *It* was very quick and always escaped before she could identify *It* clearly. *It* taunted her.

Rillessa knew that no one believed her. The isolation incurred by that skepticism did not weaken her determined vigil against *It*. Rillessa had little interest in the opinions of anyone at Hodge Farm, all of them so full of themselves that they could not be bothered with her. Only Calem mattered, her charming, handsome Calem.

Rillessa flushed slightly, thinking of her husband and of his recent dark moods. Calem used to frighten her when the dark moods came, for she was shy and sheltered when she married him. She used to think the anger in him was truly meant for her, but she had learned. Calem did not love her enough to be hurt deeply by anything she did or said. Only Birk could turn Calem so bitter and cruel.

Rillessa hated Birk Hodge, because Birk did not respect his son. She never showed her hatred. Calem would never have forgiven her for any slight against his father. She let them think she hated only the world that Birk had chosen as his home. She let Calem believe that she did not recognize envy as the cause of his frantic worry over Birk's relationship with Miss Tori Darcy.

Rillessa blinked, unable to defy the instinct of her tired eyes any longer. She thought the dark blur of *It* cast a shadow of hasty movement across her in the instant that her eyes closed. She ran to the window and searched the garden below her for any betraying motion or touch of incongruous color, but she saw nothing. *It* was much too quick.

Rillessa clutched at the memory of a streak of crimson, glimpsed once across the nebulous black blur of *It*. "Datum," she muttered, mentally manipulating the recollection of a Prili computer file, "Bori chameleons, worn as cloaks."

It wore a Bori cloak, but *It* was not Bori. The Bori cloak could not hide *It* from her, because she knew: *It* watched her and wanted her for some foul purpose, despite Calem's insistence that *It* existed only in Rillessa's imagination.

Rillessa returned to her post against the wall, and she continued her vigilant, defiant wait. She wished that the incessant, distant clicking of Stromvi teeth would cease, so that she could catch the soft sounds that might betray *It*, but the clicking comprised an inescapable part of Stromvi. Rillessa did hate Stromvi. The entire planet conspired with *It*.

"I don't care if they doubt and despise me now," whispered Rillessa with a touch of condescension. Her knowledge gave her confidence. She had served the Prili long and well, and she had encountered much information that few Consortium members ever learned. "The inquisitor will prove them wrong, when he unmasks *It*."

Calem would have believed her, she assured herself, if she had not suffered that untimely fever, truly hallucinating for many days. She had spoken too freely during the fever, rather than planning her words carefully. When she first saw *It* and realized that no one shared her perception, she had known that convincing the Hodges would be difficult. The fever had sealed their disbelief. She blamed *It*, though she did not know how *It* had caused her illness.

She would not let *It* defeat her. She would expose *It* to truth, and *It* would lose *Its* power over her. She would bring truth to Stromvi. Truth was the purpose of inquisition. *It* considered her defeated. *It* underestimated her.

She had indeed spent frantic days wondering how she could persuade an inquisitor to come to Hodge Farm and vindicate her. No inquisitor could be expected to address the unsubstantiated request of a single Level VI on a remote, peaceful Consortium planet. She could not prove that *It* existed without an inquisitor to confirm her truth, and she could not summon an inquisitor without some proof that *It* presented a real danger.

Rillessa told herself that she had gained her husband's indirect support because Calem had inspired the solution to her dilemma. Calem had taunted his sister one evening with a reference to that young man who had once been Calem's friend and tutor. The Hodges called him the Squire. Rillessa almost sympathized with the young man for a shared experience of Hodge mockery. She even felt grateful to the Squire, for his disappearance from Hodge Farm had brought Calem to the Prili data center and Rillessa.

As the researcher on duty, Rillessa had handled Calem's request. She had been nervous, her natural sense of inadequacy aggravated by the existence of a sealed file regarding the young Soli known as the Squire. Rillessa had no access to the sensitive information. She had been sure that the handsome Mister Hodge would consider her incompetent.

She had read the contents of the Squire's official file to Calem: The Squire had died in an undefined accident at a Sesserda school for Level VI aspirants. Calem's smile had faded, and he had become totally silent. Rillessa discovered later that Calem, in those first shocked moments, had actually suspected Birk of arranging the Squire's death. Calem had requested nothing more from the files, but he had asked Rillessa to send the information to Sylvie Hodge immediately.

He had astonished Rillessa by returning the next day. He wanted to talk to someone who would believe him; he talked to Rillessa. Sylvie had not accepted the truth, and she had accused her brother of manufacturing lies at Birk's behest. Rillessa had given Calem sympathy, amazed that he actually seemed to welcome her meager offering.

As far as Rillessa could observe, Calem had never tried to help his sister again. In recent spans, he had delighted in telling Sylvie that the Squire had discovered her shallowness and abandoned her—like all the disillusioned suitors who would follow. Calem's familiar, slightly cruel teasing had finally served a fruitful purpose, however, when it led Rillessa's mind from the unfortunate Squire to his unfulfilled ambition.

Rillessa shared some of Birk's contempt for the young man who had aimed his aspirations so foolishly. Very few Level VI beings had ever managed to become acknowledged Sesserda scholars. Even advanced Level VI's like the Cuui, who were actually encouraged to study Sesserda, received more pity than acclaim from average Consortium members. Rillessa knew of only one significant exception: a Soli, who had achieved actual Sesserda mastery.

That Soli had even been elevated to Level V, an unprecedented achievement for an individual Soli singled out from his species. The magnitude of transition between Levels VI and V was nearly as great as the step from Level II to Level I. Advancing beyond Level VI signified the departure from childhood.

Rillessa's musings had crystallized at thought of that odd, misfit Soli, and her fears of *It* had merged with a bit of hoarded envy toward Tori. Inquisition required cause, but the cause existed: Tori Darcy, Victoria Mirelle of Arcy, widow of Arnod Conaty. The information regarding Tori's past had seemed too valuable to squander quickly, and now Rillessa savored her own instinctive foresight. An inquisition could not be performed twice for the same crime, unless the first inquisition ended inconclusively. The perfect excuse for challenge existed. The Calongi inquisitors had failed, but an inquisitor of the subject's own species existed and had never been utilized. Such challenges were rare, of course, but quite legal.

Rillessa had cataloged enough data regarding Sesserda adepts to feel implicit confidence that this aberrant Soli would thwart *It*. She knew little about the Soli who had advanced so astonishingly to Sesserda mastery, but she knew that Calongi awarded Sesserda rank very selectively. She had summoned the Soli inquisitor in Calem's name for Calem's cause, not admitting to herself that cowardice prompted her to hide behind her husband. Rillessa told herself only that she had accepted the futility of honesty regarding *It*. Only the most devious of plans could deceive *It*.

She laughed softly, pleased with her solution to the problem. "The inquisitor will even resolve my Calem's worries, by edifying Birk about his precious Tori, and Calem will feel free to leave this accursed planet. Calem will forgive my little lie when he understands."

Rillessa had not even considered the probability that an inquisitor would react less favorably than Calem to her deception. She evaluated Jase Sleide as a necessary tool, not as a man. She would have used a Calongi just as callously, if she had found a means in keeping with her twisted logic. The certainty of her rightness shielded her from fear of anything but *It*.

The soft, tinny chime of fingernails tapping a crystal wall panel made Rillessa whirl toward the door dividers in alarm. Sylvie poked her head into the room and clucked at Rillessa's cowering. "No wonder your imagination has become exaggerated," chided Sylvie, "sitting here in this self-imposed prison all day. You're not even dressed yet."

"*It* has watched me all morning," mumbled Rillessa in disgruntlement. She did not relish Sylvie's visits. "Do you expect me to change my clothes while *It* watches me?"

Sylvie strode to the window and spread her arms. "There is nothing on this planet that could watch you from a second-floor window without a hovercraft, and I think a hovercraft suspended above the front garden would be fairly conspicuous. At least comb your hair, Rillessa. You look terrible."

With an irritated jerk of motion, Rillessa walked to her dressing table. She moved the brush slowly across her auburn hair, letting the brush sensors guide the flexible teeth in untangling the snarls. The mirror reflected the work of the brush from front to sides to back of Rillessa's head, but she did not watch her own image. Her eyes darted from side to side, seeking any glimpse of *It*.

"If you expect to retain Calem's devotion," remarked Sylvie, "you had better return to more traditional methods of holding his interest. You have stiff competition."

"Who? Birk's mercenary little assistant?" Rillessa laughed scornfully, though her eyes never paused in their nervous seeking for *It*. "Calem has better sense than Birk. Calem despises her."

"Calem doesn't have a fraction of Daddy's good sense," retorted Sylvie, sharply defensive. "Calem only worries that Tori will claim too much of Daddy's financial attention." Sylvie sighed, "Calem could be right in this case."

Rillessa jumped, suddenly turning toward the window with suspicion. "Did you see *It*?" she asked urgently.

Sylvie shivered involuntarily. "Of course not. There is plenty of watching going on around here, Rillessa, but you're not the recipient of the furtive glances." An anxious tremor began to creep into Sylvie's voice, and she buried the sign of nervousness with spite. "Daddy watches Tori. Calem watches Tori. Even the Stromvi males watch Tori. Why do you think I sent Harrow to Calqui? I have more confidence in his fidelity out of my sight than here, where temptation is a known commodity."

"I'm not jealous of Tori Darcy," snapped Rillessa, as cold in her arrogance as she had been feverish with terror moments earlier. "If Calem watches her, it's only out of concern for Birk's feelings. Calem doesn't want to see his father hurt."

"Is that what Calem tells you?" laughed Sylvie, adopting a forced lightness. "Rillessa, my simpleminded sister-in-law, Daddy has a heart of pure steel. I shall refer you to the last letters of my long-departed mother, if you want confirmation. It's not Daddy's heart to which our Tori appeals."

"Tori's type of beauty can be matched by any competent reconstructionist," murmured Rillessa vaguely. Her eyes blinked and grew wide again. She became very still, watching her mirror warily.

"If I thought Tori captivated solely because of the shape of her face, I'd have replaced my features with duplicates of hers long ago," answered Sylvie. She could not help but scan the room quickly, trying to catch a glimpse of the object of Rillessa's attention. As her eyes flickered past the door, a shadow seemed to cross the sun. Sylvie caught her breath in an audible gasp, but there was no one in the room but herself and Rillessa. "What was I saying?" asked Sylvie in a shaken voice.

"You were talking about Tori Darcy," remarked Rillessa with a trace of a contemptuous smile.

"Oh. Yes." Sylvie smoothed her hair needlessly and fingered the square neckline of her dress. She began to chatter with almost her normal briskness, "Tori's the incredibly tiresome sort of woman who collects men for no obvious reason that I've been able to discover, and I've tried endlessly to learn her secret." Sylvie studied the silver rings that adorned each of her fingers. "I only collect men by virtue of Daddy's wealth," she commented with slight bitterness.

"Irresistible sirens are obsolete in this civilized era," retorted Rillessa calmly.

"Tori seems to be unerringly effective for an extinct species. She attracts all the attention she wants without resorting to absurd tales about fictitious beings lurking in dark corners." Sylvie paced the room, stared at the window, then turned away from it abruptly. "I think you're unbearably jealous of Tori, despite your denials, and that's why you're sulking in this room and fabricating monsters."

"Mister Sleide's opinion of Tori Darcy should be most enlightening," said Rillessa with cloying sweetness, unwittingly betraying her own cherished secret, "and I doubt that he'll be swayed by a fictitious siren song. His objectivity will be refreshing."

"Who is Mister Sleide?" demanded Sylvie, snapping at Rillessa for spreading her insane nervousness.

Rillessa stared at the mirror, as if she saw demons in its depths. "A Soli. A Sesserda adept," answered Rillessa absently. She drew herself upright, retrieving a measure of dignity. "Calem invited him to your wedding," lied Rillessa. She delighted in the confusion she inflicted. It seemed a fitting vengeance to her for the loneliness of her own fear. "I'm sure you're eager to have the Consortium's most respected Soli attend such an important event as your marriage to Harrow Febro."

"I've never even heard of this man, Sleide."

"He's coming, nonetheless: a Sesserda adept, who will know all that we feel and believe, whether or not we speak. The Prili say that an inquisitor knows truths that even his subject cannot recognize, for the inquisitor can read the soul as well as the mind."

"You're raving. Daddy would never allow an inquisitor here," declared Sylvie, but her face had turned ashen.

"Any Sesserda adept is capable of performing inquisition. A Sesserda adept *must* perform inquisition when circumstances demand Sesserda Truth."

"I wish Calem had left you to the Prili," retorted Sylvie, and she fled the room in shaky haste.

"The inquisitor will come," shouted Rillessa. She added softly, "He will come to unmask our deceitful little Tori, but he will stay to vindicate me."

Rillessa resumed her guarded position against the wall. *The Soli inquisitor will understand my desperation. When a Sesserda adept believes me, no one else will dare to doubt me.* Rillessa jumped nervously, certain that she had heard *It* move beneath her window. She whispered, "The inquisitor will find you and stop you from tormenting me."

CHAPTER 12

Calem identified the sound of a hovercraft before Ngiku called to him with the clicks that spoke of a visitor's arrival. Calem headed grudgingly for the garage. He had hoped that Sylvie's guests would not arrive so soon. He was not in the mood to issue cordial hospitality to Sylvie's friends. Rillessa had kept him awake most of the night with her frantic, dream-wrought whispers that "It" watched. He wondered where Ngoi had gone. Ngoi had promised to meet him this morning to discuss the crucial second harvest.

The hovercraft that maneuvered deftly into the garage was a sleek, expensive model. Calem frowned, observing the pattern of gold curves and spirals along the hull. He had not expected any of Sylvie's guests to wear Sesserda markings, and Harrow's acquisitive acquaintances certainly didn't seem likely candidates for Calongi honors. Calem tried to calculate all the possible reasons for a Sesserda practitioner to arrive at Hodge Farm at this delicate time.

When the craft's pilot emerged, a cold shiver touched Calem despite the day's heat. *So the Squire is still alive,* mused Calem, denying the uneasy sense that a ghost had just alit on Stromvi. Calem waved in an automatic impulse of recognition. *Why is he here?* Calem asked himself with a tingling of guilt. The pilot moved, and the resemblance disappeared into elusive memory, making Calem wonder how he could have mistaken the man even momentarily for the unfortunate Squire.

Calem's relationship with the Squire had always comprised (on Calem's part) an unsettling mix of respect, expediency, envy, and awe. Calem had regretted the Squire's death, but he had been relieved to hear that the Squire had failed to become a Sesserda scholar. Even the lowest level of Sesserda training would have guaranteed awareness of Calem's self-serving brand of friendship. Realization that this stranger might possess such dreaded, penetrating awareness made Calem doubly uncomfortable and insecure.

Leaning from the hovercraft door, the stranger raised his hand in a rippling motion that copied a Calongi greeting. "I am Jase Sleide," announced the Soli in even formality, "third rank Sesserda master and inquisitor."

"Your presence honors us," replied Calem, reciting the formula with stiff uncertainty. He did not even know if the greeting were proper toward a Soli. No one had ever taught him how to address a non-Calongi inquisitor. He had not known that Soli inquisitors even existed, but he could visualize a terrible panoply of possible reasons for the inquisitor's arrival.

Jase flashed a generous smile that again recalled the Squire uncannily, but the trace of a resemblance vanished with the ephemeral expression. "I expected this planet to feel hot," Jase remarked, as he emerged onto the landing step. He tugged a bulky sweater over his dark head, burying his lean, muscular frame in layers of insulating fibers. "I should have studied the actual temperature readings instead of relying on subjective commentaries."

"Stromvi is considered unbearably hot by most Soli," answered Calem with a feeble attempt at polite conversation. "You must have adapted to your inoculation at a record pace."

"A record pace. Yes." Jase's lingering half-smile disappeared, and he murmured soberly, "You still find Stromvi uncomfortable, don't you, Calem?"

"Yes," answered Calem cautiously. "You know me?"

"Of course. That is my job."

"Of course."

The inquisitor seemed to change his mind regarding his next words, and the smile returned, but careful armor rather than any semblance of friendly spirit formed the ensuing expression. The cheerful facade struck Calem as uncommonly false, considering the inquisitors' well-known devotion to truthfulness, and the effect disturbed Calem deeply.

Jase continued briskly, "Those of us who travel too

extensively often become so filled with adaptation fluid, we can hardly tolerate stasis. We keep planet-hopping just to remain conscious." Jase jumped lightly from his craft's mount-rail and landed at Calem's side. "I was surprised to receive your summons. Few Soli know that a Soli inquisitor exists. Where did you hear of me?"

"You were surprised," echoed Calem hollowly, before he could stop himself. He could not speak; he could not think. He stared, wondering frantically, *Who would have summoned an inquisitor here in my name? Has Ngoi confided in some shortsighted traditionalist like Nguri? Nguri cannot know. He would not understand, and he would shout his anger across the valley.*

Jase furrowed his broad brow in an expression of conscious puzzlement that mingled the nervous present with the uncomfortable past. Calem decided that this inquisitor did resemble the Squire superficially, though Calem persuaded himself that the differences became increasingly obvious with every moment. Still, the narrowing of those deep eyes recalled the way the Squire used to meet Calem's most misguided declarations of uninformed, erroneous "truths."

Calem almost winced in recollection of the frequent embarrassments of those painfully youthful days and the constant effort to appear superior. He felt no better on reminding himself of the passage of time. An inquisitor was certainly a more dangerous obstacle than the Squire.

Disturbed by current concerns and unpalatable memories, Calem asked, "Why don't you look quite like a Soli to me?"

"I had an encounter with some blood plasma of an exceptionally potent brew," answered Jase. Calem frowned at the cryptic reply. Jase explained with an extreme patience that made Calem feel like an imbecile being lectured by an erudite scholar, "If some bold enemy insisted on viewing the whites of my eyes, he would have a long wait. My intemperate encounter caused some pigmentation changes." Jase turned his face slowly. As he moved, the light flashed from his eyes in brilliant sparks of aqua, gold, silver, pink, and green.

Calem nodded, acknowledging the explanation with only faint comprehension of its significance. The inquisitor's deep eyes shifted with a rainbow of colors, but the effect of the keen gaze remained intimidating. "I'm surprised that you came here so quickly," said Calem, testing his way through a maze of uncertainties. He feared to admit ignorance of a summons to the inquisitor, until the question of the reason could be satisfied. "Stromvi is hardly the most accessible of Consortium planets, and it's not a very pleasant world for Soli."

A protracted stare from the iridescent eyes made Calem feel increasingly threatened, and his own gaze fell. "An official request for an inquisitor's professional services always takes precedence over personal convenience, as you surely know," answered Jase at last. "You did send the summons?"

"You're the inquisitor. Yours is the job of discerning truth," retorted Calem, regaining a grain of courage by telling himself that this Soli could be manipulated by any appeal to the proprieties of Sesserda regimens.

"Yes," said Jase slowly. "That is my purpose here."

Calem became mocking, as always when he felt insecure. "I hardly suppose that my sister would have asked an inquisitor to her wedding." A tightness in Jase's expression encouraged Calem to recklessness. "My dear father might have summoned you, since he always likes to expand his contacts with influential friends, but he would never use my name. He despises me. I suppose that Tori has a sufficiently wicked sense of humor to have invited an inquisitor here—in perfect time to disrupt Sylvie's wedding—but Tori would not want to risk her job to my father's uncertain temper. It seems that I must have sent the message, mustn't I?"

"I did not come here to absorb the barbs of your insecurity," said Jase with mild disgust. He turned, took one firm stride to reach his hovercraft, and swung himself to the top step.

Before Jase could reenter the hovercraft, a cluster of Stromvi entered the hangar and hurried to surround his ship. They clicked excitedly, discussing him remotely, and Calem wondered at the odd fervor of their reaction to the inquisitor. They disregarded Calem completely.

Jase's frown faded into resignation in the face of the chorus of Stromvi imprecations, demanding unceremoniously that he explain his presence. "Let me secure my ship first," answered Jase, laughing at a burst of eager questions from a Stromvi child. "Your port manager, Ngahi, lectured me for neglecting my hovercraft, and I promised to improve my behavior." Several of the older Stromvi nodded sagely. Others disparaged Ngahi's effrontery with singular relish.

He has an instinctive gift for pleasing the Stromvi, observed Calem with disdain. Calem had never envied that particular skill in his father or in Tori, but he considered how awkward such rapport could become under the present circumstances. His worry became a knot beneath his ribs.

"You may find me in the main house when you finish entertaining the Stromvi children," said Calem crisply. He strode out of the garage and headed toward the house, calculating furiously, wishing more than ever that he could locate Ngoi. He observed peripherally that Jase's pensive glance pursued him.

Calem rounded the house and climbed the stairs to the patio at a run. His troubles consumed him so thoroughly that the woman who stepped out of the kitchen made him jump in surprise. "Mister Birk is looking for you, Calem," scolded Gisa, the Deetari housekeeper who had worked for Birk since Calem's youth. Gisa's high, musical voice had a ripple of impatience, which only irritated Calem further. "Go to your father now. He is in his office."

Calem had always loathed Gisa's maternal disapproval. Though the Deetari were equivalent to Soli in civilization level and broadly similar in physical construction, no one would ever mistake the one species for the other. Deetari were hairless and extremely thin with skin that varied from dark blue to pale gray, the gray tones becoming increasingly prevalent with age. Even the favored Deetari clothing seemed unpleasantly alien to Calem: long, simple, sleeveless dresses, embellished with cobweb-fine Deetari lace; bracelets and anklets of twisted wire and glossy beads; turbans adorned with mineral fragments. Deetari men generally wore bright colors, while women tended to prefer paler tones; otherwise, Deetari clothing was fairly genderless. The social distinctions between Deetari genders, however, were considerable. The Deetari matriarchy relegated their men to a position of dependency. Gisa respected Birk, but she treated Calem like a young male of her own kind.

"Have you seen Ngoi this morning?" demanded Calem, trying to sound authoritative.

"I do not keep track of that sorry example of a work leader. Your father is waiting." Gisa pushed Calem with thin, midnight-blue arms. She had retracted her fingers—seven on the right hand, five on the left—into their sheaths, giving her hands the webbed effect that had always disturbed Calem. Like most members of her species, Gisa was much stronger than she appeared, and the slight gesture nearly overbalanced Calem.

Resentfully, Calem trudged through the maze of the house to reach the barren, pentagonal stairwell, the hub from which the house's uneven wings emerged. Each of four ivory walls framed a solid door, a distinction that irked Calem. Birk Hodge allowed his family only as much privacy as translucent partitions and flimsy curtains could provide, but Birk's own rooms were equipped with the most substantial of defenses.

Glumly, Calem began to climb up the steep staircase that occupied the fifth side of the pentagon. The light fell softly through the high window above the stairs, sending pale, yellow beams into the shadowy room below. The banister felt slick, and Calem realized that his palms were damp with nervousness and Stromvi's inescapable resin. He wiped his hands irritably on his trousers before climbing the last step and turning left to face his father's office.

Calem paused in the open doorway, waiting to be noticed by the strong, stern man who stood at the floor-to-ceiling window behind the black lacquer desk. "Admiring your domain again?" asked Calem with the bitter anticipation of another disapproving lecture.

The man at the window turned slightly. His starkly white hair framed bold features. The skin was darkly tanned but tinted across one cheek with the violet hue of drying Stromvi resin. Birk Hodge was slightly shorter than his son, but Calem always felt small before him. "You did not join your sister and me at breakfast, Calem."

"I overslept."

Birk rubbed at the patch of resin on his leathery cheek.

His amber eyes narrowed in disgust. "How can you be my son? I would have believed your mother a faithless whore, if I had not performed the tests of your parentage myself."

"I am what you have made me."

"I have given you all that the Consortium could offer. I gave you every advantage of education, which you tried to circumvent by leaning on the talents of your friends." Birk scowled, as if the disappointing sequence of events had all occurred that morning. "I gave you the resources to begin your own business ventures, and you achieved nothing. I gave you some of the most fertile land in the Consortium, and what have you done with it?"

"If the land is mine," answered Calem tightly, "then let me use it as I deem best. Could you trust me even once, or must you always dictate every last detail of my life?"

"I have trusted you repeatedly. Perhaps that is where I have erred."

"I'll repay all my debts to you," said Calem, trying not to sound peevish. He was determined not to plead for his father's help again.

"I spoke to Ngoi this morning."

"What did you tell him?" demanded Calem angrily.

"He sought me, Calem. He is troubled by torn loyalties. You had no right to involve him in your scheme."

"Ngoi isn't your slave, much as you like to imagine yourself a feudal lord of Stromvi. I offered him a partnership, and he accepted."

"He did not understand what you were planning."

"Do you?" snapped Calem. "Or have you simply judged me, as always, without considering the possibility that I may actually know what I'm doing?"

"Nguri is right. I have given you too much." Birk strode to his desk. His large hands manipulated the locks with remarkable speed and dexterity, and he removed a boxy parcel from a drawer. The parcel was wrapped crudely in a gray-green cloth of finely woven Stromvi vines. Birk shook the parcel at his son. "This could destroy everything I've built. You have no idea what you're risking." Birk sat, and he shoved the parcel across the desk toward Calem. The polished lacquer of the desk's dark surface mirrored the uneven wrappings.

"I don't know what you mean," answered Calem, but the fear in him made his voice quaver. He reached toward the parcel hesitantly, but he did not touch it.

"Don't compound your dishonor by lying to me further. Not even your incompetence could cause relaweed to grow on Stromvi by mischance. I ordered Ngoi to burn and sterilize your field with chemical fire. It's better that the land be made barren than risk any chance of a surviving root stalk. Tell your customers that their crop failed to adapt to the Stromvi environment."

"Stop sounding so sanctimonious," growled Calem, his face livid with shame and anger. "You chose Harrow as dear sister's contribution to the family fortune, and you never mistook Harrow's brand of trade. When Harrow offered to connect me with his friends, you approved. What did you expect them to want from us?"

"I expected you to negotiate sensibly for legitimate products. You have neither the wits nor the nerve to succeed in illegal activities."

"You expected me to take the risks for you and earn the profits for you. You had no moral compunctions, until you decided that Ngoi was likely to talk to Nguri, who would certainly notify the Calongi."

"I shall eradicate all traces of this brief madness of yours, and we shall forget it completely. You should be grateful to Ngoi for informing me before it was too late."

"If you mean 'too late' to conceal the evidence from the Calongi, you had better reevaluate your plans," said Calem, letting his personal misery become sullen spite. "An inquisitor has just arrived. He thinks I invited him. Amusing, isn't it?"

Birk leaned back in his deep chair, and his scowl became a pensive frown. "Has he come to investigate your idiocy?" he asked quietly, and the fire of his anger had become a cold and deadly calm.

"He was very amicable."

"Then he is either ignorant of the relaweed or ignorant of your involvement. The former is most probable, since a Calongi infant could read the guilt from your wretched cowardice. Where is he?"

"Securing his hovercraft—or chatting to the Stromvi workers. How long do you think it will take him to uncover the truth? He's a Soli, but he'll obviously be much less naive than the Stromvi workers, especially where we lesser Soli are concerned. I don't know who asked him to come here or why, but I do not intend to carry the blame for your many sins."

"A Soli," murmured Birk thoughtfully, then he dropped his fist to the desk with a dull, angry thud. "I'd like to let you suffer the full consequences of your actions. You and your neurotic wife would be the better for the experience."

"Harrow's friends expect delivery soon. They will not accept a lame excuse."

"I shall speak to them," answered Birk, making the problem of dissatisfied drug traffickers sound insignificant. "This inquisitor is more difficult. Inquisitors can sense deception like an osang finding prey. However, the fact that he is merely a Soli should aid us. I shall talk to him."

The sense of relief spread strongly through Calem, though he despised himself for yielding to his father's domineering personality. *Birk Hodge will take care of Harrow's unpleasant friends. Birk Hodge will handle the inquisitor. Birk Hodge will handle everything.* "I almost hope you fail," said Calem softly. "I would like to see someone defy you successfully."

"You are not worthy to be called my son," snapped Birk.

* * *

After Calem left the office, Birk folded his hands and closed his eyes, feeling old and tired. Harrow's friends. . . . Per Walis would not attempt to establish relaweed on a confederate's planet. Growth of such a crop on any Consortium world was suicidal, and it was too extravagant a gesture to be explained as a simple effort to eliminate a rival. No one could deal with Harrow Febro without realizing that the man would serve anyone for a price, but Harrow was also too much of a coward to turn against Per Walis. Who else hated Birk enough to buy Harrow's treachery?

Birk considered various independents who might want to remove Birk Hodge as a competitor, but none of them could afford the seeds that had produced relaweed on

Stromvi. The possibilities circled back to Per Walis, who
had the means to accomplish such a plot, even if the
action seemed improbable. Birk debated sending for Tori
and questioning her, but he dismissed the idea. Per Walis
may have used Tori to obtain information, but he was
too careful to inform her of his private schemes. Per
Walis had undoubtedly calibrated Tori Darcy's surprisingly limited tolerance for lawlessness. As a legal employee—and quite possibly as a legal concubine—Tori
would always perform with exceptional dedication, but
she was not designed for conspiracy.

In any case, Birk could not convince himself that Per
Walis was actually the enemy. The instincts of a Rea
warrior did not accept that answer. Someone unknown—
someone powerful—had concocted this plan. The attack
had just begun, and immediate defense was mandatory.
By now, Calem's field had been destroyed, but other
condemning evidence might still exist.

Long laid preparations must be implemented. Appropriate treasures must be selected and made safe: various
hidden assets; significant forged papers; perhaps even
Tori Darcy, who seemed to understand the honorable
balance of strength and obedience quite well for a Soli
woman. The kree'va could be left in place, unless the
situation deteriorated to the point of demanding escape
from Stromvi. The enemy's name would be useful, but
it was not required.

Birk opened his eyes and stared at the doorway
through which Calem had departed. A Rea warrior's children should be prepared for war. They should fight at
their father's side. But it was Calem who had sowed the
relaweed, and it was Sylvie who first brought Harrow
Febro to Hodge Farm. Granted, the opportunity to solidify the links to Per Walis had made Harrow seem attractive to Birk's ambitions. . . . But no. This was not
Sylvie's first betrayal. She had also chosen the Squire
over her father. She had proved her disloyalty.

Like Akras and the Rea clan, Calem and Sylvie had
betrayed Birkaj. They deserved no mercy.

CHAPTER 13

Jase nodded as Ngeta provided a detailed update on the activities of her children for the past five spans, but he contributed few questions or comments. Abruptly, Ngeta abandoned an anecdote regarding one of Ngina's escapades. At her sudden silence, Jase's unconscious smile faded. "So," she announced firmly, "you hear a little of what I say, though you do not listen."

"Have I been drifting, Ngeta? Forgive me. I must be adapting slowly to Stromvi's atmosphere. My mind feels a little woolly."

"And you do not need a barrage of old gossip," answered Ngeta knowingly, "from a crowd of idlers who have work awaiting them." She clicked tersely to those of her people who clustered with her near Jase and his gleaming hovercraft. Reluctantly, the Stromvi began to scatter back to their interrupted tasks, until only Ngeta remained. She raised her upper torso to match Jase's height, as he leaned against the hangar wall. She extended her neck to peer closely at Jase's iridescent eyes. "I preferred blue," she remarked. "This is ostentatious, which does not suit you. Why did you change them?"

"Survival, dear Ngeta. I tested the limits of Soli adaptation once too often. Pigmentation changes are common in such cases."

"You should have remained here."

"Not possible, as you know."

Ngeta grunted, "All is possible, or you would not be here now."

"I shall not be here long. I have business to transact with Calem."

"That one is not your friend," replied Ngeta evenly. "That one is friend to no being—not to you, not to his wife, not even to himself."

"But I am his friend."

"And Sylvie's?"

"I've always been Sylvie's friend as well," returned Jase equably, but he shifted the subject with deliberate firmness. "Your hide patterns become richer and more beautiful with every passing span, Ngeta."

"Ngina becomes the beauty of the family. You will not recognize her." Ngeta paused. "Why did Calem fail to recognize you?"

"I've changed, Ngeta-li, since last he saw me. I did not expect to be recognized by any Soli here."

"You Soli rely too heavily on your limited vision." Ngeta lowered her head and began to turn away from Jase. "Sylvie will not rejoice to see you, especially now, so close to her marriage to this ambitious Soli trader."

"She will not know me, unless you edify her."

"She will see an inquisitor."

"I trust that anticipation of her wedding will over-shadow my insignificant visit."

"She stopped wanting Harrow when he became her father's choice," remarked Ngeta, and she ambled across the hangar yard and disappeared beneath the vine mass.

Jase continued to lean against the hangar wall, pensively observing Ngeta's dignified retreat. He folded his arms to warm his hands and wondered idly if he had actually managed to contract a fever. He had almost forgotten the sensation of illness, for relanine had made his immune system nearly unassailable. The less pleasant assaults of the relanine itself had never masqueraded as any curable ailment.

"I feel like the wrong side of a pummel board," murmured Jase to himself. "Calem didn't expect me. Sylvie won't want me. Birk will rightfully resent my interference in his private affairs, but someone invited me, and it was not a Stromvi. This promises to be a delightful visit."

Jase shook his head, but he laughed as he began to walk toward the main house. He had always liked Stromvi. After his rehabilitation from the accident, he had chosen to visit only one friend from his past, and that one had been Nguri. Jase had arrived quietly and left quickly, and he had not returned as often as he had originally intended, but Nguri's calm wisdom—even in those brief exchanges—had made a difficult transition time easier. The prospect of seeing Nguri again pleased Jase, despite the circumstances.

Jase had shunned business dealings with Soli for so long that the ease of approaching such interaction now surprised him. Raised chiefly by a series of Escolari tutors, he had always felt misplaced among Soli, except for that brief period of youth when the eccentric, erratic charms of the Hodge family had made him comfortable with his own species. Even now, fully aware that Birk, Calem, and Sylvie had all used him rather than befriended him, Jase approached Hodge House with a certain wistfulness. Ngeta was right. He might easily have remained here.

The sight of Gisa and Thalia scurrying to clean sticky resin traces from the porch furniture increased Jase's sense of Stromvi's timelessness. Jase whistled a rapid sequence of notes, and the two Deetari women looked toward him with wide, startled black eyes. Thalia trilled a happy greeting in return, and she continued her polishing as if a familiar worker had simply returned from a morning's efforts in the rose fields. Gisa's eartips fluttered in faint exasperation with her sister's simplicity of perspective, and she crossed the mossy yard to meet Jase.

"Thalia has no mind for time," remarked Gisa in her lisping rendition of Consortium Basic. "You are looking strong."

"As are you," answered Jase politely, but sincerity followed the automatic compliment. Though Gisa appeared very frail by most standards, Sesserda-trained perceptions recognized the Deetari strength as obvious. In previous spans, Jase had never noticed the intensity of the Deetari metabolism. The expansion of Jase's observations of Gisa brought him abruptly back to the present.

"Why have you returned?" asked Gisa.

"And I'm pleased to see you again, also, Gisa."

"My cousin cautioned me about unexpected changes in routine this month. She is a very farsighted prophetess."

"I remember. Is she well?"

"Yes. Why have you not answered my question?"

"Because teasing you gives me pleasure," replied Jase glibly, and he brushed his wrist against Gisa's forward tilted elbow. She responded automatically, clapping her hands together in a gesture that was considered flirtatious

among Deetari. "You are persuasive," laughed Jase.
"Perhaps I'll answer you, after all, but I must talk to
Calem first. He's expecting his inquisitor."

Gisa's round eyes flickered consideringly. "An inquisitor?"

"That is my present purpose." Jase tapped his chest.
"My name is Jase Sleide these days. I'm not what you
remember, Gisa."

"I had heard that you died."

"You heard a fragment of truth."

Gisa nodded, as if the resurrection of dead acquaintances were a common occurrence in the context of Deetari mysticism. "Calem confers with his father at present.
You must not interrupt them."

"Then I shall wait," answered Jase, but he altered his
frame of concentration to examine Gisa's unspoken concerns, as betrayed by her voice, movements, posture, and
manner—and by subtle factors for which only the Calongi had descriptive words. He allowed himself only a
momentary inspection of her by the difficult Calongi regimen he had learned at so much cost to his Soli nature.
"I shall not interrupt your work further," he murmured,
and he was concerned but unsurprised when Gisa hurried
away from him without further comment. He had read
the fear in her.

                    *   *   *

Gisa stood at the kitchen door, rubbing her elbows
nervously. Thalia entered, trilling a Deetari song of remembering. "You expected him?" demanded Gisa, turning from the garden view.

Thalia's trill ceased, and she regarded Gisa blankly. "I
told you of the reborn man." She resumed her song, as
she gathered the dishes for luncheon.

Gisa tried to quiet her frustration. Anger at Thalia
never helped. Like so many of the lesser Deetari pro-
phetesses, Thalia occupied her own reality. Making sense
of Thalia's prophecies was generally too difficult to be
worthwhile, but the portents had become too ominous to
ignore.

A dish had cracked with each of the last seven renew-
als of the lesser moon. Yellow-bark leaves, the ancient

Deetari tool of cursing, had appeared in kitchen jars at Hodge House, though such leaves should never be found on Stromvi at all. Miss Rillessa had developed her strange illness and now lived in the waking trance of the demon-possessed.

Cousin Evia had been unable to explain the omens, but she had advised preparation for a coming change. Now, the Squire had returned from death the morning after Thalia's prophetic fit. With careful patience, Gisa asked, "What follows the reborn man's arrival?"

"The storm," replied Thalia, never breaking her routine.

"Stromvi has no severe weather. What does the storm symbolize?"

Thalia laid the crystal dishes on the counter, and she began to arrange and rearrange them according to her own obscure rationale. "Fulfillment," she whistled softly, "of a powerful death-curse against the betrayer and all who have served him."

"Whose curse?" began Gisa, but both Deetari women became silent as Birk Hodge entered from the shadowed hall.

Birk ordered sharply, "Go and prepare the patio table for luncheon, Thalia." Unquestioningly, Thalia gathered the dishes on the tray and carried them past Birk and into the hallway. Gisa made the bow of obedience and moved to follow Thalia. Birk raised his hand to block her way. "Have you forgotten why you serve me, Gisa? I brought word of the death of your sister, who lived among the lawless, and my information enabled you to speak the proper rites to recover her soul. You repaid me with your oath of service."

"Service is the Deetari species-purpose," answered Gisa proudly.

"If either you or Thalia breaks faith with me, all of your people will suffer. My curse will override any other, and only I can save you. Do you understand?"

"The portents are evil."

"Only if you fail me. Obey me, and I shall preserve your people from harm."

Gisa twisted her bracelets, tightening the wire spirals around her wrist. "I must prepare the food for your luncheon."

"The food will wait." Birk pushed Gisa toward the stone work table, and he glared down at her as she sat upon a chair of woven reeds. "Your cousin is a powerful prophetess, who has the trust of your matriarch. You will tell your cousin of Thalia's prophecy, and you will then tell her of *my* prophecy. The storm is coming. I can protect your people, but the Consortium officials must not interfere. The Calongi do not understand prophetic wisdom, and they must not be allowed to reach Stromvi until the storm has passed."

"Deetari serve the Consortium first," argued Gisa, but her fear sharpened, for Birk Hodge spoke truly. Calongi did not share Deetari beliefs.

"I do not ask you to harm any Consortium official. You will protect our fellow Consortium members from a danger they do not understand. You can save them. No Consortium official reaches Stromvi without stopping first at the Deetari port. Speak to your cousin."

"I must read my stones," answered Gisa stubbornly, though she had seldom tried to consult the stones since girlhood lessons. She had never found much solace in casting bits of mineral. However, she had never seen so many obvious omens until the past few months.

"Your stones will confirm my orders," decreed Birk. Turning swiftly from the Deetari woman, he returned to the dark maze of his vast house.

Gisa arose stiffly and walked to the garden door. The Stromvi sky was a light, misty lavender. Stromvi weather was too benign for storms.

CHAPTER 14

Ngina teased Ngev delightedly, for she admired his intricate colors and strong features, and he responded with very satisfactory nips of her neck ridge. She would have continued the pleasant game, deriving increased enjoyment from the danger of discovery, but her father's distinctively reverberant clicking recalled Ngev to more orderly duties. As the young male returned hastily to his own fieldwork, Ngina sighed in disappointment. How would she ever win a mate if her revered father intimidated all of the appealing candidates?

Ngina tried to persuade herself to ignore her father's summons, but the roots of her respect for him twined too deeply inside of her. She raised her head from the burrow and clicked a response to tell him her location. She expected him to order her summarily to travel to *his* position, but he sent only a curt acknowledgment of her message. She concluded that he intended to berate her and did not wish to be observed at that undignified task by his fellow senior Stromvi.

Absently, Ngina cleared a sun-space for a silver-lily seedling as she waited. She liked silver-lilies with their ridged cups of resin dew and their bulbous pods that could hurl shiny seed arrows across a thorn field. She had less fondness for the thorn vines that sprouted ubiquitously on Stromvi, and she tugged ruthlessly at the tough fiber caps that protected the tender shoots of new vines.

When Nguri arrived, his posture stern despite his nearly horizontal stance, Ngina dropped the fiber cap that she had been gnawing. She rippled every skin fold of her head and body, in case some particle of moss still clung from her race with Ngev. Nguri frowned at her. "Why are you not in the fields?" he asked.

"I finished my morning work," answered Ngina primly, but she bit an inner lip in her anxiety. She hoped that her father would not ask about her assignments of the day. She did not want to feel that she had betrayed Ngoi. She had satisfied her conscience by telling Tori and leaving the resolution to the Soli woman's judgment.

Nguri waddled to his daughter's side and peered at her closely. If he perceived her nervousness, he did not remark on it. He nodded his great head thoughtfully. In the softest of Stromvi vocalization, he clicked a sound of praise, and Ngina almost slipped back into the burrow in her astonishment.

"Ngina-li," said Nguri quietly, "I have need of your youthful speed and strength. You often test my patience with your independence, but you must obey me without question in this matter. It is very important to our people."

"Esteemed father, I am always your obedient daughter."

"Not always so obedient," muttered Nguri, "but you have the seeing skills that your siblings lack." From a resin-moist neck pouch, Nguri removed a stem with five leaflets, slightly bruised from handling but fresh and intact. "Can you name the source of this leaf?" demanded Nguri.

"It is a rose leaf, my revered father."

Nguri clicked impatiently, and he thrust the leaf into his daughter's hand. "Examine it."

Concluding uncomfortably that this particular test of her knowledge weighed more heavily than usual with her father, Ngina gave the leaf a slow inspection. "It comes from one of the recent Hodge hybrids," she said tentatively, "because the veins are dark, nearly violet." When her father nodded slowly, Ngina gained the courage to continue, "It has the scent of a second blooming—early stage." Pleased with herself, Ngina stopped.

"You speak intelligently of the shrub. What does this leaf say to you of itself?"

He always questions me until I fail, moaned Ngina to herself. "I do not know, my excellent father."

"It is damaged," prompted Nguri.

"Yes," replied Ngina, bewildered by her father's intentions. "You removed it from the shrub, and you have carried it. The edges are frayed. The texture is becoming rough. The central leaflet is short. Its tip is blunt with signs of regrowth, so I suppose that it was broken while still attached to the shrub.''

"Examine the central leaflet carefully, Ngina-li."

Ngina frowned, the layers of her neck skin tightening as her jaws tensed. She moved the leaf delicately across her head knobs. "The central leaflet has an unpleasant odor at the tip," she remarked and returned the leaf to her father. She felt an urge to rub her head with root resin to eliminate the memory of the unfamiliar scent.

"Yes, Ngina-li, it is most unpleasant," said Nguri grimly. "I want you to go quickly to Calem's field."

"Ngoi forbade us younglings to go there!"

"I am Ngoi's senior, and you are my daughter. You will go to that field and search it for this scent, which you have observed correctly on the leaf tip."

"You want me to search the entire field?" asked Ngina in horror.

"I shall arrange to excuse you from your regular duties this afternoon. If you discover any traces of this scent, you will come to me immediately. You will not click the message to me across the fields. You will not speak of this matter at all, except to me."

"My most exceedingly admired father, what does this scent signify? And why do you want no one else to know of it?"

"Ngina-li, do not speculate and do not question me. Are you my obedient daughter?"

"Yes, my excellent father."

"Then go."

Propelled by her father's forceful shove, Ngina dove beneath the thick humus that covered most of Stromvi. Her eyes closed automatically, leathery lids protecting the delicate flesh, and the burrowing senses became more keen. Vine thorns skidded harmlessly from the natural armament of her hide. Fierce arrays of serrated bones emerged from the secondary mouth and shredded stubborn foliage in her path. She reached an excavated tunnel rapidly. She retracted her pruning teeth with a sigh and let her claws pull her through the root-masses and mud, glad that Ngoi had cleared these little used tunnels that led to the abandoned southern fields of Hodge Farm.

The field that Birk had allocated for Calem's use lay

at the southeastern edge of the broad Ngenga Valley. A ridge, the worn remnant of the ancient planet's youthful dynamics, marked the valley's edge, but the highest lily spike upon the crest scarcely reached above Hodge House. Despite the land's insubstantial vertical contours, the shadow of the valley rim seemed oppressively dark to Ngina as she raised her head from the access tunnel.

She remembered a story about a concentration of an unusual root resin in the southern soil making those fields unproductive for the Hodge roses. She could not remember hearing any other reason given for the abandonment of the Stromvi workers' enclave in that quadrant of the valley. Ngina squinted, trying to discern the ridge in clearer detail, but even her young eyes had trouble focusing. She could still see as far as her youngest siblings, but her distance vision had begun to lessen as she matured into adult Stromvi senses.

The prospect of defying Ngoi under the specific authority of her father might have amused Ngina if the task of searching an entire field in excruciating detail did not seem so like a punishment. Ngina listened for any indication of nearby workers, but she heard only the distant clicking from the main fields. She could not recall that anyone but Ngoi had worked the field since the first planting. This experimental crop apparently required less regular care than the other roses.

Ngina tested the air, seeking the direction of Calem's roses, but the wild, rich fragrance of panguulung lilies covered the lighter aromas. The ridge grew darker as Ngina approach it. Resin steam seemed to be rising more thickly than usual, blurring the view. A strange, harsh odor swept over her head nodules.

Ngina heard the ship only moments before she saw it. She crouched instinctively, feeling guilty for having disobeyed her work leader. The gray hovercraft skimmed the tallest lily spikes, and Ngina gasped. The hovercraft, flown so dangerously low, could easily have struck her if she had not lowered her long upper torso.

The ship paused above the dark ridge. The normally silent engines wheezed raggedly; the ship seemed to hover unsteadily. Ngina recognized that the hovercraft was malfunctioning, but she did not know how to measure the seriousness of the problem. That unpleasant

Soli, Jeffer, did not keep all of the Stromvi port vehicles in good repair. One of Miss Sylvie's guests may have rented a worn and battered vehicle. Ngina began to move as quickly as only a young Stromvi, strong and anxious, could travel through the thick overgrowth of Stromvi wilderness. The compulsion to help outweighed all other concerns.

She had nearly reached the ridge when the hovercraft dropped a large object to the Stromvi ground, rose high above the ridgeline, and disappeared into the hazy Stromvi atmosphere. Ngina raised her head above the vine tangle, and the burned expanse of the ridge assaulted all of her senses. Fire could convert various combinations of Stromvi resins into a highly corrosive gas, and Ngina winced from even the slight taint that reached her through the still air.

The brief, sharp click pattern that indicated the most extreme Stromvi distress came so softly that Ngina nearly dismissed it as imaginary. She did not want to approach the burned field more closely. Fire did not come naturally to damp Stromvi! She did not want to know what limp bundle the featureless hovercraft had discarded, for the prospect frightened her, but she moved forward without hesitation. Honor demanded that she offer aid.

Her milky inner lids closed automatically across her eyes, for the thick gas of burned resin hung heavily above the dead field. The scent of a Stromvi male's blood was strong, but too many harsher odors masked the gentle identity trace of the creature that groaned in the depths of misery. Stromvi, yes. Ngina could see that much through the hazy film of fog and her own protective eyelids. She touched him and felt the deep, disfiguring gashes in his hide. He cried aloud and tried to pull away from her clumsy effort to help. With a deep sense of shock, Ngina recognized him.

"Ngoi," she whispered, trying to sound mature and capable of dealing with whatever dreadful calamity had beset him, "it is only I, Ngina. I shall carry you to the infirmary."

Ngoi clutched at her with half a hand. "Ngina-li," he sighed in recognition. Ngina tried not to shrink from his dark, mutilated flesh, steaming with resin vapor. "I hid the parcels in the third south tunnel. Move them to the

south deep-room," he clicked, "before *they* return. Tell
the seniors: Use the parcels to defend our people."

"What parcels, Ngoi? Who burned the field?"

"I burned the stalk before *they* found me. They know
that the first harvest ripened a month ago. They know
we have the seeds. Move the parcels deeper. Safer."

"You need help now," said Ngina, and she tried to lift
Ngoi without injuring him further. His blood mingled
with the resin that had coated his hide all his life, and
the sticky blend darkened Ngina's hide in ugly patches.

Ngoi clicked a frantic negative. "Hide the parcels first,"
he pleaded. "Tell the seniors: seed of destruction."

Ngina hesitated, trying desperately to imagine how her
father would behave in this dreadful circumstance. Ngoi's
pleas seemed to become increasingly incoherent with
every moment of her inner debate, and she realized that
her indecision would solve nothing. She began to move
away from the blackened field, cradling Ngoi as carefully
as she could manage across such rough terrain. She could
not delve through the vine tangles with a grown Stromvi
male in her arms.

Ngina carried Ngoi as far as the tunnel entry, before
his agitated protests ceased completely. With a shudder,
Ngina laid him inside the tunnel entrance. She had never
seen a member of her species die before. The solemn
chattering of her hind teeth seemed remote to her, a
message only of the grief of an unknown female of her
race.

*   *   *

Akras whispered her command: "The Rea-traitor
knows we come. We have delayed too long. You must
prevent him from leaving the planet, Ares. Complete the
port takeover, and initiate the attack on the Ngenga
Valley."

"Not yet!" retorted Roake. The direct contradiction of
the clan leader made Tagran's fist tighten on his knife,
but the clan leader gave no sign that her guard should
react more firmly. If Roake observed Tagran's disapproving gesture, he disregarded it. "The Rea-traitor knows
only that relaweed was planted by his son. At worst, he
suspects Harrow Febro of betraying him to Walis, but

the Rea-traitor knows nothing of Rea involvement. He will not abandon his investment in Hodge Farm readily. He has only begun to feel the pressure of our vengeance. My plan is proceeding as I intended."

"You did not mention your plan to lose an entire harvest of relaweed," remarked Ares with thick sarcasm.

"We would already have recovered the seeds if you had questioned the Stromvi intelligently," answered Roake.

"He was dying when we found him," growled Ares. "You issued the order to discard him."

"Because you had rendered him useless, and that sorry hovercraft you appropriated could not sustain his weight."

Akras terminated their bickering: "You freed another prisoner yesterday, Roake. Are you setting a precedent of mercy?"

"Claudius acted too zealously when he took the other prisoner. The Soli's disappearance could have attracted attention, and his freedom cost us nothing."

"You should have presented your argument to me before releasing him, Roake."

"Yes, clan leader." Roake's words were humble, but the tone was unrepentant.

"Did you locate the kree'va?" demanded Akras.

The war leader grunted a reluctant negative. "That house is a maze, and I could not move freely even with the Bori to conceal me."

"Surely my brother was not so *careless* as to be observed," murmured Ares. "I collected him at the appointed time." The young warrior's bitterness caused Tagran to shake his head imperceptibly.

Roake did not even trouble to acknowledge Ares' words. "I must use the daar'va, clan leader."

"And eliminate any doubt that the Rea-traitor recognizes us?" snapped Akras. "If you underestimate him, even at this late moment, he will escape."

"Did you expect to destroy his world without him noticing?" demanded Roake with a scornful laugh. "You commanded me to make him suffer his defeat! I have complied with every rule of vengeance you have instilled in me. Do not fault me for having proven more successful than you ever imagined."

"Your part of the vengeance is done," said Ares evenly, but the fierceness of envy burned in his dark eyes. "Relinquish the traitor to me, brother, for the kill."

"Not yet," answered Roake, and he stared at his younger brother with an expression of contempt. "Your haste will dethrone our victory, even as the war prize trembles in our grasp." He whirled to face his mother, and he extended his strong hands toward her in a warrior's pledge. "I shall give you the Rea-traitor. I shall give you the Bercali who defiled the Rea home vessel. I shall give you the relaweed, the Rea-star, and the kree'va. Give me the time to complete my plans."

"Your plans?" demanded Akras, her body held stiffly straight. "Have you assumed the leadership of the clan?"

"My plans serve you and the Rea," answered Roake, and his Essenji pride glowed dangerously in the iridescent eyes of a relanine addict. "If you had wanted blind servility, Mother, you would have named Tagran as your war leader."

Tagran refused to react, but Ares rose abruptly to his feet and drew his gleaming clan-knife. "Do not mock the clan leader again, Brother, or I shall slay you along with the Rea-traitor."

"Stop posturing," ordered Roake, apparently indifferent to the hand raised against him. He bent one knee to touch the floor, assuming the position of obedience, and he addressed Akras earnestly. "Let me finish what I have begun, or the traitor *will* win again. If I fail to fulfill my sworn vows to you, if the traitor does escape, I shall offer myself willingly to my brother's anxious blade."

"The kree'va and the Rea-star are still in the traitor's hands," said Akras coldly.

Roake hesitated very briefly before replying, "The Soli, Jeffer, admitted that he had seen the kree'va, though he did not know its purpose. If you had allowed me to continue questioning him, I could have located it days ago."

"The Soli did not deserve to live," replied Akras crisply. "He disgusted me."

Tagran stared unblinkingly at the opposite wall of the clan leader's room. He knew why Akras had terminated the questioning prematurely, though Akras had not explained her reasons. Tagran had killed the Soli at Akras' command, because Akras had feared the extent of Jeffer's knowledge.

She had not berated Ares for claiming the Rea-traitor's former workman as prisoner. She had approved Ares' clean enactment of the abduction, but Tagran had recognized her unacknowledged alarm immediately. If Jeffer knew of the kree'va, Jeffer might also know of the Essenji woman who had once been Birk's lover. Akras would rather lose the kree'va than allow her sons to realize how personally the Rea-traitor had hurt her.

"Let me use the daar'va," insisted Roake.

"It is the war leader's tool. Use it as you must," answered Akras, suddenly indifferent. Her sons exchanged a glance, briefly united by their surprise at Akras' abrupt change of attitude. Tagran tried to believe that her decision reflected only her trust in Roake. His hope faltered when Akras continued, "But show me the stolen Rea treasures before this day ends, Roake, or Ares will be war leader by the next dawn, and you will personally be enacting our vengeance among the Bercali."

Roake did not reply. He rose to his feet and crossed the clan leader's chamber in a swift, lithe motion. He nodded once and vanished through the door.

"I have given you my orders, Ares," said Akras tersely. "Eliminate the remainder of the port personnel, and destroy their communication equipment. Proceed against the Ngenga Valley."

For a moment, Ares frowned. Tagran could see the conflict in the young warrior's sharply featured face. Ares was an obedient warrior, but he could hardly ignore the contradictions of Akras' instructions. "You did give Roake another day," he said, not as a question or complaint, but as a carefully respectful remark.

"He has behaved without honor, Ares. He has sold himself to the Rea-traitor."

Is it possible? wondered Tagran, knowing Roake's parentage. *It must be possible. The clan leader would not lie to Ares.*

Ares could not believe so quickly. "Roake?" he asked hollowly, though he had coveted his brother's position for so long.

"I have said it," answered Akras sternly. "You are war leader. Go."

Ambition overcame Ares' doubts—or coaxed them into hiding. "Yes, clan leader," he replied dutifully. Ares bowed and followed his brother from the room.

Ares is not a fool, mused Tagran. *He will not waste an opportunity to take his brother's place, even if the reason is a lie. But how long will his faith in his clan leader last?* Tagran halted his train of thought abruptly, as he realized the disloyalty that such ideas suggested.

Akras folded her pale, strong hands and laid her head against them. Her dark braid swung freely. Only Tagran saw her weep.

CHAPTER 15

Tori wandered slowly among the Hodge rose gardens, debating whether to speak to Birk about Ngoi's slack behavior before the dreaded luncheon. Even from the gardens, she could hear the slight clatter of Thalia laying the rose crystal dishes and rose-gold utensils in careful preparation of the patio table. Birk liked to survey his empire while he ate, and he had enforced the custom with particular adamance since Calem's arrival. The sight of the spreading, sloping acres of every shade of pink, violet, crimson, yellow, cream, and blue provided a persuasive argument for appreciation of the family business.

Tori believed, though she never conveyed her opinion to Birk, that the endless efforts to win Calem's enthusiasm achieved only intimidation and resentment. Calem lacked his father's self-confidence. That confidence had contributed more than any innate intelligence or skill to the success of Hodge Farm, for it had enabled Birk to give orders to the proud Stromvi. Only a man with Birk's supreme self-assurance could have invoked the cooperation of a gifted Stromvi horticulturist like Nguri. In common with most Stromvi, Nguri admired certainty, decisiveness, and persistence.

Birk has never yielded to discouragement, mused Tori, sharing the Stromvi admiration for that particularly outstanding aspect of Birk's character, *and I doubt that he has had an easy life, despite his current success. His is the certainty of earned affluence, not the insecure arrogance of inherited wealth in a culture that respects individual achievement far above family fortune.*

Respecting Birk's confidence was easy; loving him was quite another matter. *I loved Arnod,* thought Tori wryly, *and look where that disastrous match led me.* Birk Hodge was a much more rational selection. Tori felt reasonably certain that she could persuade him that he loved—or at least desired—her enough to sign a contract of patronage. "Following in Great-grandmama's illustrious tradition," murmured Tori, and she tried to forget how bitterly she had spurned the course she now weighed very seriously.

Disgusted with her own indecision, she made up her mind to go directly to Birk's office and confront him. She might speak to Birk about Ngoi, about herself, or about nothing in particular. She was not in a mood for detailed planning.

She emerged from the gardens, intending to enter the house through the paned doors of tinted crystal behind the patio. The route was as nearly direct as any through Hodge House, and she would be able to see if Sylvie had actually ordered another luncheon place set. Gisa always grumbled at Sylvie's spontaneous disruptions of routine.

The sight of a stranger near the front entry colonnade of the house diverted Tori from both her mental conflicts and her original destination. He appeared to be a Soli, monkishly thin with the hawk's profile and the thick, dark hair commonly preferred by elite Soli who could afford to control their offspring's genetic outcome. Tori sighed, concluding that duty demanded the man's rescue.

She had commanded herself to expect such visitors, Sylvie's pampered friends, bewildered by the initial effects of inoculations against Stromvi's brutal environment. Stromvi could be very intimidating to newcomers, and the misplaced Soli magnificence of Birk's house had made even seasoned visitors to Stromvi feel lost and overwhelmed. Tori had hoped that the wedding guests would not arrive so soon, but she had already girded herself for the inevitable.

The stranger looked more pensive than befuddled, but Tori employed her prepared welcome with practiced graciousness. "You must be here to attend the wedding," observed Tori in her most professionally helpful manner. Eyeing the man's bulky gray sweater curiously, she wondered if he were immune to the sweltering heat. She restrained herself from making any caustic comments.

As she approached him closely, she realized that his unsuitable attire was not his only peculiar feature. His eyes did not fit his classic Soli pattern or accord with any natural Soli design. An abnormally brilliant iris changed, as he moved to face Tori, from blue to green to gold. The entire surface of the deep eyes seemed to wear a shifting coat of iridescence.

Tori tried to remember descriptions of any race of sufficient biological compatibility with Soli to achieve hybridization, but she recalled only scattered stories of convergent evolution among the sub-civilized species of Level VIII and below. Uncle Per, an adamant racial exclusionist, had long sheltered her from knowledge that he considered impure. Calongi wisdom also decried the crossing of member-species, but Tori did not doubt that occasional private experiments did occur. Great-grandmama had been notorious for her alliances with other than Soli males.

The man reacted to Tori's greeting with a tightening of his expression. He studied her severely, as if making a difficult judgment. His strong features became more intense in their strict control.

His attitude seemed far more serious than Tori considered warranted by a light social exchange on a magnificent day in a spectacular setting, but she reminded herself to make allowances for the unpleasantness of adaptation to Stromvi. Tori donned a warm smile to hide her cynical mood. "The Stromvi call the house 'Hodge's Folly,' " she informed him, feeling as self-consciously simpering as a Zanwi tour guide.

He raised one hand toward the house, and he stretched the fingers backward, until the flexible digits poised nearly perpendicular to the plane of the palm. "Ostentatious displays of material wealth," he remarked curtly. "Indicative of insecurity. Very characteristic of Soli and most clothing-dependent species."

"Really," answered Tori, suppressing an urge to abandon all pretense of dignity by giggling. The thought of Birk's probable reaction to the stranger nearly overwhelmed her good intentions. She maintained enough self-restraint to stifle outright laughter, but she could not resist mocking the stranger's solemnity.

She lowered her face with affected meekness and gazed up through long, dark lashes. She reached forward to touch the man's arm, as if to reassure a mourner. The sweater felt impossibly silken after her years of contact

with Stromvi fibers, but she did not let the startling softness distract her. With a deferential fervor, she murmured, "I had no idea that fanciful architecture reflected
so badly on us. Please, sir, inform Birk Hodge of this
alarming situation. He will be devastated. He will want
to take immediate action."

"The problem," observed the man, without a trace of
humor, "is endemic in all derivatives of our species." He
stepped away from Tori's hand with a scholarly detachment that suggested preoccupation with unspoken concerns. "Such pointless insecurity has provided one of the
greatest obstacles to Soli progress." His eyes flickered in
a quick but seemingly incisive assessment of Tori, and
he turned his searing gaze back to the house. "It is significant that a man as impervious to self-doubts as Birk
should still exhibit such clear symptoms of the innate Soli
flaw."

"I'm so dreadfully sorry. Is there anything I can do to
make amends?"

Instead of replying to Tori's acrid riposte, the stranger
knelt abruptly at the edge of the white path, fashioned
of imported, polished ovoid stones. He ran his hand ca-
ressingly across the velvet pile of the blue-green Stromvi
moss. "This is all the wealth that Birk really needs: the
productivity of the land. He has created something of
lasting value, despite himself." In a complex motion of
blurring speed, the man raised his splay-fingered hand
toward the sky, as if in some ancient ritual of offering.

An underlying power in the gesture transformed him,
stealing his mask of pompous absurdity. " 'The flower
fades, but the beauty endures . . .' " quoted Tori, caught
for a moment by a spell of Stromvi loveliness seen
through a stranger's oddly iridescent eyes.

The man glanced briefly at Tori, before he lowered his
arm with a slowness evocative of regret. " '. . . to haunt
the memory of the universe,' " he said with dreamy wonder, completing the fragment of an ancient Calongi
poem. He grimaced and muttered almost silently,
"Plagues and afflictions upon your ineffable gullibility,
old boy." He rose briskly and studied Tori with a worried
frown.

"You know Calongi poetry?" asked Tori almost long-
ingly, for she had not met anyone else who knew that

bit of verse in many spans. She had not realized how hungry she had grown for someone who could understand the beauty of words she had not heard since her childhood lessons.

The man began to fidget, and Tori almost expected him to run headlong into the garden. She hardly dared to breathe, for she felt that she clung precariously to something precious. When he spoke with all his initial austerity intact, bitterness snatched Tori back into its grasp.

"I am not surprised by Birk's inability to advance beyond a materialistic philosophy," declared the stranger with haughty precision, "but the Stromvi disappoint me. Despite a tendency to excessive independence, they had so nearly advanced to Level IV. They have jeopardized the harmony of their world by letting Birk build and hybridize to excess." The stranger waved sententiously toward the fields of brilliant roses. "Birk should have added carefully selected Soli species to enhance the land, rather than eradicating so much of the natural Stromvi environment in his zealous expansion."

Tori's moment of fascination with the stranger was lost in indignation. "You must let one of the workers direct you toward the panguulung beds. You'd feel very reassured about the stability of the natural Stromvi life forms."

"Panguulung," murmured the stranger, blinking at the word, as if it had lain long forgotten in some cobwebbed corner of his mind. "The carnivorous lily that devours the carrion scraps left by osang snakes."

"The panguulung are perfectly capable of consuming live flesh as well, if you're willing to show a little patience. Stromvi life forms are very broad-minded regarding the species that they eat."

The man crossed his arms, almost as if he felt chilled. With a sigh very like resignation, he remarked, "You are obviously Miss Darcy. Calem warned me about your notions of wit."

"You're Calem's friend?" asked Tori.

"We're acquainted."

"The two of you must have a great deal in common," said Tori, experiencing a resurgent prickle of disappointment that the stranger should be so prosaically explicable after all. She regretted consigning him to Calem's ilk.

"Calem Hodge and I actually have very little in common," replied the man with the first emergence of a smile, "except that you have evidently relegated us both to the category of 'vexatious persons.' " He continued with a dry humor utterly in contrast to his earlier solemnity, "It's a better label than 'despicable villain,' I suppose, but probably less flattering overall. Bland dislike is really much more demeaning than burning hatred or furious disdain."

Startled by the man's mercurial change in attitude, Tori conceded, "You're cleverer than Calem. He spent the first month of our acquaintance believing that I found him irresistible. He's never forgiven me for correcting him." Tori related Calem's absurd mistake with flippant honesty. She wondered, however, if this strange Soli's comments about her present reaction were entirely true. Calem's angular friend seemed to inspire uneasiness more than dislike.

Tori could not determine why the Soli man unsettled her, but she was delighted to hear Birk's unmistakable tread, as unapologetically firm and forceful as Birk himself. Birk was a big man, less muscular than in earlier, hungrier years but still strong. Birk touched Tori's shoulder briefly, and Tori did not miss the stranger's slight frown.

Birk continued his gesture directly from Tori's shoulder to the stranger's reluctant hand. "Calem told me that you had arrived," said Birk. "Your presence honors us, Mister Sleide." Tori glanced curiously at Birk, his thick white hair shining in the sun, his expression forthright, enthused, and deceptively youthful. She might need to readjust her outward reaction to the visitor in order to accommodate Birk's attitude. Birk rarely greeted anyone with such a cautious show of respect and hospitality.

Mister Sleide nodded, responding enigmatically, "The season brings remembrance—and recognition of both change and constancy."

"Is that one of your Sesserda greetings?" demanded Birk with the gruffness of reluctant admiration. "I never have understood why a man delves into alien philosophies. Do me the favor of trying to speak like a Soli

while you stand on my lands." Birk made a command of
his words: friendly, determined, and absolutely assured.
"I see that my invaluable Tori has provided a formal
welcome on behalf of us neglectful Hodges."

Tori replied with a light, mocking lilt, "We never
reached the point of actual introduction." She observed
Birk carefully, gauging his expression, trying to decide
whether Birk knew this odd Soli. Birk could become jealous quickly, but Birk could also be highly protective of
a chosen few—like Calem and Sylvie. With cautious sarcasm, Tori remarked, "We became mired in philosophical piffle."

The Soli stranger murmured quietly, "Forgive me,
Miss Darcy. I am Jase Sleide. . . ."

Birk interrupted, baring his strong white teeth in a
broad smile, "Sesserda devotees enjoy their esoteric interests." He made the tribute sound dubious, and he
added with a rolling laugh, "A Sesserda aspirant once
tried to marry my daughter, before she accumulated a
roster of husbands scattered across our galaxy. I dis-
suaded Sylvie. I told her that a Sesserda scholar was too
idealistic to ever achieve anything significant."

Tori remembered the hysterical scenes that had accompanied her first arrival on Stromvi spans ago, and she
had a fair idea of the scope of Birk's dissuasion. "Were
you correct?" asked Tori with tactful restraint.

"Yes," replied Birk, and he looked at Tori thoughtfully. "The young man disappeared into well-earned obscurity." Birk pushed a strand of Tori's hair behind her
ear. If Birk intended to convey a proprietary suggestion
of intimacy, Tori felt certain that he had succeeded, and
the stranger's gaze embarrassed her. She wondered why
Birk was behaving so unnaturally, but she told herself to
accept his behavior as an encouraging sign on behalf of
her own position's security.

Birk remarked with cheerful irony, "We are boring
Mister Sleide, who has made such a long journey to visit
us. Why have you come, Sleide?"

"I was invited." The iridescent eyes closed for a
lengthy moment, and their owner became so still and
attentive that he might have been an ancient prophet
listening to inner voices. "Didn't your son tell you?"

"Calem seldom reports his activities to me," replied

Birk blandly. "He's a grown man, responsible unto himself."

Jase Sleide smiled faintly. "This is your home, Mister Hodge, and Calem Hodge is your son."

"And you appear to be my unwelcome guest, at least until we can resolve this confusion of purpose that has brought you here."

Birk's initial geniality had hardened into almost a threatening stance. Tori tried to shrug away her uneasy curiosity. She had not heard such a predatory tone of voice since she last observed Uncle Per commencing an aggressive plot against a powerful enemy.

"You must be a very unusual Soli, Mister Sleide," said Tori, and she tried to keep her voice entirely neutral. "I've heard that Sesserda study is very difficult and frustrating for members of our species."

"I fulfill my necessary purpose for the Consortium," answered Jase Sleide evenly.

Birk scoffed, "You idle scholars of alien lore function best as remote, useless dreamers."

"Your insights fascinate me, Mister Hodge."

"Did you come here for an education in practical thinking?"

Instead of responding, Jase Sleide nodded toward the thick violet and green barrier of native briers that surrounded the Stromvi workers' enclave. As Tori tried to locate the specific target of Jase Sleide's attention, the ever-present, unobtrusive sound of heavy Stromvi teeth clicking began to grow loud and frantic: the rhythm of agitated communication rather than of pruning or of clearing the fibrous vines that grew so prolifically on Stromvi. Birk frowned, for he had never mastered more than a few basic signals in the click-language. "Can you follow any of it, Tori?" he asked.

Tori waved him to silence, for the message had commenced again, and she had caught only a tiny part of it the first time. She could usually understand the Stromvi. She had a good ear for subtle rhythms. Today their message raced too fast for her to catch much more than the underlying tone of crisis.

"Ngoi Ngenga has died by violent means," interpreted Jase Sleide. His limber hand moved from his heart to the center of his forehead in a graceful gesture of respect derived from a Calongi tradition. "You'd better send the official notification to the Consortium relay on Deetari since Ngoi was found on your land, Mister Hodge. It would be appropriate for you to request inquisition."

Birk scowled, but he did not question Jase Sleide's interpretation. He moved two paces away from Tori and Jase Sleide and stared toward the workers' enclave. The vines and briers that engulfed the entries to the Stromvi homes rippled with hidden activity. "Ngoi was the first Stromvi that Calem ever befriended," Birk grumbled, as if he considered Ngoi's death an affront designed solely to preserve Calem's indifference to Hodge Farm.

Tori observed Birk's ruthless response with little surprise. It was the detachment of her own emotions that frightened her. The sense of Ngoi's death could not reach her, for she could hear only the word, *inquisition*. Although she knew that Ngoi—despite his haphazard attitude recently—was a friend deserving of an honest tribute of grief, she could not condemn Birk's coldness when her own reaction centered so predominantly on private fears. The fact that it was Ngoi who had first befriended her after her own inquisition seemed only to bind the present more grimly to the past.

"I'll find Nguri," she volunteered and hastily left the two men, not caring what they thought of her reaction.

Nguri would know the truth. Nguri would confirm or deny Ngoi's death honestly, and Nguri would tell her the manner of it. Nguri would tell her how much cause she had to worry.

*　　*　　*

"Get dressed, Rillessa," said Calem on entering his wife's room. "We have a guest."

"Sylvie has a guest," muttered Rillessa, but she relaxed her vigil and rose to obey him. She did not believe that *It* would hurt her in Calem's presence, because *It* was too cunning to act when her husband might see. *It* wanted Calem to doubt her.

"He's *our* guest," answered Calem irritably. "Sylvie certainly didn't invite a Soli inquisitor to her wedding."

Rillessa paused in untying her shoulder sash. "Jase Sleide?" she asked. At her husband's startled glance, she added with timid innocence, "There was only one Soli inquisitor when last I viewed the records. The Calongi seldom honor Soli with official Sesserda rank."

"So we're privileged to entertain a Calongi favorite," replied Calem with a grimace of anxiety. "Be courteous to him, Rillessa. Inquisitors are a dangerous breed."

"Only to those who have guilty secrets." Rillessa rubbed the back of her husband's neck. "Why are you so tense, Calem?"

"Because your nightmares kept me awake all night," snapped Calem. He paused to listen to the sudden burst of Stromvi click-language.

Rillessa recognized the frantic emotion in the Stromvi chorus, but she could not comprehend the words. She read the shock in Calem's expression, and she felt the resurgence of her fear of *It*. "What are they saying, Calem?" she asked urgently.

"Ngoi is dead—killed."

"Ngoi must have threatened *It*," whispered Rillessa. "Ngoi was too slow and clumsy to escape *It*."

Calem shook his head impatiently. "Finish dressing and join me in the family hall."

*　　*　　*

Jase closed his eyes, trying to detect elusive meanings in the panic-heavy Stromvi clickings, but his head still felt clouded by fatigue or fever or too much dwelling in the past. He had glimpsed a shadowy motion near the Stromvi enclave that disturbed him at a fundamental level. A proper Sesserda meditation would clarify his disquiet, but layers of heavier concerns would postpone such detailed cleansing.

He wished that he had time to clear and sort valid present thoughts from half-healed memories. He had not even announced himself properly to his subject, and the omission was inexcusable. He had accepted the inquisitor's role and could not abandon his task now, however grim it seemed after meeting that unfortunate young woman. Jase pulled himself forcibly from his drifting reverie in order to focus on Birk's words.

"I don't know why you're here," said Birk bluntly, "but I trust that you plan to explain yourself, especially after hearing of this tragedy. I must tell you, Mister Sleide, that I was not pleased when Calem said you had arrived. My daughter's marriage is much too important to be jeopardized by whatever bureaucratic error brought you here."

"Or by the murder of your Stromvi work leader?"

"I do not appreciate your sarcasm, nor do I tolerate outside interference in my business dealings," snapped Birk, but he controlled his flare of temper quickly. He became congenial again, and he assumed a paternal attitude. "I certainly try to be hospitable to Consortium officials, but you must realize that your arrival has curiously preceded any need for your services. I think you should return to the port and remain there, at least until I've contacted Deetari and confirmed your identity."

"You know that I cannot leave until the need for inquisition is resolved." Jase nearly added a comment regarding the peculiar summons he had received (purportedly) from Calem, but he hesitated, and Birk forestalled him.

"If you are indeed an inquisitor, the Calongi will know where to contact you."

Sylvie spoke from the doorway of the house, "Is this our prescient inquisitor?" Dressed in a satiny print of aqua water lilies, Sylvie struck a calculated pose of cool elegance. Jase had expected to feel some surge of nostalgic affection upon seeing her, but she might have been a stranger. Even the bright confidence that he remembered had vanished, replaced by unhappiness inside a placid shell.

Birk calmly informed his daughter, "Mister Sleide will not be staying with us, after all."

"Not staying? But Mister Sleide would make my wedding so much more memorable. I've never had an inquisition accompany any of my weddings, and Mister Sleide is certainly a more decorative inquisitor than some of our Calongi."

Birk chastised her mildly, "This is hardly the time for flirtation, Sylvie."

"Are you afraid that I'll abandon Harrow, and your profits will suffer? Fear not, Daddy dear. I have no taste for interspecies relationships, and an inquisitor can't quite be considered a Soli, can he?" Sylvie crossed the porch to stand beside her father, and she placed her arm around him protectively. Her arm trembled. "I do hope I haven't offended you, Mister Sleide."

Jase answered quietly, "Not at all, Miss Hodge. You're quite correct. I'm not entirely a Soli."

"I'll notify Jeffer at the port to expect your return," said Birk. He freed himself of his daughter's clinging with a brusque gesture. Sylvie shrugged slightly, as if apologizing to herself.

Jase automatically cataloged the Hodge reactions: Sylvie's nervousness, the only evidence that Ngoi's death had affected her; Sylvie's weary acceptance of Birk's rejection; Birk's overall impatience. "I cannot accommodate you, Mister Hodge," answered Jase, hesitantly employing a Sesserda technique to convey authority. "I came here for a specific purpose, which I have not yet fulfilled. Even if that purpose were to evaporate immediately, Ngoi Ngenga is dead. Until we know the circumstances, we must assume that an inquisition will be held, and no one should leave Hodge Farm. My Sesserda status does not mitigate my legal obligations; it enforces them. If I chose to exercise my full legal rights, I could assume control of the situation myself, but I shall spare you that aspect of my presence."

"I'll obtain a verbal release for you when I contact Deetari," replied Birk with a certainty that defied argument. He passed his daughter to enter the house, and she smiled at him brilliantly.

Her soft face became tense when she turned back to Jase. "Why are you here?" she demanded in an uneven whisper.

For a startled moment, Jase imagined that she had recognized him. "I thought that I was invited."

"Not by my father."

"No," answered Jase with a grimace, as his keener perceptions reaffirmed that Sylvie did not know him at all. "The summons was signed by Calem Hodge."

Sylvie's laugh had a tense raggedness. "My brother has always been a fool."

"I'm not your enemy, Miss Hodge."

"No. You're only the conscience of the Consortium," said Sylvie, regaining her tightly controlled smile. "When will you begin to question us?"

"I have not been assigned to that task."

"Ngoi Ngenga is dead."

"I know. I heard."

"I do you hope you can finish your wretched work before my wedding guests arrive." Sylvie brightened again, but the facade was brittle. "My brother and I have disappointed Daddy in many ways, but we both mastered the crucial lesson: Daddy always taught us to appreciate the satisfying rewards of selfishness."

"Your father's coldness does not become you."

Sylvie's emotionless mask folded into pain. "Stay here, Mister Sleide. Don't let Daddy persuade you to leave." She touched his chest with tentative fingers. "You remind me of someone I used to know. I've never come as near to happiness as during the time I spent with him."

Jase watched the thick wool of his sweater engulf her fingers, and the image made him think of talons sinking into his life—repeatedly. "Did you ask me to come here, Sylvie?"

Sylvie did not seem to hear him. "You don't know what they're doing to me, Mister Sleide, how miserable I've felt, waiting for this latest wedding that my father has arranged. You think I sound cold. Harrow is colder— to me, to my father, to everyone except Per Walis, who employs him. Harrow was so charming to me at first." The rounded contours of Sylvie's face made her look childlike in her tearful pain. "Then I brought him here, and he changed."

Jase felt an echo of old emotion tug at him, but he studied Sylvie by Sesserda methods, and the instant of tenderness passed. Sylvie's hurt was genuine but shallow, and confusion rather than regret inspired her to exploit a stranger's sympathies. The news of Ngoi's death had scarcely touched her. She expected an inquisitor to enact justice, and she could not perceive any justice greater than her personal comfort. *Have the spans changed her so much,* wondered Jase with a touch of self-deprecation, *or was she always this much like her father?*

He made his well-trained voice sound caustic: "Have you already forgotten your accusation, Miss Hodge? You're trying to appeal emotionally to a man who is not quite of your species. I do feel compassion for you, but you would neither comprehend nor appreciate my reasons."

Jase regretted the need to rebuke Sylvie, and part of him loathed the ease with which he set aside a cherished illusion of the past. His cynical remarks had the calculated effect. Sylvie's amber eyes widened with astonishment that anyone would actually speak sharply to her, and she ran into the house. "To seek consolation from Daddy," remarked Jase wryly, "who will give her as little love as he receives."

Jase shivered, a renewed chill besetting him in waves. The sweater did little to alleviate the discomfort, and Jase rubbed his hands, trying to warm them. For an unpleasant moment, he wondered if the implant had malfunctioned, misallocating the injection of relanine into his blood, but he banished the futile worry.

His eyes searched the gardens for the shadow that he had imagined against the thorn hedge, but he saw only a pair of Stromvi workers emerging from their home enclave and heading toward the fields. The clattering of Stromvi voices had become muddled with crossed questions and concerns, and Jase could distill only occasional, isolated words. He resisted the temptation to follow the two Stromvi workers and ask them for such information as they could provide. Instead, Jase headed for the family hall and Calem, who had some pertinent questions of his own to answer.

CHAPTER 16

Tori ran along the white stone paths, weaving through Birk's formal garden until she reached the mossy trails that marked the Stromvi realm. She slowed her pace, moving more cautiously among the native Stromvi plants that edged the rose fields. Though it was a carefully cultivated segment of the native flora, the vines could still snag the flesh from a careless Soli's tender skin.

Without hesitation, Tori followed the uneven course to the hothouse that Nguri had made his personal retreat. It was a typical Stromvi structure, embedded within the ground and delving into a root-supported cavern. Silver-lilies surrounded it, pale and delicate cups that cradled shining beads of blue and lavender resin, exuding soft mists wherever sunlight penetrated the protective shield of pulpy foliage. Tori walked carefully, avoiding the ripening silver-lily pods. The sting of seeds could be painful.

The round hillock of woven roots and matted fibers had been designed for the Stromvi people. It suited the Soli physique as badly as stairs suited Nguri. Tori untied the bindings of her sandals. She set the shoes in the dry hollow of a meter-long granite block, which Birk had imported for that purpose, and she took from the hollow a set of traction bracelets. The bracelets were an old set, worn almost smooth, but Tori fastened them tightly around her wrists and unfolded the coarse, externally barbed sheaths across her hands. Unlike the Stromvi, her hands had no natural ridges of sharp hooks beneath thick cuticles; her nails exuded no resin-dissolving acid to control the level of friction through the underground tunnels.

She crawled inside the hothouse. Propelling herself with the traction bracelet barbs, she slid along the slippery passage to the inner chamber. Steamy, resinous air enveloped her, the piercing odors so overwhelmingly disagreeable that she dug her fingers into the thick pad of a Stromvi rug to prevent herself from retreating. Her body signaled the danger that her mind knew did not exist. The room repelled her. Even Stromvi's surface air would have poisoned her Soli lungs if she had not been inoculated to survive on the Stromvi world, and the Stromvi dwellings swam in thick fogs of the potent resin gases.

Within the hothouse, Nguri had cultivated many new varieties of root stocks, experimenting with fiber types and textures, resin chemistry, biolight, and coloring. Most such Stromvi plants never saw the sun. They subsisted on the chemical byproducts of microbes in the Stromvi soil, and they converted that soil into the fertile land which enabled the roses to grow and thrive. Humid Stromvi had no native forms of fungus to produce decay. Root resins, diverse in chemistry and process, along with Stromvi teeth performed the functions that maintained the Stromvi cycle of life. Without the strict sterilization procedures of the Consortium, a few Soli spores could have devastated the Stromvi ecology.

The senior Stromvi sat in the center of the room, his upper body waving slightly, his teeth clattering in a faint echo of the rumbling of his people, heard only dimly through the thickly insulated walls of the deliberately isolated hothouse. The pallid spikes of dangling roots brushed his squat head, spreading droplets of their warm, bioluminescent efflux onto his thick skin, endlessly enhancing his body's natural armor.

Nguri continued the soft clicking of his hind teeth as he spoke to Tori in his deep outer-voice: "Ngoi is dead."

"How?" whispered Tori.

"Torn apart," said Nguri grimly.

"By an osang snake?"

"No," answered Nguri.

He paused for a moment in his clicking. Tori could not distinguish the distant, subdued rhythms, but Nguri raised his body slightly in attention. When he resumed the click speech, he forged a new element into his previous pattern: *Ngoi of Ngenga; work leader of long purpose; honored father, brother, son; many-friended; joyous light.*

Until the time of mourning ended, Ngoi's family and friends would each add new words of tribute to the message that the clan would chant. Tori recognized most of the elements as standard Stromvi praise, but she wondered at the brevity of the descriptions and the paucity of contributions. Ngoi's epitaph was a paltry, pallid effort by Stromvi standards.

"His body is riddled with the marks of Stromvi pruning teeth," said Nguri, startling Tori from her pensive reverie.

Recalled to herself, she absorbed Nguri's words with quick, cold logic. *If it is clearly a Stromvi crime, the inquisitors will not question me,* she concluded immediately. After reassuring herself of that crucial element of personal safety, Tori felt the weight of sick wonder bear down upon her fully, and her selfish instincts disgusted her. "Stromvi have never killed their brothers," she observed aloud.

"Not in all our recorded history," agreed Nguri solemnly.

Tori recalled the comments of the strange Soli visitor— that the Stromvi had jeopardized the harmony of their world by working so closely with Birk. The criticism had annoyed her on behalf of Stromvi like Nguri and Ngeta and others whom she loved, but now the words taunted her. "I mourn with you, Nguri," said Tori, contrite for the doubts that writhed inside of her. "Can I help in any way?"

"What do you know of inquisitors?" asked Nguri, and a stiffness of manner made him seem strange and unfathomable.

Chilled by the question, Tori countered it, "What is there to know about inquisitors? They are Sesserda adepts, who fulfill their civic duty by enacting Consortium law. They are nearly always Calongi. They see all truths. They ensure justice."

"I ask a question, and you recite a dictum that every Consortium infant learns," replied Nguri scornfully, but his voice clattered with the soft, rattling vibration that conveyed Stromvi anguish so eloquently. His black eyes narrowed beneath the protective outer lids of furrowed hide, and he leaned toward Tori to see her clearly. "None of my people has ever faced a serious truth-seeking, for we have had no crimes great enough to warrant Consortium justice."

She did not want to answer, but love for Nguri and sorrow for his people forced her frightened whisper, "An inquisitor interviewed me once." It was nearly the truth—nearer than any other words she had spoken on the subject in several spans. The shadows of her deception mocked her: *Many questions. One crime. No conclusive resolution, except regarding the rarity of my case.*

"Tell me," urged Nguri.

"Only one inquisitor comes, as a rule. The inquisitor asks you questions, and you answer. Sometimes the inquisitor just watches you, as you proceed with your life. The process is painless." Tori shrugged, while a cynical voice in her head continued, *Except for what it does to your heart and spirit.* "The inquisitors are very good at what they do. There are very few beings that they cannot read accurately. That is why Consortium law has proven so successful for so long among so many diverse species, and that is what has made the Calongi the dominant lawgivers." She knew that her voice betrayed her, but she hoped that Nguri would only credit her with empathy for his own anxious pain.

Nguri's hooded black eyes, milky now from the inner lids that had closed against the resinous air, studied Tori unswervingly. She hoped that he would not ask her why the Calongi had questioned her, for she did not want to lie to him. "Thank you, Tori," he said at last. "You reassure me."

He did not sound reassured, and he resumed the weaving dance that followed the pattern of mourning. The depth of his distress concerned Tori on many levels: for him, for his people, for Hodge Farm, and for herself. Nguri was senior; Nguri was much respected; Nguri would be questioned first.

In his current, dark mood, Nguri would not stand up well before an inquisitor. The questioning would last that much longer. "Have you any idea who might have killed Ngoi?" asked Tori, for the inquisitor would ask this question and others like it.

"No," replied Nguri tersely.

"Had anyone expressed particular anger against him?" persisted Tori.

"Only myself," answered Nguri faintly. "I accused him of valuing Calem above his own people."

"No one could imagine you as a murderer."

To Tori's alarm, Nguri snapped his pruning teeth at her. "Who could imagine any Stromvi in such a role?" he demanded sharply. "It is Soli who have corrupted us with laziness, foolish insecurities, and hunger for unproductive pleasures. When did any Soli ever thank us for the sharing of our beautiful planet, for yielding acres of our beautiful soil to insipid, shallow-rooted Soli plants that cannot even pollinate themselves without our help?"

"I thought you loved the roses like your children," said Tori, feeling more hurt than she could have imagined by Nguri's expressions of disdain for the roses they had tended together.

"They are worthless children," retorted Nguri, and his pruning teeth sliced a dangling, dead root casing, "like worthless Soli."

"Nguri, hear your anger," pleaded Tori, "and conquer it before the inquisitor arrives."

She tried to exit gracefully, but the slippery, resinous dew of the damp room had covered her limbs. She berated herself for the haste that had brought her to the hothouse without checking the traction bracelets. They had sufficed for the downward slope of entry, but they were much too badly worn for climbing. The skidding surfaces resisted her efforts to maneuver, and she was forced to ask Nguri's help to propel her back into the drier portions of the entry passage. The Stromvi grunted agreement and pushed her with his broad, hard hand.

* * *

"*It* killed him," muttered Rillessa. "*It* will kill us next." She frowned resentfully at the goblet of wine her husband thrust into her hands. "Is it drugged?" she demanded coolly.

"Of course not," snapped Calem. He reached toward the goblet, as if to snatch it back from his wife's white, clenched fist. Rillessa recoiled from him. The goblet fell to the floor, and the colorless wine splattered across the dull carpet, giving the dried moss a brief illusion of life. Both Calem and Rillessa stared bemusedly at the hard, unbroken crystal of the empty goblet, as it wobbled and became still.

Jase watched the uneasy family portrait, feeling intrusive but too lethargic to move. The worst of the feverish chills had eased, but they had left his body aching. He had achieved some semblance of comfort, engulfed in a well-padded chair at the side of a stiltedly formal settee. The room contained too many of Birk's expensively collected artifacts to qualify as tasteful, but it did provide an ample selection of furniture to ensure a guest's physical comfort.

Ignored by his host and hostess, Jase observed, an art in which he had been tutored exhaustively by Calongi masters of the craft. Calem had answered nothing, but Calem's nervousness was so palpable as to be embarrassing. Rillessa's emotional instability sufficed to explain a part of Calem's tension, but Jase detected currents of distress that relegated Rillessa to a position of minor annoyance in Calem's view. Jase remembered Gisa's fear and regretted that he had come. He would welcome the arrival of a more experienced inquisitor.

Calem kicked the fallen goblet beneath Rillessa's chair. He leaned against the window seat briefly and then crossed the room to gather a fallen petal from one of Gisa's elaborate floral designs. He held the pale peach petal to his nose. "Dream Spirit—or Lady Julianne," he mused. "I never can tell the two apart."

"Stop pacing," warned Rillessa. "*It* will see that *It* has frightened you."

"Be quiet, Rillessa," answered Calem without emotion. Wife and husband stared at each other vacuously.

Jase endured the tableau until the tension began to snatch at his own peace of mind. He rose from the depths of the chair and winced slightly at the resultant pounding in his head. Continued movement seemed to lessen the aches. He felt the faint tingling of a surge of relanine entering his system.

He crossed the family hall, thinking that the room succeeded too well in retaining the cold of its crystalline panel walls, despite the clutter of furniture. He retrieved the fallen goblet and set it carefully on the polished table. He rubbed the granite surface briefly, remembering how much effort Birk had exerted to bring such massive stone pieces to Stromvi.

Turning from the table, Jase said softly, "I'm very sorry about Ngoi Ngenga. I know that he was a particular friend of yours, Calem."

"A particular friend," echoed Rillessa. "*It* killed him. *It* will kill us." Her spidery fingers kneaded the fabric of her dress, a splotch of harsh orange that emphasized her alien discordance with cool-toned Stromvi.

Jase looked at her, analyzing her stark face and rigid posture by Sesserda techniques, and he nearly shuddered at the magnitude of conflicts evident within her. He willed himself into the detachment of Sesserda control, though the effort revived the pounding in his head. "What do you mean, Miss Canti?" asked Jase with a Calongi's persuasiveness.

"Ignore her," muttered Calem wearily. His light hair had fallen across his face in random tendrils, making his handsomeness appear dissolute. "She enjoys chronic distress." He filled another goblet with wine, and he stared into the pale liquid without drinking it. "She never liked Ngoi," he observed and raised the goblet to catch the window's light. "She relishes his death because it justifies her constant misery."

Calem's icily objective manner in deriding his wife did not seem to disturb Rillessa. Her tight lips almost seemed to tilt to the approximation of a smile. Jase found her indifference even more chillingly distasteful than Calem's scorn. The signs of a narcotic's interference were clear, though Jase could not identify Rillessa's particular destroyer. His own addiction made him loathe the company of other drug abusers. He could imagine his possible future too clearly when watching them.

Jase pondered the advantages of questioning Calem directly. *If you did not summon me, Calem, why am I here? I know that the reasons are more complex and troubling than I anticipated, and I did not expect a holiday.* "I would like to help," offered Jase, wishing that he had not returned to Stromvi on this day of all days, "if there is anything I can do for you."

Calem began to laugh. Rillessa's expression disapproved of her husband's levity, making her resemble the reserved, rather dignified woman Jase had expected from

her official records. However, her green eyes danced
restlessly, constantly scanning the room from floor to
ceiling in all directions. A threat of madness lay in those
eyes, and Jase frowned, suddenly sure that the threat
verged on reality.

"Will you help us by being our inquisitor, by prying
into every secret and dredging every private thought and
feeling into public view?" asked Calem with a lightly
mocking tone. He seemed to delight in the question: a
glorious joke that no one else had the wit to appreciate.

Calem sidled past the scattered chairs to stand in front
of Jase, blocking the inquisitor's effort to escape without
confrontation. Calem puckered his face with worry. He
bent forward conspiratorially, clutching Jase's shoulder.
"Will you probe us for our guilty secrets—and later disparage our Soli foibles with your Calongi colleagues?
Doesn't it bother you to serve the Calongi against your
own kind? Or don't you consider yourself as lowly as us?
Do you have a Soli family, Mister Sleide, or were you
created in some alien laboratory in defiance of your precious Consortium law?"

"I came here to help you."

Rillessa announced clearly, "He came to kill *It*."

"Can't you keep her quiet?" asked Sylvie, entering the
room with an eye-catching sweep of her aqua satin skirt.
She walked straight to Calem and pushed him toward his
wife. Calem glared at his sister, but Sylvie had appropriated his position before Jase. Sylvie faced Jase with a
defiant tilt of her head. "You upset me deliberately a
little while ago. Why did you do that to me, Mister
Sleide? I have enough grief to endure without your efforts to aggravate my pain."

Calem laughed with a loud coarseness that offended
by design. "I love to watch you work, Sylvie. Have you
ever slipped and found yourself thinking about someone
other than yourself?"

"My brother is such a model of selflessness," sighed
Sylvie, touching her smoothly upswept hair. Her amber
eyes never swerved from Jase. "Would you guess, meeting him, that Calem would be such a miserable failure at
everything, despite a fairly decent employability quotient? Of course, Calem never passed an exam on his
own merits. He stole all of his results from his friends.

Daddy selected the friends and let Calem take care of anything really illegal: the bribery and such. The friends never realized why Calem became such a devoted companion to them. They were so charmingly naive."

"I imagine that they knew," replied Jase, "eventually." He tried to retreat from Sylvie, and Rillessa grabbed his wrist.

"You must find *It*," hissed Rillessa, "and kill *It*."

"Will you stop!" shrieked Sylvie. "No one is looking at you, Rillessa. No one cares about you. Your insane jealousy of Tori Darcy is driving all of us mad. It would not surprise me to learn that you killed Ngoi, mistaking him for your phantom admirer."

In the leaden wake of her outburst, Sylvie seemed to realize the import of her words. She shrugged self-consciously and walked to the Cigni tall-harp, a very expensive, very ornate concert piece that her father had given her in a spurt of optimism. Sylvie touched the harp carelessly, and a discordant cascade of sound whined from the badly tuned instrument. Jase winced.

"Are we too uncivilized for you, Mister Sleide?" asked Calem with gloomy defiance. "Do you feel degraded and demeaned just being in this monstrosity of a house? I do. A sense of shame is my father's gift to his children, his guests, his workers. . . . Ngoi understood."

"Blaming Daddy is your answer for everything, isn't it?" said Sylvie sharply. Calem growled an unintelligible reply.

"*It* has killed and will kill again," muttered Rillessa, tugging relentlessly at Jase's hand.

Feeling besieged, Jase turned to the latest demand on his attention. Rillessa could never have possessed a particularly dominant personality, certainly nothing on the Hodge scale. Calem had probably married her only to annoy Birk. Of all the Hodge family, Rillessa was by far the easiest to ignore, and Jase regretted that she would interpret his abruptness as merely part of the normal Hodge contempt for her. He did not know enough of the Ilanovi mind methods to help her now, when she marched so insistently toward the line beyond reason.

Sylvie left the harp and crossed the room with quick, determined steps. She pushed Rillessa away from Jase and slapped her sister-by-marriage twice. Rillessa blinked, thwarting tears of pain, but she smiled at Sylvie with a complacent dislike.

Sylvie raised her hand again, but Jase gripped her wrist before she could complete the third blow. Sylvie jerked away from him angrily. "You have no right to touch me, Mister Sleide," she snapped. "You have no right to be here at all." She whirled toward her brother. "Were you really stupid enough to invite him?"

Calem sipped his wine thoughtfully. He leaned against the granite table, and the metallic mesh of his vest clattered against the stone edge. "I always love to watch my insufferably sophisticated, extraordinarily cold, and condescending sister transform herself into an hysterical shrew," commented Calem with a distorted grin. "Harrow deserves to see the tempestuous side of your dark nature, Sylvie. Harrow might actually like you this way."

Rillessa hissed, "*It* moved outside the window. Did you see *It*?"

"Wouldn't that be a rich joke?" demanded Calem, apparently oblivious to his wife. "Harrow might actually learn to appreciate you for something other than economic convenience, Sylvie. The wedding show promises to be even better than I expected, accompanied by your tantrums, Mister Jase Sleide, and a full-fledged inquisition."

"I think I shall see if your father has talked to the Deetari representative yet," murmured Jase, his throbbing head unable to endure the barrage of angry emotions any longer. He retreated from the room, under the cool gazes of Sylvie and Calem. He disregarded Rillessa's frantic, incoherent protest. He would speak to her later, he promised himself, and try to diagnose her deepest troubles away from any onlookers.

Jase felt his way through the house of trompe-l'oeil panels and deceptive crystal walls. Birk had always enjoyed shifting the floor plan as an exercise of power. Even spans ago, Jase had found Birk's fascination with control unsettling. The maze of corridors used sound and light and shadow to confound, but the deceptions could not fool relanine-refined Soli senses, trained by Calongi masters to unnatural acuity. Even in his current, hazy state of near-illness, Jase navigated unquestioningly through the house.

Jase let his mind close inward on itself, stabilizing unhealthy emotional responses and forcing clear vision. Despite weighing a substantial number of alternatives, he
could not identify any desirable position for himself in
the explosive Hodge household. Under ordinary circumstances, the rational decision would be to leave immediately. However, a possible inquisition pended, and
another inquisition demanded belated completion.

He muttered to himself, "You have managed to preserve a suitably Sesserda-calm perspective among peoples
on the brink of interplanetary war, Sleide. You should be
able to endure Hodge Farm for a few more millispans."

Jase climbed the stairs to Birk's office in an abstraction
formed of a lingering ill-ease and a deliberate, meditative
haze. The second floor of Hodge's Folly consisted of two
unequal and disjoint segments. Birk's office occupied the
smaller segment, creating an appearance of solitary re-
gality that the habitually open door did not alleviate.
Jase observed the austere changes in the office decor and
concluded that Birk's desire to dominate his environment
had not subsided with the passing Stromvi years.

Sunlight poured across the black lacquer of the broad
desk and reflected blindingly from a silver desk set. Jase
averted his eyes and saw Birk hunched over the transceiver unit at the opposite end of the room. A disturbingly familiar sense of something present but unperceived
sent a teasing warning through Jase's mind, but Birk demanded evenly, "What do you want, Sleide?"

"Have you contacted Deetari?" asked Jase. He wished
that Birk would face him. He could read little from the
glossy white folds of fabric across Birk's back.

"I'm in the process of requesting confirmation of your
identity. Is that all?"

"No." *Preposterous to imagine that Birk actually considered his visiting inquisitor an imposter! The penalties
for impersonating an inquisitor were far too severe, and
the difficulties of enacting such a deception were virtually
insurmountable. Even a Soli inquisitor, announcing his
status, might expect a reaction of surprise but never disbelief.* "We have a great deal to discuss, Mister Hodge."

"Later, please. I'm still in contact with Deetari. An
official is being summoned to speak with me directly."

"I can wait."

"Wait elsewhere," retorted Birk sternly. His eyes turned briefly toward Jase. "I've made my position clear. You're unwelcome."

The quick retort disturbed Jase. Birk was notoriously outspoken but rarely so prickly, especially toward a Consortium representative. Even if Birk did doubt Jase's official status, Jase would have expected a pretense of belief until the uncertainties were eliminated. Ngoi's death should have increased Birk's eagerness to placate a man who claimed to be an inquisitor. The nameless fear within Hodge House had not missed the house's master.

"You must understand why I cannot leave yet," said Jase.

Birk growled, "I understand that one of my workers died suspiciously soon after your unexpected arrival. I don't know if you're actually a Soli in servitude to Calongi masters, but I know that many men covet my wealth, my power, and my success as a Soli. If you're looking for a stake in my possessions, abandon your ambitions now."

Incredulous, Jase laughed. "Sesserda practitioners are generally accused of caring too little for such wealth and power." An old instinct, a remnant of a youthful hurt, enabled pride to air itself, "I need no part of your treasures, Mister Hodge. Planetary rulers offer me any prize I can name, and I'm unable to answer them: I have everything already."

"Except your own life," said Birk bleakly. "If you crave a reconciliation with your species, start elsewhere and leave my family in peace. Your subjugation of Soli nature to the Calongi's effete regimens disgusts me."

The taste of old anger filled Jase, but he detached it from any external reactions, repentant of his flare of pride. Birk had used such taunts deftly when Jase lived at Hodge Farm, delighting in Jase's ferocious reactions to sensitive subjects. Sesserda warned against the temptations of childish outbursts. Sesserda forbade such a fiery temper to exist.

The ability to defy Birk's current intent did not particularly please Jase. Sesserda discipline constrained the temper but did not make the cause seem less cruel. Jase retaliated with a coolly calculated shift of topic, "Do you know that your assistant, Miss Darcy, is known legally as Victoria Mirelle of Arcy? I'm sure that you recognize the planet's name. It is notorious, like its dominant owner, Per Walis. He is a customer of yours, I believe."

"I don't ask for credentials when I sell roses. What is your point?" Birk had become cautious.

"Miss Darcy has a positive three rating in her criminal history file. She was ranked as the most viable suspect in the murder of her husband, Arnod Conaty. The inquisition was left incomplete, largely because Miss Darcy refused to cooperate in full. She has a very low employability quotient as a consequence of her actions."

"Is that why you came here?" demanded Birk. "To investigate Tori?"

Jase stared at Birk, probing and observing by inquisitor's skills: Guilt was there, but scorn had overtaken it with the comments about Tori Darcy's past. Jase concluded uneasily that Birk's surprise was genuine. The source of the darkest fears at Hodge Farm had no bond with the inquisition of Birk's assistant.

The certainty of revelation made Jase conscious that his involvement with Birk's family was becoming unofficial again and dangerously personal. The slim self-defense of representing Consortium justice had abandoned Jase, and he realized how vulnerable he had made himself by returning to Hodge Farm. Ukitan, as usual, had predicted with wisdom. Jase left the office, giving Birk no answer.

CHAPTER 17

Tori scrambled free of the hothouse and inspected the oily resin on her hands with disgust. Radiant light would alter the resin's structure and let her dust it from her skin and clothing, but the process would take most of the afternoon to complete—even against the thin layer she had acquired in her brief visit to the hothouse. She did not share the Stromvi appreciation for resin's ability to thicken the hide and enhance the colors of skin mottling.

The Stromvi accumulated too much thick resin for sunlight ever to reach the viscous layers against the skin. The Stromvi guarded their resin layers carefully as children, until a solid foundation could be built. Infants never left their subterranean homes. Stromvi life depended on the resin, but Soli endured it uncomfortably.

Until the resin on her skin dried, Tori could only move clumsily, walk gingerly, and watch the resin's mottled patterns spread and darken from palest lavender to violet. She refastened her shoes to her feet with difficulty. The sandals' loose weave would allow the light to dry some of the resin, but only the friction of the sandals' soles would enable her to stand and walk steadily. She had never tried to master resin walking because she had always avoided entering Stromvi dwellings on any regular basis.

She debated whether to return to her loft to treat the remaining resin with the astringent drying solution. Even occasional applications of the harsh ointment had made her callused feet nearly as resin-hard as Stromvi hide. Her impatience with the encumbrance of resin vied with a futile desire to know if Birk had contacted Deetari yet. The ointment could wait. Enduring resin in its many forms was a necessity of life on Stromvi, and Tori had become inured to the associated discomforts.

When Tori reached the main house, Thalia was collecting the uneaten luncheon from the patio table. Thalia, her slim, dusky blue form bowed low over her task, whistled a brief note of sorrow and sad omens, followed by the brisk tune that meant Sylvie. Tori nodded in agreement, despite her general impatience with Thalia's Deetari superstitions. Whatever else Ngoi's death might bring, it would certainly drape the house with mourning and overshadow Sylvie's wedding plans. Tori did not need the help of a Deetari prophetess to make *that* prediction.

Tori decided that the same thought had occurred to Sylvie, for Tori could hear the woman's sharp voice reverberating through rose crystal panels. As usual, Sylvie was demanding sympathy. Sylvie's voice sounded close, though Tori had carefully avoided the family hall. Tori hated the acoustical tricks of the wall panels, even more than the visual deceptions.

Tori assumed that Birk would have chosen to escape his children's company, for Sylvie's rampages irritated him. The need to communicate with Deetari would provide him with ample excuse, although he should certainly have completed the call by this time. Following the narrow aisles that defined the changeable floor plan of Hodge House, Tori headed for the stairs to Birk's office.

She entered the pentagonal stairwell in solemn contemplation of the blue-green carpet of thick, dried Stromvi moss. She raised her eyes, hearing movement above her. The high window's light framed the lanky figure of the inexplicable Soli stranger.

Jase Sleide was just beginning to descend the stairs, and he paused on seeing Tori. "Mister Hodge has evidently been waxing persuasive with recalcitrant Deetari officials," remarked Jase with cool amiability, "which has not improved his manners, I regret to say. I presume that you found the Stromvi you sought: Nguri Ngenga, I believe." He had tucked his hands into the front pockets of his sweater. Even the sight of all that muffling wool made Tori feel the heat more keenly.

Something seems strained about his calm detachment, thought Tori, but she did not try to analyze the reasons.

She rubbed her own hand in useless irritation at the cling-ing resin. "Nguri always goes to the hothouse to contem-plate serious problems. I did not need any profound insight to know that Ngoi's death would trouble him."

A rapid upward shifting of black, heavy eyebrows ac-knowledged Tori's observation, and the iridescent eyes flickered with a golden light as Jase glanced at her. Jase kicked the stair wall in pensive distraction, but he replied briskly, "The news seems to have hit Calem rather hard as well. He's been repining in the family hall, enjoying the consoling devotion of his loving wife and sister."

"From what I could hear, Sylvie seemed to be winning most of the attention."

"Sylvie usually does," said Jase quietly.

Before Tori could think of questioning the familiarity of his comment, Jase trotted down the stairs past Tori and pressed through the nearest door to the front wing. As the door slid closed, she could see him head confi-dently down the narrow aisle, moving without a trace of the hesitation displayed by most visitors to Hodge's Folly. Tori stared at the closed door for nearly a micro-span, before continuing her interrupted journey up the stairway. Jase Sleide puzzled her, but she had deeper worries.

Birk's office, one of the few permanent rooms in the house, had a heavy, folded door, rarely closed except for access to a large, little-used cupboard. Accustomed to entering freely, Tori barely noticed opening the door, just as she disregarded the deep warning voice of a very sophisticated, very expensive security system that some enterprising Jiucetsi had persuaded Birk to buy. Tori pushed the door until it clicked into its open setting, and she entered the room. Birk closed his transceiver's cover with a quick snap. He spun toward the door with a fierce expression on his tanned face, and Tori stepped back-ward in surprise at the quick, silent fury of his reaction.

Birk seemed to relax on seeing Tori, for his scowl soft-ened, though he did not smile. Tori's own frayed nerves continued to shiver, unable to escape a staggering sense that even the indomitable Birk Hodge was frightened by the prospect of inquisition. Birk rose and strolled toward Tori. "An inquisitor will be here tomorrow," said Birk, leaning against the front of his broad, polished lacquer desk to face Tori squarely. "We're fortunate to have found a qualified Calongi in the vicinity. I was afraid that we'd need to postpone the wedding, but we should be able to clear up this mess in good time."

We certainly would not want to let Ngoi's murder interfere with Sylvie's plans or Birk's marketing gambits, thought Tori cynically. After witnessing Stromvi grief, Tori found Birk's callous practicality barbaric and revolting. She did not esteem her own reactions any more highly, and the sting of shame made her brusque, "Nguri says a Stromvi killed Ngoi. Nguri is very upset."

"Have Gisa organize a mourning feast. She knows the proper customs."

The Stromvi will not be placated that easily, thought Tori, but she saw no point in expressing the obvious. Birk was cold toward Stromvi, but he was not stupid in dealing with them. "I shall tell her to have a room prepared for the inquisitor."

"For the Calongi inquisitor. Yes," muttered Birk, rapping his knuckles against his desk in a cadence slightly skewed from the Stromvi chorus. "I suppose we must prepare for an ordeal of several days. All of the Stromvi in the Ngenga Valley have access to this farm." Birk braced his feet against the floor in front of his desk, planting himself firmly between the desk and Tori.

"Inquisitors are very thorough," replied Tori weakly. She did not like to contemplate the duration of the inquisition.

Birk leaned toward Tori with his clenched fists gripping the desk's edge. He tried to capture Tori's nervous, shifting glance with the intensity of his own gaze. "There will be no need to question Soli," he declared imperturbably. "You will not be subjected to a personal reading, Tori."

"I know," answered Tori, struck uncomfortably by Birk's pointed remark. She almost asked him why he thought she needed his reassurance, but she suppressed her dangerous curiosity. If Birk had discovered her unpleasant history and chose to accept it, she would not tamper with his reaction. If he did not know, she would not offer him any unnecessary hint that such information existed.

"You have become important to me, Tori. You have

strength, and you understand loyalty. If we had met sooner. . . ." His smile was thin. "But you were a child then."

"I'm not a child now," replied Tori briskly, but she knew that she needed to clear her thoughts in order to understand what Birk was saying.

"I'm past the age for creating dynasties."

Maneuver him now, advised an imagined voice in Tori's head. *Let him comfort you; let him feel strong, protective, and male.* "Are you even sorry that Ngoi is dead?" she asked, and she pictured Mirelle shuddering in despair. *Forgive me, Great-grandmama. I inherited your face and figure, but I lack your courage.*

"Of course I'm sorry about Ngoi," replied Birk, and he seemed more surprised than disappointed by her response. He also seemed to take her oblique rebuff as a challenge to his authority. He approached her, and his familiar expression of determination hardened into something vaguely menacing. "Ngoi served me well for many years," he said.

Tori scoffed at her own twinge of alarm. She had enough cause to worry without letting Birk intimidate her. She turned away from him, but she let him rub the tension from her back.

"You're upset, Tori."

"Yes. I am upset." She endured Birk's touch against her silky shirt, but she withdrew abruptly when his hands began to shift toward her throat. She could not tolerate another comparison from the past. "I'm covered with resin," she protested and forced herself to smile winningly over her shoulder. "I think Sylvie needs the comforting words."

"My children have little experience with unpleasantness," muttered Birk, his mood changing from tender to sharp. He creased his forehead, and his age betrayed him briefly. "Go and placate them for me. I shall join you momentarily."

Tori nodded, concealing her relief with an artfully wistful glance at Birk. She preferred the stormy squabbling of Calem and Sylvie to a continuation of this awkward conversation. "I'll try to smooth their ruffled scales."

She left the office, aware of Birk's gaze pursuing her. She hated the compulsion to perform, but she forced herself to glide gracefully despite the slipperiness of resin. When she turned the corner to reach the stairs, she let her posture relax, and she leaned for a moment against the cool, ivory wall.

She straightened and began to walk slowly to the lower floor. She had worked so hard to gain Birk's trust, and she did not altogether dislike him. She had thought her firmness of resolve could overcome innate reluctance for physical contact with anyone of any species. Mama had certainly made the rules of successful concubinage clear. Tori had thought that she could choose rationally and force her emotions to obey, because *that* was a very significant part of Mirelle's legacy. Tori wondered wryly whether her buried instincts had risen to protect her from Birk Hodge or from her own impulsiveness.

She muttered, "So much for any notion of upholding the family tradition."

A thunderous roar shook the house, and the stair beneath Tori seemed to shift perversely away from her descending foot. The hovering realization that she was falling frightened her more than the deafening reverberation. Three sharp, successive tones accompanied the suspended moment. She gripped the banister and caught herself.

Her ankle felt bruised, but she rotated her foot cautiously and decided that she had not done herself any serious injury. Her heart was pounding so hard that she fancied she could hear it as well as feel the rush of blood it pumped. She heard no other sound. No voices echoed through the crystal panels of the house. No subtle Stromvi chorus throbbed across the fields.

Tori glanced at the stairway rising behind her, tempted to return to Birk's office. The prospect of facing the steep ascent so soon after her near-fall daunted her. With the taste of fear still lingering in her mouth, she could sympathize with the Stromvi aversion to buildings that rose above ground level.

She descended the final step very carefully, fixing her eyes on the thick, leathery texture of the dense carpet of dried moss. Stromvi dwellings often wore such carpets, but in Stromvi homes the moss still lived and glowed with resin. The dead moss provided firmer footing for Soli, but it lost much of its beauty. Dead moss. Dead

Stromvi. Dead Ngoi. Tori drew her attention away from the spiral of despair.

The luminous ivory wall panels blinked into darkness, leaving only the cone of sunlight from the high circular window above the stairs. The power failure and the disconcerting silence crawled into Tori's already unsettled soul, freezing her. A door into the pentagonal stairwell slid open with a whisper of grating panels, forced by hand.

Jase Sleide strode two paces into the stairwell room before he lifted his dark head and took notice of Tori. Relief flooded her disproportionately at the sight of the peculiar Soli. "Do you know what's happened?" she asked him. She managed to sound confident, and she moved fearlessly across the stairwell. The sight of another living being restored her common-sense perspective.

"I hoped that you, most knowing native guide, could tell me, the humble visitor in these strange parts." He replied airily, but the dark skin of his face had a faint sheen. "Have you seen my cohort in vexatiousness, Calem?"

"I thought he was in the family hall with Sylvie and Rillessa."

"Not any longer. They evidently left while you and I crossed paths a few microspans ago."

"They're probably in their own rooms—or on the patio."

"Is Birk upstairs?"

"Yes. I just left him."

"I believe I'll go and seek his unique counsel," suggested Jase. He began to act on his words, but he paused beside Tori. "Care to come with me?"

Tori glanced at the stairway. Her fear of it seemed childish before a witness. "Yes," she answered, glad enough to share her disquiet with anyone. "Birk is usually the best source of answers at Hodge Farm."

The high-pitched shriek burst from Birk's office as they reached the second-level landing. The office door snapped shut, and Tori blinked to clear her eyes of a resin shadow that seemed to blur her vision for a moment. Jase stepped back a pace in surprise. He turned his head toward the stairs they had just left, and he frowned, but he moved forward quickly and laid his hand against the sealed door. "Can you open it?" he asked Tori.

Still stunned by the terrible cry, Tori raised her hand leadenly to the sensor panel. She had not used her access authority since the system installation test, but the code sequences that matched her handprint had been embedded in her memory by an Ilanovi regimen. She hesitated and touched the intercom instead of releasing the door lock. "Birk?" she asked and received no reply.

"He could be injured," murmured Jase.

Tori frowned and laid her hand against the panel, her fingers exerting the required pressure sequence. Instead of opening smoothly, the door vibrated in place. Jase leaned against it, concentrating pressure along the door's inward fold. The door shifted, and it jerked open rapidly, striking the wall. The intrusion alarms began to ring dully.

"An authorized access should not have triggered the alarm," observed Tori quietly, but she choked into silence on entering the office and turning toward Birk's desk.

She had so often stood across the desk from Birk Hodge, seated there in his massive chair. He had always dominated the room, as he dominated Hodge Farm, but he had never commanded such attention as he drew now. Beneath the gleaming white hair, Birk's well-chiseled face, contorted and discolored, rested against his desk. A thong with a silver sheen had been twisted around the tanned neck, cutting into the flesh. The muscular arms, still stretching the fabric of his silken coat, hung limply against the desk's closed drawers.

Jase muttered briefly in a language Tori did not know, then he crossed the room. He touched Birk quickly and lightly, and his fingers brushed the silver thong. "A silenen noose," he said softly, "an exceptionally useful device for gripping bulky objects with a minimal exertion of strength."

"He is dead?" asked Tori, and her voice sounded distant and strange to her. She was grateful that she had not eaten since dawn. Her body had not reacted well to the discovery of Arnod, and she doubted it would now.

"So it seems. The thong appears to have snapped his neck: a very quick, efficient process. The Xiani really ought to devise a means of excluding necks from the roster of objects to be gripped. This is how your husband died, isn't it?" Jase glanced at Tori, when she did not answer. "You're looking rather pale, Miss Darcy."

Tori tasted the bitterness of horror and resentment welling together inside her. The most compelling impulse urged her to cry in desolation that fate could destroy her universe with such cruel repetition. "My husband?" she asked, and she forced the same expression of calm innocence that she had shown to five inquisitors.

"Arnod Conaty, whose murder remains officially unresolved." Tori turned to leave the room, but Jase entrapped her wrist with a gesture that seemed almost lazily careless. His fingers felt icy against her skin. "My patience is not at its peak today, Miss Darcy, and I am not in the mood for verbal sparring. You'll need the glowing heavens' highest help if you try to lie to me now—and I will know the truth."

She stared up at him defiantly, but he accepted her anger with apparent indifference. She answered him coldly, "Someone or something shrieked. Someone closed the door. You heard. You saw. You know that I couldn't have killed Birk."

"Remote devices of many kinds exist."

"I have no such devices on me," she snapped, "and you're welcome to search or scan or throw me to a Calongi inquisitor."

"Unnecessary. I believe you. We're joint witnesses to something," muttered Jase, narrowing his iridescent eyes, "though I'm not quite sure what we've observed. We entered this room together and found it empty—of major life forms—except for him." His nod toward the desk and its grim burden was barely perceptible. "Can the door be operated remotely?"

"Not according to the Jiucetsi who installed it. Nor can the windows be opened or closed without a great deal of noise: They trigger a siren." She almost relished the impossibilities, because they taunted the man who mauled her with the past.

Jase released her arm, and she rubbed at the wrist. Jase had not held it roughly, but her skin seemed tender where he had contacted it. He walked to the softly tinted windows and examined them without touching them. He shook his head and asked in a ruminative voice, "Who defined madness as the normality of any other being's life?"

"Anzante of Persilim-2," replied Tori, though she did not think that Jase had expected an answer. He seemed to glance at her in surprise, his quick movement exaggerated by the windows framing him. Birk had installed the tinted illusion windows to magnify the strengths of his own silhouette. Against the windows, Jase seemed to grow larger. His movements appeared more harsh, his profile more predatory, his posture more threatening.

Tori pulled her gaze away from Jase Sleide. She returned to her study of Birk's distorted face, morbidly fascinated by her own detachment from pain. Somewhere inside of her, something wept with genuine grief, but this body she wore seemed to have no connection with sorrow, no relation to the death of a man who had given her refuge from Uncle Per and Arnod and Great-grandmama Mirelle. Birk had tried to comfort her only microspans ago, and Birk would surely talk to her again, greet her across a field of roses, and argue with Nguri over marketing strategies.

"It really is easier the second time," observed Tori evenly, although a crueler, more honest voice in her whispered that nothing was easier at all. Nothing could ever be easy while the past refused to free her.

She did not quite trust her own present calm. She remembered how relieved she had felt when she had first accepted that Arnod was actually dead, freeing her of her self-inflicted, life-long obligation to him—and how guilty she had felt later for her initial emotions.

"Stromvi is certainly producing a fine welcome for the inquisitor," sighed Jase. His calm did not seem forced. Tori wondered if he were maintaining a stoic pose only for her benefit, or if he were actually that immune to fear. "Who else has access to this office?"

"Only Birk was imprinted for full entry rights, and he gave me the secondary codes. He may have added Gisa and Thalia to the list, but he never used the system after the novelty waned." She drew her stare away from Birk with a reluctance that sickened her, and she forced herself to concentrate on the pale walls, patterned in bas-relief with sketchy images of Birk's favorite rose forms.

"Birk was very blunt about his intention to keep his children off the access list."

"Interesting exclusivism," mused Jase.

"You're as calm as a Calongi, aren't you?" asked Tori with distaste.

"Not quite." Jase surveyed the room once more, but his gaze barely paused on the dead man. "We should probably resecure the room while we look for the rest of the family."

"Securing the room seems a little ineffective now, don't you think?" asked Tori sardonically, but she followed Jase from the office and laid her hand once more on the control panel. She shifted her hand's pressure in an ordered sequence. The door closed with a grinding protest, but the alarm continued to ring, despite her efforts to silence it. "It's not locking, and it's not accepting a deactivation of the alarm," she muttered, pressing her fingers against the panel in a final attempt. "A squadron of Jiucetsi should descend on us soon. They monitor these signals from the Deetari port city."

"I shall welcome a squadron of Jiucetsi with embarrassing enthusiasm at this point. I would not want to denigrate your Stromvi hospitality, Miss Darcy, but discovering my host's murdered body was not a part of my plans for this visit."

"Perhaps Sylvie thought a murder or two would enliven the wedding entertainment," snapped Tori. She ran ahead of Jase and descended most of the steps, before pausing in the growing shock of realization. She kicked the stair that had tripped her earlier, wishing that she had the courage to be alone. "Forgive my sharpness, Mister Sleide," she said roughly, and the apology tasted bitter. "Birk was a friend. So was Ngoi."

Jase rejoined her at a methodical pace. "Arnod Conaty was your husband, as I recall."

"I have not forgotten!"

"No?" Jase shrugged, the bulky sweater stretching across his shoulders. "You seem to deny his existence so well."

"Birk is dead, and Ngoi is dead, and you expect me to stand here discussing my late husband with you? I don't even know you!" Tori let her furious thoughts spill forth in acidic honesty: "You're not in the mood for verbal sparring? Neither am I, Mister Sleide, much as that may surprise you. Yes, I was married to Arnod Conaty, until someone throttled him with a silenen thong, and the inquisitors never identified Arnod's murderer. I admit that Birk and Arnod died by the same inglorious method, and I admit to having known both men. Are you happy now?"

"I never thought of murder as a subject for rejoicing."

Tori did not pause to acknowledge his ironic remark. "I don't know if you're Calem's friend or a visiting trader from Glastonmoor, and I don't know why you've taken the trouble to study my past history, but I find your indelicate insinuations in extremely poor taste. Yes, I've been a subject of inquisition in the past. I would probably be the highest ranking suspect in Birk's murder—without *your* invaluable testimony of the circumstances of discovery. I have a rare combination of physiological quirks, you see, that invalidate Calongi truth scans." She stumbled slightly in speaking Birk's name, and her eyes blurred, but she allowed herself no tears. "I'll have enough trouble, as it is, persuading the inquisitors that I did not somehow deceive you into acquitting me."

Jase only murmured, "The Stromvi have resumed their click-speaking."

He truly is as imperturbable and composed as a Calongi, thought Tori, marveling a little, for Jase Sleide seemed so genuinely unconcerned by external events. She realized that her outburst had exhausted her own anger. "The pace is slower," noted Tori. She listened carefully and curiously, glad of the distraction. She frowned, for the word mix was unusual. "They are repeating one word: death-watch."

"A perceptive people, the Stromvi."

*   *   *

Thunder on Deetari preceded torrential rains and winds that carved the mountainous lands. Raising her eyes from the hovercraft's unresponsive transceiver, Gisa expected to see a sky filled with black, rushing clouds. She saw only the open garage door, the patch of mossy landing field, the back of Hodge House, and Thalia running from the kitchen. Then the storm erupted across the landing field, but the sky rained silent fire instead of water. The fire seemed to slide ineffectively from the roof of Hodge House and dissipate before it could touch the damp gardens.

Gisa whistled to her sister, but Thalia had run past the museum wing of Hodge House and headed into the fringe gardens. Thalia's path would take her quickly to the thick vine mass of natural Stromvi terrain, but Thalia was a prophetess and would sense a safe route. Only a few meters of vine mass separated the gardens from the buried back wing of Hodge House; perhaps Thalia would find one of the abandoned entries. If the intervening space had not been darkened with the fire of deadly energy beams, Gisa might have chosen to follow Thalia, rather than trust her own logic.

Gisa whispered, "The storm has come," and she knew what the prophets had ordered her to do. She feared, and her faith weakened. She tried the transceiver again, but even its displays had begun to flicker erratically.

The rain of fire stopped as suddenly as it had begun. Gisa saw the reprieve as only another omen, forcing her to presdestined action. She sealed the hovercraft door and activated the ship's power system.

The hovercraft did not respond. Through the shield glass, Gisa saw a shadow hurl itself at the craft's sealed door. She felt the thud of impact, and she heard a muffled shriek of pain as a beam of fire touched the shadow. The shadow became solid: a blurred image of a man engulfed in a strange, dark cape. He leapt from the Hodge hovercraft that Gisa had claimed, and he ran to the sleek, Sesserda-marked ship beside it. He grappled with the locked door.

Gisa tried the hovercraft systems once again. They hesitated and whined. The displays came to life.

A Soli woman ran into the landing field from the direction of the front rose gardens. Clothed in orange as bright as true fire, the woman ran an erratic course past the garage toward the dense fields of cultivated Stromvi fruit vines. Gisa did not try to identify the figure more closely. With nearly full acceleration, Gisa hurled Birk's hovercraft out of the garage and across the landing field. Below her, bright roses blurred their many colors. She raised her eyes from the hypnotic rush of ground and saw the vast silver disk that loomed above her. Gisa recoiled, as the storm of fire engulfed her view.

* * *

"Did you see where your wife ran?" asked Sylvie, emerging cautiously onto the patio in Calem's wake.

"Toward the garage," replied Calem. He walked to the end of the patio and tried to peer around the corner of Hodge House, but he stayed close to the wall. He saw only a hint of the silent fire that illuminated the rear gardens, but he recoiled and stumbled back to his sister's side.

"What is it?" demanded Sylvie. "Calem, what did you see?"

"Energy fire, I think," he answered. He did not want to say more. He did not want to think of why energy fire and sound-shock came to Stromvi. Harrow had warned him—so lightly as to make the possibility seem like a joke—that the customer for the relaweed did not express dissatisfaction mildly. "We need to find Father." Birk would know what to do.

Sylvie did not move to let her brother reenter the house. "What do you know about this?" she asked, showing that trace of Hodge strength that had once made her Birk's favorite.

"Unhappy customers," replied Calem brusquely. "I think they're firing on the house."

"And you intend to go back inside?" Sylvie's nervousness lessened the impact of her scorn. "For once, your pathetic Rillessa had the right idea. We need to take a hovercraft and get away from here now."

"Don't be stupid, Sylvie. The hangar yard is under attack."

"We can circle through the garden to reach the garage."

"Even if we reached it, do you think we could actually escape unnoticed in a hovercraft?"

"We can try. We can do something on our own for once, or would you prefer to let inquisitors and nameless enemies make us incidental casualties of Daddy's perpetual schemes? We've run out of choices, Calem."

"We can't leave him," argued Calem.

"Do you think Daddy wants *our* help? He doesn't need us. Staying here is suicidal. Escape is a chance. I'm leaving with or without you."

Calem grumbled, "You don't understand that you're facing real weapons," but he followed his sister, hurrying after her down the stairs and into the shade of crimson rose trees.

*   *   *

Ngina dragged the last of the heavy, vine-fiber sacks out of the shallow tunnel where Ngoi had stored them. The panguulung grew thickly here, and she moved carefully to avoid the anaesthetic fibers that lined the trumpet throats. She had made the journey from the tunnel to the old resin cave three times, and she was nearly exhausted. She was glad that she hadn't tried to carry Ngoi past the edge of the Stromvi gardens. The other younglings, summoned by her frantic click-speech, had taken charge of Ngoi and left her free to complete Ngoi's work.

Ngina wished that she had dared ask for help in moving Ngoi's parcels. She would have spoken if one of the seniors had come in response to her call, but only Ngare and Ngilang had been close enough to hear her across the vine-mass. Ngare and Ngilang had been scarcely able to deal with the shock of finding Ngoi. They did not even seem to realize that Ngina had already carried Ngoi to that point. She had told them to take Ngoi to the infirmary. She had not dared to wait longer to fulfill Ngoi's last, urgent order.

The southern caves had been abandoned since her earliest memories, but Ngina knew her people's methods and designs. The circles of panguulung, the patterns of silver-lily beds, the largest stands of magi reeds: These factors were controlled, unlike the rampant vines and blossoms of the natural terrain.

Ngina had no trouble finding the resin cave that Ngoi had chosen for concealment. He had prepared it for comfortable use, trimming the root stalks and hanging a few weavings. He had even cleared the old access to the wire-root network that carried Stromvi click-speech throughout the Stromvi world, and the soft, unfocused sounds comforted Ngina. The small room held root samples and splicings like those in Nguri's hothouse.

Ngina envisioned the painstaking millispans that Ngoi must have spent on his own work, hidden here from anyone who might compare it to the greater genius of a horticulturist like Nguri. All knew that Ngoi served as work leader because his mind was slow for a Stromvi. Ngina had never considered that Ngoi might wish in his gentle, timid way for the gifts that he had never possessed. She grieved for his unfinished dreams, as she pushed the last vine-sack into the corner with its fellows.

The ground shuddered, and the wire-roots transmitted a roar into the small, biolit cave. One of the vine-sacks toppled, spilling the coarsely wrapped parcels. In a stunned reflex, Ngina clutched the parcel that struck her forefoot.

Ngoi's dreams had not ended gently. Somewhere, an enemy had entered and transformed the cavern nymph into a frightening, hollow queen. A nightmare's potent horror surged in Ngina. She twisted the wire-root connections deftly, and she clicked a desperate warning to her people.

CHAPTER 18

Tell Calem. Tell Sylvie. Tell Rillessa, if any sense can penetrate that haze of self-deception she occupies. Tell the Hodge heirs that Birk is dead, and let them deal with the official consequences. Consign Jase Sleide to the attentions of Calem, and be rid of all of them—until tomorrow, when an inquisitor will find cause to question Soli very carefully indeed.

Tori thought that she had considered her plans with laudable pragmatism, under the circumstances. She had weighed the urge to cling to her species' company and discarded the impulse as infantile, since none of the available Soli prospects seemed particularly congenial. Thalia was too silly to be a comfort, and Gisa was too aloof and absorbed by her Deetari prophecies. The Stromvi were too wracked by grief to share a Soli's helpless terrors. She could surely find some useful work to occupy her in her loft.

The plans seemed sensible to her, until she failed at the first item. She could not locate Calem. She could not locate anyone.

The Hodge House furnishings all resided in their customary, slightly awkward positions, accompanied by the traces of interrupted living. A delicate green scarf lay on the floor of Sylvie's room. A half-eaten melon rested on a plate in the kitchen. In the family hall, two crystal goblets held wine, and a damp stain spread across the carpet. The few transparent windows, distributed chiefly across the front of the house, showed the usual, soft Stromvi sky and untroubled gardens.

Tori entered each room of the occupied wings of the house insistently, and she jumped at every imagined echo of a sound. She expected at each moment to find Sylvie or Calem, Rillessa, Gisa, or Thalia. Both Hodge siblings

were vocal about their aversion to hot Stromvi afternoons, and the Deetari women seldom strayed far from
the house at any time. Rillessa always had to be coaxed
even to leave her room.

Tori called the names, while Jase walked pensively behind her. Except for herself, Jase Sleide, and the dreadful mockery of life in Birk's office, she found no one.
Tori paced every route from the stairwell to the family
hall three times, before Jase persuaded her gently that
the inhabitants had departed.

On conceding grudgingly to his assessment, Tori hurried to escape the house's haunting, shadowy rooms. She
emerged from the pillared portico at a headlong pace,
undeterred by Jase's cautioning advice, and she headed
directly for the Stromvi workers' enclave. She called to the
Stromvi through the thorny hedge, for the Soli entry had
not been cleared in months, and she waited for an answer.

The distant clicking continued without break or
change. Jase joined her silently, the direct sunlight giving
his eyes an incongruously metallic appearance. "The Stromvi
are always coming and going from this enclave," she told
him. "It's the primary entrance to their home caverns and
tunnels." She resumed her impersonal, professional courtesy, defying him to revive less palatable topics.

"None of the click-speech is coming from here, unless
it's deep underground," replied Jase. "There is no one
inside to hear you."

His contradiction annoyed her because he sounded so
incontrovertibly positive. She did not believe that he had
good cause for his certainty. "The sounds are too muffled
by foliage to distinguish the origin," argued Tori, but no
answer came to prove her claim. "There are always
Stromvi in the clearing," she insisted and called again.

"I have a hovercraft in the garage," began Jase. "We
could widen the range of our effort. . . ."

Tori shook her head at him, irritated with him for his
consistent *rightness* in opposition to her, when his conclusions had no obvious logic in excess of her own. "They
cannot have gone that far." She did not try to refine
her pronoun. Soli, Deetari, or Stromvi would satisfy her
equally at this point. "Ngev will be in the garden. I asked
him to prune the nectar roses near the border path."

She resumed her search in the garden, pursuing every

twisting walkway with stubborn thoroughness. She spread her search outward to the edge of the rose fields, but the Soli accesses proved as deserted as the house, and the Stromvi resin tunnels remained as unresponsive as the workers' enclave. Her shouts and pleas fell unheeded. She found no sign of workers, not even a field rippling with hidden motion, and the Stromvi click-chorus continued without visible source.

"Nguri will be in the hothouse," she insisted, and Jase sighed, but he followed her to the entry. "Nguri, it's Tori," she called, but the Stromvi did not reply.

Jase bent to tug a host of spined silver-lily seeds from his trouser legs. He collected the sharp seeds cautiously and cast them by fistfuls across the hothouse roof. The seeds glinted as they whirled and settled among the matted vines.

"Nguri!" called Tori again. She watched a shower of silver seeds hover momentarily against the lilac sky, and the flash of beauty fanned the fright inside her. The loveliness was so fragile.

"Nguri is not there to hear you," said Jase, his keen-featured face resigned to patience. He held a single silver-lily seed, twisting it between his fingers. "This house is silent."

Tori nearly warned him of the silver-lily's propensity for causing skin irritation, but she decided to let him learn for himself. She told him crisply, "I despise pessimists."

"I am not a pessimist," he answered soberly. He observed her focus on the seed in his hand and added, "I'm also immune to silver-lily toxin. You're remarkably perceptive to have recognized my good fortune in that regard."

Tori turned away from him, embarrassed by the oblique reprimand and annoyed at herself for having indulged her petty impulse. She reached into the granite hollow and withdrew the four sets of traction bracelets that it contained. She inspected each set carefully, without admitting the doubts that goaded her. She did not want to accept that anyone had died. She did not want to believe that Nguri was gone. She did not want to admit that Jase's words echoed her own growing misgivings, because only hope could continue to muffle her raw pain.

The set of bracelets that she had used earlier in the day showed the least wear of any in the hollow. She hesitated, but she restored the bracelets to their holding box. If she entered without decent traction capability, she would be unable to return without assistance. "Too much hard usage and too much accumulated Stromvi resin," she informed Jase briskly. "I shall have to bring some new bracelets from the supply room."

Because the infirmary lay beside their path from the hothouse, she insisted on searching that building also. She did not expect to find Ngoi's sad, mutilated corpse occupying a white ceramic bier, and her gasp brought Jase quickly to her side. "Nguri told me there were marks of Stromvi teeth," she murmured, appalled and nauseated by the sight before her. Only the distinctive hide coloring across the head identified the body as Ngoi's.

Jase bent over Ngoi. To Tori's astonishment, he seemed to be sniffing the body. "Did Nguri tell you where Ngoi died?" asked Jase.

"No. Why?"

"Not sure," replied Jase. He extracted a cleaning swab from a green glass canister, and he used the swab to pry apart the edges of a deep wound in Ngoi's right foreleg.

Tori averted her eyes. "What are you doing?" she demanded, sickened by even the thought of Jase Sleide's idle delving.

"Just observing." He hummed an uneven snatch of a macabre nursery tune involving carving knives. "This was a suicide."

"Suicide?" For a moment, she believed, but she weighed the word of an enigmatic Soli on a scale of likelihood. What living being could inflict such horrible death upon itself? Recollection of Nguri's worry about inquisitors sealed her certainty: If a casual inspection could determine that Ngoi had killed himself, Nguri would have known. "Not possible," she asserted firmly.

Jase did not try to contradict her. He finished his cursory examination of Ngoi's body at a leisurely pace, while Tori waited uncomfortably, not quite willing to abandon her odd companion. Jase said nothing, but Tori soon realized that his silence constituted his most effective argument.

Jase's silence did not disturb her until she realized how deliberately he maintained it. She became uncomfortable with his unspeaking presence, but she could not fashion any conversation to ease her mood. She could think of nothing but her encroaching fears, growing as she stood idly by while he worked.

He finished his self-appointed labor and cleaned his hands carefully. He seemed surprised to notice Tori, leaning against a bench and restlessly crumpling dry resin powder from her dark green sash. He said nothing. Tori stalked from the room.

On leaving the infirmary, Tori no longer tried to call to friends. The lack of vigilant Stromvi mourners around Ngoi's body had persuaded her of the futility of her search. Stromvi did not abandon the newly dead for any reason short of catastrophe.

She paused beside the line of new roses, where she had stood that morning with Nguri. She felt the prick of conscious pain begin to replace her numbness. The blue-and-white hybrid rose had been severed at the base, below the grafting. Not even a stump remained to offer new shoots for a future rebirth. She felt the tears trying to form.

She murmured to the bared ground, "Even you?"

"What was it?" asked Jase softly, breaking his austere silence.

"Blue-and-white. Hodge's Dream. Ancient form and fragrance in combination with modern durability. We have other bushes, but this was by far the most successful. Nguri warned me that my satisfaction was premature."

"I doubt that beheading could be considered a normal threat to a rose bush on Stromvi."

His phlegmatic reaction seemed to impose its own calm. Tori felt the horror recede marginally into its fragile containment. "Why should anyone have threatened a rose at all? Why should anyone have threatened Birk or Ngoi?"

Without attempting to reply, Jase knelt and inspected the shorn root crown, and he touched the soil gently. "The bush was sheared cleanly," he said, "and dragged." He stood and pointed toward the supply cottage. "In that direction."

They found the blue-and-white hybrid easily. It had been thrown beneath the battered gong at the stairway to Tori's loft. The ivory buds and single open flower had wilted, and most of the leaves had been stripped from the canes. The skeletal bush looked enormous in its death. The breadth of it was nearly Tori's height.

While Jase stared consideringly at the hybrid's sorry remains, Tori pushed past him in order to climb to her room. She rested her head against the wall of her loft and closed her eyes to combat the whirling sense of helplessness.

The image that arose in her mind wore her own face, but its expression was sternly contemptuous: *"Show some strength of character, Victoria. Did you inherit nothing from me but appearance?"*

"I'm sorry, Great-grandmama," whispered Tori. "I'll try not to disappoint you further." Resolutely, Tori straightened and crossed her room with a firm step.

She pulled her resin-stained shirt over her head and draped it across the drying rack beside the windowsill. With the purple resin mottling the green fabric, the shirt nearly blended with the Stromvi horizon. She reached for a sleeveless blue long-blouse and fastened the shoulder sash hurriedly. She had limited concern for traditional Soli concepts of modesty, but she was in a vulnerable mood.

She rubbed the remaining patches of dried resin from her exposed skin and reapplied the protective cream shield where the resin had dissolved it. The cream solidified quickly into a clear, flexible, and porous coat, essential to Soli defense against the acute concentration of ultraviolet light on Stromvi. She replenished the eyedrops that performed a similar defensive function.

"There were three hovercrafts in the garage when I arrived," remarked Jase, arriving unceremoniously in the one-room loft, "including my own humble craft. Are you still determined to explore Nguri's hothouse, or would you consider an alternative plan?"

"I might consider an alternative," replied Tori, her mouth dry with regret for the plans she could no longer cherish. With care, she folded the shawl that she had held mockingly before her in contemplation of Birk and her uncertain intentions for him.

"In that case, Miss Darcy, could I interest you in a visit to the Stromvi shuttle port? The trip promises little in the way of scenic interest to a seasoned Stromvi veteran such as yourself, but I'd like to let Ngahi earn his port manager's pay by explaining to me the quaint Stromvi custom of vanishing to a jaunty tune of 'death-watch.' With some luck, we can also present our bright and cheerful faces to the Jiucetsi security patrol."

"Do you expect to find Ngahi?"

"We can but hope."

Tori gathered the silken folds of her long-blouse at her waist with a belt that Birk had given her, and she touched the silver links gently. Each link of the belt had been hammered into the likeness of a different rose from the Hodge collection, and pale layers of refractive shellacs captured the varied hues of the roses. "We could contact the port first and see if they've had any unusual troubles of their own."

"An outstanding suggestion, if you have a particularly powerful transceiver handy. As I recall, the Stromvi atmosphere attenuates radio signals with exceptional severity at this time of year, and Stromvi communication networks only accommodate Stromvi exchanges. I know that my hovercraft's unit failed to receive any port acknowledgment when I arrived here this morning, and my unit is considerably more sensitive than most of its counterparts."

"We've had several equipment failures recently," admitted Tori. "We normally keep three systems."

"And, of course, you have always relied on the notably efficient Stromvi for normal planetary communication. The chain of misfortunes grows ever longer," murmured Jase.

"The transceiver in Birk's office still functions."

"Do you want to try it?"

"No," replied Tori crisply. "The idea of leaving here is gaining appeal by the nanospan." She dipped her hands into a glove box and let a layer of the elastic film cling to her skin. She seated herself on the edge of her bed and began to smear resin-drying lotion on her feet. The acrid aroma filled the room.

Jase almost smiled, but he seemed to reconsider the impulse. He leaned against the loft railing, looking down into the supply room. "The Stromvi message hasn't changed. I wonder where they've gone."

Tori answered Jase briskly, glad of a momentary break in the awkward tension between them, "Underground, I should think, since they are chiefly a subterranean species. They live in deep chambers, inaccessible to Soli without elaborate excavation equipment."

"I hate to find fault with such a reasonable hypothesis, but if the Stromvi have all retreated to their deep, underground refuges, why can we still hear them so distinctly? Are they broadcasting their cryptic message to the surface simply to provide a conundrum for two stray Soli?"

Tori shrugged, because she had no answer, and she had decided that contradicting Jase was as pointless as searching Hodge Farm. "Where did you learn the Stromvi click-language?" she asked, resealing the container of drying solution tightly. She peeled the gloves from her hands and threw them back into the box for dissolution.

Jase hesitated before replying, and she glanced at him, for he seemed to be weighing her simple question with unwarranted care. He answered quietly, "I learned it here. I spent several winters at Hodge Farm with Calem, when we were students together. It was Nguri who first taught me how to listen with more than my ears, although he grumbled bitterly about wasting time on yet another of Calem's wayward friends." Jase tapped the molded railing in quiet cadence with the faint Stromvi clicks. "After Nguri and I resolved a few cultural misunderstandings, I nearly accepted the job you currently hold."

"What stopped you?"

"Birk and I had philosophical differences."

"Of course," replied Tori stiltedly. She had almost forgotten the conversation with Birk, seemingly so long ago. Less than half a millispan could have passed since that moment when she had first noticed Jase Sleide in the shade of Hodge's Folly. Nothing more onerous than lunch and Sylvie's wedding had concerned her then. Tori offered feebly, "I suppose we'd be smart to eat something."

"Have you the appetite for it?"

"No." Everything had changed since she met Jase Sleide of the iridescent eyes and eccentric manners.

"Neither do I," replied Jase. "Do you have a good knife or some pruning shears?"

"There's a machete downstairs in one of the supply lockers," answered Tori, faintly troubled by his request. "It may be too corroded to have any edge left. I doubt that anyone has used it in years, because the Stromvi have always taken care of the pruning."

"A very convenient evolutionary development, those pruning teeth; probably began as pincers rather than teeth. Unfortunately, my ancestors did not equip me so ably. Find the machete for me, please."

Tori located the machete in a box of miscellaneous tools. The blackwood handle had cracked, and the blade sported a blue-gray coat of metallic particles deteriorated by long exposure to the humid Stromvi atmosphere, but Jase hefted the blade appreciatively. He pulled a length of fine, gray cord from a pocket of his sweater and wrapped the slender strand carefully around the cracked handle for reinforcement and a better grip.

He went to the broken rose bush and used the machete to cut three of the tattered canes from the root base. He checked their lengths for thorns with professional delicacy and speed. With the rose canes in his left hand and the machete in his right, he gestured toward the door. Tori gave him a questioning look, and he shrugged.

"Given the choice, I prefer to practice my exceedingly inadequate notions of forensics on a rose rather than on former friends," he explained with a pronounced grimace, "and dissecting one friend a day is my limit. I could study the damaged canes here and now, but the current roster of perplexities has me a little rattled. Please, don't consider me ungrateful for your hospitality, Miss Darcy, but I'm more than ready to end my visit to Hodge Farm."

"I think I'm more than ready to accompany you." Tori grabbed an awl from the toolbox to make herself feel better matched to Jase's machete, and she joined him.

In silent accord, they paused at the door to survey the colorful expanse of gardens and farmland. Nothing moved. No shifting leaves among the acres of roses indicated the passage of a Stromvi or other being of significant size. The Stromvi planet had no winged life forms to fill the sky. Eddies of heated air rose lazily, unhampered by wind or strong weather.

"What do you expect to see?" asked Tori softly of herself.

But it was Jase who replied, "I have no idea."

CHAPTER 19

The garage lay on the far side of the main house, beyond the kitchen garden. Tori tried to stifle all thoughts as she passed within view of the window of Birk's office. She thought that Jase seemed to walk a little more quickly as well, until the wide expanse of tinted glass was behind them.

The green-gray garage, an undecorated, boxy hangar, was closed and silent. The garage stood in a clearing where only persistent Stromvi moss was allowed to survive. The stark lines of the garage and clearing had never struck Tori so ominously.

Tori tried the side door first and found it locked. With Jase beside her, she circled back to the front of the garage. Jase touched the control panel to open the garage doors, but the doors did not move. "Is garage access restricted?" he asked, his even voice too disciplined to betray discouragement.

"Of course not," answered Tori, allowing her own frustration to show clearly. "The main door opens and closes automatically when it senses hovercraft activity. This panel is just corroded from disuse. No one steals on Stromvi."

Jase glanced at Tori from beneath his dark, curling brows. "Birk certainly equipped his office with a sophisticated security system for a planet without theft."

"Good Jiucetsi salesmanship," muttered Tori uneasily. She pressed the ineffective manual control in frustration.

"We can hardly walk to the shuttle port," commented Jase, scanning the empty hangar yard with a faint frown. "Stromvi is not well suited to surface travel by fragile Soli." He handed the rose canes to Tori. "Stand back for a moment." He jammed the machete blade beneath the sensor panel, breaking the cover plate and flinging the pieces across the yard. He jerked the emergency release, and it yielded with a groan. The doors creaked apart just far enough to allow Jase and Tori to squeeze through the opening.

Jase laughed, the first entirely mirthful sound that Tori had heard from him. "You have a very strange sense of humor," she remarked, for the garage was quite empty of hovercraft.

"You must admit that it completes our predicament with a swift, deft blow," he observed, cutting the air with a whistling wave of the machete. "And it does make a certain amount of perverse sense. Where are all the people who ought to occupy this busy farm? I would prefer to assume that some of them departed by an obvious means of transport rather than contemplate metaphysical alternatives."

"We would have heard a hovercraft depart," argued Tori irritably.

"I wonder. We did spend a good deal of time searching the house. The acoustics of that monstrous maze can be exceptionally tricky, and at least half the windows are paned with illusion glass of various forms. I'm not sure how far I trust my finer senses at this point. They've not been behaving well today." Jase proceeded a few paces into the enormous, echoing hangar. "The most immediate flaw in my argument is my own hovercraft, which was keyed only to me, unless Ngahi made some modifications without telling me. An unauthorized entity could have moved it—but not under its own power, not easily at least."

"Identity locks can be compromised by someone who knows the methods," argued Tori. At Jase's sardonic expression, she added, "So I've heard, at least."

"You must hear from interesting sources." After a brief pause, he added, "Rose canes." Tori interpreted his cryptic comment as a request only when he extended his hand abruptly. She dropped the canes toward his open palm, and he seemed to snatch them from the air before they could begin to fall. Jase strode toward a storage alcove and inspected an assortment of spare drive belts hanging on the wall.

Selecting several of the more flexible bands, Jase knotted them together with quick efficiency into a makeshift sling, such as Stromvi sometimes used for carrying clippings. He tied the canes into the sling across his shoulder. The battered rose canes rested forlornly against his back.

While Jase occupied himself in the alcove, Tori crossed the garage, seeking evidence of anything misplaced or missing, but everything except the crucial hovercrafts seemed in relatively good order. A dark smudge across the floor might have been a burn mark, but it only suggested that a hovercraft had left the insignia of hasty passage.

Tori rejoined Jase, whose momentary humor had apparently passed. He was studying the empty garage with a dissatisfied scowl. "It looks like we need to try Birk's transceiver after all," he remarked without enthusiasm.

"The Jiucetsi could have arrived at the port by now. The trip from Deetari doesn't take long in a fast ship."

"Your conclusion presupposes that the alarm actually reached the Jiucetsi. It's an entirely rational assumption under normal circumstances, which makes it entirely suspect at the moment." He headed for the side door. He wrapped his fingers around the interior locking device, a simple, mechanical model intended chiefly to discourage Stromvi children from excess mischief. With a sharp jerk, Jase pried the lock entirely from its casing, and the door swung free. "I'm becoming suspicious of Hodge Farm locks," he explained, and Tori did not argue with him.

She followed Jase from the garage. The lilac sky had begun to turn pink, tinted by the microscopic organisms that drifted in the heated Stromvi afternoons, absorbing the blue-light wavelengths. As she pondered the delicate shift of color and the passing microspans that it represented, the clear sky boomed with thunder.

"It's beginning again," whispered Tori, but the encompassing roar drowned her words. Jase grabbed her arm and pulled her back into the garage. He pressed his hand across her mouth in an unmistakable command to keep silent, and he drew her into the dark corner behind the water tanks. Three successive tones shuddered through the humid air. They faded, leaving a wake of ponderous silence.

Tori tried to match Jase's uncanny stillness, until she felt him resume breathing. She mouthed, "Why?"

"Events that arrive in triplicate make me superstitious," replied Jase in a slow whisper devoid of any inflection. He paused before speaking again: "Why do I advocate silence when three chimes of thunder tear across the sky? Possibly from a primitive instinct to hide when confronted by the monsters of my imagination. Probably for no good reason at all." Jase shook his head. "Let's try the transceiver."

"Must we?"

"No. I must. Wait here, if you prefer."

"Alone? No, thank you."

"Amazing how a little fear vitalizes the Soli herd instinct."

"And I thought I was merely exercising common sense," answered Tori.

Jase grunted a noncommittal reply. He crossed the hangar yard by an indirect route that clung to the shadows. Tori did not question his caution.

She braced herself to return to the house. She entered slowly, but the narrow aisles and constantly startling patterns of translucent crystal walls absorbed a measure of her nervousness. The familiarity of surroundings helped her to pretend that she was merely escorting another visitor through Hodge's Folly.

Calming herself by a determined effort, even reentering Birk's office proved less traumatic than she had feared. She suffered neither a sense of physical illness nor the unnerving dearth of emotion that she had experienced on first discovering the death. She felt an urge to cry, but she had practiced stifling tears for many spans. She avoided looking toward Birk's desk, crossing instead to the black lacquer wall unit that housed the transceiver.

"The alarm has stopped," remarked Jase. "Did you notice?"

"It has a timer control," answered Tori vaguely. She removed the cover from the transceiver. She could sense Jase standing immediately behind her, watching her actions attentively. She laughed in nervous relief that the transceiver was actually present, its power indicator functioning.

"That setting is a local channel," noted Jase. "I wonder who Birk contacted after summoning the inquisitor? See what you reach without adjusting code or frequency."

"That setting is for the port, which is the default when

someone clears the coordinates," muttered Tori, and she transmitted the stored distress signal and waited for acknowledgment.

"Just a suggestion. I saw the Deetari code set earlier. Left Birk. You came. Curious timing."

"I might understand you better if you spoke in complete sentences," said Tori in sharp frustration, for she was receiving no answer to her link request. She repeated the transmission.

"I'll do my best. I've spent too much time negotiating with Cuui traders in the past decispan, and they tend to like their serious business dealings terse. I sometimes lapse into their habits when I'm distracted." Jase leaned over Tori's shoulder to observe the blank screen. "No luck?"

"None." Tori started to turn away from the unresponsive communication device, remembered what lay across the room, and closed her eyes where she stood. "Feel free to try it yourself."

"Peculiar, isn't it? We Soli always think that we can succeed where another fails." As he spoke, Jase keyed his own message, adjusting code controls. He began to scowl in concentration, though he continued to talk, "Most Consortium species reserve such distrust for alien efforts." He repeated his message attempt several times but sighed at last, "Our situation deteriorates with despicable persistence."

"The Jiucetsi may still come. They could have been delayed."

"I have more hope for the transmission that occurred before the 'death-watch' began: Birk's call to Deetari."

"Someone will arrive," insisted Tori, trying to reassure herself. "In the meantime, we can make another search. We have half a millispan of daylight left."

Jase walked back toward the grimly laden desk and remained silent for several moments. Tori refused to turn and watch him. "Assuming our pattern of dashed hopes perseveres," he said, "where on this farm would you feel safest?"

Tori answered immediately, "Nguri's hothouse. I have a case of new traction bracelets in the supply room, so we can move freely through the resinous tunnels. Nguri always keeps the hothouse stocked with manna and water, and if all else fails, the roots are edible. The heavy air is unpleasant but not toxic, and there's a narrow exit tunnel that can be opened in an emergency."

"The hothouse sounds like Nguri's preference, not yours."

"He may return there," said Tori stubbornly. She glanced at Jase, carefully restricting her focus to exclude the desk.

"You're not easily discouraged, are you?" asked Jase wryly, but he shrugged. "I suppose that I can endure the unpalatable environment for a night. I've lived in worse places simply for the cultural experience."

"Remind me never to visit you while you 'experience.' "

"Very few Soli seem to share my tastes," mused Jase. He studied the tightened end of a silenen thong.

CHAPTER 20

The heavy aroma of the hothouse seemed even less welcoming than usual, but Tori curled her arms around her, wondering how a place so physically repellent could seem comfortable. She concluded that the low, domed cavern, festooned with luminous root spikes and soft Stromvi weavings, made her feel protected and secure. "I must have acquired some of the Stromvi burrowing instinct," she murmured.

"Generally a practical defense on this planet," said Jase absently, "since most of the dangerous life forms live on the surface." He was inspecting the three plundered rose canes by the bright, focused light of a pocket torch that he had found in the garage. The resin's volatile oils steamed within the narrow, incandescent beam.

Tori finished the manna cake, observing glumly that even that universal Consortium food tasted like Stromvi resin in the hothouse. She did not dare complain since it was she who had chosen the refuge. Perhaps she should have let Jase suggest an alternative. The hothouse had mellowed her irritation enough to credit Jase Sleide with a possibility of intelligence, despite being Calem's friend. "Do you think a Calongi will actually arrive tomorrow?" she asked him.

"Very few forces in this wide universe are able to daunt a Calongi."

"I would never have believed that I could look forward to meeting an inquisitor," said Tori, grimacing at the irony of twisted circumstances, "especially considering the likelihood that I'll be accused of conspiring to arrange this day's mad roster of horrors."

Jase winced and laid aside the rose canes with care. "You're not exceptionally fond of inquisitors, I gather."

Tori laughed, less from mirth than from long bitterness. "Of all the beings that I have ever loathed from personal experience, official inquisitors must rank close to the most abhorrent on my list."

"Inquisitors perform a very necessary function in maintaining Consortium peace."

"Necessary, perhaps, but unpalatable." In the hazy light of luminous resin, Jase's eyes seemed more blue than iridescent, but the strangeness about him was perversely increased. *He has an unsettling intensity about him,* decided Tori, *as if he peers directly into the soul. What an unlikely friend for Calem!*

"You actually hate inquisitors," muttered Jase, as if the concept pained him.

"You need not sound so disapproving," chided Tori, surprised that her comments could upset him more visibly than the rest of the day's events. "I respect your Sesserda studies. I respect the Calongi. I even respect their inquisitors. I simply don't care for inquisitors entering my personal sphere of life." A drop of resin landed on her shoulder, and she suppressed a futile instinct to brush the drop away. The warm resin teased a tingling path along her skin, seeping past the silken fabric of her neckline. "If you know enough about my unfortunate Arnod to quote his means of death to me, you must understand my reasons."

"You were not found guilty."

"I wasn't declared innocent," countered Tori quickly. "The guilt is irrelevant to most good members of this great, civilized Consortium. We're too accustomed to the guarantees of absolute Calongi justice." She became fervent on a topic of acute personal bias. "Uncertainty serves as well as a conviction. For your sake as well as mine, I hope you have a persuasively innocent perspective to offer to the inquisitor. The Calongi may respect 'creation,' but the concept of privacy means nothing to them."

"They revere truth," replied Jase quietly, "in themselves as in others. Their zeal for truth can make them uncomfortable companions, but it has made them great."

"Have you ever endured an inquisition, Mister Sleide?"

"Not in the official sense, no."

"Argue with me after the experience if you still feel so inclined." Tori grimaced. "And if I haven't been sentenced to 'atonement' on some barren lump of interstellar ice."

"If Consortium justice were truly that inept, I would unquestionably accompany you into purgatory. I practice Sesserda, as well as study it, because I know that your cynicism is misplaced."

"You are an idealist."

"Since we may soon become joint subjects of a rather difficult inquisition, we shall learn which of us predicts most accurately, shan't we? I cannot match your claim of unique physical anomalies, but I do have a few quirks that impede detailed readings."

Tori couldn't restrain the sarcasm in her tone, "We always learn that Calongi scanning techniques are universally accurate."

"Fewer than one in ten billion exceptions, even including the marginally civilized Level VII's."

Tori frowned at him. "If your statistic is valid, it seems an extraordinary coincidence that two such exceptions should presently occupy this room."

"The fact may be significantly less coincidental than you think." Tori raised her eyebrows questioningly, but Jase did not elaborate. He regathered the rose canes with a sigh.

"What are you trying to deduce from those pathetic twigs?" asked Tori.

"Some clue as to what shredded the foliage so effectively."

"Stromvi teeth?"

"No. The cuts are too even. Almost identical on every remaining leaf. Someone abused the sorry bush most methodically, but I still haven't a clue as to the reason." He struggled out of his sweater, a task made difficult by the slippery resin and the room's low ceiling. In startling contrast to the shapeless bulk of wool, the shirt beneath it was an intricate patterning of gold curves and spirals on a fabric so sheer that the gold seemed to merge with Jase's dark skin.

"I wondered how long you would tolerate this heat."

"I'm just beginning to feel warm. I usually adapt to new environments quite easily, but today has been exceptional in many respects."

Tori nodded toward his thin shirt. "That's a Calongi design, isn't it?"

"Yes." He shifted position, avoiding a root spike that hung down the wall behind his back. "It's one of the more obscure patterns reserved for Sesserda practitioners."

Tori's comfortable mood dissipated. "I've met other Sesserda scholars," murmured Tori softly, "but I never heard that the Calongi would allow a Soli to practice their religion formally."

"Sesserda is a universal religious philosophy," answered Jase with slow precision. "Its complexities are tailored to the many senses of the Calongi, but its practice is not restricted by any edict."

"I know little more about Sesserda than the standard Consortium injunction to 'respect creation,' " said Tori lightly, exaggerating her ignorance. She had studied Sesserda briefly in a naive phase of her youth, before Uncle Per had discouraged her interest. She had obeyed Uncle Per without questioning his motives, for she had not yet understood the limits to a patron's care for his concubine's child.

" 'Respect creation' is the fundamental law from which all else is derived. Ideally, it's the only law required. The awesome simplicity of that law is where its power lies." Jase paused before continuing, "I'm a Sesserda practitioner at the third level."

Extraordinarily advanced training for a Soli, thought Tori, and her suspicions assumed an ominous shape. Impatiently, she told herself that she had surely forgotten the precise significance of Sesserda rankings. No Soli could possibly have the authority that she associated with third level. "Is that why an inquisitor's techniques may function unreliably in your regard?"

"Third level control is enough to interfere with the delicate senses of a trained inquisitor. An official scan of me can only reach data that I give voluntarily, which makes the reading no more accurate than my personal perceptions of truth. Deeper readings can be made, but they're too uncertain to have legal validity."

Even disregarding all that she thought she remembered of Sesserda, Tori had trouble believing that Sesserda study could enable a Soli to impede Calongi scanning. Such refinement of skill was surely implausible in any species but Calongi. Tiva disorder was a natural aberration and rarer than Jase's one-in-ten-billion statistic. Voluntary control would demand manipulation of every physiological function.

Jase could be giving her an inflated view of his capabilities, although such an indulgence of ego seemed inconsistent with what she had observed of him. Tori began to regret that she had not questioned Birk more directly about this visitor, Jase Sleide. She grimaced, considering how little she could have anticipated a need for such questions when the opportunity existed.

She pushed restlessly at the traction bracelets fastened around her arms. She folded their smooth covers across the rows of tiny hooks to preserve her hands from injury. She realized that Jase was watching her manipulation of the traction bracelets, and she stopped abruptly.

When Jase spoke again, he sounded both uncomfortable and reluctant: "I am compelled to fulfill an onerously tardy obligation, Miss Darcy. We need to discuss some unpleasant issues."

"Birk is dead," replied Tori. "Ngoi is dead. Everyone else is gone, and we appear to be stranded. I have no idea what has happened or why. I do not like the situation. I'm not sure I like what little I'm learning about you, Mister Sleide, but I intend to stay closer to you than your shadow until we find a way to escape this lonely, demented corner of the universe."

"Bluntly stated," observed Jase with a wry twisting of his mouth.

"What did you expect me to say? That I'm having a wonderful time? That your scintillating company compensates for the numb horror of losing everything that I considered solid in my life this morning? That I have any notion of what we should do if no rescue arrives tomorrow or the next day or the day after that? You don't need to educate me about the hazards of trying to travel across this planet's natural surface without a hovercraft. I know the full roster of osang snakes, carnivorous panguulung lilies, nineteen varieties of poisonous thorn-creepers, not to mention that delightful seed pod that exudes a caustic gas when it opens. Birk has a private hoard of adaptation fluid somewhere in the house. We could probably survive at Hodge Farm for fifty spans, but I don't find that prospect very attractive at the moment."

"I don't think our situation is quite that desperate yet."

"No? Tell me, Mister Sleide, is it another coincidence that you arrived and calamity accompanied you?"

"Probably not," answered Jase readily.

Tori had not expected him to concede so easily to a suspicion that she had voiced on impulse. His response dismayed her more than a little. "Birk greeted you with respect, not with particular familiarity," said Tori, feeling hollow at the thought of losing even the tenuous companionship of Jase Sleide. She did not want to be that alone.

"I knew Birk for many spans. As I said, I once lived here. However, I doubt very much that he recognized me. In your position, I think I'd be far less trusting of a stranger who arrived just prior to two violent deaths and a mass disappearance of people and pertinent equipment. I've never been a great believer in coincidence."

"And what, in my position, would you choose as your alternative? I haven't seen an abundance of volunteers for the Tori Darcy support league today." She wished that the hothouse did not impose such strict constraints on movement. She would have enjoyed storming across the room in a flurry of frustration.

"You make an excellent point."

Confronted by such equable agreement, Tori's temper cooled. She leaned against the Stromvi rest-mound, feeling the dampness penetrate her skin. She addressed a trio of thick, blue-white root spikes, dangling unevenly above her head, and she imagined briefly that Nguri was with her. "I'm not a timid, blushing Soli blossom cultivated with great care from the Hodge gardens. I don't frighten easily, and I have more experience with violent death and loss than most beings of my age and species. At this precise moment, however, the trend of this particular discussion is making me feel rather ill."

"I'm not feeling inordinately cheerful about it myself," answered Jase.

Her illusion of talking to the Stromvi elder shattered, Tori turned toward Jase beseechingly. "Then, please, let's revert to frivolous chatter or useless activity or anything to keep from talking ourselves into absolute madness. Tell me your life history, or pose some mindless social queries that I can answer without thought or feeling."

"My Soli social skills are a little weak. Despite—or perhaps because of—my constant exposure to alien cultures, I tend to communicate better with alien species than with other Soli."

"Then let me regale you with some of the fantastic stories that I learned at my dear mother's knees. Mama's favorite choice of topic was a little unorthodox for a child's hearing because Great-grandmama was a very unorthodox woman."

"Mirelle of Attia."

"So you already know." Tori felt a chill begin to eat at her from within.

"You married Arnod Conaty as Victoria Mirelle. I could hardly learn the one fact without the other."

"Mirelle is too infamous to remain a secret, I suppose," said Tori with a brittle smile, "though I seldom stop trying. I wouldn't have mentioned her now if I weren't desperate for distraction. Do you have any idea how impossible it is to escape the legacy of Mirelle? As a child, I was educated thoroughly regarding all the ghastly family power struggles. I learned all the lurid tales of stolen thrones and shattered hearts, but I was nearly fourteen spans old before I realized that the family trade was concubinage."

"Were you encouraging Birk Hodge to become your patron?"

Tori hesitated, but her private doubts had lost their meaning. "Yes," she answered, meeting Jase's keen eyes squarely.

"You would have made a disastrous pairing," remarked Jase gently. Tori looked away from him, uncomfortable with his quiet condemnation. Jase continued, "You're too independent. Birk has always had a nearly pathological need to control anyone whom he decided to claim, and I doubt that you would have cared for him in his vicious mode."

"Your warning is irrelevant now, isn't it?"

"So it seems." Jase extended his hand to catch a drop of dew that dripped from a pale violet root spike. The droplet settled in the palm of his hand, where it continued to glow faintly. He watched it, as he murmured, "You're very forthright, Miss Darcy. You embarrass me, for I've been less honest with you."

His comment surprised her, for she had thought the embarrassment all her own. "In what regard, Mister Sleide?"

"I should have clarified the ramifications of my Sesserda ranking. Calongi masters have trained me in Sesserda disciplines that few Soli recognize." He continued hesitantly, "Achieving third-level rank is very unusual for Soli, who generally have only the seven developed senses instead of the ninety-six of a Calongi."

"What sort of unusual disciplines has Sesserda taught you?" asked Tori, leery of receiving the answer.

"Every Sesserda scholar studies lessons of observation, maximum utilization of mental and physical faculties, appreciation of the value of all species, all beings. Sesserda practitioners learn to implement the theories."

"How thoroughly do you practice Sesserda?" demanded Tori, her dread increasing with his obvious equivocation.

"For species of Civilization Level III and below, I'm authorized to serve as an official inquisitor." The droplet cradled in his palm faded, and he smeared it with his opposite hand. "I was asked to come here specifically, although Birk apparently had no idea of who initiated that unlikely invitation. I came to question you regarding the death of your husband, Arnod Conaty, because I received a message in Calem's name, indicating serious concern about your relationship with Birk. I am your inquisitor, Miss Darcy."

For a moment, Tori tried to persuade herself that this moment was a bizarre joke, that the entire day had been a nightmarish delusion, but the faces of Birk and Ngoi and Arnod all arose in her mind to mock her. The sense of revulsion for both the resinous air and the circumstances that had led her to the hothouse expanded, filled her, and seemed to burst inside her like a swollen wound. The bitterness flowed through her, empowering her with the hollow strength of anger. "Can none of you let me live in peace?" cried Tori furiously. "I should always rely on my first instincts. I distrusted you when we met. Calem's friend, indeed."

"If I sounded abrupt with you . . ." began Jase contritely.

"You sounded like an arrogant prig," grumbled Tori.

". . . it was only because we were not supposed to meet informally. My shuttle apparently arrived late from Deetari, and you were already occupied in the fields. There are rules governing the interactions between an inquisitor and his subject."

"You haven't obeyed the rules very well, have you? You should have informed me of your status immediately."

"My paltry excuse is that I haven't been functioning well today." The elusive shadows of resin-light made his face, creased with worry, seem less austere. "I have trouble relating to Soli under the best of circumstances, and you were not what I expected."

"Is that good or bad?" snapped Tori.

"I'm not sure yet," replied Jase earnestly. He clenched his hands, rubbing at the traction bracelets. "As you know, even the Calongi find you difficult to read, and I'm really little more than an apprentice inquisitor without exceptional promise for advancement. I would never have agreed to return here at all if Calem's message had not seemed so peculiarly desperate, if your presence on Stromvi had not seemed so genuinely unlikely, and if my talks with Ukitan-lai had not made me realize that I needed to confront the past." His voice faded, and his attention seemed to drift, but he recalled himself quickly. "After bungling my initial opportunity to speak to you, the entire issue became buried by the intervening circumstances."

"Charming," said Tori. She met Jase's rueful gaze defiantly. "May I question the inquisitor?"

"Of course," replied Jase firmly, but his hooded eyes narrowed.

"What do you know about the deaths of Birk Hodge and Ngoi Ngenga, *Inquisitor* Sleide? What do you know about the disappearance of several hundred people from the Ngenga Valley? How much do you know about sound-shocks?"

"My explanation for today's events would be pure conjuring at this point. You and I are equally uninformed, I'm afraid."

"Thank you for acknowledging my innocence!"

"If it's any help, I doubt that Omi-lai—the inquisitor who closed your previous questioning—would have released you if he actually considered you capable of premeditated murder, but Omi is a stickler even for a Calongi. He would consider any judgment irresponsible if he could not confirm it with all senses in accord. I know him. He's a superb musician." Jase smiled, but Tori did not relinquish her proud fury, and the smile faded quickly.

"I'm delighted for you both."

"Omi-lai would be appalled at any being who would condemn you on the basis of uncertainty. I've examined the recorded evidence regarding your husband's death quite thoroughly, and the case against you had very little substance, if one discounts your neighbors' patently envious opinions. I haven't studied you enough to make any comprehensive conclusions from my own readings, of course."

"Of course," echoed Tori coldly.

"I'm also fairly confident that you didn't kill Birk, although my judgment in that regard has a shaky legal foundation, due to my personal involvement."

"An utterly impeachable witness for my defense," muttered Tori.

"I agree with your identification of the 'thunder' today as sound-shock. A number of Consortium devices can cause such a phenomenon but none of them involves murder or abduction."

"Can you drive a Stromvi tunneler?"

"Do you have a tunneler?"

"I think I can find one," replied Tori with the cool, haughty gaze that enhanced her resemblance to her great-grandmother most effectively. "The trip may not be pleasant, but almost anything is better than spending a night chatting with an inquisitor." She uncovered the hooks of her traction bracelets and used them to clamber out of the hothouse.

"All you needed was the right incentive to escape," muttered Jase with a sardonic grimace. He gathered his sweater and the machete, and he followed Tori into the moonlit Stromvi night.

CHAPTER 21

The Soli access to the Stromvi workers' enclave required constant clearing to be navigable. The tangle covering the path provided further indication of Ngoi's recent neglect. Jase used the machete liberally in order to force an entry through briers that were slightly less poisonous than most of their relatives, but could still raise fierce welts. "I hope you know where we're going," growled Jase, as a thorny branch snapped across his hand.

"You sound frustrated, Inquisitor," said Tori with derisive innocence. "Where is your Sesserda self-control?"

"Have you ever tried to enter a Stromvi deep-cavern?"

"No."

"I tried once. I repented quickly."

Undaunted, Tori retorted, "I hope that whoever stole the hovercrafts will be as easily intimidated as yourself. Nguri told me that the Stromvi store four tunnelers beneath this enclave. Tunnelers are much slower than hovercraft, but Stromvi use them to travel throughout this planet."

"Stromvi can survive for months with less oxygen than we Soli breathe in a millispan."

"The conditioning inoculations are supposed to enable our lungs to process the resin emanations like a Stromvi."

"The procedure isn't recommended for maximum comfort. Filling my lungs with toxic resin," grunted Jase, slashing the last barrier of briers with a ferocious energy, "is not a prospect that I particularly relish."

"Would you prefer to await a rescue that may never come?" snapped Tori. She pushed through the opening that Jase had cut in the hedge.

She faced the empty enclave with a heavy sense of disappointment. She had not truly expected to find any

Stromvi families here, for they would have responded to
her calls if they had been able, but busy, burrowing
Stromvi children had filled this circle on all her previous
visits. The desolate contrast depressed her, deflating
some of her angry energy.

She said quietly, "The large dome in the center leads
to the deep caverns." The emptiness made her feel a
need to whisper. The dim chorus of Stromvi clicking did
not help, for it persisted in its one mournful word-blend,
and the sounds had grown no louder here at the thickest
concentration of local Stromvi dwellings. "With a modi-
cum of luck, we may reach the shuttle port in time to
greet your fellow inquisitor. We may even locate some
of the missing Stromvi."

Tori strode toward the large dome's entrance. Jase
shook his head, raised his eyes to the sky for a moment
of commiseration with distant friends who served regularly as inquisitors, and began to cross the clearing in
Tori's wake. He stopped and looked again at Stromvi's
dominant moon. He frowned and hurried to catch Tori
before she entered the Stromvi dome. He tapped her
arm lightly and pointed at the mottled silver disk just
clearing the horizon. "Full moon," he whispered.

"Shouldn't it be?" asked Tori, impatient to reach the
tunnelers.

Jase raised his dark brows quizzically. "Not if I arrived
on Stromvi this morning."

"You arrived eight days early for Sylvie's wedding,"
said Tori, uncomfortably impressed by his cool certainty.

"Nine days early," countered Jase softly.

"Did your Sesserda honor compel you to offer me one
more puzzle that I cannot solve?" grumbled Tori, wishing
that she could disbelieve him or distrust him as thoroughly as she resented him. "You overextended your
welcome before you arrived." She pushed through the
loosely plaited door to enter the dome.

The dome's entry tunnel was large enough that Tori
could nearly stand straight, but as it began to spiral
downward, she was forced to crawl. "I should have worn
mud grubbers for the occasion," she muttered, laughing
sardonically at herself for her poor selection of attire.
Her arms would be scratched raw.

She peered into the upper chamber, a wide room

draped with the characteristic Stromvi weavings of shaded purplish fibers. The chamber resembled a slightly larger version of the hothouse, though fewer roots pierced the roughly textured walls. Plentiful rest-mounds indicated that the room had been designed for sizable gatherings. The Stromvi click-speech continued at the same soft level heard aboveground.

Tori did not enter, for the room was as vacant as every other dwelling she had inspected since Birk died, but her attention fixed on a half-open ivory bud, which lay on a low Stromvi table in the center of the room. The moist air had prevented the flower from wilting. "I wanted so much to see that blue-and-white hybrid marketed," she murmured.

"The only Stromvi I ever knew to enjoy cut roses was Nguri," remarked Jase, peering into the room curiously, "and he only enjoyed them for purposes of professional interest. Have Stromvi habits changed?"

"No." Tori frowned, for Jase's observation disturbed her, but she could not dispute its accuracy. "Nguri did enter the fields very early today, and he could have collected a sample before I inspected the roses this morning. I hadn't monitored that row for several days, and some of the Hodge hybrids produce budding shoots very quickly." She tried to find significance in any memory of that single bush, but it began to blur in her mind with all the roses she had ever inspected at Hodge Farm. "One of the canes had been cut recently, but it was a hasty, careless job—not like Nguri's work."

Jase slid into the room and examined the flower closely without touching it. "Why might Nguri have returned to the workers' enclave at dawn?"

Tori shrugged, wondering if she were betraying Nguri to the same injustice of suspicion that haunted her. "He was unhappy with Ngoi's sloppy management. Ngina told me that no one had seen Ngoi this morning, which could suggest that Ngoi had retreated from one of Nguri's famous diatribes."

"How much did Nguri say about Ngoi's death?"

"Nothing more than I already told you," answered Tori, and she looked at Jase sharply. "What are you thinking, Inquisitor?"

"Nothing very intelligible, I regret to say. Something

still bothers me about that mutilated rose—beyond the general madness of everything—and I cannot quite identify the specific reason. How much of the first click-message this morning did you understand?"

"Less than you, apparently, and I'm supposed to be the knowing resident here."

"Too bad. I would have liked confirmation of the wording. However, I've had a lot of practice at interpreting diverse Consortium languages."

"Your advanced Sesserda training requires you to speak every dialect of the Consortium, I suppose."

"Hardly," replied Jase. Gingerly, he tried to pick up the rose, but thick resin made it slip from his fingers. "I've studied a few hundred languages. Any educated Calongi knows at least a thousand."

"How limiting for you."

Jase used the traction bracelets to heave himself back up the ramp into the tunnel where Tori waited. "There seems to be considerably more resin in that room than in most Stromvi dwellings, although I didn't see an exceptional number of root spikes."

"Maybe someone pruned them very recently."

"Maybe. Poor housekeeping, if so. Ngoi's management really must have deteriorated." Jase rubbed his neck and crouched again to resume the descent through the tunnel. Slightly annoyed with him for appropriating the lead position, Tori followed. The narrow tunnel allowed only single-file progress.

"Nguri attributed Ngoi's recent lapses to the bad influence of your friend Calem," said Tori, trying to provoke a defensive reaction.

"Calem and Nguri share a long and mutual dislike," returned Jase evenly.

"I blamed Rillessa's constant, childish demands for her impervious husband's attention. For the past five months, she's been insisting that an unspecified someone was watching her for lustful purposes. She kept berating Ngoi for his failure to provide Hodge Farm with adequate Stromvi protection against her invisible nemesis."

"Perhaps someone really was watching her."

"No one on this planet, except possibly Calem, ever lusted after Rillessa. Stromvi and Deetari take no such interest in Soli. Birk and one mechanic at the shuttle port are the only Soli males who live on Stromvi permanently, and I'm the only such female. If Rillessa was being watched, it wasn't for the reasons she imagined."

"You never sensed anyone watching you?"

"Only Birk."

"I presume that his motives really were lustful," said Jase with heavy irony. He paused briefly to peer into another vacant room. "The light is becoming discouragingly dim and dismal down here."

"It should brighten again soon. The most luminous resins are grown at lower levels."

"If we don't find your much touted tunneler, we'd better prepare ourselves for a spectacular climb," grumbled Jase, and he dropped abruptly from Tori's view.

The shaft that sloped into darkness before her brought a gasp to Tori's lips and a momentary regret that she had insisted on this route. Climbing the steep length of that shaft with only traction bracelets for support would be virtually impossible for any Soli. Tori considered retreat fairly seriously for several microspans, even though Jase had already disappeared into the darkness. She shifted her feet in front of her, secured the loose fabric of her long-blouse, propelled herself to the shaft's brink, and slid.

The odor of resin became so thick that Tori choked, as her lungs tried to adapt to the rush of heavy Stromvi air. The resin made the passage slick, and the Stromvi had fashioned the tunnel smoothly, but the warmth of it, like a living, pulsing membrane, seemed to tug at her bare arms and ankles. She closed her eyes against the stinging resin and tried to restore the evenness of her breathing. She skidded to a stop.

Jase tapped her foot. Tori opened her eyes, but the atmosphere was as impermeable to Soli sight as pondwater. All of the images were distorted and blurred. She muttered, "This is the worst idea I've had since I married Arnod."

Jase pulled insistently at her ankle. "Tunnelers," he said, his voice sounding thick and ragged.

Tori could see nothing but vast dark blotches and the lighter, mobile blur that was Jase. "Can you really see tunnelers?" she mumbled, trying not to open her mouth too far in the rancid atmosphere, although the resin had already permeated her body.

"Sesserda training has many uses," replied Jase, and he prodded her toward a looming, dark monster.

Tori extended her hand to touch the black plane in front of her. The plane felt soft and slightly uneven, like carpet moss. When Jase opened the tunneler's lower door, the brightness of the resin-biolight brought tears to Tori's eyes, cleansing them of some of the accumulated resin and clearing her vision partially. Water could not dissolve the resin, but it could displace some of the surface particles. She struggled to climb into the tunneler, but even the hooks of the new traction bracelets failed to cling to the steep entry ramp.

"Take hold of the cargo pulley," said Jase, and Tori felt the leathery grip thud against her shoulder. She inserted her bent arm through the soft, strong circle of snakeskin. She was glad that the Stromvi did not use silenen thongs for their lading, for she thought she would always visualize silenen thongs as twisted around the neck of Birk or Arnod. She let the grip pull her, elbow first, up the slope and into the cabin.

"Do you prefer to navigate or drive?" asked Jase. "I should probably drive, unless you have a significant aversion to my appropriation of that choice. Handling one of these beasts requires a fair amount of physical strength, since Stromvi tend toward forcefulness, and I believe I have the advantage in that respect."

"The privilege of driving is entirely yours, Inquisitor Sleide, but I'm not sure that I can navigate very well at the moment. I can't even see clearly."

"Bite your lip. Raw resin in an open cut is a terrific inducement to lubrication of the eyes. The atmosphere in here isn't quite as thick as in the cavern. You'll adjust in a few moments." Jase jabbed his fist hard against controls designed for massive Stromvi hands. The engine began to click rapidly in an imitation of steady Stromvi gnawing, and the tunneler lurched. Tori braced herself against the mossy wall, but she still acquired bruises from the sudden motion. "Something actually functions," observed Jase approvingly. "Chart our course, navigator."

Tori bit her upper lip and winced at the sharp, stinging pain of resin mingling with her blood. Tears began to stream freely, as Jase had predicted. Tori blinked rapidly, resisting the urge to rub at her eyes with her resin-coated hands. Her vision cleared slightly. "Are there any maps?" she asked, surveying the interior of the tunneler with slow care and debating the likeliest position for a Stromvi navigator's post. Though the vine-weavings made the tunneler aesthetically comparable to any traditional Stromvi dwelling, the fibrous camouflage concealed sophisticated Consortium machinery, designed to Stromvi specifications but engineered by the same highly skilled Xiani who created most Consortium starships.

"Try that panel," suggested Jase, nodding toward a smooth fiber curtain.

Supporting herself against a low divider hung with Stromvi rugs, Tori fumbled toward the panel and pushed aside the drapery of soft, woven reeds. A three-dimensional grid formed of luminous, wire-thin root casings crossed the wall beneath it. Like the tunneler, the map was an imperturbably practical adaptation of traditional Stromvi materials and methods, implementing the ingenuity of the Consortium's amalgam of cultures. Tori identified the plant symbols of Hodge Farm and the shuttle port. "It seems to be nearly a straight course, if you take the upward fork just beyond the cavern."

"Considerate Stromvi." The tunneler groaned and slowed. "Hold on." Jase touched two controls lightly before selecting a third. He pulled his arm close against his body and held the position for a long moment, before releasing the gathered tension in a single explosive jab. The tunneler hurled itself forward through the Stromvian earth.

CHAPTER 22

Rillessa watched *It* shift and change, darkening and thickening, as the poison from her needle-gun spread throughout *Its* being. *It* stopped in mid-stride, and she knew that the pain had reached *Its* awareness. The shriek fled from *It*, racing high in anguish, though *It* did not seem as desperate as *Its* cry. *It* bent, and the darkness of *It* lifted like a growing shroud. Rillessa's mouth gaped in eager, anxious anticipation of *Its* death. The shroud heaved and writhed. The dim blur of *Its* form began to ripple with color, and the scarlet streak spread to stain the rim of an oblong gash across *Its* belly.

Rillessa began to rise to her feet, abandoning the shelter of a wickedly abrasive Stromvi lily. She wanted *It* to die. She did not want to wait any longer. She inserted the final needle into her weapon, willing to sacrifice that security of reserved assets for the sake of eliminating *It* irrevocably. Her hand began to tremble, but her grip became firmly determined as she took aim.

The shroud of *It*, brilliant now with races of ephemeral colors, emitted a second brief, shrill shriek, as Rillessa's needle plunged into *Its* scarlet mouth. Rillessa raised her needle-gun defiantly above her head. She exulted in her victory, shouting, "I have beaten you," as the colors of the shroud became ashen gray. She strode proudly toward her victim.

In a single hurtling motion, the shroud of *It* lifted from the ground and flew at Rillessa. She tried to retreat and escape, but the shroud, cold and damp, struck and clung to her. The weight of *Its* shroud was not great, but Rillessa sank to the ground beneath the irrefutable force of her own terror.

*   *   *

Death-watch, clicked Nguri, and he listened attentively for the remaining echoes rumbling through the tunnels, as the voices of his people became silent. He rubbed his jaw, for it ached from the lengthy chant. "Such songs become painful," he muttered, but he did not rejoice at the reprieve. The subsequent duties of death-watch would bring more pain than the click-chant.

With a grumble deep in his hind throat, Nguri heaved himself free of the load of thick soil, and he filled his thirsty lung-sacs. He realized how nearly he had drained himself, for he could feel the resin tingling throughout his inner cavities. He stretched his torso to its fullest extent in order to peer above the thorn-tangle and observe the softly lavender dawn. The morning beauty did not give him peace today. It refueled his anger at those who would destroy his precious world with careless greed.

Nguri's senior wife, Ngeta, emerged from her own concealment a short distance from Nguri, and she approached him with a calm dignity that scorned fear. "Husband, we must gather with our people in the hidden caverns without delay," she adjured him.

Nguri smiled at her, relishing the exquisite patterns of her hide and accepting her courage as a tribute of her faith in him. "You go, Ngeta-li. I must complete a certain task before I may join you."

"Husband, you owe nothing to any Soli."

"I know, Ngeta-li," replied Nguri grimly.

"You are as stubborn as our daughter, whose obstinacy you deride as adolescent folly."

"Ngina's behavior is consistently inappropriate to her breeding and her gender," grumbled Nguri, "and your comparison of my performance of honor-bound duties to her indulgence in headstrong whims does not merit further discussion."

"Yes, husband," answered Ngeta with wry meekness.

Nguri grunted, and he lumbered into the hedgerow without attempting to correct Ngeta's misconceptions. He wanted to complete his self-appointed tasks quickly and rejoin his family. He must find his wayward daughter and learn from her the measure of the wretched Calem's involvement in this onrush of ominous events. Death-watch would not wait while Nguri took the pleasure of bickering with his senior wife. Nguri acknowledged gruffly that Ngeta usually won such arguments anyway.

Nguri lowered his torso as he approached the open clearing near Birk's absurd house, and he kept his movements smooth and cautious. In the dappled shadows of early dawn, Stromvi hide provided exceptionally effective camouflage against the Stromvi landscape, but Nguri blended less well against Soli hedges and Soli constructs. He studied the empty garden and the silent house by careful, winding progress within the shelter of Stromvi vine wreaths. He walked as close to the ground as was possible without burrowing.

Nguri heard the rumbling voice of the Stromvi land, and he became very still. He fought an instinct to delve rapidly into the ground, for he needed to learn how his planet's enemy would proceed. He was determined to give his people whatever knowledge he could gain for their defense. He would not concede to the prophesied end of death-watch. He had let the Soli come. He owed the price. He would be martyred, if necessary, but he would not hide and wait for the end of his world. He would not live if he could not redeem the honor he had lost to Soli betrayal.

He listened closely to his planet's voice: The lesser beast walked closest, easing Nguri's decision. The larger menace might be more informative, and the path of courage dictated that the greatest fear should be faced first, but sense demanded investigation of the nearest danger.

Nguri tried to bury a secret, dishonorable hope that the "lesser beast" might be only Birk Hodge, crossing the Farm in search of vanished workers or thwarted ambitions. Nguri could not feel personal fear of a man so long respected, however selfishly that man might have behaved. Nguri did fear the beast that had caused Ngoi's death. With chilling recollection of the ragged wounds, Nguri acknowledged the viciousness of the creature that could have driven Ngoi to such a desperate self-destruction.

An alien blood-scent reached Nguri's head nodules, as a cry of aching shrillness made him seal his ear slits. He scurried forward, locked in his self-made silence, but his head nodules gained greater discrimination in the absence of any registered sound. The blood-scent had a metallic tang, unpleasant and unfamiliar. Other scents had less potency, but one was Soli, recognizable even in its heavy garb of fear. *Rillessa*? wondered Nguri, for that Soli female was not a being he had expected to encounter at the edge of the seed fields.

Cautiously, Nguri lifted his torso, and he saw the Soli male running toward him—but no Soli had such a scent, sweet as death and too clear and pure to be a mask of perfume. The man was not a Soli, then, although he had the look. Nguri ducked quickly, as the man's head turned toward Nguri's place of hiding. Nguri smelled the anger that filled the man and threatened all beings in its path.

The man's tight mouth formed a word that Nguri did not hear. The man's hand held a weapon that Nguri did not know. The man turned slowly, his weapon hunting for its target. Nguri did not move, for the man's hard challenge promised death.

The scent of searing fire, unnaturally hot and sterile to be of Stromvi origin, caused Nguri to wince in pain. A narrow swath across the seed field smoldered toward the man, and Nguri felt new vibrations of the ground as the greater beast approached. The angry man ducked into the shadow of the vine hedge, and Nguri could see him clearly: definitely not Soli. The ivory skin had a translucence that Soli lacked, and a crest of black hair shaded into a silver mane extending down the neck and arms. The man wore a leather kilt and breastplate of coppery hues, and a ruby starburst clasped the shreds of a crimson cloak at his shoulder. His legs and feet were nearly invisible, encased (Nguri supposed) in boots of light-refractive material.

The man breathed slowly, and confused scents of injury ebbed but did not quite vanish. A long, blistering scar crossed the man's head, cutting through the silver mane. The man touched the wound and scowled in annoyance.

A shadow blocked the sun's light, and Nguri looked sharply toward the new menace, a hovering silver disk much larger than any Stromvi ship. Nguri's movement drew the man's attention, but Nguri did not notice. Nguri had opened his ear slits belatedly, and the purring of the silver ship's engine disoriented him for a moment, tangling the diverse scent signals into a blur. "Ares," hissed the man, and he raised his weapon toward Nguri.

The ship dove toward the ground, and fire beams converged on the vine hedge where the man hid. Two beams struck the man's breastplate and sizzled into darkness. A third beam skimmed the man's arm, gouging flesh and charring blood and bone. The man shifted his aim toward the source of the attack, and the burning light that burst from his weapon scorched the vines that concealed him.

Nguri pressed into the humus to escape the crossing beams of fire, encircling him now, as the ship poured forth new enemies. Nguri could hear them in the pounding of the ground, though he could not see them, and too many scents now masked the individual traces. The smoke of boiling resin filled the Stromvi air, forming a thick fog. Nguri heard the sounds of choking and felt satisfied that his world could defend itself at least a little.

Hoping to escape in the resin fog, Nguri shuffled backward from the hedge. A vine ensnared his hind foot, and he snapped the tough vine impatiently with his pruning teeth. He heard the hiss of the fire beam before its scent reached him, and he tried to dodge, but the people of Stromvi had never moved quickly. The agony came in a sharp, quick jab, as fire sliced through Nguri's hide, and years of layered resin boiled from the wound. With a soft click of pain from injury and aged muscles, Nguri burrowed into his planet and lay still. He waited, and his anger against the destroyers grew.

*   *   *

Tagran squinted to see the single returning Rea warship through the glare of early morning. Yesterday, Ares had led two such ships of Rea warriors against Hodge Farm. A millispan earlier, Roake had gone alone in a personal shuttle. Rea communication devices, too unsophisticated to overcome the effects of Stromvi's atmosphere for long distances, had issued nothing but static since the brothers' respective departures. Only the daar'va had provided an indication of Rea actions in the Ngenga Valley, and sound-shock represented an uncertain message at best.

Tagran returned to the shape of the clan leader's warship, the only large Rea ship that had remained at the port. His fair Essenji skin felt burned even from the few microspans of exposure to the powerful Stromvi sun. The kilt, tunic, and breastplate of a senior Rea warrior's uniform gave little protection against such a foe.

Tagran held his position though the wind of the warship's landing buffeted him. Akras had ordered him to await Ares' return. She had said nothing about Roake.

The exit panels of the silver disk ship parted, and Ares jumped to the resilient landing pad without awaiting the extension of the exit ramp. He was little more than a blur of darkness, for his Bori cloak still covered all but his head. He crossed quickly to Tagran. "Where is she?" demanded Ares, his fine Essenji features furrowed into a scowl.

"In her room," answered Tagran, "but she asked me to meet you and tell you to await her summons." Tagran's distaste for his role as envoy increased with the deepening of Ares' scowl. Tagran did not like the games of authority. He could not altogether blame Ares for displaying signs of growing anger.

Ares' dark eyes smoldered, but he accepted Tagran's message with a curt nod. "Tell her that my brother is now my prisoner, though we were forced to destroy his shuttle in the process of capture. Even then, he nearly escaped us on a stolen hovercraft, but complex code locks slowed his access to the hovercraft's full capabilities." Ares' words about Roake were a tribute, consciously bestowed but resented. "We claimed his hovercraft and one from Hodge Farm, though the latter is unusable. One Hodge Farm hovercraft escaped, but its pilot was too obviously inexperienced to be the Rea-traitor, and we have accounted for the other significant targets of attack."

Which means we have lost Birkaj, thought Tagran grimly, but he waited for Ares to admit the crucial failure.

"Tell her," continued Ares slowly, "that we were unable to damage the Rea-traitor's house with the minimal weapons that she authorized, but he cannot have left Hodge Farm. As the clan leader ordered, none of our warriors left visual range of the warships, and we gave first priority to the pursuit of possible escape vehicles. Our third warship remains just beyond detection from the Ngenga Valley, alert to any further vehicular movements. If the Rea-traitor does not emerge within another day, I shall lure him out of hiding."

"I shall convey your report to the clan leader," replied Tagran, "if she will see me."

Ares laughed softly, a disturbing sound that lacked any mirth. "Did our clan leader enlighten you as to her further commands regarding my brother?"

"The disposition of prisoners is the war leader's responsibility," answered Tagran soberly, though he shared Ares' reluctance to consider Roake an ordinary captive.

"As always, Tagran, you recognize the proper duty of a Rea warrior. So be it. I shall fulfill my duty and punish the traitor. I have long wished that Roake did not exist, constantly reminding me of my inferiority to him." Ares did not seem to relish his triumph. He began to return to his own warship, but he paused. "Do you understand her, Tagran?" asked Ares, turning slowly back to face the elder warrior. "You have known her better than any of us."

Tagran frowned, for Ares' question troubled him. "She is clan leader, and I obey her."

Ares' smile was bitter. "Of course, Tagran. Forgive me if I seemed to doubt your loyalty."

*   *   *

Ngina wrapped her arms above her head and pressed herself disconsolately against the rest-mound in Ngoi's cave. She felt confused and entirely miserable. She had wanted to prove herself for so long, and she finally had an opportunity, but she had no idea what to do next. She carried an additional uneasy burden of uncertainty, for she feared that she had not reacted very wisely so far. Her honored father would be furious with her for behaving so independently.

She should have called for help more quickly when she discovered Ngoi. Perhaps Ngoi could have been saved. . . . No, decided Ngina firmly, she could not afford to accept that unnecessary guilt. Ngoi had lived barely long enough to whisper a few short words. No wise elder could have reached him in time to help.

After Ngoi died, however—what else *could* she have done? She should have told her father immediately, of course, instead of trying to finish Ngoi's aborted work on her own. She had not appreciated the enormity of the task until she began it. Until the roar of strange sound, she had not even considered the possibility that the creature who had tortured Ngoi might return. "Stupid," she muttered to herself, but the imprecation did not relieve her doubts. Now she feared even to leave Ngoi's cave.

She had given the warning, but she had not expected her people to begin actual death-watch at her word. She had never imagined how quickly *death-watch* could spread through Stromvi by the soft vibrations of the wireroot networks. The sense of what she had started overwhelmed her.

She knew that she must go to the major southern cavern, for her family would miss her and worry about her. Her father would expect an answer to his query about Mister Calem's field, and she would have no choice but to explain how she had failed to complete the search for that strange, unpleasant scent. She must obey the death-watch that she had begun in panic, or she must confess all of her folly, or she must salvage some morsel of honor by bringing an intelligible story to her people.

If Ngoi had lived a little longer, he might have explained so much that now bewildered Ngina. He might have described the face of the enemy instead of muttering about his pain and abjection. He might have told her why the packages had such value, and who valued them. "He might have told me whom to trust," she whispered.

A rattling startled her. Ngina lifted her strong, young body to a fighting crouch, and she peered cautiously through the tangle of root spikes that guarded the entry tunnel. She could feel movements that throbbed distantly through the ground, but she could not identify the perpetrators. She did not know if they were her people or her enemy. The dry rattling recurred, and Ngina tensed with fear, for the sound came too clearly to have traveled far.

Slowly, Ngina touched the parcel that she had clutched absently with her forefoot. She cut the twine that held it with a quick snap of her pruning teeth. Cautiously, she unfolded the vine-cloth wrapping. When the package rattled a third time, she became instantly still, but she resumed the unwrapping after only the briefest pause.

Blue sponge-moss cradled the russet pods. Each cylindrical pod wore a slim black scar down its length, where the pod had been sliced and resealed with a sticky resin paste. One of the pods jerked as Ngina watched it, and she nearly dropped the entire parcel in alarm. She touched the unexpectedly active seed pod gingerly. The leathery pod casing had begun to harden. She could feel it vibrate restlessly, as the rattling occurred again.

Carefully, Ngina removed the active pod from its mossy nest. She stared at it, engulfed in her hand. She turned it and studied it. With a sudden, sharp motion, she squeezed it along its resin seal, and the pod cracked.

Tiny, heavy, silvery seeds, almost as fine as dust, cascaded from the opening in the pod. A great beetle, its belly a sickly, luminous green, waved its clawed legs angrily as it struggled to right itself. It touched Ngina's hand with its sharp pincers. She did not feel the prick of its attack, for her hide protected her, but she dropped the beetle in revulsion. Ngina rubbed her head nodules against a root spike, trying vainly to erase the mingled scents of the seeds and the beetle. The odors made an unpleasant combination, hauntingly like that which had stained the bruised leaf tip of a Hodge hybrid rose.

The beetle regained its feet and crawled hastily across the fallen seeds. To Ngina's astonishment, the beetle stretched its black wings and lifted itself into the cave's low dome.

Ngina whispered with a chill, soft dread, "What have you done, Ngoi?"

CHAPTER 23

Dawn sky on Stromvi unfolded with unique softness. The rich, moist atmosphere, rarely disturbed by any consequential weather variations, coated the world evenly. Having long abandoned the hot furies of volcanic activity that had made it fertile in its infancy, Stromvi had achieved a stable uniformity of texture across its surface. Except for glacial remnants at its poles, Stromvi had no great concentrations of water or other liquid, no deserts, no outstanding features of deep canyons or towering mountains.

The Consortium categorized most Stromvi life forms as botanical. The thick, thriving vines, moss and lilies entwined to cover nearly the entire planetary surface, and the resin-rich root stalks permeated the planet's deep mantle. Perfectly balanced with each other and with their world, the Stromvi people needed only the products of the native plant life to survive in quiet contentment. If not for the persistent pleas of the Deetari on the neighboring planet, the Stromvi might never have recognized a desire to share the culture, protection, and economic advantages of the Consortium. The Stromvi valued self-sufficiency, even when it reached a flawed extreme.

When Tori awoke to her first Stromvi sunrise, she had struggled not to cry at the sadness that engulfed her. Neither adaptation trauma nor her determined commitment to the work of a man she barely knew caused her emotion. She had cried for the Stromvi sky.

Stromvi was an old world nearing its final era of life, but she did not share the sorrow that a Calongi might experience for a planet in its last few natural millennia. Tori did not know how to feel that strongly in a geological time-frame. The urge to weep came from her own alienism, suppressed only physically by the adaptation drugs of the Consortium. She had never seen the planet of her own species' origin. She had heard little good about it, except in the past tense. Stromvi made her feel very alone.

After the first few months, she had forgotten her initial reaction to Stromvi thanks to her work and her growing attachment to the people of Hodge Farm. She recalled that first feeling with painful clarity when she awoke on the upper surface of a battered tunneler, surrounded by a tangled disarray of Stromvi foliage. The rare intrusion of the tunneler above the surface broke the landscape's purity of line.

Tori was glad that she had not seen Hodge Farm at its inception, when the grounds had first been cleared. She felt certain that she could not have matched Birk's determination to proceed from the scouring of the land to the planting of Soli roses. The scarring of the Stromvi world would have tormented her memory.

"No shuttles rising or landing this morning," said Jase cheerfully, as he clambered onto the tunneler beside her. He blended well with the background. The mottling of resin made his dark skin almost as dusky as a Deetari's, and the golden Sesserda markings of his shirt had disappeared beneath blue and lilac resin. "The base soil seems sufficiently matted with root tendrils to support our weight, and the new growth appears marginally penetrable. There are some signs of osang passage. Old, I think."

"Old, I hope," muttered Tori. Sunlight had begun to dry the night's accumulation of resin from her skin, but her lungs still ached from the strain of forceful adaptation. "Have you ever seen an osang snake?"

"No," replied Jase. He was watching the dark, still Stromvi landscape. A lingering coat of damp resin gave his hair a violet sheen, and a series of even, blue resin lines across the high bridge of his nose resembled careful artistry. "Have you?"

"Only the skull, which sufficed to discourage further acquaintance." Tori shaded her eyes, still resin sore, to scan the horizon for signs of shuttle activity. "Nguri called it a small snake, too young to have developed true fangs, but even the immature mouth had teeth to make a Stromvi envious."

Jase pointed toward the rise that marked the edge of the shuttle port. His hands were battered from pounding the tunneler's stubborn controls, though the damage seemed less severe than Tori had expected from watching him during the night. "We may both enjoy an imminent broadening of experience. Can you see the undulation of the surface plants?"

"It could be a Stromvi burrowing."

"Without sending a click message to a fellow Stromvi? A tunneler's vibrations are distinctive, and Stromvi are sociable people."

"We may not be the only frightened creatures on Stromvi. The click-chorus has stopped altogether." Tori pulled a fragment of broken root spike from the tunneler's jaw seam. She stared at it resentfully, but she cracked it open and drank of the inner sap. She winced at the acrid flavor. "I like Stromvi food even less than I like inquisitors," she murmured with a sigh. She offered the root to Jase. "Here, you deserve each other."

Jase answered amiably, "We both serve the people of the Consortium." He accepted the root spike and drained it of its remaining sap. Tori enjoyed observing his pained expression.

Her smile faded, as she considered the path they were about to take. *No shuttles in the sky. The port is no haven. How far must we search to find safety from whatever has afflicted this world? Great-grandmama would deride that question. She would tell me that safety is always illusory.*

The port lay no farther from the tunnel's end than the length of the Hodge gardens. For a Soli, the journey would be at least as difficult as a walk through a solid hedge of old-style roses. The protection of the skin cream would thwart only the smaller thorns. *Why didn't I consider the travails of this Stromvi stroll last night? This Soli inquisitor flustered me, but he has no similar excuse for our lack of preparation.* Tori tried to forget her own adamant refusal to listen to Jase. "He could have been more insistent," she argued to herself.

"I'm still here," murmured Jase, "in case you were wondering."

"You were with me last night, but you let me run rashly into another ill-conceived plan, for which I am unfortunately famous. I thought no further than the spontaneous taking of a tunneler, and I didn't consider even that part very realistically."

"I seldom abet rashness," replied Jase, "unless I've calculated the alternatives for myself—and found them lacking. The only items of equipment I coveted last night were missing, inoperable, or otherwise unavailable due to the customary Hodge Farm reliance on Stromvi muscles and methods. Do you think I would have settled for an antique machete if I'd seen any tool of greater use during our search?"

"You could have advised me to wear something more practical for forging a passage across Stromvi wilderness." Tori lifted a clinging length of the resin-stained silk of her long-blouse.

"I do know the limits of my advisory capacity, Miss Darcy, and I try to avoid trespassing beyond their bounds."

"You make a very strange inquisitor," sighed Tori.

"So I've been told. Where would you like to enter the port?"

"If we veer slightly north," suggested Tori, "we should be able to enter from behind the control center."

"Avoiding the port radar." Jase nodded in approval of her plan. He chewed the bitter remnants of sap from the root stalk, before asking, "Did you hear Birk speak to anyone on Deetari?"

"No."

"Neither did I. The disquieting thought has occurred to me that Birk may never have contacted Deetari about Ngoi's death."

"He told me an inquisitor would arrive today," countered Tori, but she presented her argument with feeble conviction.

"Did he? His information progressed very rapidly during the brief moments between your conversation and mine. When I talked to him, he was still waiting for an appropriate official to be summoned to the transceiver, or so he claimed. I wish I'd been in better condition to read him for truth yesterday." Jase slid to the ground, gathered several of the root spikes disinterred by the tunneler, and returned to sit beside Tori. He laid the haphazard meal in the space between them. "Did anything about Birk's behavior seem odd to you in that last meeting?"

"You have the Sesserda training in observation, not I," said Tori. She selected one of the smaller root stalks and tried to brush the bits of clinging leaves and soil from its length. Sticky, half-dry resin made the cleaning task nearly impossible. "Did he seem different to you, or are you simply testing my reactions in good inquisitorial fashion?"

"Birk made several uncharacteristic remarks to me," answered Jase quietly. He gnawed at a root spike, absorbed in his own thoughts.

"What sort of remarks?" asked Tori curiously, when Jase showed no inclination to continue.

"Birk enjoyed control: people, objects, his environment." Jase glanced obliquely at Tori. "I'm a little surprised that he waited so long to solidify his claim on you. He would dearly have loved to possess the legatee of a woman who ruled kings."

"I had no intention of becoming a possession," said Tori tightly. "As for the rest, you're saying nothing new. Calem bemoans his father's domination endlessly, and Sylvie has been sinking farther into self-pity ever since Birk terminated her one 'sincere' relationship a few spans ago."

The flash of a rueful smile yielded quickly to an inquisitor's unrevealing blandness. "Birk succeeded early with Calem, producing that stultifying blend of resentment and dependency. Birk actually respected Sylvie at one time, but she committed the unpardonable sin of disobeying him."

"It's hard for me to imagine Sylvie defying her father for anyone," said Tori, trying to determine how much Jase Sleide knew about the Hodges, "but I only met her after her Squire disappeared. You must have known her earlier."

"Yes," he answered. "Her emotional calluses were less obvious then, at least to me." Jase shrugged and returned to his original topic, "Much as Birk enjoyed control, he acknowledged some limits. I never knew him to offend a Consortium official deliberately until our last conversation. He pretended to dispute my status as an inquisitor, but I don't think he actually doubted me on that score."

"I can't imagine anyone pretending to be an inquisitor. The privilege of being loathed hardly seems worth the effort of deception."

"Most Consortium members respect inquisitors highly," said Jase, pausing just long enough to make his rebuke clear, "but you're right about the unlikelihood of pretense. Birk taunted me, risking an inquisitor's condemnation, simply to drive me from his office before I could hear him contact Deetari. He didn't hesitate to tell me that I was unwelcome at Hodge Farm or that he intended to verify my status. What else would he try to conceal from me in a simple request for support?"

"If Birk had wanted privacy for his communication, he would have told you that fact very directly and waited for you to leave."

"Unless he thought that approach might take too long." Jase threw the emptied root shell to the ground. "If Birk knew more about Ngoi's death than he pretended, if he anticipated something of what was about to occur on this planet, if someone had a very real, very strong motive for killing him—we cannot be sure that he told either of us the truth about anything yesterday. My senses were behaving rather badly at the time, and I'm not sure I would have recognized an outright lie."

"Then the Calongi inquisitor, like the Jiucetsi, will not come," replied Tori with a shrug. She had abandoned hope of outside rescue somewhere during the frantic night, and she did not want to dwell on those final moments with Birk until she could feel herself safe from yesterday's fear. She had not even considered reaching a future with time enough for actual grief.

"Do you know where Ngahi stores the personal shuttles these days?" asked Jase.

"Hangar four, unless the shuttles have joined the popular disappearance." She assessed him dubiously. "Are you a qualified space pilot?"

"I can manage the smaller ships. Didn't your education include basic pilot's training?"

"Uncle Per didn't consider pilot's training necessary for me," replied Tori crisply, but her bitter thoughts added, *A concubine should not be too independent.*

"He had a rather shortsighted perspective," observed Jase. Tori sensed that Jase had somehow heard her unspoken remark. "Personal shuttles are, at least, easier to handle than that wretched tunneler." Jase shook his bruised hands. "If I ever see Calem again, I think I'll tell him to ask future favors of another inquisitor." Jase added softly, "If he requested this favor at all."

Unwilling to resume discussion of the inquisitor's status, Tori jumped from the tunneler to the ground and began to head toward the port without pausing to see if Jase followed. The terrain seemed more amenable to careful Soli progress than Tori had expected, until she raised her eyes and realized that she had traveled less than five meters. "This is hopeless," she announced, glaring at a tall thorn shrub that seemed to rise spontaneously in front of her, as the soft ground sagged beneath her weight.

Jase stepped around her to apply the machete to the twisted thorn vines. "We can't take the tunneler any farther, unless you dispute the accuracy of Stromvi maps."

"The port designers insisted on a particularly solid foundation for the landing field," grumbled Tori, "and this distance would be no more than an idle stroll for a Stromvi." She waved toward the port, now hidden by the vines surrounding her.

"You can't be discouraged yet. That wouldn't be in keeping with your profile."

"Stop reminding me of why I hate inquisitors."

"Sorry."

"You said there were signs of osang passage. Did you see a usable osang trail leading toward the port?"

"Yes. We're proceeding parallel to it." Jase stopped his assault on the thick vines, and he remained silent for a long moment. He ran his hand through his hair, pushing the straight strands from his face. "It's a risky course," he said thoughtfully.

"Not if the trail is old, as you indicated."

"I could easily be wrong. Stromvi foliage re-covers cleared ground with exceptional efficiency, and my prior experience with Stromvi has been limited to the relatively docile Ngenga Valley. I've also heard of young snakes adopting old trails. If that trail *is* active, we're virtually guaranteed to encounter its owner. Osangs respond to vibrations, such as a tunneler's movement, and they hunt accordingly. That distant undulation of the surface plants could well represent a hunt for us."

"Then we lose more by our delays than by using the snake's home trail. Anyway, Stromvi have been known to kill osang snakes without special tools or training. Surely a third-level Sesserda practitioner can achieve as much." She began the statement as a gibe, but the possibilities prompted her to continue thoughtfully, "Isn't a process of physical optimization a prerequisite to fourth-level status?"

Jase frowned at her, and his brilliant, unnatural eyes narrowed. "You said that you knew essentially nothing about Sesserda."

"I learn quickly," replied Tori, briefly regretting her implicit confession of having lied to an official inquisitor. His current reaction, confirming that he had not perceived her first deception, gave her a rather smug feeling.

"You also know—too well—how to confound Sesserda senses," answered Jase, his frown deepening into a scowl. He slashed a thorn vine. "I'm beginning to understand why Omi-lai returned to Calong-4 for renewal training after questioning you. You and your 'Tiva disorder' must have devastated his concepts of Level VI predictability." Jase stepped back to the higher ground in order to study the snake path he had spotted earlier. "This spontaneous suggestion of yours is much more rash than borrowing a tunneler."

"Tell me your alternatives, Inquisitor."

Jase raised one slender finger. "Return to Hodge Farm: That smacks of defeatism." He raised a second finger, tallying the prospects. "Continue as we've begun: As you said, we still risk encountering an osang snake, assuming that we survive the thorn poisons." He raised a third finger. "Take the tunneler somewhere else: I might consider that alternative, if I knew another destination of any possible use, but I doubt that my hands would appreciate a repeat bout of driving that beast—not at the moment anyway."

"Your options aren't very promising."

"No. Not promising at all." He folded his hand. "So, weigh the final option: If we use the snake's trail, we'll have little warning of its approach, assuming we don't walk into the beast's jaws immediately on entering its domain. After your encouraging description of the osang dental structure, are you willing to entrust your life to my Sesserda training? I'm still a mere Soli, after all, and I haven't noticed that you were particularly willing to trust me in more orthodox endeavors."

Tori shrugged, though his quiet recital of the risks had disconcerted her. She was not accustomed to hearing her impulsive ideas analyzed. "All the osang snakes on this planet may have disappeared with everyone else."

"Do you find that a particularly comforting possibility?" asked Jase wryly, but he veered toward his right in his attack on the vines.

Tori did not answer. She clutched the awl in her hand, and she stared at Jase's back, trying to measure the strength of the Soli inquisitor by his motions. Even across the treacherous vine-mass, he maintained the easy gait of centered, Sesserda control, but his build was more slight and wiry than obviously powerful. She did not like to rely on anyone, least of all an inquisitor, but she would have felt happier if he had looked less scholarly and more substantial.

Crossing the brief space of vine-mass to reach the osang's trail seemed much less difficult than their first, abortive effort at surface travel. An uncomfortable sense of being lured into a trap nearly made Tori call to Jase and suggest reconsidering her idea. Pride kept her silent. If her inquisitor was willing to accept her challenge and face an osang snake, she could at least show the courage of following him.

He slashed an opening in a sticky mass of cling vines, and the pale channel of the snake's trail took away her chance to change plans. Jase moved forward without a pause into a misty shroud. Tori stepped gingerly into the silk after him, slightly surprised by the firmness of footing that the trail provided.

The relatively smooth corridor of the osang trail did not relieve Tori's doubts. The lacy gray veils of hardened silk, which the osang exuded, kept the trail clear of thorn vines but also obscured the view beyond a few paces and deadened sounds. If an osang lay in wait, she would never be able to detect it until it attacked.

As they entered a solid tunnel of silk that pierced through the Stromvi growth, the muffling effect of the snake's pathway became even more acute. The Stromvi

valued osang silk for its insulating properties, but Tori
found the whispering resonance of the silk strands too
eerie to allow such practical considerations. She wondered how the Stromvi managed to gather the silk without developing chronic nightmares.

Slightly ahead of Tori, Jase negotiated the treacherous
footing of a series of silk hollows, fashioned around foliage that had long ago shriveled. Even as Tori watched, the
indigo fan of an osang's hood unfurled above his head. She
cried a warning, but the silk absorbed the sound.

A spray of immobilizing venom burst from bloated sacs
along the snake's wide hood. In a silvery rain, the venom
touched the hardened silk and sizzled. The snake snapped
its enormous jaws around a bubble of its own silk, and
it shook its head in a frustrated attempt to dislodge the
clinging strands from its fangs.

Tori blinked, as bewildered as the snake by the disappearance of its chosen victim. But there was Jase, crouching among the broken bubbles of silk. With the machete
held loosely in one hand and his other hand cupping his
chin, he watched the snake as if it were an oddity of only
slight interest.

Tori ran back along the trail far enough to escape the
snake's immediate range. She turned to see if she were
pursued, and she stopped. The osang's hooded head wavered, as its twin tendrils lifted and tasted the air for the
direction of its prey.

Jase stood immobile beside the snake. He seemed to
hold the machete more firmly, but he did not try to use
the blade against the snake's thick, pallid hide. The tendrils shifted toward him, and the snake's hood sacs expanded with a new rush of venom. The osang darted its
strong, pale, and sinuous neck toward Jase, but the great
jaws closed again on empty air. The snapping of the
osang's teeth sent a shudder through the osang's silk-
shrouded length.

Tori knew too many stories of the osang's deadly techniques. She expected Jase to fail. She expected to become
the osang's prey as well, but she did not intend to concede
easily. Wielding the awl, Tori tried to hack an opening in
the silken tunnel. If she could crawl outside the tunnel
through a hole too small for the snake, she might be able
to elude it. She certainly could not hope to outrun the

osang in its own entrapping trail. Jase might even manage to join her, though his chances seemed slim.

The awl drove easily through the first, soft layers, but it scraped uselessly against the buried, crystallized shell. Frustrated, Tori tried to achieve some leverage by which to pry the opening wider, but she could not find any solid fulcrum. She dared a look toward Jase, fearing what she might see.

To Tori's relief, Jase still eluded the venomous assault. The osang had acquired a frantic, jerky rhythm that had ripped most of the sheltering silk from its serpentine body. A strange, erratic vibration along the older, harder silk sharpened and diminished with the snake's agitated twists and turns. Scattered venom steamed against the silk along the trail, dissolving and reforming patches of the tunnel into sickly, malleable globs or hard, glittering crystals.

He said it was a risky course. But all courses have risks. We might have succeeded. We might not have encountered the snake.

She was nearly ready to attempt a return to the tunneler via the osang's trail, but she hesitated, disgusted with herself for feeling concerned about her inquisitor. She watched the duel, trying to imagine how she could affect its outcome. She could not even follow Jase's movements.

With a frustrated lunge, the snake seemed to lose its furious energy. Its attack, so strongly begun, dwindled and became almost lethargic. The osang's deadly hood hovered above the Soli inquisitor. Tori rose to her feet, watching with fascinated disbelief, for Jase made no effort to escape. The venom sacs expanded, but they ejected only a weak, ineffective trickle that dripped into the snake's gullet. The jaws closed slowly and weakly, and the head drooped.

Jase drove the machete against the gleaming inner surface of the hood. He barely scored the leathery surface, but the hood folded like a dark cap against the osang's head. The snake, its length three times the height of the Soli man, sank in defeat, and it lay flat and still against the ground of its eerie tunnel, its body abject and weary in surrender.

Jase poised one booted foot lightly on the snake's back, and he raised the machete above him as if declaring a military triumph. He grinned at Tori and waved her forward. Tori joined him cautiously.

"I didn't think I could dominate an osang so easily,"
he announced with perfect equanimity. "I should learn
to distinguish new snake trails from old."

"Stop posing. You look ridiculous," whispered Tori,
afraid to rouse the snake. She jumped, as the snake
hissed softly.

"Try to think kind thoughts about me. My friend here
may have protective instincts regarding his conqueror."

Leery of disturbing the snake more dramatically, Tori
waited for Jase to nod before she continued walking. She
watched the snake closely as she passed it, but it did not
move. The silver and violet streaks along its pale green
hide made it blend well with its silk-strewn domain. A
twitch of the forked tail startled her, and she hurried to
increase the distance between herself and the osang, hoping that the snake's mate had already burrowed for the
summer hatching.

"Watch for sensor posts," suggested Jase mildly. He
showed no signs that the combat with the snake had troubled him in any fashion. "The port may monitor osang
movement in the immediate neighborhood, and I'm not
sure I want to announce our arrival yet."

Tori nodded briefly. Through the webs of snake-silk,
thinning toward the tunnel's end, she could see the
murky yellow of the port wall. The wall's warm color
tended to look sickly in Stromvi light, but it provided a
necessary contrast to eyes less sensitive than a Stromvi's
at distinguishing shades in the higher end of the spectrum.

Unable to deny her curiosity, Tori asked, "Did you
defeat the osang by tiring it—or by talking it into submission? I thought I heard something unusual vibrating the
silk, and osang snakes only vocalize the hiss of warning."

"You have sharp hearing. I used both techniques actually. I was concerned that the osang snake might be too
highly evolved to respond to a Niorni command language, but the seventh variant seemed effective. I must
remember to notify the life data base."

"You're rather useful as a partner in crisis."

"Thank you," answered Jase with his crooked smile.
"If the snake was listening, I'm sure he was pleased."

Tori leaned toward Jase and whispered, "I don't believe for a moment that an osang snake feels protective
of a 'conqueror.' "

"You believed me when you thought the snake was close enough to attack."

"I was humoring you, Mister Sleide."

Jase's smile broadened very briefly and faded. "You're very gracious for a murder suspect," he responded with exquisite care.

"Such extravagant praise might turn my head."

"It's a pity that your determination and resourcefulness support the case against you. I find the traits admirable in themselves, but they confirm that you have the mental armament to have effected the execution of that unsavory man you married. Why did you ever marry a man with such obviously sociopathic tendencies?" Tori glared at Jase without replying. Jase sighed, "I just wanted to remind you, Miss Darcy—for honor's sake— that I'm still an inquisitor, and I'm still under oath to observe you accordingly."

"I never doubted that your zeal for justice would rule your every action," replied Tori crisply. "Did you?"

"Shared obstacles can inspire shared confidence. I wouldn't want you to jeopardize your legal records by trusting me too much. I have a very bad habit of remembering nearly everything I see or hear—belatedly, as a rule, but thoroughly. I'm truly sorry that I was so slow in telling you my status."

Refusing to answer him, Tori nodded toward the opening of the snake's trail into the wide access swath that encircled the port. "If we follow the port wall toward the north, we should find an opening. The Stromvi have several entrances that lead beneath the wall."

"Suitable for Soli?"

"Usually."

He thrust the machete toward the wall. "Onward!"

"Please," muttered Tori. "Don't let one victory go to your head."

"It's my victory, and I intend to enjoy it."

"You could enjoy it with a little more subtlety."

"I may compose an epic poem on the subject tomorrow."

"Immediately after my inquisition?"

Jase let his smile disappear. He resumed walking toward the port without a backward glance. He did not reply to Tori's question.

CHAPTER 24

The control center lay nearer than Tori had expected. Its open gate provided a more comfortable entrance than Stromvi routes, but the very ease of access worried Tori. No port workers were in sight. No Stromvi greeter appeared with welcome or questions. Tori stayed close to Jase, for the deserted port felt as threatening as the osang snake.

Constructed at ground level, the control center's careful design made it low enough to satisfy Stromvi tastes but high enough to support inexpensive tracking antennas on its roof. The walls of the building wore Stromvi tapestries, but the wide, white rectangles of standard Consortium factory doors constituted the entries. All of the doors of the control center were open, contrary to both local and general Consortium custom. Jase peered inside a back room, but he shook his head and did not enter. "It has a hollow feel to it," he whispered. "Where is hangar four?"

Tori led him around the control center. Two moderately large cruisers occupied the center of the port. "Other than the Deetari ferry, large ships rarely come to Stromvi," remarked Tori quietly. "Do you suppose our rescue has arrived?" She wanted to hope, but she did not quite dare to face another disappointment.

"Xiani markings," observed Jase, shading his eyes from the glare of light reflected from the mirrored backs of shielded windows.

"Which tells us nothing, since the Xiani engineer most Consortium ships."

"Most owners add personal markings for easy identification, as well as for amusement. These two cruisers are factory-bland but well used. They're also disk models: an unpopular design except for unusual applications requiring omnidirectional maneuverability."

"They wouldn't suit an inquisitor?"

"Inquisitors rarely travel officially without Sesserda markings. And the Jiucetsi have very flamboyant tastes in decoration. Unmarked ships aren't generally used by legitimate owners."

"You think those ships were stolen?"

Jase shrugged. "Stealing a sophisticated Consortium ship is difficult, but it's much easier than stealing the technology to build a duplicate."

"How many crew members does such a ship require?"

"At least three. Eight is the recommended number for extended trips. They can hold over a hundred Soli-sized passengers on a protracted basis."

"Could we be watched from those ships?"

"Possibly, although the viewing screens are probably optimized for longer range and larger objects than two tiny Soli. Of course, this landing field is designed to maximize the visibility of persons or objects moving across it. The ships could also have other sensors, acoustical, for example."

Tori bit back a comment. Jase left the possibility of surveillance dangling. They continued toward hangar four in a silence broken only by the soft tread of their shoes on the resilient surface of the landing field.

The sun burned against Tori's face. She pulled at the scarf that formed the collar of her long-blouse, and she brought it over her head as a hood. The scarf was less effective than her Stromvi work hat, but it gave more protection than her hair.

She could see the forms of a dozen shuttles lined inside the open hangar as they reached the wide entry. Jase bypassed the bulky Stromvi and Deetari vessels and headed determinedly for a small, two-person shuttle designed for Soli use. He touched the door release, but the ship remained closed. Carefully, he pried loose the cover panel from the ship's external hold. "There should be some bypass circuits in here," he remarked, as he crawled inside the tight compartment.

Tori leaned against the ship and watched the hangar entrance and the empty field beyond it. She muttered to herself, "I never heard that Sesserda included technician training," but she did not intend to dissuade Jase from any attempt that might secure an escape from Stromvi.

The heat was becoming oppressive, and its currents writhed in the heavy air above the landing field. The field's lifelessness seemed less tragic than the abandoned Stromvi caverns, but the port's barren expanse threatened implicitly. It left no place to hide.

Tori circled the ship in order to see the stretch of untrammeled Stromvi land that extended behind the hangar. The far port wall drew a thin, yellow line across the view. Tori tried to excise the incongruity of the wall from her gaze.

The slightest patch of crimson, a slender stripe between the hangar and the wall, aggravated the sense of imperfection. The blues, greens, and violets of Stromvi did not go well with such harsh, hot colors. Tori could sympathize with those Stromvi who had objected to Birk's original horticultural proposal because of the prevalence of jarring shades of red, orange, and yellow among Soli roses.

As Tori watched the crimson flaw, trying to discern its nature and purpose, the crimson disappeared. She blinked twice, assuring herself that she had not imagined it. Hurriedly, she returned to Jase, dropped to her knees, and whispered urgently, "Someone else is here."

Jase pulled himself from the crawl space. "Where?"

"Behind the hangar. It moved too quickly to be a Stromvi."

"Shall we search for it or hide from it?" asked Jase softly, but the drumming roar of shuddering sound, raw and formless, stopped him.

Tori clapped her hands to her ears, but the thunder beat inside of her. She saw Jase rise and hurl himself toward something that she could only recognize as a blur. The sole definitive line in its dark shape comprised a streak of crimson, but it passed in front of Jase and hid him from Tori's sight.

The sound grated, stretching and slowing, and then racing to a whine, almost painful in its failure to achieve any consistent tone. Tori started to move toward the blur that had engulfed Jase, but she could not find a clear direction. She turned, as the thunder stopped, and three loud, clear chimes rang above her.

"Jase," she whispered tentatively, though she wanted to shout for him. She wanted to hear him or see him walking toward her, but she saw and heard nothing. With quick, frightened movements, she stepped back to the shuttle that Jase had chosen. She crawled into the cramped hold where Jase had been working, and she propped the cover panel into place for concealment from any careless glance.

She sat very still, trying to slow her breathing and conserve the air that seeped into the hold from the imperfectly closed cover panel. She stopped an image of herself melting in the Stromvi heat and forced herself to visualize the uniformly comfortable lake on Uncle Per's estate. Resolutely, she tried to recall the soothing embrace of the water closing over her as she dove into the clear depths among the water-butterflies.

Think carefully, she told herself sternly. *Where do you stand, Victoria? Alone. Entirely alone.*

You have been alone since Arnod died. Longer. You have been alone since your self-imposed exile from Uncle Per's estate with a generous dispensation to settle you anew and buy your silence—the dispensation that Arnod squandered along with your love and trust. You picked up the pieces of your life and continued.

You know this planet almost as well as a native. You have spent five years working to understand it and its people. Where are they? Someone or something might have removed all of the Stromvi from the planet in an instant, but it seems more likely that the Stromvi are hiding voluntarily. They could easily have undocumented caverns and tunnels detached from the acknowledged routes. Death-watch, *they chanted. Was that their signal of danger?*

Tori maintained her position for as long as she could bear the stifling heat. When at last she emerged, she moved slowly. She still wished that she might see Jase returning, but she did not want to find him on her own power. She did not really believe that she would see him alive again.

The possiblity of discovering Jase rent or broken scared her more than the murders of Birk or Ngoi or even Arnod. Though every death seemed to tear a raw, unhealing wound in the vicinity of her heart, the certain deaths had seemed isolated from reality. The loss of Jase carried a more personal threat.

I suppose his Sesserda methods kept me feeling relatively stable, despite the collapse of my personal universe. He did exude something akin to the famous Calongi serenity. I don't think I could bear to find him. . . . She stopped herself from pursuing such thoughts. She certainly did not want to miss him.

She nearly stepped on the machete, its blade stained with a thick, brown paste that she did not want to identify. The knife lay near the edge of the landing field in front of hangar four. Gingerly, she collected the machete, holding it away from her body so as to avoid contact with the soiled blade. She ran toward the control center, accepting haste as a necessary alternative to concealment in crossing the open landing field.

She hesitated in the shadow of the control center, but she entered the building. None of the light panels operated, but she knew the floor plan fairly well, and the Stromvi wall weavings glowed faintly with old resin. Tori groped along the main corridor toward the office used by Jeffer, the port's lone Soli employee.

Jeffer had come to Stromvi as Birk's pilot and handyman, but Jeffer's careless personal habits had caused the termination of the arrangement shortly before Tori arrived on the planet. The office reflected Jeffer's slovenly habits, and Tori searched through the chaotic jumble with distaste. She found the log of ship arrivals and departures beside a six-span-old Cuui trade circular. She uncovered Jeffer's toolkit beneath an assortment of ration wrappers and manna crumbs.

She strapped the toolkit around her waist, after reluctantly discarding the heavy multiscope that made the kit unwieldy. The kit drooped to her hips, for the thongs had been set to encircle a much larger waist than her own. She readjusted the range of the length control and settled the toolkit more comfortably. She added the awl to the kit, and she cleaned the machete on a rag of indeterminate origin.

Leaving Jeffer's office, Tori headed toward the main control room. She listened carefully for any betraying sound of movement before she entered. Without the usual panoply of three-dimensional displays, the room looked incomplete. She tried to activate each of the transceivers, but none of the equipment in the room would function.

Absently, she brushed at her forehead to ease a slight tingling. Her fingers touched an oily softness, and she jerked her hand from her face quickly. Broken bits of a bloated, stinging insect clung to her finger, and she dislodged the unpleasant residue against a desk edge. She rubbed lightly at her face to ensure that nothing more clung there, and the translucent oval of a severed wing drifted to the floor.

Stromvi has no native winged species, she thought numbly, *and Consortium controls of life transport are strict and effective.* The implications of that fragile, broken wing appalled her.

Tori had planned to search more thoroughly for useful, portable equipment or any indication of the fate of Jase or the port workers. She stared at the oily green traces of the insect staining her fingertips. She could not identify the insect from its remains.

As idly as she had killed an unidentifiable insect, something had apparently swatted the life from Stromvi. The insect's presence in the control center accelerated her desperation to escape. She could not linger in the empty port.

She retraced the route out the gate and along the wall, making the osang trail her goal. She hoped that the snake would be too aware of its recent defeat to attack her, but she did not pause to weigh the odds against her. The prospect of facing an osang snake frightened her far less than an unknown enemy marked with a crimson streak.

CHAPTER 25

Nguri stirred reluctantly, aching in his soul as much as in his body. Destruction: He had seen its threat in the gnawed petal of a blue-and-white rose. He sensed the threat's fulfillment now, and he did not want to move ever again, but he filled his body with a deep inhalation of the resinous evening air, and he pulled himself from his sheltering, healing urge to hibernate.

His body had fared well enough, he decided, for such an aged and battered model. The enemies' rain of fire had scored him painfully, but the healing fluids of his planet's atmosphere had mingled with his blood and old resin, flowing into the hide-gaps and sealing them. Nguri lifted his upper torso carefully.

*   *   *

Rillessa shifted beneath the limp weight of *It*. She shuddered, realizing that the stench of death had begun to issue from the heavy cloak of graying animal. The Bori chameleon, light-shifting skin hopelessly impaired by needler damage, had managed to adopt a muddied image of Rillessa's features in its dying desperation to conceal itself. Rillessa recoiled in revulsion from her own distorted likeness, imprinted in the Bori's dead flesh.

She pushed at the bulky mass, trying to extricate herself from the clinging skin. She shifted her own weight. Her hands plunged blindly into the gash of *Its* scarlet mouth, and *Its* brown, acidic blood spattered her. With a brief cry of pain, Rillessa pulled back her burning hands. She struggled to crawl away from *It*.

Rillessa sat on mossy Stromvi soil and stared at the carcass of *It*. Her body heaved with fright and exertion, and blisters had risen in patches across her bloody palms.

"Bori," she muttered repeatedly, and sometimes she made the word an accusation, and sometimes she whispered it like a question.

She saw nothing around her except the dead beast that had covered her. She did not notice Nguri, until he spoke. "What is Bori?" asked the Stromvi softly. He rubbed at the marks of fire that had scored his hide. The resinous air had sealed the wounds, but such haphazard healings itched.

"Bori," repeated Rillessa with vague determination, and she continued to stare fixedly.

Nguri tested the scents of the air carefully before crossing the open patch of moss to reach the gray alien. The body had begun to spread and flatten, and its ebbing lifefluid had begun to leech into the ground. A great patch of moss had withered and turned as gray as its ashen burden. "Was this creature Bori?" asked Nguri, inspecting the carcass and its travesty-likeness of Rillessa with a grunt of distaste.

Rillessa continued her mumbling without apparent comprehension. Nguri clicked disgust. He laid his torso nearly flat against the ground to inspect the alien from all sides, but he did not touch the beast or try to turn it. With a shake of his wide head, he returned to Rillessa.

She did not react, even when he reached toward her with an open hand. Nguri touched her gently, and she continued her vacuous repetition of a single word. Nguri said soothingly, "You need to come with me, Rillessa. You are injured, and enemies may return here. Do you remember seeing the enemies?"

Rillessa's impervious stare did not waver. Nguri repeated his expressions of disgust very quietly. With a strong, determined move, Nguri collected Rillessa beneath his arms, as he might have carried one of the smallest Stromvi children. Rillessa became completely limp.

Nguri clicked a monologue of irritation as he shuffled toward the southern fields, but he did not let his senses rest from searching. The enemies had missed him, hidden by his hide's natural camouflage. They had also escaped him, but they had not left the planet. Their tainted scents still disturbed Stromvi air. Death-watch proceeded.

*   *   *

Omi, honored Calongi inquisitor and full Sesserda
master, correlated sensory information from ninety-six
independent sources and determined that his uneasiness
was indeed his own. The cilia-fine tendrils that maintained the integrity of his external nervous system relaxed
into velvety softness, but Omi did not take pleasure from
the gentle sensation of peace. Having eliminated the possibility that some careless, restless soul in the sprawling
complex beyond the meditation chamber had disturbed
him, Omi accepted that the daily meditation had fulfilled
its function well. A problem existed and must be raised
into conscious light to be eradicated.

Omi assigned each memory fragment of the previous
day to a distinct region of his multisegmented cerebrum.
While he performed the parallel tasks of sorting and
assessing the detailed events, his controlling brain region gathered the most promising items for cross-corre-
lation. He collected, discarded, and reevaluated, until
he achieved a mixture that prodded his uneasiness into
clarity.

"Your Soli student requested a case report," remarked
Omi to Ukitan, honored Calongi inquisitor and exalted
Sesserda master, who shared the meditation chamber at
this hour of the morning.

Ukitan continued his meditation with the majority of
his attention, but he replied quietly, "The Soli female
with the Tiva disorder."

Omi nodded, his outer limbs flexing and rippling like
a cape of flowing water. "An unsatisfactory case made
interesting by the female's heritage."

"The infamous Mirelle of Attia."

"Very likely another victim of the Tiva disorder."

"A probable contributor to Mirelle's singular pattern
of success in a barbaric profession."

"Why did your Soli student wish to review the case?"

"A friendship-debt."

"He did not elaborate?"

"His attention as inquisitor was requested. I perceived
the need in him to comply. Why are you troubled by
this, Omi-lai?" Both Calongi knew that the Mirelle case
had troubled Omi enough to return him to Calong-4 for

Sesserda renewal training from Ukitan and other masters. Both Calongi knew that such a personal reaction did not suffice to cause Omi's questions about the case's current status.

"A contact failure report was filed yesterday regarding the Deetari/Stromvi system," answered Omi.

"The Deetari/Stromvi system has a sporadically isolationist history."

"The Soli female, Victoria Mirelle of Arcy, resides currently on the planet Stromvi."

"I shall send a message to Jase-lai and inquire as to his progress."

"Thank you, Ukitan-lai. You restore my tranquillity."

* * *

Ngina joined her people silently. No one noticed that she arrived from the direction of a deep, long-abandoned tunnel, which she had followed from Ngoi's cave. Amid the confusion of resettling the southern caverns, most attention was focused on gathering and calming the children. Since earliest Stromvi history, every enclave had maintained a hidden, secondary cavern network, and all Stromvi had learned the procedure for death-watch. That was tradition. Few Stromvi had ever considered the prospect of death-watch as reality. Many Stromvi elders feared more deeply than their children.

Ngina felt awkward, moving among her people, all of whom seemed to have some immediate purpose. Each Stromvi's duties had been assigned at the first death-watch gathering, which Ngina had missed. She had been trying to exterminate those awful winged beetles from the parcels in Ngoi's cave. Almost a fifth of the parcels had been infested. The work had left her feeling nauseous, whether from general fear, disgust at the repeated smashing of those horrid insects, or the handling of the seed parcels. The dry seeds had not bothered her, but a very few had begun to split, and their oil had burned her fingers, more sensitive than the rest of her resin-thick hide.

She saw Ngev, but he was busy helping Ngela check the support braces. The southern caverns had been rele-

gated to secondary status for good reason. Many of them
had become unstable after long spans of overuse.

When she saw her mother sorting supplies, Ngina
nearly cried for attention like an unresined infant. Ngeta
recognized her daughter's scent even in the large, crowded
cavern. Ngeta clicked an outpouring of relief, followed
by a diatribe about the anxiety that Ngina's absence had
caused.

"I am sorry," answered Ngina faintly.

Ngeta stopped her lecture abruptly. She came and put
her strong, brightly patterned arms around her daughter.
She clicked the wordless sounds of comfort.

There was so much that Ngina had meant to say, but
all of the last two days seemed to retreat beneath her
mother's soothing care. Forgetting felt so much better.
There no longer seemed to be any urgent reason to confess, now that Ngoi was dead, and the flying beetles were
dead, and the parcels were hidden safely. Her mother
would protect her from her honored father's questioning,
at least for a little while.

*   *   *

A true Essenji warrior laughed, and the five Rea who
heard him approved with varying levels of emotion. The
prisoner's obvious injuries and the cruel thongs that
bound him did not impede the crisp melody of his mirth.
Tagran gestured sharply to recall the three younger warriors to their duties of preparing Roake for transfer, by
the war leader's command. None of the four knew
Roake's destination, but Tagran had strong, private
suspicions.

The fifth Rea, who seemed more a shifting blur of
darkness than a solid being, stood apart from the others.
His arrival, betrayed by a slight streak of crimson, had
inspired Roake's amusement. He spoke softly to the
nearest of the warriors, a broadly muscled youth. "Tiber,
go and guard the captive I left below. He is a Soli, presumably a port worker whom our first sweep missed."
Tiber saluted and obeyed. The shadowy Rea approached
the prisoner. A pale, five-fingered hand emerged from
the shadow and snatched the ruby starburst from the prisoner's shoulder.

"The badge does not contain the authority it represents," remarked Roake with contempt. "You cannot control the Rea without me, Ares. You may steal the war-star, but you will not become the war leader by that token. You will fail, as you have always failed. You are nothing without me."

Ares hissed, "You live in the past. I lead now."

"The clan leader will not tolerate your treachery."

"You are the traitor. The clan leader will honor me for the swiftness of my retaliation."

Ares does not believe his own words, observed Tagran, verifying that Roake's bonds remained secure.

Roake sensed his brother's doubt but attributed it to general insecurity. Roake attacked accordingly: "How long will the Rea respect your command when they realize that you have cost them their hope of restoration?"

"You cost us the relaweed. You enabled the Rea-traitor to escape our first attack."

"Don't waste your ambition's lies on me, Ares."

"You used the daar'va to give him warning."

"I would have used it successfully to recover the kree'va by now, if you hadn't interfered. Did you think the Rea-traitor burned a span's profits in relaweed for the sake of this miserable planet? He had begun to panic, but you chose to concentrate your attack against me instead of against him."

"Only one ship left the planet, and he was not on it. He has not escaped the Rea. He will not escape me. You chose the wrong ally, my brother."

They squabble with each other, thought Tagran, *as if they were still boys contending for a prize of sport. But they wield their clan leader's deadly schemes.*

"You let a ship escape to notify the Consortium?" mocked Roake. "You're less competent than I believed."

"The ship was too small to travel farther than Deetari, which *you* promised would not threaten us," retorted Ares. "You have fed the Deetari prophets enough omens to discourage them from meddling with any reported trouble on Stromvi—or so you claimed."

Roake grunted, for he could not admit to a weakness in his own designs. "You still don't know how to begin to search for the Rea-traitor, Ares. You only captured his wretched offspring by chance and their own ineptitude as pilots, and possession of them will do you little good."

Ares' Bori-shadowed figure laughed scornfully. "So, you witnessed their capture? It was an easy pursuit, I admit. The pitiful Calem believes I have saved him from *you*, the great, unforgiving customer whose cruelty was so extolled by Mister Febro. Miss Sylvie will be grateful to me for saving her from the wreckage of her ship, when she regains her limited senses. They will both be very cooperative bait."

"If you plan to entice the Rea-traitor into view, you would have done better to capture the Mirelle woman, but she didn't happen to throw herself in your path, did she, Ares? You are hasty and careless, and your temper robs you of competence. I know also that you will never locate the kree'va without me because you never took the time to understand the daar'va fully. You can't even find the first harvest of relaweed."

"I shall find the seeds. And there will be more—far more than you ever provided for us with your schemes that never reach fulfillment."

"There will be no more harvests on Stromvi. This planet is dying even now, though its people have not yet recognized the lethal infection. This is the clan leader's gift to the Rea-traitor."

Ares grunted, "The Rea-traitor's possessions must not survive," but Roake's retort had appalled every hearer. Destruction of a worthy foe increased Rea pride; destruction of a world honored no one, for it stole a little freedom from every being. Tagran wondered if Roake's claim were true.

Ares refused to give Roake's words further attention. Waving the bright war-star, Ares taunted, "Did I thank you for bringing the home vessel back within our grasp? The Bercali entered the planetary system this morning. No one but you, dear brother, could have negotiated with them so persuasively on their own treacherous level of comprehension. In light of recent revelations, I must assume that you intended to use their help against your own people . . ."

"You are mad."

". . . so as to reap whatever reward the Rea-traitor promised you, but the clan leader will enact the plan you presented to her. I shall give the Bercali their promised prize today."

"You enjoy the process of destruction too much. You lose sight of the purpose."

"I destroy the enemies of the Rea," replied Ares fiercely, "for I am true to my beliefs. I serve the clan leader faithfully."

"Unlike me? I'm practical, Ares. You always forget to protect your own tools of ambition."

"I protect them, until they serve me no longer. You no longer serve my needs. You no longer serve the Rea."

"Then kill me," replied Roake calmly.

Ares retreated a pace and redraped the Bori, until even the shadow and the crimson streak blended into near-invisibility. Ares' voice emerged from the Bori shroud, "You will not betray us again."

"None of the Rea will kill me for you," said Roake, as firmly as if issuing a command. "Like you, they fear the weight of my death-curse. Not even the noble Tagran here will take that risk, because the clan leader would never give such an order."

Would she not? asked Tagran of himself. *She is willing enough to risk the death-curse of Birkaj.*

"She named me war leader in your stead," replied Ares.

Roake continued confidently, despite his brother's comment, "She would not condemn me, even if she believed all the nonsense that you claim about my 'treachery.' You will have much to explain when she learns of your actions."

"When she completes the surprise welcome for the Bercali," answered Ares with the harshness of thinly restrained anger, "she will return in triumph, grateful for the service I have given her. I am sure you will enjoy witnessing the Bercali's entrapment in the snare that you conceived for them." Ares' pale hand emerged again from Bori concealment, and he pointed upward. "Your death approaches, Brother."

"I'd wager against it, but you have nothing that I'd care to win."

"Cherish your worthless conceit. We both know that I have taken from you everything that you have ever valued."

Roake smiled. "I destroyed the relaweed, Ares, and the kree'va no longer functions. You'll never find the Rea-traitor without me, for you haven't studied his history enough to understand him. You search vainly."

"That is a particularly foolish lie. In your position, I would indeed have destroyed the relaweed, but you are too practical, too cautious, and too thoroughly addicted. You could not discard the relaweed so quickly, for you would weigh its value too long. Of the kree'va, you know only that *you* failed to find it with the daar'va's first sounding. As for the Rea-traitor, I understand him well enough to kill him. You have lost."

"You haven't won. You will not have the Rea. You will not have the relaweed. You will not regain the kree'va, and you will not fulfill *her* vengeance without my help."

"I shall have all, for your treachery has placed all within my grasp."

"Without me, Ares, you will destroy everything in your path, until you have nothing left to destroy except yourself. You will not survive a span."

"You will not survive another night," answered Ares crisply. His hand gestured toward the two young warriors, both too well trained to react openly to the bitter exchange between brothers. "Take the prisoner outside to await his hosts."

Tagran led the small procession out of the warship. Tiber stood at attention beside the bound, unconscious figure of a resin-stained Soli. The approaching disk of a Bercali shuttle blocked the Stromvi sun.

Tagran watched the dark shuttle settle roughly on the port field. As soon as the Bercali emerged, the two young Rea warriors dragged Roake to the shuttle's landing ramp and thrust him into the grasp of the startled Bercali guards. *The Rea are strong*, observed Tagran with a stirring of pride, slightly troubled by the circumstances of comparison. *Our youngest warriors carry themselves with more distinction than this wretched Bercali commander, a sorry specimen of a sorry species.*

The Bercali resembled Stromvi with respect to basic body shape. However, the brown-skinned Bercali generally stood on the hind two legs, which were longer than corresponding Stromvi limbs, and they used the front legs as lower arms. The lower hands were well equipped for gripping though incapable of detailed work. The Bercali head was froglike. Tagran found Bercali faces as ugly as the erratic patches of spines that sprouted from the Bercali arms and legs.

Ares emerged from the Rea warship. He shrugged free of the stifling Bori and loosened the folds of the protective fabric cloak that helped discourage the beast from assimilating the shape and color of its Essenji owner. Ares pulled the hood of his cloak over his head, for his ivory skin was sensitive to even faint suns' light, and the Cuui's contraband adaptation fluid had been particularly weak lately.

As Ares stepped forward, his Essenji handsomeness made a striking contrast to the Bercali. The war leader's coppery breastplate gleamed brightly. Ares gestured, and Tiber carried the limp Soli away from the Rea warship and dropped him at the Bercali's feet. "A bonus for you," remarked Ares idly.

The commander of the Bercali shuttle pushed at the body with his lower arms, rolling the body to its back. His heavy lids squinted across yellow eyes. He grunted, "Soli?"

"Evidently."

"Our bargain included only one favor, and we haven't yet seen the merchandise we purchased."

"This Soli looks healthy enough to be marketable. You should be paying me for the addition to your cargo."

"I pay only for legitimate prisoners. I'll expect you to resolve your bill in kind."

"You will have your part in our relaweed trade," said Ares reassuringly. He pulled the edge of his velvet cloak away from the ruby starburst at his throat. The Bercali's uneasiness satisfied Tagran's clan-pride.

"The other prisoner," muttered the Bercali, "is an Essenji."

Ares stiffened, and Tagran sensed his surge of irritation. "You agreed to dispose of him for me," said Ares with a faint hiss of warning.

"The legends of Essenji . . ."

"Are nonsense," snapped Ares, "and merit the concern of only the inept and the cowardly. If he dies far from his people, his death-curse will be worthless. I trust that you will not be so stupid as to kill him within this planetary system."

The Bercali growled, "Do not teach me my business."

Ares relaxed from attack posture to deadly watchfulness, but his fury did not abate. *It cannot end*, thought Tagran, *while Roake lives in his mind, always condemning, always deriding*. "I am also an Essenji, Commander. Had you forgotten?"

The commander twisted his russet chin spines thoughtfully. He slapped his hands together, and one of his burly soldiers threw the Soli's body onto the lading platform. "I don't know what you *are*, Ares," said the Bercali commander, "but I know what you've promised me. I've taken a great risk to enter Consortium space with illegal cargo, and I expect to be rewarded accordingly. If this device fails to meet your claims, I'll find you again, and you'll regret the occasion of your deceit."

"The device you have purchased from us will not disappoint you. I told you: It came to us as payment for a full cargo of relaweed, and we accepted it only because its worth far exceeded our original price. We do not generally deal in such objects of exotic technology, but I think you will realize quickly that we know the value of our merchandise. The device will fulfill all of my promises."

"Remember what you've vowed because I won't forget." The Bercali barked a sharp command, and his soldiers joined him. In stern formation, they marched back inside their shuttle. An automated arm gathered the lading platform into the hold.

CHAPTER 26

Tori moved very slowly through the osang passage, realizing how much more haunting the gray-white webs and veils appeared without another Soli beside her. She was sure that she remembered where Jase had left the snake, and she approached with all the caution she could exert. Every breath and rustle seemed loud and eager to betray her. When she did not find the snake where she expected, a moment of relief overcame the grimmer implications. The osang was awake and active again—somewhere.

Tori reached the end of the passage and stumbled into an enguyang-thorn vine. One long thorn drove into her shoulder. She extracted the sharp, burning splinter and shook her arm to keep from scratching at the swelling wound.

She clambered across the last stretch of rough land, following the imperfect trail that Jase had slashed. Many of the resilient vines had already snapped back across the path. Tori struggled to evade the snatching strands of briers, but they snagged her clothing and scratched her skin with a ferocity that seemed almost malevolent.

She reached the tunneler, but she did not let herself relax her wary guard. She secured herself inside the vehicle and spent several microspans convincing herself that all of the equipment remained precisely as they had left it. She removed the force mallet from the toolkit and tested its weight in her hand. It was an imperfect fit, for Jeffer was a large man, but the tool would serve.

Tori checked the map closely, trying to commit its entirety to memory, for she knew that she would not be able to leave the controls readily once she started the tunneler. She had watched Jase and seen his concentration, as well as his bruised hands. Even using the force mallet to start the heavy Stromvi machine, the effort jarred her bones.

She did not try to push the tunneler to its maximum speed. The vibrations, even traveling at a moderate pace, made accurate aim at the direction controls very difficult. When an unexpected jerk nearly caused her to plunge the tunneler into a solid bank of core clay, she dropped the speed further. She muttered, "I should never have left Uncle Per's estate."

The resin permeated slowly, replacing the clearer air of the surface. The transition to the resinous atmosphere was no less painful at the reduced pace, but it did not produce as much of a blinding effect; the tear ducts were better able to counter the accumulation across the corneas. Tori identified the forking tunnel on the monitor well before reaching the point of decision.

She was certain that the lower fork led back to the deep cavern beneath the workers' enclave at Hodge Farm. She was less confident that the upper right fork led to a cavern beneath the farm's south fields. She was not even sure that the second cavern network still existed, for she had only heard Nguri mention it as an old enclave, abandoned due to dangerous ground settling well before Hodge Farm had grown to its current dimensions. The south fields had largely reverted to natural Stromvi terrain after the construction of the main house at the northeast corner of the valley.

The map indicated that the south caverns still existed, and Tori directed the tunneler into the upper right fork with a grim expression, hoping that the map was current. She knew that the enclave caverns beside Hodge House had been abandoned, and she knew that the access to them was too steep for her to reascend to the surface level. If any Stromvi people remained in the Ngenga Valley, the south cavern area seemed to her the most likely place to find them. It was the only nearby, sizable Stromvi habitation that Jase and she had not searched.

Unless the south caverns had collapsed completely, her position there would surely be preferable to entrapment beneath the Hodge Farm workers' enclave. At least, she might have the option of returning to the surface without facing the menace at the port. She tried not to consider the possibility of driving the clumsy, vibrating tunneler into an unstable region and triggering her own burial.

Stromvi did have other enclaves, of course, but Tori had no idea where to find them. The maps in the tunneler covered the Ngenga Valley and port regions only, and she had never thought of questioning the Stromvi about their kindred's communities. She had gathered that some of the communities had disapproved of the Soli experiment, and the Ngenga Valley had grown more isolated since the development of Hodge Farm.

The intensity of resin slowed her metabolism, staving off hunger, but accelerating the onset of fatigue. To her frustration, her actions began to slow and lose accuracy, and she was forced to reduce the tunneler's speed to a crawl in order to maintain its direction. Little as she liked the idea of stopping and restarting the tunneler in a narrow, poorly supported passage, Tori began to think that she would have no other choice.

She counted silently, repeatedly losing her place and starting again. As millispans of trudging progress passed, her concentration drifted from even that simple, self-appointed task. The tunneler coughed, faltered, and stopped.

Tori dropped to the floor of the tunneler and cradled her elbow in her lap. Streaks of red marked the trails of the poison that had spread from the enguyang-thorn in her shoulder. The upper arm had swollen, stretching the skin tight.

Soli visitors had often complained that Stromvi resin left them perpetually fatigued. Tori had privately accused those visitors of laziness, but she acquired a new sympathy for them as she sat alone in a tunneler deep within the Stromvi world. "My inquisitor was right again," she sighed. "An excess of resin in the lungs isn't healthy."

Tori closed her reddened, teary eyes, and her head lolled against a Stromvi weaving. "I'm sorry, Great-grandmama," murmured Tori, "but I never wanted to be anyone's concubine." The weaving tugged at her cheek and scratched her as she slid against the rough fibers and yielded to exhaustion.

*   *   *

The pain pounded up his spine, sending its throbbing messages into his skull. "Ukitan warned me about days like this," muttered Jase, struggling to remember the mind-cure for a fouled adaptation. "One truth, one whole, one self as cell of insignificance except within the whole." He paused, unable to complete the canticle.

Uneasily, Jase identified a strange, stale flavor amid the sharpness of Stromvi resin. It was the mildly bitter taste that characterized many of the dangerous Abalusi drugs, serving as warning to any race with sufficient sensitivity to perceive the hazard prior to ingestion. The Soli physique generally appreciated the warning too late. . . .

Where? wondered Jase, trying to feel despite the binding field that held him, trying to see despite the mask that blinded him, trying to hear despite the sound hood that reduced his universe to a field of colored noise. The scent of processed metal did not inform him of any specific location, but it provided a negative type of data: He was *not* in a Stromvi cavern, *not* on an open landing field, *not* in the company of any Stromvi native. He perceived movement around—but not of—him. He sensed anger but could not feel its focus or its source with any clarity.

"May wisdom lighten your journey," said Jase quietly. He hoped the Sesserda greeting sounded pleasantly neutral. A cold ceramic probe jabbed Jase in the ribs, but he tried again, "Worth may begin in imperfection, but an indulgence of errors does not strengthen the foundation." The jab was repeated with increased vigor, tearing the skin. Jase grunted in disapproval, "A prisoner makes a poor friend."

He felt the sting against his neck. The inoculation burned into his veins, but he did not let it steal his consciousness quickly. He cataloged his body's reactions of pain and rebellion, postponing any assessment of the probable cause until a more opportune time. The mind-attacking drug did not alarm the calm center of Sesserda-trained concentration, for Sesserda trusted that his relanine-saturated system would adapt to the intrusive element of toxin without excessive difficulty.

He sensed other recent injuries inside him, for he could feel the elevated levels of relanine teasing his nervous system. *Perhaps I did see an energy gun aimed at me*

*from a cloud of darkness. The beam cannot have struck a
vital organ, or I would not be here now. I wonder if the
resilient Miss Darcy escaped?*

As the poison spread and began to deaden his senses,
Jase muttered to himself, "To what ingenious purgatory
have you subjected your beleaguered body this time?"
He sensed a stirring of his bindings and regretted provoking his captor so hastily.

* * *

The warmth embraced her, holding her gently. Tori
enjoyed the trace of a dream that had already faded from
her memory, until the nagging irritation in her lungs
started her coughing. Tori let the blissful illusions of
sleep escape her quickly because she had wakened
enough to distrust the peace.

Radiant light. Tori blinked. Her eyelashes scattered
the blue, powdery flakes of dried resin, and she brushed
the residue from the corners of her eyes, her face, and
hands.

"Good morning," said Nguri gently. The aged Stromvi
crouched beside Tori, his upper torso nearly horizontal
and his large head almost against her face. He retracted
his head slightly to accommodate the focusing range of
a Soli. Behind him, bright Consortium light panels illuminated a low-ceilinged room carved from core clay and
accordingly dry and free of resin. "I am most glad to see
you, Tori. I feared that we had parted forever in anger,
and I grieved."

"Weigh your gladness against mine, my friend. Are we
in the south cavern enclave?"

"An offshoot of it. We heard the tunneler approach
and sent workers to find you. It is well that you stopped
when you did. You were headed for the old, unstable
region."

"I planned well, didn't I?" asked Tori wryly. She sat
upright on the pad of woven Stromvi fibers. The toolkit
had been placed on a low ledge, and the handle of the
machete peered from the kit's outer pocket. "What's
happened, Nguri?"

"Death-watch," replied the Stromvi soberly.

"I heard the click-chorus, but I still don't understand the meaning."

"You haven't studied Stromvi legends," chided Nguri. "Before our history ends, the ancient invaders will return and demand payment for all the years of peace. If they claim one living Stromvi, they will own the souls of all our people. When they come, we must keep a vigil for a month and then die as a race."

"That's one of most appalling superstitions I've ever heard," scoffed Tori, but the legend compounded her uneasiness. Under normal circumstances, she would never have considered that any Stromvi would believe such a terrible prophecy of doom, but she no longer knew what to think about the Stromvi world.

Nguri stretched his mouth in his frightening smile. "We're all very civilized members of the Consortium, credulous Soli, but the *death-watch* cry is still the most dire form of warning among our people. I do not know who started the cry across our world, and I do not know the reason, but none of us will emerge from hiding quickly or incautiously."

"Are there any other Soli hiding with you?" asked Tori, and she held her breath to await the answer.

"Only Rillessa. Perhaps she will talk to you," said Nguri slowly. "None of us has been able to extract any intelligible words from her. She sits unblinking in a nearby chamber and whispers only that 'It' watches. Her hands were burned when we found her." Nguri watched Tori with a curious, tilted gaze. "I would be most interested in hearing your own story of the past four days."

"Four?"

"You slept long."

"You know that Birk is dead?"

"Is he?" sighed Nguri with the curious sibilance of Stromvi shock. "Such a vibrant life as Birk's does not fade easily into silence. Until finding Rillessa, I expected the end of all of you Soli—except for Birk. It is hard to believe him dead." Heavy lids drooped across the black eyes.

"The port is deserted, except for something. . . ." Tori reached for the toolkit, suddenly concerned that the port logbook had been lost, but the book rested neatly beneath the kit. She fingered one slick, printed page, but she replaced the book on the ledge. "I should talk to Rillessa first," she sighed.

She tested her feet gingerly, but she felt surprisingly well, and the resin had not coated her too thickly for mobility. Only a slight discoloration of her shoulder marked the site of the thorn's infection. Her clothes had been cleaned, though resin still darkened the fabric.

"Come," said Nguri. He led her into a clay tunnel that seemed much too blank and textureless for Stromvi tastes. No weavings covered the walls, which wore no decoration but small, carved identification symbols like those on Stromvi maps.

"These are emergency tunnels," explained Nguri, observing Tori's curious inspection of her surroundings, "too dry and riddled with clay for pleasant Stromvi living but better for Soli. We don't visit this place regularly, and we don't like to hide our artworks from common view." He hunched his shoulders briefly. "The resin caves are more appealing." He gestured toward an opening along the wall. "Rillessa is there. I shall let you go alone, for I seem to frighten her, but I shall stay nearby in case you need me."

"Such gallantry," grumbled Tori. "You dislike Rillessa in general and avoid her whenever possible."

"You're quite right, clever Soli," answered Nguri with a teasing click pattern. Tori tried to return his lightness with a grin, but she suspected that her effort was as feeble as his own. She had never seen a Stromvi deeply worried before, but she did not doubt that the rapid speech, the slight protuberance of the pruning teeth, and the nictitation of the inner eyelid were signs of Nguri's tension.

Tori straightened her shoulder sash and resin-stained long-blouse, and she pushed her loose hair behind her ears, wishing that she had taken the time for better preparation. She did not want to compare herself to Rillessa, who had let fear of a faceless enemy dominate all ordinary concerns. For months, Rillessa had abandoned all interest in her once-fastidious appearance, scarcely even dressing herself without stern prompting.

Tori might now share Rillessa's nightmare, but she did not mean to imitate Rillessa's reaction. Tori did not intend to cower in defeat. With a proud poise, Tori pushed through the woven door into Rillessa's cavern room. She could hear Nguri's shuffling retreat.

Sitting stiffly upright on a block of clay in a Stromvi cave, Rillessa might have been ready for Sylvie's wedding. The lilac shift and dark green overskirt looked like castoffs meant for a Stromvi child's amusement, but Rillessa wore them with dignity, and her auburn hair fell in smooth curls to her shoulders. A fine, feathery white robe rested across her knees.

Expecting to find a shattered, hysterical woman, Tori felt surprised at how calm Rillessa appeared. Tori seated herself on a carved clay chair before noticing the resin bandages that wrapped Rillessa's hands. Above the bandages, the arms were scored with welts and burns.

Rillessa did not react to Tori's arrival. She did not seem to realize that anyone had entered the room. Tori spoke to Rillessa very slowly, hesitant to disturb a fragile veneer of calm. "I'm glad to see you, Rillessa," said Tori softly. "Are your hands severely injured?"

"I set the needler badly," replied Rillessa with perfect composure, but she did not focus on Tori. She stared at the wall, and she did not blink, though her green eyes, clouded with accumulated deposits of resinous air, must have hurt fiercely.

"Was it the needler that burned you?" asked Tori, wondering how Rillessa could have acquired anything as deadly and illegal as a needler. Prili data gatherers won fame for their skills at appropriating unusual information, but Tori had never considered the vast scope of topics that such data might include. Her respect for Rillessa increased by a hesitant measure.

"The needle burned through *It*—but *It* did not fall. I escaped *It*, but *It* waits for me."

"What is 'It,' Rillessa?"

"*It* watches."

"Have you seen *It*? Can you describe *It*?"

"No one believes me," murmured Rillessa with a moue of self-pity. She added in a secretive complacency, "But they'll believe the Soli inquisitor. *It*'s quick, but he'll be quicker."

"Jase Sleide?" asked Tori hollowly. She wished that she might turn from this tormented woman and find Jase awaiting her, even if he questioned her relentlessly for the next fifteen spans.

Rillessa whispered eagerly, "The Soli inquisitor will come to question Tori, but he'll stay to help me. He'll understand why I had to deceive him."

"*You* asked Jase Sleide to come here?" demanded Tori sharply, but she could see the awful logic of it, knowing Rillessa's state of mind in recent months.

"To find *It*," answered Rillessa with relish, "and ensure Consortium justice."

Tori wanted to shake Rillessa for raising the specter of Arnod's death merely as a ploy. The greater cost of Rillessa's lie sickened Tori. If Rillessa had summoned Jase honestly, perhaps he could have prepared a defense for Birk and Ngoi—and for himself.

Tori's mind filled with parading images of Arnod, Ngoi, Birk, and Jase. All of the images condemned her, and her sense of Jase mingled with old impressions of five Calongi inquisitors, berating her for impeding justice. *My inquisitor kept me alive*, thought Tori with a guilt-laced ache of regret, *but I could not return the favor. How could Rillessa have deceived us all?*

Tori shuddered from the effort to remain calm. *Rillessa is not at fault*, she told herself harshly. *The blame lies with "It" and with all of us who ignored Rillessa's warnings.*

"I told Calem all about you, *Mirelle*," said Rillessa dreamily. "I told Calem—and Harrow, too. They know not to trust you."

"I'm not Mirelle," replied Tori with quiet ease, but a familiar resentment tightened in her throat.

"I know who you are—and what you've done," countered Rillessa. "You brought *It* here."

"What is *It*?"

Rillessa blinked. Once started, she could not seem to stop. With her eyelids fluttering frantically, she turned her resin-clouded eyes toward Tori. She added with a petulant frown, "I never understood why Calem refused to summon an inquisitor himself. He wanted to remove you from Birk's life, and you'd made yourself so vulnerable."

"Where are Calem and Sylvie?"

Two tears emerged from Rillessa's eyes and began to

creep hesitantly down her face. Rillessa stiffened, and
her face became paler than the blue-tinged light. Tori
leaned forward to ensure that the woman still breathed.
Tori touched the downy border of Rillessa's lap robe,
and Rillessa leapt toward Tori with an incoherent shout.

Tori stumbled from the chair and stepped backward,
trying to elude the startling attack. Undeterred, Rillessa
hurled herself against Tori and beat at her with hard,
resin bandage casings. Tori tried to take hold of Rillessa's
flailing hands and still them, but it was Nguri who
clamped his great arms around Rillessa's waist and pulled
her back to the block of clay.

Rillessa sagged and sat, hunched and weeping. Nguri
clicked a brisk call for aid, and two young Stromvi females ambled into the room. They acknowledged Tori
with gentle, impersonal graciousness, and they stationed
themselves on either side of Rillessa without touching the
sobbing woman.

Nguri waddled from the room with all the haste that
his ungainly body could manage. Tori watched Rillessa
for a long, bitter moment. She turned and reentered the
corridor. She could see Nguri moving at a determined
pace ahead of her, and she hurried the few steps to reach
him. Tori asked grimly, "Has Rillessa attacked anyone
else?"

"No," answered Nguri with a slow, singularly sober
click sequence. "Perhaps she's emerging from shock."

"Is that what you call it?" said Tori dryly. Reaching
the room where she had awakened, she tugged at Nguri's
hand. The Stromvi joined her with an obvious lack of
enthusiasm. "Where did you find Rillessa yesterday?"

"In a field."

"She said she shot 'It' with a needler."

"So I heard. Interesting, is it not? I hadn't believed
her capable of such a violent action."

Tori crossed her arms and strode across the room to
face the stark wall, trying to quiet her temper. "You
were listening to my little talk with Rillessa."

"Of course. I am a very nosy old Stromvi." Tori
laughed curtly, but the sound had an acrid taint. She
could not escape a suspicion that Nguri had been well
aware of Rillessa's unstable state.

Nguri lowered his head to inspect the toolkit closely.

He pulled the machete from the kit and seemed to give exceptionally acute attention to the gray cord that Jase had wrapped around the knife's cracked handle. Nguri clicked his hind teeth quietly and remarked, "I had wondered who summoned Jase Sleide back to this world. You knew that Jase once lived here?"

"He told me."

"I hadn't thought that Birk or Calem would choose to risk any inquisitor's probes, and Sylvie certainly would not have wanted to see this particular Soli again. She cared for him once, but Birk disapproved. Sylvie never forgave herself for surrendering to her father's materialistic arguments."

"Jase was Sylvie's Squire?" asked Tori in surprise. "I thought the Squire died spans ago."

Nguri blinked his wide eyes at Tori with thoughtful care. "Translations from the Calongi language can be misleading. The Calongi have many words for death, several of which imply a degree of philosophical rebirth."

A memory of a meticulous ship's cabin on her first flight to Stromvi made Tori shiver. She had visualized the Squire from the traces of his habits and his impact on the Hodges. She had never imagined him as her own inquisitor. "I always thought I might have liked the Squire," she murmured ruefully. "I didn't picture him as a third-level Sesserda adept."

Nguri demanded bluntly, "You have secrets to hide from a Sesserda adept?"

Tori's cautiousness revived. "Not at the moment," she replied with a manufactured smile.

Nguri clicked a brusque comment on the unpleasant complexity of Soli schemings. "You had secrets to hide from Birk."

"Do you tell Ngeta every detail of *your* life?"

Nguri grunted. "The scent of Jase Sleide covers this machete," he said, lifting the knife and passing it several times above his head nodules. The Stromvi head nodules served a function only remotely akin to the Soli olfactory sense; their sensitivity was renowned. "There are other odors that I cannot identify." If Nguri could not identify the source, then it did not belong to Stromvi.

"I was with Jase Sleide when your death-watch began." Tori tried not to let her fear revive, but its threat made

her recital brusque. "We traveled to the port in the tunneler, and he disappeared. He dropped the knife. I think
he had wounded something."

"Jase Sleide is a most resourceful being."

"Something else was apparently more resourceful than
he." Tori opened the logbook and began to flip through
the pages, trying not to consider what might have overtaken Jase. "The entries end the day before death-watch:
no unusual traffic; only a Stromvi surface foray and the
regular trade run to Deetari." She turned a few pages
and frowned. "Jase told me that he arrived on Stromvi
a day before coming to Hodge Farm. There should have
been a ferry arrival recorded, since Jase brought his own
hovercraft."

"Jase has long kept a ship at the port. He entrusted
its maintenance to that scoundrel, Ngahi, who had no
stronger friend-spirit than to accept payment."

Tori smiled wanly at Nguri's disparagement of the port
manager. The two Stromvi had shared an amicable rivalry for many years. She hoped that Ngahi still lived to
continue the harmless feud, but she had serious doubts.
"That seems a little extravagant, considering that Jase
Sleide hadn't visited the Hodges in the six spans that I've
lived here." She expected no comment from Nguri on
Jase's spending habits, for Nguri had neither interest nor
aptitude for economic concerns. She weighed a new possibility and voiced it: "Did Jase visit you?"

Nguri clicked acknowledgment. "He came after his accident. It was a troubling time for him, before he accepted the change that disassociated him from the past.
Storing his own ship on this planet gave him a needed
sense of connection to that past, I believe."

"What sort of accident?"

"He may tell you if he chooses."

If he still lives. "You knew Jase Sleide well, didn't you,
Nguri?" She was not sure what she was seeking to learn.
There seemed to be little point in trying to understand
Jase Sleide now.

"We spent much time together when he lived at Hodge
Farm. Unlike Birk's useless son, Jase worked the fields
and studied our methods diligently. As a youngling, he
was far less than he has become, but the seeds of his
life-purpose were there within him."

Far less than he has become. . . . The gulf that separated Sylvie's suitor from a Calongi friend certainly does seem vast. "Did you know that Jase had studied the Calongi methods of inquisition?" *Why does it matter now? Because Jase Sleide, alive or dead, is part of the strangeness that has overtaken us. And because I never realized before how deftly Nguri keeps a secret. Nguri and I have talked about the Squire in the past, and Nguri always let me believe that the Squire had died.*

Nguri hunched his knotted shoulders. "Jase studies many subjects. Calongi honor him with their trust."

"Jase told me that he couldn't account for a full day between his arrival on Stromvi and his arrival at Hodge Farm."

"Disturbing," said Nguri thoughtfully. "His time perceptions are generally quite acute."

"He indicated that his Sesserda senses were malfunctioning."

"That would be consistent with his inability to remember a period of time. Memory lapses are common in such cases."

"Loss of memory is common for a Sesserda practitioner?"

"Jase is an uncommon Sesserda adept."

"Obviously," agreed Tori, "but an inquisitor can hardly afford to be forgetful." Nguri's evasiveness disturbed her.

Evidently recognizing Tori's growing impatience, Nguri relented, "A severe external force can hamper anyone's skills. If Jase arrived on this world and disappeared for a day. . . ." Nguri shrugged.

"He didn't appear to be injured."

"Perhaps he was simply detained."

"Who would risk the repercussions of abducting an inquisitor, even briefly?"

Nguri clicked exasperation. "I'm not good at understanding alien motives, Tori Darcy. I know Stromvi, but we are simple people. I know a little about Deetari, but they are a gentle race, quite civilized except for their peculiar matriarchy and odd obsession with prophesying. Most Soli confuse me, and I have never tried to study other Consortium members. I am content with my plants. They have mysteries enough to enthrall me."

"We need to understand what caused this 'death-watch,' Nguri. I need your ideas."

Nguri straightened his upper torso, raising his head above Tori and glaring at her sternly. "I am a horticulturist."

"You're a wily and opinionated old Stromvi, and you love this world as deeply you love your people, though you're too cantankerous to admit to such sentimentality."

The click of pain was almost inaudible. Nguri lowered his head back to Tori's level. "The ability to analyze and recognize alien needs and motives is one of the rarest gifts of any Consortium species," declared Nguri gruffly. "The great leaders, who must interact with many species, defer to trained advisers for such difficult considerations, and those advisers are in great demand."

"I don't happen to have a Calongi adviser available to me."

"You had a Soli adviser until you misplaced him."

"Jase?"

"I've heard that he excels at his profession, and he is less obvious than a Calongi for clients who prefer not to intimidate their customers."

"So," mused Tori, impressed despite her aversion to the inquisitors' arts. *Poor Sylvie, if she recognizes her former suitor: Harrow would seem a sorry substitute for Jase. Poor Harrow, if he ever learns the nature of his competitor. . . . I wonder when Harrow is expected to return here?* "Did Rillessa want an inquisitor's help against her nightmare-foe? Or did she want Jase specifically because she knew that her enemy belonged to a species she didn't understand?"

Nguri clicked a thoughtful assent. "She has gathered many facts in her confused mind."

"Someone might have preferred to eliminate the advantage of Jase's advice." Tori shook her head, refuting her own premise. "But if his captors knew that much about him, why would they have allowed him to come to Hodge Farm at all?"

She realized immediately that she had struck a sensitive subject, but she could not retract the words. With a surge of anger, Nguri snapped, "Why did we allow any Soli to come and despoil our beautiful planet? Why did Ngoi and Birk die? Why have Birk's worthless children disappeared at this time of pain? I do not know these answers, Tori, and I do not enjoy the probing of such turbulent events. Ask of the younglings. They have many wildly imaginative theories."

More alarmed than she wanted to admit, Tori replied contritely, "I didn't mean to imitate our lost inquisitor, Nguri." She knew Nguri well enough to distinguish his present seething temper from his usual half-teasing gruffness. "I ask questions only out of respect for your wisdom."

The Stromvi clicked a scornful comment regarding the hollowness of Soli flattery, but he lowered his great head and tapped the logbook with his massive hand. "What do you seek in this book?"

"Identification of two cruisers that I saw at the port landing field."

"Have you found such reference?"

"Not yet."

"You read. I shall be in the root garden. I cannot think in this sterile atmosphere." Nguri ambled toward the doorway, muttering, "It would have been much easier if you had not lost Jase."

"Sorry," answered Tori. She felt uncomfortably sure that Nguri referred to Jase as a vanished asset rather than a departed friend. Such cold practicality was not at all consistent with her concept of Nguri, but nothing on Stromvi seemed to be as it had appeared a few days ago.

In lonely silence, she continued her conversation with Nguri, *I am not sure that I still feel safe with you, my friend. I even felt safer with Jase Sleide—safe from all but the pitiless justice of the Calongi. Your anger against Soli festers and grows, and I think you could be a very dangerous foe.* Tori touched the machete and wondered sadly if she would ever feel safe again.

CHAPTER 27

Harrow ground his teeth together nervously. Ares scoffed at the tall Soli, whose swarthy coloring looked sallow under Stromvi light, "You sound like one of these pitiful Stromvi."

Harrow made an effort to relax his tense jaw. "The Stromvi harvest was supposed to be a clean purchase," said Harrow tightly. "No deaths, no clear destruction to attract the inquisitors, no obvious disruption of the law. You promised to triple my investment in the relaweed, and you promised that Per Walis would be repaid so well that he wouldn't care where the relaweed was grown. He'll be furious if you've let anything happen to Tori Mirelle."

"We do not aim to satisfy your *other* employer, and disruption of the puerile Calongi law is our purpose. We Rea serve a higher freedom, and you gave your pledge to us."

"I gave my pledge to Roake. Where is he?"

Ares replied in a mocking tone that Harrow did not question, reaffirming Tagran's low opinion of Harrow Febro, "My brother fulfills many vital tasks in our glorious cause." Ares pushed a limp edge of the Bori away from his eyes with an irritated gesture. He kneaded the Bori's soft belly, and the creature wailed in a soft, high cry of pleasure. The Bori's edges firmed and did not droop again beyond the boundary that Ares had dictated.

Ares is in a cynical mood. His taunting of Harrow Febro reflects only general frustration, thought Tagran, sharing some of the same emotion. The "attacks" against Hodge Farm and its inhabitants were simply vandalism against the Rea-traitor, and such petty harassment did not make a Rea warrior proud. Nor could a Rea warrior derive much sense of honor from chasing a war-prize that was already lost. Searching the burned field seemed a futile exercise at this point, an indicator of how aptly Roake had assessed the situation.

Ares clearly did not know how to locate the relaweed, and his plan to coax the Rea-traitor from hiding troubled Tagran. However, Tagran doubted that Roake would have fared significantly better. Misfortune had plagued the Rea since coming to this uncomfortable planet. *As if the present Rea cause dishonored the clan*, mused Tagran, *and merited defeat.*

"Where are the Hodges?" grumbled Harrow. "Where are the Stromvi? Roake didn't tell me anything about this."

"Tell you?" laughed Ares. "You play your minor role at our clan leader's command, Harrow Febro. Do not imagine that you have achieved greatness in our ranks." Across the field, a dark figure rose from the pit where the Rea searched, and the warrior waved a gesture of emptiness. Ares muttered, "I should let you search in the muck of this planet with my warriors, if you are so eager to consider yourself a clan member."

Harrow retorted smugly, "I'm more useful to you as a contact with Per Walis. Roake understands my value."

Ares hissed with the ferocity of the cunning beast he wore as a cloak. "Be grateful that Roake was not here to welcome your return. He does not like disobedience." Ares' clan-knife glinted from beneath the Bori concealment.

Retreating several paces in alarm, Harrow spread his hands in a conciliatory plea. "How was I to know that you'd chosen this time to initiate a full assault on Hodge Farm? I was only away for a few days. Sylvie insisted that I go to Calqui."

"Naturally, your Sylvie should be obeyed above the Rea war leader." Ares sighed, his fury vanishing as quickly as it had come. "You annoy me, Harrow. We Rea eliminate the creatures that annoy us too frequently."

The rapid shifting of Ares' temper disturbed Tagran, who had seen such instability grow to a killing madness in other clan cousins. The pressures of the last few days had made Ares increasingly dangerous. Tagran nearly acknowledged a private anger against the clan leader who could use her sons so ruthlessly.

Harrow seemed to sense the same danger, "Pay what you owe me, and I'll leave. I loathe this planet."

"I shall pay you when I am finished with you."

"I completed my job when I connected you with Calem Hodge." Greed emboldened Harrow. "I'm not responsible for your personal failure to collect the seeds. You owe me a great deal of money to compensate for the relaweed you lost."

Harrow is regaining his cockiness, observed Tagran. *He is not astute enough to survive long among the lawless. He does not know that he is merely a pawn.*

"Tiresome Soli," muttered Ares, "have you no interests beyond yourself?"

"Your brother made promises to me. If you try to renege, I'll make sure that Per Walis collects from you."

"You threaten feebly," mocked Ares, "contradicting your own accusations against the Rea. Would you tell Per Walis that we placed you in his employ? Would you admit that you planted *his* relaweed on a Consortium world, instead of in some remote greenhouse under his control? Would you tell him also that you planted relaweed on the world where his own Mirelle was living? As you reminded me moments ago, she is herself a treasure of exceptional worth."

"*I* haven't done anything to jeopardize her," grunted Harrow. "Per Walis let her work for Birk Hodge for his own reasons. I haven't done anything to hurt Per Walis' operations. I've even helped eliminate Birk Hodge as a rival."

"Foolish, weak man, my brother bargained poorly in recruiting you." Ares turned and strode across the burned swath of a dead field toward a hovercraft that bore Sesserda markings. Concerned, Tagran followed him.

Ares nodded very slightly, acknowledging Tagran's company. "My brother nearly escaped us in this vessel," said Ares, and he sounded calm and amiable, "but one of the internal code locks apparently forced him to land it prematurely." Ares ran his hand along the scored side of the hovercraft, feeling the roughened shield-skin that his own command had caused to blister. Despite the damage, the hovercraft remained sound, its layered walls stout enough to support interplanetary travel. "It is a fine ship. We shall take it to the home vessel and see if we can overcome the rest of the code locks." Ares' touch lingered on a pattern of gold.

Tagran murmured, "Those markings signify Calongi honors." *And Calongi honors signify Consortium officials.*

"I know," agreed Ares, and he laughed loudly. "There is a delightful irony in it: Calongi honors embellishing a Rea's vessel!"

"Where is the ship's original owner?" asked Tagran, hoping that Ares would not take offense at Tagran's prodding. Surely, Ares must realize the dangers suggested by the presence of an official Consortium vehicle at Hodge Farm. Even the most confident of the lawless were careful to recognize Calongi markings and avoid them.

Ares' smile faded. "I don't know. This craft was stored at the Stromvi port, but I don't know who brought it to Hodge Farm."

A Rea shuttle crossed overhead, and Ares saluted the passing ship. Tagran felt slightly reassured by Ares' return to a rational mood, until Ares continued in a strange, uneven voice, "My brother fought well. Even after he was forced to land, he might have escaped, if his Bori had not died."

"Your brother has always been a capable warrior," answered Tagran cautiously.

"Capable and expensive. Without Roake's addiction to drain us, the supplies available to the rest of the clan will become far more plentiful. I shall be able to obtain adequate adaptation fluid, for once, and prove that I can match my brother's skills, given an equal chance. I shall not repeat Roake's mistake of costly addiction. I shall use only enough to gain the freedom from environmental constraints that a Rea leader requires."

He recites Raskannen's specious reasoning, observed Tagran uneasily. *Is this what Akras has taught her sons?*

"You disapprove, don't you, Tagran? I can see it in the tensing of your jaw. You never speak your mind directly, though you certainly observe a great deal and form opinions. Tell me, noble Tagran: If Roake betrayed us and gave warning to the Rea-traitor, why did he wait for our actual attack before trying to escape? Delaying was a foolish, arrogant mistake. Roake is generally arrogant but seldom foolish."

"He thought he had at least another day."

"Yes, that was the clan leader's statement to him," mused Ares. "Why wasn't he conspiring with the Rea-traitor when we arrived? One might almost think that he expected us to arrive in his support, and he used the daar'va at a prearranged signal from the clan leader. That would have conformed very closely to *his* stated plans for reclaiming the Rea treasures: Locate and recover the kree'va, disable any methods of escape, and leave the Rea-traitor to suffer knowledge of our victory. Roake even left the daar'va for our retrieval."

"The clan leader gave no such signal," said Tagran staunchly, though Ares' logic seemed uncomfortably sound. "Long-range communications were disabled."

"A simple confirmation code could have reached from the port to the Ngenga Valley," answered Ares. "The clan leader has been spending much time alone. She has even sent you away from her." Ares walked the length of the hovercraft, pointedly giving Tagran time to weigh unsettling conclusions. Ares returned to where the senior warrior stood. "Stop frowning, Tagran. I'm only airing my own ignorance relative to our clan leader's greater wisdom. We both know that my brother betrayed us. The clan leader said it."

Tagran could not reply. Ares left him and rejoined the sulking Harrow Febro beside the Rea shuttle.

*   *   *

Ukitan, honored Calongi inquisitor and exalted Sesserda master, studied the small, neat book in which his incoming messages had inscribed themselves, and he admired the simple elegance of the Xiani design. He felt the polished casing of the book with thirteen senses, and he lauded the Xiani subtlety. "It is most challenging," murmured Ukitan, "to please senses that are alien to one's self and one's species."

"Xiani understand their proper functions as a race and as individuals," answered Omi, honored Calongi inquisitor and full Sesserda master, "and they achieve greatness accordingly."

"Lower species rarely succeed at a true exchange of alien concepts. Exceptions are noteworthy and admirable."

"You no longer speak of the Xiani," observed Omi politely, and he waited. A Calongi did not question his host when seated at table in his host's birth-home.

"My Soli student has not acknowledged my greetings."

"Courtesy is subservient to opportunity."

"Share your concern, Omi-lai."

"Focal points of conflict often coexist with individuals of apparent insignificance and relative innocence—the catalysts of conflict."

"Suato's principles of historical analysis are well known to me."

"Mirelle of Attia was a focal point of much turbulence during the spans of her adult life. Since her genetic records were destroyed in the Nitian revolution, before Nitia accepted Consortium membership, I am unable to make a precise correlation. However, I have estimated that the Soli who calls herself Victoria Darcy is Mirelle's duplicate within a two point deviation—or less."

"A clone?" asked Ukitan, startling his visitor, for the host's privilege of questioning was rarely employed.

"Perhaps," answered Omi, and his vast brain began to process the significance of Ukitan's inquisitorial probe. "The crime of cloning, if present, is attributable to a woman long ago dead and subjected to the final justice. It is a more recent crime that causes my disquiet."

"The death of Arnod Conaty?"

"The historical precedent suggested by that event alarms me. A Soli male should not have been allowed inquisitor's status in this matter. The potential for compromise, Ukitan-lai, is horrifying."

"The potential for truth, Omi-lai, is paramount. I do not doubt Jase-lai's honor, and this journey was necessary to his growth."

"He has not responded to your greetings."

"The planet of Deetari has not responded to my greetings," answered Ukitan, and he caressed the Xiani message book with the soft tendrils that performed the most delicate functions of his sensor cape. "The journey to Stromvi is too arduous for this ancient body of mine, but I owe a friendship-debt. You will understand my dilemma."

Ninety-six Calongi senses united in understanding, and Omi regretted that he could not claim the privileged ignorance of a lesser race. He made note to atone for his unworthy reaction of dismay. "I cannot judge impartially," argued Omi with implacable Calongi honesty, "for I have questioned Victoria Mirelle on a previous occasion."

"We have received no new request for her inquisition, Omi-lai. That function is still assigned to my worthy Soli student. I seek only to ensure that justice is afforded to him in his difficult undertaking. I thank you for bringing this matter to my attention."

"You are too wise," answered Omi, and he began to plan an additional course of meditations to banish his disgruntlement. "I admire your skill in causing me to probe the issue of your concern."

"Your insightful tribute honors me. I have arranged your itinerary for your greatest comfort."

"You have always been generous."

CHAPTER 28

Roake surveyed the confines of his cell. He commended the Bercali for upholding their reputation for thoroughness so effectively. The small, bare room contained no implement that could possibly be construed as an aid to escape.

The stark white walls shimmered each time the ship lurched, providing an unpleasant reminder of the lethal rays of energy that played across the skin of the cell. According to a common rumor, no being of any species had ever escaped from a Bercali prison. A standard Bercali cell contained only a fraction of the features incorporated to ensure the Essenji's confinement.

Imprisonment had not dulled the sheen of Roake's ivory skin or lessened the brightness of the keen eyes, strikingly iridescent from the excess of adaptation fluid that had filled his veins since infancy. Since the Rea men preferred to keep their thick manes long, the Bercali had shaved Roake's head, neck, and upper arms, but enough of the fine, dark hair remained to cover the obvious scars across the dome of his skull. The silver hair of the lower mane would regenerate more slowly.

He retained the air of pride and strength that characterized his rare and eerily beautiful people, but he did not seen fearsome enough to intimidate the sturdy Bercali. The ship contained many prisoners of more threatening aspect than the Essenji, but only he had earned the Bercali's particular care and caution. The Essenji legend preceded him.

A siren rang as the Bercali guards opened the cell to enter and administer the day's nutrient injection to the prisoner. Most cells included automated mechanisms for such functions, but the Bercali had stripped even that simplistic gear from the Essenji's cell. Roake did not flinch as the stinging nutrient liquid entered his veins.

It might have seemed cruel to have bound the Essenji within the cell: bound him tightly with fused silenen thongs. It might have seemed cruel, had any impartial witness observed the act, but an observer might have perceived more strangeness in the evident fear with which the armed Bercali entered the cell to tend their prisoner's minimal physical needs.

If the Bercali feared so much, the observer might have wondered, why had they removed the robotic equipment that would have eliminated the need ever to enter the cell? Surely, the legends exaggerated grossly in describing a Rea warrior's effect on photonic circuits or electromechanical devices. Surely, the legends of the Essenji death-curse were absurd.

The ship lurched violently. One of the guards fell against the Essenji. He emitted a sharp whistle of pain, and he scrambled across the floor on all six limbs, the undignified form of his movement indicative of his extreme distress. The dull, dark skins of the other Bercali guards paled.

The unfortunate fallen man blinked his heavily lidded eyes slowly and ponderously to clear the lenses. The defensive film of mucus was a legacy of a rival species. The long-extinct enemy had attacked by spitting acidic fluid into enemies' eyes. The Bercali guards dragged their shamed fellow out of the cell and resecured the door.

Roake twisted his full lips into a wry smile. Since the Bercali had removed all equipment from the cell, they had deactivated all means of observing the prisoner remotely. Hence, Roake did not bother to control his expression of disgust. He closed his iridescent eyes, and his breathing deepened and slowed. A roar of formless sound rippled through the ship, shaking even the insulated cell. Roake's brilliant eyes snapped open.

He felt the change pervade the ship: The daar'va spread its deadliness swiftly, though its effects would dissipate much faster than the kree'va's similiar work. As the tainted air circulated through the cell, Roake's lungs burned, and a constriction of his heart stole his outer senses, abandoning him in black silence.

The faintest trace of awareness lingered, as relanine

reacted to the alien elements that would have killed a healthy Essenji instantly. The toxins altered, even as the cellular functions of the Essenji shifted slightly to neutralize the invaders. Each cell, infected for spans by the relanine content in massive doses of illegal adaptation fluid, lost a little more of its original character. Each cell became a little hungrier for the relanine that sustained it. A few cells, robbed of needed relanine by stronger neighbors, died.

When his senses returned, Roake knew that he had lost a brief measure of time, but he allowed himself no regret or fear. Adaptation fluid gave him life; adaptation fluid gave him freedom. Akras had never permitted him to equate his constant use of adaptation fluid with dependency, despite the enormous quantities of the extrapotent Cuui fluid that Roake required regularly. She had nearly persuaded him that he had chosen the course of his life, for the truth lay somewhere in one of those relanine-damaged pools of memory.

Rea warriors esteemed Roake for surviving addiction, and they praised his courage. Roake could not remember any warrior ever seeking to emulate him, but strict Consortium controls, after all, did make large-scale use of adaptation fluid a very expensive habit to maintain. Obtaining a regular supply of contraband fluid in addictive quantities and concentrations had frequently stretched even Roake's considerable limits of lawless ingenuity.

Roake relaxed individual muscles that very few members of his race could control consciously, and he slipped his slender hands free of the silenen bonds. He stretched his arms, easing the stiffness from his shoulders and back. With a sharp breath and a rapid jerk, he extracted his feet from the shackles enclosing his ankles. The motion tore wide strips of flesh from his feet, but Roake concentrated briefly to accelerate the clotting of his blood and seal the wounds.

Roake laughed softly as he stood, savoring the freedom to pace the tiny cell. He tugged at the discarded thongs of silenen, but they refused to separate from the prisoner's chair. The ship jerked, and Roake stabilized himself by delicate muscular control, though he could easily have relied on the chair's support. Patiently and expectantly, Roake observed the rippling sheen of the walls with each shudder of the assaulted ship.

Many alarms began to ring, while Roake continued to watch the walls. The lights faded and brightened several times before darkening completely. Only the occasional shimmer of the energy beams lit the room, casting pale shadows across the Essenji's naked body and delineating the intricate muscular structure. With a final, hurtling lurch of the Bercali prison ship, even the energy beams failed, leaving the cell dark and void of any energy but Roake's life force.

Roake walked directly to the sealed door, navigating effortlessly by a relanine-tuned echo-location skill. He began to tackle the hard, ceramic door by thrusting his powerful shoulders against it in a carefully considered pattern of assault. With the locking fields deactivated, the door would eventually yield. Roake was confident, for Akras had taught her sons all she knew of the design of the home vessel, and the Bercali seldom altered basic architecture. Roake progressed very slowly, despite his strength, but he persisted. Above all, the son of Birkaj and Akras had learned to value patience.

*   *   *

Sitting cross-legged in the middle of the common cell's floor, Jase observed his fellow prisoners surreptitiously, while pretending to doze. The dominant prisoners, massive Cluvi and lithe Jiucetsi, had claimed the few berths and the choice locations against the walls. The weaker or more submissive species sat as far as possible from any territorial prize. A feverish Zanwi, its ruddy skin covered with dark boils, shuddered alone in a huddle.

The Bercali guards apparently issue adaptation fluid sparingly, mused Jase, for several of the prisoners showed the early effects of illness, starvation, or contamination. From the queasiness that had accompanied his own inoculation upon imprisonment, Jase suspected that the Bercali fluid was impure. The impurities probably impeded adaptation of the genetic patterns of the more specialized races.

The Bercali are not wise enough to realize why they are one of the few nonmember races authorized to buy fluid from the Consortium. They serve a valid species-purpose when they take legitimate prisoners to work centers, but they slip into habits of cruelty and neglect. It seems that they are due for another Consortium lesson. I hope I have an opportunity to place the recommendation!

Jase was not immediately concerned by the poor quality of the inoculations, except as evidence of the Bercali disdain for agreements with the Consortium. He could feel his implant issuing the purest, most potent cousin of adaptation fluid directly into his bloodstream. His supply should still be ample. If his supply exhausted itself before he could return to a Calongi world. . . . Well, the most concentrated adaptation fluid would not help salvage the genetic structure of a true relanine addict.

He studied the other prisoners carefully: an informative task for species identification, since each prisoner had been stripped bare before incarceration. No extraordinary pigment appeared to color the sensitive regions of any other prisoners' anatomy, but that certainly did not imply universal ignorance of the meaning of such pigment changes. Jase kept his eyes narrowed, hoping to avoid the unwelcome attention that their peculiar coloring might attract. He doubted that a recognized relanine addict on an unauthorized prison ship could expect a long lifespan. Even the use of addictive doses of adaptation fluid was a singularly expensive habit to maintain, and pure relanine was unattainable without Calongi consent.

All of the prisoners in the cell were males, a fact that Jase found culturally noteworthy, since the Bercali rarely troubled to observe alien variations in gender. He pursued the Bercali's probable reasoning with an ironic sense of encouragement. If the adaptation fluid were impure, the fertility control could be equally imperfect. Bercali concern about possible reproduction among the prisoners suggested a long incarceration rather than immediate execution: time enough to devise an escape.

The cell contained no other Soli. Jase was grateful that his captors had stripped him of his Sesserda shirt while resin still disguised it, though the relanine would escape his system that much more rapidly. The Bercali would tolerate relanine addiction more readily than such obvious affiliation with Calongi as Sesserda gold. The prison guards would certainly not want to keep a captive inquisitor alive to condemn them.

He wished that he knew who had captured him. He could remember almost nothing that had occurred between the sound-shock at the Stromvi port and his arrival in this cell. Only the most traumatic of relanine adaptations impaired the memory. He could blame the impure Bercali fluid, but the significance of his latest lapse became grimmer in recollection of a full Stromvi moon and the loss of time that it represented.

The ship lurched, and the prisoners muttered imprecations in many languages. Jase listened and watched attentively for those prisoners who employed the Cuui dialect known as Basic, the universal trade speech of the Consortium. Both courtesy and common sense recommended Consortium Basic among such a motley assortment of beings, and its usage generally conveyed something about the social attitude of the speaker.

Jase identified twenty-six represented languages, twenty-two of which were vocally based. He could have conversed fluently in most of the languages within the limitations of Soli anatomy, but he maintained a stoic silence. He was unwilling to admit his knowledge of the wicked plots encircling him.

The roar drowned the prisoners' voices. *Sound-shock*, thought Jase and wondered why he was not surprised. He needed a solid millispan of Sesserda meditation to collect all his piecemeal observations and conclusions into consciousness.

In the wake of thunder, his fellow prisoners became loud in their complaints. The ship shuddered abruptly. Several of the prisoners lost their footing, and arguments erupted.

Jase shifted his concentration from the prisoners to the larger environment, and he concluded that the ship's simulated gravity had lessened almost imperceptibly. The orientation of "vertical" had also drifted slightly. Malfunctions of the ship's simplest functions did not bode well for the reliability of the overall system.

Attempting interstellar travel in a poorly maintained space barge could be more lethal than any Bercali prison farm. Even presuming that the source of the sound-shock spared any of the ship's unwilling passengers, the odds against survival were still uncomfortably low. Jase decided that the urgency of escape had just increased significantly.

Despite the recent discontinuities of his memories, Jase still trusted his fundamental time-sense: He did not believe that the ship could have left the Deetari/Stromvi system yet. He had intended to wait until the ship stopped for supplies or the collection of another prisoner. He could not escape easily while the ship was in flight, unless he could recruit considerable aid for his cause.

None of his fellow prisoners appeared strikingly well qualified to commandeer a prison barge, and the guards seemed little better. The ship's automated systems would most probably be unusable without authorized access. Jase frowned, wondering if he could train and coordinate unskilled laborers into performing all the operational functions required. Controlling a large, damaged ship manually within the complex gravitational fields of a planetary system was not an ideal exercise for learning.

"Assuming I can apply the theories well enough to control the ship myself," he muttered very softly, but the improbability of escaping a Bercali prison did not daunt him. A stern Sesserda litany had stifled discouragment. "A ship this size could carry individual shuttles," he mused, pondering new possibilities.

The ship's gravity changed subtly again, disturbing Jase more than the jarring motions that wracked the prison cell. He dodged three hurtling prisoners who had embroiled themselves in a wrestling match and lost their collective balance. He decided that the time for remaining quietly unobtrusive had passed.

Moving carefully amid a rolling, chaotic sea of frightened, angry men of many species, he headed toward a wall berth held by a wary Cluvi. Before Jase could reach the wall, the primary lights went dark. The emerald eyes of the primitive emergency beacons encircled the door and the ceiling.

A dark mass of prisoners attacked the door, pounding its panels without effect. Jase claimed an abandoned berth and clung to it absently as the ship's line of gravity tilted sharply, throwing the majority of the room's inhabitants into a scrambling mound atop the cell door. He heard the crack as the door opened, and shouts accompa-

nied the ebbing of the prisoners out of the cell and into
the body of the ship.

The prisoners' shouts and screams dwindled and
stopped. Jase waited, grimly contemplating the reasons
for the silence. Comparison to the events on Stromvi did
not make his conclusions more pleasant.

He swung himself from his perch and used the row of
tilted berths as a ladder. He dropped carefully to the
edge of the door and peered beyond the cell. The ship
rolled in a rough, wide oscillation.

Jase gripped the rim of the entry lock tightly, waiting
for the ship to stabilize—with or without a definitive
sense of gravity. When the wracking motion finally
stopped, the floor had resumed nearly its original orientation. The repetitive thuds of shifting bodies in the
corridor let Jase count more casualties than he could
see in the dim light. The total exceeded his expectations alarmingly.

He moved cautiously into the corridor, observing uneasily that none of the bodies moved, and few of the
bodies were Bercali. Dead prisoners were plentiful, and
not all of them had come from his cell: He found two
females and a genderless Cuui.

He pursued the dim vibration of the ship's engines,
reasoning that the course would lead him out of the
prison quarters. The ship was unusually large—a converted colony base, Jase concluded. The air had acquired
a metallic tang that did not conform to any of the standard atmospheric blends. Jase studied a few of the prisoners' bodies, trying to decide if toxic air had killed
them, but the bodies were unmarked and uninformative.

The bodies of the prisoners did not extend beyond the
shattered ceramic doors of the prison vault. Jase contemplated the doors grimly. Such ceramics did not shatter
without exceptional and deliberately destructive force.

Jase could not determine if the air became purer as he
climbed from the prison wards to the crew levels of the
ship, but he no longer noticed the metallic scent. His own
body, burning now with relanine, adapted too eagerly
to the new elements to detect the subtle environmental
changes. He recognized the nearness of relanine over-
dose, imposed by the excessive stress of repeated adapta-

tion, but the danger carried its own euphoria. So close to relanine madness, he could not feel imperiled.

The cold did not penetrate quickly, but even the purest relanine had limits of temperature tolerance. Jase began to shiver, and he wondered if the ship's heating system had failed altogether. The air still circulated. The pseudo-gravity functioned, albeit erratically. The engines still beat an orderly cadence.

The rhythmic drumming grew louder. The temperature grew increasingly chill, and lacy fingers of ice formed on the narrow, horizontal pipes that lined the corridor walls. Individual heating elements still operated beneath the floor, but the distribution system had failed. Patches of the black flooring seared the flesh, and patches burned with cold. Along the ramps that joined the worker levels, dark, frosted stalactites had formed at odd angles between the railings. The touch of a frozen railing melted into a smear of umber blood on Jase's hand.

Jase ducked quickly into the shadow of a crossing ramp above him, and he raised his eyes to study the maze of mesh-enclosed walkways that filled the cylindrical chamber. The pseudo-gravity had shifted nearly to its original orientation, but the majority of the stalactites pointed at an angle ten degrees from current vertical.

Jase traced the directions of the stalactites visually. The mesh of the walkway two levels beyond him wore the same dark sheen as the bloody railing. The dull blue light from the engine room glowed spottily through the mesh, outlining the motionless figures of six Bercali.

As Jase watched, a globule of thick Bercali blood seeped through the mesh and splattered on the ramp beside Jase. The drops of blood crystallized as they struck the rubbery surface.

With cautious patience, Jase climbed from the shadow to the surface of the ramp above him. The skin of his fingers clung to the icy railing as he vaulted to the next level, but he commanded his own blood to circulate hotly within his hands long enough to free his grasp. With a heated ramp again beneath his feet, he allowed his body to resume a normal, protective concentration of self-contained warmth. His fingers became numb, yielding precedence to life-crucial organs.

As he climbed, the ramp became more consistently

warm, and Jase began to feel the flow of heated air imprisoned in the upper levels of the ship. He entered the system of mesh corridors near the source of the Bercali blood. He tried to sense any motion beyond himself, but he felt only the tingling of his own blood slowly resuming its normal flow.

The first Bercali body that he found had no arms; the second had no legs. The head of the third had been sliced by a broad, burning beam that had left the mottled skin puckered and brown. The fire that had failed to complete its gruesome job had cauterized only the lesser blood vessels, and the seeping blood had spread from the floor to the mesh. Jase rubbed at the traces of blood on his own hand, contemplating the dead Bercali.

Each Bercali body had been brutalized distinctly, as if by a grisly ritual. Despite his revulsion for the carnage and his distaste for the brutal Bercali culture, Jase touched each body in respect for the departed spirit. He whispered the Sesserda words of passage to each of the dead, regretting belatedly that he had not thought to provide a similar service for the dead prisoners. When he had completed a tribute that few, if any, Bercali would have appreciated, he made a second circuit, systematically appropriating any useful gear.

A padded vest and breechcloth fit him badly, but they gave warmth and some sense of protection. Jase slung a cord of unidentified metal keys across his shoulder and belted a Bercali dagger at his waist. He examined the Bercali boots with regret; they were useless to a Soli. He did not touch the energy weapons or any of the powered devices. He disliked intentionally lethal tools at any time, and he did not trust them at all on this ship of death.

He felt the shift of air—a brush of breeze that did not conform to the larger flow. He held very still, trying to detect the motion's source, and he knew that he had delayed too long. Motions swirled the currents from both ends of the mesh corridor. Jase turned toward the lesser source and walked quickly and quietly in its direction. The corridor ended in darkness, the blue glow barely illuminating the serrated edges of the mesh, where it fused to the larger wall of the ship.

The sonorous hum of the engines stopped, and the room seemed to spin as the pseudo-gravity swung through a circular cycle. The mesh scraped Jase's arms, his skin less durable than Bercali hide, before he managed to brace himself. Metal rattled in the corridor behind him, and the Bercali bodies thudded heavily, shaking the walkway.

The engines resumed their pulsing beat, but the frequency of the rhythm seemed lower to Jase, and he wondered how much longer the ship's systems would continue to function at all. *Not even Ukitan predicted this much trouble from my effort at formal inquisition,* he mused. *If I ever complete the process of judgment, I may need to add a note of warning to the records of Miss Victoria Darcy. The bitter tribute given to the legendary Mirelle might belong equally to Mirelle's descendant: A woman who inspires unto death.*

Where is she now? he asked himself and frowned on considering the possibility that Tori might have been placed on this same Bercali ship.

"No," he whispered, arguing inwardly. "She has a much greater aptitude for self-preservation than you, old boy, despite her apparent recklessness." He derided himself for envisioning her in a reciprocal state of concern regarding her inquisitor's safety.

Jase felt the shifting air and hurled himself toward the edge of the corridor. The red-gold trace of an energy beam cut the space that his head had occupied the previous instant. He rolled to his feet and ran into the lightless hall, hoping that a solid surface would remain beneath his feet. He dropped through the current "floor" into an adjacent corridor before he could complete the thought. The body of another dead Bercali broke his fall.

"Soli, would you like to leave this tomb?" demanded a deep, rich voice in flawless Consortium Basic.

"The idea has a certain appeal," answered Jase cautiously. He could not see the source of the voice, and he could not name the species. He could eliminate a few races, including Bercali, by the perfection of the pronunciation. "Where are you?"

"Continue along the corridor, as you were headed, but be more attentive to your footing. The gravitational orientation has shifted. If you feel threatened by me, realize that I did not need to alert you to my presence here."

"That thought had occurred to me," replied Jase, and he walked toward the voice with a deliberately unhurried pace, avoiding obstacles with a carefully controlled appearance of ease. He sensed no pursuit from the wielder of the energy gun, but he did not relax his attentions. After a few steps, he could see a shadowy figure standing beside a side opening in the corridor, but Jase continued to peer into the darkness as if he had not yet managed to discern any definable shape.

"My name is Roake," announced the figure curtly, when Jase came within a meter of him. "I control the only escape from this dead ship. I shall take you with me, if you will carry certain equipment that I require."

Jase allowed himself to look at Roake directly. "What sort of equipment?" asked Jase, weighing Roake against the menace of the unknown entities behind him.

Roake gestured abruptly toward an open storage locker, inside of which five large, cubic crates had been stacked. "All that you find in that locker. The shuttle bay is at the end of this hall. I shall prepare the shuttle while you bring my equipment. We have very little time."

Roake lifted a crate from the locker and carried it down the hall with swift strides. A door opened before Roake, and yellow light silhouetted him against the interior of an escape shuttle. *Roake could easily be mistaken for a Soli*, mused Jase, *if the muscular structure were hidden beneath Soli clothing instead of scavenged Bercali motley, and if exertion had not emphasized the strangeness of his scent*. Jase collected a crate from the locker, grimaced at the unexpected weight, and followed Roake to the shuttle.

"Place it in the hold on the opposite side," ordered Roake sharply. "I have released the lock for you."

"Considerate gesture," murmured Jase. He tapped the side of the crate as he loaded it, but the contents had been sealed too securely for such casual inspection. "Now you can add smuggling to your diverse accomplishments, Sleide," he muttered beneath his breath.

He returned to the locker and paused before the remaining contents. He felt the distinctive vibrations of bipedal movement in the prison ship—close enough to warrant concern. With a grimace, he collected another of Roake's heavy crates in his arms and moved hurriedly to the shuttle.

He packed one more crate securely into the hold, but he carried the last crate, lighter than its fellows, directly into the pilot's bay and secured the box with transport straps. Roake demanded dryly, "Did you think I would claim the cargo and abandon you, Soli?"

Jase shrugged and seated himself in a berth that adapted slowly to his size. "Does the Bercali commander know that you've appropriated his escape vessel?"

"The Bercali are dead."

"The other prisoners?"

"Also dead. They were inferior. I did not need them." Roake touched the control console to open the outer doors of the shuttle bay.

"You need me?" asked Jase.

"No. You are a convenience, seized at an opportune moment." An alarm blinked, warning that the bay's inner door had not sealed completely, and energy beams exploded across the vision screen.

The shuttle rocked beneath the force of fire, and a siren began to shriek a plaintive protest. An angry voice emerged from the shuttle's communication system: "Do you actually expect to escape, Bercali scum? The death-curse of our fathers will never free you."

Roake drove his fist into the comsystem's receiver, but he smiled, though his hand's blood streaked the smashed equipment. He reached into a small Bercali pouch that hung around his neck, and he withdrew a hard and glittering crimson capsule. He held the capsule high, and dimly luminous beads of his blood rolled down his arm from a gouge at his wrist. "Take this to the aft lock. Break it in the outer chamber." He tossed the capsule to Jase. "Seal the inner door quickly."

Jase turned the capsule rapidly in his fingers, studying it for identifier markings. He found not even a maker's symbol. The omission struck him as ominous. "Lethal chemical fire?" he mused speculatively.

"Lethal to the unprepared, certainly. Warriors in protection suits should, at least, be incapacitated when the fire eats through their seals."

"How quaintly barbaric of you," observed Jase mildy, and he made no move to obey Roake's order.

Roake snapped at him, "If you're useless to me, I'll

kill you with those others who defy me." He pointed an energy pistol at Jase's head. "Obey me now."

To die at the hands of Roake or at the hands of Roake's enemies, thought Jase grimly; *the options are poor*. With a tight expression, Jase enclosed the capsule in his hand and propelled himself through the narrow entry to the aft lock. He slammed his fist against the control panel to open the inner door, nearly as furious with himself as with Roake.

Jase threw the capsule against the air lock's floor, smashing the crimson shell. He smelled the gas that burned without flame: bitter and metallic. He resecured the inner door and leaned his back against it, cursing himself for contributing to the plague of death.

The shuttle jerked and rolled, throwing Jase against the floor, and sending the blood rushing to his ears. Changing pressure tugged at his skin, but he dragged himself painfully toward the pilot's bay. He pushed himself back to the berth behind Roake, who held the shuttle controls with too much hard intensity to observe Jase's return.

The vision screen showed the shuttle bay, cold and stark and deadly. Dark figures clung to the half-open door of the inner bay, but Jase could see no detail of them. Their lack of clear features puzzled him, and he made a note in the rigorous file system that comprised his normal memory. He had little time to contemplate the strangeness in the present. While the Bercali ship continued its helpless warning that the inner door had not been secured, Roake exerted an override with vicious determination.

The shuttle hurtled into the vacuum along with a rush of the prison ship's escaping atmosphere. Jase tightened his grip on his berth, hoping that the shuttle's structure could survive the rash method of escape. The vision screen became dark.

CHAPTER 29

The shuttle engines whined with stress, but Jase could feel the slow damping of vibrations that signified the achievement of a controlled acceleration. When the shuttle steadied, Jase asked with carefully measured irony, "Whom did we murder, Roake?"

"Credulous fools," answered Roake, and he continued to concentrate on the control console.

Jase disciplined his infuriated senses in order to suppress a scathing retort. Any of the comments clamoring in his mind could only aggravate an already tense stand-off. He began a detailed observation of his surroundings, sorting and filing data via trained Sesserda rhythms. The Sesserda masters generally advised the process as a means to promote calm. It also prepared the mind for demanding tasks, such as an inquisition or the evaluation of an enemy.

The shuttle was a standard lawless craft, stripped of insignia but probably well used before the Bercali acquired it. The controls had the burnished look that only developed after spans of wear. A thick, knotted hide covered the padded surfaces.

Roake is decidedly not standard, concluded Jase with grudging appreciation for the magnificence of the man's form and bearing. A Bercali rope-vest left bare large patches of Roake's back, corded with muscles that would have indicated the most exceptional strength in a Soli. Roake's head had a set of slight, parallel ridges that Soli lacked, but the short, black hair nearly covered that difference. *Only an attentive Soli*, thought Jase, *or a keenly observant alien would notice the differences in structural patterns*.

Despite the obvious similarities to the Soli physique, Jase could not categorize Roake's species immediately.

Concentrated effort would bring less common species'
traits to the foreground of Sesserda awareness, but the
inability to fit Roake to a familiar pattern perturbed Jase.
Jase had encountered representatives of a wide variety
of civilizations. However, the most informative aspect of
Roake (to Jase's mind) did not involve a racial characteristic. To Jase, Roake's most striking features were his
eyes: a golden hue underlay a bright iridescence that Jase
knew exceptionally well from his own reflection.

"Where are we headed?" asked Jase quietly.

"To a planet called Stromvi. It's the closest port."

Roake conceals his reasons for selecting Stromvi, observed Jase, his inquisitor's training alerted by signs of
deception. *I wonder why he bothers to lie to me?* "Are
you familiar with Stromvi?"

"Are you?" snapped Roake.

"We have a passing acquaintance."

"Good."

Since any immediate process of inquisition seemed
likely to antagonize Roake, Jase relaxed into his berth
and closed his eyes to the point of apparent sleep. He
tried to dispel the lingering disquiet within him, but he
could feel the biding anger, cold and bitter in a corner
of his mind. The soothing of this wound would take time.
Roake pushed me, but I made the choice to kill.

Jase frowned at Roake's stark profile and the edge of
the iridescent eyes. Every member of the Consortium
could obtain the diluted relanine mixture that was used
to manufacture adaptation fluid, but the carefully measured doses of adaptation fluid did not contain enough
relanine to sustain full addiction. Even if the legal preparations were hoarded for spans, the quantity of inert in-
gredients, inseparable from the relanine they carried,
would outweigh the addict before addictive levels could
be reached.

The Calongi maintained strict control over the distribution of the pure relanine. Roake was certainly not a recipient of such dubious treasure. The only true relanine
originated in Calongi blood, processed to impersonal purity under direct Calongi supervision. Even in the improbable event of a Calongi's capture, the pure relanine
could not be extracted involuntarily. A Calongi could not
be rendered unconscious short of death, and a conscious

Calongi could alter his blood to make it useless. Death contaminated the Calongi blood immediately.

Weaker relanine variants could be obtained from a few plants of Calongi origin. Anyone with a large streak of recklessness and a willingness to pay extravagantly could acquire illegal concoctions of relanine's essential oils from select Cuui merchants, but few survived that fluid's use for more than five spans. Other sources unquestionably existed, but Jase doubted that their products were any more reliable than the Cuui's.

"The port on Stromvi may be occupied by friends of the Bercali," murmured Jase.

"You came from the Stromvi port?" asked Roake, and he looked directly at Jase for the first time. Jase opened his eyes fully and stared without blinking. Roake frowned.

"My arrival surprised you because you didn't expect the poison to spare anyone except yourself," mused Jase softly. "Even then, you considered my survival anomalous. You intended that I should die with your 'other enemies' when I threw the final capsule, because inhalation of such potent gaseous chemical fire is nearly always lethal."

"You've been adapted for survival," muttered Roake. "How?"

"The adaptive gifts of relanine, obviously."

"From whom?"

"A friend."

"Calongi?"

Jase shrugged, but he made a mental note of the rapidity of Roake's conclusion. "Relanine is obviously the reason that you and I survived when the other prisoners died. You should have realized immediately that I was an addict—like you."

Roake returned his attention to the shuttle's controls. "Yes," he admitted finally, "I should have given the matter more thought. Your survival is an unexpected factor, Soli."

"What is your species, Roake?"

A subtle straightening of posture betrayed excessive pride, but Roake responded without emotion, "I am Essenji."

Jase raised his dark brows, as regimen-embedded memories surfaced in a rush of information regarding the rare Essenji. "Consortium data banks record your people as effectively extinct—almost completely absorbed back into the Soli genetic pool from which you originally mutated."

"What other misinformation does your Consortium data bank contain about Essenji?" demanded Roake with unabashed arrogance.

"I cannot seem to recall anything pertinent," replied Jase evenly, though the brief, violent Essenji history paraded itself disquietingly in his head.

"A convenient memory lapse?" asked Roake with the disbelief of the chronic deceiver.

"The Consortium contains thousands of extant species, and the species' variants number in the millions. You should be impressed that I recognize the name 'Essenji' at all."

"Impressed by Bercali prison-dung?" sneered Roake.

"You were their honored guest, no doubt," observed Jase dryly.

When he sensed Roake's anger seethe anew, Jase called himself a fool in several exotic languages. *Where is your much-lauded tact today, Sleide? Still reeling from a surfeit of unexplained circumstances and a relanine-high, I suppose. I never expected an inquisition of the troubled, troubling Miss Darcy to lead me into this barrage of madness, even if she did inherit more than an unacknowledged name from her notorious great-grandmother. . . .*

"Sorry, Roake. Be patient with an ignorant Soli, please, and educate him about the mythical Essenji."

"I shall refresh your memory, Soli, since it functions so erratically. We Essenji are much stronger and more cunning than our weak Soli ancestors. We are intensely passionate—and we do not cringe from violence, like you. We have many gifts that lesser races do not understand but often covet. I am the most dangerous being that you have ever met, Soli."

"Thank you for the warning," answered Jase very solemnly. He congratulated himself for resisting any comment about the obvious dearth of humility as an Essenji asset. "What makes you so exceptionally dangerous?"

"Freedom from petty laws, inquisitive Soli."

"My name is Sleide."

"You ask too many questions, Sleide."

"Insatiable curiosity."

"It is an irritating habit, which you should attempt to cure immediately."

"The planet of Stromvi has been experiencing some trouble lately. It's not an ideal destination for a stolen escape shuttle."

"Bercali could not hold me. Bercali *friends* cannot conquer me."

"And I've heard people call the Calongi immodest," murmured Jase.

* * *

Omi settled into his ship berth with great dignity. "May I provide any increase in your comfort, Master Omi?" asked the Teurai navigator with solicitous concern.

Omi flicked the short tendrils above his eye ridge in a polite acknowledgment of the Teurai's respectful behavior, but he answered aloud, unsure of the young Teurai's sophistication, "You have provided well. I am content."

The Teurai bowed, an elegant motion from such an ungainly, ursine figure, and Omi observed that the young Teurai would be beautiful in its aquatic breeding phase. The rough, gray-furred hide had already begun to loosen, contributing to the current impression of clumsiness, but Omi perceived the slim, graceful form that would emerge, shining with a brilliant rainbow of color. The Teurai had enhanced the promise of its approaching femininity with a light salt scent. Omi nodded appreciatively for the artistry of the race.

"I regret that my journey has delayed your sea stay," remarked Omi.

The wide, green Teurai eyeband registered startlement, but the navigator replied promptly, "When a navigator pair chooses to mate, sacrifices must occur. We chose with knowledge."

"Gifted offspring will reward your sacrifice."

"This is our great hope."

"The promise lies within you both. I have perceived it."

The Teurai bowed again, and the gesture reflected a deep respect for Calongi judgment. Omi perceived the excited emotions that the Teurai tried to contain. The long, narrow Teurai snout twitched. The folds of skin above the eyeband flexed. The sea stay must have been imminent for the Teurai's emotions to be so sensitive. "My thanks to you, Honored Master. Your encouragement gives me strength, which I shall share joyfully with my husband."

Omi nodded regally, and the Teurai retreated from the passenger chamber. Omi contemplated the surge of hope that he had sensed in the Teurai, and he felt satisfaction. He enjoyed his skills most poignantly when he could provide pleasure to such youths.

On contemplating the youth of the Teurai, Omi recognized that he had allowed personal perspective to mislead his time-sense. He scolded himself for the inaccuracy of thought. The Teurai navigator pair had ranked among the finest navigators in the Consortium for many spans. The soon-to-be-male had even bred in a previous cycle.

Ukitan had certainly exerted his renowned skill of influence to draft the Teurai from the brink of their sea stay. These Teurai were mature members of their species and undoubtedly more experienced in space flight than their Calongi passenger. Omi had never relished travel of any extended variety. He nearly always confined his performances to a few, highly civilized planets. A particularly regretted exception had placed him in proximity to the planet of Arnod Conaty's murder.

Respect the Teurai skills, said Omi to himself in a litany of discipline. *Innocence does not indicate ignorance, nor does it imply lack of intelligence or civilized advancement. Innocence comes first and last, at beginning and end of the journey. Innocence may thrive in the ancient's wisdom as in the infant's purity.*

Having satisfied his inner need for balanced judgment in regard to the Teurai, Omi observed that he felt no great improvement in peace of spirit. He would have scowled if the Calongi physique had permitted such a contortion of facial muscles, but the Calongi had bred themselves too carefully toward a perpetual aspect of calm detachment. The lesser member-species required the reassurance of that calmly superior Calongi appearance in order to solidify their confidence in Calongi justice, but Omi occasionally found himself wishing for the freedom of his ancestors to react openly and instinctively.

I am unsettled, Omi informed himself, *because I do not enjoy dealing with Soli, and I do not appreciate Ukitan's efforts to correct that bias via confrontation.* Having acknowledged his unworthy emotions, Omi felt very slightly better, and he decided to dredge his full reactions into conscious viewing, however painfully humbling the process might prove.

My unsatisfactory inquisition of Victoria Mirelle aggravated my innate distaste for her conceited, self-indulgent species. A lesser being, especially of a race as prone to destruction as the Soli, ought not to control that much unconscious power over the external sensory signals. Her existence disturbs my tranquillity, and I do not wish to encounter her again. Ukitan has recognized her adverse effect on my ability to judge Level VI beings impartially, and he has acted to correct my flaw. I sought him after the unpleasant inquisition specifically because of his wisdom in such matters, and I must not resent his teachings. His justice is true.

"Many thanks to you, Ukitan-lai, for guiding me to the course of correction," murmured Omi, but his gracious words ended in a rueful whistling. *Imagine authorizing a Soli male as inquisitor of Mirelle's legatee! Ukitan judged less clearly in that issue. Ukitan-lai requires a clarification of perception in the matter of Jase Sleide.*

Acceptance of a Soli as a Sesserda adept does not negate the essential nature of the Soli. By strict Sesserda wisdom, mastery of the highest mysteries entails the fulfillment of species' essence in equal balance with the individual achievement. Ukitan must accept his student as Soli, both for the sake of truth and for the sake of the student himself.

Satisfied with his analysis of Ukitan's weakness, Omi relaxed that portion of his brain. He continued to digest the recorded information regarding the planet Stromvi, as the data implant progressed within his second lobe. A similar implant provided his fourteenth lobe with a detailed level of instruction regarding the Stromvi/Deetari system. Other brain lobes pursued standing problems of long interest, recreational studies or enhancement disciplines.

Omi's outer senses acknowledged the initialization of flight mode, and he began a selective shutdown of sensitive physical functions in preparation for the flight transition phase. The bypass of anomalous velocity settings always made him queasy. He hoped that the Teurai navigator-pair would not try to impress him with the perfection of their calculations. He would eagerly sacrifice a meter's accuracy in final destination for an easy passage.

*   *   *

Jase watched the violet half-disk of the Stromvi planet grow in the viewing screen. The thin rim of atmosphere enhaloed the world with a gentle glow of life. Roake had piloted the shuttle in silence since the escape, and Jase had not chosen to interrupt the unstable peace. Jase had used the time to sort the surge of facts and apparent facts that had bombarded him since he received Calem's terse request for help. As the truths diverged into numerous skeins of extrapolation, Jase began to wish that he shared the enormous capacity of the Calongi brain for parallel-task analysis.

The Stromvi world had filled the screen when Jase concluded that his concentration needed a rest. He observed Roake's selection of route coordinates and remarked quietly, "You have visited Stromvi before."

"Have I?"

"You have visited Hodge Farm."

"Hodge Farm?" echoed Roake with specious surprise.

"A rather incongruous Soli rose farm in the Ngenga Valley. Do you like roses? The bush of a large blue and white rose had an extraordinary accident at Hodge Farm recently."

"You seem to know the planet well for a man who has only a 'passing acquaintance.' "

"We might both benefit from a bit more openness, Roake. We're in trouble, you and I, and we both know it. I think that each of us holds a part of the picture, but neither of us alone knows enough to survive the schemes of whatever enemy incarcerated us."

"You claim my 'enemy' as your own?" mocked Roake. "Then why were you so reluctant to slay our mutual foes?"

"A quirk of mine: I dislike killing." Jase fingered the dagger that he had taken from the Bercali guard. "Observation: Despite your evident experience as an agent of death, I don't believe that you converted the Bercali ship into a tomb single-handedly. I eliminated no more than six attackers with your encapsulated onslaught, and those six certainly didn't constitute the majority of your opponents. They were simply the few who happened to be placed inconveniently. *You* did not destroy and brutalize the Bercali. You simply anticipated the invasion and took advantage of it because you knew the plans of your own enemy."

"So, the enemy is again mine alone. You are indecisive, Soli. That is a tiresome characteristic."

"Indecision doesn't happen to be one of my flaws. You were imprisoned for a specific purpose," drawled Jase, noting with amusement that Roake's attention had sharpened, "whereas I was merely an incidental inconvenience. The Bercali obviously bound you, rather than throwing you into a common cell with the rest of us rabble, and the distinction would seem to have been personal. The Bercali may have been exercising a general species prejudice, although to Bercali eyes, you and I must appear almost identical. Of course, your endearing personality might have won their special attention."

"You concoct imaginative fables, Soli."

"I could tell you others—about deception and murder, about the intriguing Stromvi legend of death-watch, about sound-shocks and stolen ships, and about a very unpleasant band of Essenji known as the Rea, who were considered formidable space pirates at one time. The Rea began as a formal organization of political anarchists, abandoned Consortium law altogether for more lucrative forms of rebellion, and dwindled suddenly into obscurity. A rumor—among very select circles—recently placed them in the vicinity of Stromvi. Little is known about the present composition of the Rea, except that the war leader is purported to be a relanine addict."

"Personal freedom does not imply anarchy."

Jase continued imperturbably, "A number of philosophical extremists consider relanine the means to releasing the true freedom of the individual spirit, but few of them are so dedicated as to ingest the concentrated fluid and risk the consequences. They work gradually toward their goal of full addiction, I am told, but rarely survive to achieve it."

Roake guided the shuttle into the Stromvi atmosphere before he responded. "Since you advocate an open exchange of knowledge to our mutual benefit, you might begin by explaining your own purpose and allegiance."

"I am a humble member of the Consortium, who apparently chose an unfortunate time to visit old friends on the planet Stromvi." Jase prepared himself to read Roake's reactions carefully, despite the distraction of senses caused by continuing surges of relanine. "Someone had the execrable taste to murder my host shortly after I arrived. I don't suppose you have a fondness for neck-breaking as well as poison?"

"Who was your host?" demanded Roake sharply. With a faint twinge of disappointment, Jase concluded that the oblique accusation had truly startled Roake.

"Birk Hodge."

"You're certain that he's dead," said Roake slowly, as if a burden of impossibilities had just descended upon him.

Am I certain of anything about Hodge Farm at this point? wondered Jase. "I didn't perform an autopsy on the body," he replied dryly, "but I witnessed either Birk's death or an improbably elaborate deception—for a breeder of roses."

Roake scowled, and the twisted cords of his muscles rippled dangerously. "Unfortunate."

"I imagine that Birk would concur with you," murmured Jase. He exerted his full range of trained inquisitor's skills, holding Ukitan's serene image in his mind as a grounding point. The relanine in him, hyperactive from the strain of recent survival, blurred the very senses that it fed, but Jase forced strict bounds upon his rampant, erratic perceptions. He dispelled his private antipathy toward Roake with a blow of a mental dagger that hurt nearly as much as a physical weapon, but he had no time for the gentler methods. Impartially, Jase acquitted Roake of any direct part in Birk's murder.

Jase regretted the judgment as soon as he eased the stern inquisitor's control of mind and emotion. He did not doubt Roake's guilt of manifold crimes, but Sesserda justice forbade him to condemn on the basis of general suppositions. The only specific acts of violence that Jase could actually attribute to Roake involved the escape from the Bercali ship, and Jase's participation negated a valid assessment of that evidence.

Sesserda demanded respect for Roake, whose true circumstances were as yet undisclosed. Jase adjusted his attitude toward Roake with reluctance. He acknowledged that Ukitan would require him to correct a lingering, negative bias.

"The death of Birk Hodge," said Roake with the tone of weighty deliberation, "if it occurred as you claim, increases the urgency of my goal. We must proceed quickly."

"You've become very inclusive suddenly. Do you find me convenient again?"

"Yes," replied Roake without any attempt at dissembling. He glanced at Jase very briefly, but he appeared to finalize his decision in that instant. "I have need of one who is familiar with Hodge Farm. I must locate a certain valuable commodity before it is found by others. You must advise me in the search."

"I must advise you?" laughed Jase, genuinely amused by Roake's arrogance. "Are you appealing to my honor—or possibly claiming a friendship-debt? Our long, devoted relationship seems to have eluded my recollection."

"The valuable commodity," said Roake crisply, "includes a full harvest of unprocessed relaweed."

"Raw seeds?" asked Jase in a sober whisper.

"Enough to addict every creature on the planet."

"Or kill them."

Roake shrugged. "Nothing of great value is gained without risk. You must share my understanding of this truth, at least."

"Never judge a man by the color of his eyes."

"You may undermine my fragile respect for you."

"Respect? You astonish me."

"I have allowed you to live, have I not?"

"I appreciate your generosity."

"If I decide that you are merely a fool, addicted by mischance, I may become less generous."

"Who else seeks the relaweed?"

"My brother."

"Sibling rivalry can be so cumbersome. Is he addicted?"

"No. He is young."

"But ambitious."

"He is, as you might say, a dedicated fanatic of the most determined variety. He is Rea."

Jase turned the Bercali dagger in his hands, studying the serpentine pattern of its hilt. "Are you Rea?" asked Jase.

"Not in my brother's current view."

Truth, concluded Jase, but a prickle of instinctive fear crept along his spine. *Did Roake part from Rea company by his own choice or by theirs?* wondered Jase, but he did not voice the question. He did not doubt that Roake would take extreme offense at any suggestion of submission to another's will.

Jase chose his words with care and wielded them with precision. "Was the relaweed grown on Stromvi?"

"Of course," replied Roake scornfully, as if the answer should have been obvious. "The planet's environment is perfectly suitable. My brother intends to establish relaweed as a permanent element of the Stromvi ecology. I intend to see that he fails."

"From your noble concern for the people of Stromvi?"

"Would you consider such concern a sufficient motive?" asked Roake, assessing Jase with open curiosity and obvious self-interest.

Jase smiled faintly, but the prickle of fear had become a certainty. "Uncontrolled growth of relaweed could only be achieved on Stromvi via the introduction of a natural means of pollenization," he mused, observing Roake's unconscious physical affirmations with resigned dread, "such as an appropriate insect population. The planet's entire ecosystem would be disrupted—perhaps disastrously. If the Stromvi resins absorbed any of the natural relanine oils from the weed—a highly probable circumstance—the destruction would be complete, because resin is the life-source of every native Stromvi species, and the raw relanine oil is as ubiquitously lethal as any substance in the known galaxies."

"Lethal, except to those who achieve addiction."

"Uncomfortable, even for an addict," countered Jase.

"Where shall we begin our search," asked Roake complacently, "my loyal ally?"

CHAPTER 30

The field was dead. Every nodule on Nguri's head felt the horrible, unnatural emptiness as a harsh prickle of recrimination. *You let us die*, accused the broken canes and the papery husks of lily leaves and resin stalks, burned by chemical fire.

Nguri lowered his body toward the earth. He scooped lifeless soil into his hand and tasted its barrenness. Even core clay, rigid and hard, held more promise of fruitfulness, more prospect of future nourishment and life. The hollow crusts of insect larva sifted from the particles of dead leaves and blossoms, and Nguri felt a chilling tightness of his resin sacs. *Voracious alien insects, greedy alien plants, foolish alien meddling:* Nguri knew the name of his planet's death-watch now.

Nguri surveyed the ravaged field and hardened his resolve—without despair, without the futile recriminations that came too late, without even anger. The course was set, badly but irrevocably. The disaster must be faced and met. If the fragile beauty of a planet's life could ever be restored, once broken, the process must begin from an honest base. *It will not be the same*, sighed Nguri to himself. *My precious world will never be as perfect as it was before we let the aliens come.*

Nguri turned stiffly, his body feeling aged and leaden. *When the poison has pierced the hide, it cannot be withdrawn. It must be taken into the heart if it is to be endured and survived.*

The means exists. Take the enemy's poison into yourself and make it your own. Nguri lifted his broad head, unconscious of the somber nobility of the pose. *Exterminate the infestation with its own terrible momentum.* Nguri let his head drop back amid the folds of his ridged neck skin. He moved slowly away from the devastation, but he moved with purpose.

*   *   *

Tori reread the port logbook from beginning to end, still dissatisfied with the meager information she had found. She had flagged the most curious log entries with short segments of magi reed. She reviewed the questions again, reserving her conclusions until the end.

At least once a month, Jeffer's broad scrawl had cited unnamed deliveries to Birk Hodge. Tori had handled all the normal Hodge Farm receipts during that time, and she was reasonably sure that none of the dates corresponded to her own records. All of the logbook's notations of standard supply shipments included itemized descriptions that confirmed her recollections.

During six distinct periods of time, the log entries occurred in Ngahi's cramped writing. Jeffer had always been irresponsible, disappearing for millispans without explanation. His last disappearance, however, had transpired three days before death-watch. The logbook contained no indication that he had ever returned.

Ngahi had made the final entries. Only one small supply ship had come from Deetari on the day of Jase's supposed arrival, and it had left the same morning. No specific reference to passengers was made, but a note about readying a hovercraft might well have applied to Jase's personal vehicle. Nothing further had been recorded until that night, and the nocturnal entry was scribbled in the margin of an empty page: *Ngikik claims to have detected our unauthorized visitor again. Deetari cannot confirm.*

Tori rubbed her eyes, resin-sore from too many millispans of entombment beneath the Stromvi surface, and she deactivated the light panel for the night. The resin would gather more thickly in the darkness, but her eyes craved the rest, even if other parts of her body remained too agitated for peaceful sleep. "What visitor?" she whispered into the darkness, then laughed softly. "Probably one of Sylvie's wedding guests, reluctant to be announced as the first arrival."

Sylvie's marriage to Harrow seemed unlikely ever to occur now. *Many thwarted plans, my own among them. . . . I*

*hate this equivocal state of waiting for the fulfillment of a
dreadful Stromvi legend—or for the next turn of fortune's
unpredictable, inexorable wheel. Great-grandmama never allowed external events to dominate her. She created fortunes
and destroyed them, according to her will.*

"But Great-grandmama always knew what she
wanted," sighed Tori. "I only know what I don't want."
She had formed a goal over the past few days, but she
had begun to regret it as soon as she realized its existence: She wanted to leave the southern Stromvi caves.
The caves had ceased to feel like a refuge as soon as
Tori realized that she had no freedom to depart.

The tunnels that she, as a Soli, could negotiate all
seemed to end in perpendicular shafts or in suffocating
holes of crumbling humus. She had seen no tunnelers.
The Stromvi maintained their death-watch faithfully and
stoically, and they had no advice to offer her. When she
requested information on reaching the surface, the
Stromvi replied only with the click sequence of death-
watch, and they refused to pursue the subject further.

None of the Stromvi seemed to mourn Ngoi now, and
no one had mentioned retrieving his body. Such behavior
toward the Stromvi dead was unprecedented and lent unnerving credence to Jase's observations about the means
of Ngoi's death. Ngeta and Tori's other Stromvi friends
scarcely acknowledged her. They always seemed legiti-
mately busy, but Tori sensed that they felt awkward in
her presence. A Soli had no proper role in death-watch.

Except for Nguri, no one would discuss with her the
incidents surrounding death-watch, and Nguri behaved
more oddly than anyone. He asked questions of apparent
irrelevance regarding Birk and Jase, and the most trivial
answers preoccupied him disproportionately. Uneasily
comparing Nguri's questions to an inquisitor's probes for
Sesserda Truth, Tori had even found herself wondering
if the Stromvi people had conspired toward the eradication of Birk Hodge's influence.

Birk had died in a second-floor room that no Stromvi
could have reached or exited quickly. Ngoi had died by
the power of Stromvi teeth: Ngoi's own, according to
Jase. An elusive something—Rillessa's unknown
enemy?—had killed or captured Jase. Sylvie, Calem,
Gisa, and Thalia, as well as surly, slovenly Jeffer and

the other port workers, had disappeared. Someone cried death-watch, and a civilized people reverted to their most primitive cultural habits.

Tori had not confronted Nguri with her concerns about remaining in the caverns. If Nguri replied as uselessly as the rest of his people, she knew that she would feel more frighteningly alone than ever. Even if he replied reasonably, she could only embarass herself by admitting that she did not know where she wanted to go. She valued Nguri's opinion too much to confess her irrational anxiety to escape.

"Escape is your answer to everything," she muttered to herself, "and it hasn't served you well yet."

She tried to tell herself that this occasion differed from her past mistakes. A rising sense of claustrophobia had begun to outweigh sterner reasoning, making her feel that she had been incarcerated with Rillessa in a ward for the mentally deficient. Tori credited the Stromvi with too much intelligence for enacting such a travesty of judgment, but she had less confidence in the purity of their present motives. Stromvi respected Consortium law, but Stromvi lived on the outermost fringes of the Consortium in more than a spatial sense. Birk Hodge, with his questionable ethics, had not settled on Stromvi strictly because of its horticultural provender.

Nguri promised continually to give his attention to the matters that concerned Tori, but he always found a valid excuse for procrastinating. His visits had become increasingly brief with each passing day. The Stromvi people in general appeared entirely content to stay in their deep caverns.

Courage was not considered a strong racial trait among the Stromvi. Still, Tori expected more from them. She esteemed Nguri particularly and knew that he was capable of great courage, as well as great ingenuity, in the matters that he valued.

Tori had thought she understood Nguri's values, but she had begun to appreciate that the scope of differences between Stromvi and Soli did not end with appearance. In his gentle and congenial fashion, Nguri had imprisoned her. Tori did not know why, but she did not intend to accept his decision meekly.

Tori rolled over on her cot and pressed her forehead

against the cool clay of the wall. "Nguri is right. It was inexcusably careless of me to have lost my expert on alien relations," she murmured, "even if he was an inquisitor."

However, ignorance of alien thought processes could help as well as hinder. Nguri also judged from a limited perspective, or he would have realized that Tori would rebel, if only from a Soli instinct against the oppression of too much subterranean living. As long as she did not confront him openly, Nguri allowed her the illusion of companionship.

He expects me to submit publicly, like Ngeta, or to avoid him altogether, like Ngina. He expects me to react like a Stromvi female. I suppose I have learned more sympathy for Ngina recently: Nguri has begun to intimidate me.

"Poor Ngina-li," whispered Tori, contemplating the young Stromvi speculatively, "you have too much of your father's intelligence not to respect him, but too much of his independence to be able to obey him easily." She had not seen Ngina in the caverns, but she had made no specific effort to seek the Stromvi girl.

If Nguri *had* positioned the walls of Tori's gentle prison, few Stromvi would defy him. Ngina, however, often argued against her father's "unreasonable" restrictions and might well consider the prospect of helping Tori a delightful exercise. On the other hand, death-watch was hardly a suitable occasion for prank-playing. Tori's persuasive force might well require a twisting of logic and a substantial dose of lies. Tori grimaced, wishing that she were less confident of her own ability to deceive Ngina into conspiracy.

In the darkness, Tori pressed her hands against her aching eyes. The prospect of abusing Ngina's trust sickened Tori, but the idea of remaining dependent on *anybody*—Nguri or Birk or Uncle Per—grated to the point of terror. Tori still dreaded a crimson-streaked shadow, but that fear had receded into a memory in the last few days. If she fought or fled or faced her unknown enemy, she wanted to make the choice for herself.

Tori thought of Great-grandmama Mirelle and tried to make her emotions as steely as that memory. Ngina would recover and become stronger from the lesson Tori taught. Guilt served no purpose except to hinder. After all, Stromvi had betrayed Tori first.

"That argument, Victoria, would give your inquisitor friend the shivers." Tori smiled ruefully to herself, though the tears that cleansed her eyes required no conscious prompting. She stretched to the length of the cot, forcing herself to savor a revived sense of freedom, refusing to ponder the ramifications of her decision. If Ngina could be found in this Stromvi maze of dead-end tunnels and layered chambers, Tori would regain her liberty—to do what, she did not know, but she would not let uncertainty stop her.

* * *

Ngina sat alone in one of the recovery caves. She had claimed to be ill, and her mother had pretended to believe her. Ngina had requested seclusion because she had not yet summoned the courage to go to her father. She had expected him to summon her. She had expected other visitors, as well. No one had come. No one but her mother seemed to remember her, which relieved Ngina even as it made her feel more alone.

Ngina needed advice, a commodity that she had always been loath to request, but she feared to admit the extent of what she had done already. She could not bring herself to tell her mother because Ngina imagined that the magnitude of her folly would turn even her mother's patience to anger. In silence, Ngina could pretend—for the moment—that she had not found Ngoi, that she had not learned of Ngoi's secret, that she had not cried deathwatch. . . . Ngina sat, feeling sorry for herself, trying not to think beyond the moment, because if she thought at all, she feared that the impact of Ngoi's horrible death would become unbearable.

How can such pain exist? she wondered, her mind sliding unwillingly into the shadowed halls of mourning. She had known Ngoi all her life. She had taken his slightly solemn presence for granted. Even when his inconsistent form of leadership faltered and annoyed her, she had not considered a world without him among the elders.

Ngoi was a fixture, like her honored parents, and his loss made her dearer family seem vulnerable. *If I can ache so deeply for Ngoi's death*, concluded Ngina, *I shall surely die of grief if ever I lose my honored mother or my esteemed father.* Ngina's thoughts pursued an extravagant course of personal dejection, which acknowledged only dimly that death had established a very real and solid presence on gentle Stromvi.

When Ngina heard a woman's voice ask for permission to enter, Ngina clicked affirmative without even trying to identify the visitor. Tori Darcy entered Ngina's room, pressing through the lacy veil of resin roots, and Ngina's brief spurt of eagerness became tainted by alarm. She had not considered the Soli reaction to death-watch. She had not considered Mister Birk's reaction.

Ngina envisioned a torture of questions and punishments from Mister Birk, and she imagined Tori as his emissary. After all, Tori was Mister Birk's assistant— or maybe something more, if Ngetil's wicked ideas were correct.

Oh, dear, moaned Ngina to herself with an added dose of guilt, *I have made Ngoi's trouble that much worse.* She greeted Tori with a click of mournful anticipation.

"You don't care for this vigil of doom?" asked Tori with a smile of sad sympathy.

Ngina clicked a troubled negative, wanting the distraction from her solitude but mildly resentful of the intrusion on her grief. "Why are you here, Miss Tori?"

"Your mother said that you haven't been feeling well, and I thought you might like a visitor."

"But why are you here in the southern caverns at all?"

Tori did not respond immediately, and Ngina decided that the Soli woman must be feeling ill from too much resin. *Too much resin*: It was a difficult concept for Ngina to grasp, and she derived a little forlorn pride from her clever deduction about Tori.

"I needed to talk to your father," answered Tori at last. "I hope I'm not tiring you, Ngina-li."

"No. I'm not feeling that bad." Ngina did not want to be questioned, but she did not want to be left alone again either.

"When I'm troubled, sometimes I feel better if I walk. Would you like to walk with me for a little while?"

"I suppose," answered Ngina hesitantly. It *would* be pleasant to leave this little room, and no one would be likely to stop Ngina in Tori Darcy's company.

Tori smiled warmly. "Perhaps we could walk toward

the exit tunnel, in case I develop a sudden craving for the outside air."

Ngina shrugged. One direction was as good as another. Her honored father seldom entered this part of the cave network. Ngina raised her lithe torso and stretched her strong hind legs. She had crouched too long in her somber study, and her firm, young muscles had tightened and grown cold.

Tori stood back to let Ngina lead the way through the narrow entry tunnel of the recovery cave. When they reached the wider passage, Tori walked at Ngina's side, but Tori paused periodically to balance herself against the tunnel walls. "Despite all my practice, resin still makes me clumsy," admitted Tori with a laugh. The scent of Tori Darcy's mood seemed strange to Ngina, but Ngina felt too encumbered by her own burdens to question Tori in such personal fashion.

"How did you manage the entry slope?" asked Ngina, finding Soli restrictions as bizarre and inconsistent as the diversity of Soli moods.

"I had some help."

"Of course," answered Ngina mechanically.

Ngina guided Tori into one of the less frequented tunnels. *Miss Tori will not mind the longer route*, reasoned Ngina with sardonic candor, *for Soli have no sense of direction in the caverns*. Somewhat to Ngina's surprise, the exercise of walking had already made her feel a little less gloomy. She was reluctant to let Tori leave, for fear that the full weight of depression would redescend.

"I'm glad you came to visit me, Miss Tori," admitted Ngina with unaccustomed shyness. "I think I was needing a friend."

The troubling scent of the Soli woman's mood intensified. "I'm glad I could help," answered Tori. Ngina wondered why Miss Tori's smile seemed strained.

*   *   *

Sylvie choked on the dusty air of the ship. Much as she had always hated Stromvi, her body still craved its moistly resinous atmosphere. She always suffered the illness of adaptation poorly, for she resented the cause. If her father had only settled on some civilized Soli world, her life would have been much easier. Stromvi was the only serious point of contention between Sylvie and her father—except for the Squire, of course, but that argument had staled long ago.

Sylvie paced the small, closed cell, where she had spent—how many?—days. The conditions of the cell were fully adequate for humane life sustenance, but Sylvie demanded rather more of her environment than basic survival. She had not seen anyone. She had not heard a voice or felt another being's touch. She wished she could remember why she had entered this horrible isolation cell. She did not recall any illness that might have warranted such a severe form of hospitalization. The scabs on her arms and legs were inexplicable to her, but they did not seem to indicate severe injuries.

Sylvie kept dreaming about Rillessa frantically waving a flaming torch and hurling herself ferociously against a horde of faceless foes. Sylvie dismissed the image as unbearably ridiculous, but it recurred with annoying persistence. None of the dreams included Calem, who ought to have stood at his desperate wife's side, but Harrow was there. Harrow seemed to be standing, too sophisticated to show concern, at the burning center of the opposing army.

Where was Harrow, now, when his Sylvie most needed him? Not that Sylvie minded a postponement of the wedding. She would have been glad if Daddy had decided to cancel the entire abominable scheme. Harrow's initial charms had paled.

"Why did I let Daddy stop me from marrying the Squire when I had the chance? No," muttered Sylvie, "that's unfair to Daddy. I stopped myself. I was a fool." Sylvie swirled toward the cell's small mirror and grimaced at her tired reflection.

*　　*　　*

"Tending that Soli discourages me," sighed Perekah, a fleshless woman who had once been a prized Rea clan breeder. Five of Akras' finest warriors were Perekah's issue, and the youngest was Tagran's child as well. "If she is indeed the daughter of Birkaj, he has destroyed all Essenji spirit in her."

"She's to be released soon," answered Tagran.

"Into Ares' care? In his present mood, he might kill her for stepping on his shadow. She is not a worthy foe, and she is our own kin. Why must we torment her? Birkaj has defeated her already."

"The clan leader ordered us to detain her," replied Tagran, for he would not voice his personal misgivings. "We do not need to know the clan leader's reasons."

"But you and I do know her reasons, Tagran, because we remember. Akras hates this daughter—and the son, who is equally defeated—because Birkaj gave them life by a Soli woman. How can we continue to serve Akras' jealous anger?"

"Akras is clan leader," snapped Tagran. "Each of us has vowed to serve her, and no honorable Rea would break such an oath."

"I have been loyal for a lifetime," mumbled Perekah. "When my brothers left the clan, I derided them for their dishonor. I wish now that I could see them again and retract my bitter, wounding words." Tagran frowned, for Perekah and her brothers were his own close cousins. Perekah pressed her moment of advantage: "Akras is leading us to destruction, Tagran. She condemns her own son as traitor, and you and I both know that his only clan-crime is his birthright!"

"Brother-feuds produce many accusations," answered Tagran, dismissing the matter with a shake of his head. "The words are meaningless. Strength measures the final victor."

"And you believe that Ares could ever best Roake without the clan leader's direct sanction? Ares is like his father, Zagare: A capable subordinate but a poor leader."

At this remark, Tagran nodded reluctantly. "Birkaj would have made a stronger war leader."

"*You* made a better war leader than Zagare," grumbled Perekah, "even if Akras never had enough wisdom to grant you official clan-status." Tagran stiffened because resentment of his long, equivocal rank could be tapped too easily, and such feelings were dishonorable. "Zagare led the Rea to the most bitter defeat of our history, and Ares will complete the deathblow to us. *This* is what our clan leader offers us. Not victory. Not honorable vengeance. Self-destruction, like the scarring of her face in a pattern that represents a final, futile vow and not the proud retaliation of Rea strength."

"Our clan leader has never dishonored us. We *must not* dishonor her." Tagran clenched his fist around the hilt of his clan-knife. He might question Akras' judgment privately, but he became protective when he heard such outright criticism. Even Ares' uncomfortable speculations had maintained some level of respect. "*Her* strength, *her* determination enabled the clan to survive after the loss of the home vessel, when most of our warriors were dead, dying, or injured to the point of helplessness. *You* remember, Perekah. Your lungs burned with the contamination, until Akras provided enough adaptation fluid to heal you. She bought the Cuui's fluid with her clan-jewels, her father's weapons, and her own service, and she has never failed to maintain our supply of such fluid, which gives us freedom."

"The fluid's quality is poor enough for the price we pay," muttered Perekah. "Raskannen provided better."

"We were more prosperous then, but we have nearly regained our status as a recognized force among the independents. Do you realize how few independents are able to obtain adaptation fluid of any sort? The three suppliers can charge nearly as much as they please."

"Only two Cuui and a Soli have ever managed to conceal enough relaweed crops from the Consortium to produce fluid," agreed Perekah dryly, "and we are their servants—we, who should serve no one but Essenji. Like our clan leader, you have forgotten what Rea honor means."

Tagran's eyes narrowed with anger. "You have forgotten respect. When the clan leader selected Harrow Febro and began to mold him, you predicted her failure to make use of him. You said he was too weak to be able to infiltrate Per Walis' service. But he served the clan leader's purpose."

"He *is* weak. He serves our clan leader only out of cowardice, and he will serve anyone who threatens him. He thinks himself clever and valued because he has been entrusted with a single crop of relaweed, but Per Walis expends such small crops to search for possible competitors—like us. Harrow Febro disgusts me. He reached his position in Per Walis' organization only because of a well-placed cousin and a well-known eagerness to sell anything to anyone."

"His cousin and his weaknesses were the reasons the clan leader chose him."

"I do not dispute Akras' ability to select her tools capably," retorted Perekah. "But *her* tools serve *her* purposes."

"You doubt her only because she does not share her reasoning with you. She has never failed us."

"Tagran, where are we headed? Per Walis must know that Febro is serving dual masters, and he surely knows where the relaweed was planted. By now, Walis knows where to find us and would have every mercenary in this galaxy hunting us, except the relaweed was planted on a *Consortium* world, and Walis does not need to destroy us. By our clan leader's command, we attacked the Stromvi port, we caused the deaths of *Consortium* members, and we are jeopardizing others. The Consortium does not tolerate such actions. Our clan leader knows this as well as Per Walis, but *she* does not care."

"We shall leave Consortium space for a time," answered Tagran, "and with the home vessel restored to us, we shall be strong enough to defeat Per Walis' mercenaries. There will be *four* sources of adaptation fluid outside the Calongi's control."

"Is that what you truly believe?" asked Perekah, her expression softening very slightly, for she admired loyalty. "Akras has used your devotion, Tagran, to retain her other warriors. She has used Roake's skills, honing them with too much relanine, but I think he began to see too clearly, and Akras turned Ares against him."

"Roake has always been the son she wanted," sighed Tagran, conceding only a fragment of his private doubts, "but she only worked to earn Ares' loyalty."

"She abuses even Ares now. Akras cares nothing about the future, except as a pretense that helps her fulfill her death-vow. She wants her vengeance against Birkaj, not because he nearly destroyed his clan, but because she loved him and he betrayed *her*. Can't you see what must happen to the clan? Even if the Consortium does not steal our freedom, we cannot survive. Per Walis—and his Cuui counterparts—cannot afford to tolerate even a hint of competition for the relaweed trade, and we have no hope of defeating so many powerful enemies. Birkaj himself is Per Walis' ally, and even Birkaj's death will cause trouble for the clan."

"Would you let Birkaj go unpunished?" asked Tagran. It was a question that had long troubled him.

"I would have slain him outright thirty spans ago, when he was merely another wounded refugee—like us— trying to use Rea knowledge of smuggling routes and smuggling bases to establish a new life for himself. Instead of concealing the clan's survival from him, I would have made sure he learned quickly of his failure to destroy us."

"Patient vengeance is more complete and more appropriate to the magnitude of Birkaj's crimes. His death and the resources that he bequeaths will restore Rea greatness. The clan leader understands honor." Tagran finished grimly, "Such honor must be respected."

Perekah raised her head proudly. She had never possessed Akras' beauty, but she was Essenji, and age had not coarsened her features or dulled her striking coloring. "One of my daughters died in that fiasco of an attack on Hodge Farm because our clan leader forbade the use of any weapon of decent range and power. After all the spans of surveillance, our clan leader surely knew that Birkaj had shielded his house from standard energy beams. But she intended only to make Birkaj suffer in anticipation of the coming vengeance. She wants to kill Birkaj *personally*, and so my daughter has died at the hand of a pitiful, frightened Soli woman with a needle-gun. Explain this honor to me, Tagran. I no longer seem able to comprehend it."

"A warrior's death in battle should not be mourned," said Tagran, but he touched the short silver fur on Perekah's shoulder with gentleness.

*   *   *

Nguri opened the panel cautiously, repeatedly peering above, beyond, and behind him. He did not like Soli devices, for he found their design cumbersome, but he understood the use of every tool that Birk had ever imported. Nguri had made a point of understanding, as he had made a point of pretending disinterest. He had respected Birk Hodge and valued Birk's eagerness to market Stromvi creations, but he had never completely trusted anyone not born of Stromvi.

Nguri had his own priorities and his own concept of rightness. If the justice of the Calongi coincided with Nguri's notions, that was well and good. If not. . . . Nguri shrugged. Calongi did not know all. Calongi did not know Stromvi.

The panel creaked as Nguri freed it, for Stromvi humidity had corroded the old metal. The crate had lain untouched in the hidden cellar beneath Hodge's Folly since that monstrous building's construction, but Nguri had not forgotten. Nguri forgot nothing that the soil of his world encompassed as its own.

Birk had never adequately comprehended the inverted logic of Stromvi's subterranean perspective: Stromvi people concealed their secrets from each other by disinterment, not by burial. Nguri grinned ferociously, observing that the contents of Birk's guarded treasure remained untarnished by the years.

Bending to inspect his prize, Nguri felt the ache of age, and he clicked a quiet plaint. The hard burrowing through root-bound tunnels beneath the foundation of Hodge's Folly had aggravated the inflammation of joints too arduously abused in the past few days. A sharper pain ran the length of his torso, building to a throbbing tension beneath the neck ridge.

For a panicky moment, Nguri wondered if he had overtaxed his weary body. He dared not summon help. He dared not share Birk's secret prematurely—better that it remained forgotten.

The tightness in his resin sacs eased, and Nguri moved with slow care to loosen the stiffened muscles. He would not join the final death-watch yet, but he felt the press of a new urgency. If time ended too soon for him, it might end too soon for all his world. Nguri bent grimly to his task.

PART III

Scythe of Conspiracy

CHAPTER 31

Roake landed the shuttle at Stromvi's single port, undeterred by the port's shroud of silence. The port's traffic
monitor confirmed the location codes only passively, re-
flecting the shuttle's own signals in the appropriate pattern. The aberrant arrival conditions did not appear to
concern Roake; nor did Jase's suggestion to employ a
cautious approach. The descent was abrupt, the landing
rough though solid. Jase forbore to comment on the unnecessary discomforts incurred by Roake's piloting, the
style of which seemed disturbingly consistent with the
Essenji's character.

Roake freed himself from the safety bonds as if the
confinement had seared his skin, and he burst through
the shuttle's outer doors as soon as the panels parted to
free him. Jase reacted more warily, still doubtful of the
port's status as a sanctuary. Roake's resolute confidence
did not measurably allay Jase's suspicions.

The milky sun of Stromvi afternoon beat through the
doorway, lighting the ship's smeared and sullied floor,
displaying each stain and patch as badge of a grim history. Roake's bleak shadow raced across the entry sill
and vanished. Jase listened, feeling the stillness reach
through the core of him. Roake moved, and Jase traced
the Essenji's course and every gesture by the inner
senses, the senses that relanine both honed and
tormented.

Jase felt Roake pause and turn his head back toward
the ship. Before Roake could speak, Jase rose and went
to stand in the sunlit doorway. After the chill of the
dying Bercali ship—an atmosphere that the purloined
shuttle had nearly matched—the warmth of Stromvi
poured into Jase, his bones and sinew welcoming the
healing comfort with an eagerness to respond. The sud-

den flow of energy, its path eased by elevated levels of relanine, made Jase feel nearly as rash and confident as the Essenji.

"No," remarked Jase amiably, "I didn't take advantage of your momentary distraction." Jase enjoyed the brief flash of Roake's reaction. The pleasure of disconcerting by anticipation always amused Jase more than his Calongi masters considered proper. Ukitan had often advised him to curb such impulses, for Sesserda discouraged actions that might seem unduly uncanny or alarming to the uninformed. "You forgot about me for a moment, Roake," chided Jase airily. "If I were less or more than I am, your lapse could have cost you a Cuui's hive-price." Jase felt sure that Roake had little, if any, appreciation of Sesserda skills. He suspected that Roake had rarely dealt with anyone whose senses exceeded even the erratic enhancements that relanine imparted to an untrained addict.

Roake glowered. The potent Stromvi sunlight clearly pained him, but acknowledgment of Jase's words inflicted a deeper wound to his pride. "You are an easily forgettable entity, Soli."

Jase hopped from the shuttle to the spongy surface of the landing field. "Your former friends appear to have left the port to us." The silver disk ships had gone, and the landing field looked forbiddingly barren.

"A wise man never lingers openly in his enemy's house," said Roake. His eyes had narrowed in suspicion. "I gave you the opportunity to escape me. You did not use the gift well." Already, the Stromvi sun had brought a flush to the Essenji's ivory skin, but Roake did not flinch from the burning. He stood boldly in the open light, declining any shade of the shuttle or the nearby hangars.

"Your generosity honors me," replied Jase wryly, "if indeed it was a sincere offering. As you noted, however, I do have an interest in preserving Stromvi from the very dubious blisses of relanine."

Roake nodded once. "I require a smaller craft for the journey to your Hodge Farm. Direct me to the appropriate hangar."

"Hangar four is my personal favorite." Roake had landed at the end of the port opposite the control building and hangar four. Jase waved toward the distant building with a bent hand, wondering if Roake appreciated the gesture's ambiguity. The bent hand meant concession to a Cuui but implied a warning on Escolar, where Jase had spent most of his childhood. "Delightful afternoon for a stroll, isn't it?" added Jase. "I love a brisk walk after exterminating all life from a Bercali prison barge."

"You are either mad," commented Roake with a scowl, "or very cunning."

"Both traits—in excess—make relanine addicts, and relanine often aggravates both traits."

Roake gestured sharply with the Bercali pistol for Jase to lead. Jase glanced at the open shuttle they were abandoning. "What of your cargo?" asked Jase mildly.

"I shall return for it, when I have chosen my next ship. In the meantime, let the unwary try to steal from me." The crests of Roake's skull seemed to firm in anger, and a vein pulsed vividly at his shorn temple.

Jase shrugged. The Stromvi air might sweeten the shuttle's stale interior, and the cost in corrosion could not mar it much more greatly than the abuses of its previous owners. Jase began to stride confidently across the field.

He exerted much more care of movement than he allowed Roake to observe, for he did not trust the unseen enemy, he did not trust Roake, and he did not trust a silent Stromvi world. The resin-thick air, the misty rose sky, and the even, easy stillness of the violet horizon did not satisfy his restless senses. The energy of the planet itself beat furtively beneath him, and within that earthen realm lay the core of life on Stromvi. The planet did not share the peace of its surface level's heated afternoon.

By the time the two men reached the shade of hangar four, Roake's fair skin had a raw, red crust across the shoulders and the upper back, where the traces of a shaven, silver mane had scarcely begun to regenerate. Jase observed the effect curiously. The rapidity of burning seemed extreme, even for unprotected, nearly albinic skin under Stromvi ultraviolet. The inner force of relanine should have adapted an addict more rapidly, unless an impurity in the addict's fluid was itself accelerating the damage.

Roake did not appear to notice his swelling blisters. He assessed the lines of hovercraft and personal shuttles critically. He ensured openly that Jase did not stray too far from the reach of the Bercali weapon, but his attention was inconstant. When he bypassed the ship that Jase had nearly appropriated with Tori, Jase slowed, and Roake continued his own inspection.

After so many days, Jase expected to learn nothing. His meager discoveries pleased him disproportionately, for success at any civilized endeavor had begun to seem like a forgotten art. The traces of Tori Darcy had nearly faded beyond the perception of his most focused senses, but he could still recognize that she *had* stood here, touched this panel, held this bit of brace. The number of intervening days, though still more than Jase could consciously count, must be fewer than he had feared.

After assuring himself that Roake remained preoccupied, Jase knelt quickly beside the ship's cargo hold. He shifted the cover very slightly, and an intense perception of Tori filled the depths of Sesserda *awareness*. She had hidden here for a protracted time and departed voluntarily. She had escaped the trap that had taken her incautious inquisitor.

Jase firmly pressed the cover back into place, but his fingers lingered on the cold ceramic plates. *If she did escape, where would she have gone, having lost her chance to leave the planet? Back to Hodge Farm, back to the territory she knows? Yes, if she could find the means. That is where I would go.* Jase glanced toward Roake with a mingling of resignation and dark humor. *That is where I am going.*

Jase assumed an idle, impatient pose as Roake looked toward him, but inwardly he savored a faint taste of encouragement. Little enough had gone well since his arrival on Stromvi, and a weight of guilt regarding Tori Darcy still teased him. After all, an inquisitor did carry a special responsibility for his subject of inquisition. If nothing else, Jase owed Tori Darcy a verdict.

*   *   *

Ngina helped Tori climb the steep portions of the long, sloping access. Traction bracelets could not negotiate the slippery growth regions, and no fumbling Soli could sustain a Stromvi's pace through even the driest of resin tunnels. Ngina showed no signs of her reported ill-health, except that she scarcely spoke. Like the planet itself, Ngina seemed to have lost her voice to death-watch.

Tori did not try to pierce Ngina's unusual reticence. The silence suited Tori's intentions, though it made her feel more guilty and foolish. The Stromvi people were her friends and refuge. Having regained them with such difficulty, why was she trying to position them as antagonists?

Because I had forgotten how thoroughly the people and the planet are one, answered Tori's sterner voice, *and I am not a proper part of their whole. In a time of crisis, they do not want me, and they will not protect me.*

"And I've always run when I felt frightened," muttered Tori in cynical self-contempt for her truer motivation.

"Are you frightened, Miss Tori?" asked Ngina sharply, though the young Stromvi had not seemed to be more than peripherally aware of Tori's continued presence beside her.

"I was only thinking aloud," answered Tori quietly, "of another time and place."

Ngina clicked an incomplete pattern, which left Tori wondering what the Stromvi girl had decided not to say. "I think I should go back to my room now."

"Of course," replied Tori, disturbed by the suddenness of Ngina's decision. "I should be getting back, as well. I hope I didn't tire you too much." Tori did not let her uneasiness show in her smile. "I'm afraid I've rather lost my sense of direction with all the twists and turns down here. Could you point me to the exit?"

"It's not far down this tunnel. The passage is quite level and direct. You shouldn't have any trouble managing your way." Ngina clicked a curt farewell, but she did not begin the return journey to her room. She drooped to a position of rest, her long torso flat against the ground, her arms crossed above her head nodules.

"Thank you, Ngina," murmured Tori, troubled by Ngina's despondency and by an unwelcome yearning to help.

While Tori hesitated, Ngina raised her head and gazed at Tori with wide, unhappy eyes. "Have you ever been really afraid, Miss Tori?"

*Great-grandmama would divert such a question with a
laugh and continue on her way, forgetting a troubled
Stromvi adolescent, forgetting any part of Stromvi that did
not aid her own well-being. I have troubles enough of my
own,* argued Tori within herself, but she answered soberly, "Ngina, I'm afraid now—for all of us. I don't understand this 'death-watch,' but I know that it signifies
an end of a time and purpose that I valued."

"That isn't the same at all. That is *shared* fear. That
is selfless fear."

Ngina, innocent child, thought Tori bitterly, *if you
could read my selfish heart, you would despise me!*

"When I feel fear, I cannot think beyond myself," said
Ngina with the surging, rushing force of a desperate confidence. "I can hardly speak to anyone at all, not my
honored mother, not Ngetil or Ngoli or even my most
gentle sister, Ngiada. You never seem to fear anything
or anyone. I have seen you stand against Mister Hodge
and win his greater respect, and even my most honored
father has never intimidated you. How can I become
brave, Miss Tori?"

"By doing what is necessary, despite your fear, and
becoming greater than your limitations." Tori smiled in
rueful memory. "That is something my great-grandmother told me, the only time I met her. I was very
young, but she made an impression. She excelled at making impressions."

"Was she very brave?"

"She was very extraordinary in many respects. I suppose you could call her brave. She certainly achieved
more in her lifetime than anyone ever expected of a Soli
woman of extremely unpromising origin."

"What did she achieve?"

"Infamy, dear Ngina, which is a fearsome burden in
itself." Tori knelt to touch the resin-slick skin of Ngina's
serious face lightly. "You're an honorable daughter of
your people, and I esteem you and the promise of your
youth. You're too filled with life to let an ancient legend
defeat your inner joy."

"I don't fear an ancient legend," whispered Ngina,
"but a horror of the present. Miss Tori, *I* began the
death-watch cry. I cannot tell my father how I have
shamed him with my foolish behavior, but you must tell

Mister Hodge. Miss Tori, Ngoi planted a strange crop in the southern field, and he died for it."

Shock displaced Tori's anxiety to escape. She asked softly, "Do you know who killed him, Ngina-li?"

"No. But someone very dangerous and cruel must have wanted the harvest that Ngoi withheld. Ngoi died horribly, Miss Tori."

"I know. I saw him in the infirmary."

"Will you tell Mister Hodge for me, please? Tell him that I began the death-watch without thinking because I was so very much afraid when the terrible sound came, after all that had already occurred. I didn't mean to make the troubles worse. I didn't realize that my people would actually begin the final vigil."

"You heard the sound-shocks, Ngina: An enemy *has* come to Stromvi." *And I am preparing to leave the sanctuary of my Stromvi friends to face it again, after escaping it so narrowly. . . . What are you trying to achieve, Victoria? What are you trying to escape? You are letting claustrophobia—and paranoia—drive you back into the hunting grounds of a formless darkness streaked with crimson.* "You didn't cause the death-watch, Ngina. You only recognized it more quickly than the rest of us." *And Birk Hodge is dead and cannot decide anything for either of us. I may regret leaving the tunnels as soon as I emerge, but I shall suffocate if I remain.*

Ngina clicked her hind teeth pensively, and she hunched one shoulder in a gesture very reminiscent of her father. Her melancholy expression had faded, and solemn puzzlement replaced it. "You never told me why—and how—you knew to seek my honored father in the south caverns."

"Your father found me and brought me here."

"He sought you?"

"We had much to discuss, but I've stayed too long. Your resin tunnels are very hard on a poor Soli." *I won't be any happier or less fearful above ground, but at least I shall feel free again for a little while, until my restlessness makes me run from the next great dread of my life. Ngina-li, I'm more cowardly than anyone. I simply fear all the wrong things.*

"I don't think I understand you, Miss Tori."

Tori sighed, "Take care of yourself, Ngina. Thank you

for your company." Tori began the slow, slippery journey through the last resin tunnel dividing her from sunlight.

* * *

Per Walis studied the report on Harrow Febro thoughtfully. He had known from the start that Harrow Febro was a competitor's agent. That aspect of the data held no surprises. Per had also guessed that the mysterious competitor was associated with his own organization.

Per had not expected his mysterious competitor to fashion such a drastic trap against Birk Hodge. Per had never considered Birk Hodge that significant, except as a useful patron for Victoria, until she matured into more sensible ambitions. Per had wondered why Harrow cultivated Sylvie Hodge, but the attraction might have been sincere—at least, as sincere as Harrow could be.

Per Walis was too professional and too practical to let his pride be injured by externals. Nonetheless, he was slightly disconcerted to realize that the mysterious competitor had not targeted him at all. Per Walis had been no less a pawn than Harrow: a pawn used solely to reach Birk Hodge.

It was a disturbing report, not least because it came so tardily. By now the first relaweed crop had certainly been harvested, unless the Consortium had already moved to intervene. Victoria had not replied to the last three letters that Rosalinde had sent, but that lack did not signify particular trouble in itself. Victoria was notoriously erratic in her filial attentions. Like Mirelle, Victoria was too independent.

But, of course, Victoria *was* Mirelle. As an experiment in environmental influences, the cloning could be considered a success. As an investment, the results were disappointing. Per had hoped that a few spans with a lawless rogue like Birk Hodge would have undone some of the damage of Victoria's expensive Consortium education, provided at the insistence of the original Mirelle. At least, Birk Hodge should have stopped Victoria from moping over the circumstances of Conaty's death. Per could understand why Victoria might have killed Conaty, but he could not fathom why the failure of inquisition had left her so distraught. Some devious Calongi trick was no doubt a factor.

The reasons for tolerating Birk Hodge's ambitious conceits no longer mattered. Birk Hodge had not only outlived his usefulness to Per Walis, Birk had allowed himself to be made hopelessly vulnerable to Consortium justice. Hodge Farm was essentially a ruin. The question remained: How much could the fatal misfortune of Birk Hodge harm Per Walis?

Connections did exist. A list must be made of individuals who actually knew the scope of Birk's work for Per. The list would be short, since few had firsthand information about Per Walis' business. Hearsay from the lawless would not hold much weight with an inquisitor. However, anyone vulnerable on that list must be eliminated. Most such individuals were easily accessible.

Ideally, Birk and Harrow should be removed first. That situation might take care of itself, or it might require delicate handling to avoid Consortium entanglements. The immediate need was to ascertain the current status. Considering the apparent boldness of Birk's Hodge's enemy, Birk and Harrow might both be dead already.

Was Victoria worth the risk of retrieval? If the Consortium had already interfered in the Stromvi matter, then the fewer connections that the inquisitors could make to Per Walis, the better. However, Victoria's fundamental connection to Per Walis would inevitably be recognized. Victoria's Tiva disorder protected her family and associates from her direct testimony, but her mother's patron was named on official Consortium files. Victoria's employment on Stromvi was equally impossible to conceal, even if she could be removed immediately to a neutral world. The issue was troublesome.

A claim of estrangement from Victoria seemed to offer the safest approach, since it represented truth in a narrow sense. Perhaps Rosalinde would not be too distraught to lose Victoria. Mirelle's cloning experiment had always distressed Rosalinde, and there was always Lila. Per Walis grunted, debating with himself. He did hate to displease his concubines.

                    *   *   *

   Omi approved of Deetari. The simplicity of architec-
tural design, the immaculate condition of every wall and
walkway, the precision of service contributed to a serene
sense of effortless Deetari control. The Deetari displayed
their planet's mineral wealth without ostentation. Lus-
trous natural fragments of metallic galena, pearly stilbite,
and silky chalcedony could be found in hidden corners,
made precious by the surprise of discovery.
   Omi approved of the planet Deetari, and he respected
the people who had made it a cleanly balanced, comfortable, and welcoming home. He set aside any irritation at
the ponderous Deetari processes of communal reaction
by observing the planet's placid healthiness, but he recognized how keenly the Deetari port personnel irritated
the Teurai navigators. Because Omi also respected the
Teurai pair and the sacrifices they had made in order to
bring him here, he gestured to indicate his willingness to
assume the negotiator's role.
   Both Teurai accepted his offer with a spirit of humble
surprise verging on awe. Calongi masters rarely tackled
such a mundane problem as a minor administrative conflict regarding an itinerary filing. The Deetari official did
not attempt to conceal her astonishment at being addressed by the revered Calongi master and inquisitor.
She waved her blue-gray arms in excitement and trilled
the news to her companions in the office, a process that
effectively halted such little progress as the Teurai had
begun with her. Omi waited patiently.
   After expressing many polite refusals to enjoy the fullest of Deetari hospitality, Omi reiterated his desire to
take a private shuttle to the planet of Stromvi. The Teurai had expressed the same request on his behalf and
encountered blank resistance. Even with his senses limited by the restricted scope of the ship's communication
system, Omi could detect the intensity of Deetari consternation.
   The Deetari official chirped a nervous apology, and a
decorative, uninformative hold pattern replaced her image
on the viewing screen. Within microspans, another Deetari appeared: a solemn elder, whose skin had turned silver with age. "Wise Calongi master," she sang in a reedy

approximation of the Calongi first-language, "I am Akila. Your attention honors my people."

"Matriach," replied Omi with a tendril gesture indicative of respect for a planetary leader, "I esteem your people and regret that I have troubled them. Explain the cause of their concern, please, that I may understand and alleviate their distress."

Akila bowed rigidly to acknowledge the Calongi request as a command. "Our enormous esteem for you, Calongi master, makes us eager to satisfy you. Our inability to satisfy causes us great pain."

"Why are you unable to authorize an itinerary to your neighboring planet? This port is the recognized point of access to this planetary system."

"It is by the example of wise Calongi justice that we respect our neighbors' customs. With much regret, we acknowledge Stromvi death-watch. We cannot authorize intrusions into their grief. We are very sorry to bring such sad news to the Consortium."

Knowing that Deetari operated in their own scale of time, Omi did not condemn them for their slowness in informing the Consortium of such a significant occurrence as Stromvi death-watch, in whatever form that mythical event might actually take shape. He observed the surge of his own anxiety with some distaste. Anxiety was kin of fear, a primitive emotion that Omi considered unenlightened and uncivilized.

"Share with me, please, such information as you hold regarding the death-watch," said Omi quietly.

"If the Calongi master will allow us to honor him with our hospitality, I shall investigate and inform him." The matriarch clasped her hands in front of her, the crinkled skin of her finger sheaths emphasizing her age and the stature that age granted her.

Recognizing Deetari stubbornness, Omi offered compromise, "The ease of an evening of your gracious hospitality will make my journey brighter tomorrow morning. I accept your offer with thanks, Matriarch."

"We shall make every effort to please you, honored Calongi master."

"I do not doubt your ability to please me promptly in all requests," answered Omi. The matriarch hesitated

only briefly before bowing in implicit concession to Calongi wisdom.

*   *   *

"All will end," sighed Thalia to the darkness.

"I will end your complaining," snapped the shadowy
form of a man, reaching across a shrouded table for the
food that she had brought him. Thalia's mindless whistling irked him, but he hated most her occasional, seemingly irrelevent comments. She sounded so lucid in such
moments, until one tried to decipher her actual meaning.

"Death, once summoned," she assured him, "does not
depart unpaid."

"Why couldn't you have disappeared instead of your
sister? I shall be as mad as you if I wait here much
longer with only your company." For the tenth time, he
growled, "A ship will come soon. You must welcome it,
as your sister taught you."

"Beauty is hollow, but she destroys," answered Thalia.
She resumed her carefree trills of Deetari melody.

CHAPTER 32

Tori folded aside the final woven-vine layer that concealed the Stromvi tunnel entry. The long strands of evening sunlight felt glorious. Air that held more oxygen than resin filled her lungs and exhilarated her. She shook her head delightedly at the violet hue of her arms because the color would fade as the resin peeled from her skin.

The drying process could take days, despite the light panels that had minimized the resinous accumulation in her Stromvi dry-cave. Tori grimaced, although she recognized the resin's value both as camouflage and defense against the Stromvi sun. She clambered out of the tunnel and replaced its fibrous door. Familiar rows of yellow roses blended into shades of orange a few meters from her position among the silver-lilies. "I've walked past this garden a hundred times," she whispered, impressed anew at Stromvi skills of concealment.

Maintaining a cautious survey of the nearby hedges, Tori ensured that she had not lost any item from her equipment kit. She withdrew Jase's machete from the fiber scabbard she had made for it. "*Jase's* machete," she murmured with acrid irony, acknowledging the sense of his possession, "as if he laid a permanent claim in his brief use of it."

Tori replaced the machete carefully. She had borrowed a cloak of rough Stromvi cloth, and she wrapped herself in its folds, an uncomfortable precaution against unseen, unfriendly eyes. She moved slowly through the silver-lilies, avoiding their ripe pods of sharp seeds. She slipped only once, for her confinement in the Stromvi caves had forced her to improve her resin-impeded sense of balance. Once she reached the mossy path that fringed the rose fields, she managed to walk almost normally.

Her unexpectedly rapid progress forced her to stop after a microspan. "Where now?" she whispered. Facing the main house across the brilliant beds of the Hodge gardens, she pretended for an instant that Birk would soon emerge onto his patio and wave at her. She indulged the shadows of evening, allowing them to play tricks on her resin-blurred vision. She could see Thalia laying the elaborate table settings for supper. Sylvie arrived on Harrow's arm, the two of them smiling at each other with very civilized detachment. Calem, his face furrowed in a sulk, walked behind his sister. A stranger moved smoothly at his side.

Tori frowned, for the stranger's presence made the illusory picture become real and solid. She blinked repeatedly, telling herself that resin and fatigue had combined to deceive her, and she bit her lip sharply to bring the cleansing tears. With the sweet taste of her own blood in her mouth, she sank unsteadily to a crouching position in the shadow of a scarlet tree rose.

Calem, Sylvie, Thalia. . . . Even Harrow. Welcome home, wandering Victoria. All is well.

Except Birk and Ngoi are still dead. And a silent Stromvi maintains its death-watch with Rillessa in its cavernous grip, while Nguri holds his own counsel too thoroughly. And a Soli inquisitor named Jase Sleide has vanished.

Tori gripped the machete handle for reassurance, and she fingered the fine cord that Jase had wrapped around it. She glanced briefly at the sliver of a setting moon, a lesser moon that confirmed only that she had lost track of the days. In good Stromvi fashion, she settled herself into a hollow among the dense garden growth. "Never make a major decision when you're exhausted, Victoria." She thought wistfully of the comforts of her downy bed in her room at Uncle Per's estate house.

*   *   *

Omi wished for the pleasure of a soothing Farii bath and promptly felt shame at his weakness of spirit. In a devastating instant of self-revelation, he observed that his spans of contented isolation from lesser Consortium species had eroded his ability to respect them. He actually resented this latest Deetari delay and had considered—briefly but seriously—exerting a direct form of Calongi power that few Consortium species ever witnessed. Such an exercise might have made the Deetari fear him more than their prophets, but it would not have been civilized.

His intolerance was inexcusable. The matriarch had been cordial, despite her attempt to conceal Deetari's source of information regarding Stromvi death-watch. She had yielded the name of Gisa Ald reluctantly, but she had not demurred from summoning the woman. Only the morning had been lost while the Deetari bureaucracy searched for Gisa. Impatience was unwarranted.

In a severely humbled mood, Omi observed the approach of the Deetari daughter whom he awaited. As wire-thin as most of her sisters, the Deetari still managed to convey a sense of solidity. She did not bow on arriving, but Omi detected no arrogance in her: only self-certainty. "You wished to see me, Master Omi," she remarked without hesitation. She spoke Consortium Basic with little trace of Deetari accent, and Omi observed the slight Soli influence. "I am Gisa Ald."

Omi answered in the same language, "You came from Stromvi very recently and brought word of that people's death-watch."

"I have lived on Stromvi for many spans," replied Gisa evenly. "I know the planet and the people well."

"You have long served a Soli master." *A master who is not registered as a Consortium member*, thought Omi, restraining his disapproval by an inner litany. "Has he joined the Stromvi death-watch?"

"Mister Hodge is master of himself. I do not rule him or know his mind."

"You have left his service?"

"I have escaped a great tribulation in order to bring warning to my own people." Gisa touched the point of her narrow nose. "A prophet has told me not to speak of the deeds of demonic enemies. I may tell you only that the death-watch is real."

"Do you know a Soli named Jase Sleide?"

"I know him."

"Is he on Stromvi now?"

"He came, and the death-watch began."

The confirmation of an unpleasant theory caused Omi to reevaluate the priorities of several mental tasks. He regretted the constraints imposed by a Deetari prophet, but he respected the Deetari culture and would not coerce information from the troubled, reluctant Gisa. Nonetheless, answers must be obtained. The Consortium had a responsibility to Stromvi, and Omi represented Consortium justice. Extended observation was critical.

"Your sister remains on Stromvi," remarked Omi mildly, and he observed the deepening of Gisa's anxiety. "As a Deetari, she is not bound by the isolation of death-watch. Have you attempted to contact her?"

"Thalia is simple. She does not understand the use of communication devices."

"She must concern you."

"She is not unprotected. She has prophetic abilities."

Omi inclined his head thoughtfully. "You do not believe that she is protected adequately. You believe that she will die with Stromvi. You abandoned her, but you feel guilt."

"The matriarch is wiser then I," replied Gisa stiffly. "She has said that we must await the outcome of death-watch before sending a ship to Stromvi."

"Respect is wise. Ignorance is folly. I intend to go to Stromvi now," countered Omi. He assessed Gisa's quietly suppressed turmoil and made judgment. "You will accompany me, Miss Gisa. You have warned your people. You must now complete your obligations to your sister."

Gisa's fingers fluttered briefly, but the obvious signs of consternation faded quickly. *She has inner strength*, observed Omi with approval, tempered by the certainty that Gisa's fear was very great.

"The wisdom of the Calongi master is greater than my own," she acknowledged with a sigh.

Omi accepted her compliance as the natural response to a Calongi master's direct instructions. "Inform your matriarch, please. My personal shuttle has been readied and will leave within the millispan. She will please allow my navigators to remain in orbit here until my return, since their vessel is unsuitable for intrasystem travel."

Gisa bowed and withdrew. Omi experienced the warming of intense satisfaction that accompanied a sound judgment. Gisa's reactions to places, people, and objects would inform Omi without betrayal of prophesied Deetari warnings. Such observation was a subtle form of inquisition, a form that detractors of Calongi often labeled devious, but Omi intended only to maintain honor. He respected creation too deeply to do otherwise.

* * *

The gray hovercraft purred in the Stromvi evening, as it brushed the tall lily spikes in its passing. Roake steered a direct course, making no effort to hide from any watchful foe. Jase moved his fingers lightly across the surface of the crate wedged beside him in the crowded cabin. The five crates that Roake had taken from the Bercali ship filled nearly all of the available space.

With a menacing tension, Roake growled, "It is time, Soli, for you to earn the life I have granted you. Locate the relaweed quickly, unless you wish me to retract my gift."

Jase responded mildly, "Threats are childish, Roake, and impress neither of us. I've already agreed to help you recover the relaweed, but I cannot form sound conclusions without data. If you want the results, you must aid the process."

Roake clenched his jaw. His anger was palpable, but he did not let it rule him. "What aid do you request?"

"Information: Tell me about the relaweed harvest."

"The seeds were grown in the southern field of Hodge Farm," grunted Roake. "The first pods were harvested and packaged by a Stromvi, who subsequently destroyed the field."

"How long ago did this occur?" asked Jase. He was fairly sure that Roake could not answer, but the question should provoke Roake to an informative emotional reaction. A loss of mental faculties was arguably the most dreadful of relanine poisoning's potential byproducts, and not even Sesserda training could preclude an occasional worry in that regard.

"I'm uncertain," admitted Roake, and the confession of ignorance was clearly painful for him. "The Bercali curs use contaminated relanine for their adaptation fluids."

"I lost track of some time myself," replied Jase, well able to empathize with Roake's particular discomfort. He was mildly impressed that Roake had answered honestly. "Impurities can cause unpredictable reactions."

A curt nod, coming from Roake, amounted nearly to approval. "My brother intervened too late to salvage the field's last crop, but he prevented the Stromvi from completing his intended tasks. My brother is impetuous and learned nothing from the Stromvi, except that the first pods remain intact." Roake added with contempt, "My brother let the Stromvi die."

"Did you question the Stromvi yourself?" asked Jase with a deadly softness that would have alerted any less arrogant hearer.

"The Stromvi chose to alleviate his dishonor by incurring his own death. An unfortunate choice," sighed Roake, "but understandable. I could learn little from him, for all sense had left him before I arrived."

"How disappointing for you."

"Yes," replied Roake seriously. "It has caused me much inconvenience."

Jase nodded in mocking sympathy. "I can see only one solution for your problem. You must trust me to find the relaweed—in my own way, under my own authority."

"You cannot expect me to trust you away from my sight," answered Roake with scorn.

"I think you recognize expediency, or you wouldn't be talking to me now. The natives of this planet know me, but they will say nothing of value if you accompany me. You wear violence openly. No Stromvi would confide in me with you as witness, and I do need Stromvi advice."

Roake began to speak, but Jase forestalled him with a sharp, imperative gesture of his open hand and the subtle shiftings of voice and presence that touched the subconscious. Jase had seldom exercised the sophisticated command techniques, for such methods offered too much power for careless use, but he had rarely fought for the life of an entire planet. "Understand, Roake, this planet belongs to its people in a much deeper sense than most cultural concepts of ownership. You will locate nothing on this planet without Stromvi aid. You will achieve nothing on this planet without Stromvi cooperation."

The fine Essenji features had sharpened attentively. A

faint frown indicated Roake's suspicions. Jase waited in quiet readiness to see if Roake discerned the persuasive method used. A Rea warrior might consider such command techniques the equivalent of direct attack.

Roake turned to stare pensively at the viewing screen. Apparently impressed by Jase's stern assurance, Roake remarked, "You speak eloquently, Soli."

"I speak the truth. If you have been equally honest with me regarding the relaweed, then you have no reason to distrust me."

"Will you swear to this," asked Roake solemnly, "by your honor?"

Jase forced himself to maintain a serious expression, untainted by the doubts inside him. "I will," answered Jase, "if you make a similar contract." Jase doubted Roake's ability to appreciate Sesserda honor, and the exchange of honor's vows seemed farcical under such circumstances. *However*, mused Jase, *Sesserda teaches that the most apparently villainous of beings may respect their own personal ideals. Every judgment must weigh the culture and civilization level of the individual involved. Roake could be considered honorable in the context of a warlike Level VII society.*

"By my honor," said Roake with quiet pride, "I swear not to kill you unless you fail in your vow to me. I have spoken truthfully to you about the relaweed. I have no interest in harming Stromvi."

Roake's edged promise had a pompous ring and a dark implication of deception in unspecified regions, but Jase sensed unexpected sincerity in the Essenji. "I need to examine the southern fields, but I need some equipment first. Land me as near as possible to Hodge House, please."

"Soli, do not give me orders."

"Sorry."

"I'm an exceptionally capable tactician."

"Of course."

"You will allow me to inject you with tracking fluid, which will ensure that you do not stray too far from my attentions. I do have many resources, Soli. I will find you if you betray me."

"An alliance based on mutual trust is so reassuring."

"Find the relaweed quickly."

Jase began a facetious reply, but his deeper senses stopped him. "When will you require an injection again?"

Staring fixedly at the vision screen, Roake answered tightly, "Soon. I'm unaware of any hallucinations as yet, but I'm becoming feverish. And you?"

"I have some time yet." *Although I may have less time than I expect*, mused Jase, uneasily pondering a question that he had been avoiding. *Contaminated relanine consumes its purer relative at an alarming rate.*

"Fortunate," said Roake crisply.

"Quite fortunate." With sensitive fingers, Jase traced the prominent veins in his forearm. The pressure made the relanine-saturated blood glow softly even through the skin. "I don't happen to like you much, Roake, but I do understand what you may be facing, and I could not wish that level of pain on anyone. I've seen relanine deaths. I've experienced relanine poisoning. I can give you a little more margin, if you need it."

"If I spill your blood, Soli, it will not be for the sullying of my own," snapped Roake, but the stern set of the Essenji's magnificent features relaxed fractionally. Jase observed wryly that his offer had truly astonished Roake, but it had hardly increased Roake's respect for Jase's intelligence. "Bring me the seeds."

* * *

Midway through the Stromvi night, Tori awoke for the seventh time and felt the repellent sliminess of a dew worm crawling across her ankle. She used a leaf to catch the wrist-thick worm, and she flung the creature into the darkness. She crawled from her hiding place and sighed to the misty stars, "I've had a surfeit of Stromvi naturalism. I never coveted a primitive lifestyle. I *enjoy* decadent luxury."

She walked cautiously toward the supply shed, but she doubted that any obstacle less than an army of osang snakes would have deterred her from reaching her loft. Someone had disposed of the dead rose bush, but the shed—as much as she could see of it by misty starlight—seemed otherwise untouched. She climbed the stairs wearily, dropped the equipment kit and machete on the window ledge, and, too tired to think about further precautions, collapsed in an exhausted huddle on her bed.

She awoke shortly before dawn. Without touching the room's lamps, she arose and cleaned a dozen layers of flaking resin from her skin. She scrubbed at slick patches, knowing the futility of the effort, and she used the corrosive resin cleanser more extensively than experience recommended. The cleanser burned sensitive skin, but at least the air reached Soli pores too long encased by the Stromvi resin.

When she had dressed in a clean, deep violet blouse and skirt, she felt much more ready to tackle Stromvi's spreading mysteries. She pulled the thick Stromvi draperies across her window and risked lighting one small globe. She found a box of food rations in a downstairs cupboard and made a very satisfying meal of sweet manna and clear water.

As she ate, she turned the pages of the port logbook. She had read it repeatedly, but she still grumbled softly at its uninformative entries. "This log either represents a tribute to Jeffer's inefficiency," she muttered, "or it indicates a deliberate effort to obscure truth." She brushed the manna crumbs from her hands and swept them into a tiny mound on the blue clay table. She stared at the crumbs without seeing them.

Calem and Sylvie Hodge have apparently resumed normal life. Do I dare join them? The only true argument against that course is uncertainty. I have no better plan.

"Great-grandmama, what shall I do?" whispered Tori, but the ploy of visualization did not help. With a flick of her finger, Tori scattered the crumbs across the table. She grumbled at the logbook, "I wonder what my favorite Soli inquisitor would advise."

A half-sensed sound made her extinguish the light and rise from the table. She approached her window carefully, lifting an edge of the curtain with slow stealth to confirm that the main house remained dark. Tori dropped the curtain. It caught on a rough edge of the casement, leaving a crack of dim light.

Tori did not move to restore the darkness. She became entirely still. She sensed a silent visitor behind her, and knew that the Stromvi people did not climb stairs with such ease and delicacy.

With a rapid twist of motion, Tori grabbed the machete from the ledge. She pressed her back to the wall and aimed the machete at the figure she could barely see in the pale stripe of dawn-glow. The figure stepped from the stairs into the room with a long, loping stride and stopped abruptly.

"This is a very unpromising welcome for your favorite Soli inquisitor," remarked Jase softly, and he nodded toward the machete. "I'd hate to be any lower on your popularity list." He reached past her to tug the curtain back into concealing placement, and he tapped the small globe into life. "However, you have satisfied my lifelong desire to make a melodramatic entry on cue."

"At the expense of my nerves," muttered Tori. She wondered briefly if she could conjure such a vividly outlandish dream. She concluded that she would never have imagined a Soli inquisitor in ragged scraps of clothing that made him resemble a barbarian soldier who had lost too many battles. Despite the exotic and impractical costume, he looked reassuringly healthy.

Tori decided that an inquisitor could surely sense the relief inside of her. She did not even try to bury her reaction more deeply. Despite his alarmingly surreptitious entry, she *was* elated to see him. "I thought you were dead," said Tori. She derided herself immediately for issuing such an uninspired greeting. Her nervousness was showing, and her inquisitor was the last person to whom she should allow herself to appear so fragile. She was finding it difficult to equate this savage apparition of a man with the very civilized Consortium status of a Sesserda adept.

"Speak a bit more quietly, please," warned Jase in a hush, "just to humor your paranoid inquisitor." He stepped close enough to her to divert the hand that still held the machete. The texture of his skin, distinctly Soli rather than Stromvi, felt warmly real and very comfortably alive, but the brief touch of his fingers carried a peculiar tingling that was almost painful. "Would you mind pointing that knife away from me? It makes me feel too much like a criminal, which is a very sore subject at present."

For a curious moment, Tori imagined that her skin glowed where his fingers had pressed it, but the glow faded so quickly that she doubted whether she had seen it at all. The tingling, where he had touched her, persisted and seemed to spread and numb the resin cleanser's nearby burns. The minor puzzle was outweighed by much larger concerns. "Where have you been?" demanded Tori with a softness that robbed her agitation of its intended bite.

"Sojourning on a Bercali prison ship. Dreadful ambiance. I really cannot recommend the accommodations."

"Bercali?" An inquisitor in a Bercali prison presented such an incongruous image that Tori nearly laughed, but she observed Jase's coarse attire with renewed speculation. The ragged holes at the bottom of the long, padded vest might well have been designed to suit a Bercali's lower arms.

Jase forestalled any further questions about Bercali incarceration with a curt gesture of dismissal. "I have very few explanations to offer you yet, Miss Darcy, and a few more complications have arisen, but I should like to defer that discussion until a more opportune moment. At present, I need the benefits of your experience and keen insights into the Stromvi psyche."

Refusing to let him dominate the conversation so quickly, Tori interrupted him, "How did you find me?"

"You live here."

"And you were in the neighborhood?" asked Tori, exasperated by his flippancy.

Jase shrugged, but he pointed at the gray cord that he had twisted around the knife's grip. "Tracking wire on the machete," he murmured in answer to her previous question. "It's an expensive variety used for training the rather delicate Sesserda senses that are able to detect it." He grimaced. "I thought I was being extravagantly wasteful in using it to bind a broken knife handle, but the wire was all I had in my pocket at the time."

Tori rubbed the handle's binding thoughtfully. "You took a risk in assuming that *I* had the machete."

"I was wagering on your resourcefulness." A faint rustle behind him caused Jase to whirl nervously toward the stairs, but he relaxed as a page of the open logbook turned, issuing an echo of the first soft sound. "Actually, I was searching for my hovercraft, which has coils of the same type of wire embedded in its walls. However, I'm afraid my ship has left Stromvi. Finding you is an unexpected consolation."

"You make me feel so wanted." The wry acknowledgment of the inquisitor's priorities did not slow the renewal of Tori's much-battered hope. She was beginning to feel slightly giddy from the release of too much long-held tension. "First you abandon me at the port. Now you rank me below your hovercraft. How quickly they forget. . . ."

"I think we'll both find our time together indelibly memorable, my dear, but the reasons don't flatter either of us." He took the machete from her gently and laid it carefully on the ledge.

Watching him place the knife just beyond her reach, Tori asked sardonically, "Are you still afraid that I may try my murderess' skills on you?"

"I'm simply keeping caution as my close companion, though you might not believe it if you met my new conspirator. He's a rather temperamental gentleman who apparently likes to kill people. I agreed to locate some parcels of relaweed for him. Ngoi grew the seeds and probably hid them as well. Can you suggest where I might look for either the parcels or a helpful Stromvi?"

Tori's momentary lightness of spirit dimmed before acrid memories. "Ngoi's 'strange crop,' " murmured Tori leadenly.

"You knew he was cultivating a new product?"

"I thought Ngoi and Calem were experimenting with Soli herbs, until Ngina told me yesterday that the crop was more dangerous than we knew. She found Ngoi dying. She began the death-watch."

Jase's luminous eyes widened. "You are a fount of information. Where is Ngina?"

"With the rest of the Ngenga Valley's Stromvi. They're holding vigil in those southern caverns that were supposedly abandoned spans ago. I don't intend to go back there, Mister Inquisitor. I'm quite ready to leave this planet."

"Lovely goal," answered Jase with grim humor, "if you've found a means of achieving it."

"Don't you have a ship yet?" asked Tori cuttingly, because she did not want her inquisitor to think she expected his help.

"I told you: I looked for my ship and found you instead. Anyway, I can't leave until I locate the relaweed and decide what to do with Roake—my fiendish cohort in crime."

Tori shook her head at him. "You're a very poor sort of rescuer." She returned to the chair that she had left on hearing Jase's arrival, and Jase claimed the place opposite her. He reached across the table to turn a page of the logbook. "Jeffer's logs," said Tori, "punctuated by Ngahi's sporadic notekeeping. None of the entries are very enlightening. They fail to mention that you arrived on Stromvi at all."

"Jeffer wasn't at the port when I arrived," answered Jase absently, then he frowned. "Ngahi met me, but he disappeared soon after the Deetari shuttle departed."

"You didn't tell me. . . ."

"I didn't remember," snapped Jase with a startling flash of irritation. He clenched his hands before him, and he fixed his iridescent gaze on the logbook. His arms tightened, and a dark luster suffused his skin, making the tendons and sinews appear to have been sculpted from some strange burnished stone.

Tori began to push away from the table slowly. Inquisitors were disturbing at best. This temperamental Soli in gladiatorial garb presented a truly alarming prospect.

As swiftly as his frustration had flared, Jase observed her hesitant retreat and became again the detached Sesserda scholar, "I'm sorry. I'm not maintaining Sesserda tranquillity very well, am I? I need a few days of uninterrupted meditation. I don't enjoy losing pieces of my life."

Tori asked cautiously, "What else have you remembered about your arrival here?"

"I landed at the port. Ngahi greeted me normally and sent me to inspect my hovercraft. He wanted me to tell him if his workers had prepared it to my satisfaction. I don't remember anything else, until I approached Hodge Farm. I can't even be sure of what I've just told you. My perceptions from that period are hopelessly garbled. I lose time fragments on occasion." He shrugged. "It's part of the price for the Sesserda senses that serve me under normal circumstances."

Tori weighed the seriousness of his words against

Nguri's remarks about the Soli inquisitor. She decided that pressing Jase further in regard to his own problems would be more disquieting than helpful. She asked instead, "Do you know that Calem and Sylvie are back? I saw them at the house yesterday evening, though I don't think they saw me."

"Calem and Sylvie? I did not know," answered Jase thoughtfully. "That could make a difference. Were they alone?"

"No. Thalia and Harrow were with them—along with a stranger. Rillessa is with the Stromvi. She's not very rational."

"Did the stranger look like a Soli?"

"As far as I could tell with resin-bleary eyes and from a vantage point in the middle of the lily garden."

Jase frowned, the intensity of his calculating thoughts almost palpable for that instant. "I need to assess them. Both Calem and Sylvie are fairly easy to read."

"What do you intend to do?" scoffed Tori. "Walk up to the front door and announce yourself as a guest?"

"That seems like a courteous notion, don't you think?" replied Jase, and a slightly devilish grin spread slowly across his face.

"The notion might be considered either courteous or very stupid."

"Tsk, tsk. Is that a proper attitude for the Hodge Farm welcoming committee?" He had regained his Sesserda poise, and Tori could feel him casting his nets of forcible calm across her. "Lurking surreptitiously in my host's shrubbery is hardly recommended etiquette, nor is it particulary comfortable. I think we should join the Hodges for a sociable morning meal, after which we can chat with Ngina."

"And a lovely time was had by all," said Tori scornfully, despite the very similar trend of her own thoughts before Jase's arrival.

"Why not?" he asked, but Sesserda training spoke more eloquently in the ensuing silence.

For a moment, Tori stiffened, hating his inquisitor's skills, hating all that pertained to inquisitors. She rose restlessly and paced back to the window. She touched the glow globe into darkness and opened the curtains to admit the strengthening morning sun.

Jase came to stand beside her. "I don't suppose you could find any civilized clothes that would fit me? I hate to pay social calls in a costume that I stole from a dead Bercali."

"Some of Birk's discards are stored downstairs." Tori turned to face her inquisitor, and she wrinkled her nose with affected disdain. "You're certainly not the most presentable of escorts, Mister Sleide."

"And you look delightful too, my dear. Lavender resin adds such a fetching aura of ill-health."

"Are you trying to adopt manners consistent with your present rude attire?" Tori tapped Jase's vest lightly. She found the solid feel of him very comforting after so many recent doubts. "For a Sesserda adept, you're a little too convincing as a barbarian."

His smile twisted slightly. "Have I mentioned how glad I am to see you again, Miss Darcy?"

"No, Mister Sleide. I was beginning to wonder."

"Do I need to remind you to distrust me because of my inquisitor's status?"

"Please don't." She let his Sesserda spell of calm enfold her, too grateful for its soothing influence to maintain resentment of its invasive nature.

CHAPTER 33

Walking toward the sunny patio of Hodge House, Tori felt that she had slipped into some unreal fragment of a distorted dream. She had shared many meals with Birk on that patio. He had shared many of his hopes for the future with her. Birk's predictions had always been optimistic, albeit from a self-centered perspective. The continued existence of Hodge Farm after Birk's death seemed disrespectful.

Tori glanced at Jase, who watched his goal unswervingly, his iridescent eyes narrowed and remote. Birk's suit fit the inquisitor too loosely. The creamy linen had been tailored for a much broader frame. The effect of a cast-off garment might have detracted from a less assured wearer's bearing, but Jase seemed unaware of any such possibility. Not even the inadequate Bercali rags had truly seemed to disturb him.

He has the confidence of a Calongi, mused Tori with unsought respect, *and the persuasiveness, as well. Why did I defer to his Sesserda judgment now, when I watched him walk into a trap once before? This is madness. I ought to have remained with the Stromvi, or I ought to have found a means of escaping this planet on my own.*

The scene on the patio could not have appeared more peaceably domestic. Sylvie clutched Harrow's swarthy hand across the table, and she chattered about the wedding arrangements. Calem made deprecating comments about his sister's extravagant tastes.

The table wore the silver, star-shaped clothes that rarely emerged except for the most honored guests. Instead of the rose crystal dishes of daily usage, Thalia had set the cut blue corundum that scattered watery light. Thalia moved quietly, serving Sylvie, Calem, and Harrow first, then offering a pastry shell to a stranger. Rebuffed by the stranger's sharp gesture, Thalia carried her tray of partially emptied dishes into the house.

An incongruous element in the summery scene, the stranger wore a hooded cloak of a velvety pile and burgundy tone. His pallid face, all sharp bones and strength of line, was partially hidden by cloak-cast shadows. Successful Soli businessmen often accompanied Harrow, but the stranger resembled death's distinguished reaper more closely than a tradesman.

It was the stranger who first observed the approach of Jase and Tori, while the rest of the little group on the patio continued their oblivious enjoyment of their breakfast. The stranger's dark eyes flickered, but he did not speak. His pale fingers moved stiffly and unnaturally in a grasping reflex. Tori found the motions disquieting.

Jase called jauntily, "Good morning. Is this the fortunate bridegroom, Sylvie?" Jase bounded up the stairs ahead of Tori.

Sylvie released Harrow's hand with guilty speed, and she clutched at her own smooth hair. She seemed to be mouthing Jase's name helplessly, trying vainly to be heard. Harrow had risen, giving himself the full advantage of his height and powerful build. He met Jase's carefree greeting heartily. Calem stared into his goblet. The stranger smiled grimly at Tori, as if sharing with her an evil secret, and Tori joined the others on the patio with the stranger's gaze still on her.

While Jase murmured sympathetic acknowledgments to Harrow's idle calumny against the Stromvi environment, Tori walked directly to the stranger. "We haven't met," she informed him, meeting his challenging stare boldly. "I'm Tori Darcy."

The stranger replied with brusque impatience, "No. Let us, at least, be honest in our meeting, Miss Mirelle."

"You're mistaken."

"Is it so? Then I apologize." The stranger's sly smile lingered, proclaiming disbelief. "I am Ares."

As if the name carried a spell, all other speakers paused to hear it. Sylvie broke the quiet with a nervous laugh. "Ares is one of Harrow's partners," she announced too brightly. Her bland eyes had a feverish glow. Her skin was flushed in irregular bands that spread across her cheeks and over the bridge of her nose. She nearly resembled the unstable Rillessa.

"I didn't know that any Essenji still traded with Consortium members," remarked Jase with an amiable easiness. He tilted his head in a child's gesture of innocent curiosity. The shadow of his straight shock of hair hid the iridescence of his eyes.

"You know of the Essenji?" asked Ares, shifting his attention to Jase with a spark of suspicion. The velvety cloak rippled over shoulders that had tightened into a rigid line.

"Your people have a remarkable history, do they not?" replied Jase lightly, and he turned to Calem. "Do you enjoy your liberty as much as you expected, Calem? Or does responsibility for your own life, unfettered and undefended by your father, weigh too heavily? You're not looking well."

Calem pushed his goblet away from him. The liquid sloshed across the rim and splattered the table. "Stop jabbering like a Ziltsi idiot," muttered Calem. "Where have you been?"

"Here and there. Seeing sights. Renewing old acquaintances and developing new friends."

"We thought those murderers had killed you both," said Sylvie, her voice escaping her control with a shrill tremor. "I cannot bear to think what might have happened to us all if Harrow hadn't arrived and frightened the cowards."

Jase claimed a chair at the table and snatched a sweetplum from the sapphire center-bowl. "Harrow must be more intimidating than I've yet appreciated. How many murderers did you scatter with your appearance, Harrow?" No one answered Jase.

Tori wondered what Jase was attempting and what the others thought of his game. She realized that Ares still watched her. Ares had called her Mirelle. Ares knew. . . . Tori severed the nervous thought. Ares knew nothing more than Jase Sleide knew about her, nothing more than Rillessa had evidently learned from Prili data files. Ares still made Tori exceedingly uneasy.

Thalia emerged from the house, whistling almost soundlessly. She looked at Tori and promptly let the serving tray slip from her thin, blue hands. Sylvie and

Calem both jumped nervously at the crash of spilled dishes.

A pool of amber juice spread across the cool, white deck of the patio. A sphere of crisp, sugary dough tumbled from its basket and rolled to Tori's feet. Twittering apologies, Thalia collected the bits and pieces of scattered food.

Tori knelt beside the Deetari woman, murmuring, "Let me help you, Thalia." She reached for a fallen serviette and brushed Thalia's arm. The Deetari shrank from Tori's touch with a perceptible shudder.

"Thalia can manage on her own," said Calem gruffly. "That's her job, Tori, not yours."

Tori rose to her feet, discouraged from her task by Thalia's panicky reaction rather than by Calem's peevish intercession. Tori faced Calem with a faintly contemptuous expression. "Do I still have a job, Calem?"

Calem frowned, and Tori almost believed that he truly did not understand the reason for her question. Harrow did not convince her at all, though he gathered his full sycophantic charm to reply, "Of course, Tori. Why do you ask?"

Sylvie muttered anxiously, "What does she mean, Calem?"

Thalia scurried into the house. Jase inspected the remaining fruit in the center-bowl and remarked with apparent carelessness, "I assume that you notified Deetari of the attack."

"Of course," answered Ares softly, "although the attack produced no significant damage. This planet is unfortunately close to the lawless regions."

Jase nodded. "I heard a rumor that placed the Rea in this vicinity. Are you familiar with the Rea, Ares?"

Ares answered very seriously, "The Rea are a group of roving warriors, I believe."

"A group that evinces some very uncivilized behavioral patterns," replied Jase, prodding a cluster of plump, green wilaberries. "They were originally a cultural sect, proclaiming individual freedom with a regimented zeal, while enslaving themselves to an unswervingly autocratic leadership. The Rea appear to retain some of their confused ideals, but they seem quite unconcerned by the freedom they steal from their victims. They suffer somewhat from hypocrisy."

Ares' fingers repeated their clutching gesture. Harrow glanced at him uncertainly, but Ares only enveloped himself more tightly in his cloak. Harrow said briskly, "You appear to be quite knowledgeable about these Rea, Mister Sleide."

"I read a file about them once."

"The Deetari officials assured us," said Ares with dry precision, "that we shall encounter no more trouble here."

"How comforting," answered Jase.

Tori wished that someone would at least mention Birk, but she could not bring herself to name him first. Instead, she muttered, "The official assurance has not comforted the Stromvi, it seems."

Ares' cynical smile stretched thinner. "The Stromvi appear to be as superstitious as their Deetari neighbors."

"They cut our profits with every day of their infantile hiding," grumbled Calem. He laughed, surprising Tori with his depth of bitterness. Calem seldom wore his pain so openly in front of strangers. "Where would you look for them, Mister Sleide?"

"Are they lost?" retorted Jase.

"Workers can be so unreliable," said Harrow. He plunged into a meandering dissertation on business practices that Tori found absurd in its irrelevancy. Only Sylvie pretended to listen to Harrow, and even she kept glancing at Jase as if the Soli inquisitor were an uncomfortable specter that she hoped would disappear. Calem and Jase seemed to be measuring each other against a dubious rod of commonality, and Ares seemed to find the entire spectacle amusing and contemptible.

With a roar of overloaded engines, a hovercraft swept over the house, skimming just above the roof and plunging toward the patio table. Tori recoiled instinctively, but the gray ship climbed back into the air just short of striking the ground. The hovercraft circled over the garden at a dangerous speed, and its warning lights flashed blindingly across the patio.

In the blinking aftermath of the glare, the ship darted out of view. The roar did not fade gently. As abruptly as it had come, it ended.

"Unusual weather phenomena this year," commented Jase. Harrow muttered a curse.

"Pranksters," snapped Calem. Sylvie leaned across the table to whisper a question in her brother's ear. "Nothing," growled Calem. Ares left his chair and disappeared into the house in a single fluid motion. Jase pursed his lips and nodded thoughtfully.

Tori watched all of them, certain only that she did not trust any of them completely. *Great-grandmama said that catastrophe was the precursor to opportunity*, she recalled grimly, *and chaos abets the resourceful*. Tori laughed. She received curious looks from the four Soli seated at the table. With an enigmatic smile, she took several of the wilaberries from Jase's hand and followed Ares into the house.

* * *

Ngina tried to bury her fear, but she trembled. "Most honored Father," she whispered timidly. Her father, concentrating deeply on his inspection of a magnification plate, did not hear her. The projected image was a fierce, spined beast that covered the wall of the sterile lab, a cold room by Stromvi standards. Ngina scarcely noticed the menacing image that engrossed her father. That dreadful creature, likely smaller than a dust mite, only made her task more difficult by consuming her father's attention.

Procrastination had only made the prospect of confession more difficult. Ngina whispered again, only slightly louder than before, "Honored Father, I must speak with you." She expected his anger, and she wished that she had not come.

Nguri glanced at his daughter distractedly. He peered at her for a moment, as if trying to remember her identity, then he laid aside the magnification plate and hurried toward her. His hands cradled her face in a gesture of great warmth, but he chided her, "Ngina-li, do you fear me so much? Your mother told me you felt ill, but I know my Ngeta: You asked her to keep me away from you, didn't you? Did you think I would berate you for failing to complete a task I set for you, when so much

evil has occurred since that time? I rejoice that you are
well."

Astonished by her father's gentleness, Ngina touched
his shoulder ridge tentatively. He did not know what she
had done, and he did not question her. She could remain
silent and accept his forgiveness, but he had given it for
the wrong reasons. Having resolved to be as strong as
Miss Tori, Ngina admitted, "I did not fail you in that
task, honored Father. I found the scent."

Nguri studied her closely. A pall of deep concern settled over his warmth. "Then what do you fear to tell me,
Ngina-li?" he asked slowly.

"I found Ngoi, honored Father, just before he died."

Nguri's broad head shifted backward, stretching gnarled
neck ridges. Aged Stromvi bones cracked in protest of
the startled gesture. "Did he speak to you?"

"Yes, honored Father. I was frightened, and I think I
behaved unwisely, but so much happened. Ngoi died,
and I moved his seed parcels for him, and then a parcel
opened and a beetle flew from it." Almost inaudibly,
Ngina clicked, "I began death-watch."

"You moved the seeds," echoed Nguri. To Ngina's
amazement, her father clicked approval. "So, we may
have time."

"Time for what, honored Father?"

"Time for our world," answered Nguri sharply, but his
impatience did not seem to be directed at Ngina. "Tell
me the rest," he ordered.

Ngina clicked in dutiful compliance.

                    *   *   *

Akras walked slowly through the sullied corridors of
the vessel where she had once been young. The Bercali
swine had vandalized the original furnishings but had discarded little. Those Rea warriors who marched ahead of
Akras raised their knives in silent tribute to each faded
sign of the Rea past.

The work of clearing the ship of its cargo of dead proceeded swiftly, bowing to the determination of pent years
of Rea frustration. The sterilization that the daar'va had
begun would be complete before Akras would reclaim
the home vessel formally. Akras wished that she could

share her people's joy of conquest. Returning to the site of so much pain brought her only a renewal of anger.

She had recognized Roake's escape with the daar'va proudly—and cursed herself for considering the traitor's son her own. She hoped that Ares would not share her weakness of respect for Roake. She wanted Ares to be enraged by his brother's escape from the daar'va's programmed deadliness, the lethal gift of the Rea to the ignorant Bercali. She intended that Ares turn full Essenji vengeance-lust against his own brother, and Akras would see another fragment of her shattered honor restored. She did not doubt that Ares would obey her, but she did not like to make him suffer over her commands.

The *traitor* had made her own deceptions necessary. The *traitor* forced her to wield one son against the other, allowing each to think himself favored, encouraging all Rea to believe that the feud lay only between Roake and Ares. One son would die, and the other would despise her, but the *traitor* would be destroyed, and Akras would be avenged.

Akras entered the cold control room of the vessel that had once been the Rea home. "Strip all Bercali furnishings from this place," she ordered tersely, "and sterilize all that remains." Two young warriors raised their knives in salute, and they begin to pry the Bercali markings from the command console.

CHAPTER 34

The ivory wall panel felt cool, as Tori's fingers traced the etching of a budding rose. She leaned against the panel, as she stared up the stairway that led to Birk's office. The upper window let its light fall gently on her face.

A door into the stairwell slid open. "You exceed my expectations, Mirelle," said Ares quietly, and he walked toward Tori, but he stopped and faced the stairs. "You do justice to your legend. I had feared otherwise, since you wasted yourself here, but I realize now that you must have a powerful reason. What did Birkaj offer that could entice a woman of your regal standards?"

"I'm not Mirelle, and I'm nothing more than a paid assistant." Ares had thrown back the hood of his cloak, but the black and silver mane only enhanced the deathly aspect of his sharp features. A ruby starburst at his throat resembled a mark of glistening blood.

"And I am a simple trader!" laughed Ares, his dark eyes shining with scorn, his pale hands active again in a disturbing, grasping gesture. "You and I do not need to wear the courteous, cowardly masks of those Soli fools who sit outside and pretend that catastrophe never strikes. You and I know what we seek. I respect you, Mirelle. I have read every legend of you, and I know that you are cunning."

"I don't know you," said Tori, irritated by his insistent use of the name she loathed, "and I don't know your purpose here."

"My purpose is one with your own, and I shall succeed. You might persuade me to accept you as an ally. You will not have Birkaj's treasures without me. Consider my offer, Mirelle."

Birk's treasures? wondered Tori, and she forced herself to smile at Ares, as if she understood him. "What about your partner, Harrow?" she asked. "Would he want me as an ally?"

A rapid crackling startled Tori, until she realized that Ares had merely snapped his oddly jointed fingers. "I acknowledge no partnership, least of all with such a weak fool as Harrow. Those whom I accept may serve me or receive my enmity. It is their choice."

"You expect me to serve you?"

"I expect you to recognize that I am worthy of you, as you are worthy of me. Such a balance is rare. We could be extraordinary together, and our power would be as the sun above a cringing world."

Ares withdrew as he had come, and Tori shook herself in relief at his departure. With firm determination, she climbed the stairs. The door to Birk's office was open, and she entered. The office was pristine and orderly. No sign of death or violence remained. A fresh pink rose occupied an emerald vase on Birk's lacquer desk.

Tori went to the wall unit and opened the transceiver cover, but the cubicle was empty. Only a slight silver scratch suggested that any equipment had ever occupied that vacant space. Methodically, Tori began to search the cupboards and drawers of the office. Ordinary supplies, orderly file references to customers and delivery schedules, a mimovue of Sylvie as a bright-faced girl. Nothing exceptional or untoward presented itself.

With a cautious glance toward the door, Tori tapped the wall beneath the rose prints, and she placed her fingertips on the patterned wallpaper in a practiced sequence. Acknowledging her fingerprints and body chemistry along with the order of her touches, the wall safe opened. Tori extracted the bundled contents and scanned them quickly. All of the major Hodge contracts and patents were present, but all of Birk's personal documents were gone.

Tori thrust the contracts back into the recess, and she closed the safe hurriedly. She walked to the door again and ensured that she was still alone. She did not want anyone—particularly her inquisitor—to ask her why she had access to Birk's safe. She could have answered that Birk had never used the wall safe for anything of significant worth, but the explanation sounded feeble even to her. She suspected that Birk had offered her such tokens of trust in an effort to increase his control of her, but she was not that certain of her conclusion.

She frowned, trying to recall any document in Birk's safe that could have value to anyone but Birk. Birth registrations for Calem and Sylvie, an unreadable marriage agreement, and old trade licenses from the spans before Birk settled on Stromvi had little obvious value to anyone but Birk. All of a Consortium member's necessary records resided in Prili data files, and even those records lost meaning with the death of the owner.

Tori turned to the door frame and began to trace the indentations that marked the sensors of the security system. She touched one of the shadowy circles. It was quite cold and obviously inactive. She made a thorough inspection of the room, touching each indentation within her reach, and she discovered no warmth, no vibration, no reassuring indication of activity. She recalled the glowing promises of the enthused Jiucetsi salesman, and she grimaced. The expensive Jiucetsi security system appeared to be entirely inoperative, and only Birk should have been able to deactivate it completely.

Returning downstairs and entering the wide east hall, Tori glimpsed Thalia peering from a stairway that led to the larger segment of the second floor. The Deetari woman chirped unintelligibly and turned away quickly. Tori called to Thalia and took a few steps after her, but Thalia clutched her bundle of linens and hurried up the steps.

Having been so clearly avoided, Tori allowed Thalia the privilege of escape. The slim chance that Thalia could give a coherent explanation of her actions did not seem to merit pursuit.

Thalia had never possessed the clear, practical wits of her Deetari sister, Gisa. Although Thalia always performed the actual labor of serving the Hodge meals, Gisa normally maintained a very visible presence as supervisor. Tori preferred not to consider why Gisa remained so glaringly absent on this peculiar morning.

Disturbed by Thalia's retreat and equally determined to avoid the dining patio, Tori retraced her steps as far as the stairwell. She turned the sharp corner into the next large wing, choosing to exit the house through the long display rooms, where the tributes accorded to various Hodge roses formed a museum of Birk Hodge's accomplishments. Porcelain renditions of several of the most significant Hodge hybrids bloomed under glowing orbs that imitated the blue-toned Stromvi sunlight. Tattered golden prize-banners of Consortium competitions looked sickly and sad.

None of the awards or testimonials mentioned contributions of the Stromvi people. Nguri had never allowed his own name to appear, and his people had followed his precedent. Birk had been glad enough to accept full credit for the genius of Hodge Farm.

Tori had once chided Birk for taking undue rewards, but Birk had silenced her with a smiling reply: "I may have taken advantage of other beings in my life, Tori, but I've never abused the Stromvi. No one can take anything from a Stromvi that the Stromvi doesn't choose to give." His unusually insightful remark had impressed her.

Tori touched the broad, chill petals of a Golden Ardor rose, releasing the fragrance that accompanied the display. She tilted her head and closed her eyes to savor the rich, fruity aroma that had become a favorite ingredient of Mequisti perfumers—and a personal trademark of Tori's mother for a few spans. Uncle Per had purchased two dozen of the Golden Ardor rose bushes from Birk Hodge. It was during the planting of them that Tori had first met Birk.

Birk had always spoken freely about the economic significance of establishing a garden for a Soli of Per Walis' wealth and influence. Tori had refused to recognize any aspect of their business together except Hodge Farm roses. She had imagined that Birk had come to accept her on that basis, accepting the limitations of her access to Uncle Per in light of her proven value to legitimate Hodge Farm concerns.

However, if Birk had hidden "treasures," as Ares had indicated, perhaps Birk's other ambitions had extended even further than Tori's reluctant speculations. Perhaps Birk had known about his assistant's past scandals from the start. Perhaps he had wanted even more than the daughter of a rich man's concubine. Perhaps he had wanted *Mirelle* all along.

Feeling the old hurt tighten inside of her, Tori stepped quickly away from the rose display and its haunting fragrance. The rear door resisted her, for it was seldom

used, and violet flecks of encroaching Stromvi plant life
dotted the shuttered door's edges. With a firm shove that
creaked and rattled, Tori pushed open the door and
stepped into the shadowy yard at the rear of the house.

A few scattered rose beds, less orderly than those at
the front of the house, bloomed against a violet backdrop
of Stromvi's natural terrain. None of the rose colors were
harsh, here where Stromvi fields were clearly visible.
Plans to cultivate all of the property surrounding Hodge
House had never been completed. The north side of the
museum wing rested like a frail bastion against eternal
Stromvi land. Beyond it, the closed back wing of the
house formed a nearly-forgotten mound, almost completely buried beneath Stromvi vines.

Tori crossed the empty yard toward the garage, listening for any sound of life other than her own. She
could hear nothing from the house and nothing from the
fields. Bereft of Stromvi clicking, windless Stromvi was
a very silent world.

Someone had taped a protective membrane across the
garage lock that Jase had broken. The hangar door was
closed tightly, but the side door stood open, and Tori
hastened toward it with a sudden, anxious yearning to
discover whether the hovercrafts had returned along with
the Hodge siblings. Under normal circumstances, she
would not have considered trying to fly a hovercraft without a more experienced pilot beside her, but the prospect
of escaping—to anywhere—brought a familiar, reckless
urgency into her heart.

The hangar lights, triggered by her motion, flared into
brightness as she entered. Two port rental units resided
placidly in their allotted spaces. A robotic maintenance
arm extended from the ceiling and polished the weathered surface of the farthest hovercraft with wide, slow
circular motions.

Tori tried the nearest ship first. It fulfilled her expectations by remaining impervious to her access efforts.
Rental ships were not intended to make unauthorized
use easy. The second ship sat as cold and unyielding as
its sister. Tori thumped the ship's green-and-silver side
in frustration.

"Having trouble?"

Tori's nerves jumped, until she recognized Jase leaning

against the frame of the side door. She pushed the robotic arm out of her way and slid from the rental hovercraft to the floor. "Can you enter either of these ships?" she asked him.

"Not lawfully. My own ship is still missing."

"Legal niceties are not my highest priority at the moment."

Jase raised one dark brow, and he gave her a tilted smile. "The warm atmosphere of good fellowship at breakfast didn't make you feel at home?" he tutted. "And I thought Sylvie and Calem were concealing their grief so effectively. You should have stayed longer. Thalia's pastry skills really are exceptional."

"Did you learn anything useful?"

"Bits and pieces. Calem and Sylvie think they've been here all along, which we know to be untrue. Harrow is quite conscious of having arrived at Hodge Farm only yesterday. Your friend Ares is clever enough to avoid confronting me. He recognizes me, though he only suspects me of being a minor Consortium official." Jase ambled across the hangar toward Tori as he spoke, his hands plunged deep into the pockets of Birk's linen coat. He stopped in front of her, but he watched the labors of the robotic arm above him.

Exasperated by his impassiveness, Tori snapped her fingers to take his attention from the automatic maintenance. "I still intend to leave this planet, Mister Inquisitor. Do you plan to help me, or do you prefer Hodge hospitality?"

"I intend," he answered, "to locate some relaweed, as I believe I mentioned, and that little effort takes precedence over the stealing of a hovercraft. The latter, I might add, is not a trivial task for me either, since I'm hardly a practiced thief." He lowered his gaze from the robotic arm to Tori. "You did offer to take me to Ngina, if you recall."

"A hovercraft could facilitate the journey," countered Tori, unwilling to accept Jase's reluctance easily, "as I believe you advised me some days ago."

"Retaliating with my own advice is an unkind tactic, but it's also ineffective in this case. Intervening events have changed my perspective significantly. A hovercraft, Miss Darcy, brings a dearth of privacy as its price, in

addition to placing me in a very awkward position with
both my hosts and my absent conspirator, Roake. I already know that you walked the distance from the
Stromvi tunnel once, so it cannot be too arduous a journey for a Soli."

"The hovercrafts are here now. They may disappear
again, while we conduct your search and inquisition."

"He who has the relaweed is not likely to be abandoned, I think."

Sesserda calm really is marvelously contagious, mused
Tori. "Perhaps not," she conceded, her nervousness easing enough to let her feel intrigued by the idea of relaweed as the treasure that Ares sought. "I'll take you
to the tunnel where I left Ngina."

"Thank you," murmured Jase.

He followed her lead into the garden with docile graciousness. He strolled beside her with every indication of
easy peace, but he did not speak, and he only smiled
and nodded absently at Tori's few crisp comments and
questions. Tori concluded wryly that his attention was
not on her. If he watched the garden for observing eyes,
Tori could neither blame him nor regret his vigilance.

Tori led him without hesitation toward the roses that
bordered southern Stromvi fields. She knew the Hodge
gardens. She knew the path she had walked from the
cleverly hidden tunnel entrance. She felt perfect confidence, until she neared her goal and saw a level expanse
of twisted cling vines that she did not remember. She
paused for only an instant, but Jase stopped.

"You're unsure," he accused her.

"No." She bent to the ground and reached cautiously
through the vines. She touched the soft soil beneath them
and felt its spongy warmth. "The moss path has been shifted
and covered very recently. These vines weren't growing
here yesterday. They cling by emitting a trail of very thick,
sticky resin, which hasn't even dampened the ground yet."

Tori pulled at the nearest vine, and the tendrils lifted
easily away from the surface. Jase stepped past her and
took hold of the thickest section of the matted growth.
It shifted without resistance. "Where is the entrance?"
he asked.

"Nearly where you're standing, I think. It cannot be
more than three meters from you, because I saw the

color shadings of that line of roses from this angle. I remember the placement of these five lily spikes, and they're rooted solidly." Tori pushed at the referenced spikes in proof.

Jase began to search, kicking the soil and digging into soft patches with his hands. After a few futile microspans, Tori began to help him. She could see his doubts increase, as her own certainty became frustration. She had emerged here. She trusted her memory.

They searched, but they found no trace of a tunnel entrance. "They've closed the access," sighed Tori, acknowledging defeat at last. "Someone must have questioned Ngina about my absence, and Nguri didn't want me to come and go too freely." She met Jase's peculiarly inconstant eyes defiantly. "I've told you the truth, Inquisitor. I did leave Ngina here."

Instead of answering, Jase sat on the mossy ground where he had begun his search, and he laid both hands flat against the earth beside him. He sat in silence for a full microspan, his eyes closed and his expression intense. "Hear me, people of the Ngena Valley," he whispered in a voice that vibrated with deep emotion. Though the persuasion was not aimed at her, Tori could feel its penetrating force, a trembling of air that transcended Soli-recognized sound. "You know me. You know that I'm not your enemy." He ended with a string of rhythmic clicks that could almost have issued from a Stromvi throat. It was a Stromvi plea for forgiveness.

"They cannot hear you," said Tori quietly. She felt an unexpected sympathy for him. At that moment, he seemed so innocently convinced that his Sesserda faith could overcome all barriers of distrust and fear. *As Birk said, Jase Sleide is an idealist*, thought Tori, faintly dismayed by her compassion for an inquisitor. "They wouldn't believe you if they did hear, because you're a Soli. They knew Birk, and he betrayed them." Jase relaxed his splayed hands and regarded Tori with a solemn attentiveness. "Stromvi have the tenacity of an old cling weed," she continued, trying to smile, "and they trust wholeheartedly or not at all. If they've decided to condemn the Soli species, your pleas will not persuade them to change."

Jase rubbed resinous moss from his fingers, and he

pried a prickly leaf from his straight, dark hair. He
turned a very serious expression upward to Tori, who
still stood before him. The sunlight gave the iridescent
shadings of his eyes the metallic brilliance that made him
seem most alien. He leaned forward, resting his hands
on his crossed ankles, where the lua-leather straps of
borrowed sandals bound the loose trouser legs. "You
have too much insight to spend your life fighting your
own history," admonished Jase severely. "Warring with
yourself is a poor life-purpose."

"I'm not a Sesserda follower," replied Tori, startled by
his earnest indictment, "and I don't need an inquisitor's
advice."

Jase merely nodded, but the gesture seemed more indicative of resignation than of agreement. "Where is the
relaweed?" he asked softly of the sky. "Does Ngina have
any idea of the danger of what she found?"

"She knows that it caused Ngoi's death."

"Ngoi's guilt caused his death." Jase wrapped his
hands behind his neck and bowed his head. "The drug's
inherent danger terrifies me, Tori. When the seeds begin
to burst, the drug will contaminate the air. The relanine
oil will attach itself to the resin particles, and it will infiltrate every life-form on this planet. Death-watch encom-
passes all of Stromvi by now. We may already be too late."

Jase's grim attitude troubled Tori more than his words.
She pushed aside a clump of rootless vine strands, and
she seated herself on the warm, loamy ground, facing
her inquisitor. She touched the linen that covered his
knee, sharing an ache of honest fear for a world and a
people that mattered to her. "What happens to the people of Stromvi if the relanine spreads?" asked Tori.

"They achieve death, mutation, or addiction," replied
Jase with crisp irony, "in that order of preference. Having been acutely addicted to relanine for the past five
spans, I can attest to the unpleasant effects with considerable authority."

Deeply shocked, Tori withdrew her hand from him.
Jase smiled wryly. "You're an addict?" she demanded,
trying to discern some hint of strange, inquisitorial
humor or deliberate provocation in his words. Drug addiction seemed antithetical to all she knew of Sesserda.

Such abuse of a natural creation could hardly be considered respectful of the creation's original design.

Jase asked with dry, almost scholarly curiosity, "How many other Soli do you know whose eyes glow in the day or night, with or without an external light source?"

"I've never made a point of gazing into your eyes," said Tori briskly, though she could not help but stare at the iridescence now. His dire predictions for Stromvi frightened her, but they seemed unassailable. His personal revelation distressed her on a fundamental level: Inquisitors should surely be above such frailties as addiction implied. Her cynical views on Consortium justice became a measure more disturbing, and her opinions of Jase Sleide became a measure more complex. Every time she thought she had him categorized neatly, he overturned all of her expectations. He was as mutable as the substance that apparently filled him. "Isn't relanine the primary component of adaptation fluid?"

"It's the only active component."

"Everyone who travels in the Consortium uses adaptation fluid—without becoming addicted."

"Legal adaptation fluid is processed, blended, and weakened to a point of being nearly unidentifiable as a relanine derivative. An average addict's body absorbs more relanine in a millispan than you're likely to encounter in a lifetime—although you're absorbing an extra dose by just being with me. My personal habit demands far more than average measures."

Unconsciously alarmed, Tori edged away from him slightly. "You mean that you're as dangerous to Stromvi as the relaweed?"

"No," he answered with a somewhat bleak smile. "Unadapted relanine is much more volatile than hosted relanine, and the oils in relaweed move into the former category if the seeds die."

"Why haven't I seen you taking extra inoculations?" asked Tori, still uncertain of whether to believe him.

He tapped his chest above the heart. The cream-colored shirt clung to his dark skin. "The Calongi equipped me with an implant that allows me to maintain my relanine supply without external replenishment for almost a span at a time, given a normal level of environmental changes." He sighed, as if reaching a long-avoided decision. "You may believe me, Miss Darcy. I'm not attempting to provoke a reaction for purposes of inqusition. I am indeed a relanine addict. I survive only because I have sympathetic Calongi friends and sufficient assets to afford my very expensive habit."

What did I think had caused the strangeness of his eyes? mused Tori, accepting slowly: *Cosmetic enhancements to make a Soli inquisitor more intimidating? How better for a Soli to become a third level Sesserda adept than by adopting the traits of his Sesserda masters?* "The Soli inquisitor," murmured Tori pensively, "who is half Calongi."

Jase shrugged, as if he had heard her description too often to contradict it. "The Rea are quite right about relanine's capacity to enhance the senses and increase the body's durability, but they're mad to covet the gifts that command such a price."

"You apparently made that choice."

"Not voluntarily."

Tori studied the luminous signs of relanine's impact with wonder. "How did you become addicted?" she asked.

"An accident," replied Jase tersely. "Do you know of any other access to the southern caverns?"

She almost retorted regarding the brevity of his answer, but instead she shook her head. "None that I could find again. Many of the old tunnels are unstable. Others have been filled. I wouldn't know where to begin a search."

Jase nodded in acknowledgment and jumped to his feet. "The southern field, Calem's field. Where the relaweed was grown, where Ngoi died. I'll see you later, I hope. Thank you for your help." He began to stride along the path to the Stromvi fields, his long legs covering the ground swiftly, and he turned where the path forked toward the southern portion of Hodge Farm.

Tori watched him until he disappeared behind a row of tall, violet magi reeds. She laced her fingers and rested her chin on her hands, her elbow propped against her knee. The Stromvi sun felt hot. She twisted her long hair into a knot and pulled the sun-hood over her head.

CHAPTER 35

Roake pried the last inoculation patch from his arm, leaving a raw, iridescent stain where the skin had absorbed far more adaptation fluid than prudence dictated, even for an addict. The fluid used by Roake was a dangerously potent blend even in recommended dosage, for he had bought it at great cost from a particularly avaricious Cuui. He still owed much of the promised price in service to the Cuui. He had also pledged a harvest of Stromvi-grown relaweed, knowing even as he made the desperate bargain that the deal could not be kept. If the Consortium did not confiscate the relaweed, Per Walis would eventually claim it. Roake had never believed his own fervent proclamations about establishing the Rea as the fourth independent relaweed source, but he obeyed the clan leader and told no one of his doubts.

Roake's breathing began to lose the raggedness of incipient relanine illness, as the adaptation fluid flowed through him, enacting its subtle changes. The resinous Stromvi atmosphere, instead of hovering on the edge of deadliness, became merely unpleasant again. Roake had nearly crossed the line of permanent damage this time, waiting so long to replenish his supply.

He still resented the uncertainty that had tormented him, tempting him to consider for even a moment the insolent offer of a Soli to share blood like an Essenji brother. Roake flexed his arm. The raw wound of inoculation had nearly disappeared already, and his sunburned skin had regained most of its suppleness. Roake seldom expended futile energy on regrets, but his recent doubts disturbed him. The clan leader had promised to cache his adaptation fluid at the prearranged deposit point. Now that the tingling traces of relanine had restored him, he admitted to himself that he had disbelieved her.

If she had allowed him the promised day, Roake remained convinced that he could have retrieved the Rea treasures and submitted the Rea-traitor to Rea justice. Roake understood, of course, that the clan leader had anticipated his intention to kill the Rea-traitor himself. Why else would she have allowed Ares to usurp the war leader's privileges?

This twisted plan of hers required much faith. Ares was a worthy foe—too worthy to be encouraged to label his brother a traitor, even temporarily—and Roake could not discern the clan leader's reasons for maintaining the extra layer of deception. Remembrance of the clan leader's warning about Ares' jealousy made the present burden of isolation no easier. The clan leader had also ordered Roake to endure whatever actions Ares took, until the larger plan could reach fruition. She had not mentioned the scope of Ares' ambitions. Perhaps she had taken it for granted that Roake shared her understanding of Ares. Roake did not like to admit that his brother had always been a mystery to him.

With a grudging sigh, Roake concluded that his recent tendency to dispute the clan leader's wisdom had undoubtedly caused her to design her plan for multiple purposes. She demanded absolute faith and obedience, as was her right as clan leader. Not even the war leader could be spared the hard lessons of Rea discipline. Roake wondered if even loyal Tagran had the clan leader's full confidence.

Roake assured himself that his current ostracism would soon be righted by the clan leader. However, this business of deception among the Rea troubled Roake. He had not quite recovered from the shock of being attacked by his own clan. *They behaved properly,* Roake assured himself: *Rea warriors are trained to obey the clan leader above all, and she obviously conferred authority to Ares for the Hodge Farm sortie.* But the idea that Rea warriors might believe Ares' claims of Roake's treachery still grated. All Rea, even Roake's wives, were as ignorant as Ares of the clan leader's orders to Roake.

Roake glanced at his stolen ship's message panel, but the awaited signal had not yet appeared. He reverified the codes, while deriding his obsessive repetition of that simple action. The clan leader would contact him, as ar-

ranged, and his doubts were dishonorable as well as foolish. She could not have had time yet to complete even
the recovery of the home vessel.

As he reapproached the Ngenga Valley, Roake set the
controls of his stolen craft for battle status, for he liked
to be prepared, and he did not entirely trust any plan
that involved his brother. With care, he set his fingers in
the indentations of a heavy crate's locking mechanism,
and he slid open the lid. He removed a layer of thick
insulating foam, and he gathered the sheltered device
into his hand with great delicacy.

It was the controlling mechanism of the last great Rea
treasure, the final vestige of a larger power that once
had nearly justified the immensity of Rea pride. It was
the programming unit of the daar'va, the war leader's
tool that Ares—and presumably Akras, as well—had
been willing to sacrifice in order to destroy the Bercali.
The Bercali had paid for it with both trade goods and
service, believing themselves clever, and they had paid
for their conceit with their lives.

When Roake had laid the basic plan to recover the
home vessel, he had intended to make recovery of the
daar'va the first Rea priority after boarding. The ritual
destruction of the enemies' bodies could certainly have
waited. *He* would never have allowed another agent to
remove the daar'va first. Granted, only the Rea and the
Bercali had any concept of the daar'va's value, and the
Bercali would be dead. Only a Rea would have known
how to locate the daar'va by its sound patterns.

Roake did not need to see the Rea cleanse the home
vessel to know that Akras had succeeded in reclaiming
it from the Bercali interlopers. Roake's satisfaction at
her achievement was as real as his buried fury against
her decision, which had denied him the right of walking
beside her in reclaiming that vital segment of lost Rea
honor. He had stolen the daar'va as much from that
anger as from a real concern for his personal survival.

The clan leader had placed the daar'va in his care. She
had never retracted that order to him. He had every right
to claim it.

Roake was less able to rationalize his escape from the
boarded vessel. Despite the conflict on Stromvi, despite
Ares' ambitions, Roake was still Rea. If the clan leader

had appeared, he would have trusted her to acknowledge him as war leader still. But she had not come. Rea warriors, men he knew, had pursued him through the vessel as if he were indeed a traitor.

He resented most that the clan leader's deception had forced him to attack Rea warriors in escaping the prison ship. The warriors had worn the light-distorting protection suits, but those suits were not designed to withstand strong chemical fire. If Rea warriors had died from that skirmish, the Soli had absorbed the death-curses, but the wastefulness of Rea resources offended Roake at a fundamental level.

In imprisoning Roake in the Bercali tomb, Ares had apparently underestimated his brother's ability to survive the preprogrammed shift in environment. Roake wondered if his mother knew of Ares' greatest treachery— or if she had concocted it for her own deep purpose. If Akras had known of Roake's incarceration, she might have tolerated it as another element of discipline. She would have known that he could survive. Perhaps she had intended that he take the daar'va.

Then why did Rea warriors chase him through the prison corridors, until he evaded them long enough to escape? If he had not encountered that ubiquitous Soli, he would not have been able to take more than a segment of the daar'va.

Roake despised the doubts that seemed to rise within him at every turn. The sacred authority of the clan leader could not be disputed. The clan leader had vowed to Roake that his position was secure, that any evidence to the contrary served only as a brief deception necessary to the redemption of Rea honor. Nothing had required her to give Roake even that meager hint of her intentions. The Rea-traitor must suffer and be destroyed: That was paramount.

But the Soli claimed that the Rea-traitor was already dead. "No," growled Roake softly. The Soli lied, or he was mistaken, deluded by some trick of the Rea-traitor. The Rea-traitor could not have died so easily. The Rea-traitor, despite spans of denial, was still Essenji, and only another Essenji could kill him. The clan leader had sworn that only Ares would be allowed that privilege, and the death would occur with her as witness. Ares would not choose to sit with the Hodge offspring except to lure the Rea-traitor from hiding. The Rea-traitor still lived— unless the clan leader deceived again. . . .

Roake shook his head, impatient with himself and the questions that a tenacious Soli had added to an already uncomfortable load. The Soli was an irritation, aggravatingly adept at using his addiction to advantage, but he was too well connected to dismiss. He was clearly a Consortium official of some minor sort. He had worn Calongi-marked silks when Claudius first captured him, and he had obviously taken that Calongi-marked hovercraft to Hodge Farm.

Even if the clan leader failed to acknowledge the danger of killing a Consortium official, Roake could not sanction an act that would virtually ensure the end of any Consortium tolerance regarding the Rea. Roake assured himself repeatedly that respect of the Consortium's power did not imply cowardice. Such respect represented only good sense, for the Consortium *was* immense, and the Rea *were* small.

Roake did not regret having freed the Soli after the initial capture, despite the clan leader's subsequent anger. He did not regret the Soli's survival of the daar'va attack on the home vessel, though the Rea *might* have managed to escape blame for a minor official's death in a Bercali prison. Roake continued to believe that the Soli was too insignificant to comprise a danger in himself. The Soli would be much more threatening if he died at Rea hands, for Consortium inquisitors had uncanny skills at learning the perpetrators of such deeds. Additional Calongi attention was not what Rea needed. The Rea had already assumed too many risks.

No, the Soli's death was not yet ordained, whatever Ares and the clan leader might profess. If nothing else, the Soli provided Roake with an extra measure of insurance regarding his own restoration of rank and honor: The Soli might actually locate the relaweed. The Soli had already proven unexpectedly resourceful—and intriguingly prompt—in finding the Rea-traitor's concubine, who might well have knowledge of the Rea-traitor's whereabouts. If the Rea-traitor were hidden among the Stromvi, the gullible Soli might be useful in transferring that information to Roake. With the Rea-traitor, the relaweed, the daar'va, and the kree'va in his possession, Roake would be able to redeem his Rea honor even without the clan leader's aid.

Roake unpacked the contents of three more crates, uncovering only the miscellany of excess Rea tools that had made the daar'va seem more impressive and valuable to the credulous Bercali. Roake opened the final crate, which held the second key element of the daar'va, the tracking module that Ares—despite his rashness—had wisely separated from the larger system. The atmospheric disruption that had destroyed the foul Bercali had required only the daar'va's primary module. Use of the daar'va in its entirety produced effects that could too readily be exploited by the possessor of the kree'va.

The tracking element regulated the daar'va's effects into particulate lattices at a programmed array of distances and orientations. The ordered lattices formed a series of remote virtual systems that enabled the daar'va to derive the location of its sister system from the multipath returns of the scanning tones. The tracking process became reciprocal if the kree'va were active.

Roake did not mind announcing himself to the Rea-traitor. Let the clan leader deceive Ares; let Ares deceive the Hodges. Roake intended to fulfill his own pledge to the Rea, and he would not endure a passive role. He had offered his brother fair warning, sweeping the stolen hovercraft ostentatiously across the Hodge gardens and house.

Roake tailored the daar'va's programming to the Stromvi environment. With sober care, he connected the tracking system to the rest of the daar'va and activated the whole. The waves of sound-shock, the overt manifestation of a multifaceted system, rippled over Stromvi. The first results appeared on the daar'va's compact screen, displaying where the heat of susceptible electronic devices had been rendered cold by the daar'va's interference with internal cells of selected gaseous media. The identification traces of deactivated photonics were less detectable, but the confidence indicator measured high. The first function also registered the location and mass of warm-blooded life-forms, but the inadequacy of data below the Stromvi surface made such information useless to Roake at present.

The second function proceeded, and Roake became more attentive. Each of three submodules issued a tone of triangulation, discerning the target as if from three distinct locations. The fourth submodule remained silent, denying the daar'va the information needed to add a precise time reading to the three position variables.

Roake muttered at the device, "Even you refuse to accord me the rights of Rea war leader." He did not need the fourth tone to locate a stationary target, but the signal's absence troubled him. Instead of solidifying the conclusions of Roake's first attempt to use the daar'va, just prior to his brother's unexpectedly personal attack, the current results only reiterated Roake's private uncertainty.

Roake overlaid the parameters of the position fix on the Stromvi survey grid, and his frown deepened. The kree'va still registered at a location below the planet's surface, but it had moved substantially since the last fix. It no longer lay beneath Hodge House.

"Someone knew about the kree'va and recognized the use of the daar'va to search for it," whispered Roake, nodding to himself in slightly sour satisfaction. "Not the clan leader, for Ares would have gloated over finding the kree'va, and the Rea have had no opportunity to recover it since handing the daar'va to the Bercali." He concluded grimly, "The Rea-traitor still lives." Roake began to repack the daar'va with quick, efficient care. "So much for the annoying Soli's claims," he said with scorn, but he found himself making the Rea sign of protection against a fallen foe's death-curse.

*   *   *

Tori felt and heard the sound-shock, and she did not even dare to breathe until it had faded. Her ears seemed to ring with the lingering tones, until she shook her head to free herself from the surge of terror. For a quiet moment in the aftermath of fear, she pondered the possible new catastrophes that might await her.

She realized only gradually that the normal sounds of Stromvi had resumed. No single voice began. All of Stromvi seemed to return to interrupted life by common consent. The usual array of soft, clicking chatter spread across the fields, speaking of the state of this or that planting, gossiping cheerfully about the latest pairing of younglings. Instead of reassuring Tori with its normalcy, the prosaic resumption of routine seemed to seal the chill unreality that had settled across the world.

"I'd even welcome Uncle Per at this point." At her ironic murmur, a black-and-gold shuttle sped across the sky, slowed above the Hodge landing field, and dropped out of view beyond the intervening hedges. "Sesserda markings," she murmured, almost disbelieving what she had just seen. The black-and-gold vessel had been too large to be called a hovercraft, which was definitely the label that Jase had given to his own missing ship. Another Sesserda adept had come to Stromvi: another inquisitor.

A surge of terror displaced all saner reactions of joy or relief, but Tori refused to acknowledge her own emotions. "I don't care who you are," she informed the unseen new arrival, "as long as you can provide passage off this planet." She clambered to her feet, pried a clinging seedpod from her skirt, and headed toward the house.

She told herself that she was behaving with the same rashness that had embroiled her first with Arnod Conaty, then with Birk and the current chaos, but she did not slow her pace. Rashness had not killed her yet, and Great-grandmama Mirelle had never shied from taking risks. Mama and Lila could keep Tori's share of caution if the safe course meant the likes of Uncle Per.

*   *   *

Omi allowed the shuttle's ramp to lower him gently to the ground, while his diverse senses examined Stromvi in minute detail. The apparently normal conversations of Stromvi field workers did not support the premise of death-watch. He searched for other inconsistencies.

He compared his perceptions with the Prili data that he had examined and concluded that an alien element had been added since the data's last update. Perhaps it was the Soli presence; perhaps it was a less obvious alteration. The new data would require analysis and comparison against many possibilities. Omi dedicated one brain segment to the immediate task of correlating the data with his internal records.

An obvious aberration in the atmosphere was a minor excess of relanine. The measured value was still too slight to merit concern. Perhaps adaptation fluid had been spilled, or physical stress had caused relanine to escape its unnatural Soli-addict host in abnormally large quantities. Self-adapted relanine generally remained affixed to its living tissue, as opposed to the supremely volatile habits of the pure fluid, but predictions were uncertain regarding a Soli.

By the time the ramp had deposited Omi on the planet's surface, Omi had discarded nine hundred and thirteen species from his list of potentially contaminating life-forms. His own memory records contained the details of over six hundred thousand species known to the Consortium, and he continued his process of correlation of his Stromvi perceptions with calculated species' effects on the Stromvi atmosphere. His ship's records might contain another two million, but a thorough assessment would require access to the Prili data base. The magnitude of the task did not daunt Omi, but he was disappointed that his first selections had not proven statistically viable.

Omi bowed slightly in acknowledgment of the approaching male, wrapped in a dark cloak. At a slightly greater distance, Omi identified the Hodge children and a Soli man. Omi noted the extreme nervousness of Sylvie Hodge, along with a plethora of lesser details that suggested drug-induced agitation, in the already-vast compendium of his inquisitor's observations for this unofficial assignment. "I am Omi, honored Calongi inquisitor and full Sesserda master," he announced evenly.

The unidentified man stepped forward, and Omi admired the quick control of reaction that the man demonstrated. "We are honored by your presence, noble Calongi. May I inquire as to the reason for the singular privilege of your visit?"

"An inquisitor was summoned to this place," answered Omi. He observed closely and determined that the man had detected the equivocation of the answer. "You are an Essenji." The stranger bowed, smiling very slightly. "Your name is not associated with the files for this location, respected Essenji."

"I am Ares, a guest of the Hodges."

Omi noted the underlying scorn that accompanied Ares' use of the Hodge name. Omi heightened the remote senses that examined Calem Hodge: Fear and uncertainty pervaded the young man, making more refined readings difficult. "How many other guests are here at present?"

Ares answered, "I am the only guest, at present, unless you count Harrow Febro, who is here to marry Miss Sylvie Hodge. There was a stranger here earlier: a Soli. I believe he came to visit Mister Birk Hodge, who is away from this planet on business. Have you come in pursuit of this stranger? I wondered about him, but I had not considered that he might be dangerous."

Omi sensed the presence of a much larger number of non-Stromvi beings than Ares indicated, but the fragments of data would require further assessment to provide specific numbers and locations. "My ship perceived a peculiar sound pattern moments before my arrival. Did you enact it?"

"I heard nothing unusual," replied Ares innocently.

He lies in every detail, mused Omi, *trying to deny me a precise gauge of truth. He will be difficult.* Omi issued a brief, lyrical whistling of the Deetari language, and Gisa emerged cautiously into the open doorway of the shuttle. Omi stepped off the landing platform and let it rise to Gisa's level. "You will both accompany me," commanded Omi, and he moved smoothly across the landing field toward the house.

Gisa jumped from the shuttle and ran to join Omi, though she remained a pace behind him. Ares followed unhurriedly. Omi observed a similar anxiety in both Deetari and Essenji, despite the difference in their outward behavior.

When he reached the garden area in view of the patio, Omi paused to note how the Hodges and their companion observed his arrival. Harrow's reaction verged on terror, though his expression remained fixed and confident. Calem seemed resigned and defeated. Sylvie was puzzled, but her attention was not on Omi.

"Gisa?" whispered Sylvie uncertainly, before Harrow gripped her arm tightly and angrily.

"Miss Ald has been most helpful in preparing me for

this visit," remarked Omi. Gisa reacted to his statement with alarm, but she said nothing.

"Master Omi is an inquisitor," offered Ares helpfully. "I assume that further introductions are unnecessary."

He is calculating his options for eliminating me if I threaten him, observed Omi with distaste. *He is a Level VII primitive.*

"Why are you here, Master Omi?" asked Harrow tensely. "Has someone reported a crime?"

"I am here in pursuit of truth," replied Omi mildly. "Please, calm yourselves. I intend you no harm."

"Of course not," murmured Ares dryly.

Thalia emerged onto the patio, glanced toward her sister and Omi, and proceeded to clear dishes from the table. "Go to her, Miss Gisa," said Omi in response to the Deetari woman's unspoken plea. Gisa did not hesitate to comply. She took the tray of dishes from her sister and whistled a command to enter the house. Thalia trilled in contentment and obeyed. The two Deetari women disappeared into the shadowy hall.

Omi resigned himself to face a situation that would certainly be distasteful. He announced impassively, "I should like the following individuals brought here promptly: Mister Birk Hodge, Miss Rillessa Canti, Miss Victoria Darcy, Mister Nguri Ngenga, and Mister Jase Sleide. Please endeavor to see that all requested persons are present."

Omi moved toward the gardens with great dignity while his audience watched with varying degrees of irritation and concern. Even Ukitan-lai would agree that a brief meditation was appropriate. Dealing patiently with so many primitives would require stern discipline.

* * *

Jase rubbed the burned stalk thoughtfully between his fingers, absently counting the gritty particles of carbon dust that he dislodged. He did not raise his glance when Roake approached. "I rather thought you'd find me here," remarked Jase quietly.

"I have been observing you, as I promised."

"I know," replied Jase equably. "You have a serious dearth of patience, my friend."

"I reserve my patience for worthy causes."

Jase dropped the burned stalk and knelt to wipe his fingers on the single patch of surviving moss. "You can't quite decide what to do with me, can you, Roake? You need allies, and I'm the only candidate you've found, but you really don't trust me in the slightest."

"Trust can be built on many bases." With pointed menace, Roake added, "Your lady friend is very beautiful."

"Miss Darcy? Yes, she is exceptional in many ways." Jase discounted the implied threat, but he pondered Roake's intentions curiously. "She would not, however, enjoy being accounted my possession. The lady doesn't care for my philosophy of life."

"She has discerning taste as well as beauty. Perhaps she could aid my search more capably than you."

Jase dropped the burned stalk and dusted the clinging carbon from his fingers. He stood and faced Roake squarely. With clear, exaggerated enunciation, he demanded, "Then why didn't you stop to question her when you first saw her with me? She's hardly intimidating, at least not in a confrontational sense." Sesserda perceptions fastened on an evasiveness of reaction. He asked softly, "What—or whom—does she represent to you?"

"She makes you expendable, Soli."

Jase only shook his head, recognizing hollow bluster. He extended one arm toward the dead field, his hand spread and opened to the sky. "Did you know how much relaweed was planted here, Roake? This one field, had it been allowed to reseed, could have contaminated the entire Ngenga Valley. You know enough about relanine to understand the magnitude of danger."

Roake retorted sharply, "Relanine gives freedom." He showed no sign of realizing that Sesserda influence had prodded him to speak.

"Excessive relanine gives lingering, agonizing death, as you and I both know." Jase continued grimly, "I'm pleased to see that you've managed to replenish your personal supply, since you were perilously close to exhaustion when last we met. Did you take your part from the Stromvi harvest, or did you bring your own fluid for the occasion?"

"Perhaps I was less 'exhausted' than you imagined, weak Soli. Did you expect to endure more capably than an Essenji warrior?"

"An Essenji warrior? You still claim the life-purpose of a member of the Rea. You haven't truly parted from them. You're a warrior, and you're Rea, and you're metaphorically blind. You, who consider yourself an advocate of personal freedom, were willing to condemn an entire world to the shackles that enslave you. I cannot believe you were stupid enough to abet this mad scheme to grow relaweed on Stromvi—or did you concoct it?"

"You cannot understand," replied Roake tersely. He clenched one fist. "It is a matter of honor."

"When 'honor' becomes an excuse for idiocy," snapped Jase, "it merits shame and not respect."

"Events can begin their own existence, independent of intention or control. Such events neither lessen nor increase a man's honor. They simply continue."

"I'm not that fatalistic. Accept your own responsibilities, Roake, and you may find that you have more allies than you think."

"Allies," muttered Roake, and he turned his back to Jase and raised his face to the sky. "Do you perceive the vastness above you, Soli? That is my domain—all of it. I do not need you. I require no one's permission to claim that which is rightfully my own."

"You've never felt alone before, have you? You're overcompensating for an unfamiliar sense of personal inadequacy. That 'vastness' belongs to no man, not to you and not to the Rea. Ownership is a cultural fiction, a convenience of social order, and your claims are more hollow than most."

"What did you learn from your fellow Soli?" growled Roake, folding his arms before him.

"They all have secrets, as does the Essenji with them. The Essenji calls himself Ares. Do you know him?"

"He is my brother," muttered Roake.

"I should imagine that he makes an unpleasant enemy."

"He is Rea," answered Roake, smiling thinly.

"And you both want more than relaweed from this world. Did you cause the sound-shocks?"

"No."

Yes, concluded Jase, but he gave no indication that

he had recognized the lie. "Do you know the Stromvi language?"

"A few words," admitted Roake.

"A sound-shock occurred a few days ago, and the Stromvi spoke of death-watch, then grew silent. They have resumed a semblance of normal life since the most recent sound-shock. Since their speech recommenced almost in unison, I suspect that they had predicted the occurrence of the latest sound-shock and planned for it."

"What is your point, Soli?"

"The Stromvi have the relaweed. Neither you nor your brother will be able to take it from them."

"That is the only reason I still tolerate you, Soli. You will retrieve the harvest for me. That was our agreement."

"I agreed to try to recover the relaweed before further contamination could occur, and you agreed to let me proceed as I deem best. I don't expect you to value my advice, but I shall give it, nonetheless: Cooperate with me, Roake. You're standing in the path of a torrential flood, and I'm the only high ground in sight."

"You waste my time." Roake turned abruptly toward his ship, resting half-concealed at the edge of the vine-mass.

"Do you hear a particularly regular, repetitive sequence of Stromvi clicks?" demanded Jase, before Roake had taken a step. "The Stromvi announce a summoning to Hodge House for the purpose of inquisition. While you were busy assessing the results of your sound-shock, a shuttle, bearing a Calongi inquisitor, passed over the rose fields." Roake stiffened. "He'll learn the truth about the Rea and the recent events here. Come with me, and you'll have a chance to survive the next few days. Otherwise, I think your enemies may win."

For a microspan, Roake did not answer, and Jase sensed the tug of forces that warred inside the Essenji: pride and uncertainty and unwilling belief in a Soli's perceptions. Jase felt the Essenji pride achieve its triumph via anger. "You understand nothing," growled Roake. "I've tolerated enough." Many frustrations found a focus. Jase gathered Sesserda energies, anticipating what was to come. With a roar of fury and a swift, furious leap, Roake aimed a powerful kick at Jase's head.

Jase let his body react according to Sesserda training,

unfettered by conscious design. The increments of time became ponderous. Roake seemed to hang suspended in the air. Jase moved away from the descending blow, peripherally aware of his own speed of action.

When he reached the bank of thorn vines, Jase paused to look back at Roake. Sesserda perceptions of time resumed their normal reckoning. Roake whirled in surprise, realizing that his target had eluded him. With a bit of deliberate showmanship, Jase strolled out of Roake's view at a leisurely pace.

CHAPTER 36

An unusually subdued Sylvie met Tori near the circular bed of white roses. "We're expected to gather at the front of the house immediately," announced Sylvie. "Where is that man you brought to luncheon?"

"I don't know," answered Tori briskly, and she wondered if Sylvie had actually forgotten Jase's name or feared to speak it. An unwanted pity for Sylvie nudged at Tori. Without Birk Hodge as her support and strength, Sylvie's pretensions seemed like empty gestures, an insecure woman's efforts to seem significant. "Where is Birk?" asked Tori, more gently than she had intended.

"Arranging some business dealings on Deetari," muttered Sylvie. She shaded her eyes from the glare of afternoon sun and stared toward the rose fields.

Birk has died, thought Tori with a pang of futile regret, *but it is Sylvie who resembles a ghost. She carries on the motions of life, unaware that the foundation of her brittle, dependent existence is gone.*

"No sign of the others arriving," said Sylvie, letting her hand fall limply to her side, "but I've filled my quota with you. Let him find his own subjects."

"What subjects?" asked Tori, though she feared that she knew the answer.

"Inquisitor's subjects, of course," replied Sylvie wearily, as if the prospect of inquisition constituted merely a tiresome, daily routine at Hodge Farm. "Do you think I run errands for anyone less than a Calongi?"

Determinedly, Tori pushed her instinctive terror beneath a bleak, defensive curtain of denial, repeating to herself endlessly that the Calongi would restore the peace to Stromvi. She could wear a mask of composure, but she could not make herself feel comforted. She resumed walking toward the house, and Sylvie kept pace with her.

Tori barely recognized that Sylvie still existed. Together, they emerged from the garden in front of the colonnade, where Calem and Harrow waited.

Omi stood silently at the base of the stairs, a dour icon robed in a mantle of his own sinuous outer-arms. Tori knew him at once, though she could distinguish few Calongi as individuals. The blue sense triangles along each side of Omi's head were unusually pronounced and slightly asymmetrical. She forced herself to speak his name calmly, "Master Omi. I did not expect to see you again."

Omi replied evenly, "Unusual circumstances follow you, Miss Mirelle."

Sylvie glanced at Tori with a vague show of curiosity but did not speak. Ares stepped from the shadows near the front door, and he nodded at Tori in ironic greeting. Thalia hovered near the far corner of the colonnade, as if eager to escape. Tori thought she could see Gisa as well, standing still and silent, close against the wall behind her sister.

Nguri arose from the nearest rose trench, and Tori took a step toward him. He turned his black gaze upon her forbiddingly, and Tori felt as suddenly ashamed as if he had caught her stealing manna from a child. She remained where she stood, but she observed the pallor of Nguri's hide colors with reluctant concern.

Distracted by private worries, Tori did not notice that Jase had appeared on the path beside her, until he spoke: "Omi-lai, the tides of truth rejoice at your arrival."

"Truth often flows at the side of the deep current, Jase-lai," answered Omi.

Ares' dark eyes had narrowed, assessing Jase. He said to Omi, "We have met your request, Master Omi, but you have still not told us what particular facet of truth you seek. Is it not time that you remedied your omission?"

"Birk Hodge and Rillessa Canti are not present," observed Omi mildly.

Nguri rumbled, "Rillessa is too ill to be moved yet." Calem remained imperturbable in face of the comment about his wife. Ares and Harrow both displayed more evident interest in Nguri's news than Calem, but no one questioned Nguri further.

"And Mister Birk Hodge?" repeated Omi.

"He's on Deetari, conducting business," answered Calem.

Tori would have contradicted Calem, but Jase spoke first, asking crisply, "Omi-lai, were you summoned here to perform a specific, official function?"

The directness of the question startled Tori, for few beings had the temerity to probe a Calongi inquisitor so sharply. Granted that Jase was himself a Sesserda adept, his brusqueness seemed no less odd, and Tori imagined that the Calongi himself was surprised. Omi answered consideringly, "No, Jase-lai."

"Then join me in the house, please. My position here is official, and I would speak to you. Miss Darcy will join us in the family hall in ten microspans. Nguri, you will come fifty microspans after Miss Darcy. The rest of you will wait here or in the dining room until I summon you." Jase crossed the yard and passed Omi to climb the stairs to the porch. With every indication of absolute confidence, Jase faced Ares at the door. Though Ares, as ominous and darkly shrouded as Omi, presented a far more intimidating image than the wiry Soli in borrowed clothing, Ares bowed without hesitation and stepped from Jase's path.

After Jase had disappeared inside the house, Omi moved with unperturbed dignity in his wake. Ares remarked to the remaining group, "Such nerve is not uncommendable."

Calem grumbled, "But such conceit makes a joke of the Soli race."

Nguri clicked a comment on the blindness of those who see no deeper than the vine-mass, but only Tori seemed to hear him. Nguri trudged back into the gardens, and Tori pursued him hurriedly. Not even bothering with the trade speech, Nguri clicked at her that she would be late for her inquisition.

"Nguri, old friend, I'm sorry if I've offended you."

"Apologize to Ngina," grunted Nguri, "if she should realize how you misled her."

"You've deceived me equally. You didn't mean for me to leave the caverns while death-watch continued, but you never once spoke openly! What's happening to this world, Nguri? Why did your people hide? And don't recite another death-watch legend to me. Why have your people returned suddenly to life, as if nothing had occurred?"

"Ask of your inquisitor. He awaits you."

Nguri bent low and dove into the soft vine-mass beneath a hedge, where Tori could not follow. Glumly, she retraced her steps to the house, wishing she could as easily return to the old, easy friendship with Nguri. She had acted rashly again, escaping the Stromvi caverns as if they were a prison, as if they were Uncle Per's estate. "I never learn to be grateful for my sanctuaries until I lose them," she reflected, though even the thought of the southern caverns made her shiver in memory of their suffocating atmosphere. "Why couldn't I have been born with Lila's contented form of selfishness?"

Tori circled through the gardens to enter the house from the patio, enabling her to avoid the uncomfortable company that lingered near the front colonnade. She stared at the panel-clock just inside the folding door. On principle, she would have liked to flout any inquisitor's peremptory order, but these inquisitors controlled her future in a particularly immediate, inescapable sense. She estimated the elapsed time since her allotted ten microspans had begun, eager to end the ordeal of facing Master Omi once again. The fact that Jase Sleide had apparently usurped the dominant inquisitor's role did not allay her nervousness. It only made the truth of his Sesserda status more unpleasantly evident.

The rippling of sudden, discordant music made her jump, and she proceeded directly through the dining room to reach the family hall, her last hesitation overcome by unsettling curiosity. The sun's misty light crossed the floor, the pale path her only greeter. Omi sat at the harp, tuning it with dexterous hands and tendrils. "This fine instrument," he remarked, "loses its proper purpose to neglect."

How typically Calongi, thought Tori with faint exasperation, *fretting over a musical instrument in the midst of murder and mass madness.* "If I may inquire of you, Master Omi, where is Mister Sleide?" asked Tori, as all her restless memories arose of other times alone before Omi, honored Sesserda master and full inquisitor.

"He will return shortly." A rush of clear, pure notes cascaded from the harp. At first, Omi's voice merged almost indistinguishably with the music of the instrument, but the Calongi's song rose quickly into a shivering, multilayered harmony.

The unexpectedness of sound tried to whisper a warning within Tori, but she could hear only the vastness of the music. The astonishing Calongi song poured through her, nudging buried joys and sorrows, overwhelming her fears with an almost unbearable awareness of an exquisite moment. She forced herself to remain silent, though she wanted to cry out in agony against the hurtling depth of emotion the song conveyed.

Omi did not let the music fade. He snuffed it into silence, jerking Tori from its spell. Still shaken by the inner echoes of a song that she could not even define by the rules she knew, she whispered feebly, "I had no idea that Calongi music could be so intense."

Omi replied impassively, "The composer of the piece you heard is a much respected songmaster, Mintaka-lai. A well-crafted honor-song evokes its subject vividly." He adjusted a string, and Tori jumped at the slight whisper of vibration, quickly damped. "If such a song is played properly, the listener feels the music with all the senses."

"Your playing is deservedly renowned," admitted Tori, filled with uneasy wonder at the deep, lingering impact of that complex melody, composed of seemingly ordinary, individual sounds. She knew that Omi coerced a reaction from her, but for the moment, still carried by the music's spell, she did not care. "If I listened too often to such a song," she whispered, "I might never break free of it. Already, I want to hear it again—endlessly—but I'm afraid to hear it at all. I think that the music of your people holds too much power, Master Omi, for a creature as uncivilized as myself."

The golden cilia above Omi's eyes flickered. "You perceive your limitations wisely, Miss Mirelle."

"Few Soli can tolerate Calongi music," said Jase quietly, and Tori wondered how long he had sat engulfed in that overly-padded chair beside the stilted gold settee. She found his silent comings and goings disquieting.

"Few Soli hear Calongi music," responded Omi.

Jase drummed his fingers on the chair's padded arm, and the hollow sound seemed loud and magisterial. "I wonder, Omi-lai, why you chose to expand Miss Darcy's cultural boundaries at this particularly sensitive time."

Omi shifted his outer-arms, almost draping the harp with his living cloak. "Miss Mirelle is a particularly unusual subject. Tiva disorder is a rare condition."

"Enlighten me further, Omi-lai, that I may learn from your wisdom."

Omi's neck cilia shifted. "Her reaction to the song was much more informative than any evidence I might have perceived from her via the traditional methods of inquisition."

Silently, Tori reiterated her loathing of inquisitors. Neither man acknowledged her presence at all. They dissected, and they judged, and their detachment infuriated her.

Jase said coolly, "Your choice of that particular song, Omi-lai, was intrusive, and the use of it was inappropriate under the present circumstances." His apparent defense startled Tori, and she looked at him curiously, but the iridescent eyes stared only at Omi.

"Disavowal of the truth, Jase-lai, does not alter truth's substance." Omi nodded gracefully toward Tori, who stiffened, expecting condemnation. "She reacted wisely. She recognized the alienness of the subject and its disharmony with herself." For a moment, Tori felt the shock of receiving a Calongi's praise, but long-honed cynicism made her question Omi's true intent almost immediately. "Can you match her wisdom, Jase-lai?"

"The issue does not require any judgment," answered Jase with even, unruffled calm, but his expression had tightened markedly, "because the issue does not exist."

What issue do they discuss? demanded Tori in silent frustration. *Are they judging me or each other?*

"Your reaction belies your claim," replied Omi imperturbably, "and does not reflect the Sesserda wisdom that Ukitan-lai attributes to you. Speak no further to me, until you have repaired your serenity." The Calongi returned his attention to the neglected harp, adjusting strings in uncanny silence.

Tori said, "I never saw inquisitors bicker before. Should I feel privileged?"

Omi plucked one string and let its tone dwindle into a faint resonance. "I did not come here in an official capacity, Miss Mirelle," he answered after a lengthy pause. "Jase-lai reminded me quite correctly that his service as your inquisitor was requested specifically, and further cause for inquisition has not yet been established."

"Didn't Birk Hodge summon you here to inquire about the death of Ngoi Ngenga?" asked Tori in surprise, for she had assumed that the inquisitor's arrival had merely been delayed.

"No, Miss Mirelle."

"I wish you'd stop using that name," replied Tori almost automatically, for she knew the Calongi perspective on encouraging falsehood of any sort.

"A legal change of name must be justified, Miss Mirelle."

"Did you come here simply to reiterate your disapproval of me?" asked Tori stiffly.

"No, Miss Mirelle. A wise Calongi master sensed that Jase-lai had encountered difficulties."

Tori glanced uncertainly at Jase, but his lean frame slouched in the chair. He had closed his eyes and might have been asleep from all appearances. "I assume that Mister Sleide has told you what's happened."

"He has told me a story that appears to contradict all other testimony and evidence. The Hodges maintain that their father is still alive, and they believe firmly in the truth of this fact. A Deetari contact report from Mister Birk Hodge confirms their claim. He placed a request for data six millispans after he was purportedly killed."

"Reports can be falsified. I saw Birk. He was murdered." Tori suppressed a shudder. "I know that you have no reason to trust me, but you can't actually believe the Hodges and their unpleasant friends above one of your own Sesserda adepts." The absurdity of defending one inquisitor to another heightened her sense of helplessness.

Jase murmured from the depths of the chair, "I'm not sure *what* we actually saw in Birk's office, particularly in light of Omi-lai's information from Deetari. I cannot request Omi-lai's official aid in inquisition when I'm personally uncertain of the crime. I'm sure of very little: Ngoi committed suicide. The Stromvi chose to disappear for a time, but they have now returned. The Rea have an interest in Hodge Farm. I was imprisoned briefly by

Bercali, who are now dead. Calem and Ngoi grew a harvest of relaweed in the south field."

"Your list seems fairly indicative of a lapse in Consortium peace," observed Tori.

"Truth," said Omi, "is often draped in many layers of darkness."

Jase continued, "Level VI species' members commit nearly all Consortium crimes. When Level VI members involve themselves with Level VII's, the results are inevitably troublesome. Sesserda justice isn't meant to be a substitute for personal responsibility. We don't attempt to thwart determined self-destruction. At present, the only certain victim is the planet of Stromvi, but we have no lawful authority unless the Stromvi people request Consortium intercession."

"Did you enjoy being imprisoned?" asked Tori pointedly.

"I have caused more damage to the Rea clan," answered Jase softly, "than they have caused to me."

"What about all your worrying over the relaweed?"

"As Omi-lai has reminded me, the Stromvi are Level V members, who have every right to keep the relaweed, as long as they don't use it for illegal purposes."

"I don't believe any of this," said Tori, and she paced between the two men, glaring at them alternately. "Is this the famous Calongi respect for absolute truth and justice? The two of you can sit here debating legal minutiae and the propriety of playing a song, while a murderer wanders free, and an entire planet may be facing destruction."

"Emotionalism aids nothing," murmured Omi blandly.

"I'm not advocating a maudlin show of sympathy!" Tori stared down at Jase, her frustration further incensed by his continued refusal to display any sign of significant life. "You tell me that Stromvi is in danger of relanine contamination, but you don't seem overly concerned." She whirled toward Omi, so swiftly that her full skirt wrapped her legs. "Do you know that I found a flying insect at the port, despite the well-known dearth of winged life on Stromvi? Massive ecological disruption defies Consortium law, as I recall, and I think an investigation might be warranted. I realize that my official credibility is extremely low, thanks to your lingering suspicions that I killed my husband, but couldn't either of you acknowledge that I might feel some concern for the survival of this planet?"

"Please explain your premise further," requested Omi mildly, "and tell us how your husband's death relates to your other allegations." Tori turned from both men in disgust. She tried to think of nothing but the colors of the roses beyond the window.

Jase murmured, "Omi-lai, she is a very experienced subject of inquisition. *She* knows that you are trying to provoke a reaction. *You* know that she believes what she is saying about Birk Hodge and Stromvi. *I* know that you respect Ukitan's judgment too much to believe that I'm gullible enough to have conspired with a murderess." Tori glanced sharply at Jase, but his eyes remained closed, and his bland, remote expression told her nothing.

Omi answered, "I am pleased that you have resumed thinking, Jase-lai. However, the original Mirelle inspired treachery in less likely individuals than yourself, and Miss Victoria Mirelle of Arcy is exceptionally similar to her predecessor in many respects. The probability of your corruption may be low, but I cannot discard the possibility when no clearer truth yet presents itself."

"I understand, Omi-lai, and I am honored by your frankness. I must, however, pursue my own perceptions of truth." The iridescent eyes opened and fixed on the Calongi.

"The most acute perceptions may be deceived, Jase-lai, if expectation imparts a bias."

Jase shifted to the edge of the deep chair. "I shall incorporate your wise comment into my meditations on the past few days' events." He rose smoothly and crossed the room to stand in front of Tori, near enough to force her to look up at him. "You're quite wrong in thinking that we're unconcerned about Stromvi. Omi is currently calculating our best options. Unfortunately, he has limited data on which to work, since he and I are in full accord about one conclusion only: Neither of us has talked to anyone who knows more than a tiny segment of the truth of what is happening here and why."

"You and Master Omi aren't very reassuring," replied Tori. "I'd still welcome a squadron of armed Jiucetsi."

Omi plucked a fragment of melody from the harp, and Tori shivered.

"I shall speak to the Stromvi man alone," said Omi, as the echo of the vibrating strings faded. "Alone, I shall be more likely to obtain his cooperation, considering his recent display of antagonism toward Soli."

"I shall explore the incomplete factors in my Soli perspective," answered Jase, nodding in agreement with Omi's declaration. "Please accompany me, Miss Darcy." He gestured briskly toward the door.

Still frustrated but unwilling to argue further, Tori marched into the hall and turned toward the main entry without allowing her inquisitor a chance to issue other orders. Jase stopped her with a firm grip on her arm. "Wrong direction," he chided quietly, "since I'm discouragingly familiar with that part of the house. We need to investigate the less frequented rooms. Any suggestions, most knowing native guide?"

"What are you trying to find?" she countered, wondering uneasily if she imagined the relanine tingling of his touch even through the fabric of her sleeve.

"Something of value," he replied, releasing her.

Birk's treasures again, concluded Tori with a prickling of interest, but she only commented, "That's not a very specific description."

"Alas, it's the best I have at the moment, because I'm only extrapolating. First, I'm looking for a cellar."

"Didn't our deep-cavern tour discourage you from subterranean living?"

"It inspired me. This house is suspiciously close to the Stromvi workers' enclave. Do you actually believe that Hodge's Folly was *not* built on a foundation of Stromvi architecture? The Stromvi may tolerate a Folly in the open air, but they're very particular about the character of their underground neighborhoods."

"You could be right," mused Tori.

"You needn't sound so incredulous. I have been right on occasion in my life."

"You haven't been doing too well recently." She tilted her head pensively. "I think I preferred you as a barbarian. Fallible inquisitors make me nervous."

"You're digressing rather obviously."

"The floor plan of the back wing is even more convoluted and deceptive than the rest of the house. There are rooms in that wing that I'm not sure anyone has entered since they were built. A cellar access might be hidden in any of them."

Jase frowned, as if weighing her answer on an internal balance. "Why didn't you search those rooms when death-watch began?"

"I never think of them as living quarters, I suppose, and at that time I still expected to find normal answers and normal residents in normal places. You lived here, too. Why didn't you suggest searching the back wing more thoroughly?"

"Because Birk's uniquely dynamic floor plan has one persistent characteristic: It manipulates the inattentive, and I wasn't functioning at my peak that day." Jase headed into the maze of Hodge corridors at a pace that made Tori rush to keep up with him. "The back wing bends away from the workers' enclave, doesn't it?"

"Yes. As far as I know, the wing is entirely surrounded by natural Stromvi terrain, except for a fairly narrow entry from the house."

"I don't think I've ever entered the back wing at all. The extension is inconspicuous even from the outside, buried behind all those hedges and vines." He paused where the hall turned back upon itself. "Where's the entry?"

"Inside an alcove at the northwest end of the museum wing."

"I think you've already earned your pay, native guide." He turned toward the pentagonal stairwell and resumed his rapid strides.

"Reward me with some answers."

"Regarding death-watch, Rea raiders, and the ever-shifting truths of Hodge Farm? I have little enlightenment to offer yet, unless you have a fondness for the sharing of confusion."

"Offer me some answers regarding your verdict about me, Inquisitor."

They had reached the stairwell, and Jase paused and gazed at the high window. He glanced at Tori obliquely. "What happened to your selfless zeal for helping Stromvi? Does it manifest itself only in a Calongi's presence?"

"Omi isn't my inquisitor now, as he told me himself."

"Omi-lai intimidates you."

"Yes."

Jase laughed. "I didn't think you considered my verdict worth hearing." He turned on her a quizzical gaze, his urgency to seek Birk's treasures apparently displaced by her request. With his hands in his pockets, his hair straying across his forehead, he presented a very harmless, amiable picture.

Wishing that she had not raised the subject of her private fears, Tori persevered sharply, "The matter of my personal future may seem relatively insignificant, given the turbulence of recent events, but I still have a rather substantial interest in the matter. I may not agree with your opinions, Mister Sleide, but you obviously have the official blessing of the Calongi. Assuming we ever manage to leave Stromvi, are you planning to hand me to a reformation crew?"

"Certainly not," replied Jase. Tori tried not to show her relief too plainly, but she felt one knot of fear loosen fractionally inside her. Jase continued gently, "You really don't have much faith in me, do you?"

"Five inquisitors failed before you, including Master Omi." Lack of condemnation did not constitute acquittal. Nothing had changed, but at least her situation had not worsened.

"Those five inquisitors didn't share my rare opportunity to observe you under such unique conditions of external, independently generated stress. Recent events have provided a marvelous set of reactional stimuli. How could an inquisitor ask for more?"

"Sarcasm is not an inquisitorial prerogative." Tori pressed the nearest door to the museum wing, and it slid open silently.

"You requested a verdict, Miss Mirelle," said Jase in a suddenly toneless voice that sounded eerily like every Calongi who pronounced dispassionate judgment. "Do not make assumptions regarding that verdict's content until you have heard me."

Tori waited uneasily, but she could not make herself look back at him. She had endured formal judgment five times, and a Soli inquisitor made the ordeal no more palatable. She imagined the words before he spoke, for she had heard them so often.

He astonished her, saying crisply: "You did not kill Arnod Conaty, but you did obstruct Consortium justice, for you know the truth of his death and have withheld the facts deliberately. You felt guilty, because you had indeed considered killing your husband, though I doubt that you would ever have acted in so violent and uncivilized a manner. In what I fear was a typically rash gesture on your part, you assumed the blame, knowing that you had Tiva disorder to protect you from any substantial punishment. You convinced yourself that you *should* have killed Conaty before he hurt the wretched girl who finally murdered him. Hence, you shielded her."

"The Calongi cleared all the other suspects," replied Tori evenly, but shock huddled inside of her. A Soli—relanine addict or not—could not possibly discern so much from observation and old records, when even Calongi had been defeated.

"As I have remarked previously, you are resourceful. You made sure that the young woman escaped the planet before the inquisitors arrived. She was obviously a recent visitor, since no one else recognized her existence in your husband's life. Her name should be easy enough to derive from the planet's visitor logs."

"You actually think you can perceive more than a Calongi," said Tori with a careful imitation of disdain, though her mouth tasted as dry as the dust of Arcy.

"No. I simply have a *little* more empathy for your perspective. Considering your husband's well-documented habit of collecting attractive young Soli women, I am quite sure that the other inquisitors deduced the truth equally. They could have acquitted you, despite the Tiva disorder, but since you had worked so hard to defy the law, the inquisitors let you punish yourself with the uncertainty. You see, they *were* merciful to the girl whom you protected so valiantly and needlessly. I imagine that they have quietly arranged for her unofficial rehabilitation."

Tori passed through the door, aching to escape all memory. That girl, that wretched girl, had cried and begged for forgiveness. Across Arnod's dead body, Tori had heard her and watched her and hated her. The girl had looked a great deal like Lila. Helping her had seemed the only possible course.

Jase followed Tori into the museum wing, allowing her no chance to assimilate his verdict in solitude. He resumed his normal, lightly mocking tone. "You could have spared everyone a great deal of trouble by trusting Calongi justice to treat the girl fairly, but I don't suppose the outstanding example of your Uncle Per instilled in you a tremendous confidence in Consortium law."

"Uncle Per keeps his own law, and no one ever lodges official complaints against him." The statement was as much of a concession as Tori intended to make.

"Like you, his victims hurt themselves by refusing to trust Sesserda justice."

"Stop preaching." She pushed aside the cream damask curtains that concealed an oddly shaped alcove. She gestured limply toward the narrow, shadowy entry to the back wing.

"Not exactly the welcoming portal of the third heaven, is it?" Jase paused beside Tori. She refused to look at him. He told her quietly, "You're guilty of protecting your husband's murderer, of course. I haven't decided yet how best to handle that aspect of the judgment." Jase pushed through the dark, swinging door and held it open, waiting for Tori. "I'd like to acquit you officially of the larger crime, but I'm not sure that I'm still eligible for that honor. Circumstances have made my involvement with you more personal than the law recommends. Omi-lai has already expressed his disapproval."

"The only personal involvement we share is mutual annoyance," replied Tori, passing Jase to enter the dim back wing. Smoky light panels, flickering from age, made an inauspicious pall for the empty, windowless corridor. "Why were you so angry at Omi for playing that honor-song?" she asked, trying the inquisitors' own methods against him in retaliation for the shock his judgment had given her.

Jase smiled faintly at her well-crafted effort to provoke him, but he answered evenly, "It was the sort of typically indirect gesture that can irritate even the Calongi's staunchest supporters. He insulted us both by playing that particular song, even as he honored us with the music itself." They entered a circular room, and Jase raised the edge of gray protective drapery from an oval marble table. He let the drapery fall back into place. "I give him credit for his cleverness. I would never have thought of using an honor-song to elicit deep reactions from a Soli, but he let your ignorance of the music's nature counteract the conscious control that Tiva disorder normally gives you."

"The music was unexpected," murmured Tori, continuing through the room to rejoin the twisting corridors.

"Even those who know what to expect often react strongly. The Calongi use honor-songs among themselves as a sort of filter for predicting the success of both personal and professional relationships."

"They gauge compatibility from a song?"

"The reaction to the song represents the reaction to the song's subject, if the honor-song is well crafted. The best Calongi honor-songs are said to express the souls of the individuals whom they honor."

Tori could only stare at him, as the significance of the earlier conversation struck her. "Omi played your honor-song, didn't he?" she asked with an acrid amusement aimed largely at herself. Whatever Master Omi had expected to prove, he had certainly succeeded in eliciting an honest reaction.

Jase nodded, busily inspecting a wall that seemed to serve no purpose but obstruction. "Omi, honored Calongi inquisitor and full Sesserda master, has an unseemly sense of mischief. I should be grateful that he played the finest of the songs written of me." Jase shrugged, abandoning his study of the jutting wall segment. "Some honor-songs are significantly less flattering than others, for they depend on the perceptions of the song-master. Mintaka-lai is a good friend, and she's very gifted at her craft."

"Was Omi trying to determine whether you and I are conspiring together to destroy Stromvi?" asked Tori with faint cynicism. She tried to revive her earlier irritation. Present anger was much safer than old regrets, nebulous fears, or excessive contemplation of inquisitors' devious methods.

Jase replied quietly, "Omi-lai assessed your very ambivalent feelings toward me, and he recognized the obvious. We have a chasm of differences between us culturally and personally." The iridescent eyes met Tori's, defying her reluctance. "But our basic natures are complementary in many respects. You have the practicality and initiative that I too frequently lack. I have the patience and the advantages of Sesserda training. If we chose to conspire, we could work together very successfully."

"It was a beautiful song," said Tori, pondering her inquisitor from yet another perspective. She could see the blush despite the darkness of Jase's skin, and she laughed with only a teasing trace of mockery. "Now you know how it feels to have your soul bared by an inquisitor."

"Omi is right. I've gone too long without a proper meditation agenda to balance my spirit." He stopped in mid-stride and stared at the opaque crystal walls of the curving corridor they followed. "We're walking in a circle. Where are the doors to the rest of the back wing?"

"You are rattled, aren't you?" asked Tori, selfishly pleased by the slight retribution of disconcerting her inquisitor, whose verdict had shaken her so thoroughly. "Look at the walls again."

"I don't know if I should blame you, this house, or the entire planet, but I haven't even been observing as thoroughly as I was taught," muttered Jase. He stepped forward to touch the nearest panel. The light shifted to engulf his hand, and his fingers seemed to disappear inside the wall. "It is an effective illusion," he murmured, "covering more than visual senses alone. Did Birk show you this?"

"No. I discovered it myself. Uncle Per had some similar architecture on his estate, which may have been where Birk acquired the idea. I don't think this wing was originally designed with such elaborate tricks. Thalia once mentioned something about structural changes, but you know how difficult it is to make her speak sensibly."

"Could these renovations have been made since you came here?"

"It's very unlikely."

"I thought you started working for Birk shortly after he met Per Walis, which would seem to make Per Walis a tardy source of inspiration."

Tori frowned, a fine crease of worry appearing between her dark eyebrows. "I've never been sure, but I think Birk may have met Uncle Per before the development of Hodge Farm. They certainly weren't friends, but Birk seemed to know a great deal more about Uncle Per than the sale of a few roses would require, even allowing for Uncle Per's economic significance to Hodge Farm."

"Intriguing premise," remarked Jase, "considering Per Walis' dubious reputation." For a long moment, Jase simply stared at the barely visible door. He began to move down the corridor by careful increments, pausing to face various points along a series of slowly curving walls. "I'm becoming increasingly curious about Birk's unmentioned antecedents." Jase nodded to himself, walked seven more paces down a narrow hall, and entered one of the inconspicuous doors.

The room was small and square, white and empty. Jase crossed to the far wall and pressed it just below his shoulders' level. The wall segment shifted and slid, opening onto a dim alcove.

"How did you know this was here?" demanded Tori.

"I started paying attention."

"That's a very inadequate explanation."

Jase only shrugged. Tori joined him at the brink of a small, irregular hole in the floor. The edges of the hole were unfinished and ragged, showing the fibrous layers of flooring, insulation, and structural mesh. "Not very characteristic of Birk's overly decorated architecture, is it?" asked Jase quietly.

"It can't have been designed this way."

"I'd guess that someone created this access very recently and very hastily."

"Then where's the original entrance?"

"Perhaps it was sealed." Jase knelt at the edge and inspected the black depths. "It's not a very prepossessing treasure chamber." He shifted himself to the brink and dropped into the room below. Tori could hear the muffled sound of his landing. A moment later, he propped a ladder against the edge, and a dim light flickered into existence in the hole. "It's quite well equipped for excavation, however."

"Is there anything worth seeing?" asked Tori, but she climbed down the ladder to join him without awaiting a reply.

The cellar was larger than she had expected. The dim biolight of a Stromvi lantern, which Jase had uncovered, showed a second chamber beyond the first. Both rooms were cluttered with skeins of dry, unwoven vine fibers, plastic crates filled with the same imported white rock that Birk had used throughout his garden, and a variety of rusted implements of Soli construction.

"Jeffer must have been in charge of cleanup," observed Tori. "This room looks as chaotic as his office."

"It's chaos or well-ordered camouflage."

"You think Birk hid something down here and sealed the access so not even he could reach it easily again?" asked Tori doubtfully.

"I prefer not to speculate too rashly at the moment. I'm still accumulating data."

Tori felt her way cautiously among the clutter, but she stubbed her toe on a fallen tool. "Why did I let you drag me into another pit of darkness?" she grumbled.

"My irresistible charm must have overwhelmed you."

"You have the charm of a tidal wave. What are we trying to find?"

"A treasure to tempt the angels," murmured Jase, pensively appraising the resin-caked contents of a toppled seed barrel. The pale, tentative wands of young root tendrils crept from the clotted seed balls.

"We've witnessed a shortage of angels recently," observed Tori. She gathered one of the seed balls in her hand and probed the new root stalks gently. The papery seed husks, riven by the emerging shoots, were too fragile to be of Stromvi origin.

"Then seek a treasure to tempt a would-be demigod."

"Ares?" asked Tori. She replaced the seed ball carefully, though she presumed that the seedlings represented some of Birk's original, experimental imports and had little chance of surviving long on resin biolight alone. The seed barrel must have toppled very recently.

"Either Ares or my friend Roake. Or any of their kindred souls in zealous self-advancement. Birk Hodge, for example."

"Birk."

"You provide a superlative chorus, Miss Darcy." Jase had shifted his attention to an empty crate, a focus that struck Tori as singularly uninspiring.

"I think I'll let you revert to a solo. You certainly don't need my help to stumble through a neglected storeroom."

"Now that I've given you my verdict, you don't feel any particular compulsion to help me," replied Jase soberly, "because you still don't trust my judgment. It's an unfortunate truth, since we do share the same enemy and feel the same concern for Stromvi. As usual, your lack of faith in Sesserda wisdom hurts you most of all because you force me to reciprocate your uncompromisingly independent attitude."

Tori hesitated, stung both by his words and by the gravity with which he spoke. "How did you expect me to help?" she asked, wishing that she did not feel so suddenly abandoned.

"Since you were as close to Birk as anyone, you should be able to recognize his concept of a 'treasure,' " answered Jase. He donned a carefully controlled smile, as if a shutter had fallen across the dire reality of his private thoughts. "The Soli cultural reality epitomized by your Uncle Per—and obviously coveted by Birk Hodge—generally mystifies me." Jase lifted a tarnished coatrack from its damp corner. "I might mistake a deteriorating coatrack for a priceless idol wrested from the Ghianhworshipers of Avyli during a lost, dark century." He turned the coatrack and replaced it. "The Avyli idols actually look rather worse than this coatrack. The Ghianh high priest might appreciate the upgrade."

"Stop prattling. Aren't you considered an expert in the delicate art of alien relations? Surely, you've dealt with more subtle psyches than Birk's."

"I think you're practicing to become an inquisitor yourself," replied Jase. "Did Nguri also tell you that I have more difficulty relating to my fellow Soli than to any other beings in the Consortium? I've often been accused of mistaking myself for a Calongi."

"If you're trying to tell me that you're abnormal to the point of insanity, Sleide, spare yourself the trouble. I've already made that deduction for myself."

"That's an awfully hasty verdict. There are currently half a hundred Consortium research projects centered around the subject of my sanity. I function more fruitfully in my current life, which is one definition of sanity.

But if I'm sane now, what was I previously, for I was certainly very different? In my misspent youth, no one openly questioned my sanity, but if I was sane at that time, is it possible that I can still be sane with such a radically changed perspective? It's all a rather circular philosophical debate at this point."

"Do you enjoy provoking pointless research and speculation?"

Jase's smile twisted slightly, but he did not reply. He carried the lamp into the second chamber. "Nguri has been in this room recently."

Tori abandoned her inspection of a crate of pipe fittings to join Jase. "If so," she answered thoughtfully, "this cellar must be connected to the Stromvi cavern network. Nguri certainly didn't climb down that ladder we used." With a curt nod, Jase tugged a woven curtain free from its thorn pins, leaving the tunnel access bare. The tunnel sloped downward quickly into darkness, and the dim light could not penetrate far. The scent of resin hung heavily in the still air near the tunnel. "I should have brought traction bracelets," murmured Tori.

"I doubt that traction bracelets would help. If Nguri wants us to know the purpose of this room and his visit here, he'll tell us. Otherwise, not even Omi will be able to pry the truth from that stubborn Stromvi. Nguri knows his planet too well."

"Nguri didn't create the entry that we used."

"No. I can't identify that party. Too many conflicting signals bury the truth."

"I feel like I'm falling behind in a race for my life."

"At the moment, we all seem to be losing that particular race."

"You're so encouraging. Now that Master Omi is here, can we finally leave this planet and ponder its mysteries from Deetari?"

"The Stromvi port isn't equipped to refuel a Calongi shuttle," said Jase with a slight shake of his dark head, "and Omi's ship wasn't designed for long journeys. Omi instructed his Teurai navigators to meet him between here and Deetari in fifteen millispans—about five local days—unless summoned earlier. Of course, Omi arrived in the wake of sound-shock, and his transmitters failed. We're still without a means of making outside contact.

We must hope that the Teurai manage to return, as planned, but five days appears to be the minimum wait."

"There are other shuttles at the Stromvi port. Master Omi could certainly take us that far."

"I think we're safer here than flying a low-capability rental unit all the way to Deetari, when we know that Rea warships are prowling nearby. In any case, Omi and I have a moral obligation to remain here until we've assessed the Stromvi perspective on death-watch. You might ask your friend Ares to take you to Deetari. You've made such an impression on him."

Before Tori could voice her caustic opinion, Jase gestured brusquely for silence, and he covered the lamp, leaving darkness. Tori sank to a position behind one of the enormous fiber skeins, feeling her way cautiously. She had detected nothing to cause alarm, but she trusted the inquisitor enough to rely on his perceptions above her own.

After a full microspan, Tori could hear the faint sound of footsteps in the room above the first cellar chamber. Uneasily, she recalled the ladder that still protruded from the hole, but she heard no indication of descent. The footsteps departed hurriedly.

After a dozen microspans, Jase spoke. "Someone is more eager to hide from us than to confront us. There's something unsettling about becoming a cause of fear on this benighted planet."

"Could you tell anything about our near-visitor?"

"A Deetari female," answered Jase crisply, and he allowed the lamp's brightness a slim opening.

"Thalia?"

"Or Gisa. Or an unknown. Did you know that Gisa accompanied Omi-lai from Deetari?"

"How did she reach Deetari in the first place?" demanded Tori.

"She confiscated one of the missing Hodge hovercrafts and took it to the port, where she transferred immediately to a personal Deetari shuttle that she had prepared for a prophesied emergency. She told Omi-lai that she was standing in the kitchen garden near the hangar at the time of the first sound-shock. By the time the sound-shock ended, she was already headed for the port, because her Deetari prophetess had predicted the arrival of catastrophe in a 'storm of thunder.' I can't vouch for the prophetic voice of Deetari, but Gisa believes what she says, according to Omi-lai."

"Perhaps I should have chosen Gisa as my ally in escape."

"She didn't seem inclined to wait for anyone."

"Not even Thalia," mused Tori. "I'm surprised that Gisa would abandon her own sister."

"All Deetari women are closely related, by their reckoning. Gisa has always been practical, and Thalia could hardly be considered a substantial asset in desperate circumstances."

"My head is spinning from an excess of disconnected theories," said Tori and headed for the ladder, making her way along the thin beam of lamplight. She felt each of the cold, smooth rungs before trusting her weight to them again, vaguely suspicious of sabotage from an unseen source, and she began to climb.

The ever-present scent of resin sharpened with a waft of sweet, harsh pungency. Tori gripped the edges of the ladder tightly, her formless suspicions coalescing in a frightening rush. She glanced below her, realizing that the only light now came from the room above. She hesitated, torn between continuing her ascent and rejoining Jase in the darkness. She could not discern either the source or the direction of the new resin aroma.

The pressure against her ankle had a cool, slick force that departed as quickly as it came. Tori flung herself up the remaining rungs and rolled away from the edge of the ragged entry hole. A drop of blood trickled from a puncture in her ankle, but the entire area surrounding the wound was numb. She tried to stand, but the foot would not support her weight.

She squeezed the flesh above her ankle, trying to coax the blood to flow freely and cleanse the poison from the wound. A few more drops emerged, but the price of her effort was a gouging pain that seemed to reach into the bone and tendons. She bit back a cry and curled her nails into her hands to keep from tearing at the injured area.

She heard the crash of conflict below her, and a heavy tread seemed to stumble among the clutter of abandoned tools. The sounds ceased, as she dragged herself toward the door. The ladder shifted slightly. She scanned the

room for any makeshift defense, but the emptiness
mocked her.

She began to breathe again when Jase's head appeared. He climbed rapidly, pulling the ladder after him
and casting it to the floor against the wall. A long gash
parted the fabric of his borrowed shirt, but he moved
swiftly, showing no indication of injury. He carried a
bronze-handled knife, the blade of which glistened with
a darkly iridescent stain.

He extended his free hand to Tori, though his eyes
still watched the basement access, and all of his attention
seemed focused beyond the small room. Tori accepted
his grip quickly. She winced as she rose, and she nearly
fell after taking the first step, but she was glad enough
that Jase did not slow his determined pace on her
account.

Grimly silent, Jase supported most of her weight, enabling her to hobble back through the tortuous corridors.
Despite Jase's help, Tori's ankle began to throb with rising intensity at every step. The distance seemed to have
become endless. *How much farther?* she demanded of
herself, trying to endure the pain stoically, knowing that
there was no true refuge to be found and wondering why
they even bothered to attempt escape from the unseen
menace.

When they reached the pentagonal stairwell, the burning hurt and the futility persuaded her that she could
walk no farther. Jase murmured, "I know," before she
could speak. He led her to the stairs and released her
hand.

Tori sank gratefully to the bottom step. Jase leaned
heavily against the wall, as if equally exhausted. There
was little of the imperturbable Calongi-like coolness
about his resolute expression.

Tori extended her damaged leg in front of her stiffly.
"Be careful where you wave that knife," she muttered,
as a chill swept through her. "I think the wound in my
ankle is poisoned."

Jase nodded and seemed to reassemble his strength by
concentrated will. He abandoned the wall's support and
came to sit beside Tori on the stair. He held the knife
like a beacon in one upraised hand. He shifted the edge
of her skirt impersonally in order to examine the wound,

and he frowned at the swelling skin surrounding the puncture. He touched the injury, but Tori could not feel the contact. "Did you see what attacked you?" he asked in a strangely muted voice.

"No," replied Tori through gritted teeth. "Did you?"

Jase spoke again, but Tori could not focus on his words enough to understand him. His fingers traced a streak of crimson that had traveled from her ankle to her knee. He continued to speak softly and incomprehensibly. With a queer detachment, Tori watched him lay the curved edge of the knife against her leg and slice with a single, quick motion through the swollen skin. Her blood oozed reluctantly from the wound.

She recognized the compounding of pain, but the sensation seemed remote and unimportant. The traces of iridescence on the knife colored her own seeping blood, the iridescence spreading with the immediacy of a Suviki fast-dye. A prickling ran the length of her extended leg. For a moment, the pain intensified to a level that she would not have believed possible. Before she could cry aloud, the pain was gone. Jase pressed the flat of the blade against the open cut and held it.

"One of the very few advantages of keeping company with a relanine addict," he remarked, his voice again clear and comprehensible, "is the ready availability of a nearly universal antidote to toxicity. For rapidly absorbed poisons, relanine is virtually the only useful defense." He removed the blade. The cut had already sealed, the fine crimson line of it marked with the same iridescent sheen that had coated the knife.

Tori shifted the ankle gingerly, but aside from a strange tingling, it felt nearly as strong as normal. Almost disbelieving that the injury had hurt so unmercifully microspans earlier, she touched the fine line of smooth scab. The skin remained tender where the poison had spread, but the ugly streaks of inflammation had already faded. She leaned cautiously against the stair banister as she stood. Jase offered his hand again, but Tori shook her head. "I can walk on my own," she told him, regarding him with something between uneasiness and awe.

"Good," he replied. His cheerfulness seemed slightly forced. "Let's rejoin Omi-lai, before we land ourselves in any more trouble."

Tori moved haltingly from the stairwell into the room
that served currently as an informal library of horticultural texts. The document reader in the corner was an
old model that had not been used in Tori's memory. She
glanced at it with a sense of guilt because she could have
used it freely, but she had always felt confident that her
fine, expensive education had encompassed more than
Hodge House could teach. With relanine's strange, potent fire tingling in her leg, she appreciated how little
she knew about even the common Consortium sciences.

She circled the partition that divided the library room
and had often bewildered straying guests. Jase followed
just behind her, ready to support her if her ankle failed
again. She glanced at him obliquely, unable to decide if
his presence made her feel safer or more nervous. "It
was your blood on the knife that counteracted the poison?" she asked, trying to sound nonchalant and sophisticated, though she had seldom felt more overwhelmed by
the scope of Consortium diversity and skills.

Jase nodded slowly, as they reentered the corridor
maze. "Our faceless attacker scored against me before I
could snatch the weapon," he replied finally, as if making
a reluctant admission. He fingered the sliced shirt, and
Tori could see the thin, darkly iridescent line of the
sealed gash that crossed his chest. Even half-hidden by
the pale fabric, the cut looked severe. It made a longer,
slightly broader line than her ankle's scar, and the iridescence was more pronounced, shifting color as he moved.
"Our attacker escaped, I'm afraid, leaving me with nothing more useful than a confusion of camouflage scents
and a glimpse of a crimson streak in a mass of darkness."

"*It*," observed Tori in grim recollection of Rillessa's
warnings.

"Rillessa certainly saw something to justify her
paranoia."

"When she despaired of persuading anyone to believe
her, she summoned you here to confront 'It,' " said Tori,
bitterly conscious of the irony of her effort to justify Rillessa's deceit. "My inquisition was an easy excuse."

"Unfortunately, that excuse forced her to settle for a
Soli instead of a Calongi." Jase's terse laugh sounded
unexpectedly ragged, and Tori glanced again at the riven
shirt, wondering if the injury troubled him more than

he indicated. He continued strongly, "I appreciate the confirmation of one of my numerous theories about who summoned me here." Deciding that her nerves were concocting problems too zealously, Tori put aside her unwelcome moment of worry about her inquisitor.

Tori stopped at the door of the family hall, delaying the prospect of facing her Calongi nightmare again. "I don't know if you could read anything from Rillessa in her current state of derangement, but you might ask Nguri where the Stromvi are keeping her. You might at least discover whether I imagined the existence of the south Stromvi cavern network." She entered the family hall, expecting to see Omi, and she sighed at the room's emptiness, "I hope we're not repeating recent history. Being stranded with you once was quite sufficient."

"Is that a kind comment for the man who wants to acquit you?"

"Where's your Calongi friend, Inquisitor?" demanded Tori stiffly, ignoring his gibe. She drooped into a chair, feeling exhausted by the combination of the attack and Jase's peculiar method of healing.

"Omi-lai probably asked Nguri for a tour of some points of local interest, so as to provide a basis of observation." Jase stared out the window, but only the mute beds of roses were visible. "Omi is in a difficult situation, being forced to choose between my unsupported claims and the logic of his own perceptions and reasoning. His difficulty is compounded by the fact that he's consciously prejudiced against me for being both a Soli and a Sesserda adept, and his discourteous thoughts in that regard torment him."

"I'm devastated for him."

Jase rubbed at the knife wound across his chest as if its presence irritated him. "Omi is a very honorable man, acutely aware of his own flaws but not yet able to overcome them. The current situation is aggravating his emotional bias, and he hates himself for his weakness."

"If you're so sympathetic to his perspective, I wouldn't think you'd exert yourself to humble him as you did earlier."

"You're judging hastily again."

"Maybe," conceded Tori, wishing she could decide whether to like this strange Soli, despite his official posi-

tion in her life. "Do you actually intend to lead the inquisition of the Hodges and friends, assuming you decide
that such inquisition is appropriate?"

Jase answered slowly, "I shall do my best to complete
what I have begun. In her twisted way, Rillessa reached
the right conclusion: Because I lived here, because I
know Stromvi, because I am fundamentally of the same
species as Birk, I have a much-needed advantage." He
walked to the harp but touched only its gilt frame. "Omi-
lai agrees with my perception in this matter—under the
conditional premise that I haven't allowed my Sesserda
honor to be compromised."

"By me," added Tori, smiling faintly at the thought of
an inquisitor being afflicted by Mirelle's persistent legacy.

"Yes."

Tori rubbed her ankle. The sealed puncture had begun
to itch. "Will he claim that we conspired to attack each
other with a knife blade?"

"Omi-lai knows that unknown factors still exist in the
equation of Hodge Farm." Jase raised the knife and
turned it in his hands. "This knife is a remarkable piece
of primitive craftmanship. It's very old and very well-
used." He sat in the chair beside the harp to study the
knife more closely.

"Why didn't you tell me that you were Sylvie's
Squire?"

Jase shook his head very slightly. "I'm not the same
man. The appellation is ridiculous. The subject was irrelevant. Would you like any more answers?"

"Can you play your own honor-song?"

Jase raised his eyes to her without shifting position in
any other visible way. "I can play only an approximation.
I obviously lack the complex Calongi vocal equipment,
which is where most of the music's power is produced."
He dropped his gaze back to the knife and addressed
it fixedly, "Don't encourage impossible fantasies, Tori.
You've hurt yourself enough by attaching your emotions
to the wrong men, and a relanine addict is as wrong as
they come."

"Your ego is showing," remarked Tori dryly.

Jase answered quietly, "As you've recognized from inquisition, Sesserda observation doesn't allow its subjects
much privacy. I'm sorry."

"Stop being insufferable, and go scan someone else. You're not even a very comforting protector since I seem to encounter more trouble with you than without you."

Jase arose and departed without further comment. Tori pulled her chair forward and propped her feet on a small, stone table. "Great-grandmama would never have tolerated such conceit," she muttered. "Impossible fantasies, indeed. If we survive until the wayward Teurai ship returns, I may teach you to respect Mirelle's legacy, my cocky Soli inquisitor." She dropped her head heavily against the back of the chair. "Five more days." She tried not to think of an unseen enemy that had struck in the dark.

CHAPTER 37

Omi observed the Stromvi horticulturist with a concern that verged on disapproval. While Nguri talked amicably of roses and root clippings, Omi sensed the Stromvi's underlying anger as a palpable source of danger. The origin and focus of the anger remained unclear.

Omi recognized many possible reasons for the fury that smoldered in the usually peaceable Stromvi. The inquisitor had viewed the dead field where relaweed had been grown, and he knew that contamination could be severe. He had not personally encountered any winged insects, but he considered the likelihood of their import as relaweed pollinators to be significant. Omi evaluated the entire Hodge Farm establishment as an oppression of the Stromvi people.

None of the answers satisfied Omi completely. The relaweed had been grown with Stromvi help. The Stromvi had invited Birk Hodge to exploit their world, despite Consortium recommendations against the decision. Nguri himself had played the most vocal part in support of the Soli presence.

Guilt might have intensified slow Stromvi anger, but not even that explanation gave Omi the necessary sense of *rightness*. Omi could not escape the unpleasant impression that a wily Stromvi elder was toying with Calongi analysis as if it were an experiment in rose hybridization. The most aggravating aspect of the interview was that Nguri Ngenga refused to be provoked into truth by either direct questions or subtle comments. Since Omi had no official inquisitor's status at present, the law forbade him to employ the most powerful Sesserda techniques to derive an accurate reading.

An official status could not even be established by citing emergency circumstances. Ngoi Ngenga had died by suicide. The direct inspiration of the desperate act might be suspect, but none of the Stromvi's relatives would sanction an official inquiry, and Consortium law would not forcibly supercede local justice in such cases. According to Ukitan-lai's impossible Soli student, Birk Hodge might have been murdered, but the contradictory evidence was far too solid to discard.

The need for justice blared with aggravating clarity to Omi, but the world belonged to the Stromvi people, and the Stromvi people had shown neither eagerness nor willingness to request inquisition. By the nature of Sesserda beliefs, Consortium law could not be forced upon the obviously innocent, especially when the innocent comprised an entire populace.

That Essenji man, Ares, could benefit from extensive reformation, but he was not registered as a Consortium member, and no Consortium complaints against him existed. The Soli trio of Harrow and Hodges made an almost equally unprepossessing unit, but none of the three had courage enough even to orchestrate their own destinies. The two Deetari women represented uncertainty. Both withheld information for hidden reasons.

The Mirelle woman was simply a complication that Omi wished did not exist at all. He berated himself for his immature attitude upon completing his uncharitable thought of her. All creatures had purpose, including this young Soli woman who remained so brazenly disrespectful of Consortium justice.

While Omi assessed the Hodge Farm situation with one busy segment of his brain, he focused his vast array of outer senses on Nguri Ngenga and the surrounding fields of roses. The Stromvi air did taste of impure elements, but the traces were too faint for a satisfactory source identification without extended analysis. "You have created a remarkable botanical blend in this place, Master Nguri," observed Omi. "How will you accommodate the new contaminations?"

Nguri lifted his head and met the Calongi's eyes, though the Calongi stood half a meter taller than the Stromvi at full height. "That which is beautiful must be preserved. That which destroys must be removed in order to preserve the balance. When an infestation threatens, natural enemies must be created, if they do not already exist. The cling weeds are trimmed from the silver-lily shoots. The panguulung must not grow beside an enclave. When a natural form encroaches beyond its proper sphere, it must be restored to discipline."

"You answer with philosophy rather than method."

"I understand the needs of my people and my world."

"You must have known that the relaweed was planted in your valley. Why did you allow it to become a threat?"

"When a new creation is discovered, it must be evaluated. So your Sesserda wisdom teaches us," remarked Nguri, and Omi admired the Stromvi's skill at indirection, even as he regretted the Stromvi's independent attitude. "If the new element upholds or enhances the perfection of the large world of creation, it is accepted and made a part of the whole. If its alienness makes it antithetical to the proper world, it must be excised. It must be made to know its boundaries." Nguri lowered his head and snipped a stray shoot that had risen between two nearby roses. "Intruders must be pruned."

"I respect you, Master Nguri. I regret that you do not trust my judgment." Omi bowed, before he turned and moved with smooth Calongi dignity toward Hodge House.

"That which is beautiful is Stromvi," murmured Nguri very quietly. "All that is not part of Stromvi must be excised."

Omi did not pause or turn to indicate that he had heard the faint, grim whisper. He knew that he had not been meant to hear the words. He knew also that Nguri would not care greatly whether the words were heard or not—and that indifference filled Omi, honored inquisitor and full Sesserda master, with a deep sorrow.

* * *

Ngina shifted tentatively, trying to avoid any sound that might reveal her presence. Despite her care, she bumped one of the corroded Soli tools, and it rolled against a crate with a clatter that made her drop low against the floor in alarm. After a microspan of silence, she realized that she was alone, and she raised her upper torso to peer across the tops of the fiber skeins.

Nothing moved in the room except herself, and her scent nodules detected no other hidden beings. Still, she moved cautiously. The strange, dark creature that she had now glimpsed twice exuded virtually no detectable aroma. It seemed to blend with its background in all respects.

Relieved to be alone, Ngina also felt guilt that she had allowed the creature to escape her observation again. Her honored father had warned her not to lose scent of it for an instant, but he had not even suggested the possibility that the creature might attack. It had certainly tried to harm Miss Tori, until Mister Jase had grappled with it and frightened it.

Why were the Soli here at all? Her honored father had said nothing about the Soli access that made these rooms a basement of the Hodge house. He had not told her how swiftly the creature could move, nor had he informed her that the creature could climb as quickly and easily as a Soli. He had provided very inadequate information, and Ngina did not see how he could possibly blame her for losing the creature's trail again.

Ngina drooped in discouragement. Her honored father would condemn her, even if he said nothing. His disappointment would be a sufficiently unbearable punishment. He had trusted her again, despite all her recent failures. She had succeeded at nothing.

Ngina wished that she had dared speak to Tori Darcy, but the creature had been too near. Ngina wanted to believe that Tori Darcy was still her friend, despite the bitter words of her honored father. Ngina did not know how to share such suspicion and distrust of the Soli people, whom she had respected all her life. She did not like to ponder the nature of secrets that her honored father held so close to himself. Ngina did not want to understand the hopeless fear that had driven Ngoi, but she was learning quickly.

*　　*　　*

Akras wrapped her arm tightly to staunch the flow of blood. She did not waste time recriminating herself for the carelessness that had caused the injury and cost her the satisfaction of slaying the Rea-traitor's concubine. The death of the Soli woman would have served little purpose, except to assuage the anger of a momentary impulse. Akras simply vowed to repay the man who had dared to keep her from her prey. That Soli man would suffer for taking her Rea clan-knife, the very personal weapon that had belonged to Raskannen.

The Bori whined as it fed, greedy for more of the freshly butchered osang snake. Akras hacked another slab into digestible segments and threw the pieces to the Bori. The Bori would be useless throughout the night, but she had delayed the feeding as long as possible. A hungry Bori could not be trusted near a recent blood-wound, such as marked her arm where her own knife had been turned against her.

He had fought well, that unexpected opponent. The deceptions of her Bori cloak had not provided the customary level of advantage. For a Soli, he displayed considerable perceptiveness and agility.

He had also proven to be irritatingly tenacious of life. Akras had now ordered this Soli's death twice, and both of her sons had failed her: Roake in defiance, insisting that the Soli bearer of Calongi symbols could be endured better than the Calongi who might come to question his disappearance; Ares in arrogance, discarding the Soli into doomed Bercali hands to show contempt for Soli and Bercali both. Perhaps she had erred in withholding the facts of Roake's reasoning from Ares. The association of Calongi symbols with this Soli appeared to be more significant than she had at first assumed.

Where was Ares? He should have reported by this time. He knew how little his clan leader liked to linger on this abominable planet of the Rea-traitor's lair. Ares had much to explain. While Tagran led the Rea reclamation of the home vessel, Ares should have waited, guarded, and watched covertly for any sign of the Rea-traitor. By releasing the prisoners and presenting himself openly as companion of that greedy Soli, Harrow Febro, Ares might lure the Rea-traitor into visibility, as hoped— or ensure that the Rea-traitor remained hidden for the next ten spans. A Calongi had indeed arrived, as Roake had predicted. Perhaps Roake was equally correct in assessing Ares as too reckless and unstable for leadership.

Or perhaps, Akras decided, *I have forced Ares to suffer his brother's domination too long. It is time for the traitor's children to die: all three.*

She sighed faintly, unwillingly troubled by a reluctance to complete her own determined plans. She could not afford weakness. She could not delay the final vengeance any longer. She must not think of Roake as her son but as a creation of the Rea-traitor.

Still, Roake has prepared a fitting, lingering form of death for the Rea-traitor. How the traitor must be suffering, watching all that he has built dissolve around him! It is well that the traitor disappeared before Ares could capture him. If Ares had brought him before me, I would have ordered Ares to kill the traitor immediately, and this way is better. The traitor remains, after all, my prisoner, and I shall let him experience some part of my own spans of torment before I grant him death's oblivion.

Akras refastened the bindings of her lua-hide vest. She fed the last of the snake, caught and killed by two Rea warriors, to the ravenous Bori. The Bori paused in its frenzied feeding, its color and form becoming nearly indistinguishable from the rough Stromvi ground on which it lay.

Sound-shock rumbled through the air and through the planet. Three sharp tones rang, and Akras knew that her eldest son still served the Rea clan. He still trusted his clan leader. She had hoped to let him die in battle, but he had proven more resilient than Akras had expected. He must be retrieved and attacked unexpectedly.

Did Ares truly believe his brother a traitor? It was always difficult to be sure of Ares' thoughts. However, Akras had no doubt about the crucial issue: Ares trusted his clan leader. Roake had always required leashing against excessive independence, but Ares had never disobeyed.

The thunderous tones faded into heavy silence. The Bori resumed its interrupted meal, thrashing and gnawing the snake meat noisily, but the cavern's walls muffled the ordinary sounds, the sounds that neither shook the ground like sound-shock nor propagated, like click-speech, along the Stromvi's cunningly designed network of wire-roots. Akras pondered the Bori, as its flaccid body shaped itself erratically, trying to assimilate the characteristics of both the snake it consumed and the ground on which it lay. Akras had selected her Bori for its effectiveness at light-distortion. Her Bori cloak had only a trace of the shape-shifting instincts of the most expensive Bori, the rare simulacrums.

The Bori were vicious and unintelligent, but they had a very sophisticated capability as chameleons. Bori skin and internal organs were extremely flexible, and the composition of Bori skin allowed the Bori to adjust properties of light reflectivity or absorption on a cell by cell basis. Some Bori could adjust each skin cell to match a given pattern of shape and color, while others could only adjust their skins to a single overall camouflage pattern. The most common Bori, such as those that the Rea wore for "cloaks," were the unskilled Bori. The simulacrums could resemble anything within the size range of the specific Bori. The skill level could be enhanced to a limited extent by training, but no consistent method of breeding simulacrums had ever been developed.

Akras' father had brought the first Bori, a war prize, to the Rea. The creature had revolted her, its inconstancy an offense to Akras' concepts of Rea honor. The Rea-traitor had appreciated the Bori's value immediately.

They are alike, mused Akras grimly, *treacherous and deceptive, blending innocuously into their surroundings until they turn against their masters. Foolish Consortium, believing that the Rea-traitor observes any law but his own; foolish Akras, believing that the Rea-traitor ever loved anything but his own power.*

Akras touched her scarred cheeks, tracing the hard ridges of deliberately mishealed flesh. "He will die," she whispered, "with all that he has valued."

She gathered the sated Bori around her shoulders, and she headed back to the house access to complete the task that the annoying Soli had interrupted. She activated a small, personal transmitter, a fairly primitive electronic device that the Rea had selected empirically for its imperviousness to the daar'va's field. When she climbed from the ragged hole into the traitor's house, she issued a pre-arranged, encrypted message to Roake.

*   *   *

Nguri clicked softly in satisfaction, as the *treasure* responded to the sound-shock with a sequence of vibrational symbols. He incorporated each carefully gathered bit of data into the Xiani analyzer. He forced the device to accept the incongruity of pattern. The analyzer expected botanical life-forms and questioned inconsistent entries, but it could extrapolate the composition and characteristics of nearly any cohesive system from the tiniest fragment sets of information. Decryption of the symbolic language that controlled Birk's *treasure* differed only in scope from the genetic code derivations for which the Xiani had designed the analyzer.

Nguri could have given other names to the *treasure:* Birk had used it as a weapon; others, less destructive than Birk but less respectful of existing environments than the Calongi, had designed it as a planetary adapter. Nguri understood. He had trusted Birk once, but he had learned. Nguri did not repeat his errors.

CHAPTER 38

Calem searched his father's office with a sense of guilt that irked him. He found nothing more informative than rose-breeding records on thin sheaves of storage film, each embossed with Nguri's verification seal. No small, personal token announced Birk Hodge's domination. The monstrous house and Hodge Farm attested to that certainty of Stromvi life, where no lesser emblem would suffice.

When he sat in his father's chair, Calem took pleasure from his feeling of defiance. He imagined for a moment that Jase Sleide's preposterous premise at breakfast was true, that Birk Hodge had died in this very room at this very desk. Calem laid his hands on the desk's smooth, gleaming surface, enjoying the touch of the cold, black expanse. The stark, startling austerity of the office suggested Birk. Calem drew his fingernails across the desk, the shrill, unpleasant sound echoing Calem's bitterness toward his father's contemptuous attitude. Long resentment had seethed into new life with this latest slight, this unannounced departure on business that was confided to Harrow but not to Calem.

The most irritating aspect of the entire family mess was this inability to remember when Birk Hodge had left—and when Harrow had arrived with his uncivilized companion, Ares. The arrival had apparently halted a lawless raid that had caused Ngoi's death, but Calem's memories of that significant event consisted of only the acrid scent of burning resin.

Calem could recall distinctly the microspans after Sylvie's tantrum in the family hall, when Rillessa had run outside, babbling incoherently about "It." Calem seemed to remember arguing with Sylvie about whether or not to follow Rillessa, but somehow the outcome of the argument had become blurred. In Calem's murky memory, Harrow and Ares were suddenly part of the discussion, and the decision had been made to let Rillessa sulk by herself. Calem resolved to avoid any future sampling of those noxious alien liquors that his father stocked.

Calem did not particularly regret his wife's prolonged absence. He had lost all patience with her delusions. However, he wished that he could recall having made some active decision in her regard. Despite Ares' slippery assertions, Calem had an annoying impression that Harrow had usurped Calem's rightful authority once again.

Calem grasped his father's silver light-pen and threw it against the patterned wall. The concussion jarred loose the pen's cover and activated the mechanism, and the thin, pale beam of visible light spilled across the dark moss floor. Calem aimed the heavy pen holder carefully before casting it, and he smiled when the silver ovoid smashed the pen and stifled the light. "You haven't lost your aim, son," he muttered, "only your inheritance. These inquisitors can't be too clever if they think Harrow would kill his new partner in nastiness, when such a promising family rapport is developing."

Calem jumped to his feet immediately on hearing the polite knock of a visitor at the open door. Jase Sleide glanced at the broken pen and holder. "You ought to learn to control your obvious outbursts of temper, Calem, especially with two Sesserda adepts in the house. Why do you imagine that I'd suspect Harrow of murdering Birk?"

"Is this an official inquisition?" demanded Calem, irritated that his quiet comment had been overheard by the Soli inquisitor. Calongi were known to have extremely acute senses, but a Soli had no business being able to hear a whisper from another room.

"Your father's death has not been recorded officially," replied Jase.

"Then I'm not obliged to talk to you."

"Is that why you declined to wait in the dining room, as I requested?"

"I don't owe you any obedience. You may issue commands all you like, but don't expect me to jump like your Calongi cohort—certainly not in my own house."

"You are a member of the Consortium, Calem Hodge,

sworn to uphold and obey Consortium law and its representatives."

"I obey the law," grumbled Calem. "I only came upstairs. You didn't have any trouble finding me." When Jase did not reply, Calem added uncomfortably, "Where is the Calongi?"

"Omi-lai walks his own path," answered Jase, blithely uninformative. "When did you last see your father?"

"I haven't seen him since the day you arrived," snapped Calem. He did not recognize the inquisitor's influence that prodded his frustration. "I think you should be answering the questions. Why did you come here? I didn't summon you. What did you say to my father that made him leave here so hurriedly? What are you and your Calongi friends doing to this planet? You've nearly terrified the Stromvi workers back into their barbaric origins. I'm assuming that you really are an inquisitor, since your tame Calongi defers to you, but unless you start providing a few explanations, I shall lodge a formal complaint against you with the Consortium representative on Deetari."

"Standing in your father's place seems to have given you new courage," observed Jase evenly, "but it hasn't improved your logic." He bent to collect the broken bits of the silver desk set and dropped them absently in his jacket pocket. "By all means, contact the Consortium representative, if you doubt that I am a mere servant of justice. What happened to the transceiver that was here earlier?"

"I suppose it failed," grunted Calem, "and my father sent it to Jeffer for repairs."

"You have another transceiver?"

Calem shrugged irritably. "I presume there's one on Harrow's ship."

"Shall we go use it?"

"I'll use it alone when I'm ready."

"I do hate having my honorable intentions doubted. Blots on the family escutcheon are so tiresome."

Calem did not move. The vague, uncertain sense of recognition fixed on a familiar style of speech and manner. Physical changes had occurred: The face was thinner; the coloring had shifted into darker tones; the eerily inconsistent eyes drew a disproportionate share of the attention and made other, more ordinary Soli characteristics almost unnoticeable. Calem did not know what gave him such sudden conviction that he knew this man, but he hissed, "Squire," with exasperation but no doubt.

Except for a faint, rueful smile, Jase showed neither surprise nor dismay. "That ridiculous epithet has not improved with age."

The crazed, skewed reality of recent days stabilized for Calem, fastening on an easier past. "What in the seven icy hells happened to you?"

Jase answered amiably, though he fixed his unnatural gaze on Calem with an unblinking, unnerving resemblance to a stern Calongi. "Relanine addiction, I'm afraid. In excessive quantity, relanine adapts the genetic structure of its host for much more than a temporary shift of environment. My appearance really hasn't changed nearly as much as the rest of me."

Calem had little interest in any facet of a man that could not be identified by sight. "Did Sylvie or my father recognize you?"

"Not as far as I could discern."

Calem sank again into his father's chair, but he no longer appreciated any significance in the gesture. For the first time in days, he felt a measure of confidence growing in him. The inquisitor was only the Squire, improbably alive. The relaweed had disappeared, and though the profits might be lost, no one could prove that the illegal weed had ever been grown on Stromvi. Harrow's arrival had apparently discouraged that barbaric Rea war leader, Roake, from returning to claim either relaweed or the promised vengeance for lack of delivery. Birk Hodge had taken care of everything, as always, and the fact that he had not confided in his son was irritating but hardly catastrophic. "Why did you come here, Squire? For Sylvie?"

"Your wife invited me, using your name and an excuse that no longer matters. She had learned about the existence of a Soli inquisitor, and she had some confused idea that I could find the 'creature' that was spying on her. Did you ever see it?"

"She imagined 'It.' " Calem shook his head, the fair hair remaining imperviously still. "How did you ever manage to connive the Calongi into accepting you as a

Sesserda practitioner? You must have learned more cunning from my devious father than I thought."

"Don't become too comfortable with me, Calem. You are guilty, at least, of arranging a harvest of relaweed, conspiring with known drug smugglers, and exploiting Ngoi Ngenga so thoroughly that he died of his involvement with your scheme. I don't know who tampered with your wife's sanity, but I'm betting that your Rea chum, Ares, has a good idea of how to mix a truly mind-shattering cocktail."

"Ares is not Rea," countered Calem, his fragile sense of security weakening slightly, for Ares' disdainful attitude and penchant for obscure remarks did suggest some resemblance to the dreaded Roake. "He's one of Harrow's friends."

"How many Essenji have you ever met?"

The question struck Calem as irrelevant, and he growled his retort: "How would I know? Ares calls himself an Essenji, but he looks indistinguishable from a Soli to me, except for an affectation of hair color."

"You never were a very keen student of racial biology. Do you know a man named Roake?"

"No," replied Calem quickly.

"Please, Calem, don't waste our mutual time by lying to me. Obviously, you do know him, and you fear him. He's not a very congenial character, I must admit. He claims to be Ares' brother. He also claims to be trying to recover your relaweed—for the good of Stromvi, of course. Was he your intended customer?"

Calem began to shake his head, but Jase snapped at him, "Do not lie again to me, Calem Hodge." Jase continued in a softer voice, but a compulsion to listen and hear clearly made Calem again feel as small as if he faced his father. "I shall know the truth before you can begin to circumvent it," said Jase. "I am an inquisitor, as surely as Omi-lai, and I shall be no more tolerant of deception than he."

Intimidation crawled along a familiar, bitter path, and Calem squirmed uneasily in his father's chair. "I never met the actual customer. Roake presented himself as an intermediary," acknowledged Calem gruffly. "Harrow arranged the deal on behalf of his own employer, a man named Walis. I didn't even know what crop the Rea wanted, until my father had committed me to Harrow's project."

"You were ignorant and innocent of everything," remarked Jase dryly, "as always."

"Question Harrow or Ares—or my father—if you want to discover your supreme Sesserda Truth and enact justice. I can't help you. If you need a formal request for investigation of Ngoi's death, I'll place it. As his employer, I have that right. I can't offer you anything else."

"No one grovels as well as you, Calem." Jase touched the remaining elements of the silver desk set, a writing-film dispenser and an embossing seal that wore a silver Hodge rose. "I hope your father's enemies are more impressed than I with your degrading performance. Otherwise, I must believe that they are still using you unmercifully for their own nefarious purposes." Jase retrieved the broken pieces of the light-pen from his pocket and dropped them on the desk. He retained the pen holder. "Beware of guests wielding silenen thongs."

Jase left the office. Calem shoved the intact portions of the desk set furiously. The seal rolled to the edge of the desk and teetered at the brink, scattering reflected light from the silver rose. The dispenser crashed to the floor, spilling its contents. The roll of writing film began to writhe, uncurling in the light, as sound-shock filled the air.

*   *   *

Jase pressed his back against the cool, translucent crystal wall, trying to regulate his racing, erratic pulse by conscious effort, but the relanine sickness had advanced too far to tolerate such discipline. The knife-score across his chest had sealed, but it throbbed unmercifully.

He smiled grimly, thinking of Tori's hesitant remark that her injury *might* have been poisoned. Having absorbed the majority of the knife blade's poisonous oil, Jase had no doubts on the subject at all. The Rea poison, a final invader after all the injuries of recent days, had nearly drained him of relanine. He barely noticed the sound-shock.

Sesserda perceptions began to surge and fade. Jase struggled to retain control, but he could feel himself drifting between hallucination and fact. Stromvi resin tasted sweet but turned bitter in his blood. A blackness filled with anger exploded in his skull, but his skull had become a Stromvi cavern, and the blackness seeped through its tunnels, darkening the biolight and destroying the life-giving roots.

Birk Hodge loomed tall in front of him, mocking him and demanding to know his life-purpose. Rea warriors swarmed around him, and some died at his hands, staining him with guilt. Y'Lidu threw exploding vials of relanine at him; the shards cut him.

Jase unfolded his clenched fingers from the broken pen holder in his pocket. He stared at his hand and the thin lines of blood that crossed it. His blood was almost colorless now. He tried to feel the simple pain of the cuts, but the piercing agony inside of him refused to acknowledge lesser nerve signals.

He sensed Ares' approach and roused himself enough to duck behind the crystalline partition. *The Rea must not see weakness in you,* he snarled to himself. *You have no time for weakness, Sleide. You are a Sesserda adept. Maintain your discipline.*

He restrained his breathing until Ares had passed. He felt Ares move toward the family hall, and he cursed his inability to follow and diffuse the danger that Ares presented. The dangers *were* spreading. Relanine hallucination contained the elements of truth, which could possibly be sorted by Sesserda techniques. He could do nothing without at least a few microspans of concentrated Sesserda meditation. He could do little without additional relanine, but that problem, too, required meditation.

Jase closed his eyes and forced other senses to turn inward. A pure and compelling light, fashioned by his mind, blazed through him, cleansed and revived him. The belief in Sesserda strength would sustain him for a short time, but the cravings of a relanine addict would not be denied for long.

*   *   *

"Instead of a Calongi and the Soli who commands him with such delectable arrogance, I discover again the enchanting Mirelle." Ares spoke with such pretentious emotion that Tori suspected him of satire. She raised her eyes slowly and did not remove her feet from the low table. The echoes of sound-shock seemed still to reverberate along her nerves. She wished that Jase would return. She wished that she had not asked him to leave. Even Omi would be more welcome than Ares.

"Are you so eager for inquisition?" she demanded crisply.

"Inquisition is irrelevant. The Consortium is irrelevant."

"A very large number of people would differ with you."

"But you are not among them, are you, Mirelle?" he asked with sudden, unexpected gentleness. "You and I do not need Calongi reassurances of our worth—at the price of accepting their definitions and designs. You and I forge our own truths."

Tori smiled, though Ares' suggestion of commonality chilled her. *This* was Mirelle's legacy: this infernal, inescapable illusion that she admired the beliefs and feelings of every man she met. Even Arnod had fallen prey to that impossible delusion for a time. Even an unlikely Soli inquisitor showed some traces of susceptibility.

Tori shifted her position in the subtle ways of her family's training, conveying approval rather than the initial disdain. She felt no great compunction about misleading Ares, since the alternatives seemed pronouncedly more dangerous. "How long do you intend to wait, Ares?" she asked, emulating his own boldness. She had no idea how he would interpret her question. She wasn't even sure why she sensed that he *was* waiting for something.

He hesitated only a moment. "No longer than necessary," he answered with a faint, slightly cynical smile, "and the time of the final conflict seems to be growing imminent." He continued sharply, "Do you know where Birkaj hid his treasures?"

"Perhaps," replied Tori evenly. She wondered at Ares' odd pronunciation of Birk's name.

"Then lead me to the kree'va—now," demanded Ares. He approached her with the strong, graceful strides of the great hunting felines of Soli legend. When he stood above her, his deep eyes intense and hard beneath the black-and-silver mane, he needed no weapon in his hand to prove his deadliness. "I shall deal honorably with you, Mirelle, but I do not tolerate betrayal."

Tori moved with extreme care, feeling unusually grateful for all the begrudged spans of Mama's coaching. Even in inquisition, she had seldom appreciated the value of maintaining poise in the face of the most uncomfortable situations. She did not allow herself to react to the momentary twinge of her recently injured ankle.

"I can help you, Ares, because Birk trusted me more than anyone else, but I cannot afford to give my information freely. I have no patron now, for Birk is dead: I saw him." Ares did not question her confident words, but his thin expression tightened appreciably. "I invested too much time on Birk to leave here without recompense. No one else knows where he hid his 'treasures.' I could keep them myself, as I think you realize."

Ares narrowed his eyes. "I am willing to believe that you know Birkaj more intimately than anyone else on this planet, but I distrust your sudden eagerness to bargain." His detached sophistication, a caustic mimicry of Harrow and Calem and every member of their speciously civilized society, sloughed from him like an osang's rejected skin, and he spoke angrily. "Let us stop this empty banter and make clear the subject that we are discussing. My time is short, because I have a very ambitious, very dangerous brother who is seeking the kree'va now. If you have what I seek, I shall reward you appropriately. If you are merely toying with pretty words, I shall also take appropriate action."

The abrupt shift from calm to fury startled Tori, forcing upon her an uneasy awareness of Ares' spontaneous temper. Visualizing Ares as Birk's executioner made the event seem real and terrible again. The denials made by Calem and Sylvie had almost persuaded her battered emotions that the events accompanying death-watch had never occurred. The concept that such dispassionate murder might choose her as its next victim horrified her, but it also made her feel ashamed. Fear of death became very imminent, but the prospect of its violent form made her realize how deeply she had believed that her husband had earned his own end.

The daylight still streamed in the window. The harp still stood as Omi had left it. The moss carpet remained stained, for Thalia had not yet cleaned it. Death did not descend, and Tori disciplined herself to say coolly, "Remember that I have considerable value to you for more reasons than Birk's little legacy. I am Mirelle, and that name is legendary. I have never disappointed my patrons."

She rose languidly from her chair, and Ares stepped back to allow her to pass. She entered the hall confidently, as if she knew her destination precisely. She listened for indications of any other, safer living beings than Ares, but the sounds that darted among the crystal panels were elusive and misleading. She turned toward the main entry, and Ares moved swiftly to block her path. She sighed inwardly at the repetitive thwarting of her intentions.

"You are trying to deceive me," muttered Ares, "as I should have expected from a woman who chose Birkaj." He pressed her forcibly away from the outer door.

He drove her at a rapid pace through the house and into the back wing, unconsciously retracing the steps that Tori had taken so recently with Jase. Ares did not hesitate before the illusion-hidden doors. He clearly knew his destination well.

He shoved Tori into the room with the gaping, wounded floor, and he did not relent at the edge of the ragged hole. Tori did not waste effort trying to avoid the fall. As Ares pushed her, she jumped toward the clearest space in the lower room, tucking her feet beneath her and hoping that she could manage to roll away from harm.

Her ankle protested the pressure of an awkward landing. By the time she could regain her footing, Ares had joined her and gripped her neck chokingly with his sharply muscled arm. The edge of his metal armband cut into her skin, and the force of his hold denied her even the voice of argument or plea.

"You know this room well," accused Ares, "though I cut the house access to it myself only yesterday. How did you enter? What did you steal from here?"

In the pale halo of light that fell from the upper room, a figure moved. The shape was indeterminate, a shadow more than an obvious entity, but an abrupt, powerful motion sent a thin slash of scarlet flickering across the black uncertainty. The shadow stepped close to Tori, and a chill, slick darkness gripped Tori's chin.

Tori repented of every ill thought she had ever cast against an inquisitor. She prayed fervently that either Jase or Omi might arrive immediately. When neither inquisitor appeared, she berated them inwardly for leaving her alone in a house that had already witnessed murder.

The blackness released Tori's face and hissed, "She entered earlier, as you entered just now, Ares. She does not have the kree'va or the relaweed, and she did not escape with the traitor. While Rea searched for her, she was with that Soli inquisitor, whom you thought the Bercali would finish for you. Have you been wasting your attention on *her* instead of reporting to me?"

If the voice had not betrayed the speaker as a woman, the jealousy would have sufficed, thought Tori. She imagined the woman's cold, keen inspection, but the shadows remained darkly unrevealing.

Ares' grip loosened fractionally, as he answered, "She confirms that Birkaj is dead. If Mirelle, whom Birkaj trusted, does not have the kree'va, then it is Roake who has already taken it with the daar'va and the relaweed, and he is only wielding the daar'va now to taunt us. If Roake has killed the Rea-traitor, then they were never allies, and my brother did not betray us. Please explain to me, great Clan Leader, which brother has acted dishonorably: he who defied you, or he who obeyed?"

The shadow retreated a pace, pushed its dark shroud roughly, and became the slender Essenji clan leader, whose stern features might have been chiseled from ivory: pure, unapproachable, and imposing. Even the white scars that ran along her cheeks belonged on a damaged artifact and not on the face of a living woman. Akras breathed deeply, not quite allowing herself a sigh. "This woman has filled your mind with nonsense, Ares, but I shall stop her scheming. Bring me the drug that served so effectively with the other Soli. I shall let the traitor enjoy the wreckage of his concubine in his final moments."

"And will we steal the Calongi's mind similarly, so that he will wait idly while you enact further vengeance against a dead man?" demanded Ares. "The drug did not even suffice to affect his Soli counterpart."

"You might have considered the inquisitors before you brought this woman to me."

"The Calongi has surely sensed our warriors already. We have no more time to wait, Clan Leader, and we have no more reason to stay here."

"The inquisitors will not move against us until they are sure of that great Truth that they value above all else." Akras added quietly, "We have sufficient time to complete our plans."

"I am war leader, and I serve you loyally," retorted Ares, the unpredictable fury bursting forth again, "but I am finding Mirelle more believable than you."

Akras actually recoiled from him. "What has happened to you in these past few days, Ares?" When Ares did not reply, she snapped, "You are becoming as disrespectful as Roake, but you are slower to understand. This woman lies. The Rea-traitor is not dead. The Rea-traitor hides from us, but he knows that we succeed in destroying his cherished domain. *She* probably believes that he will emerge to rescue her." The bitterness of too many spans filled the words and made them cruel.

Akras fixed her hard gaze on Tori. "I understand why you try to turn my son against me. You are fighting for survival. I bear no malice toward you," said Akras without the warmth to make her claim ring true, "but the traitor values you, and nothing of his must be allowed to survive intact: not you, not his home, not his servants, not his children." Her thin lips tightened, as she repeated, "Not his children."

The cruel pressure against Tori's throat lessened to leave a throbbing wake, but Ares did not release her. "Mirelle is as valuable as the relaweed," he said, as if discussing a trade of comparable merchandise.

"We are Rea warriors," declared Akras with angry pride, "not panderers of Soli flesh."

"You taught me well, Mother. We trade in anything that brings a profit." Ares' voice nearly duplicated the clan leader's bitterness.

"I taught you to pursue a purpose," answered Akras. Her voice softened almost to a plea. "Our vengeance is nearly complete, Ares. Our honor is nearly restored, and we shall not sully it again. Do not lose your trust in me now, so close to the culmination of all that we have worked together to achieve."

Tori could feel Ares' frustration in the shift of bruising pressure against her throat. He threw her abruptly against the fiber skeins, and he bent to bind her hands and feet with the same tough fiber strands. "I am truly sorry that we could not find a way of working together, Mirelle," he whispered, his voice as tender as a lover's, while his hands tied ruthless knots. "But I am a Rea warrior, and I must obey my clan leader." He nodded toward the grim woman, who watched him silently. "You chose your final patron badly, Mirelle," he sighed. His voice became harsh again, as he spoke once more to Akras. "I shall bring the drug, Clan Leader, but I will not administer it."

He crossed the shadowy chamber to stand beneath the access hole. With an impressive agility and strength, he bent and jumped upward, grasped the edge of the floor above, and swung himself into the upper room. His departing footsteps sounded loud and angry.

The clatter of falling metal echoed from the inner cavern, startling Tori and causing Akras to whirl and drape herself again in darkness. Before Akras' shadowy figure could merge back into its near-invisibility, a sleek, resin-mottled battering ram of young Stromvi energy lunged at the Rea clan leader, toppling her with sudden force. Ngina tore at her opponent's living cloak with sharp pruning teeth, and the Bori's wail of pain pierced the heavy air.

A blinding beam of fire shot from the dark, adjacent room. Tori cried a warning, but the fire moved too quickly, tearing a resin-seething scar across the back of Ngina's head. The Stromvi youngling collapsed upon the Rea clan leader, only to be shoved aside indifferently as the clan leader regained her feet.

"I've warned you to be more cautious, Mother," said the man who entered, holding a black energy gun in obvious readiness. "You're becoming as reckless as Ares. I'm sorry I heard only the end of your conversation with him. It sounded fascinating. I could almost believe that my little brother was arguing with you. Will you treat him to the same discipline that you have given me?"

Akras countered with impatience, "You do not seem

to have learned your lesson as well as I had hoped, Roake. Have you recovered the kree'va?"

"I've located it. The Stromvi have it, as well as the relaweed, but we seem to have acquired a basis for negotiation." He turned Ngina with his booted foot. "This is the daughter of the senior Stromvi, Nguri Ngenga. The Stromvi are not a people to sacrifice their young for the instruments of power. This is a fortuitous acquisition, since we have little time left to us." Roake walked to where Tori sat, bound by Ares' harsh twines. "Ares should not have taken this one. He's right about her value, but we can't afford her."

"I'm delighted to meet you, Roake," murmured Tori, wondering furiously if she might twist the mockery of this alarming Essenji into useful divisiveness with his clan leader. Roake seemed at once more rational than Ares and less easily influenced.

"Your Soli inquisitor has spoken of me," replied Roake, bowing toward Tori with a rakish flair. "I hope he didn't malign me excessively." He glanced at his mother. "You know that she is under Per Walis' protection?"

"Per Walis is not here."

"He has a long reach," said Tori, snatching at a frail, new hope.

Neither Akras nor Roake acknowledged her remark. Roake pursued his own argument, "The Consortium *is* here. The Calongi might be willing to sacrifice her to the cause of Sesserda Truth, but my Soli comrade is fond of her."

"One Calongi and his Soli follower do not concern me," answered Akras. "The daar'va has prevented them from communicating with their Consortium leaders. We shall eliminate them."

"Kill a Calongi?" laughed Roake. "Do you know of anyone who has actually survived such an attempt?"

Akras retorted coldly, "You could have eliminated the Soli already. Why didn't you leave him to die with the Bercali?"

"He's a relanine addict. The daar'va doesn't affect him." Roake continued tonelessly. "And I wasn't sure where I stood with you at the time. I might have needed the good will of a Consortium official. He claims that Birkaj is already dead."

"He lies, or he is himself deceived."

"As you say, Clan Leader." Roake nodded compliantly, but his ironic expression did not convey agreement. "These inquisitors are too preoccupied with deciphering their ideal justice to move swiftly, which will give us a little extra time. We must use this Stromvi girl to persuade her people to give us Birkaj, the kree'va, and the relaweed promptly, before the Consortium arrives in sufficient force to deal with us seriously. We must not stay on this planet for more than another day. Will you command your warriors yourself, Clan Leader, or will you permit me, as war leader, to complete the plan myself?"

"Your brother seems to consider himself the war leader," remarked Tori.

The quiet barb proved disappointingly ineffectual. Roake agreed quietly, "Ares is a capable warrior, but he has some difficulty dealing with his inferiority to me. He forces me to reeducate him periodically."

Akras snapped, "Enough, Roake."

"No, Mother. It's not nearly enough. He must have believed that he had your blessing to betray me."

"I was not on this planet when he mistook your disobedience for evidence of treason," said Akras, and Tori's momentary hope chilled at Akras' firmness of denial. "I would have told him that you would not serve the Rea-traitor for any price."

"So," said Roake without evident emotion, "my brother was mistaken in considering me a traitor, as you are mistaken in believing that the Rea-traitor still lives. Birkaj is already dead, or the Soli inquisitor would have found him by now."

"You overestimate this Soli."

"He has the full relanine perception skills, where I have only the rudiments."

"Then the Soli realized what you truly sought and deceived you."

"No. He is as naive as the religious drivel that he espouses. He is consumed by a single, dominant worry—about the relaweed, as I intended. He feels sympathy for me in my addiction." Roake's contemptuous laughter made Tori wish that she could slap him.

"If Birk is dead," asked Tori quietly, "who killed him?" She finally gained the clan leader's attention.

Akras let her cloak fall away from her face again, and she took two steps toward Tori with the abrupt, unsteady tension of shock. Roake shrugged, answering with a faint scowl of irritation, "His pathetic son finally reacted to the pressure of self-interest."

"Calem and Sylvie both think their father is still alive," retorted Tori quickly. "Two inquisitors have read that truth in them."

Akras crossed almost hesitantly to Tori and stared down at her, bound at the clan leader's feet. The pale ivory face hovered like a waiting moon. "Did you kill him?" demanded Akras with the first sign of deep feeling.

Tori could not determine if Akras' taut, haunted expression signified fear, anger, or anxiety, but Tori concluded that the clan leader sought a very personal vengeance against Birk Hodge. While the odd, suspended moment lingered, Akras seemed to resemble the pathetic girl who had killed Arnod. The same unwanted mix of pity and disgust tried to engulf Tori.

Tori let her own gaze become vacant, and for once she summoned specters from the past deliberately. "A silenen thong tightens so quickly and so irresistibly," she murmured. "There is a gurgle of pain, as strangulation begins, but the thong snaps the neck." The old haunts rose too easily; the horror became real. "The sound is terrible because it's so simple and final. There's hardly time for the blood to begin to suffuse the face."

"Did he betray you?" whispered Akras, her pale, strained face barely moving to form the words.

"From the day we met," answered Tori dully, and she spoke of Arnod, but she knew that the Rea clan leader heard a condemnation of Birk.

Ngina clicked a sound of pain. Akras ordered her son crisply, "Bind the Stromvi's hands, feet, and jaws." Roake moved slowly to obey, but he watched his mother curiously, as if she had suddenly turned into a stranger.

Akras threw her cloak from her, and the Bori lay shuddering on the clay floor, still complaining of the wounds that Ngina had inflicted. Akras lowered herself gracefully and sat cross-legged in front of Tori. Blood's dark stain

seeped slowly through the bandage around Akras' arm.
"He betrayed me, also," said Akras with solemn earnestness. Tori barely nodded. She did not need to feign the
agony of memory.

"Clan Leader," began Roake warningly.

"Silence," snapped Akras. "You have laid the claim
before me that the Rea-traitor is dead. If your claim is
true, then this woman is the most likely instrument of
his execution. If your claim is false, then Ares is correct
in calling you unworthy, and I do not wish to see you
again." Roake made a stiff half-bow of obedience. He
leaned against the cavern wall, still holding his weapon
in readiness.

"My father, Raskannen, was a great clan leader,"
began Akras. "Birkaj killed him, as Birkaj killed my husband, Zagare. Did Birkaj swear his love for you?" Tori
did not try to respond, but Akras did not seem to care.
"He makes such oaths lightly. He took the honor from
my people, and he took everything from me." She
touched her scarred face. "I have vowed to destroy him."

Ares returned, leaping nimbly from the upper room,
and he stopped to stare at his brother in disbelief. Roake
saluted his brother in a silent, irreverent welcome, but
Akras did not pause in her recital. "I watched him for
many spans," murmured Akras, "and he did not know.
Even when I killed his Soli wife, he did not recognize
his enemy. I had hoped the inquisitors might question
him and uncover his vileness, but he disposed of his wife
before anyone else knew that she had died. He pretended
that she had simply left him."

The revulsion that Tori felt for the clan leader's confession could not distract her from the immediate threat.
Ares had drawn a long, bronze-handled knife, the twin
of the weapon that Jase had taken. Roake had raised his
gun. Akras seemed oblivious, but before either brother
could fulfill his deadly gesture, Akras raised one slim,
battered hand imperiously. The knife seemed to hover in
Ares' grasp, thinly restrained but anxious to embed itself
in Roake's heart. The clan leader's slender fingers
twitched in emphasis of her unspoken command.

Ares' arm dropped heavily to his side, and he sheathed
his knife with the sharp force of resentment. Roake
maintained a wary stance, but he returned his weapon to

its indefinite aim. Ares glared at Roake with blazing fury, but neither man spoke, and Akras continued her quiet, desperately bitter outpouring of recriminations and regret for all that she had lost. "The traitor has forced me to live in his own deceitful image," said Akras, allowing her own hand to fall gracefully to her lap, "but I will restore my honor when I cut the heart from him, for it was by the heart that he committed his greatest offense."

The attention of both brothers became fixed on their clan leader. Ares leaned slowly against the wall beside Roake. The brothers seemed to forget their personal feud.

Tori risked a glance at Ngina and met the young Stromvi's frightened eyes. Ngina clicked a quiet pattern of shared predicament, but Akras showed no sign of hearing the Stromvi words. "You understand," continued Akras, "that I must apportion the Rea-traitor's remains with my clan-knife. The Soli should not have taken it from me. He will pay for that dishonor. I have ordered my warriors to capture him once more. This time, I shall ensure his elimination myself."

Roake growled incomprehensibly and sprang toward the access. He lifted himself into the upper room as adroitly as his brother had done, and his footsteps raced into the distance. "While the clan leader speaks," murmured Ares in quiet chastisement, "no interruption should exist."

Akras never slowed. "You understand that I must have the Rea-traitor's body. There are rituals to be performed to complete a death-vow. You must return his body to me, or I must use a substitute, and the latter would be far less satisfying."

"In the gardens," said Tori swiftly, for she could think of no better reply, "by the blue-and-white rose." The search for a nonexistent rose might at least buy a little more time. She had an unpleasant suspicion that her own body was the substitute that Akras referenced.

The clan leader nodded graciously. "Find it, Ares," she ordered.

"Yes, Clan Leader." Ares smiled thinly at Tori, making her wonder if he already knew the futility of his undertaking. "With your permission, I shall send warriors to collect our prisoners."

"As you wish," answered Akras. When Ares had gone, she fastened her melancholy gaze directly on Tori. "He does not understand."

"No," agreed Tori, though she had no idea of what Akras meant.

"You have changed everything. I must reconsider the course of honor. Did you love him?"

"No," replied Tori, wondering if Akras referred now to Ares or to Birk.

"You were wise."

CHAPTER 39

Omi stood alone in the garden. He observed without moving. He assessed, and he experienced a feeling that very rarely assailed a Calongi. Omi feared.

When Jase joined him, Omi yielded the right of first address that his seniority merited. In the silence, Jase closed his eyes in evident pain, but he spoke calmly when the stretch of time made Omi's intention clear to him. "It is the Stromvi's world," said Jase, "but not all have chosen with understanding."

"They have chosen where to place their trust," answered Omi in a shallow voice. "The law defends their decision."

"Beyond the Ngenga Valley, death-watch continues, but the Stromvi who enact it have little comprehension of the truth."

"They will not listen to us above their own elder. We can do nothing more for them." Omi's regret layered his quiet words so sharply that Jase winced. "We cannot prevent completion of the calamity already begun."

"We can reduce the damage. Nguri will listen, if we make him realize what he has started."

"He will not listen," answered Omi.

"The Rea do not share your doubts."

"They understand nothing."

"Nonetheless," replied Jase with the hardness of determination, "I can persuade them to share their resources with me."

"Will you also adopt their uncivilized methods, Jaselai? Even if you chose to intimidate the Stromvi, you have adapted too often and too acutely in these painful days. The relanine sickness has begun within you."

"The symptoms remain relatively mild." Jase added

with a twisted smile, "I am still conscious and reasonably rational."

"You know the illness will progress rapidly, once the environmental changes accelerate. Your people are too fragile. You have no time, and I have no will to contribute to destruction. Name even one victim whom I may defend with honor and clear conscience, and I will aid you as you wish."

"Sylvie Hodge is a victim. Rillessa is a victim. Even Calem is a victim."

"You may as well ask me to defend the Rea, whose unlawful drugs impaired the minds of these three. All whom you have named have contributed to the evil. They pay no more than the necessary dues of their selfishness, which has negated even the friendship-debt that brought you here. The two Deetari women will suffer likewise, for they have both abetted the destruction with their lies, forcing their own prophecies of death to become reality."

"Victoria Mirelle is a victim."

"She has lived her allotted life already."

"Tori doesn't even know that she's a clone. She's a Consortium member who would be horrified to know the scope of Mirelle's legacy to her."

"You are judging with emotion, Jase-lai. Miss Mirelle has already begun to repeat her original's defiance. She chose again to set herself apart from the law. The law cannot protect her now." Omi paused. "You are thinking that I am a cruel and cold man, the type of Calongi who pleases the Consortium's detractors by providing an example of the injustice wrought by dispassionate truth."

"Absolute truth condemns us all, Omi-lai."

"Yes," agreed Omi. "And in such truth, I find myself a coward, afraid to risk my own life for beings whom I cannot truly respect. You judge truly: These 'victims' do not merit condemnation unto death, but I cannot feel compassion for them. I am flawed, Jase-lai, and it is for this reason that I have been seeking counsel from Ukitan-lai. I am ashamed."

"Your shame aids nothing," said Jase with a sharp impatience that failed Sesserda doctrine as thoroughly as Omi's confessed weakness. "Ukitan-lai sent you here to overcome your prejudice. Extend my time, Omi-lai."

"You will be more likely to survive if you allow the

sickness to run a natural course. Artificial delays will aggravate the eventual pain and increase the chances of permanent nerve damage. External contamination will accelerate while the new infusion of relanine adapts to you."

"I know all of the standard warnings, Omi-lai. I probably have more experience with relanine poisoning than anyone in this galaxy."

"Your sarcasm indicates a lack of Sesserda peace. You should correct this flaw."

"I'll meditate on the subject tomorrow, if I still happen to be alive." Jase removed the jacket that he had borrowed from Birk's discards, and he hung it from a thorn branch. He opened the torn shirt above his heart. "I trust that you can see the heat patterns well enough to strike the implant directly."

"Enemies gather."

"You know perfectly well that we have sufficient time, if you stop arguing."

Omi's tendrils shifted slightly in offense, but he calmed his own reaction quickly. "Lie on the path. The pain will be brief but acute."

Jase complied, the smooth, white stones grinding beneath his weight. The Calongi's dark, velvety outer-arms coiled tightly. When the outer-arms lifted, the lower limbs—the two slender legs and the numerous true arms—appeared in all their gold and iridescent shadings. Some arms had hands with varying numbers of fingers. Some were more specialized, ending in a single sheathed needle or combs or nearly any shape that Omi found useful, for the Calongi often grew limbs by conscious design.

Omi lowered himself to the Soli's side. Omi raised one of his *irivi*, a thin, flexible, tubular limb, from beneath the shortened cloak of his outer-arms. Jase murmured, "I need as much as you can give me without killing me outright, Omi-lai."

"Be still. Focus on the peace, or you will die from the first shock of my blood in your heart." Omi began to whisper in a wordless pattern of Sesserda healing. He soothed himself as well as Jase into the near-trance that would enable them both to endure the exchange, for the voluntary bleeding of the *irivi* required the painful re-

routing of many nerve impulses. Omi shuddered, and a
hollow, needle-fine bone emerged from a fleshy pocket
at the end of the tubular limb. Omi drove his bone-tipped
appendage into the Soli's chest.

Jase jerked reflexively, and he murmured a nearly
soundless echo of Omi's healing litany. Omi's needle
pierced more deeply, until the implant's seal was
breached, for the fiber that guided Jase's normal supply
would not support live relanine. The transfer began. The
Calongi blood that filled Omi's hollow limb glowed with
iridescence through the dusky outer skin, and the living
blood sizzled as it merged with the remnants of purified
relanine within Jase's implant. Omi's blood began to
burn indiscriminately through Soli bone and sinew, but
the needle of Calongi tissue guided the largest part into
the deeply embedded, deeply protected implant.

Omi withdrew the *irivi* slowly. The deliberate denial of
so many sensory commands strained even the Calongi's
phenomenal resources of stamina. A single drop of iridescent blood marked the dark skin of Jase's chest. The
scab hardened almost immediately into a thin, flexible
shell.

"You may experience increased illness while adapting
to my blood," said Omi softly. "I cannot yet predict how
rapidly the atmospheric changes will work against you,
for the changes are complex."

Jase raised himself cautiously to a sitting position. He
touched the tiny wound that pierced to his heart. "Already, I feel the strength of the extra relanine you have
given me. The rewards outweigh the pain. I thank you,
Omi-lai."

"Relanine does not make you a Calongi. Remember
your Soli weaknesses if you wish to survive."

Jase laughed, but the sound was strained. "I am unlikely to forget, under the circumstances. I regret that
others sometimes fail to recognize the same truth."

"I understand, Jase-lai. I have not credited you with
sufficient wisdom."

"I have never tried to be anything but a Soli. I shall
not pretend that my judgment of my fellow Soli is as
impartial as your own."

"The Hodges are not of your species."

Jase nodded minimally. "Birk was an Essenji, chemically altered to masquerade as a Soli. He was a Rea clan member."

"You were never fully convinced that he was dead."

"As usual, you perceive clearly, Omi-lai. I may have seen Birk. I may have seen a dead simulacrum of exceptional quality. I've tried to replay the events, but I doubt the accuracy of my memories. I suspect the Rea of instigating a physical trauma that caused relanine to interfere with my awareness. Perhaps they administered a mind-impairment drug to me when I first arrived on this planet. They seem to have used such drugs freely against Rillessa, and to a lesser extent against both Sylvie and Calem. I cannot recall any details of my own brief incarceration."

"The Rea will be no gentler if you allow them to imprison you again."

"They are preparing to leave the planet immediately, and I have no better way to follow them and persuade them of the truth. I would admittedly have preferred to have more time to pursue safer options, but neither Nguri nor the Rea clan leader consulted me."

"By capturing Miss Mirelle as well as Miss Ngenga, the Rea have already forced you to readjust your intentions. Because of Miss Mirelle, the Rea leave prematurely, believing that Birk Hodge is dead and believing that their Stromvi hostage can gain them all else that they desire from this world. You have antagonized the clan leader personally. Your plan is rash."

Jase smiled crookedly. "You are too astute, Omi-lai. You could make the credulous believe that Calongi read minds."

"Only the most blindly credulous would believe that two Sesserda adepts could remain ignorant of crimes occurring almost in their presence."

"The Rea believe that they can dictate justice. They have a very limited understanding of truth."

"They have no respect for creation," said Omi-lai, rising stiffly. "They destroy and deceive even each other."

"The Essenji are only civilized to Level VII, Omi-lai. We must judge them accordingly." Jase refastened the shoulder clasp of his shirt, and he jumped to his feet with abrupt, carefully focused energy. He collected the jacket. "They do have their own sense of honor, and they are trying to uphold it. I really don't think they want to kill me—or Tori or Ngina. It's Birk who matters to them. They won't leave Stromvi until they're sure that he's dead."

"Incidental destruction does not disturb them. The clan leader has already attacked you once, and you injured her and her pride in return."

"Because I thwarted her spontaneous, impassioned gesture of jealousy against Miss Mirelle. The Essenji react emotionally, and I shall appeal to their very powerful emotions of clan protection."

"If they take you from this planet, they will take you with full intent of killing you, Jase-lai. You plan in terms that you consider heroic, but such plans are self-destructive and self-deceiving."

"You made the choice for me, Omi-lai," answered Jase soberly. "I am a mere Soli, after all, and the methods of judgment available to me are few."

Omi's neck tendrils shifted in consternation. "I do not force you to become a victim."

"Ukitan-lai sent us both here for reconciliation with the past. As Sesserda practitioners, we are obligated to teach each other. You have caused me to recognize truths about myself, and I must return the favor."

Omi did not reply. Jase delved into his jacket's pocket, withdrawing the cracked silver pen holder. He held it in front of Omi. "This was on Birk's desk." He handed it to Omi, who pried apart the silver halves with six thin, dexterous fingers that emerged from beneath the rippling cloak of outer arms. A starburst of rubies gleamed from the broken shell of the pen holder. "The version that Ares wears is smaller. This is the dominant Rea emblem."

"Vengeance is most uncivilized," sighed Omi, "even for a Level VII." Omi's heat patterns shifted, warning without words.

Jase nodded. "Most uncivilized."

The beams of Rea fire crossed between Jase and Omi, bruising the ground and raising a thick cloud of resin steam. Six Rea warriors, leather-armored for barbaric glory but armed with the very deadly products of stolen Network technology, met to claim their prisoners. The steam thinned, stirred by the warriors' approach.

The senior warrior, a man as dry and tough as his lua-leather vest, kicked the prone Soli, but Jase remained as still as death. "Find the Calongi," ordered the warrior tersely, pointing at three of his men. "Take the Soli to the warship."

In his self-imposed trance, Jase's Sesserda senses remained alert. He recognized Calem's distant whine: "You said they wouldn't attack us again, Harrow!"

Harrow grumbled, "They're not attacking us," but he was unsure.

Sylvie cajoled with an acidic undertone, "Run into the garden, Harrow, and scatter them for us."

Somewhere among the southern rose fields, a pair of Stromvi females led Rillessa into daylight. The Soli woman blinked blindly at the brightness, and her eyes ran with cleansing tears. The Stromvi left her alone.

A young Rea warrior approached Omi, who was seated quietly beneath an overhang of Stromvi vines. The young warrior returned as he had come, unaware of the whispered command word that had deflected him.

Gisa pleaded with the Deetari spirits for a lifting of all curses on her people. Thalia offered food to a shadow. The shadow inspected an energy pistol, smuggled from the lawless Soli civilization known as Network.

A Rea warrior attempted to confiscate Omi's shuttle, while his Essenji brothers watched. Roake shouted from the edge of the landing field, "Order your legion to stop this attack, Tiber. We can't combat the Calongi! Listen to me, Tiber, and not to my brother's jealous lies." Omi's shuttle emitted a shrill siren of warning, and startled Rea warriors fired on the shuttle to silence it.

"Obey my brother, Tiber," ordered Ares bitterly, "for he is war leader. Claudius, go to the clan leader. She has two prisoners with her."

The people of Stromvi completed the final, loving preparations of their fields. Slowly, they retreated back into their caverns. The final phase of death-watch had commenced.

CHAPTER 40

"Will they kill us?" asked Ngina quietly. She lay on the thin mat on the floor of the cell, her head resting on her forearms. Her skin had lost some of its sheen and depth of color, for the atmosphere of the Rea shuttle was dry and harsh by Stromvi standards. Ngina's first use of adaptation fluid had not transpired easily, and she still moved sluggishly from the fluid's initial effects.

Tori rolled to her side and leaned over the edge of the cell's single bunk to see Ngina's sad face. "Don't dwell on depressing possibilities, Ngina. The Rea haven't harmed us yet." Akras' haunting anguish, like the despair of the girl who had killed Arnod, had fed Tori's guilt and made her almost indifferent to her plight of captivity. She had scarcely resisted when Ares confined her in the shuttle that had brought her in turn to the Rea ship.

"I feel half-dead already," groaned Ngina.

"That's part of adaptation. Now you know how we Soli feel on arrival at Stromvi. The feeling passes." *Adaptation sickness ends—like everything else,* thought Tori, her mood no more cheerful than Ngina's. *Everything ends, like Arnod and Birk Hodge and inquisition.*

"You're not sick now."

"It's relatively easy to adapt to one's own natural environment," answered Tori, trying to convince herself more than Ngina. The adaptation *should* have been easy. The shakiness of her senses was doubtless a product of fear and the final loss of hope. "The Essenji are physically very similar to Soli." Tori swung her slender legs over the edge of the bunk, and she stared at the undecorated white door. "Unmarked Xiani design," she muttered, recalling Jase's description of the disk ships at the port.

"What?"

"Like Stromvi caverns without weavings: It isn't home, if it doesn't reflect the people." Tori did not know why the comment seemed significant to her. Homeless herself now, she found the barren nature of the prison cell grimly appropriate.

"It's not my home anyway," sighed Ngina, and she clicked a soft, sad passage from a Stromvi song of family.

"Don't mope, Ngina. It's contagious." Chastising Ngina, Tori tried to shake herself free of the same clinging, debilitating sense of futility. She shoved her loose, dark hair away from her face and straightened her violet shoulder sash. "I need to think, if we're to escape this mess," said Tori, forcing an unfelt briskness into her voice. "We're alive now only because you're potentially useful as a hostage, and I'm a marketable commodity in certain circles of unsavory affluence."

"And because you helped the Rea clan leader to destroy Mister Birk," said Ngina in quiet, lonely accusation. "I heard you speak to the clan leader, Miss Tori. All of you—Soli, Essenji, or Deetari—scheme against each other, while Stromvi work. I'm not very wise, but I think I'm sick from more than adaptation fluid."

Tori started to voice a proud rebuttal, but she remembered caution and bit back the words. Sharply as Ngina's recrimination hurt, Tori realized that she would have found a complete denial difficult even without fear of listening ears. She had earned Ngina's accusation of guilt, albeit for a different cause. Tori said only, "For once, you've paid too much attention to your father."

"I know. The truth lies somewhere between his present bitterness and my naiveté. The truth is still without beauty."

"Never say that to a Calongi," remarked Tori with a sigh, for Sesserda's idealistic truths seemed far removed from the cruel intricacies of Rea justice.

"The Calongi may keep their great Sesserda Truth. I don't like it."

"Absolute truth can be very painful," admitted Tori. Absently, she scratched at the taut skin of her forearm, where a slight discoloration showed the effects of Roake's rough application of the inoculation patch. "Every time

I begin to believe in Consortium justice, it disappoints me anew."

"Do you think the Rea killed Mister Jase and Master Omi?" asked Ngina slowly, as if she had just considered the idea that her misfortunes might not be isolated.

"No," replied Tori tersely. *Please, no.* "The Calongi are an uncommonly durable race, and our Soli inquisitor. . . ." She did not finish the sentence aloud, but she continued in her head: *Jase warned me that he dared not trust me fully, and I thought he referred only to his inquisitor's theories about the deeds already done. He was apologizing for the future.*

The sense that she had been betrayed by a man she had begun to respect hurt most of all. "Our two inquisitors allowed the Rea to take us," said Tori wearily. The weight of regret pressed hard upon her. "Master Omi must have known that a shipload of Rea warriors had come to Stromvi with threatening intent. Even our Soli inquisitor must have recognized the imminence of danger." She shook her head irritably, her dark hair swinging back across her eyes. She pushed at the hair, wishing she had a brush. "Obviously, you and I were less important than loftier Sesserda concerns. Inquisitors identify crimes' perpetrators. We cannot expect them to overstep their legal authority and prevent a crime's occurrence."

Ngina considered Tori's sharp outpouring slowly. The Stromvi girl's black eyes mirrored the barren room's cold light. "You're angry with Mister Jase? I am more than angry with you." Ngina clicked a terse, rapid sequence. "Consortium language has no words for my anger. I thought you were my friend, Miss Tori, but my friend could not have killed Mister Birk or anyone else."

If I had known how he treated Akras, more cruelly than even Arnod treated me, I might have killed Birk. Great-grandmama would have killed him, but Mirelle's revenge would have fallen swiftly instead of lingering in the Rea fashion. Why must I believe Akras, who seeks my own destruction, rather than Birk, who was always kind to me? Because I have seen how Birk used the Stromvi, though I chose to be blind. "I am your friend, Ngina-li."

"Only when you need my strength. I begin to understand my father at last."

"I'm sorry that you understand only his loss of faith."

Tori arose from the bunk and crossed the small room, stepping carefully around Ngina, and she examined the locked door for the tenth time. She turned her gaze to the wall beside the door and continued thoughtfully, "We need to ensure that the Rea appreciate our very real value to them." Thinking of Jase's accusations against her, she added softly, "We must trust each other, Ngina-li."

"I shall never trust anyone again." Ngina's words sounded like childish excess, but her tone had become confident. "I have come to understand Ngoi most of all. He sacrificed himself honorably. I must find his courage in myself."

Shocked, Tori turned from the wall and stared at the Stromvi girl. Ngina's tranquil fatality seared Tori's own self-pity from her. Tori said haltingly, "As my great-grandmother once told me, honor is a poor substitute for life." She continued more firmly, "I don't think Ngoi's circumstances were the same as our own. Even if he did kill himself, he may have reacted only from terrible pain that his captors inflicted." Tori stopped herself, realizing that such words would only fuel Ngina's depression. "Please, don't even talk about emulating him, Ngina-li. You have too much sense. Adaptation sickness is making everything seem overly bleak to you."

More shaken than she wanted to admit, Tori returned to the bunk and sat cross-legged upon its thin, gray thermal cover. The soft fabric of her skirt spread a violet circle around her. The color, so natural to the Stromvi world, seemed too garish for the sterile cell.

"I'm not as brave as you, Miss Tori, or as clever." The statement carried a trace of cynicism.

"You're nearly as clever as that wily father of yours," said Tori almost pleadingly, "and necessity creates the 'courage' you and I need now."

"Your position isn't like mine. You're alone, and the Rea can't use you to threaten anyone else." Ngina's innocent honesty stung. "They want to use me as a weapon against my people."

"I know," answered Tori, feeling a frantic need to dispel Ngina's desperation. Both Stromvi and Soli sat in uneasy silence. Tori wracked her memories for some clue as to how Great-grandmama Mirelle would salvage herself from such apparent hopelessness. . . . And the answer was clear, if unpalatable. Mirelle would use the most susceptible man who could aid her cause. Mirelle would use Ares. The greatest prizes always necessitated the largest risks.

Having named her goal, Tori thrust aside all interfering emotions. As she had once worked to misdirect the Consortium's chosen inquisitors, she now wielded against the Rea the mental armor bestowed by Tiva disorder. Addressing the unadorned wall, Tori began to concoct a deception that she hoped would make her great-grandmother proud. "You can't dwell in the past, Ngina. You must move forward. You're right about me. I am alone now, but I don't intend to remain alone for long. I wasn't designed for solitary, monastic life."

"I don't know what you mean," muttered Ngina.

"I mean that I'll have a new patron soon. Ares wants me too much to keep me imprisoned for long, and he pleases me. I shall help him to fulfill the greatness that is within him."

"Why do you say such things to me?" asked Ngina forlornly. "Do you want me to know more sorrow?"

Tori's thoughts ran at a hurtling pace, controlling her own actions with complete dispassion. *Turn Ngina's discouragement into outrage and revive the rebelliousness that now may save her life. Let Ares know that you're aware of him, for Ares can provide freedom—for you, for Ngina, for Stromvi. Use every method you were taught, overt or subtle. Use every method you remember.* Tori delved into memories of similar desperate performances, and she did not let herself care that those memories, which she had never before acknowledged, had belonged to another life, embedded in her by artifice.

"Consider it my own form of honor. You deserve an explanation: Birk betrayed me. He used me only to reach my mother's patron, Per Walis. I don't blame you or your people for what Birk did to me, but I cannot help you, and I must think of my own future. A man of Ares' strength is rare, and he desires me. I'm moving forward, Ngina, as you should."

"I don't understand you, Miss Tori."

Tori sighed artfully, "Sweet child, no one has ever understood me, except Great-grandmama Mirelle, because

I am like her." Tori smiled at the blank, uninformative wall beside the door. "I am like her in every way."

*   *   *

"She knows that we observe her," muttered Roake, "and she wields her words accordingly." He silenced the recording device, allowing it to continue its spying voicelessly.

"Of course, she knows," snapped Ares, but his dark eyes still followed every gesture of the Soli woman. "She is not a fool."

"And she isn't the original Mirelle. Remember *that* truth, Brother, when you covet her legend." Roake hesitated very briefly before deactivating the visual projection of Victoria Mirelle and Ngina Ngenga.

Tagran could not help but admire the siren's skill at her craft. Even recognition of the treachery she wove did not make her less fascinating to observe. She had also chosen her victim well. Akras had treated both her sons harshly, but Ares was more sensitive than Roake, and Roake had his devoted wives to console him.

Roake added, "Miss Mirelle becomes a liability to the man who admires her without sensible detachment."

Even Roake is impressed, thought Tagran. *He berates himself as well as his brother.*

Roake swept from the control room, his dark cloak flowing from the bright war-star at his shoulder. His brother watched him and remained silent until the door had closed behind him. Akras observed both her sons thoughtfully. Tagran wondered if she had any idea how fragile her control of them had become. He was certain that she did not know how many of her warriors had begun to share Perekah's mutinous opinions.

"At least Mirelle considers me worthy of her deceptions," muttered Ares. He tugged the copper clasp from his own shoulder, and he threw it with his short cloak to the empty chair beside him. "Roake denies me any honor at all."

"Accept this burden, Ares," said Akras, her stern eyes distantly focused, "by trusting *my* honor."

"You let me declare myself war leader, knowing that

Roake still served you. You helped him make a mockery of me before all the Rea. Teach me the honor in *this*.''

She answered, "The weight is heavy, while the vengeance remains incomplete."

Tagran wished that Akras would free him from his duties as her personal guard. He defended her readily when he spoke to the other warriors. In her presence, he had trouble disbelieving Perekah's accusations of Akras' growing madness.

"The traitor is dead," said Ares, "executed by Mirelle. We have regained our home vessel, and we still have the daar'va. We do not need the kree'va, for Rea honor can never be restored. We have sullied Rea honor ourselves for too many spans." His words were softly spoken, but they shocked Tagran, who expected such defiance from Roake but not from Ares. "The relaweed's cost has already been too high, and my incomparable brother can surely find some other means to feed his addiction. You have squandered my honor and many spans in your great, futile vendetta, Mother. Waste nothing more on the traitor's servants and useless children. Let us kill them or sell them or abandon them, but be done with them and with this planet we encircle endlessly, before the Consortium and all of Per Walis' hirelings descend upon us!"

"We must be entirely sure that the traitor is dead," answered Akras, but she sounded weary. "You found no body."

"With the home vessel restored to us, we could destroy the entire Ngenga Valley from space," argued Ares impatiently. His mother frowned, as if surprised by the realization that the Rea vessel's weapons could be turned against a planet. Tagran felt his warrior's instincts shiver into alert. "We know that the traitor never left his farm. Only the Deetari woman escaped us."

Akras inclined her head. "Fortune served us there." Akras' hard eyes held contempt for all Deetari. "The Deetari woman shared her awe of us with her planet so effectively. Their fear of us survived even in a Calongi's presence."

Ares conceded grudgingly, "Roake evaluated them accurately. Superstition is their weakness."

"Destroying with weapons of broken leaves and overturned pottery. Yes, Roake excels at such schemes of guile."

"None can outshine our war leader." Angrily, Ares reactivated the visual surveillance. He glowered at the flat, erratic image projected by an unsophisticated device, stolen from a smuggler who had crossed the Rea. As Ares watched the Soli woman, however, his expression began to smooth slightly. Tagran wished that the woman were Rea and sincere in her admiration for Ares.

Akras observed the focus of her younger son's attention, but she did not acknowledge his cynical comment. "Roake believes that he can still locate the kree'va. He will use the Stromvi girl to reach it, and he will initiate the planet's destruction before the Stromvi can realize their danger. He will endeavor to obtain the relaweed first, but he knows the priorities."

"You deprive me of even a role in the final battle. Will you leave me no honor at all?"

"To you I give the greatest honor," whispered Akras, "the traitor's first-born child." Tagran inhaled sharply, but neither Akras nor Ares appeared to notice.

"Calem Hodge is unworthy of an honorable death. Let him die with his home."

"The first-born is worthy," said Akras. *Say no more*, Tagran wanted to plead with her, but he did not speak. "The first-born is your brother." Ares raised his head slowly. "Do you understand now?" hissed Akras bitterly.

Ares neither moved nor changed expression, and the lack of obvious reaction cried a warning to Tagran. The hidden feelings were often the most dangerous. "I began to understand," said Ares smoothly, "when you spoke of Birkaj to the Soli woman." He nearly smiled. "You expected me to kill Roake in the first foray against Hodge Farm. He was your intended victim all along."

"He was always secondary. I wanted you to bring the Rea-traitor to me for his long delayed execution."

Ares touched the control console thoughtfully. "For all these spans, you have honored Roake above me always, so that I would learn to share your hatred for him. After Roake escaped the Bercali, you let him believe himself still favored, so as to magnify his defeat when I steal his life at your command."

Is it so? wondered Tagran sickly, though he knew the answer.

"Yes," whispered Akras. Her voice wavered very slightly as she added, "You will take your brother's life at my command." Tagran closed his eyes, unable to bear the sight of his Akras issuing such a dishonorable order.

"I have always been loyal to my clan leader," answered Ares softly. Tagran reopened his eyes to see if Ares could truly react so mildly to a command of fratricide. Ares stared fixedly at the projection, and Tagran could discern nothing of the young warrior's emotions. "I thank you, Clan Leader. You have indeed enabled me to understand."

Akras folded her arms and nodded. After a microspan of silence, she arose and nodded at Tagran to follow her. He obeyed mechanically, and they left Ares alone. The door sealed behind them with a hiss.

When they had walked nearly the length of the newly scrubbed corridor, Akras stopped. She leaned her straight, strong back against the ship's cool wall. "The prospect of final vengeance tastes no sweeter than the long spans of anger," she said to the air. She looked at Tagran. "You do understand? You remember what we lost?"

We lost honor, pride, and glory. We lost Akras of the laughter, Akras whom we all loved. "I remember, Akras."

CHAPTER 41

"I know that you're conscious, Soli," said Roake impatiently. "You're entirely aware of what I am saying and doing, and you would be well advised to cease this pretense."

"I could call your bluff," replied Jase, opening his eyes lazily, "as you have called mine, but you and I could circle each other endlessly, couldn't we? We're a dreadful pair of schemers, I fear."

"What is your purpose, Soli?"

"Truth."

"You uphold your noble purpose badly," accused Roake, and Jase shrugged. "You are an improbable inquisitor."

"Legal inquisition is a prerogative and responsibility that comes with Sesserda's third level, which is my rank. Are you hurt that I didn't notify you of my official status? I'd apologize, except I have terrible manners where my captors are concerned."

"You were not imprisoned here on my order. I have upheld my vow to deal with you honorably."

"Have you come here to release me? No? How disappointing. Your warriors have made outstanding progress in eradicating the evidence of the Bercali and their guests, but this hold still carries an unpleasant fragrance of decay. Do you suppose the decay recalls victims of the Bercali or of your recent meddling with the atmosphere?"

"If you irritate me, Soli, I shall forget that you are here."

"As you seem to have forgotten your business arrangement with Calem Hodge and Harrow Febro? You arranged for the relaweed to be grown on Stromvi, didn't you?"

"I obeyed the clan leader," grunted Roake.

"I doubt that Per Walis will forgive you on that basis, since Harrow is his employee, and you've lost the relaweed. You're highly effective as an instrument of coercion, Roake, but you're in a precarious position at the moment. Your clan leader has been using you to enact her vengeance against Birk Hodge, and she's been using your brother to control you, but she's taken large risks in the process."

"You oversimplify."

"Probably, but you're not visiting me in jail for the purpose of hearing a recital of your own plots and motives. How are you planning to use me?"

"You promised to locate the relaweed for me. I hope you haven't failed me."

"You never expected me to give you the relaweed. You freed me in the hope that I might lead you to something of even greater interest: Birk Hodge."

"I freed you once because I respect a survivor. Why have you chosen to become a Rea prisoner again?"

"Your cheerful company makes me feel so welcome. I can't tell you how much our friendly little chats mean to me, especially when I consider the attractive alternatives available to you. Please don't feel insulted if I admit that Mirelle's legatee would be my own first choice for company at the moment. For that matter, I'd much rather talk to Ngina Ngenga than to you."

"You gave our captives to us," retorted Roake.

"Did I? The incident eludes my memory."

"You consciously jeopardized them."

"You certainly give me credit for a great deal of foresight."

"Where is your Calongi colleague?"

"On Stromvi, I should imagine. After attacking me, your people damaged his shuttle, I believe. Both moves were bold but self-defeating. For various reasons, Omilai is reluctant to take an active part in the Hodge Farm troubles, but you've pushed him closer to a commitment. Attacking those whom a Calongi protects is seldom wise, since Calongi retribution is as pure and perfect as Sesserda Truth. The Rea may not acknowledge Consortium law, but you've made yourselves its object by interfering with a Consortium planet and Consortium members."

"You're not in a position to register a formal complaint against us, Sleide." Roake smiled thinly. "Your feeble attempt to make my brother a victim of inquisition was not even lawful by your own Sesserda standards. We don't need to defy your Consortium to achieve our goals. Greed for what we offer kills. Fear of us kills. We don't need to destroy the slaves of weakness."

"None of your people has ever been a subject of official inquisition, but I have every right to change that status. True Sesserda justice supercedes legalistic quibbling."

"At Calongi convenience."

"Inquisitors are too few, I grant, to address all unregistered wrongs that afflict the less civilized regions of the Consortium, but we can hardly ignore flagrant violations in front of us. The Rea chose peaceful, isolated Stromvi as a focus for their viciously convoluted schemes, and the preservation of Consortium justice is the oath-bound business of every inquisitor. I should be more specific: The Rea chose to attack Hodge Farm, because Birk Hodge was Rea, wasn't he?"

"He was a traitor," answered Roake crisply, "and he was ours to condemn or acquit, not yours."

"I don't suppose you ever considered requesting extradition. No, that might be considered an acknowledgment of Consortium authority, which does not conform to the Rea style, does it?"

"You saw him killed."

"I saw a dead man."

"Did my brother kill him?"

"No."

"The Mirelle woman?"

"No."

"Who?"

"Much as I'm enjoying this little chat, I have some reservations as to why I should continue to answer you."

"You are my prisoner, Soli. You show signs of relanine sickness. I can let you die by relanine's agonizing, nerve-by-nerve mutations, or I can kill you mercifully."

"Since you're so persuasive, Roake: The murderer was Birk Hodge."

"Don't be insolent with me. I've nearly lost patience with you."

"No, Roake. You've gained respect for me, or you wouldn't be here. You asked for my verdict, and I've given it. You asked why I allowed your Rea warriors to recapture me so easily, and I shall tell you. Stromvi is changing, and you will help me salvage some lives, some justice, and some hope. Nothing that lives on Stromvi will survive intact, and nothing that has left Stromvi recently will survive at all unless you do as I say."

"Your conceit astounds me, Soli."

"Tell me the nature of the Rea treasures that Birk Hodge stole, and tell me that a planetary adapter was not among them." Jase spread his hands to the length of the chain that bound them together. "You freed me because you trusted that I wasn't a party to any schemes of Birk Hodge or your own people. Enough relanine flows in your system to tell you what flows in mine."

"It is an unusually pure fluid," acknowledged Roake.

"It is entirely pure, as a rule. You recognized my potential as an extension of your own awareness when you saw me on this very ship." Jase relaxed against the wall as much as the chain allowed. "Imprisoning me threatens to become a favorite Rea habit. I assume that you were involved in my first capture, but your people had already rendered me unconscious, and you observed only the Sesserda markings and not the source of my Sesserda skills. You trust me to behave honorably with you, because the Calongi have 'favored' me with their own pure form of relanine."

"You know nothing of *Rea* honor."

"The examples provided by your people have not impressed me. I know you distrust your brother, and he envies you to the point of hatred. I know that Birk killed a Bori simulacrum of himself to deceive you and escape your clan's vengeance, though someone evidently removed the simulacrum before it could achieve its intended purpose."

"A simulacrum," echoed Roake thoughtfully.

"In death, a good quality simulacrum cannot be distinguished from its image without an autopsy. Killing such a rare and expensive simulacrum is as wasteful as it is cruel, of course, but I imagine that Birk considered the cause worthwhile. Birk is still alive; he is still on Stromvi; and he is probably seeking *your* destruction now. Between Birk Hodge and your bad-tempered brother, you're not in a very enviable position, are you?"

"I am the Rea war leader."

"That was your brother's claim yesterday."

"He was mistaken."

"Or you are mistaken now. The perspective is critical, I think, since each of you believes his claim implicitly."

"I am the chosen of the clan leader," said Roake.

"Let me judge for you." Jase's voice softened, invoking the Sesserda arts of persuasion cautiously. "Let me speak to your clan leader."

"She will see you when she is ready."

"She will see me quickly or not at all. You will both listen to me, or you will both be very dead very soon. You perceive relanine sickness in me. What do you feel within yourself, Roake? I shall tell you, in case you haven't identified the nature of the problem yet. Your body is consuming relanine at a vastly accelerated rate, and your supply will soon exhaust itself, because you've been poisoned, Roake, by the changes that have begun on the planet Stromvi. We've all been poisoned. Everyone who was on Stromvi within the last three millispans has been infected with a self-replicating toxin that feeds on any trace of relanine in the body. This is my perception, and it is Omi-lai's perception."

"Then you are dying with us."

"Possibly, unless you have the good sense to trust me a little further. Bring your clan leader to me, and bring my two fellow prisoners to substantiate my story. I'll prove my claims." When Roake remained silent, Jase leaned forward as far as the chain around his neck permitted. "Feel the relanine surging through your veins. You've taken a full measure within the past millispan, haven't you? But you still feel the onset of the sickness. The chills and aches have begun. Your own mind becomes suspect, as trivial mental tasks elude your ability. Perhaps you try to read a command on your ship's console screen, and the words become suddenly incomprehensible, though all else seems normal to you. Perhaps it's the arithmetic skills that vanish. Perhaps it's the memory of where you spent the past microspan or why you came into this cell block."

"Stop," growled Roake.

"The poison may kill the others quickly, but you and I will linger, Roake. You and I will remain conscious of every lessening of our selves, every incremental failure of our minds and bodies. Such is the gift of relanine addiction. I know that you feel this truth within yourself."

"The kree'va," said Roake tightly, "was long the great weapon of the Rea clan leader. The Rea-traitor used it once before, tainting the atmosphere of this ship, the Rea home vessel, but the strongest of us survived."

"If your kree'va is a sophisticated planetary adapter, it is surely programmable. It has been programmed with enormous cunning on this occasion."

"The Rea-traitor would not program it against himself."

"Nor does he have the skills to create such a complex toxin, so ingeniously designed to defeat all standard, relanine-based Consortium cures. One must appreciate the biological sophistication of the result. Even the Suviki have difficulty formulizing the live variants of relanine. No, Birk-in-hiding is as thoroughly poisoned as the rest of us aliens to Stromvi."

Roake rocked back on his heels, though he remained crouched before Jase like a great cat ready to spring. "A Stromvi commands the kree'va?" demanded Roake slowly.

"A Stromvi who has outschemed all of us, I'm afraid, by fulfilling death-watch in his quiet, unobtrusive way. Nguri respects Consortium law, but he epitomizes the flaws of his species as well as the gifts. He respects his own planet first. We need to persuade him to compromise."

"His daughter," murmured Roake with a nod of grudging comprehension, "now has adaptation fluid in her body."

"Since she received the inoculation after leaving Stromvi, she's not infected, but she cannot return to her home, unless her father develops an atmospheric antidote."

"You would be a worthy opponent, Soli."

"If you didn't need me as an ally."

"Why did you wish us to capture the Mirelle woman, if she's now jeopardized by having left that accursed planet?"

"She was jeopardized already, but her capture was your brother's inspiration, not mine."

Roake narrowed his gleaming eyes. "Are you speaking the truth, Soli?"

"Don't you know?"

Roake's pensive expression conceded the Soli's point. "I shall bring the clan leader."

"And the others," whispered Jase with the full force of Sesserda persuasion. He awaited Roake's answer uncertainly, for this added request surely stretched the Essenji's trust and could break the entire, frail rapport. *Omi-lai would tell me that I am yielding to my emotions again,* thought Jase, *for I cannot help Tori or Ngina by bringing them here. I can only reassure myself of their status.*

Roake nodded his shorn head slightly. "I shall send for Miss Mirelle and Miss Ngenga, as well."

Concealing his relief, Jase tugged lightly on the chain that held him. "I'll be waiting eagerly."

Roake smiled darkly. "So I should imagine."

* * *

Birk struck the Deetari woman, deliberately hitting the tender front lobe of her ear. Across the room, Thalia flinched in sympathy for her sister, but Gisa made no acknowledgment of the pain. "It was an abomination," repeated Gisa sternly, "and I destroyed it."

"I bought and trained that simulacrum for a purpose, which your superstitious folly defeated. Did you think I locked my office door as an invitation to *you*? I have enemies, Gisa, and your interference has ensured that they still pursue me."

"The image of a man's death becomes the man. The death of your simulacrum becomes your death. You do not understand what you have done, Birk Hodge. You have brought Death to us, and he will not rest until he has justified his journey."

Birk reined his temper, faced with the futility of correcting the past. Gisa's confession, prompted by Thalia's thoughtless comment about carrying the simulacrum to the panguulung bed, changed nothing. His attempt at deceiving the Rea into believing him dead had failed, and they had evidently excavated the kree'va. Rea warriors marched unchallenged across Hodge Farm.

The sight of the proud Rea warriors stirred more bitter regret in Birk than any loss involving Hodge Farm. He saw the least of the Rea warriors command the Stromvi with more confidence than Calem had ever mustered, and the Stromvi obeyed without question. The Rea were worthy, and no one but the Rea had ever met that standard in Birk's life.

In witnessing his own children's pathetic weakness and submission to Rea control, Birk's shame grew nearly intolerable. He would have slain Calem and Sylvie himself for their embarrassing performance under threat, but he did not wish to draw attention to himself. He had only one Bori left to conceal him, and the Rea might yet return to complete their vengeance. Birk understood Rea perseverence. "How many of the Rea have left Stromvi?" demanded Birk.

Gisa answered sullenly, "All. Two of their three warships were seen departing to join their home vessel, and the dawn-sounds suggested that the third followed them. Mister Harrow remains, issuing orders boldly now that Mister Ares is gone."

"Harrow enjoys bullying those who are even weaker than himself," grunted Birk. "Has he spoken of the Rea since they left here?"

"He speaks of the next crop of relaweed and the price the Rea will pay for it."

"Has he spoken of me?"

"Only when your daughter inquired about your return. He repeated the story of your business dealings on Deetari. Your son accused him of conspiring with the Rea to steal Hodge Farm, and Mister Harrow replied that he was merely acting under your instructions."

"And I suppose that my spineless son accepted that explanation without challenge," growled Birk.

Gisa inclined her head gracefully. The bruise along her ear lobe painted her dusky skin as violet as the darkest Stromvi resins. "Mister Calem is drinking too heavily," replied Gisa. "Miss Rillessa returned to him this morning. Miss Rillessa lives in emptiness, for her soul has been taken from her, as my sister foretold."

Birk muttered a curse against Deetari superstition, but Rillessa's fate did not concern him. Rillessa was an unlamented casualty in Birk's private battle with the Rea. "You're certain that the Rea captured both inquisitors?"

"That is Mister Harrow's stated belief, though he terms the imprisonment a 'visit.' I have learned nothing to contradict his premise. I last saw the inquisitors entering the garden-of-blue-roses, and the Rea warriors fired directly at them. I did not wait to see the outcome, but there were no indications of ensuing struggle. The inquisitors may have been killed outright."

Thalia whistled softly, then murmured, "Death of a lawgiver brings evil to the place of death. We shall suffer for this deed."

"You will suffer more keenly," snapped Birk with impatience, "if you betray me, whom you have vowed to serve. Do not be tempted to act against me." He glared at Gisa. "You deserve my curse already for having destroyed the simulacrum, but I'll give you the opportunity to redeem yourself. The daar'va's interference should have cleared by now. I want you to contact your Deetari sisters and learn whether the Rea home vessel has left this planetary system yet."

"You will leave, when it is gone, as you promised us, and free my people from your curses?" asked Gisa.

"I fulfill my promises honorably, when I'm served well. I'll lift all curses, and I'll go and not return. However, you must not fail me again. I shall not forgive another betrayal—from any of your people."

"We have hidden your transceiver in my room, as you instructed. We shall use it to speak to our wise sisters, who understand the prophecies and will agree to aid your escape."

"You haven't found Tori for me?" Birk asked the question almost hesitantly, for he was still torn in Tori's regard. He could not eliminate the possibility that Tori had betrayed him to the Rea, either for her own ambitions or at Per Walis' orders. He needed to learn the truth from her. He did not want to think he had misjudged her so completely.

"She has not been seen since the Rea departure."

"She also disappeared after the first Rea attack, but she returned unharmed," muttered Birk, troubled by the indications that Tori had spent that time with the Soli inquisitor. How much had that inquisitor learned from her? "Has Harrow spoken of her?"

"He speaks of her with regret and causes Miss Sylvie much envy. He says that Miss Tori went with Mister Ares."

"Ares couldn't afford her," grunted Birk, "unless the Rea have prospered far more than their battered armor suggests." But the Rea had managed to gain influence within Per Walis' own organization. They could not be as defeated as they appeared. "Continue to question the Stromvi about her."

"You value her above your children," observed Gisa.

"I value her access to her uncle now above all." Birk smiled thinly. If Tori had betrayed him, he would return her to her Uncle Per in pieces. "And she would ease the loneliness of my exile. I *can* afford her better than she has ever realized, far better than my sorry children have ever realized. Remember that, Gisa. I have hidden assets that make the loss of Hodge Farm insignificant, and they feed my power and make my curses strong."

Gisa nodded, and Thalia shivered against the wall of the narrow room, a slyly inconspicuous chamber where conspirators could easily meet unnoticed. "We serve you, Mister Birk," said Gisa. She took her sister's arm and led her from the room where they secretly met Birk on alternating days. Relieved to see them go, Birk wrapped himself again in his Bori cloak. The creature made him feel safer from unexpected visitors.

His plans, so carefully laid, had gone awry. He had changed identities several times throughout the spans, "killing" his previous self by various means. He had bought the simulacrum when he became the Soli, Birk Hodge. Its death should have bought him more time, especially with such a ready suspect as Tori to distract either that Soli inquisitor or Per Walis.

He had not identified his enemy correctly. He had not recognized the Rea until the sound-shock, when the simulacrum was already placed and ready for the silenen thong. When he realized the magnitude of his danger, there was no time to make other arrangements. There was time only to flee, hide, and hope that the roof-shield would escape the daar'va's influence.

If he had been able to reach Jeffer at the port, he

could have escaped the planet by now. Trying to negotiate with the Deetari was frustratingly slow even under normal circumstances. He wished that he had dared to appropriate the Calongi's shuttle before the Rea damaged it. A hovercraft lacked the speed and power necessary to evade the Rea in a determined pursuit, but the Calongi's shuttle might well have sufficed.

Birk sank heavily into a draped chair in the narrow room of ghostly, covered furnishings. He had remade his life often enough to feel confident that he would succeed again, but the challenge of starting anew no longer invigorated him. Nothing would restore him to the clan. Nothing would bring Akras back to him.

*　　*　　*

The Deetari sisters moved quickly through the house, escaping the back hall anxiously and returning to the more familiar wings. Though they could excuse their presence in any quarter of the house by citing a need to clean or straighten, the guilt of secrecy made each sister nervous.

They walked side by side in apparent calm and dignity down the zigzag length of the main second-level corridor. Their eartips fluttered at a rustling from Rillessa's room, but they did not pause. Most of the bedrooms were empty; the panels that formed their walls served only to confound.

In Gisa's room at the end of the corridor, above the front colonnade of the house, each woman drooped into a cushioned chair. "I am sorry, Sister," trilled Thalia mournfully. "I have no courage."

"You had courage enough to destroy the hulk of that wretched creature that molded itself into Mister Birk's likeness," answered Gisa. "I am proud of you, Sister, and glad to accept Mister Birk's anger on your behalf."

"He would not have known to accuse either of us if I had not spoken thoughtlessly again. I am sorry, Sister. I should not have entered Mister Birk's office at all, but I had dreamed of Death."

"I know," replied Gisa, though she worried that Thalia might forget another warning and speak too freely in front of Mister Birk's enemies.

"His curse is powerful," whimpered Thalia, perceiving Gisa's concern, "as our sisters warned."

"It cannot spread its harm to our people, if we are faithful to our vows," said Gisa confidently, but Thalia had demonstrated enough prophetic ability in the past to make her fear persuasive.

"If a lawgiver died here. . . ."

"Then *here* will suffer, but *here* is not Deetari."

"The omens all are evil," whistled Thalia, and Gisa could not contradict her. "Death has been summoned, and She must be satisfied."

With the brusque motions of nervousness, Gisa lifted the heavy, stone-topped bedside table. She tried to move it carefully, but she creased the upper casing of the transceiver hidden in the hollow of the table's thick-walled base. Anxiously, she bent to assess the damage.

Thalia whistled in shock, "The dead avenge themselves." Her whistling soared into a high frequency wail. Gisa turned without rising. She tried to cover the transceiver with her pale saffron skirt.

"Please, Miss Thalia," murmured Omi blandly, "the frequency of your voice is painful to me, and the fear that prompts your distress is unjustified. I am not an avenging ghost." Thalia's wail faded into silence. "Miss Gisa, please place your call to your matriarch, as you intended. I doubt seriously that the Rea vessel has even left orbit, but I always welcome substantiation of my perceptions."

Gisa whispered, "Is Mister Jase with you?"

"You conspired against him," answered Omi, and he observed Gisa's torn and troubled reaction. "Children," he murmured, "why have you so little ability to discern what is right and just?"

"The lawgivers discern the truth," said Thalia in a high, clear voice devoid of her usual trills, "but they cannot change its past course. They perceive right and wrong, but good and evil wage an independent battle, and each of us alone must choose a part."

"She is prophesying," said Gisa with awe.

"Yes," replied Omi soberly. "She knows her true purpose."

CHAPTER 42

"Are you so impatient for your death, Soli?" demanded Akras, entering Jase's prison room alone. She wore the same uniform of red tunic, leather kilt, and coppery breastplate that distinguished her senior warriors. No special emblem of her authority marked her, but Jase knew her beyond doubt. "I would have visited you soon without Roake's request. I have a debt to repay." Akras raised her bandaged forearm.

Jase lifted his eyes slowly to meet hers. The chains bound him to the wall at an awkward level, allowing him neither to sit nor stand straight. He forced himself to maintain Sesserda calm, as his senses fed him their relentless data. The clan leader was as irrational as y'Lidu and at least as dangerous. "Where are your sons, Clan Leader?"

"They are serving my will, of course." Akras took hold of the riven fabric of Jase's shirt, and she examined the fading scar that her knife had inflicted. "You heal quickly, Soli. Roake told me that you were addicted to a very potent level of relanine."

"The Rea need my help, Clan Leader." As soon as she entered the room, Jase knew that Akras would not be persuaded even by Sesserda skills, but he had no choice other than to make the effort.

"We need nothing from you." Akras struck him with her gauntlet-clad hand. "How many injuries can you endure, Soli?"

"I shall heal almost as quickly as you can wound me."

"Relanine accelerates healing only until the relanine is exhausted. Then your addiction will become your greatest torture." She began to flog him methodically.

"Is that why you addicted Roake?" asked Jase without

473

permitting himself even a tremor of pain. "To give you
a means of controlling him?"

"Don't waste your energy in trying to manipulate me,
Calongi-slave. I'm not as easily influenced as my sons."

"Roake is wise enough to trust me. You've lost your
power over him, Clan Leader. Listen to me, or you will
lose your entire clan."

"Where is my clan-knife?" hissed Akras.

"On Stromvi. With Birk Hodge."

"Liar! Birkaj is dead, slain by a woman he betrayed."

"Birkaj is waiting for you, mocking you for destroying
your own clan's future."

The prison ward's battered door opened to admit a
powerfully built, senior Rea warrior, whose mane had all
turned to silver. Roake was visible just beyond the door,
where he frowned impatiently. The senior spoke: "The
war leader asks permission to enter. Shall I admit him,
Clan Leader?"

"I am not finished," answered Akras.

Roake snapped, "Let me pass, Tagran. That Soli is a
Consortium official." Roake shouted past the determined
Tagran, "Clan Leader, you agreed to listen to the Soli."

"I have listened to his lies already." Akras turned from
Jase to face her son. "I ordered you to return to Stromvi
and negotiate the recovery of the kree'va and the relaweed. Why are you still here, Roake?"

Jase answered firmly, "He understands that he must
trust me if he is to save the Rea clan."

"Be silent, Soli," ordered Akras, but Jase's words had
already had their calculated effect. They had reached Tagran and made him hesitant. Roake used the moment to
push past the guard and interpose himself between his
mother and Jase.

"Tagran," said Akras, staring coldly at her son, "call
Ares here."

"Don't bother, Tagran," countered Roake. "I've already asked Ares to join us. He needs to hear this Soli
as well."

Akras murmured with deadly sweetness, "I shall be
fascinated to hear how this Soli effected such a miracle
of persuasiveness against you, Roake. Stand guard, Tagran. We shall await my son."

The prison door slid closed. Tagran stood impassively

at attention before it. The turmoil behind the warrior's placid face told Jase more than all that he had learned from Roake, Ares, or Akras. Jase began to plan accordingly.

* * *

When Ares came to the cell that Tori and Ngina shared, Tori's immediate reaction was dread that he might have accepted her tentative bait. She wondered if she could actually complete the plan that she had laid, or if she would discover herself too intimidated at the last. Losing her nerve with Birk had been merely disappointing; losing her nerve with Ares could be fatal.

The two doughty Essenji warriors who entered the room in Ares' wake reassured her in a perverse fashion. She did not relish being dragged to her feet by the most senior of the warriors, a man whose snowy mane provided an unsettling resemblance to Birk. The second warrior fettered Ngina's arms and legs, as if she were a mindless beast to be led to a slaughterhouse.

"Gently, Remus," ordered Ares, though there was nothing of gentleness in his own stiff manner.

Ngina snapped furiously at her captor, but she managed only to rip the hard leather of his breeches, eliciting a curse and a blow from his metal-banded forearm. Leaving Tori to Ares' custody, the white-haired Rea joined his fellow, and together they managed to subdue Ngina and complete her binding.

Ares gripped Tori's arms tightly, pushing her awkwardly before him into the dizzying, metal mesh corridor of the Rea vessel. He whispered across her shoulder, "Let your pace submit to mine. I do not want to damage you, Mirelle."

Tori tried to comply, and the walking did become easier, but her resolve became only more bitter. She asked gently, "Where are we going, Ares?" She tried not to hear Ngina's clicks of distress, but she knew that the young Stromvi stumbled behind her in shame and misery.

She could feel Ares' trembling of anger. "My brother has commanded that I bring you to another cell area. I have not been privileged to hear the reasons."

"He taunts you, Ares, because he fears you."

"Rightly so," replied Ares softly.

They left the mesh walkway, and descended ten steps into a solid corridor. Tori could hear the Rea warriors mutter in frustration, trying helplessly to lead Ngina down the narrow stairs. Ares turned his head and snapped at the warriors, "Take the Stromvi via the lift, Remus. I shall meet you at the cell block."

The sounds of Ngina's painful, fettered walk diminished, and the vast emptiness of the Rea vessel echoed with the footsteps of Ares and his prisoner. Tori made an effort to move with apparent ease and confidence. "You are a treacherous creature," mused Ares, "but you have courage."

Tori answered evenly, "I don't like prisons."

"Are you not afraid that I may kill you?"

"Should I be more fearful of you alone than of you and your warriors together?"

"Most creatures would tremble before either prospect."

"I don't seem to have been designed for nervous tremors and fainting bouts." Tori tried to turn her face enough to see him. "I'm not sure I like being called a 'creature.' "

"You are a magnificent creature, a legend." His hand grasped her already-bruised throat. "Why are you alive, Mirelle?"

"The alternative has never appealed to me," whispered Tori.

"You lived before my father's father. Did you think I did not know? Did you think you could deceive me?"

"Not you, Ares," answered Tori with difficulty, and she wondered what this mad Rea warrior actually believed. She searched for words that would seem to conform to Ares' reality. "The others."

Ares began to caress the bruises that he had caused. Tori refused to flinch. "Yes, the others. They are trusting fools, like my brother, who thinks himself so clever." His thin smile broadened with disquieting warmth. "My half brother, the traitor's son. Did you know, lovely Mirelle? Your late patron was my mother's lover."

"I did not know," answered Tori, but she could not feel surprised, not after the odd, twisted misery that Akras had shown in speaking of Rea betrayal, honor, and love. Still, it was impossible to think of Roake as brother to Calem and Sylvie. It was far easier to imagine that Roake was the only true heir of Birk Hodge.

"My brother is defiant, like Birkaj. Such denial of the clan leader's authority proves his lack of honor."

Tori leaned against Ares. "You have honor, Ares, and strength. I would be proud to serve a patron such as you."

His laughter was harsh. "Just as you alone would give me Birkaj's treasures?"

"I was Birk's greatest treasure, Ares. That treasure is yours to take now."

He did not answer, but his breath had quickened against her. They had stopped in front of a dark metal door that seemed to have suffered many hammer blows from its opposite side. Ares turned her toward him. He kept her arms locked in his inescapable grasp. His cloak enfolded them both.

"You and I obey our own laws," whispered Tori. "We don't need anyone else." Tori accepted the Essenji's kiss as if she shared his hunger for its fulfillment.

The clumsy sounds of Ngina's passage, accompanied by the loud grumblings of her Rea escort, reverberated through the corridor. Ares pushed Tori to arm's length, and he frowned at her. When the Rea led Ngina around the corner and into view, Ares pressed the control for the battered door. The door opened onto a Rea guard, who saluted and stepped aside. Ares dragged Tori with him into the dismal remains of a Bercali prison cell. The two Rea warriors followed, leading a stumbling Ngina.

Akras and Roake stood together in front of the solitary prisoner, chained against the long wall. When the prisoner, his shirt hanging in bloodied strips, turned his brilliantly iridescent eyes to Tori, she shrank against Ares, only half for artful effect. She had not believed that even Rea would knowingly abuse an inquisitor of the Consortium.

Her revulsion for the Rea man who still held her sickened her. She imagined that Ares' kiss had stained her lips with guilt that an inquisitor would read clearly. She was not sure that her fretful notion was untrue. Mustering her flagging courage, she said dryly, "You've looked better, Mister Sleide."

Jase answered with perfect Sesserda calm, "I'm glad

you noticed, Miss Darcy. I've been meaning to speak to the management about the accommodations." The young warrior, Remus, fastened Ngina's bonds to the row of shackles, designed for securing dozens of Bercali prisoners.

Akras said quellingly, "You have presented Roake with a preposterous story, Soli, yet he defies me on its behalf. Curiosity at this phenomenon of persuasion has allowed you to survive the past few microspans. I shall soon lose patience, however, unless you give me a far more plausible truth than you offered him."

"Truth is my purpose, Clan Leader," said Jase. "I am a Sesserda practitioner."

"Where is Birkaj?"

"On Stromvi," replied Jase. None of the Rea reacted with more than grim silence. Tori showed only a flickering of her surprise; Ngina remained unresponsive. "He's quite alive, if not entirely well."

Ares hissed against Tori's ear, "Have you lied to me again, my Mirelle?" Tori tried to shake her head, but Ares' hold made even that slight movement difficult.

"Miss Mirelle believes that Birk is dead," said Jase sharply, "but she's wrong." Ares eased his grip, and Tori breathed more easily; both of them bowed unconsciously to the persuasive confidence of a Sesserda adept. "Clan leader, will you permit me to confirm some elements of truth before I enlighten you with them?"

"Cautiously," answered Akras.

"Ngina-li," said Jase gently, and the young Stromvi raised her troubled eyes to him. "You know me, Ngina-li. You know that I'm your father's friend."

"I know that he has been your friend," replied Ngina, lifting her head very slightly.

"And you know that I am an inquisitor, and you must answer me. As a Consortium member, you know that this is the law."

"Yes," answered Ngina weakly, and she glanced uneasily at her captors.

Jase commanded her firmly, "Ngina-li, please give me your attention. The storage chamber, where you watched the clan leader fight me, connects to the tunnel network of your people's home caverns, does it not?"

"You saw me?" asked Ngina.

"I perceived you. Answer me, please."

"Yes, the chamber connects to the worker enclave."

"Where did your honored father take the device that he removed from that chamber?"

"I do not know."

"When you gave him the seeds harvested from Mister Calem's field, did he identify them for you?"

"No."

"It was relaweed, the primary relanine source for commercial adaptation fluid. Do you know that relanine is a very dangerous drug?"

"No."

"When your father sent you to Mister Calem's field, did he tell you what to seek?"

"Only a scent—like that carried by a ragged leaf of one of the hybrid roses."

"Was it the scent of the seeds from Calem's field?"

Ngina clicked pensively, beginning to rouse from her torpor. "It was similar but not the same. The odor of the seeds was not so unpleasant."

"Relanine adapts to its host, as it adapts the host. The rose leaf may have been exposed to relanine carried by an insect, which would differ from the relanine of relaweed, just as relaweed differs from the relanine in a Calongi's veins."

"Yes," murmured Ngina, "there were insects in some of the pods, and that scent was very like the first."

Jase barely nodded. "Your father is very familiar with the properties of relanine because he and I have discussed them at some length, debating the theoretical possibility of curing relanine addiction. As I recall, he once proposed creating a mutative virus that would feed on the relanine. His idea was not original, as I told him, but no one has ever discovered a method of eliminating active relanine without destroying the host."

Ares said crisply, "You prove nothing, Soli." But Tori could feel Ares' tension increasing.

"The proof manifests itself," retorted Jase, "in your brother, in myself, in each of us according to the quantities of relanine within us. Nguri has the kree'va, and he has the relaweed to provide the pattern for the change. Roake and I show the symptoms first, for we are the addicts, but we shall outlast the rest of you for the same reason. How many Rea did *not* spend some time on Stromvi within the past few millispans? Not enough to sustain the clan, I suspect. Birk Hodge will have the final vengeance, for the Rea clan will die with him."

"Unless I relinquish command of the Rea to you," finished Akras scornfully. "Do you believe that I am so credulous?"

"We must return to Stromvi now," said Jase, undaunted by Akras' cynical comments. "You intended to trade Ngina for Rea treasures, but you will trade her instead for Rea lives. Only Ngina's father knows how he programmed the kree'va to attack relanine, and only he can invert the process in time to save us."

"Her father serves the Rea-traitor," argued Ares, and he glanced at his brother, as if seeking confirmation. Roake smiled archly and said nothing.

"Nguri serves his people. I assure you, Nguri never intended to sacrifice his daughter. Like the rest of her people, she had no significant amount of relanine in her to feed the virus. However, you took her from her world and adapted her to this environment. She will not contract the lethal infection from us because the virus is contagious only under the kree'va's influence, but she cannot return to her own people while the atmosphere remains tainted. To regain her, Nguri must help us all."

Akras said calmly, "The Rea would not need your help, Soli, in negotiating such a trade, even if we deemed your story true." She knelt before Jase and withdrew a bronze knife from the scabbard at her waist. "This was my mother's clan-knife. It is not the equal of Raskannen's blade, which you stole from me, but its edge is just as sharp." In a swift motion, she grasped Jase's hair and dragged her knife along his throat. Tori cried a wordless protest, but the Rea reaction drowned her own.

"Clan Leader!" shouted Roake. He reached forward to stop her attack, but she thrust the knife at him, scoring his arm. He stared from Akras to his wound with an expression of shock. Ares jerked, as if the cut had marked him equally. The senior Rea guard at the door took hold of his fellow, Claudius, to deter any form of intervention, and the young Remus averted his eyes.

"Do not defy me again, Roake," ordered Akras furiously, "or you will join this Soli." Roake spread his hands in cautious appeasement, and Akras turned back to Jase, whose neck wore a thin, iridescent trail. "You took Raskannen's knife from me, Soli. You earned your death for that misdeed alone." Akras touched the longest scar along her cheek. She began to trace its likeness onto Jase's face.

Jase answered her with a careless calm, seemingly impervious to the vicious disfiguring of his flesh, "I don't think you can wield that knife fast enough to kill me, Akras. I received a particularly potent relanine transfusion quite recently."

Roake said gruffly, "He speaks the truth, Clan Leader: about the relanine within him and about the Stromvi man's vile poison."

Akras let her knife tear a narrow strip of skin from Jase's shoulder. The blood barely oozed to the surface, and a faint relanine glow disputed the seriousness of the wound. Akras arose from her position in front of Jase and announced coldly, "Your brother is a traitor, Ares. Bind him with the other traitor's servants." Akras strode from the room, leaving stunned silence in her wake.

Roake ordered angrily, "Follow her, Tagran, and see that she does herself no injury. She has lost all capacity to reason."

Tagran glanced at Ares, but Akras' younger son had become flaccid, even his hold on Tori relaxed and limp. Tagran waved in sharp command, "Claudius, Remus, obey the clan leader." Bemusedly obedient, the two warriors turned on Roake, grappling him to the floor.

"Your blind loyalty, Tagran, will condemn us all," growled Roake. "Ares, stop this madness!"

"The clan leader must be obeyed," murmured Ares. Claudius and Remus chained their erstwhile war leader between Jase and Ngina, and they saluted Ares. "Go," snapped Ares. The two warriors repeated their salute, but they hesitated to leave, watching Tagran. Ares added almost gently, "You go, as well, Tagran. Our clan leader needs you beside her." Tagran nodded once. He gestured, and his two subordinates followed him out of the cell. The battered door slid closed behind them, and the rush of air escaping the door's seals sounded hollow.

Tori touched her aching throat gingerly, recalling her repugnance for Birk's hands just before his death—which may not have been his death at all, if Jase had told the truth to Akras. Tori did not know what she believed, what she should believe, what she was causing others to believe. Nothing made sense to her any longer.

Ares no longer held her, but he still stood uncomfortably close. She laid one hand on the bare collar of his shirt. "What do you believe, my Ares?" she whispered tenderly.

"My brother is not the war leader," muttered Ares, pushing Tori away from him. Ares crossed the room in three long strides and tore the war-star from his brother's vest.

Roake said coldly, "I'm sorry that you won't live long enough to suffer the full weight of my death-curse, Brother."

"You cannot actually accept this Soli's claims of an insidious Stromvi-concocted poison," retorted Ares. "The Stromvi people are as meek and compliant as any race in the Consortium." Ngina clicked a brief, resentful denial.

"Can you be as blind as Tagran?" snapped Roake.

Ares did not reply. He stood motionless, studying the war-star in his hand. Tori approached him cautiously and touched his arm gently. When he seemed to accept her tentative appeal, she extended the gesture with slow care. "Why would your brother support a Soli's lies?" murmured Tori.

"Roake confounds himself with excessive scheming," answered Ares.

Tori waved vaguely toward Jase, who smiled slightly but allowed her to continue her coaxing alone. "He's a Sesserda adept, Ares. I don't like the breed, but I respect their perceptions."

"My Brother," urged Roake, switching from threats to an appeal of kinship, "you know me too well to believe that I would betray Rea honor. You've called me a traitor to gain your own power, and I respect your ambition, but you know your claim against me is false. You know that I would defend the Rea to my own death, and I swear to you that this poisoning is real. Trust me once more, little Brother, and let me save our people."

Ares answered with a mocking laugh, "Shall I trust the Rea-traitor's son? My father did not trust *yours*."

"What is this lie?" demanded Roake, but his firmness of voice had faltered.

"This is the clan leader's word to me," replied Ares. "You are the son of Birkaj. How can I believe you above her?"

Jase interrupted softly, wielding Sesserda persuasion with every syllable, "Your clan leader seeks only death, Ares: Birk's, Roake's, her own. She will lead you to your death, and she will destroy the Rea clan. She believes Roake about the poisoning. She believes me. She doesn't want to survive. She doesn't want any Rea to survive."

Tori murmured carefully, "You heard how she spoke to me, Ares, when she thought that I had killed Birk. She reduced her life to a bitter hope of vengeance, and without it, she has nothing. Why did she delay repeatedly, restraining you for so many spans from the restoration of Rea honor? She didn't want to achieve her single goal, because she knew that it would mean the end of everything she had made important to her."

Ngina had raised her head in the sober dawn of understanding. "She is hollow," said Ngina, "like a regal image on a swollen balloon."

Ares grasped the chain that bound his brother by the neck. "Swear to me by Rea honor: The Soli's story is true, and the poisoning is real. Swear that you have not and will not betray the Rea."

"I swear all these things by Rea honor," answered Roake. "I swear, also, to lay aside my just vengeance against you, Brother, until such time as the Rea future is secured, if you will make a similar vow of truce."

Ares threw the length of chain from him. He crossed to the door and paced back to the stand in front of Tori. His smile was cynical. "I would loathe to see our alliance end so soon, lovely Mirelle." He turned to manipulate the wall controls that released the prisoners' chains.

* * *

Akras deactivated the surveillance monitor with a weary gesture, and she laid her head against the console. One of the youngest of her guards reached toward her out of concern, but she roused herself to snap at him, "Leave me."

"Shall we resume guard of the prisoners?" asked Tagran, gesturing a sharp condemnation of his subordinate, who had dared to touch the clan leader.

"No," replied Akras. "My sons are with them. Let them go back to the Rea-traitor's planet, if they wish. They cannot escape." With the furrowed edge of her fingernail, she scraped a dull patch where a Bercali symbol had been removed from the console. "Go and help with the cleansing of the ship. I want the purification completed within the millispan." The young guard moved reluctantly toward the door. Even Tagran hesitated for an instant, before saluting the clan leader and bowing from the room.

Perekah waylaid Tagran in the hall. She wore a leather kilt and vest, instead of the silks of a breeder or a nurse. She had bound her long hair in a warrior's braid, and her clan-knife was sheathed at her side. "Is it true?" she demanded. "Has Akras imprisoned Roake again?"

"Yes," replied Tagran curtly.

"And what of Claudius' story of Stromvi poisoning? Is it true, Tagran?"

"It is the Soli's claim," grunted Tagran, fingering his own knife's hilt impatiently. He did not want to talk to Perekah. He did not want to hear a Soli's warnings echo in his head. He did not want to imagine why Akras had bidden him carry the daar'va to her private room.

"Tagran, how long can you pretend that she is sane? We must free Roake. Where is she holding him?"

"Take your complaints to Ares," answered Tagran, and he shrugged free of Perekah's hand and continued down the long, cold hall.

"For how long will you support her, Tagran?" shouted Perekah after him. "Until the clan is dead?"

Tagran whispered to himself, "Until she no longer needs me, Perekah."

PART IV

The Pruning

CHAPTER 43

Tori walked beside Ares in frustration, wishing that she could escape him for even a moment to try to elicit some real answers from Jase Sleide. Apparently, Roake intended to return to Stromvi with Jase, and the two of them had agreed—very *chummily*, thought Tori grimly—to employ Ngina as a hostage against Nguri. Ares would presumably contend with Akras' anger over the release of her prisoners. No one had mentioned Tori's disposition.

Ares continued to hold Tori's arm—less tightly but just as firmly as when he had first taken her prisoner, and she felt no freer. They followed Ngina, who still moved awkwardly from pain, though the cruel shackles had been removed. Jase accompanied Roake, who led the small, inharmonious band by Ares' implicit concession of present authority. The great Rea vessel seemed even larger and more strangely empty, as they past through corridor after corridor without encountering another Rea.

The three men seemed to have developed a peculiar understanding among themselves, a three-way rivalry that had settled into a formidable alliance of temporary convenience. Some subtle transformation of Jase had made him one of *them*, and Tori's confidence in the Soli inquisitor suffered a severe case of ambiguity. She could not help but admire whatever skill of innate personal force or Sesserda training had won the Rea brothers' joint respect. However, watching a Soli inquisitor negotiate so equally with Rea warriors was fundamentally disquieting.

Jase Sleide, the infinitely adaptable alien relations expert, thought Tori with a certain cynicism, *proving his Sesserda life-purpose by walking at the side of the enemy, offering advice on defeat of a friend*. Despite her own hopes of enlisting Ares' sympathies, she could not readjust herself so quickly to the idea of Roake and Ares as allies against the common threat of *Nguri*. The contradictory passions of Rea violence and honor seemed irrational to her; the possibility of Nguri posing a threat to anyone would have made her laugh under less tumultuous circumstances.

Beneath the drumming of the ship's engines, Tori could not even hear the soft words that Jase spoke to the Essenji beside him. She saw Roake shake his head, the shorn mane making the motion a blur of stark black and pale, emerging silver. Jase gestured expansively with both arms, clothed again in Birk's discarded coat, a tatter now. The inquisitor's supple fingers seemed to bend at odd angles, making him resemble some strange hybrid of Soli and Calongi.

Roake stopped, scowled, and faced the Soli. Ngina sagged prone against the floor, exhausted and eager for any brief respite. Roake called his brother tersely.

For an oddly sustained moment, Ares studied Tori. She met his dark eyes squarely, but she wondered what twisted thoughts transpired in his handsome, troubled head. She would not have been astonished to see him draw his wicked knife and drive it through her or Jase or Roake or Ngina. She was surprised to find herself feeling a measure of pity for him.

Ares smiled thinly, released her and joined his brother. So abruptly freed, Tori felt the full strangeness of her shifting circumstances. She sighed, concluding wryly that Jase must indeed be gifted at his job if he could actually comprehend Rea motivation well enough to manipulate it.

Tori took a cautious step forward, not wanting to be omitted from the discussion, but Jase raised a cautioning hand toward her. The small gesture stopped her. By the time Tori could resent his Sesserda command technique, Jase had left the two Rea to argue alone. Pausing momentarily to give encouragement to Ngina, Jase continued past the Stromvi girl to Tori's side.

The raw, skinless strip along his cheek glistened with an iridescence nearly as uncanny as his eyes. Sensing the direction of Tori's glance, he touched the dreadful injury lightly. "Only the surface is still impaired, and it will heal soon," he murmured, "if we live that long."

His rueful smile and his inclusive acknowledgment of danger made Tori set aside her doubts about him. Beneath his potent influence, her mind restored him as ally. "Is it true?" asked Tori in a whisper filled with fear and horror and wonder that the man before her could endure the ghastly, mutilating attentions of Akras' knife.

"About Nguri's poisonous plot? Yes," answered Jase. He turned his head slightly toward the Rea brothers, who argued in soft, harsh words that Tori could not quite distinguish. "They're debating the reasons for Akras' release of us," explained Jase. "The complete lack of resistance to our escape has alarmed them more than my warnings. They're beginning to realize that their mother has her own formula for revenge, and its contents are not what either son has been led to believe."

"Can you stop the poison's progress?" asked Tori, significantly more concerned by the immediate prospect of death than by the Rea's family squabbles.

Jase answered thoughtfully, "Nguri can stop it, I hope." The qualification made Tori's fragile spirits plummet.

Ngina lifted her head at her father's name, but she hunched her shoulders helplessly. "My honored father is much wiser than his daughter," said Ngina, and she clicked her sad confusion.

Roake interrupted the brief conversation sharply, "Sleide, what do you sense on this ship?"

"Death," replied Jase evenly.

"From the Stromvi's poison alone?" snapped Roake.

"No."

Roake growled an Essenji curse. "That is why we encounter no guards, no resistance to escape. She has activated the daar'va."

"Of course," agreed Jase, conveying his complete lack of surprise with a shrug. "She is at war." All of his listeners regarded him with acute, unsettled attention.

We all watch him as if we await the inquisitor's redeeming word to restore Consortium justice, thought Tori, *but he is a man and not the Consortium's juggernaut.* She wondered sickly whether anything could actually make the current outlook worse.

"She would not destroy the clan," argued Ares, but his voice held no conviction. His pale hand tightened on his knife's hilt.

"There was no sound-shock," said Tori, staring up at Jase with an irrelevant memory of his honor-song and its effect on her.

Somewhat to Tori's surprise, it was Roake who answered her. "The sound-shock is necessary only to the daar'va's locating mode," grumbled Roake, "or to intimidation of the ignorant. Our clan leader will complete her vengeance against the Rea-traitor even in death." He paused and amended bitterly, "Her vengeance against my *father*. She will destroy the Rea on behalf of a lovers' feud."

Ngina roused herself to click puzzlement. She tilted her head toward Jase. "I don't understand these things, Mister Jase. How will our deaths aid the clan leader's vengeance against Mister Birk?" Her frankness of curiosity almost resembled the attitude of her normal, confident self, but her wan voice evoked the helplessness of a child trapped in the incomprehensible schemes of alien adults. Tori felt considerable sympathy.

"She intends to ram your planet with this ship, destroying both," answered Jase gently, the Sesserda peace of his voice at odds with the violent content of his response. "I imagine that she's currently programming the ship's controls. She's using the daar'va against her own warriors, because she's not so mad as to believe that her people will join her eagerly in suicide. By now, the upper levels of this ship have been contaminated." Jase made one of his odd, quick hand gestures in Roake's direction. "You'll need to wear a protection suit to reach her, Roake, and to deactivate the daar'va. If you move immediately, you may be able to save your people. They're not dead yet, though a rebellious few have been disabled. I'd accompany you, but I need to reach Nguri quickly."

Both Rea men stared at Jase, visibly weighing his words against a heavy load of urgency. Roake conquered his hesitation first, hissing another curse, and he turned toward the stretching corridor and began to run.

Ares glanced from his brother's rapidly departing silhouette to Tori, and he nodded slightly. Tori wondered if the gesture was meant to acknowledge her or Roake's decision. The drumming of the ship seemed to quicken.

"I need to reach Stromvi promptly," said Jase, and his voice resonated with persuasion. "I've stayed here too long already. I cannot wait for a Rea revolution, if I'm to convince Nguri to program an antidote."

"Your antidote cannot salvage the Rea," answered Ares with a slow, strange tranquillity. He smiled at Tori with a gentleness that seemed improbable from him. "I fear that you are more faithful to this inquisitor, my Mirelle, than to me. Perhaps you have chosen well, for his is the only victory. His honor is intact." His comment astonished her, even as it made her wonder if Ares was really as mad as he often appeared.

Ares' smile tightened as he shifted his dark gaze back to Jase. "Your own hovercraft seems to be a sturdy enough model to sustain a cross-orbit trip," said Ares with a trace of his old mockery. "You will find it in the third bay down that passage." He pointed with his knife blade. "Use your Sesserda omnipotence and take it." Without another word or gesture, Ares turned and followed his brother down the long, echoing corridor. Ares moved strongly but unhurriedly.

When Ares had disappeared into a far, branching hall, Jase exhaled a long-held breath. Tori said softly, "You're certainly a persuasive man, Inquisitor. You talked yourself from torture to freedom in a matter of microspans."

His smile flashed briefly. "I'd like to take credit for arranging all the brighter aspects of our present predicament." He sighed again. "But I hadn't predicted that Akras' realization of failed vengeance would plunge her into suicidal zeal, until I met her. I just hope Roake and Ares can stop her from achieving the final gesture of despair." Jase helped Ngina climb the steps that led into the side passage indicated by Ares. "How are you feeling, Ngina-li?" he asked solicitously.

"Terrible," replied the young Stromvi, stumbling back onto a level floor.

"You still haven't adapted completely," replied Jase. "Miss Darcy? I assume you're still feeling fairly healthy, since you're so reluctant to believe me about Nguri's nifty little plan."

"You don't make trust easy," sighed Tori. The necessity to move at Ngina's slow pace was nerve-racking. The distance between the shuttle bays appeared to be considerable. The third bay door wasn't even visible yet. "When you left me in Hodge House, how much of all this did you know?"

" 'All this' is not very specific."

"Don't quibble."

"I knew that the Rea warships were returning, and I knew that Ngina was about to be taken hostage, since she was wandering perilously close to our unseen enemy in the dark. I knew that I was in no condition to stop the Rea *en masse*, but if I let them take me along for the ride, I hoped to find an opportunity to talk convincingly to Ares about the advantages of keeping Ngina alive and well. I wasn't sure of Roake's standing." He shrugged. A trace of iridescence stained the coat across his injured shoulder. "I still hope that my personal abduction will solidify Omi-lai's position, but I don't dare to count on his help. We're not exactly his favorite species."

"You already knew about the toxin, didn't you?" asked Tori, impatient with any mention of Omi. "If you'd told me, I could have looked for Nguri immediately and tried to talk to him."

"He wouldn't have listened to you. He didn't listen to Omi."

"But you think you can influence him?"

"With Ngina's help, yes. He's probably worried about her already."

"I failed him again," clicked Ngina wearily.

"Will we have enough time, Jase?" asked Tori.

"I don't know, Tori."

She retorted sharply to hide her fear, "I thought you knew everything."

Jase answered with a whisper, "I don't even know how to save my best friend."

His best friend. My best friend, too. "Nguri only protects his world," murmured Tori staunchly. Her defense of Nguri brought a soft, sad click of surprise from Ngina.

"Or he destroyed it," replied Jase. "No one could admire Nguri more than I, but he has made a terrible error of judgment in this instance."

"If I return to my planet now," asked Ngina, "will I die because of the adaptation fluid in me?"

Jase became brisk in words and motion, "I don't intend to expose you to the Stromvi atmosphere until I'm sure that your father can counteract the effects of his ingenious virus." The constraint of Ngina's pace seemed to have become suddenly frustrating even to Jase, for he paced the corridor as they traversed it, but he continued earnestly, "I have faith in his ability to produce an antidote, or I wouldn't have accepted this ordeal of Rea hospitality. I'm sorry to use you this way, Ngina-li, but your father made the choice of you inevitable, when he chose you as his conspirator—and when he decided that he needed to defend his world against the Consortium as well as the Rea. By helping him, you earned a small measure of his guilt and its price."

"I'm only his errand runner," sighed Ngina.

Tori countered gently, "You're his favorite, his most esteemed child. He wouldn't have enlisted your aid in a cause less than his world's survival. He wouldn't risk you lightly, Ngina-li."

"Is it true?" clicked Ngina, but her phrasing directed the question only to herself.

Finally reaching the door to the third bay, Jase manipulated the lock controls swiftly. Ngina covered her ear slits with a click of pain, though Tori heard nothing as the door opened. "These sonic systems," remarked Jase, "are easy to bypass if one can hear the right frequencies. They're not much use against interspecies interlopers, but the Bercali have never been known for their sophistication in alien relations." He grimaced at the sight of his own ship, the graceful golden Sesserda swirls scratched and burned. He shook his head at the fused mass that had once been a lock mechanism. "The Rea sometimes show a terrible lack of subtlety."

"There's a lading platform here," called Tori from the side of the bay. "It should support Ngina's weight."

"Good. Ngina, use the platform while I inspect the flight controls." He swung himself into his ship without troubling to draw out the recessed stairs. Ngina climbed gingerly onto the lading platform. She clutched its edges nervously as it made its graceful ascent to the wide rear entry of Jase's ship.

"Who will open the shuttle bay doors for us?" asked Tori. "I don't see a command console."

"This is a secured bay. It accepts signals only via physical link from a preprogrammed control room," replied Jase absently. "But I don't think we'll have a problem." He began to rearrange the interior of the hovercraft, explaining as he worked, "I'm reasonably sure that Ares directed us here in good faith, which says there's a way to escape. Perhaps the system has been programmed to open the bay when a shuttle is activated."

"You trust Ares?"

"Up to a point, yes. Don't underestimate Rea honor. It's the origin of everything we've endured in the last few days."

"If Akras intended suicide, why did she bother with all the torments of sound-shocks, abortive attacks, and abduction?" asked Tori, climbing into the ship and examining the gold-swirled walls dubiously. A hovercraft, however well made, seemed insubstantial for space travel.

"She didn't plan the suicide until after she'd imprisoned us. She had failed to find Birk, alive or dead. Roake had started listening to me. Ares was becoming increasingly besotted by you. Akras realized that she had lost control of both sons, as well as her vengeance, so she defined a new scheme, a very thorough and final scheme." Jase waved Tori toward the center of the ship, and a sheath of inner walls emerged in a smooth curve from the floor, reducing the interior volume nearly by half. "Extra protection for space mode," explained Jase, as Tori tapped the new wall pensively. He touched another control, and the tracery of an outline became a paper-thin door that slid aside to reveal Ngina and the lading platform. "A slightly elasticity accommodates storage requirements, but the walls are really very durable."

"They look as flimsy as your answer about Akras," replied Tori.

"What more did you expect me to say? I convinced Roake to have you and Ngina brought to my cell along with Akras, but Akras tolerated my request. She let Ares escort you personally, though she's fiercely jealous of you. She let me talk, instead of executing me for the crime of having crossed her. None of those events would have occurred if she'd been reacting according to normal Rea behavior. She was indulging her sons, preparatory to killing them both. You were very astute, Ngina-li, in recognizing her as hollow. I might have distributed the truth with a little more caution if I'd recognized that hollowness more quickly."

"I once dreamed of a cavern nymph," said Ngina with a shudder, "a hollow, mocking queen like Akras."

"You shouldn't let a dream intimidate you," chided Jase, claiming the pilot's chair and directing Tori toward the seat beside him. Ngina tried to fit herself comfortably within the remaining space. She clicked irritation as she fastened stiff cloth straps around her battered ankles. "I'm afraid the Soli chairs make the cabin a little cramped for Stromvi," apologized Jase. "I had the design made adaptable to the Stromvi physique for Ngahi's sake, but I never planned on transporting two Soli and a Stromvi together in space mode."

"I'm fine," said Ngina, sounding thoroughly miserable. Both layers of the ship's door closed, abruptly muffling the rattle of the retreating lading platform.

Tori caught her breath quickly, as the ship's console indicated that the inner bay doors had opened. "Isn't that a little quick for an automated response?" she asked Jase. "You haven't activated the ship yet."

"I have now," he replied, making his words true. "Akras may have been monitoring us after all. If so, she wastes no time."

"Are you sure she doesn't intend to 'purify' us out of existence as soon as we're off her vessel?"

"No," replied Jase crisply, activating the ship's view screen, "I'm not *sure* of anything at the moment." The Xiani machinery purred nearly soundlessly, even in the low-speed mode that carried the ship through the narrow opening into the outer bay. The ship barely cleared the storage tethers, when the inner bay doors snapped closed.

The outer bay doors opened rapidly, and the vacuum of space accelerated Jase's ship, transforming its smooth, apparently horizontal progress into a rough, rushing exit. Swept abruptly from the Rea vessel's artificial gravity, a roller-coaster sense of disoriented equilibrium made Tori grip her chair's arms tightly, while Ngina clung to her restraining straps. Jase activated the full propulsion as soon as his ship cleared the Rea defense sphere, and a second shock of acceleration assaulted his passengers.

"We might have been safer staying with the revolutionaries," observed Tori with a slightly strained grimace. "Are you sure this ship of yours was designed for interplanetary travel?"

"The Xiani recommend using space mode only under emergency circumstances, but I still trust this ship more than misused Bercali shuttles. It's an uncommonly fine model." Jase managed a fairly normal smile. "And uncommonly valuable. In returning it to me, Ares made quite a gallant tribute to 'his Mirelle.' You impressed his Essenji romanticism, Miss Darcy." Tori averted her face to hide embarrassment's bright stain, though she knew that any inquisitor could sense such a pronounced reaction without looking at her.

Ngina groaned, "I used to think space travel might be fun."

"The Stromvi physique doesn't relish unstable gravity," said Jase sympathetically. "That's why your father rarely leaves the planet."

"He always delegated the major travel to Ngoi," answered Ngina with a glum, expressive clattering of her hind teeth. "I wish I'd never gone to Calem's field."

"I just wish you'd left the relaweed for the Rea, instead of contributing it to your father's experiment in relanine eradication. The relaweed would have been safe enough in Roake's jealous care until a proper Consortium envoy could arrive to confiscate the drug." After a moment of silence, Jase emitted a sigh that seemed composed of long-restrained exasperation. "I could have concentrated on locating Birk and removing him to a less vulnerable location than Stromvi for his well-earned inquisition."

"Don't bestow your stern lecture on Ngina," berated Tori, stung by the added hurt that Jase's sharp words brought to Ngina's mournful eyes. "Save it for Birk."

Jase answered grimly, "Birk Hodge has earned much more than a lecture."

"Careful, Inquisitor," murmured Tori. "You've been so busy relating to the Rea, you're beginning to sound as vindictive as Akras. That hardly suggests a suitable attitude for a Sesserda adept."

"You're right, of course," he replied stiffly. He narrowed his iridescent eyes to slits. "Having my skin stripped from my body in ribbons tends to make me unconscionably irritable."

Feeling as if she had just been deservedly slapped, Tori replied with deep contrition, "I'm sorry, Jase."

The rigid set of his shoulders relaxed slightly. "I know," he said. "We're all having a rotten day."

Ngina sighed, lost in her own unhappy musings, "I wanted to show my honored father that I am a worthy daughter, and instead I condemned my people by involving them in Rea vengeance. Death-watch forced everyone into conflict, and it magnified everything terrible."

Tori realized that she was staring again at the glistening wounds on Jase Sleide's face and neck, and she shifted her gaze hurriedly across her shoulder to Ngina. "Never speculate too long on the alternatives of your personal past," advised Tori, herself feeling somewhat overwhelmed by results of her own recent choices. "It's a disheartening exercise, and it rarely improves either the present or the future."

Jase remarked quietly, "You're beginning to sound like a Sesserda philosopher, Miss Darcy."

"You're a bad influence, Mister Sleide."

"Frequently," he murmured, "as I'm about to prove by negating one of your Uncle Per's injudicious restrictions. Do you have any piloting experience, Ngina?"

"Piloting?" asked Ngina, and the stirring of interest brought a healthy violet flush to her hide. "A ship like this? No. Could I learn?"

"Very easily, since most of the ship's functions are automated, and the rest follow Xiani standards that I'm sure you know already. I'll demonstrate and let each of you practice in turn before we reach the Stromvi atmosphere. I plan to fly directly to Hodge Farm and use the ship's broadcast system to click a message to Nguri, explaining his daughter's difficult circumstances."

"Your plan sounds a great deal like common blackmail," commented Tori, for the terse acknowledgment of Nguri's position as opponent roused all her stubborn loyalty to the old Stromvi. She wondered if Jase would claim credit for the influence that made her judgmental.

Jase nodded, but his jaw tightened perceptibly. "The Calongi may strike me from the Sesserda rolls and submit me for criminal rehabilitation, if I survive long enough. Or they may give me an award of merit. It's a difficult call."

"Not for you, apparently," answered Tori, sorely torn. She hated to abet her inquisitor in using Ngina against Nguri, but she appreciated the necessity of such a drastic plan. She knew Nguri's stubbornness.

"That's why only a first level adept is trusted to make a true Sesserda judgment about himself," replied Jase. "Personal bias is so difficult to eliminate."

Jase is not my inquisitor any longer, Tori reminded herself. *He gave me his verdict: personal bias and all. Which makes him only a man. Of my own species. More or less.*

"I hope you're voting in my favor," continued Jase, "because I'm depending on you and Ngina to complete the 'persuasion' of Nguri if I fail. I could be wrong about the toxin's relative effects on a relanine addict, or I may have miscalculated the rate of relanine deterioration. In either event, I might not remain coherent long enough to locate Ngina and convince him to undo his work against us. I intend to prepare you both to complete my plan, if you're willing."

Ngina murmured, "I would like to hate you and consider you my enemy, but I believe you, Jase Sleide. You are favored by the Calongi, and my honored father has long called you a friend. I will do what you ask of me."

Tori shrugged somewhat self-consciously, wishing that she could duplicate Ngina's ready offer of faith. Ngina's immediacy of reply, despite all that she and her people had suffered recently at alien hands, made Tori feel like the frightened, cowardly youngling that Ngina had proclaimed herself. Ironically, it was Tori who now envied Ngina's courage.

Jase did not press Tori for a more meaningful reply, and Ngina merely watched his manipulations of the ship's controls. Jase and Ngina both seemed so much at peace with their respective decisions. Tori found herself feeling suddenly unworthy before them, and the fact that the

Consortium's official civilization rankings concurred with that assessment did not help: Consortium Soli were Level VI; Stromvi were Level V; Tori did not know how to categorize Jase Sleide, but a Sesserda adept surely ranked above his species' norm. Tori had learned early to value herself by what she considered a reasonably honest scale, irrespective of official categories that were intended only as guidelines for interspecies relations. She did not enjoy concurring with Calongi judgment.

She gave her answer slowly, "I won't try to pretend that I trust you completely, Sleide. You'd probably recognize such a pretense anyway. You know that I don't like inquisitors at best, and I have reservations about Consortium law in general. In your particular case, I have some personal biases of my own to overcome, such as a suspicion that you're as twisted as Ares, Roake, and Akras. I've never met anyone who straddled deception and Sesserda Truth as well as you."

Jase retorted mildly, "I didn't ask you how you gained Ares' particular regard."

"What does that prove?" asked Tori, refusing to allow her cheeks to regain their heated tinge.

"That I trust you."

"Which makes you crazier than Ares."

With a wickedly knowing smile that fueled Tori's embarrassment, Jase gestured toward the console. "This is the navigation panel. Can you see it, Ngina? Orbital destinations may be specified directly by Teurai coordinates or by any planet-centered inertial reference frame within Consortium records. . . ."

CHAPTER 44

Omi's neck tendrils shifted silently, sensing the creature's approach. The Bori's terror of its owner made its pulse rhythms irregular and facilitated Omi's ability to observe the man who hid beneath the Bori's very effective camouflage. Vastly adaptable via its own resources, the Bori did not require adaptation fluid's gifts on Stromvi and remained unimpaired by the spreading toxin that hampered Omi.

Omi had acknowledged an unpleasant likelihood that this Stromvi pseudo-virus would impair his own nervous system permanently. His senses already seemed dulled to him, and he was finding his multi-tasking abilities seriously diminished. Virtually all of his vast inner resources were engrossed in battling the invading elements, for the natural Calongi defense of adapting and absorbing served only to encourage this relanine-hungry army. Even the identification of this Essenji's basic species characteristics, suppressed as they were by physical reconstruction and permanent chemical adjustments, taxed Omi and forced him to reevaluate his intentions. A full inquisition would be impossible under the present circumstances.

Gisa stepped forward with a firmness that Omi lauded, for he knew how deeply her conflicting fears ate at her. Omi had not tried to discourage her dread of prophets' warnings and Hodge curses. Her cultural perceptions were her own, and Omi would not dispute the tenets of Deetari faith. Omi had simply offered her Calongi justice and reminded her of Deetari's obligation to uphold Consortium law or accept the necessary sacrifices of Consortium protection and trade. She had led him grudgingly to the concealed room across the hall from Birk's office.

"Have you contacted your Deetari sisters, Gisa?" demanded Birk softly, though the sound of his voice could not have been heard beyond the shielded room except by a Calongi. Birk tugged the Bori away from his face as he spoke. Omi stepped through the illusory wall. Birk retreated one pace but no further. "So, Omi," murmured Birk, "you finally pay your respects to the master of the house."

Omi bowed very properly. He observed the shifts of Birk's hand weapons carefully, despite the concealment granted to Birk by the Bori cloak. "I requested your presence at an inquisition. You did not respond, Mister Hodge."

"I thought you yielded your inquisitor's title to that impudent Soli of yours."

One of Birk's hand weapons had risen to a position preparatory for attack, but Omi did not choose to recognize the threat overtly. "Why did you allow Ngoi Ngenga to plant relaweed on this planet?"

"That was my son's decision." Birk shifted the Bori cloak, freeing his arm. Gisa ran from the room.

The searing beam of a nerve disrupter crossed the space between Birk and Omi, and the Calongi's layers of velvety outer-arms seethed and thickened at the point of contact. Birk panned the beam quickly across Omi, but the Calongi's outer-arms moved in protective synchronism with the beam. Birk aimed the weapon at Omi's head, but the Calongi's arms rose equally, baring an iridescent panoply of specialized limbs in the brightly veined sheaths of relanine sacs. A sinuous arm that ended in a six-fingered hand snapped from its sheath, snatched Birk's weapon, and crushed its firing mechanism into darkness.

"Barbaric Network weapons," said Omi, allowing his outer-arms to drape back into place above his other limbs. Birk's broken gun disappeared likewise beneath Calongi flesh. "Mister Hodge, you necessitate a harsh judgment against you." At Birk's slight movement, Omi added, "Do not trouble to use your knife, unless you wish to see how easily I can take it from you. I could disable you similarly, and I hope you will not force me to take such distasteful action."

"Arrogant Calongi," muttered Birk, "in my youth, you would not have beaten me."

"Uncivilized man, you do not understand me. We are

not dueling, and my purpose is not to defeat you. My purpose is truth and the just treatment of Consortium members. You are not a member of the Consortium, and you do not merit our protection or the benefits of our civilization. You have made clear to me your disrespect for Consortium law, which renders you ineligible to apply for Consortium membership now or in the future."

"I didn't plan to stay here much longer," offered Birk with a trace of a sneer.

"You will leave here with the Rea, who are your people," answered Omi, "and you will submit to their justice." After a brief pause, Omi added, "Or you may die here from the changes in the Stromvi atmosphere."

Birk's expression shifted rapidly from hauteur and anger to calculation and wary comprehension. "Changes?"

"The planetary adapter that you brought to this world has been activated with intent to destroy all those who have adaptation fluid in them. The use of the adapter is a remarkable tribute to Master Nguri's skills at biological programming."

"No Stromvi would have the initiative to take the kree'va," said Birk, shaking his head in a denial directed only at himself. The Bori recoiled from his sharp motion, and Birk's white-maned head seemed to float above the crimson edge of an insubstantial darkness. Birk turned a cunning look toward Omi. "Master Calongi, I admit that I was once Rea, but I sought to abandon their violent ways long ago. I stole their greatest weapon and hid it on this world to prevent further harm, for I have witnessed the terrible potential of the kree'va. The Rea have found me after many spans and used trickery and intimidation to manipulate the Stromvi into helping them against me. The Rea, not I, have injured your great Consortium's members. You must take me to the kree'va, for only I know how to deactivate it safely."

"You know very little," observed Omi, "but your ignorance clarifies truth for me. You sustained a position of influence as Birk Hodge by believing in your fiction of honor. You fail to recognize your own hypocrisy."

"Where are the Rea now?" demanded Birk, refusing to hear the Calongi's insights. "Where is the kree'va?"

"Accompany me, Mister Hodge."

* * *

Akras watched the images of her sons leading three proud Rea warriors, all encased in protective suits, through the home vessel's great mesh corridor. The warriors moved unsteadily, for they had been nearly unconscious when Roake reached them. He had been unable to revive any but these three: Remus, Dannen, and Tiber. Akras knew that her sons sought to deactivate her ability to monitor them, and she was unsurprised when her console screen became blank. She regretted the Rea treason, but she blamed only Birkaj for its enactment.

She wrapped herself concealingly in the Bori cloak and waited beside the control room door. When the door opened, Ares, his dark gaze intense and grim, strode into the room first. For a brief, hesitant instant, Akras considered reaching out to touch him in a last gesture, an abject apology for having failed to restore the honor stolen by the Rea-traitor. She did not yield to the impulse. She slipped past her Rea warriors toward the shuttle bays.

She stopped, for Roake stood in her path. "Your Bori is exhausted, Mother," said Roake. "I see the crimson of its gasping mouth."

Akras turned, and Ares stepped into the hall behind her. "Where is the daar'va, Mother?" demanded Ares.

"Return this vessel to us," ordered Roake, "for we will not let the clan die."

His arrogance, his hateful resemblance to Birkaj, canceled Akras' last regrets. Roake should have gone on the ship with the other prisoners. All contaminating elements should have been purged from the home vessel. Roake had defied his clan leader once again, and that Mirelle woman had corrupted even Ares.

Akras shouted at the traitors, "You are all dead already, for Birkaj has stolen your honor." *Zagare, we shall triumph together*. "This ship is *mine*. The kree'va is *mine*. The Rea-star is *mine*. Raskannen gave them to *me*, and you will have none of them, Birkaj." She hurled her Bori at Roake, and she jumped past him, tearing at his reaching arm with the blade of Damona's knife. Akras ran.

She heard her sons pursuing her. They were slowed by

the poison and discouragement that consumed them
alike, but they were strong and young. She needed to
elude them by cleverness. She knew her home vessel better than the younger Rea, despite Bercali efforts to eradicate the past. Surely, she could find a way to evade her
sons, until they were too exhausted even to search for
the daar'va.

"Clan Leader," called an urgent voice. "This way."

Indomitable Tagran, thought Akras, accepting his summons through a door into one of the dark, side corridors.
He fired at the door, fusing it impassably. *Of course,
Tagran would survive. He knew enough to wear a protective suit. He knew I'd use the daar'va.* She proceeded
quickly down the hallway, sure of her destination now.
She heard Tagran run to catch up with her.

She bypassed the wide bays where the shining Rea
warships were stored. She had already made her choice
of a particular Bercali shuttle. Its stench offended her,
but the Bercali captain had equipped the ship capably as
his own escape vehicle. He had also keyed the bay doors
to the ship's control. Akras smiled coldly, considering the
Bercali captain's inability to evade the daar'va despite his
careful plans. How could a Bercali hope to best the Rea?

No one defeated the Rea, no one except the Rea-
traitor. Grimly, Akras climbed inside the shuttle. Tagran
accompanied her. She saw no reason to acknowledge
him. He was her personal guard. Where else would he
be but beside her?

She set the destination coordinates for Hodge Farm.
The execution of the Rea-traitor awaited her. "Your
death-curse will be fulfilled, Father," she said calmly.
Tagran removed the hood of his protection suit, and he
rubbed his head as if it ached.

*   *   *

"Nguri, listen to me," muttered Jase quietly, though
his ship sent a much louder, longer click-version of the
message vibrating through the Stromvi tunnels.

"Nguri likes the deep, isolated caverns for his private
work," said Tori. "Your message may not have reached
him yet." She tried not to notice the shudders that racked
Jase. She tried not to recall the corrosiveness of his skin

when she brushed against him in climbing from his ship. Her own skin blistered from the momentary contact.

"He has heard me," answered Jase. He pushed damp hair away from his face. "He knows that if I can speak to him directly, he will have difficulty arguing with me. I have taken too much of what he values."

"Ngina's offer to go to him herself. . . ."

". . . is still suicidal."

Tori looked across the burned field to Jase's ship, where Ngina had remained, protected from her own world's atmosphere and her own father's creation. "I thought you trusted Nguri."

"I do trust him," replied Jase, "but he's a stubborn man, and he thinks he's fighting to save his world."

"Isn't he?"

"No. His world has already been sacrificed. Whatever survives will not be the original Stromvi."

"If anything survives," added Tori. The desolation of the burned field disheartened her, but Jase had wanted to land near the southern caves and away from Hodge House.

"How are you feeling?" asked Jase, glancing at her.

"A little dizzy. My ears are beginning to ring, but it's not troublesome yet. You're not doing so well, are you?"

"I've felt better," he admitted, "but no serious damage starts until the first bout of pain stops. Accept that as the observation of an expert in relanine sickness."

"You still don't seem like a probable candidate for relanine addiction."

"I have a propensity for being in the wrong place at the wrong time." He turned his head, as the ground unfolded and a Stromvi head emerged. Jase stood and greeted the Stromvi woman warmly, "Ngeta-li, I am inexpressibly delighted to see you, but where is your obstinate husband?"

"Where is my daughter?" countered Ngeta. Jase nodded toward his ship. "She is still uninfected?" demanded Ngeta.

"Yes. We used the air lock to exit. The purity of the ship's internal environment has been maintained."

"But Ngina cannot return to her people?"

"Not unless Nguri amends the process he has begun." Ngeta stared at the ship in which her daughter was

confined. "He says that you must come to him, Jase."
Ngeta began a stately descent down the ramp from which
she had reached the surface. She did not trouble to re-
close the concealing doors, nor did she wait to confirm
that Jase entered behind her.

Tori inserted, "I'm coming with you."

Jase laughed briefly. "I thought you were tired of following me into lightless holes beneath the Stromvi
surface."

"I'm giving you one more chance."

Jase squinted into the darkness of the Stromvi tunnel.
"It's not the smoothest passage."

"I'll manage. Hurry, or we'll lose Ngeta."

"She's not rushing."

"Neither are you." Jase sighed, but he ducked to enter
the cave. He half turned. "Don't offer me a hand,
please," said Tori, displaying her blistered forearm.
"You're as bad as a Suviki acid bleeder."

Jase grimaced. "Sorry. I should have been more cautious. I'm filled with live Calongi blood cells at the moment. The effects can be uncomfortable."

"Just keep moving, Mister Sleide."

*   *   *

As Thalia served the supper beneath a softly lavender
Stromvi sunset, Rillessa watched them: Calem as limp as
his ecru linen suit; Sylvie maintaining a brittle facade in
vivid green skirt and long-blouse; and Harrow preening
himself in his immaculate gray shorts and vest. Rillessa
despised them all, even Calem, her Calem. She did not
try to speak to them. She did not try to express her
disgust at their blithe unwillingness to *understand*. She
did not care that they thought her mad, for she had concluded that she alone was sane.

When she saw *It* come, wearing the head of Birk
Hodge as *Its* crown, Rillessa only smiled. She had killed
It once, but *It* would not die, and the part of her that
recognized the use of the Bori acknowledged that Birk
and his enemies were too numerous and too well-armed
to be conquered by her alone. She had done her best to
warn the others, and she could not be blamed for their
refusal to hear. She did not dread the Calongi who fol-

lowed *It* closely, because she knew that she alone at Hodge Farm had upheld Consortium law. She alone was without guilt.

Harrow had jumped to his feet. Calem had dwindled in his chair, his face pale with astonishment. Sylvie had reached for her brother's hand and clutched it, though Calem did not seem to notice her. Thalia began a low, mournful keening.

Rillessa pushed her tangled hair from her eyes with an impatient gesture of her scarred hands. She ordered briskly, "Stop wailing, Thalia, and sing of joy. The master of the house returns to his loving family."

Birk removed the Bori and dropped it inelegantly onto the patio floor. His children's eyes followed the Bori, and they continued to stare at it, as it acquired obvious, shifting colors in its effort to readapt. Birk retained his dark under-cloak, though he cast it rakishly over one shoulder. All of his rumpled clothes were shadow-colored. He seated himself at the table. "Bring my supper, Thalia," he commanded.

The Deetari woman ceased her dirge of mourning. "I do not serve the Dead," she said in a hollow voice. She removed her blue silk turban, baring the delicate tattoos across her skull, and her thin arms raised the turban toward the lowering sun. "The sacrifices will be made, Lady Death, as you decreed." Thalia turned swiftly and disappeared into the house.

Sylvia stared after her and murmured, "Her people call her a prophetess."

Calem said quietly, "I didn't hear your ship arrive, Father."

"You should learn not to talk so much, Calem," grunted Birk. "You only emphasize your stupidity." Instead of grumbling one of his usual retorts, Calem nodded slightly. Birk frowned, more clearly disconcerted by his son's calm reaction than by Thalia's small rebellion. He turned from Calem and fixed his cold gaze on Harrow. "Leave my house."

"I don't understand your anger, Birk," responded Harrow, but he fumbled nervously as he resumed his seat at the table.

Birk took the untouched plate of crisped fruit from Harrow's place and began to eat. Between bites, Birk

remarked, "Neither the Rea nor Per Walis are here to
defend you, Harrow, and you're pathetic without a protector to give you courage and concoct convincing lies
for you. I don't need the senses of a Calongi to see your
trembling." Harrow glanced uncomfortably at Omi's
darkly silent figure.

Omi walked to the patio edge and faced the shadowy
gardens of evening. "A ship is approaching very rapidly," he remarked, "too rapidly for safety."

"Is it Rea?" demanded Birk, as if he still dominated
his world, instead of being imprisoned by it.

Rillessa answered, "It is justice, isn't it, Master
Omi?"

"No," replied Omi, "it is retribution."

The amber cone became visible even to Soli eyes, and
it glistened in the long light of fading day. The distant
sounds of gentle Stromvi click-speech acknowledged the
ship's approach without question and returned to mundane concerns. Birk Hodge continued eating, while his
children watched him. Rillessa, Harrow, and Omi stared
at the incoming ship.

Within an upstairs room of Hodge House, Gisa and
Thalia huddled together, as Thalia prophesied of Death.
In a deep, thickly resinous Stromvi tunnel, two Soli followed a Stromvi woman, who moved at an unhurried
pace. In a deeper cavern, Nguri Ngenga stared at the
kree'va, the lost prize of the Rea warriors which strove
frantically to surmount damage wrought by the kree'va's
lesser cousin, before the Rea vessel could plummet into
the Stromvi world. Ngina watched the display screen of
Jase's ship, where a line of steep descent stretched at a
frightening pace from the Rea home vessel toward Hodge
House; softly, she mouthed Jase's instructions as she activated the hover system.

The wind of the shuttle's arrival buffeted Hodge
House, scattering the table setting and flinging broken
bits of crisped fruit against the ivory walls. Omi stood
impervious. Calem and Sylvie moved closer to their father. Rillessa hunched against the rose-and-resin-scented
wind and held her place. Harrow opened his eyes hesitantly, as the shuttle settled heavily atop the bed of scarlet roses. Birk wiped a trace of fruit from his mouth.

The slim, weathered woman who emerged from the

shuttle caused Birk to stop his idle motions. Akras crossed the yard, disregarding rose thorns that snagged her lua-hide boots. Tagran followed her. Akras' dark braid swung freely, eluding the clutching branches. "Calongi," she called, and she pointed her hard, thin hand at Birk, "this man murdered my father and my husband. I am his lawful executioner. Give him to me."

Birk whispered, "Akras."

Omi answered evenly, "You are an uncivilized people, and your private feuds do not concern the Consortium." He did not move.

Akras smiled thinly. "Come, Rea-traitor, and fight me, or have you grown too soft to duel?"

"I don't want to kill you, Akras," replied Birk, rising and staring at her unswervingly. Akras' lips thinned in contempt. "I never meant to hurt you."

"The death-curse of Raskannen has destroyed you," shouted Akras with clear, ringing pride. She pointed first at Calem, who flinched slightly, then at Sylvie, who tied nervous knots in the end of her shoulder sash. "Look at them, Birkaj, and feel your shame. You defiled yourself to create them." She spread her arms. "And to create this, which I have taken from you. Raskannen is avenged, and the death-curse of Zagare now ends your life."

Akras raised an energy gun from its binding at her slim waist. With a savage growl of fury, Birk fled into his house. Calem and Sylvie stumbled over each other to follow their father. Akras' peal of laughter held all the merriment that had once captivated young Rea men. "What glory!" said Rillessa with a smile, and Harrow gave her a look of pure loathing.

With the light agility of her stolen youth, Akras ran and leapt to the patio. Harrow extended a beseeching hand toward her. "We had an agreement, Clan Leader," he said, trying to sound charming. Akras ignored him and continued into the house. "Clan Leader!" called Harrow after her. Tagran pushed him aside roughly and entered Hodge House in Akras' wake.

The shriek of an overextended energy weapon echoed from crystal walls. The odor of burning moss floated from the door. Still, Omi did not move.

"Are they not a pretty spectacle?" asked Rillessa gaily. "Even you, Master Inquisitor," she added slyly, "trying to disguise your helplessness and cowardice as wise detachment. You are as comical as the rest of us." Omi's neck tendrils shifted slightly. "You hear me, don't you, Inquisitor? I tell you Truth, and you like it as little as anyone here."

Harrow had edged cautiously toward the patio's side stairs. "If you leave this planet now, Mister Febro," remarked Omi without turning, "you will die within three millispans. You are reaching a most dangerous phase of contamination."

"You're all mad," said Harrow nervously. He took courage from the Calongi's calm indifference. He threw himself down the stairs and dashed toward the rear of the house. Microspans later, his hovercraft raced across the garden.

"He didn't believe you, Calongi," said Rillessa with her supercilious smile. She smoothed her lilac skirt complacently. "No one at Hodge Farm knows how to believe."

"You have a twisted life-purpose, Miss Canti," observed Omi.

CHAPTER 45

Jase walked strongly into Nguri's presence, despite the fever that wracked him, the resin that invaded him, and the exhaustion that dragged at him. Watching the stiffness of his movements, the obvious effort he exerted to continue walking, Tori had scarcely expected him to survive the arduous journey through the slick resin tunnels. She had begun to feel an unnatural chill herself, which made the poisoning alarmingly real to her.

"Destruction solves nothing," said Jase.

Nguri raised his large head slowly from the specimen plate he had been studying. "Pruning is not destructive," he replied. The thick layers of milky resin film made his eyes seem blind, but he scanned the distance between Jase and Tori. An abundance of the brightest root varieties made the cavern unusually bright for a Stromvi room, but intricate weavings draped the walls and most of the tables, concealing the nature of Nguri's work. "You brought them both, Ngeta-li," he clicked.

"She followed," answered Ngeta in clear Consortium trade speech.

"Clever Soli female," said Nguri in a tone reminiscent of his old teasing, "always attaching yourself to the most dominant male of available, compatible species."

Nguri's familiarity bit into Tori, and she felt a sting of tears, but she responded briskly, "I should have had six limbs, three hundred teeth, and a hide that would dull a diamond saw." Nguri nodded his great head.

Jase touched the pruned tip of a root spike thoughtfully. With terrible calm, he said, "Nguri, unless you reverse the kree'va's actions, I will have no choice but to judge you guilty of calculated murder. You've fallen prey to the classic error of those who deal incautiously with beings less civilized than themselves. You've become

tainted by Birk's behavioral standards. You jeopardize
the civilization ranking of your entire people." Jase
ducked past a row of trimmed root tendrils to stand with
an unobstructed view of Nguri. The shifting biolight
touched relanine's iridescence and gave Jase a glowing
aura, resin blue and relanine rainbow-and-gold.

Nguri answered with a stiff shrug, "I do not accept
that the preservation of my world makes me uncivilized."

"Deliberate destruction of fellow beings, even lowly
Level VII's, indicates a severe lack of respect for
creation."

"Stromvi will be whole."

"Your Stromvi will not be whole without Ngina."

Nguri clicked a rapid expression of frustration, and
Ngeta clicked of pain. "You have learned cruelty, Jase-
li," said Nguri in the trade speech, "which is as uncivilized as any crime of mine."

"Sesserda justice only appears cruel to those who
abuse it," snapped Jase, coiled fury in his well-trained
voice. He moved to the seating mound in front of Nguri
and perched himself on it awkwardly. He leaned forward,
both hands held outward in that strange, Calongi-
reminiscent flexure that condemned the guilty. "Did you
expect me to accept death graciously, Nguri? You know
that I am an exceptionally difficult man to kill."

Tori shivered—from illness or from instinctive fear of
the lash of Consortium justice. Jase argued for her life
as well as his own, but she wanted to shout at him to
leave Nguri in peace. She knew the depths of torment
that an inquisitor could tap with apparent ease and innocence. She glanced at Ngeta, whose tapestried hide had
paled with grief and strain, and she remained silent.

Nguri grunted, "I seek no one's death." His words,
his bearing, all of his serene Stromvi strength seemed
suddenly diminished by the full, oppressive weight of the
soil and sky above the Stromvi caves. "Birk Hodge
brought death here."

Jase did not relent: "Birk Hodge came at your
invitation."

"He deceived us."

"He challenged you and awakened ambition in you."
Jase hissed, "*You* created Hodge Farm, Nguri, and you
enjoyed the praise that Hodge roses earned." Nguri

clicked of Soli folly, but Jase barely paused. "Not my folly, Nguri. I'm judging clearly. You knew that Birk was a selfish, lawless schemer, but you tolerated him, because he was the perfect, unwitting servant to you. The pretense of his ownership preserved Stromvi anonymity and spared you from the ardors of marketing your marvelous products throughout the Consortium."

Nguri clicked softly, "Birk promised to restrict his illegalities to the lawless. He promised to keep Stromvi untouched by his uncivilized fellows. He betrayed us."

"*He* betrayed the Rea. *You* betrayed yourself. You have no right to condemn the Hodges to death. You have no right to condemn Tori, and you have no right to condemn me."

Nguri shifted his head indignantly. "Hodges planted relaweed," he said with ponderous assurance. "They infested my lovely Stromvi with ugly alien beetles and the larva that devour my blossoming children. *Hodge's Dream* he called my blue-and-white, but he destroyed it. I examined it cell by cell, hoping to discover that the relanine had not yet begun its contaminating work, but the insects had already carried the poison too far." Nguri raised his torso proudly and glared down at Jase. "The *kree'va*, this thing that Birk treasured above his own people, will save my world. That is *Stromvi* justice, my Sesserda-obsessed friend, and I would like to hear you explain how it defies Sesserda law."

Jase did not reply. He moved his hands from head to heart, as a Calongi might have shifted neck tendrils. It was the sign of tribute to the dead.

Ngeta lowered her head. "You are a horticulturist and not a Sesserda adept, my husband," she said somberly. "You have banished our daughter with your misguided justice."

"This *friend* stole her from us," countered Nguri, snapping his pruning teeth in Jase's direction. Jase did not flinch, and still he did not speak.

The calculated silence of an inquisitor, observed Tori, knowing the effectiveness of such techniques, but her own threshold of tolerance was lower than Nguri's. "You can't argue with him, Nguri," she said nervously. "He's subjecting you to inquisition, and he'll achieve whatever he wants."

Nguri clicked softly, "I do not fear inquisition."

"Because you don't understand it!" replied Tori. She crossed the room carefully and knelt on the woven mat between Jase and Nguri. "Look at me, Nguri," she demanded.

"You do not have six limbs or adequate teeth," sighed Nguri, but he lowered his torso hesitantly to see her at her level.

Tori grasped his neck ridge and pulled his head close enough to her to blur him in her sight, but she knew that Stromvi eyes saw her most clearly at that narrow range. "You once asked me about official inquisition, and I told you that it was painless. I lied to you, Nguri. I've never known such pain, not even now with your wretched poison eating at my veins. The inquisitors did nothing to me except allow me to condemn myself."

She drew a ragged breath, her lungs tormented by resin and by the adaptation that Nguri's virus had fouled. She forced herself to continue, "I shall always be a Consortium member, but I've been associated with a terrible crime, and I haven't been acquitted. That official blemish makes me unwanted and unwelcome anywhere that I would care to live. No one punishes more effectively than the inquisitors, Nguri, because the inquisitors know what hurts *you* most. I feared loneliness, and they gave it to me in shiploads. Don't offer yourself to such punishment, Nguri."

"I do not matter, Tori-li," replied Nguri gently.

"You matter to us," said Jase, friend again and not inquisitor. Tori could feel the warmth of him behind her, a controlled outpouring of physical and mental influence. "You matter to your people. They do not want you to sacrifice yourself for them."

Ngeta clicked, "He speaks truly, Husband."

Nguri blinked at Tori and withdrew from her. He rearranged his position slowly to regard his wife. "Because he speaks in accord with you, Ngeta-li," he grumbled.

Jase remarked simply, "Ngeta is wise."

"Don't be smug," grunted Nguri. He raised himself to his feet with painful care. "You always were too clever, Jase-li. You stole from me the one flower that could make my sharp-tongued wife your strongest ally. I should have protected my Ngina-li better, but I needed to affirm to her that she is valued by me and by her people. You are clever, Jase-li, but you do not know everything." Nguri limped across the room and drew a beautifully woven curtain away from a table cluttered with root samples and wrapped seed parcels. A small ruby starburst marked the side of a box in the center of the table.

Defying relanine sickness and slippery resin, Jase rose swiftly and went to Nguri's side. Tori grasped a wisp of hope and clung to it desperately. "It doesn't conform to Xiani design standards," murmured Jase, frowning at the kree'va.

"An independent culture obviously produced it," retorted Nguri. "The Rea undoubtedly stole it, since the Essenji people lack technical sophistication. Consortium civilizations adapt people, not planets."

"So I've heard," replied Jase dryly. "How did you program it?"

Nguri pushed aside another weaving to reveal the Xiani botanical analyzer. "You were right about the relanine instability," admitted Nguri with a click of regret. "I didn't intend to kill the adapted hosts. I only wanted to force all aliens to leave us. I have been working on an evaluation of the flaw." He clicked gruffly, "Did you think I had no better friendship-spirit than to plan your death, Jase-li?"

Jase only shook his head in reply, for he spoke with the detached appreciation of a Sesserda scholar, "You used a botanical analyzer to create a botanical virus, based on relanine, on a world that is primarily botanical in its focus of life, technology, and culture. You embody your species-purpose, my obstinate friend, even as you betray it."

Tori came to look over Nguri's shoulder at the cluttered table, and she laid her hand gently on the aged gnarls of his neck ridge. *Stubborn, irascible, brilliant Stromvi. No wonder your people esteem you; no wonder they love you.* "Can you reverse the damage to us, Nguri?" she asked, unable to feel anger against him, unable to feel anything but regret for a friendship that must be lost.

"You are a troublesome people," was his only answer. His torso wove slightly in eloquent sorrow.

*   *   *

"He called her Akras," muttered Sylvie to her brother, as they rummaged frantically through lacquered storage chests. "You remember that name, don't you? Mother warned us about her."

"That vague warning didn't help her, and it doesn't help us," answered Calem. He dumped the contents of a large drawer on the mossy floor of the alcove. "I know there's another needler here. Rillessa only took one of them." He lifted folded rugs and weavings, shaking them for hidden contents.

"Be careful, Calem. You don't want to damage it."

"I don't even know how to use the thing."

"I do. My second husband taught me. He wasn't much more sincere than Harrow, but he had a few useful skills."

"If we had any sense, we'd take Harrow's hovercraft and get away from here."

"We can't escape, Calem. We tried that already, and we failed." Sylvia frowned and paused in her search. "Didn't we?"

"Harrow arrived. I think." Calem shook his head. "What's the difference? We have to stop her, or she'll kill him."

"Why do we care so much, Calem?" asked Sylvie wanly. "He's manipulated us all our lives. I thought I wanted him hurt. I thought I wanted to be free of him."

"I wanted him dead," answered Calem, "until I saw him out there on the patio. He was defeated, Sylvie."

"Yes," she sighed. "I could hardly bear to watch him."

"We both thought we needed him, and we hated him for making us dependent. But we were wrong. He needs us."

"I hear her coming," whispered Sylvie desperately. "Where is that needler?"

"Here!" Calem lifted the weapon triumphantly from a hidden pocket in the drawer.

*   *   *

Uncivilized beings enacted their own punishments, but Omi experienced no satisfaction at witnessing the results.

He regretted that Miss Canti was correct in condemning him, though she spoke from drug-induced madness more than from any rational process of thought. Ukitan-lai had warned that the seed of prejudice would grow and spread, if it was ever allowed to be sown.

Botanical metaphors come easily in this place, observed Omi. *But it is a fitting characterization of Ukitan's words. I thought I had acquitted myself by acknowledging my need of Ukitan's counsel and devoting myself to renewal studies for the past five spans. Ukitan was wise to send me here amid these most uncivilized beings, for I cannot continue to deceive myself among them. Here, the truth is all too evident.*

I punished Miss Mirelle harshly to appease my emotions rather than to uphold Sesserda Truth. Five processes of inquisition was the first judgment against her, and that would have sufficed as a punishment. I should have acquitted her, despite the uncertainties that Tiva disorder creates.

I have denied my own guilt by criticizing her and the child-species that she represents to me, where I should respect what such beings may become. The Stromvi are sufficiently civilized to make their own choices, but these others are only children, unaware of what they do. Sometimes children must be allowed to make their own mistakes, but sometimes they must be led by the hand to safety.

Omi weighed the dangers that he sensed, counting the lives that would be lost to each facet of the evil that had been loosed. He could not stop it all, but he could salvage a part. He could redeem himself a little. And if he survived, perhaps he would feel worthy again to perform his music among his own people.

He assessed his own damaged shuttle. Its fuel would suffice to reach the great Rea vessel, but even a brief repair time would be costly. The small Bercali shuttle offered a faster access. It was fitting that the clan leader should provide the means of saving what remained of her clan and the world that she had tried to destroy.

Omi did not bow to Rillessa. He drifted past her, gliding smoothly down the stairs into the garden. His cloak of outer-arms lifted and fell in easy rhythm, as he crossed the tumbled roses on which Akras had landed her shuttle. He climbed the shuttle's ramp with the same even dignity that had carried him without evident effort through the tangle of thorns.

Perhaps even Jase-lai would judge Omi more kindly. "Ukitan-lai was too lenient with me," murmured Omi, as he adjusted bindings to secure himself within the Bercali shuttle. "We are unaccustomed to judging against our fellow Calongi, for the need is so rare. Ukitan-lai was wise to make me face condemnation from a Soli adept. Jase-lai's extravagant gestures lack refinement, but they are not without wisdom." Prodded by a Soli's example of self-sacrifice, Omi evaluated the shuttle with his many senses, and he prepared himself to defend the lawless from themselves.

*   *   *

Tagran ran into the house after his clan leader. He found her standing before a bewildering choice of door-ways and crystalline halls. Akras was silent and attentive, a huntress seeking the direction of her prey. She began to move forward.

"Move cautiously, Clan Leader," whispered Tagran, but Akras showed no sign of hearing his warning.

Tagran turned sharply toward an echo of movement, only to hear a clear voice from the opposite direction. "You're the woman my mother hated," said Sylvie Hodge, "the woman whose name my father whispered in the night." Sylvie's voice shook from the effects of Rea drugs, but Tagran heard a trace of Essenji pride, and he grieved at the waste. He scanned the corridor, but he could not locate the speaker. He tried to catch hold of Akras to make her take cover, but she shook free of him angrily. Sylvie continued, "I know that you're the reason she left us."

Tagran saw Sylvie just as she stepped from an alcove and fired a needler at Akras. Tagran ducked quickly. Sylvie's shot struck and shattered a rose crystal panel behind him.

Akras fired her own weapon, and the scent of the scorched flesh and fabric reached Tagran before he could rise from among the crystal shards. "Bloody murderess," snarled Calem Hodge, emerging from the same concealing alcove that had sheltered his sister. Tagran saw the Soli man launch himself at Akras, knocking her energy gun from her hand.

Tagran did not hesitate. He tore Calem away from Akras. Tagran was not as swift as in his youth, but he was an Essenji warrior battling a man who had never tried to fight for anyone before today. The struggle ended quickly. Tagran never even drew his weapon, for he knew the quick, effective blow that killed. He stood above his victim, hating what he had done.

Tagran wiped his brow, sticky with resin traces. Akras had not waited to see the outcome of the conflict. She had retrieved her gun and continued her pursuit of the only prey that truly mattered to her. In silence, Tagran gave both Calem and Sylvie Hodge a kinsman's salute.

Tagran proceeded down the hall, but it bent and branched without any obvious logic. When he did not find Akras, he feared that he had chosen the wrong path. When he passed through a door and found himself in a pentagonal room, confronted by three more doors and a staircase, he stopped in frustration.

"Traitor, face me!" shouted Akras, but her voice issued from amid the maze of oddly angled halls and alcoves. "Or have you abandoned your courage as well as your honor?"

Tagran chose the door that seemed closest to the sound, but he found only more of the endlessly deceptive crystal panels, rose and ivory and gray. He tried to follow Akras' voice, as she repeated her challenge, but each direction that Tagran turned in led to another cluttered, lifeless room like all the rest. The sound of Akras would fade, and he would start to turn, thinking that he had moved farther from her, only to hear her so clearly again that even her footsteps seemed close. The house conspired with its creator, and Tagran feared that Akras would recognize her danger too late.

"I do not fear you, my Akras," answered Birkaj softly. He sounded closest of all, and Tagran hurried forward blindly.

"Then you have become a fool," retorted Akras.

"I am neither a fool nor a coward," answered Birkaj. "I am a Rea warrior who has never loved anyone but you."

"What of your wife?" sneered Akras. "What of your concubine?"

"What of Zagare?"

"Where are you?" demanded Akras, but frustration had overcome her coldness. At least, Tagran hoped that it was frustration that he now heard.

"I am here, my Akras."

Tagran awaited the sounds of conflict, but the house had become silent. *He knows she means to kill him,* thought Tagran, *but he does not believe that she will be able to resist the old lies. Perhaps he is right. She hesitates, as I would never have expected. Birkaj always understood her better than any of us. They were indeed well matched.*

Birk spoke again, and he had become tender. "We gave our pledges to each other, my Akras. I did not betray you. It was you who turned from me, for you believed the lies about me. How could you imagine that I would ever harm our clan leader?"

"You murdered him," she hissed, but she did not fire her weapon.

Tagran hurried anxiously past another stairway, telling himself that the voices could not have come from the second level, though he was unsure. He was sure of nothing except the immediacy of danger to Akras. He entered a room that seemed to be a museum, and he saw them.

Birkaj stood against the far wall, extending his hands to Akras. Unnoticed, Tagran viewed them both in profile. Despite the whitened hair and affected Soli tan, Birkaj had not changed significantly. He was the rival of Tagran's youth, the envied Roake to Tagran's Ares. He was the destroyer of the beloved Akras, and Tagran hated him.

Akras held her weapon limply, and her ruined face was wet with tears. She was shaking her head, the braid swinging against her back. Birk moved toward her very slowly. Tagran called to him, "Birkaj!" Startled, Birk turned his amber eyes toward Tagran. Birk frowned, as if wondering whether he should recognize this Rea warrior. Akras watched only Birk. She did not seem to be aware of Tagran at all.

Tagran raised his gun. Birk lunged toward Akras to shield himself behind her. "Akras," cried Birk, "order him not to fire!" Akras recoiled only fractionally, but the shift in position sufficed. Tagran burned a hole through Birkaj's chest.

Birkaj sank slowly to his knees. He touched the charred fabric of his shirt with wonder. He raised his disbelieving eyes to Akras. He fell forward, his head brushing Akras' feet, and Akras screamed, "No!" She aimed her gun at Birk's back. "Stand and face me, traitor," she ordered in a shaking voice. "Face me, coward!" Akras kicked Birk's prone body, but he did not move. "Coward," she shrieked. She began to fire wildly at the room, igniting award ribbons and destroying sculpted roses.

"Akras, he is dead," shouted Tagran, backing into the corridor to avoid her random aim. "The traitor cannot hurt you again."

Akras' destructive frenzy stopped, and she stood immobile among the smoke and slowly spreading flames. "Tagran?" she asked, as if the name were strange to her.

He answered with relief, "I am here, Clan Leader. We must leave quickly. This room is unsafe."

"You had no right to kill him," whimpered Akras, weeping with her voice as with her wide, golden eyes. She raised her gun once more. The blazing beam fired a swath of dry moss to Tagran's feet, igniting particles of resin in a sparkling, crackling display. As the energy beam sizzled through his breastplate, Tagran could not feel shock. Akras had disappointed him too often. He loved her no less.

*   *   *

Caustic smoke seeped through the Hodge House ventilation system, even as the heat penetrated to the upper floor. "Death will be satisfied," said Thalia.

"Mister Birk's curse against our people will die with us," agreed Gisa solemnly. "I was selfish to try to escape the prophecy. The Calongi was wise to force me to return."

The Deetari sisters sipped their tea. They had made their room immaculate. They wore their finest lace. They waited to die.

*   *   *

Rillessa watched Omi's borrowed ship rise into the deepening twilight. She pried a chunk of crumbling saffron bread from a loaf that she had retrieved from the patio floor beside a limp, quietly heaving Bori. When she had consumed the last crumb, she reached for the Bori. Only mildly surprised at its lightness, she draped the creature around her shoulders. She did not notice how it stung her bare arms. She stroked the Bori's motile flesh, as the first moon rose above the far, faint curve of Stromvi's horizon.

"I defeated *It*," murmured Rillessa, as another crystalline segment of Hodge House shattered from the heat with an explosive sound. In her drug-damaged mind, she saw Calem beckon her inside the house. He was smiling at her. She pushed the Bori from her and ran to her Calem.

*   *   *

"You created a virus that could attack relanine," said Jase pensively. He bent to examine the kree'va closely without touching it. "You should be able to use the same fundamental method to create a second virus that preys on the first. Given half a chance, relanine will reassert itself." Jase hefted one of the seed parcels and raised his dark brows. "Calem's harvest?"

"Yes," answered Nguri with a trace of pride. "I have measured the relanine content. It is almost completely neutralized."

"No," answered Jase, his frown deepening. "The seeds are mutating. The relanine level is increasing." He stared from the seed parcel to his hand that held it, and he stifled a tremor with obvious effort.

Nguri took the parcel from Jase and peered at it closely. He passed it across his head nodules. "Perhaps . . ." he clicked softly.

Jase raised his face toward the root tendrils above him. "Even if the kree'va's field is programmed to a constant, the ultimate effect depends on the environment and entities that the field impinges. As those external elements change, the kree'va's effects are intended to diminish and leave a new stability."

"Clearly," replied Nguri with a Stromvi senior's arch approval of an apt student's learning.

"You have attached the kree'va's programming to relanine, a most deviant variable. The kree'va cannot stabilize."

Nguri nodded in slow concession. "Instability preceded the kree'va and interacts with it. The risk of widespread mutation existed as soon as relaweed and resin mingled. The kree'va will stabilize, but Stromvi must change. I have known this since the death-watch began." Both Tori and Ngeta stared at him.

Jase continued in an odd, remote voice, "I underestimated you again, didn't I, Nguri? The kree'va has already initiated the second plague for you. Here, where the force is strongest, the effects are already apparent. Relanine is being produced faster than it's being consumed."

"The speed of the kree'va's initial effects continues to astonish me," replied Nguri, dropping the seed parcel back on the table. "I wish that the full cycle of change could transpire so efficiently."

"Stromvi will stabilize," said Jase slowly.

"Eventually," agreed Nguri with a click to emphasize concurrence.

"When you realized how rapidly and destructively the kree'va altered the relaweed, you began to modify your original programming. You intended to give those of us who are infected with the first virus our own opportunity for stability."

". . . if you leave Stromvi soon."

". . . and escape the kree'va's ongoing work here."

"You were always a satisfying student, Jase-li."

Ngeta demanded sharply, "Stop congratulating each other, please. You have both done what you have done, but you are not alone in the results. What of my daughter? Honored Husband, if you have not made plans for her safe return to us. . . ."

Nguri's momentary brightness settled back into gloom. "How could I have anticipated the deviousness of a Soli inquisitor's mind?" he retorted, and he shrugged free of Tori's touch. Tori had a terrible sense that his brusque retreat signified an end to whatever closeness they had once shared. "I do not know, Ngeta-li. I do not how many of us will survive, but *nothing* of Stromvi would have endured if I had *not* used this *thing*." He laid his broad hand on the kree'va.

Jase shook his head. Tori asked him softly, "You don't agree?"

"Like Nguri, I don't know," he replied. "I would not have used the kree'va myself, but my reluctance might be mere cowardice."

Nguri said with familiar testiness, "Agree or disagree with my judgment honestly, Jase-li. Stop taking credit for a weakness that you lack. You had courage enough to risk your life to save someone else's world."

"I made a needless gesture, trying to protect those who did not require my help. Perhaps I learned my lesson," answered Jase. Nguri grunted.

The cave shuddered, and the ground roared. "Soundshock?" mouthed Tori, afraid to speak above a whisper, though she knew that her silence helped nothing but her nerves.

Jase contradicted her quickly, "Surface explosion." A wide crack had opened in the cavern wall. The roar had faded quickly, but a low rumbling replaced it. The floor of the cave seemed to roll, and Tori braced herself against Nguri.

"Unfortunate timing," said Nguri, pushing the kree'va into Jase's hands. He gathered the botanical analyzer into his own arms. He was clicking very rapidly even as he spoke to the Soli, and Ngeta echoed and enhanced the spreading Stromvi message. "Parts of the southern caves have long been unstable," he explained grimly, as he prodded Tori to precede him from the now-crumbling room.

Weavings had slipped from the tunnel walls, revealing cracked clay. One section of the tunnel had collapsed, and three young Stromvi men were already burrowing to excavate it. The rolling motion of the ground began again, and a panicky click chorus accompanied a shriek of pain from beyond the muddied opening.

"Ngesen's hind legs are crushed," translated Ngeta hollowly, and she moved to join the frantic burrowers.

"Don't try to bring him through!" ordered Jase with

the full, stunning impact of urgent Sesserda authority. His listeners struggled against the lethargy that his words imposed. He continued earnestly, "This part of the tunnel is ready to fall. Ngeta, let them reach Ngesen from the southern side. It's not the south cave network that's collapsing. It's Hodge House and all the surrounding support structure." Ngeta and the three Stromvi youths beside her withdrew cautiously from their burrowing, as Nguri clicked a pensive confirmation. "Nguri, is there another south exit from these tunnels?"

"None that Soli could negotiate," replied Nguri.

One of the young Stromvi men offered quickly, "We can carry them, Master Nguri," and he bent low to place his strong back in front of Tori. One of his friends imitated the gesture with slightly less eagerness before Jase, who accepted the offer wordlessly.

"You're Ngev, aren't you?" asked Tori, as she tried to settle securely against hard Stromvi muscles and a youthful neck ridge that offered little room for a solid grip.

The Stromvi youth seemed momentarily surprised. "Yes, Miss Tori."

"Ngina has told me a lot about you."

Ngev hunched slightly in embarrassment, nearly dislodging Tori. "Has she?" he asked shyly.

"My daughter knows this youngling?" demanded Nguri, pausing briefly in front of them. He transferred the analyzer from his weary arms into the strong, young grasp of Ngev's as yet unburdened friend.

Tori could feel Ngev tense beneath Nguri's intimidating gaze. The young Stromvi clicked nervously and incoherently. Tori almost regretted that she had spoken. Yet the ordinariness of the exchange was so typically, endearingly Stromvi. She could see Jase smile a little sadly.

"Our daughter knows him quite well," said Ngeta over her shoulder, rescuing Ngev from a need to reply, "as you would have observed if you were less embedded in your work." Nguri clicked a rapid sequence that Tori could not follow, but he left Ngev and joined his wife. Ngev relaxed.

The young Stromvi moved ahead more smoothly than Tori had expected, though the ride was hardly pleasant. Root tendrils and drooping weavings slapped her. She slid against Ngev's slick hide, retaining her grip at the expense of the painful jerking of her wrists within the traction bracelets. She did not look forward to the truly difficult regions of travel.

The walls of the tunnel seemed to sway, but Ngev proceeded without hesitation into a steep, dark passage. The few pale, dangling root spikes trembled with the ground that held them. Tori closed her eyes against the thick, stinging resin. She could not tell if the dizziness was from the actual motion or the biochemical conflicts inside of her. She hoped that the Stromvi hide of Ngev's friend could withstand the Calongi-potent chemistry of Jase Sleide.

The ground shook so strongly that even the young Stromvi stumbled. Thin sheets of clay-colored casings fell from the tunnel walls, and the networks of Stromvi's sophisticated botanical technology became visible—the various, highly specialized root varieties that served as structural support, communication media, environmental regulators, and the source of every Stromvi necessity and luxury from food and clothing to medicinal supplies and artistic inspiration. The tunnel began to resemble a complex nest of Xiani wiring rather than the rough-hewn diggings of an amiable, pastoral people, and Tori realized how much she had always taken for granted about Stromvi knowledge and efficiency.

Tori clung tightly, as Ngev began the ascent of a nearly vertical shaft. Root spikes dragged against her back. Ngev's nails squeaked in piercing the gleaming resin layers that gave him purchase. A door folded downward, moving from Ngev's path as he heaved his weight and Tori's past the final rise and into the level access. The relative dryness of the surface air rushed into eager Soli lungs, aching from the slowness of adaptation caused by insufficient relanine.

Ngev's pruning teeth snapped the tangle of vines that had covered the little-used entry. The sudden shaft of light made Tori blink, and she heard Nguri mutter irritably against the painful brightness. She felt the heated wind before she recognized the light's source as fire. She climbed awkwardly from Ngev's back and stood among the cling weeds beside Ngev and Ngeta, and they watched Hodge House burn.

The pillars of the front porch blazed like candles, flames rising most brightly from the room that had been Birk's office. The fire danced in orange, green, and turquoise, snapping with resin, slow to ignite but fiercely hot to burn and nearly impossible to extinguish. The sounds of shattering crystal rang from the inferno. Dark, deadly smoke billowed upward.

Nguri clicked of bitter folly, though he specified no single perpetrator. Jase forged through the cling weeds to stand several paces ahead of Tori and the Stromvi. The shadows of other clustered Stromvi dotted the nearby fields.

An explosion loud as sound-shock erupted in a fiery fountain from the back wing, and a rain of searing colors fell across the gardens and spattered the violet night sky. The Ngenga Valley shook again, as a large segment of the Hodge gardens sank. The remaining walls of Hodge House fell outward, smashing against the white stone paths and crushing the blossoming roses.

The fire had already hollowed the house, always less substantial than it had appeared. The flames that had loomed so high fell with the walls and began to creep outward, becoming a darker fire that seemed to absorb the blue and violet colors of the Stromvi resin that fed it. Another burst of gold erupted from the remnants of the house, popping and bubbling with fused bits of metal and glass.

Jase rejoined the little group that he had left. He laid the kree'va in front of Nguri. "Deactivate it, Nguri," he said sternly. "It feeds the flames and spreads the tremors of explosion to the planet's very core." The planet trembled as he spoke, as if to echo his command.

"Birk kept weapons in that monstrosity of a house," answered Nguri stiffly. "He traded them, and now they burn. When all that he brought here is gone, the valley will have peace again."

"The resin is already burning, Nguri," insisted Jase, and the night's terrible light turned his eyes to brass. "The kree'va is enhancing the instability, because you keyed your changes to relanine, and relanine mutates indefatigably. You are adapting your planet to that inferno." He swung his arm, still clothed in Birk's discards, toward the seething, smoking mass.

"The program must be completed. Do you understand the scale of destruction that premature termination could cause?" demanded Nguri sharply.

"I understand relanine," replied Jase, and the trained iciness of an inquisitor passing harsh judgment made him seem as ominous and inescapable as the coldest Calongi. The trembling that had wracked him earlier had passed, or he had mastered it, and the uncanny iridescence cast by relanine glowed from his face and hands, dusted blue by resin mottling. "You've already set in motion a massive change in your world's ecology. As an inquisitor, I could condemn you on that basis alone, Nguri Ngenga, but I perceive some justice in your reasons. You tried to salvage a wretched, nearly hopeless situation, and you may have succeeded, but do not mistake one desperate act of heroic scope for a right to dictate the future of this Consortium planet. I have always esteemed you, Nguri, but *I* am the Sesserda adept, and I tell you that the kree'va is a treacherous tool. It has caused enough calamity already."

"If I stop the kree'va now, you might well be the first casualty," said Nguri, still strong and firm in voice, though his shoulders sagged with fatigue. "You are the relanine addict. I do not know if the secondary viral pattern has achieved adequate effect to restore you."

"We have no time for certainty. In your confounded independence, you tackled too much, Nguri. Even Birk—in all his arrogance—buried the kree'va far from temptation's sight. It destroyed the world that he wanted to protect. Don't repeat his mistake."

Nguri drooped a little further. His hide seemed to grow a trifle more subdued by age, but he clicked stubbornly, "I have done what was necessary. I know my planet." He bared his many teeth in his pseudo-Soli smile. "I shall miss you, Jase-li, even if you are sometimes as sanctimonious as the most annoying Calongi. I have valued our friendship." Nguri turned his great head toward Tori, as he added, "And ours, Tori-li."

With a gesture full of weariness, Nguri bent to the kree'va. His great hand traced the spirals of its controlling mechanism, until each bright spiral dimmed and became dark. Wordlessly, he turned from Jase and dove into the vine-mass behind the tunnel access. The undula-

tion of his passage made a slow, erratic course. After a
hesitant moment, Ngeta followed him.

Tori watched the hypnotic motions of the two retreating Stromvi. A pressure that she sensed only in its
absence had ceased its pitiless beating as the kree'va's
field faded. Tears carried resin from her eyes, but she
could not recall having initiated the cleansing consciously.

"Resin fire doesn't quench itself," said Ngev, stirring
Tori from a near-trance. "It must be suffocated."

"The problem is not new to your people," replied Jase
stiffly. "Ngela already clicks the summons. Go and aid
him in saving the southern fields. Let Hodge's Folly burn
down to the core clay."

Ngev's friends, heeding Ngela's call, had already disappeared into the vine-mass. A glimmer of silver from
Nguri's analyzer caught the firelight briefly and vanished
with the Stromvi.

Ngev alone hesitated, glancing from the two Soli to
the interlaced vines that surrounded them on all sides.
"You shouldn't stay here," warned Ngev uncertainly.
"The fire will spread beyond the Soli gardens soon, and
the silver-lilies will fuel it. This land may collapse."

"You can't carry us through vine-mass and surface burrows," said Jase with implacable Sesserda honesty, "and
your life-purpose no longer lies with us. Go with my
gratitude and my respect, Ngev Ngenga."

Ngev started to bend obediently toward the burrowing
trail, but he paused to ask, "Will Ngina be able to return
to us?"

Jase answered, "The choice will be hers." Ngev waited
no longer. His burrowing made a strong, swift trail. Jase
sank to his knees and pressed his hands against his
temples.

Tori knelt beside him cautiously. The kree'va lay between them. All of her accumulated fear and loneliness
bade her touch him, comfort him, or seek comfort from
him, but she felt the sting of her blistered arm and restrained the impulse. "Why don't I learn to stop following you into trouble?" she asked in sad irony.

His laugh was short and shallow, but he raised his eyes
to meet hers. "Don't give up on me yet," he said with
a twisted smile. "I'm almost as hard to kill as a Calongi."

"I was thinking along somewhat more selfish lines,"

she retorted, but even his indirect encouragement made
her posture firmer, her hope stronger.

Jase dropped his hands to the kree'va and rested his
nimble fingers delicately along the device's edges. "As
your inquisitor, Miss Darcy, I accepted a certain responsibility in your regard, and I wish you'd stop implying
that I'm so irresponsible as to risk your life needlessly. I
do try to plan intelligently on occasion." With a swift
sequence of motions, he stripped the traction bracelets
from his wrists and delved into the pockets of his coat.
His hands emerged, one with a transceiver, one with a
coil of tracking wire. He tapped the transceiver and addressed it. "Ngina-li, your passengers are waiting." An
excited clicking burst from the transceiver, and Jase lowered the volume hurriedly, as he reassured Ngina in a
slightly limp version of Stromvi click-language. "She's
coming," he finished with a glimmer of complacency.

"I heard her," countered Tori. "What about the
Rea?"

Jase looked across the garden of flame to the second
moon. "I think Omi-lai has finally resolved his personal
biases, at least enough to help Roake and Ares regain
some degree of control."

"I'm thrilled for them all. Are they about to land on
top of us?"

"If anyone can keep the Rea ship from crashing into
this planet, Omi-lai will manage it. His perceptions are
unusually sensitive, even for a Calongi. That's the crux
of his intolerance problem. He's too thoroughly aware of
weaknesses in general." Jase added quietly, "I'd wager
a Cuui fortune that Akras began the fire."

"Do you think anyone from the house survived?"
asked Tori with a tightening of her voice.

Jase answered slowly, "I sense eight dead." Tori tried
not to attach the possible names to his terse statistic.

The Sesserda-patterned hovercraft drowned further
conversation. Jase used the transceiver to shout orders
at Ngina. The ship did not land but settled lightly above
the tunnel access. Jase motioned for Tori to enter first.
As she climbed into the lock and turned, she saw Jase
raise the kree'va above his head and hurl it toward the
encroaching waves of resin-fire.

When he had joined Tori in the air lock, and the outer

door had closed away the fury of Hodge House aflame, she asked him, "Why did you destroy it? Planetary adapters aren't evil in themselves."

"Planetary adapters are abominations," he replied forcefully.

"The Sesserda adept has spoken," mocked Tori, unwilling to admit that she agreed with him. She had never even liked the artifice of Uncle Per's estate. "Do we need to remain cramped in this air lock?"

"We can't risk contaminating Ngina or anyone else, until Nguri's battling elements stabilize in us. I'm not that certain of the cure yet."

"I'm stuck with you again?"

"Until we reach Deetari or a friendly traveler with good isolation facilities." Jase seated himself against the inner wall, his knees bent to fit the constrained space. The thin, elastic wall flexed slightly where his back pressed it. He tugged a securing strap around his waist.

Tori braced herself as the hovercraft moved sharply upward. "Are you sure you trust Ngina to fly us that far?"

"In comparison with recent events, the danger of Ngina's piloting seems fairly insignificant. However, I'd recommend against standing much longer."

"Should I move to the other side of the ship to prevent your Calongi influence from sizzling my skin?"

"Your choice. I'm past the volatile phase." He added with a grimace, "In fact, I'm probably exuding less relanine than usual because I'm barely managing to remain conscious."

Tori slid to the floor beside him, trying not to let the resiliency of the wall disconcert her. Quickly and tentatively, she touched the back of her hand to his face, avoiding the track of Akras' knife. When his skin did not burn her, she fastened herself into place with a securing strap.

Jase said dryly, "You could at least trust me about my personal biochemistry."

"I'd hate to set a precedent." She raised her hand again to his face and repeated her first gesture more slowly.

He raised an eyebrow, but he made no other motion. "Am I harmless?" he asked.

Tori sighed and leaned against him. "I'm too tired to think of a witty response, Jase," she whispered.

"So am I," he answered softly. She pulled his arm around her. For once, he cooperated without Sesserda commentary.

*   *   *

Omi reached his many senses through the enormous Rea vessel, helpless in its decaying orbit. He focused all but one segment of his brain on the Rea vessel and its contents. He allowed that single brain segment to continue its effort to develop an inner antidote to the Stromvi virus that corrupted his blood. He had recognized Nguri's initiation of a secondary viral design, but Omi had left the kree'va's field of influence well before the corrective factor could take hold.

With the majority of his brain, Omi felt the daar'va. He felt the imbalances that Akras had initiated. He felt the conflict and confusion of the Rea, deprived—by their own grim choice—of the clan leader whom they had followed for so long. Most of the Rea remained at least partially conscious, though few could stand. Omi sensed their frustration, for many had reached the point of mutiny, and they cursed themselves for waiting too long. Akras had not set the daar'va to kill. She had allowed her people the freedom to confront death in honorable Rea awareness.

Omi felt the spreading sickness in Roake and the hesitation in Ares, daunted now by the reality of the leadership that he had coveted. It was a measure of Rea desperation that the brothers had admitted a Calongi to their home vessel almost eagerly. They were Essenji warriors, unaccustomed to a sense of helplessness, but the daar'va and the Stromvi virus had made them weak despite protection suits. They watched Omi with suspicion, anxiety, and hope.

When he had sorted his perceptions to his satisfaction, Omi said evenly, "The daar'va is only one element of your present difficulty. Sabotage to the vessel was inflicted via the navigational data base, and you may correct that damage quite simply by restoring the last section of the Stromvi orbit file."

Ares waved an unspoken command to Tiber, who hurried to the nearest control console to act on Omi's advice. Roake growled, "If you are deceiving us, Calongi, my death-curse will haunt you through eternity."

Omi disregarded the bravado of a frightened man. "You will be more comfortable if you wait for me here." Omi headed for the daar'va. Only the young Rea warrior, Remus, obeyed Omi's suggestion to wait in the shuttle bay. Both Roake and Ares followed Omi, despite the pain that rapid movement caused them.

The corridors were long, but Omi evaluated each possible course and selected the optimum. Time was very short. Omi saw no reason to inform the Rea that the daar'va and the relanine-afflicting virus had lessened his own functionality to a critical degree. He was unsure of both the accuracy and the thoroughness of his assessments. Omi moved silently, though he abandoned the customary, measured Calongi pace and proceeded very swiftly. Roake and Ares struggled to keep up with him.

When Omi opened the door at his destination, Ares muttered, "This is the clan leader's room."

"We've searched here already," argued Roake.

Omi ignored Roake's comment. Omi walked directly to an apparently solid wall behind the narrow cot. He sang the tones that released the lock, and the panels of the hidden cupboard slid apart to show the daar'va. "If your senses were trained properly, Mister Roake," announced Omi evenly, "you would not require such overt indicators as sound-shock to locate this device." He deactivated the daar'va calmly.

Omi felt a surge of his perceptions immediately. His mental processes resumed nearly their normal level of efficiency. Omi nodded to himself, satisfied with his accomplishment. He could feel orbital stability returning, as Tiber restored the navigational files. Omi manipulated his inner antidote until it met his criteria of effectiveness, then he programmed it into every part of his body. Relanine reasserted itself.

"You will take me to Deetari now," said Omi mildly. "Unless you wish to accept the obligations of Consortium membership, I recommend that you subsequently take your people far from the Consortium and remain there. Sesserda law does not punish an entire culture for the choices of its leaders, and I have judged that your clan leader and Birk Hodge bore the primary guilt for Rea crimes against Stromvi, Soli, and Deetari members of the Consortium. However, any future offenses against Consortium members will not be tolerated. If you choose to live without the law, you must live outside the law's protected space as well."

"Calongi," grunted Roake, leaning weakly against the cabin's wall, his finely trained body trembling, "we are dying. Your Soli friend promised us a cure."

"He has a streak of rashness," remarked Omi blandly, "but he is an honorable colleague." With a flickering speed, Omi darted one of his *irivi* toward Roake. The long, iridescent limb punctured the skin of the Essenji's throat. Roake recoiled, but his reactions were painfully slow. Ares watched the exchange without comment.

Omi retracted his arm and recoiled it calmly. Such a process of inoculation was far less stressful than the extensive transfusion that Jase-lai had required. "You have been provided with an antidote, Mister Roake, which will counteract the first shortly. I based the antidote's design on a secondary virus that Nguri Ngenga had begun to develop. It is infectious rather than contagious, but you are now capable of distributing it among your people. I have accelerated your personal healing, since you are the most severely affected."

"Inoculate me as well," said Ares. "There are many Rea to be healed."

For a moment, Omi felt impatience stir at these helpless, uncivilized beings who dared make demands of him. He laid aside the unworthy emotion. "As you wish," agreed Omi. He repeated his rapid gesture, but Ares did not even flinch.

"Thank you, Master Omi," said Ares, his voice slightly strained. "The Rea clan shall honor you in our histories." Roake grunted a wordless assent.

Omi inclined his head, approving the Rea's sincerity of gratitude. Perhaps these uncivilized beings were not entirely devoid of worth. "You need not worry about lingering effects of either virus, since they were both designed to reproduce for a very limited number of generations." Omi added, "Within their parochial perspective, the Stromvi have an unusually advanced respect for creation."

CHAPTER 46

"I wish I could return to my people now," sighed Ngina, idly tracing the silver mineral veins that decorated the white Deetari bench beside her. She shrugged uncomfortably. "My hide itches from the dryness of this atmosphere."

Tori nodded, but she could not force herself to answer. Her ice-blue Deetari shift was soft, but it seemed to chafe her skin in sympathy with Ngina's comment. Not even a trace of resin remained to color Tori, and she actually missed that irritating slipperiness.

Stromvi seemed so far removed from this quiet, structured garden with its sculpted shrubbery and dainty fountains. After ten days here, Tori felt increasingly misplaced. The old longing to escape was becoming strong again, but this time a definite destination summoned her. However, Hodge Farm no longer existed.

Tori could hardly fault the Deetari hospitality. The Deetari had welcomed the Stromvi refugees into one of the matriarch's own manor houses. Everything had been provided to ensure the comfort of the guests from Stromvi, but the ten days had seemed interminable.

Ten days. Thirty millispans. Less than a third of the full extent of death-watch. Ten days form an interlude. Death-watch formed a lifetime.

Except for distant glimpses, Tori had seen Jase only once since their arrival on Deetari. He had informed her coolly that he was quite well, and he had expressed a slightly distracted interest in Ngina's health and Tori's own recovery. Ngina had bombarded him with questions, most of which he had parried deftly, some of which he had refused to answer at all. Tori had an uneasy suspicion regarding the reason for his preoccupation.

"Why are you frowning, Miss Tori?" asked Ngina,

clicking a gentle, wheedling sound that Stromvi mothers often used to coax their children. "Are you thinking about the Hodges?"

"I was thinking about your father."

"Yes," said Ngina, clicking comprehension and regret. "I saw Master Omi, too. The inquisitors are judging my esteemed father, aren't they?"

"That is what inquisitors do," said Tori crisply. "They assess. They judge. They condemn."

"My father is a very honorable man, Miss Tori."

"I know, Ngina-li."

The wrought-iron garden gate squeaked open. Through the mist of the intervening fountains, Tori could see the Sesserda gold and the familiar shock of straight, dark hair. Jase came quickly to where Tori and Ngina sat, though he looked at neither of them. In the cool voice of Consortium officialdom, he said, "Miss Darcy, I need to speak to Miss Ngenga alone."

If Omi had come, if anyone but Jase had come, Tori would have snapped a retort in Ngina's defense. Tori wished that Jase would let her stay, but she did not argue. She knew that he loved Stromvi and Nguri Ngenga as much as anyone.

*   *   *

Jase watched Tori retreat into the house. He felt Ngina's anxiety, but he did not hasten to speak. He wished that he did not need to speak at all, but judgment was the duty of a Sesserda adept.

He garbed himself in the proper calm detachment, though he ached inwardly. "We have judged your father guilty of inflicting deliberate injury on Consortium members," said Jase, reciting words that he had practiced with pain, "and causing the death of Harrow Febro. We have notified your people of our decision. The Stromvi seniors have likewise made a judgment. You must now make your own choice."

"My father has always served his people and his world," answered Ngina, but her strong young shoulders sagged as if accepting a heavy burden.

He has served them valiantly, thought Jase, *and he has destroyed himself.* "So your people have declared, also.

They have chosen to accept Consortium sentence as a whole world rather than submit your father to us for individual justice." *They have made the wise choice, the inevitable choice. They fulfill death-watch, and perhaps I helped to ensure their rebirth. Or perhaps all my manipulations saved only Tori, and Rea, and myself. I failed in my friendship-debt: I failed to save Sylvie and Calem. I failed to save Nguri.* "In light of this decision and the severe changes that are still transpiring on Stromvi, we have concluded that both Stromvi and Consortium justice would be served best by a period of quarantine."

"How long?" asked Ngina faintly.

"One hundred spans."

Ngina's torso wove back and forth in the pattern of mourning. Jase did not let her see how deeply he felt her grief. "I wanted to see the Consortium," said Ngina with sorrow, "like Miss Tori."

"You have a choice," said Jase with proper calm. "You may stay with us and have that freedom."

"And not see my people again?" demanded Ngina, and she snapped her pruning teeth rebelliously. "Do you think I would leave them?"

Jase breathed deeply, and at last he looked at Ngina directly. "Ngina-li, your people are changing. Your world is changing. By Omi's calculations, a hundred spans will barely allow Stromvi to restabilize. If you return, you will change also, but you will begin at a different stage, and you may become very different from your family. For my part in causing you this grief, I am truly sorry."

Ngina bared her fierce arrays of teeth in a brief Stromvi smile. "You endured a terrible change, Jase Sleide, but you are still a Soli. I shall still be a Stromvi."

Jase extended his hand to Ngina, and the rubies of the Rea-star blazed in his palm. "Give this to your father: a gift from Birk."

Ngina took the Rea-star from him and furled her long nails around it tightly. The starburst's sharp edges scored her palm, for her resin layers had thinned. "My honored father thanks you."

*   *   *

The broad Deetari room opened onto craggy mountain vistas on three sides, and the graceful arches of the windows framed carefully selected views: an obsidian dome, a silvery peak, an orderly stand of tufted, celadon Deetari trees. Inside the room, the furnishings were gathered in comfortable, intimate clusters, each focused on a particular segment of the distant landscape. Tori had pulled a white wicker chair away from its grouping and turned it toward the patio door. Even if Jase tried to leave without speaking to her, she would see him from here. She would question the inquisitor if she had to tackle him bodily.

Tori jumped to her feet as soon as Jase approached. She opened the glass door to admit him quickly. "Where is Ngina?" she asked.

"Preparing to return to Stromvi," answered Jase. He crossed the jade-tiled floor and sank into a deeply cushioned yellow lounge, propping his feet on the low, padded bench before him. He leaned his head back and stared at the starkly simple design of mineral fragments embedded in the ceiling. "The planet will be under a hundred-span quarantine. Omi and I had no real options in judgment. The kree'va's changes must stabilize. With so much of the design composed around relanine, every new element complicates the results. Even without a quarantine, there is very little that the Consortium could do to help the Stromvi through their necessary transformation."

Hearing only what she had dreaded for the past ten days, Tori nodded. Any solid verdict was easier to endure than the intangible process of inquisition. "Will there be any judgment against Deetari?"

"Gisa and Thalia might have earned a disciplinary regimen, but they chose to appease their prophesied Lady Death. Their sisters were merely the victims of Birk's coercion and his cruel misuse of Deetari religious beliefs. I should have predicted that Gisa and Thalia would consider their own deaths necessary to the preservation of Deetari." Jase's Sesserda detachment vanished for the duration of a sigh, and Tori liked him better for the indication of remorse. "As judgments go, it's not quite as satisfactory as Omi's condemnation of Roake and Ares to each other's company."

"It was well judged, Inquisitor," said Tori in grim,

resigned accord. The dead had punished themselves. Like Arnod, they could no longer be helped. Tori wondered if her bittersweet memories of the Hodges would haunt her as inescapably as her brief, misguided marriage.

"Thank you for the approval," replied Jase, but his voice remained remote and devoid of satisfaction. The Deetari had embroidered the Sesserda gold of his shirt from metal thread, and it gleamed against the sapphire silk. Tori wondered if the Deetari had chosen the fabric for him. They had tailored the shirt and trousers for Soli tastes, but the bright hue was the color worn by Deetari men in mourning.

"What about me?" asked Tori softly.

Jase raised his head. "I'm afraid that Omi's original judgment still stands officially. I can't exonerate you legally, due to acute personal bias."

"If that's meant to be a compliment, I'd have been happier without it."

"Another inquisition could be arranged at my request."

"No, thank you." Tori wrapped her shawl's pale Deetari lace around her more tightly in a futile effort to feel warm. Sleeveless Deetari shifts seemed more suitable to humid Stromvi than to mountainous Deetari, but the Deetari metabolism ran faster than the Soli counterpart.

"Your temperature adaptation is still lagging," noted Jase with a faint frown. "You should have your relanine level checked. Your system has endured considerable strain, after all."

"I don't think any amount of adaptation fluid will warm me." She laughed, a forced brightness to mask grim thoughts. Ngina was preparing to leave. The last bond with Stromvi would be lost. "Everything that mattered is gone again, just like after Arnod's death. I suppose I must crawl back to Mama and Uncle Per once again. Did you know that I received a summons from him this morning?"

"Per Walis evidently has an informer on Deetari," grunted Jase.

"Uncle Per is a very cautious man."

"His concern for you is a little tardy, but it's a small sign in his favor." Jase tapped a silent rhythm thoughtfully. "However, your Uncle Per's remaining days of prosperity may be few. Omi-lai has begun to analyze the involvement of Per Walis in the unlawful aspects of Birk Hodge's business dealings, and I suspect the correlations will prove to be fairly high."

"You're a fount of cheerful news."

"You didn't want to return to Arcy. Your relations with your family are strained at best."

Irritated with him for telling her what she knew too well, Tori answered sharply, "I don't have many palatable options. Thanks to your purity of Consortium justice, I'm not very employable."

"Except in the infamous family business, of course."

Tori glared at him. No inquisitor would strike so many painful subjects unintentionally. "Are any of your influential friends in the market for a reluctant concubine?" she asked with thick sarcasm.

"That's a difficult question. I don't know many Soli—I'm assuming you'd prefer a man of your own species—and he'd need substantial resources to keep you in the style that your family would expect."

"I'm about to throw something at you, Mister Sleide." She actually looked around her for an appropriately damaging object.

Jase said mildly, "Suppose I offered you a contract of patronage."

Despite her irritated, generally discouraged mood, Tori began to laugh. "Doesn't Sesserda forbid such uncivilized practices as concubinage?"

"Absolutely, but you're the one who was so entranced by my honor-song."

"You're the conceited twit who told me not to encourage impossible fantasies."

"I didn't say the fantasies were yours," replied Jase, a trace of a grin beginning to form. "However, I merely presented the hypothesis. I made no offer."

"You were merely provoking a reaction in good inquisitorial style."

"It's part of my job description. Always attack the difficult subjects from unexpected directions, and you are a very difficult subject indeed."

Tori began to pace, not sure if she wanted to hit him or seduce him. "I understand why Great-grandmama never involved herself too closely with inquisitors of any species."

"It was probably a prudent practice, considering her breadth of dubious interests."

"Great-grandmama knew how to take care of herself."

"So do you, Miss Darcy. I think you have a talent for the field of alien relations. Would you like to work for me?"

"You're trying to provoke reactions again," grumbled Tori.

"Not this time. I only prodded you on the subject of patronage to be sure that we understand each other. I don't want you imagining that I'm simply one more worshiper of the legend of Mirelle."

Tori stopped her pacing and stared at him. "I never saw that as a major worry in regard to you. You're too busy dissecting my psyche."

His dark brows tilted above the iridescent eyes. "Having thus dissected you, I'd be in betrayal of my Sesserda oaths if I didn't try to direct you wisely. You already know that you can inspire lust, and that's not much of a life-purpose for a civilized woman anyway. You need to realize that you have other gifts as well. I believe that you can make a very valuable contribution to the Consortium in my employ. If you don't like the work. . . ."

". . . or can't tolerate your inquisitorial sense of humor. . . ."

". . . you can at least add the reference of a third level Sesserda adept to your future employability quotient."

Tori turned away from him and confronted the transparent wall that edged the fountain garden. Beyond the garden was a gate, a bench, a grieving Stromvi girl, and a past that would fade into memory. "Aren't you defying your own advice by trying to hire me?" she asked, still forbidding herself to believe him too easily. Sesserda precision could be very misleading to the untrained. "You could jeopardize your Sesserda rank by associating with someone as uncivilized as me."

"I'll be cautious."

"You'd be encouraging my involvement with a relanine addict."

"As you remarked, your current prospects are not auspicious. You might as well be miserable in my company."

"That's a charming sentiment." Tori faced him again, pondering him in his Sesserda gold. His iridescent eyes did not blink, and she wondered what manifold Sesserda perceptions he was processing. "I hate trying to make calculated decisions."

"Then react rashly, according to your usual custom."

"Restrain your sarcasm, please." She joined him on the lounge, though she barely perched on the edge of the cushion beside him. "I still loathe inquisitors."

"You don't loathe me."

"You're not sure of that or of anything else about me." She bent toward him, trailing Deetari lace against his thigh. "I don't believe you can read me at all. Tiva disorder is not that simple to ignore, and you inquisitors are too well trained to let a personal perspective interfere so easily with your all-encompassing Truth."

"Tiva disorder is much easier to handle than the personal feelings you inspire, Miss Darcy." Jase fingered the lace edge of Tori's shawl pensively. "As a matter of academic interest, the burning passion of a relanine addict tends to have an unpleasantly literal effect."

"Is burning passion part of the job description?"

"No." He slouched further into the chair and closed his eyes. "You'll need some extra inoculations to visit Calong-4. The travelers' bureau can direct you to the appropriate specialist. We'll be leaving on a private Teurai ship tomorrow. The Teurai navigators are anxious to leave, since they're on the verge of sea stay."

"Sure of yourself, aren't you?"

"No, but I'm sure of you."

"Conceited," muttered Tori. *Deservedly so*, she added to herself and hoped that Tiva disorder kept the comment private.

EPILOGUE

I have never accustomed myself to death. I once believed that age would make the partings easier. Perhaps it is so for some, but for me, each pain is as sharp as the first. The pain does fade in time, but its terrible, wrenching depth is so much vaster than any recounting can convey.

The personal deaths steal a piece of oneself, a small segment that belonged to all the good and bad of a relationship that had no opportunity to fade quietly. Even the most clearly anticipated deaths carry shock with them. Something is gone, and the entire universe must reel a little to comprehend that an element is missing.

My honored father did not live long after the change. He knew that he had wrought from necessity, and he was wise enough not to feel guilt over events that he had not caused. The many deaths among our people hurt him, but he had provided the cure and not the sickness.

Nguri Ngenga did not die from his terrible sorrow for his people. He died of loneliness because the planet that he had loved above himself no longer knew how to welcome him. He had made his planet and his people alien to himself, and my honored father refused to ingest the extra relanine that would have enabled his aged body to sustain the final adaptation. He was a very stubborn man.

His inquisitors undoubtedly anticipated his end. They judge and they condemn according to their subject's deepest fears. Such is their Sesserda justice.

Compared to my honored father, they seem so child-like now, these Consortium officials who greet my people as fragile members of their sturdy, changeless Consortium structure. They are very wise in their own ways, I know, but they do not understand my Stromvi. They brought me flowers as a tribute to my seniority here. They brought me Soli roses.

I have given them my records. My job is done, even if only one more being eventually learns and understands that my honored father served his people nobly. If I were obedient to my honored father's bravely poetic spirit, I would now fade gracefully into death. I am so old. Even the Calongi representatives seem young to me.

Alas for the dignity of my forebears, I learned too well from a young Soli woman with a passionate recklessness in her heart and mind. Tomorrow I shall take the Consortium representatives on a tour of the northern continent. I shall show them how the greatest Stromvi horticulturist bred roses. They will be embarrassed by their paltry offering to me, and I shall speak with graciousness and dignity of the value of their intentions. I shall enjoy teasing the Calongi from the impunity of my senior status. I am the last Stromvi who remembers, but I shall not be the last to be remembered: That is a truth that even an inquisitor would acknowledge.